Helen

BAHRAIN -

U.K. BRAMHALL   0161- 440-9026

D1390950

OTHER TITLES
· FROM ·
SERPENT'S TAIL

DAVID BRADLEY *The Chaneysville Incident*
MICHEL DEL CASTILLO   *The Disinherited*
ISMAIL KADARE *Chronicle in Stone*
DEA TRIER MØRCH   *Winter's Child*

· *DONA FLOR* ·

AND HER TWO HUSBANDS

· *DONA FLOR* ·
AND HER TWO HUSBANDS
Jorge Amado

Translated from the Portuguese by Harriet de Onís

SERPENT'S
TAIL

BRITISH LIBRARY CATALOGUING IN PUBLICATION DATA

Amado, Jorge
Dona Flor and her two husbands.
I. Title   II. Dona Flor e seus dois maridos. *English*
869.3 F   PQ9697.A647

ISBN 1–85242–103–7

First published 1966 as *Dona Flor e Seus Dois Maridos* by
Livraria Martins Editora, São Paulo, Brazil.
First published in English by Alfred A. Knopf, Inc.
© 1969 Alfred A. Knopf, Inc.

This edition first published 1986 by
Serpent's Tail, 26 Westbourne Grove, London W2.
Published by arrangement with Alfred A. Knopf, Inc.

Printed in Great Britain by
Billing and Sons Ltd
Worcester.

· DONA FLOR ·

AND HER TWO HUSBANDS

"God is fat"

REVELATION BY VADINHO ON HIS RETURN

"The earth is blue"

AFFIRMED BY GAGARIN AFTER THE FIRST SPACE FLIGHT

*"A place for everything
and everything in its place"*

SIGN ON THE WALL OF DR. TEODORO MADUREIRA'S PHARMACY

"Ay"

SIGHED DONA FLOR

Dear Friend Jorge Amado,

The fact of the matter is that I do not really have a recipe for the corn cake I bake. Dona Alda, the wife of Mr. Renato of the Museum, told me how to do it, and in that way I learned, racking my brains until I got it right. (Was it not by loving that I learned to love? Was it not by living that I learned to live?)

Twenty individual muffins, or more, depending on the number you want. I would advise Dona Zélia to make a big cake to start off, for everybody likes it and asks for a second helping. (Even those two, so different, were in agreement only on this: both of them were crazy about corn or manioc cake. About another thing, too? You let me alone, Mr. Jorge; don't tease me or talk about that.) Sugar, salt, grated cheese, butter, coconut milk, the thick and the thin, both are called for. (Would you who write for the newspapers tell me why one always needs two loves, why one alone does not satisfy the heart?) The proportions depending on the taste; each person has his preference—some like things sweeter, some saltier, isn't that so? And the batter very thin. A quick oven.

I hope I have satisfied you, Mr. Jorge, with this recipe which is hardly a recipe, barely an outline. Taste the cake I am sending with this, and if you like it let me know. How is your family? We are all well. We have bought another share of the drugstore, and are taking a house for the summer in Itaparica, very nice. As for the rest, as you well know, that which is crooked cannot be made straight. I don't want to tell you what goes on with me in the morning hours; it would be a lack of respect. But the truth of the matter is that the person who sets the day aglow as it rises from the sea is your faithful servant,

Florípedes Paiva Madureira—Dona Flor dos Guimarães

(A recent note from Dona Flor to the novelist)

DONA FLOR

AND HER TWO HUSBANDS

The strange and moving account of the experiences of Dona Flor,
professor emeritus of the culinary art, and her two husbands,
the first known as Vadinho; the second, Dr. Teodoro Madureira
by name, pharmacist by profession,

or

THE FEARSOME BATTLE BETWEEN SPIRIT AND MATTER

Narrated by Jorge Amado,
public scrivener located in the Rio Vermelho quarter of the city
of Salvador da Bahia de Todos os Santos, in the neighborhood
of Largo de Sant' Ana, where Yemanjá,
Our Lady of the Waters, dwells.

I

THE DEATH OF VADINHO
THE FIRST HUSBAND
OF DONA FLOR,
HIS WAKE AND BURIAL

(To the guitar accompaniment of the incomparable Carlinhos Mascarenhas)

COOKING SCHOOL
OF SAVOR AND ART

WHEN AND WHAT TO SERVE AT A WAKE

(Dona Flor's answer to a pupil)

Not because it is a confused day of grief, sadness, and weeping is this any excuse for a wake not to be held with due ceremony. If the mistress of the house, sobbing and fainting, beside herself, or dead in the coffin, cannot assume the duties herself, then some relative or friend should take charge of the rite, for one is not going to turn out into the dawn, at times in the winter cold, the devoted friends who have spent the night with the deceased, without eating or drinking.

For a wake to have life, and really honor the demised for whom it is held and lighten his first and confused night of death, it must be carried out with all solicitude, giving thought to the morale and the appetite.

When should refreshments be served?

All night long, from the beginning to the end. Coffee is indispensable, continually, that is to say, plain coffee. A complete breakfast, coffee with milk, bread, butter, cheese, crackers, couscous with poached eggs, is served only in the morning and to those who have spent the whole night there.

The best thing is to keep the kettle on the boil all the time so there will be no lack of coffee, for people will be coming in continually. Cookies and crackers to go with the coffee; from time to time a tray of cold cuts, sandwiches of cheese, ham, sausage, simple things, for the deceased is sufficient cause for worry and concern.

If, however, the wake is more sumptuous, one of those where money flows like water, then a cup of chocolate at midnight is called for, thick and hot, or a tasty chicken broth. And codfish balls, croquettes of different kinds, assorted sweets, dried fruit.

When the family is well-to-do, in addition to the coffee, beer may

be served, or wine, just one glass to accompany the broth and the croquettes. Never champagne; that is not considered in good taste.

But whether a rich or a poor wake, what is indispensable is a
steady supply of good rum; everything else may be lacking, even
coffee, but not rum. Without the comfort it lends there is no wake
worth mentioning. A wake without rum shows a lack of respect
for the dead, implies indifference and disaffection.

1

Vadinho, Dona Flor's first husband, died one Sunday of Carnival, in the morning, when, dressed up like a Bahian woman, he was dancing the samba, with the greatest enthusiasm, in the Dois de Julho Square, not far from his house. He did not belong to the group—he had just joined it, in the company of four of his friends, all masquerading as *bahianas*, and they had come from a bar on Cabeça, where the whiskey flowed like water at the expense of one Moysés Alves, a cacao planter, rich and open-handed.

The group was accompanied by a small, well-rehearsed orchestra of guitars and flutes; the four-string guitar was played by Carlinhos Mascarenhas, a tall, skinny character famous in the whorehouses —ah, a divine player. The men were got up as Gypsies and the girls as Hungarian or Romanian peasants; never, however, had a Hungarian or Romanian, or even a Bulgarian or Slovak, swung her hips the way they did, those brown girls in the flower of their youth and coquetry.

When Vadinho, the liveliest of the lot, saw the group come around the corner and heard the skeleton-like Mascarenhas strumming his sublime four-string guitar, he hurried forward, and chose as his partner a heavily rouged Romanian, a big one, as monumental as a church—the Church of St. Francis, for she was a mass of golden sequins—and announced:

"Here I come, my Russian from Tororó."

The Gypsy Mascarenhas, who was also bedecked with glass beads and spangles and had gaudy earrings hanging from his ears, pulsed his four-string guitar still more sonorously, the flutes and Spanish guitars groaned, and Vadinho took his place in the samba with that exemplary enthusiasm he brought to everything he did except work. He whirled in the middle of the group, stomped in front of the mulatta, approached her in flourishes and belly-bumps, then suddenly gave a kind of hoarse moan, wobbled, listed to one side, and fell to the ground, a yellow slobber drooling from his mouth on which the grimace of death could not wholly extinguish the fatuous smile of the complete faker he had always been.

His friends were under the impression that it was the result of the load he had taken aboard: not the whiskeys the planter had treated them to—those four or five doses would have had little effect on the class of drinker Vadinho was—but all the rum imbibed from the evening before until noon when the Carnival was officially inaugurated at the Triumph Bar, in the Municipal Square —all of it hitting him at once and knocking him out. But the big mulatta was not fooled; a nurse by profession, she knew death when she saw it; it was a familiar sight to her in the hospital. Not, however, to the point of giving her belly-bumps, of winking its eye at her, of dancing the samba with her. She bent over Vadinho, laid her hand on his neck, and shuddered, a chill running through her stomach and up her spine: "Dear God, he's dead."

Others touched the body, too, felt his pulse, raised his head with its fair hair, listened to his heart. It was useless, a waste of time. Vadinho had taken leave of the Carnival of Bahia for good.

2

There was a hubbub in the group of dancers and in the street, a rush through the neighborhood, a God-be-with-us sending a shiver through the merrymakers—and on top of everything Anete, a romantic and hysterically inclined young teacher, took advantage of the occasion to have an attack of nerves, with squeals and the threat of fainting. All that act for the benefit of the vain Carlinhos Mascarenhas, for whom that affected creature sighed, always on the verge of swooning, describing herself as hypersensitive, twitching like a cat having its hair rubbed the wrong way when he strummed the guitar. A guitar that was now mute, hanging uselessly from the hands of its player, as though Vadinho had carried off its final notes with him to the other world.

People came running from every direction; after the news had circulated through the environs, it reached São Pedro, Avenida Sete, Campo Grande, rounding up the curious. A small crowd had gathered around the corpse, jogging one another, overflowing with comments. A doctor who lived in Sodré was commandeered; a traffic policeman took out his whistle and blew it uninterruptedly, as though informing the whole city, the entire Carnival, of Vadinho's end.

"Why, it's Vadinho, the poor thing!" remarked one of the disguised revelers, his mask slipping off, his gaiety gone. All recognized the dead man; he enjoyed great popularity, with his sparkling joyousness, his hairline mustache, his profligate's pride, especially well-liked in places where drinking, gambling, and carousing were the order of the day; and there, so near his home, everyone knew him.

Another masked man, this one dressed in burlap and wearing

a bear's head, pushed his way through the tight group and managed to approach close enough to get a good look. He pulled off his mask revealing a doleful face, with drooping mustache and bald scalp, and murmured: "Vadinho, my brother, what have they done to you?"

"What happened to him, what did he die of?" people asked one another, and someone answered: "Rum." This was far too simple an explanation of such an untimely death. A stooped old woman gazed at him for a long time and remarked: "Still so young. Why did he have to die so early?"

There was a crossfire of questions and answers, while the doctor laid his ear on Vadinho's breast. His report was definitive and extinguished all hope.

"He was dancing the samba, having a wonderful time, and without a word to anyone he fell over completely dead," explained one of his four friends, sobered up as though by magic, and deeply touched. He stood there looking somewhat foolish in his drag, his cheeks red with rouge, his eyes deeply shadowed with burned cork.

The fact that they were wearing the typical dress of Bahian women should not give rise to any doubts about the five friends' masculinity. They had dressed up in that fashion the better to fool around, to enjoy themselves and have fun, not because of any deviant inclinations laying them open to suspicion. There was not a faggot in the whole lot, praise be to God. Vadinho had even tied under his white starched petticoat a huge cassava tuber, and at every step he raised his skirts and displayed the outsized, pornographic trophy, causing the women to cover their faces with their hands and let out malicious giggles. Now the tuber hung over his bared hip and elicited no laughter. One of his friends noticed it and untied it from Vadinho's waist. But not even so did the dead man look decent and modest; he was a Carnival casualty; yet, he did not even show the blood of a bullet wound or a dagger thrust running down his breast, which would have redeemed him from his air of masquerader.

Dona Flor, preceded, naturally, by Dona Norma issuing orders and clearing a path, arrived almost at the same moment as the police. When she came around the corner, resting on the supporting arms of her friends, everyone divined that she was the widow, for she was sighing and moaning, not even attempting to control her sobs, a cataract of tears. Moreover, she was wearing a rumpled house dress, which she used when she was cleaning, had on felt bedroom slippers, and had not yet combed her hair. Even so she was pretty, pleasant to look at; small and plump, but not fat; bronze of color; her straight hair so black that it looked bluish; voluptuous eyes; and full lips slightly parted over white teeth. A tasty morsel, as Vadinho himself was in the habit of calling her in his outbursts of tenderness, rare, but for that very reason unforgettable. Perhaps it was owing to his wife's culinary activities that in those idyllic moments Vadinho referred to her as "my little corn fritter, my fried bean cake, my fat little pullet," and these gastronomic metaphors gave a clear idea of a certain housewifely, sensual charm in Dona Flor hidden beneath a calm, easy-going nature. Vadinho knew her weaknesses, brought them out in the open: that banked-down desire of the timid person, that restraint which turned violent and positively unbounded when given free rein in bed. When Vadinho was in the mood, there was no one more charming, nor could any woman resist him. Dona Flor was never able to hold out against his fascination, not even when she had made up her mind to do so, boiling with indignation and recent affronts. Time and again she had even come to hate him and to curse the day when she had linked her fate to that wastrel.

But her anguish as she approached Vadinho, so unexpectedly cut down, left Dona Flor in a complete daze, empty of thought, recalling neither those moments of intense tenderness, nor, still less, those cruel days of suffering and loneliness, as though death had divested her husband of all his shortcomings, or as though he had not been guilty of them during his "brief journey through this vale of tears."

"Brief journey through this vale of tears" was the phrase of the respectable Professor Epaminondas Souza Pinto, touched and confused as he came forward to greet the widow, to express his condolence, even before she had reached her husband's body. Dona Gisa, a teacher, too, and also respectable up to a point, restrained the haste of her colleague and also her laughter. If it was true that the journey of Vadinho through this life had been brief—he had just rounded out thirty-one years—Dona Gisa knew very well that the world had not been a vale of tears for him, but rather a front seat for all the pranks, merrymaking, lies, and sins in sight. Some of them painful and troubling, undoubtedly, putting his heart to severe tests and trials: debts that had to be paid, notes that fell due, cosigners who had to be won over, obligations assumed, payments that could not be put off, complaints, threats of being hauled into court, banks, money-lenders, frowning faces, friends turning their backs on him, not to mention the physical and moral sufferings of Dona Flor. Because, thought Dona Gisa in her garbled Portuguese —she was vaguely North American, had become a Brazilian citizen, and felt herself a Brazilian, but that devilish language, she never could master it!—such tears as there had been during Vadinho's brief span of life had been shed by Dona Flor, and plenty of them, enough for both.

But in the face of his sudden death, Dona Gisa thought of Vadinho only with sadness and regret: he had been agreeable, in spite of everything, had had his pleasant, attractive side. Nevertheless, not because he was lying there, stretched out in the street in Dois de Julho Square, dead, masquerading as a Bahian woman, was she going to twist the truth, invent another Vadinho out of the whole cloth. She said so to Dona Norma, her neighbor and close friend, but did not receive the assent she had expected. Dona Norma had time and again told Vadinho just what she thought of him, had quarreled with him, preached him sermons that would have touched a heart of stone, one day even threatened him with the police. But at that sad and final hour, she did not want to comment on the outstanding and unpleasant facets of the late lamented; she wanted only to praise his good qualities, his innate good manners, his invariable sympathy, always quick to manifest itself, his loyalty to his friends, his unquestionable generosity (especially at somebody else's expense), his carefree and boundless *joie de vivre*. Moreover, she was so taken up with helping and looking after Dona Flor that she was not even listening to Dona Gisa's harsh truths. Dona Gisa was like that: the truth above everything else, at times to the point of making her seem unfeeling and callous. Possibly this was a defense mechanism of her own trusting nature, for she was credulous beyond belief and had faith in everybody. No, she was not recalling Vadinho's misdeeds to criticize him or blame him; she had liked him and they often had had long conversations together, Dona Gisa interested in acquainting her self with the psychology of the underworld in which Vadinho moved and had his being, he in telling her tall tales and peeping down the front of her dress at the curve of her full, freckled breasts. Possibly Dona Gisa understood him better than Dona Norma; but quite the opposite of her, she was not going to scant a single one of his defects, she was not going to lie just because he had died. Dona Gisa did not lie even to herself, unless there was no other way out. And that was clearly not the situation in this case.

Dona Flor made her way through the crowd in the wake of Dona Norma, who went clearing a path for her with her elbows and her great popularity: "Come, step aside, folks, let the poor thing get by . . ."

There lay Vadinho on the mosaic paving blocks, a smile on his lips, blond and fair, the image of peace and innocence. Dona Flor stood for a moment, looking at him as though she had trouble recognizing her husband, or perhaps, and this was more probable, in accepting the fact, now indisputable, of his death. But only for an instant. With a scream that came from the very depths of her being, she threw herself upon Vadinho, clasping his motionless body to her, kissing his hair, his rouged face, his open eyes, his jaunty mustache, his dead mouth, forever dead.

3

It was Carnival Sunday, and who did not have an automobile parade in which to participate that night, a celebration at which to amuse himself into the early hours of the morning? Nevertheless, and in spite of all this, Vadinho's wake was a success, an "outstanding event," as Dona Norma proudly pronounced and proclaimed.

The morgue attendants laid the corpse on the bed in the bedroom, and afterwards the neighbors carried it into the parlor. The employes of the mortuary were in a hurry, their work increased by the Carnival. While others were amusing themselves, they had their hands full with the dead, the victims of accidents and fights. They pulled off the dirty sheet in which the corpse was wrapped and handed the autopsy report to the widow.

Vadinho lay there as bare as he had come into the world, on the iron double bed with wrought headpiece and feet which Dona Flor had bought secondhand at a furniture auction six years before, at the time of their marriage. Dona Flor, alone in the room, opened the envelope and read over carefully the opinion of the doctors. She shook her head incredulously. Who would ever have said so? Seemingly so strong and healthy, still so young.

. Vadinho boasted that he had never been sick and that he could go eight days and eight nights without sleeping—gambling, drinking, carousing with women. And at times didn't he really spend a week without showing up at home, leaving Dona Flor beside herself, out of her mind? Nevertheless, there was the report of the doctors of the School of Medicine: a man whose days were numbered, his liver not working, his kidneys worn out, his heart useless. He could drop dead at any moment, as he had done, without warning. Rum, nights in the casinos, drunken sprees, running every which way to find money to gamble with had played hob with that handsome, strong body, leaving it nothing but its outward appearance. And that was a fact, for who, judging only by its looks, would have dreamed that it was totally burned out?

Dona Flor gazed down at her husband's body before calling in the helpful and impatient neighbors for the delicate task of dressing it. There he was, naked, as he loved to lie in bed, a golden down covering his arms and legs, a thick growth of golden hair on his chest, the scar of a knife wound on his left shoulder. So handsome, such a man, such an artist in bed. Once more the young widow's eyes filled up with tears. She tried not to think what she was thinking about; that was not fitting on the day of a wake.

But on seeing him thus, stretched out on the bed, completely naked, Dona Flor, try as she would, could not help remembering him when, taken by desire, he could not bear to have a stitch of clothing on their bodies, nor a modest sheet covering them. Decency was not Vadinho's strong point. When he called her to come to bed, saying: "Let's do a little balling, babe," love was for him a celebration of infinite joy and freedom, to which he gave himself with that enthusiasm he was known for, which went hand in hand with a competence recognized by a legion of women of various condition and station. During the early days of their marriage, Dona Flor had been utterly embarrassed, not knowing what to do, for he wanted her completely naked.

"Who ever heard of anyone screwing in a nightgown? Why do you hide yourself? Screwing is a blessed thing. It was invented by God in Paradise, didn't you know that?"

Not only did he undress her completely, but, as though that was not enough he touched and played with her body, the long curves and deep angles where light and shadow crossed in mysterious play. Dona Flor tried to cover herself up, Vadinho pulled off the sheet between laughs, revealing her firm breasts, her handsome backside, her belly almost hairless. He took her as though she were a toy, a toy or a closed rosebud which he brought into bloom each night of pleasure. Dona Flor began to lose her timidity, giving herself over to that lascivious union, growing in response, turning

into a heartsome, spirited lover. She never, however, completely
lost her modesty or shame; she had to be conquered anew each
time, for as soon as she came to herself after her boldness and her
sighs of satisfaction, she was once again the timid, modest wife. ·

At that moment, alone with the death of Vadinho, Dona Flor
took in, completely and with full awareness, her widowhood and
the fact that she would never have him again, never again lose her
senses in his embrace. For from the moment the tragic news spread
by word of mouth until the arrival of the mortuary van, the
cooking teacher had been experiencing a kind of nightmare not
without a certain excitement: the impact of the news, the tearful
walk to the Dois de Julho Square, the sight of the body, the crowd
surrounding her, caring for her, offering her solidarity and comfort, the return home almost carried by Dona Norma and Dona
Gisa, Professor Epaminondas and Méndez, the Spaniard who
owned the tavern. All that had been so quick and so confused that
it had not her time to give full though and realization to the death
of Vadinho.

The corpse was carried from the Square to the morgue, but not
even so did she have a moment of quiet. She had suddenly become
the center not only of her street, but of all the adjacent thoroughfares, and this on a Sunday of carnival. Until they brought him
back, wrapped in a sheet, the Bahian woman's dress he had been
masquerading in folded into a small, bright-colored bundle, Dona
Flor had been the object of a pilgrimage of neighbors, acquaintances, friends offering their condolences, giving proof of their
friendship and sympathy. Dona Norma and Dona Gisa had lost all
thought of their household duties, already somewhat neglected
because of the Carnival, with lunches and dinners left completely
to the judgment of harried housemaids. Neither of them left Dona
Flor's side, each outdoing the other in devotion and consolation.

Outside the Carnival went on with its masqueraders, its groups
and clubs of merrymakers, its rich or gay floats. The music of the
many orchestras, the chants, the bass drums, the groups, the clubs,
with their tambourines and kettledrums. From time to time Dona
Norma could not restrain herself from running to a window,
leaning out, taking a peep, exchanging a pleasantry with some

masquerader she recognized, giving the news of Vadinho's death, applauding some unusual float or pretty group. At times she called Dona Gisa if some particularly lively club appeared around the corner. And when, toward the end of the afternoon, that of the Sons of the Sea came into the street, with its unforgettable design and measurements, accompanied by a huge crowd dancing the samba, even Dona Flor, hardly able to hold back her tears, came over to the window and peeped out at the club the papers had talked so much about, the outstanding feature of the Carnival of Bahia. Just a peep, without showing herself, hidden behind Dona Gisa's broad shoulders. Dona Norma had forgotten about the dead man and the demands of the occasion, and was clapping enthusiastically.

This had gone on all day, ever since the news had arrived. Even Dona Nancy, a shy Argentinian new in the neighborhood, married to the owner of a ceramics factory, one Bernabó, who was not easy to know, came down from her fine house and her aloofness to offer her condolences and help to Dona Flor, showing herself to be an agreeable, well-bred person, who exchanged philosophical comments with Dona Gisa on the brevity and uncertainty of life.

As is apparent, Dona Flor had not had time to reflect upon her new state and the changes in her existence. Only when they brought Vadinho back from the morgue and left him naked on the bed where they had made love so many times, then and only then did she find herself face to face with the death of her husband and feel herself a widow. Never again would he tumble her in that iron bed, pulling off her dress, slip, and more intimate pieces of attire, throwing the sheet over the dressing table, and then storm her entire being, making her frenzied with pleasure.

Ah, never again, thought Dona Flor, and she felt a lump in her throat, a weakness in her legs, as she realized that all was over. She stood there, without words and without tears, benumbed, devoid of all the dramatic enactment that goes with death. Just she and the naked corpse, she and the definitive absence of Vadinho. She would never again have to wait for him well into the morning, or hide from him the fees paid by her pupils, or keep an eye on him where the prettiest of them were concerned, or tolerate his slaps when he had had too much to drink and was in a bad humor, or hear the disagreeable comments of the neighbors. Or roll in bed with him, giving herself completely over to his desire, divesting herself of clothes, sheet, and modesty for the rites of love, those unforgettable rites. The lump in her throat was choking her; the pain in her breast was like a dagger thrust.

"Flor, isn't it time to dress him," the voice of Dona Norma echoed urgently in the bedroom from the living-room. "It won't be long before visitors start coming . . ."

The widow opened the door, composed, silent now, without sobs or groans, cold and austere. All alone in the world. The neighbors came in to help. Mr. Vivaldo, of the Paradise in Flower funeral parlor, had come to deliver the cheap coffin in person—he had made a considerable reduction, having been a companion of Vadinho's at the roulette and baccarat tables where he had gambled away coffins and tombstones—and collaborated with efficiency and experience to make a presentable corpse of the wastrel. Dona Flor watched everything without a word or a tear. She was alone in the world.

4

Vadinho's body was laid in the coffin which was then carried into the living-room, where a platform had been improvised of chairs. Mr. Vivaldo brought flowers, a gift from the funeral parlor. Dona Gisa had placed a purple live-forever between Vadinho's crossed fingers. To Mr. Vivaldo it seemed a silly gesture: what they should have put between the dead man's fingers was a poker chip, and if instead of the music and laughter of the Carnival, the noise of the gaming tables were to be heard, the hoarse voice of the croupier, the rattle of the dice, the nervous exclamations of the players, it was more than likely that Vadinho would arise from the coffin, shake death off his shoulders, the way he shook off, in a gesture typical of him, the complications that snarled up his life, and go to place his bet on 17, his favorite number. What could he do with a purple live-forever? In a little while it would be wilted and faded; no banker would accept it.

Mr. Vivaldo did not waste any time; a devotee of the Carnival, he had only opened his funeral parlor that holiday Sunday to take care of a friend like Vadinho. If the dead man had been anyone else, he would have had to look after himself as best he could; he, Vivaldo, would not have sacrificed his Carnival fun.

Many were those whose Carnival plans were upset. There was a procession of visitors late into the night at the wake of that bohemian. Some had come because Vadinho was a descendant of a poor, wrong-side-of-the blanket branch of an important family, the Guimarães. One of his forebears had been a state senator, a political bigwig. An uncle of his, nicknamed Chimbo, had held the post of Assistant Police Commissioner for a few months. It was this uncle, one of the few Guimarães who recognized Vadinho as a legitimate relative, who had got him a job at City Hall: inspector of parks, a most menial employment, with a miserable stipend which did not cover one night's expenses at Tabaris. It is hardly necessary to comment on the total neglect of duties on the part of the young municipal employe: he never inspected a park of any sort, but appeared only to collect his monthly chicken feed. Or to attempt, without success, to get his head officer to sign a note for him, or to put the bite on his colleagues for twenty or fifty cruzeiros. Parks did not interest him—he had no time to waste on plants and flowers. All the parks in the city could disappear and he would never miss them. He was a night bird; his flower beds were the gambling tables, and his flowers, as Mr. Vivaldo had so rightly thought, chips and decks of cards.

Those who came because they were members of the Guimarães family could have been counted on the fingers of two hands, remote relatives and loath to linger. All the rest, that endless procession, came to take their leave of Vadinho, to have one last look at him, to smile at him in pleasant remembrance, to say good-bye to him. Because they had liked him, excused his follies, set store by his good qualities.

One of the first to arrive that night, in full dress, for afterwards he had to take his daughters, three young eye-fillers, to a dance at an important club, was Commander Celestino, a Portuguese by birth, a banker and exporter. He did not come for just a minute, like one fulfilling a disagreeable obligation. After embracing Dona Flor and offering her his services, he sat on in the living-room, recalling incidents connected with Vadinho. What was the reason for his regard for this insignificant City Hall employe, this frequenter of second-class cabarets, this gambler who had always been in debt?

Vadinho had the gift of gab, and how! On one occasion he had managed to get the prosperous Portuguese to sign a promissory note amounting to several contos. He did not forget to pay, for he never forgot the dates on which the various notes he had signed, scattered about banks and in the hands of loan sharks, fell due. He could not pay, which was another story. As a rule he never could pay, and he didn't; nevertheless every day the number of IOU's increased, the number of creditors grew. How did he manage to do this?

Celestino had never signed another note; he never let the same bee sting him twice. Nevertheless, he peeled off notes of a hundred, two hundred, even five hundred mil-reis when Vadinho showed up in despair, without a cent to bless himself with and certain that that was the day he was going to break the bank. There were others who had signed two and three times, as though Vadinho were the most reliable creditor or had the best financial rating. All of them were taken in by his cunning, his dramatic and convincing talk.

Even Zé Sampaio, the husband of Dona Norma, who had a shoe store in the lower part of the city, a person of few words, grumpy, who did not cultivate visits or close relations with his neighbors, the very opposite of his wife—even he was taken in on several occasions, and, nevertheless, this did not detract from his appreciation of Vadinho or his credit at the store.

Not even when he discovered an unbelievably shady trick. One morning Vadinho had bought on credit in his store several pairs of shoes, among the best and most expensive, and had immediately resold them, almost under the horrified eyes of Sampaio's employes, at a scandalously low price to a competitor who had just opened a store in the neighborhood. Cash in hand, for Vadinho had a strong hunch about a number that he wanted to play.

The merchant undoubtedly took into account, in spite of the trickery involved, certain extenuating features which explained and excused the misdemeanor.

A gay, carefree Vadinho told him that same afternoon that he had dreamed all night long about Dona Gisa turned into an ostrich, pursuing him over a boundless plain; he did not know exactly whether to have a toss with her in the green pastures—it was a female ostrich and there was a foxy gleam in her eyes—or to peck him to pieces, for she was pursuing him with her enormous beak open and menacing. He woke up in a cold sweat, shook off the dream, tried to go back to sleep thinking about something more pleasant, and there was the dogged teacher running after him again with lustful eye and threatening beak. Had Dona Gisa been in her usual bodily form, Vadinho would not have fled; he would have taken her on and would have tumbled that devil of a *gringa* there among the bushes, in spite of her accent and her vaunted knowledge of psychology. But seeing her covered with feathers, turned into a monstrous ostrich, he had no choice but a shameful retreat. The nightmare had come back four, five times, and in the morning, worn out with so much running and covered with sweat, Vadinho found himself with an absolutely certain hunch and without a penny. He ransacked the house, but Dona Flor was flat broke; he had cleaned her out the night before. He set out hoping to put the bite on some acquaintances, but the endeavor was completely fruitless. Vadinho of late had been taking too much advantage of his limited credit. It was then, as he passed the Casa Stela, the well-stocked shop of Zé Sampaio, that the luminous and amusing idea had come to him of devoting himself for a brief space of time to the honest job of selling shoes, his only way of coming quickly by a little change.

If he had not undertaken this commercial operation, outwardly dishonest and deplorable, though in fact shrewd and profitable, he would never have forgiven himself, for the number of the ostrich came up—Dona Gisa did not lie even in dreams—and Vadinho made a killing. Grateful and dignified, he went straight to Zé Sampaio's store, and in front of the amazed employes paid him for the merchandise he had bought that morning, laughing heartily at his wonderful foresight, and invited him to have a drink to celebrate. Zé Sampaio declined the invitation, but did not get mad at Vadinho, and went on seeing him and selling him shoes at a discount and on credit. Ten per cent off the bill, credit limited to one pair of shoes at a time, and only after the previous pair had been paid for.

Even more astounding proof of Vadinho's prestige was the fact that Zé Sampaio had put in an appearance at the wake. For only a few minutes, true, but it was the first one he had gone to in ten years. He had a horror of any and all social obligations, especially funeral ceremonies, wakes, cemeteries, rosaries, which made Dona Norma upbraid him when he refused to accompany her to one of her several weekly funerals: "You just wait and see, Sampaio, when you die there won't be anyone to act as pall-bearer . . . It's going to be a shame."

Zé Sampaio turned a glowering eye on her, made no answer, the thumb of his right hand between his teeth, in his habitual gesture of resignation at the continual commotion made by his wife.

The important people showed up, such as Celestino and Zé Sampaio, the relative Chimbo of the Guimarães family, the architect Chaves, Dr. Barreiros, an outstanding member of the bar, and the poet Godofredo Junior. Vadinho's colleagues in the government bureau, to all of whom he owed small amounts of money, appeared in a group. At their head, oratorical and solemn, the illustrious Director of Parks and Gardens, wearing a black suit. The neighbors came, the rich and poor, and middlingly well-off. And all who during those years in Bahia had frequented casinos, cabarets, the numbers banks, the gay brothels: Mirandão, Curvelo, Pé de Jegue, Waldomiro Lins and his younger brother Wilson, Anacreon, Cardoso Pereba, Arigof, Pierre Verger, with his bird's profile and his knowledge of Afro-Brazilian cults. Some, like Dr. Giovanni Guimarães, doctor and journalist, belonged to the two groups, relatives of the important and the insignificant, of the respectable and the irresponsible.

The important ones recalled Vadinho amid laughter, his picaresque adventures, his amusing sallies, his barefaced swindles, his muddles and confusions, and his good heart, his politeness, his droll antics. The neighbors, too, recalled him in similar fashion, a bohemian without schedule or responsibility. Both groups embroidered the truth, inventing details, ascribing to him incidents and episodes, with the result that the legend of Vadinho began to take on form there beside his corpse, almost at the hour of his death. The aforementioned Dr. Giovanni Guimarães invented tales out of whole cloth, added to those which had a basis of truth, even going so far as to make up lies based on precise dates and places:

"One day, four years ago, in the month of March, I met up with Vadinho at the House of the Three Dukes, playing number 17. He was wearing a rubber raincoat, without a stitch underneath, naked. He had left everything at the pawnshop, had borrowed on everything he owned, pants and coat, shirt and shorts, so he could play. Ramiro, that miserly Spaniard of Seventy Seven, wanted to take only the pants and coat as security; what in the devil was he to do with a shirt with frayed collar, an old pair of underpants, a worthless tie? But Vadinho foisted off on him even a pair of socks, keeping only his shoes. And with that honeyed tongue of his he managed to get Ramiro, that bloodsucker you all know, to lend him a rubber raincoat that was almost new, for he could not go out in the street naked to the House of the Three Dukes."

"And did he win?" asked young Artur avidly, the son of Mr. Sampaio and Dona Norma, a high-school student and an admirer of Vadinho, listening open-mouthed to the journalist's story.

Dr. Giovanni looked at the boy, waited a moment, and smiled broadly:

"Win? By morning he had lost the Spaniard's raincoat on number 17, and had to be taken home wrapped in a newspaper." The smile turned into a ringing laugh which was contagious. There was nobody like Dr. Giovanni to enliven a wake.

And as at that moment the peerless Robato came into the room, the journalist added the final proof, his words still steeped in laughter: "There is the person who will bear me out. Do you still recall, Robato, that night when Vadinho went home naked, wrapped in a newspaper?"

Robato was not one to vacillate; he ran his glance about the group gathered in a corner of the dining-room, fearful of indiscreet, female ears, and that the bereft widow might be mortified by such recollections. But vacillate he didn't; he never failed to pick up the gauntlet, he had a quick tongue, and he caught his cue instantly: "Naked, wrapped in a newspaper? Do I remember!" He coughed to clear his hoarse voice, and give wings to his imagination. "Why, the newspaper was mine. It was at the cathouse of Eunice the One-Toothed; besides us two and Vadinho, I remember Carlinhos Mascarenhas, Jenner, and Viriato Tanajura. We had been drinking all night, what a binge . . ."

This Robato was as habitual a night owl as Vadinho, but of another breed. Gambling did not attract him, nor did he flee from work; on the contrary, he was a jack of all trades, and had the reputation of being industrious and competent. He made dentures, he repaired radios and Victrolas, he took identification photographs, he was handy with any kind of machine, always eager to learn. His roulette wheel was poetry, well measured and well rhymed (beautiful rhymes), his casino, the bars and cabarets where he spent the night in the pleasant company of other litterateurs and light ladies who admired the muses and their cultivators, declaiming odes, hymns extolling freedom, lyrical and lascivious poems, love sonnets. All from his pen. He called himself the "world's king of sonneteers," he had beaten all known records, was the author to date of 20,865 sonnets, what with decasyllabic and Alexandrine, octosyllabic, sestina, and those reading the same from left to right as from right to left. An incipient baldness was threatening his dark poetic looks but without detracting from his warm charm.

He resumed his conversation and once more Vadinho crossed the room wrapped in newspapers. Young Artur would never forget him: wrapped in the pages of *A Tarde*, Vadinho, hero of a fascinating and forbidden world.

The stories followed one another while Dona Norma, Dona Gisa, the nubile young Regina, and other girls and women served coffee and cake, glasses of rum and of fruit liqueurs. The neighbors saw to it that nothing was lacking at the wake.

The important visitors, seated in the dining-room, in the corridor, at the door, recalled Vadinho amid anecdotes and laughter. The others, his gaming and vagabondage companions, recalled him in silence, serious and abashed, in the living-room, standing beside the corpse. As they came in, they stopped in front of Dona Flor, pressed her hand, embarrassed, as though they were responsible for Vadinho's shortcomings. Many of them did not even know her, had never seen her, but they had heard so much about her, how at times Vadinho took from her even the housekeeping money to gamble it at the Palace, in Tabaris, Abaixadinho, in the joints of Zezé Meningite, of Abilio Moqueca, on the countless illegal roulette wheels of the city, including that of the den of the Negro Paranaguá Ventura, where, on principle, only the banker could win.

A forbidding, frightening figure that of the Negro Paranaguá Ventura, with his innumerable entries on the police blotter, a list of accusations never completely proved, his reputation as a thief, rapist, and murderer. He had once been tried for murder and had been absolved, more because of the cowardice of the jury than for lack of proof. There was talk of other murders, not to mention the woman stabbed on the Hill of São Miguel in broad daylight, who had escaped death by a miracle. Paranaguá's joint was patronized only by professional sharpers who played with marked decks, pickpockets, purse-snatchers, swindlers, people with nothing more to lose. Well, Vadinho went even there, with his meager funds and his gay laughter, and possibly he was one of the few who could boast that he had occasionally won with the crooked dice used by Paranaguá. It was said that from time to time the Negro allowed one of the players for whom he had a weakness to win a pot.

Dona Flor's pupils came too, nearly all of them. Pupils and former pupils, as one in their desire to comfort their esteemed and competent teacher, so kind, the poor thing. Every three months a new class began in general cookery (in the morning) and in

specialized Bahian cookery (in the afternoon); they were trained
at the stove and the oven. And graduated with a diploma printed
and framed in a shop on Seventh Avenue—that was the idea of a
member of an older group to which Dona Oscarlinda had belonged, an outstanding nurse, on the staff of the Portuguese Hospital, slender and a busybody, meddlesome. She had demanded a
framed diploma, had stirred up her fellow students, had raised the
roof, had collected funds, had found a good designer, had raised
Cain. Under this pressure Dona Flor had yielded, even accepting
the designer, an acquaintance of Dona Oscarlinda, though not
without mentioning the name of her brother Hector, who had
designed the sign with the name of the school, when it was still on
Ladeira do Alvo, but who now unfortunately was living in Nazareth das Farinhas. In any case, it filled her with vanity to read on
the diploma and graduation certificate, in large printed letters:

COOKING SCHOOL OF SAVOR AND ART

and underneath, in flowery letters:

Director—Florípedes Paiva Guimarães

Vadinho, on the infrequent days when he woke up early and
stayed at home, hung around the students, meddling in the cookery
lessons, disturbing them. Gathered around the teacher, eager and
cute, they were copying down recipes, the exact amount of
shrimp, of dendê oil, of grated coconut, a pinch of black pepper,
learning how to deal with fish, how to handle meat, how to beat
eggs. Vadinho would interrupt with a wisecrack about the eggs,
with a double meaning, and the brazen things would laugh.

Brazen, nearly all of them. Lots of friendship and fawning on
Dona Flor, but with their eyes following the rascal. There he was
with his sly, conceited air, stretched out in a chair, or sitting on one
of the kitchen steps, not missing a trick, looking them over from
head to foot, running his eyes over their legs, their knees, the
visible parts of their thighs, their breasts. They affected embarrassment, lowered their eyes, but not he.

Dona Flor prepared the hors d'oeuvre and the cakes, cookies,
and desserts during the classes. Vadinho passed opinions, made

dirty jokes, sampled the dishes, moving about among the students, striking up conversations with the prettiest, laying a bold hand on such as seemed willing to allow it.

It made Dona Flor nervous, upset her to the point where she made a mistake in the amount of melted butter for a tricky corn-meal cake. She begged God that Vadinho should go into the street for his usual knavery, his vice of gambling, but to let the students alone.

Now at the wake they surrounded Dona Flor and comforted her, but one of them, that little Ieda, with her face of a sly cat, could hardly keep her tears back and did not take her eyes off the dead man. Dona Flor quickly noticed this exaggeration of emotion, and felt a misgiving. Had there been something between them? She had never noticed anything suspicious, but who could guarantee that the two had not met outside the school, had not wound up in some brothel. Vadinho, ever since the episode with that hussy of a Noemia, had apparently stopped hanging around the students. But he was a wily one; he could very well have waited for that bitch on the corner, struck up a conversation with her, and where was there the woman who could resist Vadinho's gift of gab? Dona Flor's eyes followed Ieda's, and she noticed the girl's quivering lip. There was no doubt in her mind; ah, that good-for-nothing Vadinho . . .

Of all the sorrows her husband had occasioned her, there was none comparable to that of Noemia, a demi-rep of good family, and engaged in the bargain. But Dona Flor did not want to recall that humiliating incident on the night of the wake as she was looking for the last time on Vadinho's face. All that was over, far in the past. The slut had got married, she had gone off with her fiancé, some so-and-so with journalistic ambitions, so young and already with a set of horns, Alberto by name. Besides marriage had turned the hussy ugly overnight; she had become an outright whore.

When on that occasion everything had come out well almost by a miracle, Vadinho had said to her in the warmth of bed and reconciliation: "The only woman I really love and for good is you. The others are just haybags to while away the time." There at the wake, surrounded by so many people and so much affection, Dona Flor did not want to recall that forgotten episode or watch the gestures and looks of little Ieda with her barely restrained weeping, her secret brimming over in tears. With Vadinho dead, nothing mattered. Why investigate, try to find out, accuse him and hurt herself? He had died, he had paid for everything, and with interest, for he was so young. Dona Flor felt at peace with her husband, had no accounts to settle with him.

She bowed her head, and stopped observing the girl's movements. All she saw, as she lowered her eyes, was Vadinho running his hand over her body in the iron bed, whispering in her ear: "Nothing but haybags to pass the time. The only one I truly love is you, Flor, my sweet basil Flor, nobody else." What the devil was a haybag, Dona Flor suddenly wondered. What a pity she had never asked him, but it couldn't be anything good. She smiled. All the others haybags, the only one he really loved was she, Flor, a flower in Vadinho's hand from which he stripped the petals.

5

The next day, at ten in the morning, the funeral procession set out with a huge cortege. No samba group or club of celebrants on that Carnival Monday could compare in size and animation with Vadinho's funeral. Not by a long shot.

"Look . . . at least look out of the window," said Dona Norma to Zé Sampaio, having given up hope of dragging him to the cemetery. "Look and see what the funeral is like of a man who knew how to make friends, not a wild animal, like you . . . He was a rascal, a gambler, a good-for-nothing, worthless, and yet look.

And mind you, on a Carnival day. When you die, Mr. Sampaio, there won't be a single pall-bearer . . ."

Zé Sampaio neither answered nor looked out of the window. In bed, in a pair of old pajamas, with yesterday's papers, he merely gave a faint sigh and put his thumb between his teeth. He was a hypochondriac. He had a terrible fear of death, of visits to hospitals, of wakes and funerals; at that moment he felt that he was on the point of a heart attack. He had been like that since the night before, when his wife had informed him that Vadinho's heart had given out suddenly, without warning. He had spent a terrible night, waiting for a coronary explosion, turning this way and that in bed, his hand clasping his left breast.

Dona Norma, covering her pretty chestnut hair with a black scarf, as befitted the occasion, added heartlessly:

"Me, if there are not at least five hundred people at my funeral, I will consider my life a failure. At least five hundred . . ."

From this point of view Vadinho could consider himself completely triumphant and fulfilled. Half of Bahia was at his funeral and even the Negro Paranaguá Ventura had left his gambling den and was there, his white suit gleaming with starch, wearing a black tie and armband on his left sleeve, with a bunch of red roses. He made ready to take one of the handles of the coffin, and as he expressed his condolences to Dona Flor he summed up the feelings of all in the briefest and most beautiful funeral oration for Vadinho:

"One swell guy!"

INTERLUDE

BRIEF REPORT (APPARENTLY UNCALLED FOR)
OF THE CONTROVERSY THAT SPRANG UP CONCERNING THE
AUTHORSHIP OF THE ANONYMOUS POEM THAT CIRCULATED FROM
TAVERN TO TAVERN, IN WHICH THE POET LAMENTED THE
DEATH OF VADINHO, WITH THE TRUE IDENTITY OF THE
UNKNOWN BARD, FINALLY REVEALED ON THE BASIS
OF CONCRETE PROOFS

(Declaimed by the one and only Robato, Jr.)

No, certainly not, with the passing of time it did not become transformed into an indecipherable mystery of literature, into another obscure enigma of world culture, which centuries later would challenge universities and scholars, researchers and bibliographers, and turn into a subject of investigation, exchanges, theses engaging the activities of fellows, institutes, professors, historians, and all kinds of academic bums out for an easy and pleasant life. It would not become another Shakespeare problem, it would not go beyond the doubt, as insignificant as the event which gave it its theme and inspiration was slight: Vadinho's death.

In the literary circles of Salvador da Bahia, however, the question arose and a polemic sprang into being: which of the poets of the city had composed—and put into circulation—the ELEGY TO THE FINAL DEATH OF WALDOMIRO DOS SANTOS GUIMARÃES, VADINHO TO WHORES AND FRIENDS? The discussion grew, and it was not long before it acquired bitter overtones, became the motive of enmities, retaliations, epigrams, and even a cuff or two. The arguments and animosities, doubts and certainties, affirmations and denials, quarrels and blows were limited to the tables of bars, over cold beers, where the unappreciated young literati foregathered late into the night (demolishing and razing all literature and all art prior to the fortunate emergence of this new and definitive generation) and the stubborn subliterati, hard-headed, resisting all innovations, with their plays on words, their epigrams, their rolling phrases; defying one another—the beardless geniuses and the belletrists in need of a shave—with the same violent determination to read their latest productions in prose and verse, each and every one of them designed to revolutionize Brazilian literature, God willing.

Nor was this limited to the confines of the state of Bahia (the state and not merely the capital, for the debate aroused echoes throughout the cacao-growing area). In the *Annals* of the Academy of Letters of Ilhéus indisputable references can be found to a meeting devoted to a study of the problem; or, hampered by not finding space in reviews and magazines, dissipating itself in oral discussions, not because of all this does this strange and at times bitter debate lack interest and fail to deserve attention in the account of Dona Flor and her two husbands, in which Vadinho is an outstanding character—as a matter of fact, plays the role of hero.

Hero? Or would he be the villain, the scoundrel responsible for the sufferings of the heroine, in this case Dona Flor, the devoted and faithful spouse? This is another problem, having nothing to do with the literary question that was worrying poets and prose writers; perhaps it is even more difficult and serious, and it will be up to you, the reader, to decide the answer, if patience and determination lead you to the end of these modest pages.

Of the elegy there was not the slightest doubt that Vadinho was the indisputable hero. "Never was there another so close to the stars, the dice, and the whores, a buffoon of genius" blethered the verses, in praise beyond words. And if the poem—like the discussion—did not find room in the literary section of the newspapers, it was not for lack of merit. One Odorico Tavares, a nationwide poet soaring far above the so-called state poets—all of them eating out of his hand, fawning on him, for the despot controlled two newspapers and a radio station—when he read a typewritten copy of the elegy, lamented: "What a pity not to be able to publish it . . ."

"If it were not anonymous," remarked another poet, Carlos Eduardo.

This Carlos Eduardo, making capital of his looks, something of an authority in antiques, was an associate of Tavares in a somewhat shady venture having to do with old statues of saints. The most frustrated subliterati and the most vehement of the youthful geniuses, those without any hope of ever seeing their names in the Sunday supplement of Odorico, accused him and Carlos Eduardo of being fences for old images stolen from the churches by a group of specialized thieves headed by a person of questionable reputation, a fellow by the name of Mário Cravo who, incidentally, had been a friend and boon companion of Vadinho's. Gaunt and heavy-mustached, the much-discussed Cravo spent his time monkeying with old automobile parts, sheets of iron, broken-down machines, twisting and patching up all that mess, attributing artistic worth to the results, to the applause of the two poets and other cognoscenti, unanimous in calling that old iron modern sculpture and in terming the blackguard an innovator in the field of abstract art. There you have another problem the discussion of which has no place in these pages, that is to say, the real value of Master Cravo's art. We are not going to analyze it here. We shall merely state for the record the fact that the critics have since acclaimed his work, which has even become the object of study by self-serving foreign journalists. In those days, however, he was not considered an artist; he was only beginning, and if he had achieved a certain notoriety, it was due mainly to his dubious activities in sacristies and altars.

Vadinho himself, so it was said, had on an occasion of total penury taken part in a stealthy nocturnal pilgrimage to the old Church of the Recôncavo, a pilgrimage organized by the heretic Mário Cravo. The sack of the church gave rise to much talk, for one of the pieces that had been filched was a St. Benedict, attributed to Fray Agostinho da Piedade, and the friars raised a great hue and cry. Today the image is to be found in a museum in the south, if the viper-tongued subliterati are to be believed, thanks to the efforts of those two—at the time—lean associates of the lyric muse and devout enterprises.

That morning, before lunch, talking in the editorial room about saints and paintings, Carlos Eduardo pulled out of his pocket a copy of the elegy and gave it to the poet Odorico to read.

Grieved at not being able to publish it—"not because it is

anonymous, we could use any non-de-plume"—but because of the
dirty words, Tavares repeated: "It is a pity," and reread aloud
another verse:

The gamblers and the Negresses of Bahia are black with mourning.

Then he asked his friend: "You found out who the author was,
didn't you?"

"You think it was him? Nevertheless, it seems to me . . ."

"It leaps to the eye . . . Listen: 'A moment of silence at all the
roulette wheels, flags at half mast in the whorehouses, asses in
despair, sobbing.' "

"It could be . . ."

"Not it could be. It is, beyond doubt." He laughed: "The old
whorehound . . ."

This certainty was not felt in the literary circles. The elegy was
attributed to various poets, well-known bards or young laurel-
seekers. They felt it might be from the pen of Sosígenes Costa,
Carvalho Junior, Alves Ribeiro, Hélio Simões, Eurico Alves. There
were many who thought Robato was most probably the author.
Wasn't he the one who declaimed it with wild enthusiasm, his
sonorous voice rich in modulations?

With him dawn departed mounted on the moon.

It did not enter their minds that Robato would recite the verses
of another, something highly uncommon in those circles. They
had forgotten the generous nature of the sonneteer, his capacity
for appreciating and applauding the work of others.

The date of the beginning of the success of the elegy and the
polemic to which it gave rise could be set as that gay night in
Carla's cathouse—"Fat Carla," a competent practitioner of her
profession imported from Italy, whose culture exceeded the
bounds of her métier (at which she excelled, according to Nestor
Duarte, a distinguished citizen of outstanding intelligence who had
traveled, a connoisseur), a reader of D'Annunzio, crazy about
poetry. "As romantic as a cow" was how the mustached Cravo,
who had been intimate with her for a while, described her. Carla
could not live without a dramatic passion, and she drifted from

one bohemian to the other, sighing and moaning, consumed by jealousy, with her enormous blue eyes, her breasts of a prima donna, her immense thighs. Vadinho, too, had enjoyed her graces and a little lagniappe, even though she preferred the poets. She herself versified in the "beautiful language of Dante with great originality and inspiration," Robato remarked flatteringly.

Every Thursday evening, Carla held a kind of literary salon in her ample parlors. Poets and artists put in an appearance, bohemians, certain outstanding personages, such as Judge Airosa, and the girls of the brothel were quick to applaud the verses and laugh at the jokes. Drinks and refreshments were served.

Carla presided over the soirée, reclining on a divan covered with pillows and cushions, wearing a Greek tunic or junk jewelry, a Greek from a fashion magazine or an Egyptian from Hollywood, just stepped out of an opera. The poets recited, exchanged phrases full of *esprit*, epigrams, plays on words, the judge uttered an axiom he had spent a hard week's work preparing. The culminating moment of the gathering was when the madam of the house, the massive Carla, arose from among the cushions, that ton of white flesh covered with false jewels, and in a reedy voice, so out of keeping in a woman of her dimensions, declaimed in syrupy Italian verses her love for her latest fancy. While this was going on, the artist Cravo and other gross materialists took advantage of the semi-darkness which reigned in the room—the lights turned low, the better to hear and feel the poetry—and without respecting these lofty sentiments, pawed the girls shamelessly, trying to obtain their favors for free, rooking the cathouse of its profits, real scoundrels.

The soirées always concluded with the decline of poetry and the upsurge of dirty stories toward the end of the night. It was then that Vadinho, Giovanni, Mirandão, Carlinhos Mascarenhas, and, above all, Lev, an architect who was just beginning his career, the son of immigrants, as tall as a giraffe, and the master of an inexhaustible repertoire, a good story-teller, came into their own. He had some unpronounceable Russian name, and the girls had nicknamed him Lev the Silver-Tongued, perhaps because of his fund of stories. Perhaps.

At one of these "elegant meetings of sensibility and wit" Robato declaimed in a quavering voice the elegy on the death of Vadinho, introducing it with a few moving words about the late departed, the friend of all those who frequented that "delicious den of love and poetry." He remarked in passing that the author had "preferred the mists of anonymity to the sun of publicity and glory." He, Robato, had received a copy of the poem from the hands of an officer of the Military Police, Captain Crisostomo, who had also been a bosom friend of Vadinho. The officer, however, had not been able to give him precise information concerning the poet's identity.

Many attributed the verses to Robato himself, but in the face of his stubborn refusal to acknowledge them, their choice fell on any poet who turned a verse in the city, especially those of noctambulous and bohemian reputation. There were those, however, who never believed Robato's denials, attributing them to modesty, and continued ascribing the elegy to him. Even today there are those who think that the verses were his work.

The argument grew so heated that on one occasion it overstepped the bounds of literature and good breeding and turned into a fistfight when the poet Clóvis Amorim, with a snake's tongue reeling epigrams out of a mouth perpetually chewing on a stinking cigar from the Model Market, denied that the bard Hermes Clímaco could possibly be the author of the disputed verses, inasmuch as he lacked the gift and grammar required.

"Clímaco's? Don't talk nonsense . . . Putting everything he has into it, he might turn out a seven-syllable stanza. A cruddy poet . . ."

As luck would have it, the poet Clímaco appeared in the door of the bar in his eternal black suit, his waterproof cape, and umbrella, which were also eternal. He lifted the umbrella in a fury:

"Cruddy is the whore who bore you . . ."

They came to blows, amid insults and fisticuffs, with all the advantage on Amorim's part, the better versifier and athlete.

Strange, too, and worth narrating was what happened with a certain individual who had written two booklets of verse, on whom some of the less knowing conferred the authorship of the poem. First he emphatically denied it. Then, as they kept on, his denials grew weaker, and finally he reacted in so confused and timid a fashion that his denial seemed a diffident affirmation.

"It's his, there's no doubt about it," they said, as they watched him rub his hands together, lowering his eyes, and smile as he murmured:

"It's true that they resemble my verses. But they're not . . ."

He invariably denied them, but, at the same time, he would never allow the disputed verses to be attributed to another. If anyone did this, he made every effort to prove the impossibility of such a hypothesis. And if anyone was hard-headed enough to persist in the argument, he would grumble firmly and mysteriously:

"So you're trying to tell me? As though I did not have my reasons to know . . ."

And when he heard the elegy recited, he listened with the closest attention, correcting any change in the words, as jealous of the poem as though it were his own. Only later on, when the name of the real author came to light, did he divest himself of his unearned glory. He then immediately began to anathematize the poem, denying it the slightest value or beauty—"poetry of bawdy-house and dungheap."

Notwithstanding all this discussion, the elegy made its way, read and memorized, recited around the tables of bars in the morning hours when rum releases the noblest emotions. The declaimers changed adjectives and verbs, at times mixed up or left out stanzas. But true to the original or garbled, dripping with rum, dragging itself over the floor of cabarets, Vadinho's elegy went singing his praises.

Whoever had composed it reflected a general feeling in that underworld where Vadinho had had his being since boyhood, and of which he had become a kind of symbol. The elegy was the apogee of praise bestowed upon the youthful gambler. If he had been privileged to hear all that adulation and regret, Vadinho would not have believed it. During his lifetime he had never been

the object of encomia and eulogies; quite the contrary. His ears
had always buzzed with reproach and advice, sermons having to do
with the errant life he led and his low tastes.

However, this indulgence toward his rascality, this public exhibition of his supposed virtues, transforming him into the hero of
the poem and an almost legendary figure, was short-lived. A week
after his death things were already slipping back into their places.
The opinion of the conservative classes, the custodians of morality
and decency, began to express itself through the women of the
neighborhood who had known him, endeavoring to superimpose
itself on the anarchic and dissolute panegyric created by the subversive scum of bawdyhouses and casinos, in a criminal attempt to
undermine time-honored laws and the regime.

And thus another and impassioned problem arose, as though
that created by the composition of the verses were not enough. In
connection with the latter, proof was promised of the true identity
of the author, finally revealed and forever inscribed in the golden
book of national letters.

When, years after the death of Vadinho, the poet Odorico
received his copy of "Impure Elegies"—one of the three given as
gifts by the poet—a magnificent deluxe edition, of which only one
hundred copies were printed, autographed, illustrated with wood-
cuts by Calazans Neto, he turned to Carlos Eduardo, holding out
the precious book.

The two friends were seated in the same editorial office in
which, on a day long past, they had read and discussed the elegy
together. The difference was that now they were fat and respectable and rich, very rich, owners of an art collection and real estate.

Odorico recalled: "Didn't I tell you at the time? It was by
him." And he finished with the same smile and the same phrase as
the other time: "The old whorehound . . ."

Carlos Eduardo, too, gave his cordial laugh, the laugh of a man
who had achieved his goal and was at peace with himself, and
admired the handsome edition. On the cover, in wood-cut letters
the name of the poet: Godofredo Junior. Slowly he turned the
pages, asking himself (with a certain envy): "What hidden streets
and slopes, what darkling twilight paths, what fragrant grottoes

had the beloved and illustrious poet and the poor wastrel discovered together, to the point of bringing into flower between them the rare bloom of friendship?" Slowly, as he turned these enigmas over in his mind, Carlos Eduardo touched the paper as though he were stroking the soft skin of a woman, black, perhaps, velvety like the night. The fourth elegy of the five which made up the volume was the one dedicated to the death of Vadinho, "the blue chip forgotten on the gaming table."

In this way a problem was solved, as had been promised. Another, however, raises its head, demanding a solution which it may not be possible to find. It is left to your discernment, this mystery of Vadinho.

Who was Vadinho? What was his true nature? Which his real dimensions? Was his face lighted up by the sun or shadowed by darkness? Who was he, the gay comrade of the elegy, the "some guy" of Paranaguá Ventura's remark, or the contemptible scoundrel, the incorrigible deadbeat, the bad husband, according to the neighbor women, the friends of Dona Flor? Who knew him and could define him better: the pious frequenters of the early morning mass at the Church of St. Theresa or the incorrigible habitués of Tabaris, "the ball spinning in the roulette wheel, the cards and dice, the last port of call"?

II

OF HER EARLY WIDOW-
HOOD, A PERIOD OF TRIAL,
OF DEEP MOURNING

WITH THE MEMORIES OF HOPES AND DISAPPOINTMENTS,
OF COURTSHIP AND MARRIAGE, OF THE WEDDED LIFE
OF VADINHO AND DONA FLOR, WITH CHIPS AND DICE
AND THE SAD, NOW HOPELESS WAIT (AND THE
ANNOYING PRESENCE OF DONA ROZILDA)

*(With Edgard Cocô at the violin, Caymmi at the guitar,
and Dr. Walter da Silveira with his magic flute)*

COOKING SCHOOL
OF SAVOR AND ART

DONA FLOR'S RECIPE FOR MARINATED CRAB

INGREDIENTS *(for 8 servings)*

- 1 cup of coconut milk, without water
- 1 cup of dendê oil
- 2 pounds of tender crabs

SAUCE

- 3 cloves of garlic
- salt to taste
- juice of one lemon
- a pinch of coriander
- a sprig of parsley
- a shallot
- 2 onions
- ½ cup of olive oil
- a red pepper
- 1 pound of tomatoes

GARNISH

- 4 tomatoes
- 1 onion
- 1 red pepper

PROCEDURE

Grate two onions, crush garlic in mortar;
Onion and garlic do not smell badly, ladies,
They are fruits of the earth, perfumed.
Mince the coriander, the parsley, several tomatoes,
The shallot and half the pepper.
Mix all with the olive oil
And set aside this sauce
Of aromatic flavor.

(Those silly women who dislike the smell of onion,
What do they know about pure smells?
Vadinho liked to eat raw onion
And his kisses were like fire.)
Wash the crabs whole in lemon juice,
Wash them well, and then a little more,
To get out all the sand without taking away the taste of the sea.
Then season them, dipping them, one by one,
In the sauce, and put them in the skillet,
Each separate, with its seasoning.
Spread the remaining sauce over them
Slowly, for this is a delicate dish!
(Alas, it was Vadinho's favorite dish!)
Select four tomatoes, one pepper, one onion,
And slice them over the crabs
As a garnish.
Let them stand at room temperature for two hours
To absorb the flavor. Then put the skillet on the stove.
(He went to buy the crabs himself,
He was an old customer at the Market . . .)

When almost done, and only then,
Add the coconut milk, and at the very end
The dendê oil, just before removing from the stove.
(He used to go and taste the seasoning every minute,
Nobody had a more delicate palate.)

There you have that exquisite dish, of the finest cuisine,
Whoever can make it can rightfully boast
Of being a first-rate cook.
But, lacking the skill, it is better not to try it,
For everyone was not born a kitchen artist.
(It was Vadinho's favorite dish,
I will never again serve it at my table.
His teeth bit into the crab,
His lips were yellow with the dendê oil,
Alas, never again his lips,
His tongue, never again
His mouth burning with raw onion!)

1

At the mass of the seventh day after Vadinho's death, at which Dom Clemente Nigra officiated in the Church of St. Theresa, the beautiful nave enveloped in the bluish, transparent light coming from the sea across from it, as though the church were a boat on the point of weighing anchor, the sympathy and the solidarity manifested in whispered comments were addressed to Dona Flor, kneeling in the first row before the altar, all in black—wearing a black lace mantilla lent her by Dona Norma, which hid her hair and her tears—a rosary between her fingers. The whispers did not express pity because she had lost her husband, but rather because she had had him. Bent low, Dona Flor heard nothing, as though there were nobody else in the shrine, only she, the priest, and the absence of Vadinho.

A murmur of the professionally devout, of old church mice, of spiteful enemies of fun and laughter, arose with the incense in a sour susurration:

"He wasn't worth a ha'penny's prayer, the renegade."

"If she wasn't a saint, instead of a mass she'd be having a party. With a dance and everything . . ."

"For her it was a release from slavery."

At the altar, Dom Clemente, gaunt with nights spent over ancient texts, saying a mass for the soul of Vadinho, felt in the magic atmosphere of the dawning morn a certain disquiet, a maleficent emanation, as though some devil, Lucifer or Exu, more probably Exu, were loose in the nave. Why did they not leave Vadinho

in peace, allow him to rest? Dom Clemente had known him well;
Vadinho had liked to come and chat in the patio of the monastery,
sitting on the wall, telling stories not always entirely in keeping
with those venerable stones, but to which the friar listened with
attention, curious and interested as he was in every human experience.

In the corridor, between the nave and the sacristy, there was a
kind of altar, and on it an angel carved in wood, some anonymous
and popular carving perhaps of the seventeenth century, and it was
as though the artist had chosen Vadinho as his model; the same
innocent and shameless face, the same insolence, the identical tenderness. He was kneeling before a later and more baroque image of
St. Clare, and toward her he stretched his hands. On one occasion
Dom Clemente had taken Vadinho to see the altar and the angel.
He was curious to see if the bohemian would notice the similarity.
Vadinho had burst into a laugh as soon as he saw the two images.

"Why are you laughing like that?" asked the friar.

"God forgive me, Father . . . But doesn't it look as though the
angel was trying to make the saint?"

"What's that? What kind of language is that, Vadinho?"

"Excuse me, Dom Clemente, but that angel has the face of an
out-and-out gigolo . . . He doesn't even look like an angel. Take a
look at his eye . . . The eye of a chaser . . ."

Turning from the altar to pronounce the blessing, his hands on
high, the priest saw the old women whispering among themselves:
that was where the disturbance was coming from, the malefic
atmosphere, oh, mouths of slime and evil, oh, rotting and sour
virginities, mean and envious old maids, and at the head of them,
Dona Rozilda. "May God in His infinite mercy forgive them!"

"How the poor thing suffered at his hands. She ate bread
kneaded by the devil."

"Because she wanted to. Not because I didn't tell her what I
thought . . . If she had not been so crazy about him, she would
have listened to me. I did all that was in my power . . ."

It was Dona Rozilda who was holding forth in these terms,
Dona Flor's mother, born to be a stepmother, devotedly doing all
she could to fulfill her vocation.

"But she had ants in her pants about him, she couldn't live without him, God help me, she wouldn't listen to me, she rebelled. And she found those who encouraged her, a house in which to take refuge . . ."

As she said this she looked out of the corner of her eye at her sister Dona Lita, who was kneeling in prayer. And she wound up:

"To have a mass said for that vagrant is like throwing money into the street, it just goes to fill the friar's belly."

Dom Clemente took up the thurible and swirled incense against the foul breath of the devil coming from the mouths of the devout. He descended from the altar, stopped beside Dona Flor, laid his hand affectionately on her shoulder, and said so the sinister chorus of venemous old hags would hear him:

"Even the wayward angels are seated at the side of God in His glory."

"Angel! Get thee behind me, Satan . . . He was a devil from hell," growled Dona Rozilda.

Dom Clemente, his shoulders somewhat stooped, crossed the nave, on his way to the sacristy. In the corridor he stopped to look at that strange image in which the unknown artist had combined grace and cynicism at one and the same time. What feelings had moved him to do this, what was the message he was trying to convey? Possessed of human passions, the angel was devouring the poor saint with lecherous eyes. The eyes of a chaser, as Vadinho had said in his picturesque language, with his indecent smile, his brazen face, without a trace of respect. Just like Vadinho; he had never seen such a resemblance. Hadn't he perhaps gone a little too far in his hasty affirmation about Vadinho being at the side of God in His glory?

He went over to the window cut in the stone, looked out on the patio of the monastery. There was where Vadinho used to sit on the wall, at his feet the sea dotted with fishing skiffs. Vadinho had said to him:

"Father, if God wanted to really show His power, He would make number 17 come up a dozen times running. That would be a real miracle. Boy, would I fill this church with flowers . . ."

"God doesn't get mixed up in gambling, my son . . ."

"In that case, Father, He doesn't know what is good and what is bad. That agony of seeing the ball whirling, whirling in the roulette wheel, people betting their last counter, their hearts thudding fit to burst . . ."

And in a confidential tone, like a secret between only him and the priest: "How is it possible for God not to know, Father?"

In the atrium Dona Rozilda raised her voice: "Money thrown into the street . . . All the masses in the world would not save that wretch. God is just!"

Dona Flor, the mantilla covering her suffering face, appeared in the background, resting on Dona Gisa and Dona Norma. In the blue clarity of the morning the church was like a ship of rock about to weigh anchor.

2

It was not until Shrove Tuesday of Carnival, at night, that the news of Vadinho's death reached Nazareth das Farinhas, where Dona Rozilda lived with her married son, who worked for the railroad, and embittered the life of her daughter-in-law, a slave to her bossiness. Without losing time, she betook herself to Bahia on Ash Wednesday, a day to which she had a marked resemblance, according to another son-in-law of hers, Antonio Morais: "That's not a woman, she's an Ash Wednesday, who kills happiness in anyone." The desire to put all possible distance between his house and that of his mother-in-law was undoubtedly one of the reasons why Morais had been living for several years in a suburb of Rio de Janeiro. A skilled mechanic, he had accepted the suggestion of a friend and gone to try his fortune in the south, where he had

prospered. He refused to return to Bahia even on a holiday as long
as "that virago poisons the atmosphere."

Dona Rozilda, however, did not detest Antonio Morais, just as
she did not detest her daughter-in-law. The one she detested was
Vadinho, and she would never forgive Flor for marrying him,
flouting her authority and her warnings. In the case of Morais and
Rosalia, her older daughter, though the marriage did not exactly
please her, neither did she put obstacles in the way of the courtship
nor oppose the engagement. She did not get along either with him
or with his wife, because it was Dona Rozilda's nature to make life
a hell for those around her. When she was not tormenting someone, she felt empty and frustrated.

With Vadinho things were different. She had taken an aversion
to him when he had started courting Flor and she had discovered
the web of tricks and blandishments in which the undesirable
aspirant had entangled her. She conceived such a hatred for him
that she could not even bear to hear his name. "If the police in this
country were worth their salt, that devil would be in jail," was her
answer if anyone asked about her son-in-law, made any reference
to him, or sent him regards.

On the rare occasions when she visited Dona Flor, it was to
ruin her day, talking about nothing but the swindles of Vadinho,
his licentious life, his shameless behavior, a daily and unending
scandal.

Even from the railing of the ship she began shouting her
acrimonious comments to Dona Norma, who was waiting on the
dock of the Bahian Line, at Dona Flor's request.

"So that scapegrace finally kicked the bucket!"

The ship was tying up, full of an impatient load of passengers
laden with packages, baskets, bags, every imaginable parcel containing fruit, manioc meal, yams and cassava, salt meat, chayote,
and squash. Dona Rozilda came ashore vociferating: "The devil
carried him off; he should have dropped dead long ago."

Dona Norma felt defeated. It was typical of Dona Rozilda to
leave her helpless, utterly discouraged. The obliging neighbor had
been at the dock since before dawn, her kindly face radiating

sympathy, all prepared to console a mother-in-law in mourning and tears, to take her part in a duet lamenting the precariousness of the things of this world: today one is alive and full of hope, tomorrow stretched out in a coffin. She would listen to the lamentations of Dona Rozilda, serve her up the palliative of accepting the will of God—He knew what He was doing. They, the mother and the close friend, would discuss Dona Flor's new state, a widow, alone in the world, and still so young. Dona Norma had come prepared for all this: gestures, words, attitudes, all sincere and heartfelt, for there was never a trace of putting on an act in anything she did or said. Dona Norma felt herself somewhat responsible for everybody; she was the guardian angel of the neighborhood, a kind of first-aid station. From the whole vicinity they came to the door of her house, the best in the street—only that of the Argentines, the Bernabós, perhaps a little more luxurious, could be compared to it—to borrow salt, or pepper, or china for lunches or dinners, and articles of dress for parties: "Dona Norma, Mamma sent me to ask if you could lend her a cup of white flour for a cake she is baking. Later she will pay you back . . ."

This was Aninha, the youngest daughter of Dr. Ives, a close neighbor whose wife, Dona Emina, sang Syrian songs, accompanying herself on the piano.

"But, child, didn't your mother go to the market yesterday? Lord, she'd forget her head if it wasn't fastened on. Will a cup be enough? Tell her if she needs more to send for it."

Or it was the boy who worked for Dona Amelia asking in his shrill voice: "Dona Norma, the mistress would like to borrow Mr. Sampaio's black bowtie, for the moths ate up Mr. Ruas's . . ."

Or else it was Dona Risolta who entered dramatically, with her ascetic air: "Oh, Norma, come quickly, in God's name . . ."

"Whatever has happened now?"

"There's a drunk at the door of the house, and there's no way of getting him to leave. What shall I do?"

Off with her went Dona Norma, smiling as she recognized the cause of the problem: "Well, if it isn't my friend Bastião Cachaça.

Come away, Bastião, get out of there and come and have a snooze in our garage . . ."

And so it went all day long, notes asking for money, an urgent call to help someone having a fit, to look after a sick person and those wanting injections—Dona Norma carried on a competition which earned her nothing with doctors and drugstores, not to mention veterinarians, for all the mother cats in the neighborhood came to have their kittens in the rear of her house, where they never lacked for help and food. She distributed samples of medicines—provided by Dr. Ives—, she cut dresses and patterns, being a graduate of an academy of sewing and design, she wrote letters for the maids, gave advice, listened to lamentations, helped out matrimonial plans, arranged courtships, settled the most diverse problems, always in a state of great excitement, which led Zé Sampaio to this conclusion:

"She is a flying turd, she doesn't have the patience to sit down on the toilet . . ." and he put his thumb in his mouth resignedly.

The good Samaritan was prepared to receive a suffering Dona Rozilda, and take her to her breast and comfort her. And then to have her come out with that spate of nonsense, as though the death of her son-in-law was a joyful piece of news! There she came down the gangplank, in one of her hands the classic package of manioc meal of Nazareth, well roasted and fragrant, in addition to a basket in which a string of crabs she had acquired aboard stirred restlessly; in the other her parasol and suitcase. Even so, thought Dona Norma, it was not the big suitcase that threatened a protracted visit, but a small wooden one for brief trips, a few days, and good-bye. She came forward to help her and to give her the ceremonial embrace the situation called for. Under no circumstances would she have failed to fulfill the sad duty of expressing her condolence.

"My sympathy . . ."

"Sympathy? To me? No, my dear, don't waste your good manners. As far as I am concerned, he could have croaked a long time ago, and I would not have missed him. Now I can hold up my head and say once more that there is no stain on my family. And what a shame! To choose the middle of Carnival to die, dressed in masquerade . . . on purpose . . ."

She stopped in front of Dona Norma, put down her suitcase, basket, and parcel, the better to look her over from head to foot, and say in belittling praise: "Yes, ma'am . . . It's not to compliment you, but you have put on weight . . . You look pretty, young, nice and fat, God bless you and keep you from the evil eye . . ."

She settled the basket from which the crabs were trying to escape, and went on obstinately: "That's what I like, a woman who doesn't go in for the latest fashions . . . Those who diet to stay thin and wind up consumptive. Whereas you . . ."

"Don't say that, Dona Rozilda. And I who thought I was thinner. I want you to know that I am following the strictest sort of diet . . . I have given up eating dinner, for a month I have not known what beans taste like . . ."

Dona Rozilda gave her another critical glance: "Nobody would ever think it."

With Dona Norma's assistance she collected her parcels, and set out for the Lacerda Elevator, Dona Rozilda harping on: "And Mr. Sampaio? Always in bed? I never saw such a dull man. He reminds me of an old dog . . ."

Dona Norma did not relish the comparison, and smiled in protest: "It's his nature . . . low-spirited . . ."

Dona Rozilda was not a person to excuse human frailties: "God help us . . . A husband as foolish as yours must be a cross to bear. Mine, the late Gil . . . now, I'm not going to tell you he was anything special, he certainly was far from a saint, but compared to yours . . . Ah, my child, if I were in your shoes I would not stand for it . . . A man who never goes out of the house, never visits anyone, always sulking, inside four walls . . ."

Dona Norma tried to bring the conversation back to its normal course; after all, Dona Rozilda had lost her son-in-law, for that reason she had made the trip to the capital; it was about that moving and dramatic incident that they should talk; it was for this that Dona Norma was prepared: "Flor is very sad and depressed. She took it awfully hard . . ."

"Because she is a fool, a nitwit. She takes after her father, you did not know my late Gil. Not that I am trying to make myself out important, but the man of the house was me. Never a peep nor a helpful word from him; the one who had to decide everything was your humble servant. Flor took after him, a milksop, no mind of her own; otherwise, how could she have stood that husband she picked for such a long time?"

Dona Norma thought to herself that if the late Gil had not been a milksop, completely wishy-washy, he could certainly not have stood a wife like that very long, and she pitied the poor man. And Dona Flor, now threatened by frequent visits from her mother, who might—who could tell?—even be thinking of coming to live with her widowed daughter, destroying the cordial atmosphere of Sodré and its environs.

In Vadinho's day, when Dona Rozilda had come it had been for the briefest kind of visit, hasty, just long enough to say all the mean things she could about her son-in-law and set off for home before the devil showed up with his coarse jokes and wisecracks. Because Dona Rozilda had never been able to get the upper hand of Vadinho, had never even managed to upset or irritate him. He no more than laid eyes on her, whispering and muttering, than he was overcome by laughter, showing the greatest pleasure, as though his mother-in-law was his favorite visitor, the coarse wretch!

"Just see who's here, my beloved mother-in-law, my second mother, that heart of gold, that angelic dove. And how's the tongue today, well honed? Sit over here, my blessed saint, beside your beloved son-in-law and we'll rake over all the garbage of Bahia . . ."

And he laughed that gay, ringing laugh of a scoundrel who was pleased with life. If all the promissory notes and debts he had scattered about, if such tightness of money for his gambling did not manage to sadden or exasperate him, how could Dona Rozilda hope to? She hated him because of that, and because of what he had done during the early days of his courtship.

With a furious swish she always had fled the battlefield, followed by Vadinho's laugh, to avenge herself on Dona Flor, hurling insults at her to the astonishment of the bystanders: "Never again will I set foot in this house, you unnatural daughter! Stay with that dog of a husband you married, let him insult your mother, forget the milk that suckled you . . . I am leaving before he hits me . . . I am not like you who enjoys having him beat you up."

With Vadinho's laughter following her around the corners, exploding in the alleys, a bagpipe of derision, Dona Rozilda lost her head. Once she lost it completely; forgetting her status as a circumspect widow, she stopped in the middle of a street full of people, and turning toward the window where her son-in-law was writhing with laughter, she rolled up her sleeve, and with arm bare made the most obscene gesture. She accompanied the gesture with curses and insults, in a croaking voice: "Take that, you foul thing, you indecent skunk, take it and stick it up . . ."

The passersby were scandalized, serious Professor Epaminondas, high-minded Dona Gisa: "A woman without any self-control," the professor deplored.

"She's hysterical," explained Dona Gisa.

In spite of knowing Dona Rozilda well, having been a witness to this and similar outbursts, aware of her cantankerous disposition, her inborn sourness, even so, at the steps of the Elevator, Dona Norma suffered a surprise. She could not have believed that this dislike of her son-in-law would persist beyond death, that Dona Rozilda would not utter a single word of regret, hollow though it might be, devoid of feeling, mere lip service. Not even that. "The very air one breathes here is better since that dirty dog cashed in his chips."

Dona Norma could not restrain herself: "Good Lord. You really hated him, didn't you?"

"What a question! Didn't he deserve it? A worthless vagabond, a lush, a gambler, good for absolutely nothing . . . And he had to get mixed up in my family, turn my daughter's head, beguile the poor thing away from her home and let her keep him . . ."

Gambler, drunkard, vagabond, bad husband, it was all true, Dona Norma meditated thoughtfully. But, nevertheless, how hate beyond the grave? Shouldn't one clear one's conscience and inter with the coffin any resentment or quarrel? This was not Dona

Rozilda's opinion: "Old busybody, he used to call me; he never respected me, laughed at me in my face . . . He fooled me from the start, he made a fool out of me, he dragged me through the street of bitterness. Why should I forget this just because he's dead and buried? Just because of that?"

3

On departing this for a better world, the aforementioned Gil, the nincompoop without any backbone, had left his family in a very tight spot, in a precarious situation. In his case the phrase "departing this for a better world" is not just a cliché, but the literal truth. Whatever the mysteries that might await him in the beyond—a paradise of light, music, and glowing angels; a murky hell with boiling cauldrons; damp limbo; circling through sidereal space; or nothing, simply not being—anything would be better by comparison than his life with Dona Rozilda.

Lean and taciturn, day by day more lean and taciturn, Mr. Gil supported his tribe by acting as agent for modest commercial products of not too wide sales, earning barely enough for expenses: the daily bread, the rent of a first floor on Ladeira do Alvo, clothes for the children, the pretensions of Dona Rozilda, with her social ambitions to rub shoulders with important families, to be accepted among the circles of the well-to-do. Dona Rozilda had a violent dislike for most of her neighbors, outcasts of fortune—clerks in stores and warehouses, office workers, bookkeepers, and seamstresses. She looked down on this riffraff unable to hide its poverty; she put on airs, boasting and bragging, acting deferential only toward certain residents of the Ladeira, "families that stood for something," as she angrily repeated to the late Gil when she caught him in the act of having a beer in the undesirable company of Cazuza Funnel, a numbers runner and sponger, a homespun philosopher, one of the most questionable tenants of the neighborhood. It hardly seems necessary to explain that "Funnel" was not his family name, but a nickname based on the fact that his gullet was always wide open, his thirst insatiable.

Why didn't Gil seek out the company of Dr. Carlos Passos, a doctor with a numerous clientele, the engineer Vale, a big wheel in the Transit Authority, the telegraph operator Peixoto, getting on in years, on the point of retiring, who had reached the apex of his career, the journalist Nacife, still young but doing very well for himself with the *Modern Storekeeper*, a publication devoted, if one could believe its motto, "to the uncompromising defense of Bahian commerce," all of them residents of the Ladeira, who "stood for something"? That nitwit of a husband didn't know how to select his friends; when he was not with Funnel in the Punto Fino of Baixa dos Sapateiros, he was stuck off in Antenor Lima's house, playing backgammon or checkers, probably his one pleasure in life. Antenor Lima, a storekeeper with a shop in Taboão, and one of Gil's best customers, would have deserved to be included in the list of worthwhile neighbors if it had not been for his public and notorious concubinage with the Negress Juventina, originally his cook. Now set up in the storekeeper's own house, with a maid to sweep and clean, impudent and rude-spoken, she had verbal exchanges with Dona Rozilda which marked a high point in the annals of Ladeira do Alvo. Well, in front of the house of that scum of the earth Gil seated himself, bowing and scraping, treating that piece of trash as though she were a respectable wife married by bell, book, and candle.

All Dona Rozilda's efforts to cultivate the worthwhile friendships: the Costa family, descended from a famous politician, owners of an immense plantation in Matatu—the politician had even changed the name of the street, and his grandson Nilson was a banker and an industrialist; the Marinha Falcãos of Feira de Sant'Ana, in whose warehouse Gil had received his training when young—it was Mr. João Marinho who had lent him the money to set himself up in the capital; Dr. Luis Henrique Dias Tavares,

director of a government bureau, a person of exceptional endow-
ments, who published signed articles in the newspapers, a sonorous
name to roll under your tongue giving it a flavor of relationship:
"He is the godfather of my Hector."

As she referred to connections of this nature, ridiculing those
of Gil, she dramatically asked her interlocutors, neighbors, the hill,
the city, the world, what had she done to God that He should
punish her with a husband of that kind, incapable of giving her the
standard of living she was entitled to, in keeping with her background and upbringing. Not one salesman was there who did not
prosper, increasing his clients and staff, watching his monthly sales
go up, securing new and valuable accounts. Many of them bought
a house of their own, or at the very least land on which to build
later. Some of them even indulged in the luxury of an automobile,
like one they knew, Rosalvo Medeiros, an Alagoan who had come
from Maceió only a few years before with nothing but what he
was standing up in, and was now driving a Studebaker. So stuck-up
had this Rosalvo become that one day, on Chile Street, he had not
recognized Dona Rozilda and had almost run her down when she,
afoot and all smiles, had stepped in front of the car in her eagerness
to greet this prosperous colleague of her husband's. Not only had
he scared her out of her wits with the blast of the horn, but he had
then bawled her out, shouting insults at her: "Trying to commit
suicide, you centipede?"

In three or four years, selling pharmaceutical products, with his
gift of gab and charm, that clod had an automobile, was a member
of the Bahia Tennis Club, the close friend of politicians and the
rich, ladies and gentlemen, a grandee, all puffed up, swollen with
pride. Dona Rozilda ground her teeth. And that nincompoop of a
Gil?

Ah, Gil vegetated on foot or on the streetcar with his samples
of shoe laces, suspenders, stiff collars, and removable cuffs, a specialist in articles that were out of fashion, for the limited customers
of suburban shops, antiquated dry goods stores. This was as far as
he ever got, marking time his whole life long. Nobody believed in
his capabilities, not even himself.

One day he got tired of all the complaints and nagging, of trying so hard without results or happiness. Porto, his wife's brother-in-law, the husband of Lita, Rozilda's sister, was having a hell of a time making a living, too, teaching drawing and mathematics in a manual arts school way over by Paripe. Taking the train every day, early in the morning, getting up at daybreak, coming back late in the afternoon. But on Sundays he went out in the streets of the city with a box of paints and brushes to paint bright rows of houses, and that hobby gave him so much pleasure that nobody had ever seen him in a bad humor or melancholy. To be sure, he had married Lita and not Rozilda, and Lita, the opposite of her sister, was a saint who never opened her lips to speak unkindly of anyone.

Gil didn't even make any progress at backgammon or checkers, and Antenor Lima accepted him as a partner only when none better showed up; as for Mr. Zeca Serra, the champion of the Ladeira, not even under those conditions, not even to pass the time —there was no fun in playing with such a mediocre, careless, and absent-minded adversary. And on top of everything Dona Rozilda demanded that he break off once and for all with Cazuza Funnel, when his friend, at a very low ebb of fortune, just out of jail, persecuted and tried for illegal book-making, was most in need of moral support. And he, Gil, a complete scoundrel, scurrying around corners to avoid him, submitting to the orders of his wife!

He came to the conclusion that his sacrificial drudgery availed him nothing, and took advantage of the damper days of winter to pick up a cheap pneumonia—"not even double pneumonia" was Dr. Carlos Passos's ironic observation—and depart for heaven. Silently, with a discreet, timid cough. Anybody else would have shaken it off; it was little more than grippe. Gil, however, was tired, so tired. He was not willing to wait for a serious illness. Moreover, he had no illusions; a fashionable sickness, important, expensive, mentioned in the newspapers, was not for him; the best thing to do was to content himself with his petty pneumonia. So he did and, without taking leave of anyone, defaulted this life, rested.

4

For a long time Dona Rozilda had controlled with an iron hand the scanty income from her husband's commissions, giving him the weekly nickels he needed for carfare and for the pack of Aromatics—one every two days. But even so the niggardly savings barely paid the expenses of the funeral, the mourning, the multiple aggravations. Commissions from his latest sales were practically nonexistent, a mere trifle, and Dona Rozilda found herself with a son still in high school and two young daughters—Flor was barely an adolescent—and without any source of income.

Not even being as she was, sour and acrimonious, so difficult and disagreeable to deal with, not on this account should her positive qualities be denied: her determination and strength of will, and all that she did to finish raising her children and keep herself at least in the position in which the death of her husband had left her, without rolling down Ladeira do Alvo to the street corners or the sordid tenements of Pelourinho.

She clung to the two-story house with all her violent stubbornness. To move from there to cheaper quarters would mean the end of all her hopes of social ascent. She had to see Hector through high school, find him a job, marry off the girls, marry them well. And for this it was essential not to descend the ladder, not to let herself be dragged down by unmasked poverty, in full view and open to the sight of all, without modesty or shame. She, Dona Rozilda, felt shame of poverty, a great shame, as though it were a crime that deserved punishment.

She had to stay in the apartment on Ladeira do Alvo, at all costs, as she explained to her brother-in-law when he saw her borrowing Dona Lita's savings (later repaid by Dona Rozilda,

nickel by nickel, be it said in her honor). Neither a reasonably
priced house at the end of the world in Plataforma, nor a livable
basement in Lapinha, nor a bedroom and living-room under the
entrance to the Church of Carmo; she was staying on in the house
in Ladeira do Alvo, at a rental that was comparatively high,
especially for a person who, like herself, had no means, great or
small.

There, from the wide balconies of the first floor, she could face
the future with confidence; not all was lost. She would modify her
earlier plans without giving up her aspirations. If she were to
throw in the towel right away, relinquish her well-furnished,
well-run house, with carpets and curtains, going to any kind of
tenement, she could no longer have even hopes or illusions. She
would see Hector behind the counter of a grocery store or, at
most, a dry goods shop, a clerk for the rest of his life; she would
see the girls with the same future, unless they wound up as
waitresses in a bar or café, fair game for the owners and customers,
the straight road to the red-light district, the horror of the streets
of the prostitutes. From the house where she lived she could resist
all these threats. To give it up would be like yielding without a
fight.

For that reason she turned down the offer of a job as clerk for
Hector arranged by Antenor Lima. Just as she refused even to
discuss the matter with Rosalia, when her daughter came up with
an opportunity to act as a kind of receptionist and secretary at the
Elegant Photography Studio, a flourishing establishment in Baixa
dos Sapateiros, where Andrés Gutiérrez, a dark Spaniard with a
clipped mustache, exploited the art of photography in its most
varied aspects; from 3 x 4 snapshots for identity and professional
cards (developed in 24 hours) to "incomparable enlargements in
color, real wonders," not to mention portraits of the most varied
sizes, and of baptisms, weddings, first communions, and other festive occasions, worthy of the yellowing eternity of family albums.
Wherever there was a photograph to be taken, there appeared
Andrés Guitiérrez with his machine and his assistant, a Chinese
who was so old as to be ageless, wrinkled and suspect. There were
rumors in circulation, which had reached the ears of Dona Rozilda,

always alert to talk of this sort, about Andrés, his Elegant Photography Studio, his assistant, and the volume of his business. They said he was the producer of certain postcards sold by the Chinese in sealed envelopes, which were the last word in naturalistic art, "artistic nudes" whose success was phenomenal. For photographs of this sort, according to the gossips, poor girls of easy virtue acted as models in exchange for a few cents. And, on the side, Andrés undoubtedly laid them, and, who knows, maybe the Chinese did too; the old harpies told horrors about the photographic studio. Small wonder her mother had flown into a rage when the daughter, thrilled and naïve, told her about the Spaniard's offer:

"If you mention that to me again, I'll skin you alive, I'll give you such a beating that you won't be able to sit down."

She threatened Andrés with having him sent to jail, throwing into his face her standing and connections; just let him try any funny business with her daughter and he would see what would happen, dirty Galician not worth the powder to blow him up with his indecencies, his debauchery; she, Dona Rozilda, would go to the police . . .

Andrés, too, got all steamed up, having a hot Spanish temper, and he repaid her in kind. He began by saying that the Galician was Dona Rozilda's cuckolded father. This was the thanks he got when, deploring the situation in which Mr. Gil's death—a well-bred, kindly person who deserved a better wife—had left the family, he had offered a job to the girl whom he hardly knew with the sole intention of helping her, and now this hysterical cow was bellowing at the door of his studio, threatening and calling everybody names, making up stories, miserable calumnies. If she did not shut up that privy she used as a mouth, she could go to hell and fast, and the one who would call the police would be he, an Andalusian of good family, whom that witch was insulting by calling him a Galician . . . Indifferent to the argument that was going on, the Chinese continued cleaning his nails as long as claws with a matchstick, nails which, according to gossiping tongues . . .

Whether those exciting stories were true or not, Dona Rozilda had not brought up her daughters, accomplished and well-bred, for the delectation of any Andrés Gutiérrez, Andalusian, Galician, or Chinese—it was all the same . . . Her daughters were now her fulcrum to change the course of her destiny, her ladder to rise in the world. She rejected other jobs, of less dubious intent, for Rosalia and Flor: she did not want the girls exposed to the public and to danger. In Dona Rozilda's opinion, a girl's place was in the home; her goal, marriage. To send them to a store counter, the ticket window of a movie, the waiting-room of a doctor or a dentist, was to give in, confess her poverty, exhibit it, the most repulsive and noxious scar. She would put the girls to work, that she would, but in the house, at domestic skills they had acquired with a view to matrimony and a husband. If formerly skills and marriage had been important details in Dona Rozilda's plans, now they had become transformed into the very foundation of her projects.

While Gil was alive, Dona Rozilda had planned to send her son to college, make of him a doctor, a lawyer, or an engineer, and with the support of the sheepskin, the diploma, have him climb the ladder of the elite, shine amid the mighty of the earth. The class ring on Hector's finger would be the key that would open the doors of high society, that closed and far removed world of Vitória, Canela, and Graça. In addition to this, and as a consequence of it, good marriages for the daughters with colleagues of her son, doctors of family and future.

Gil's death had invalidated that long-range plan; Hector was still in high school, with two years left to finish—he had lost a year, failed his examinations. How could she support him for five or six years in college, prolonged and expensive studies? With an effort and at a great sacrifice she could keep him in high school— he was studying in the public school of Bahia, a free state institution—until he finished. Being a high-school graduate he would be able to evade the miserable jobs open in trade, marking time, with yardstick in hand. Possibly he could find a place in a bank, or— why not?—some official sinecure, a public appointment, with guarantees and rights, raises, promotions, bonuses, and fringe benefits. For all this Dona Rozilda was counting upon her influential connections.

She could no longer, however, count on the title of doctor—the graduation ring of gleaming emerald, ruby, or sapphire—to help him scale the heights she had dreamed of. It was a pity, but there was nothing she could do; once again that turd of a husband had ruined her plans with his idiotic dying.

Now, however, he could no longer ruin her revised plans, ripened during her days of so-called mourning. For these new plans the master key, which would open the doors of comfort and well-being was marriage, that of Rosalia or Flor. To marry them ("settle them," as Dona Rozilda put it) as well as possible, with young men of position, scions of outstanding families, the sons of planters, or businessmen—wholesalers, preferably—with money and credit in the banks. If this was the goal on which she had her sights set, how was she to expose the girls to the dangers of third-rate jobs, reveal their poverty to the public gaze, where their charm and shabbily attired youth would arouse in the wealthy and important only their worst instincts, their sinful desires, propositions, of course, but no honest offers of courtship and marriage?

Dona Rozilda wanted her daughters at home, shielded, helping her with their work and behavior to keep up that appearance of comfort, to buckle on that mask, if not of wealth, at least of decent position and good breeding. When the girls went out to visit at the house of friends, to Sunday matinées, to some festivity at the home of people they knew, they were always elegant and well dressed, giving the fictitious impression of heiresses accustomed to the best. Dona Rozilda was very thrifty, counting pennies in her effort to balance the budget and keep her head above water, but she would not tolerate slovenliness in her daughters' attire, not even in the intimacy of the house. She demanded that they keep themselves like new pins, ready to receive at any moment the prince charming when he appeared without warning. On this Dona Rozilda spared no effort.

On one occasion Rosalia was invited to a birthday dance of the oldest daughter of Dr. João Falcão, a big shot, with a mansion, crystal chandeliers, silver table service, more waiters than you could count. The other guests, all people of quality, filthy rich, of the best society, real swells, you had to see it to believe it. Well,

Rosalia was the belle of the ball, the best dressed, the smartest, to the point where Dona Detinha, the kindly hostess remarked: "The prettiest of them all . . . Rosalia, a pet, a doll . . ."

And truly she seemed the richest and most aristocratic, among all those more favored by fortune and of highest local standing, the blue-blooded offspring of professionals and doctors, of government employes and bankers, merchants and tradesmen. With her pale skin, smooth and camellia-like, she was the purest white among all those elegant "whites" of Bahia, running the gamut of every shade of brunette—here, between ourselves, and let nobody overhear us —mestizas of the most delicate and beautiful mulatto mixture.

Nobody seeing her so well turned out would have said that that dress, the most admired at the party, was the work of her and Dona Rozilda, the dress and all the rest, including the transformation of an old pair of slippers into a work of art in satin. Among Rosalia's accomplishments sewing was the most outstanding; she could cut, sew, embroider, and knit.

Yes, they, the girls, under the iron rule of Dona Rozilda were the performers of that miracle of survival: Hector finishing high school, the rent of the first floor paid on the day it fell due, as well as the installments on the radio and the new stove, and even something put aside for finishing up the trousseaux, the wedding dresses, the veils, the wreaths; sheets and pillowcases, nightgowns and underwear were little by little accumulating in the hope chests.

It was they, the girls. Rosalia, at the sewing machine, pedaling away, sewing for people, cutting dresses, embroidering delicate blouses. Flor, at the beginning, in the preparation of trays of hors d'oeuvre and pastries for intimate gatherings, small celebrations: birthdays, first communions. If sewing was Rosalia's forte, the kitchen was the younger sister's field: she had been born with a knowledge of how to cook, with the gift for seasoning. From childhood on, she had baked cakes and prepared special delicacies, always hanging around the stove, learning the mysteries of the supreme art from her Aunt Lita, who was very exacting. Uncle Pôrto had no other vice, aside from his Sunday painting, than the love of good food. He was a gourmet of fish with mustard greens and lights and liver stew, crazy about black bean feijoada or a boiled dinner with a variety of vegetables. From the trays of cakes and patties, from the orders for lunches, Flor would go forward to recipes and classes, and finally a cooking school.

With one at the sewing machine, cutting and basting, the other in the kitchen, at the stove and the oven, and Dona Rozilda at the helm, they managed to get by. Modestly, drably, waiting for the knights-errant to appear at some festivity or during a walk, covered with money and degrees. The first making off with Rosalia, the second leading Flor away, both to the strains of the Wedding March, to the altar and the gay world of the rich. First Rosalia, who was the older.

Stubbornly Dona Rozilda peered around corners, waiting for the appearance of this son-in-law of silver and gold, studded with diamonds. At times discouragement got the better of her: what if the prince charming did not appear? It was time for him to come; it was impossible to wait a lifetime for him; the girls had reached the restless age when they needed a man. Rosalia, who had spent twenty years sighing at the window, tired of the treadle of the sewing machine, was urgently demanding that duke, that count, that baron—when was he coming to her rescue? Such a long delay, such a tiresome wait—what if Rosalia should suddenly find herself left an old maid, a petrified maiden, with that sour smell of superannuated virginity, to which kindly Uncle Pôrto referred with a smile as he poked fun at his sister-in-law's aristocratic airs.

From time to time Rosalia caught a glimpse of him, the desired suitor: at rare dances, on visits to the house of her aunt in Rio Vermelho; in afternoon movies, or at the wheel of a roadster, all dressed in white on a Sunday when there were boat races, an academic wag or a scholar carrying thick volumes of knowledge under his arm, or curved in the painstaking acrobacy of an Argentine tango; or romantic to the sound of a serenade at night.

Dona Rozilda was waiting too, and her patience was wearing thin; when, when would he show up, this foreordained son-in-law, this millionaire, this hidalgo, this doctor in cap and gown, this wholesaler, this planter of cacao or tobacco, this merchant, or even this storekeeper, in the last analysis, this sweaty gringo with a little grocery store, when?

5

So long they waited, weeks, months, years, so well groomed, so nicely behaved, and no hidalgo appeared, nor any aristocratic youth from Barra or Graça, nor the son of a cacao colonel, nor outstanding merchant, not even a Spaniard who had made his money in the sweat of his brow in stores and bakeries. The one who appeared was Antônio Morais, a mechanic by profession with his self-acquired training, his honorable overalls black with grease. He arrived at the right time, and for that reason he was well received. Rosalia was already weeping an old maid's tears, seeing a future of loneliness and morning masses stretching before her. Dona Rozilda felt powerless to oppose the match. It was not the son-in-law she had foreseen in the long vigils at the sewing machine treadle or over the heat of the stove. But she could no longer restrain with considerations, or arguments, or angry threats the headstrong impulse of Rosalia, whose twenty-odd healthy years longed for a husband.

Besides, if Antônio Morais was not rich or important, at least he was not in anyone's employ, he had his own small, well-patronized establishment, he earned enough to keep a wife and children. Dona Rozilda bowed before fate, reluctantly, but she bowed. What choice did she have?

By that time Hector had found himself a job with the railroad of Nazareth, thanks to the help of his godfather, Dr. Luís Henrique, and went to live in the city of the Recôncavo, rarely visiting the capital. His job had a future. Dona Rozilda did not have to worry about him. Flor, too, was beginning to give cooking classes to girls and married women, earning a little money and making a name for herself as an able teacher. Now she took over most of the expenses of the house, among other reasons because Rosalia, frightened at the way time was flying, spent her earnings in beautifying herself, on dresses and shoes, perfumes and laces.

Antônio Morais happened to notice Rosalia at a matinée in the Olímpia Cinema one day when there was a show and Mr. Mota, the owner, in addition to the two films and the serial, added a performance by artists who happened to be passing through Bahia, the ragtag of third-rate companies that had run aground on trips through the interior, fading stars of wan light. While "Mirable, the sensual dream of Warsaw," a venerable Pole, a victim of battle fatigue, weary of the lights and the beds of the cat houses, waggled an ancient bottom worn out by the vehemence of young bucks who received their education on it, Antônio Morais spied in the next seats Dona Rozilda and her two daughters—Rosalia waiting excitedly, Flor with burgeoning breasts and thighs.

The mechanic no longer had eyes for the worn-out shimmying of the "dream of Warsaw." The petulant gaze of Rosalia and his supplicating glances crossed. When they left, the young man followed mother and daughters at a prudent distance, fixing their bourgeois domicile on Ladeira do Alvo in his mind. Rosalia appeared for an instant on the balcony and left a smile fluttering in the air.

The next day, after dinner, Antônio Morais wore himself out walking up the hill, down the hill, finally taking up his place on the sidewalk across from the house. Out of the window Rosalia peeped encouragingly. The mechanic strolled up and down, his eyes on the high balcony, whistling *modinhas*. In a little while Rosalia, accompanied by Flor, appeared at the foot of the stairs. With a slouching gait, Morais leaned against the steps.

Dona Rozilda, always on the alert, had noticed the beginnings of the love affair at the matinée. And seeing Rosalia so eager and unmanageable, she had gone out to see what she could learn about the fellow. Antenor Lima knew him, and gave her definite and favorable information: a competent mechanic, with his own shop in Galés, a glutton for work. At the age of nine Antônio Morais had lost his father and mother in a bus accident; he had been left a waif, but instead of joining the street Arabs and turning into a vagrant and delinquent, he had apprenticed himself to Pé de Pilão, a Negro bigger than the Cathedral, a mechanic and a good guy. In the shop the kid was a natural, handy at everything he touched, skillful as could be. Without any fixed salary, but with the privilege of sleeping there, not to mention the tips, some of them big. He had taught himself to read and write, and with Pé de Pilão had learned his trade. While still young he began to work on his own, charging very little. He had agile hands and a quick mind; automobile motors held no secrets for him. To be sure, he had no degree, nor did he come from a rich family. But few mechanics could compare with him. He had a steady income, he would make a first-class husband, and what in the devil more did Rosalia expect, being no princess or heiress to a cacao plantation, the rude Lima asked his presumptuous, grumbling neighbor.

Other acquaintances confirmed the storekeeper's detailed account, and Dona Rozilda, after consulting with Hector's godfather, Dr. Luís Henrique, a veritable Ruy Barbosa, whose advice was invaluable, and much weighing of pros and cons, decided in favor of the mechanic.

He was not, she repeated, the son-in-law she had dreamed of, the prince of noble blood and coffers of gold. The only noble blood Morais could claim was that of a remote forebear, Obitikô, the prince of an African tribe who had been brought to Bahia as a slave, mingling his blue blood with the plebeian strains of Portuguese peasants and Dutch mercenaries. Out of the mixture had come a light mulatto, with a quick smile, an agreeable dark-skinned person. As for the coffers of gold, the mechanic's savings did not even make it possible for him to set up housekeeping at once. But Rosalia was completely infatuated, head over heels in love, and she would not listen to a word against his obscure origins, his low station, his meager resources, and in the face of this bristling Rosalia, her insolent answers and sullen silences, Dona Rozilda lowered her flag. And so it was that after the fifth or sixth nightly appearance of Morais—in a starched white suit, his hat tilted over his eyes, two-tone shoes, irresistible!—she questioned him.

The two lovers were really rapt, eye to eye, hand in hand, talking twaddle, when out of the shadows of the stairs Dona

Rozilda emerged, unexpectedly and inquisitorially, saying in a harsh voice that inspired terror: "Rosalia, my child, will you introduce me to the gentleman?"

When the introduction had been made, Rosalia muttering the names, Morais ill at ease, Dona Rozilda immediately took over, without ceremony or consideration: "A daughter of mine is not to be courted at the foot of a stairway nor on a street corner, nor does she go out alone with a suitor. I did not raise my daughter for some loafer to while away his time . . ."

"But I . . ."

"Anyone who wants to talk with my daughter must first state his intentions."

Antônio Morais declared the purity of his innermost thoughts, that his object was matrimony—he was not the sort of person to take advantage of people's daughters. He answered unhesitatingly and modestly the detailed interrogatory, Dona Rozilda checking the information she had already come by, especially that having to do with what he earned.

The mechanic received the seal of her approval and his nightly visit to the door of the house beside which, after that interview, Rosalia waited for him, sitting in a chair, was officially authorized. From the window Dona Rozilda controlled the family morals; a daughter of hers was not for the diversion of any bum. And so when Morais stretched out his tender hand toward the tender hand of the girl, the reproving grunt of Dona Rozilda fell over them: "Rosalia!"

In this way she speeded up the courtship, for Morais was longing for greater liberty, less vigilance. As a declared suitor, he was allowed to come into the house, take Rosalia to a matinée on Sundays, with Flor as chaperone, with strict orders to watch over and control the lovers, preventing kisses or caresses; Dona Rozilda demanded the most complete respect. But Flor had not been born to be an informer; understanding and sympathetic, she turned her back on her sister and future brother-in-law, absorbed in the picture, chewing caramels, leaving the couple to their needs, their hands and mouths busy.

During the courtship and engagement, Dona Rozilda behaved

as pleasantly as it was possible for her to do, concealing the sharper edges of her nature. She had to marry off the girls. Rosalia had reached the age, and more; there were swarms of girls looking for a husband, and a shortage of young men interested in matrimony. It was a hard struggle, this business of marrying off daughters, as Dona Rozilda knew from sad experience. Her acquaintances, almost without exception, considered the mechanic a good match. One of them, Dona Elvira, the mother of three dull, bleary-eyed daughters definitely condemned to celibacy, even had the three hags making up to Morais, all smiles and sheep's eyes; the only thing they had not done was to drag him off to bed. Moreover, Morais was hard-working and of decent habits, and it would not be hard for his mother-in-law to boss him, to bend him to her will after they were married. In this she was mistaken; the son-in-law was to surprise her.

So the mechanic only came to know the whole truth about Rozilda after marriage. They had decided to live in the first floor of Ladeira do Alvo, an economical and sentimental solution, for in this way they would spend less and be together, and neither Morais nor Dona Rozilda gave evidence of wanting anything but always to be together. Rosalia was the one who demurred at these foolhardy plans. "No house is big enough for two families," she pointed out, but how could she oppose this honeymoon between her mother and her fiancé?

The honeymoon lasted less than six months: the plan collapsed for, as the son-in-law explained to his acquaintances: "Nobody but Jesus Christ could stand living with Dona Rozilda, and I am not even sure He could; we'd have to see if the Nazarene had the patience. Maybe not even He could take it."

They moved to the end of the world in Cabula, practically in the country. Morais preferred the endless trip, the slow, crowded streetcar, off the rails half the time, always late; he preferred to get up at daybreak to reach the shop located in the vicinity of Ladeira dos Galés; make his way through the surrounding woods where rattlesnakes whirred and where the evil spirits of the many *candomblés* of the neighborhood ran about loose wreaking all kinds of mischief rather than to live with his mother-in-law. Better the rattlesnakes and the evil spirits.

On the first floor of Ladeira do Alvo lived only young Flor, turning into a pretty girl—sweet-faced, high-bosomed, proud-haunched—and Dona Rozilda, a Dona Rozilda who grew sourer by the day, limited now to the charms and accomplishments of that daughter, her last trump in the battle for social status, a battle lost so many times.

She did not, however, lose her determination, her firm will to climb the steps leading to the world of the rich. In her weary nights of insomnia (she slept little, always turning plans over in her mind) she decided not to give her last-born to another Morais. She would find a better match for Flor, a young man of standing, a white man of distinction, a university graduate or a wealthy businessman. She would defend that last trench tooth and claw. What had happened with Rosalia would not take place again. Not only was Flor far more docile and sensible, but she was not worried about staying an old maid, she did not talk about marriage, she did not rise up against her mother when the latter forbade her to have anything to do with office workers, clerks, Spaniards selling bread at the bakery. She obeyed without complaint, she did not turn mutinous, shouting, locking herself in her room and threatening to commit suicide in one of those moods that Rosalia got into when Dona Rozilda, thinking of her future, forbade any trivial love affair. And the result was that Rosalia had married that nobody of a Morais, not even a clerk, a mere mechanic, an artisan, what a horror! Socially even lower in the scale than they were. He might be a wonder at his work, he might make money, be a good husband, a gay companion; but the truth was that her daughter, instead of rising in the social scale, had descended. This, at any rate, embittered Dona Rozilda, whose sights were set on higher levels. With Flor things would be different; she would not repeat the same mistake.

While Dona Rozilda forged her plans, Flor was becoming an accomplished cooking teacher, her specialty the cuisine of Bahia. She had been born with a gift for seasoning; ever since childhood she had been interested in recipes and sauces, learning how to make delicacies, sure-handed in her use of salt and sugar. For a long time she had been receiving orders for Bahian dishes, and was always called upon to help with *vatapás* and *efós*, *moquecas* and *xinxims*, even the famous *carurus* of St. Cosme and St. Damian, like those given at the house of her Aunt Lita or Dona Dorothy Alves, where dozens of guests gathered, and there was enough left over for as many more. Annual *carurus*, vows made to the twin saints, the *ibejes*. With time her reputation grew, people came to ask her for recipes, took her to the homes of rich people to teach the fine details and seasoning of this or that exacting dish. Dona Detinha Falcão, Dona Lígia Oliva, Dona Laurita Tavares, Dona Ivany Silveira, other "outstanding" ladies on whose friendship Dona Rozilda so prided herself, recommended her to their acquaintances. Flor had twice as much work as she could do. It was one of those rich ladies who gave her the idea of a school, for, having asked for recipes and practical demonstrations, she had insisted on paying her for her work, to make clear that she was remunerating the excellent teacher and good friend, and not giving a cook a gratuity. Delicate subtleties of Dona Luísa Silveira, a great lady from Sergipe full of guile and very proud.

Flor began professionally, with the school set up, only after Rosalia and Morais had left for Rio de Janeiro. The mechanic had come to the conclusion that the distance between the heights of Cabula and Ladeira do Alvo was not enough: he wanted to put the ocean sea between his house and his mother-in-law, such an aversion had he taken to Dona Rozilda, that termagant, as he called her, "plague, famine, and war."

The school had prospered, ladies from Canela, Graça, even Barra itself had come to unveil the mysteries of olive oil and dendê oil; one of the first was Dona Magá Paternostro, rich and well connected, who was an enthusiastic propagandist of Flor's gifts.

Time went by; the years ran their course, Flor was in no hurry to look for a sweetheart, and now it was Dona Rozilda who began to worry; after all, her youngest-born was no longer a child. Flor shrugged her shoulders, interested only in the school. Her brother, on one of his trips from Nazareth, had designed a poster in red ink

—he was highly praised for his gift for drawing—which hung from the balcony:

COOKING SCHOOL OF SAVOR AND ART

Hector had read in the papers a long article about a school of "Knowledge and Art," the experience of someone who had come from the United States, a certain Anisio Teixeira. With the change of certain letters in the title, he had adapted it to the needs of his sister. Alongside the fanciful letters, there were a spoon, fork, and knife crossed in an amusing tripod, completing the work of the artist (if it were today, Hector could be thinking about an exhibit of his own and the sale of some pictures at a good price, but that was a long time ago, and the employe of the railroad was satisfied with the praise of his sister, his mother, and a certain pupil of Flor's, with moist eyes, who answered to the name of Celeste).

The cooking classes provided what was needed to keep the house going and care for the small expenses of mother and daughter, and also to put aside some money with an eye to the expenses of a future wedding. But, above all, they occupied Flor's time, they liberated her, up to a point, from having to listen over and over again to Dona Rozilda and how many sacrifices she had made to bring up and educate her children, bring up and educate that youngest-born, and how it was imperative for her to find a rich husband who would take them away from there, from Ladeira do Alvo and the cook stove, for the delights of Barra, Graça, and Vitoria.

Flor, however, did not seem to give much thought to courtship or engagement. At the parties she danced with one and another, listened to their compliments, smiled gratefully, but went no farther. She did not respond to the impassioned pleas of a medical student, a gay young chap from Pará, full of fun and a dandy. She gave him no encouragement, in spite of Dona Rozilda's excitement: at last, a student, almost a doctor, aspiring to her daughter's hand.

"I don't like him," stated Flor categorically. "He's as ugly as a dog . . ."

And no advice nor scolding of an infuriated Dona Rozilda could make her change her mind. The mother was seized by panic.

Would this be a second Rosalia, with Flor behaving like her sister, stubbornly determined to handle sweetheart and marriage by herself? Here she had thought that the youngest daughter took after the late Gil in nature, compliant to her bidding, and she was refusing to have anything to do with the young doctor about to receive his diploma, the son of a father with vast holdings in Pará, the owner of ships and islands, rubber plantations, forests of Brazil nuts, tribes of savage Indians, vast rivers. Set in gold. Dona Rozilda went out in search of information, and, on her return, after listening to various acquaintances, she already saw herself in Amazonia reigning over leagues of land, giving orders and countermanding orders over caboclos and Indians. At long last the prince charming had appeared: her wait had not been in vain, nor her sacrifice useless. In a ship of the Amazon River she would sail into port in the proud houses of Barra, the bolted mansions of Graça, the owners fawning upon her and seeking her favors.

Flor smiled with her delicate round face, matte in color, smiled with the lovely dimples in her cheeks, with her surprised eyes, and repeated in a weary voice, uninterested and apathetic: "I don't like him. He's as ugly as poverty."

"What the devil is she thinking?" Dona Rozilda shouted, getting on her high horse. Flor was acting as though marriage were a question of liking or not liking, as though it mattered whether a man was good-looking or homely, as though suitors like Pedro Borges were to be had for the asking on Ladeira do Alvo.

"Love comes with living together, my Countess of Turd, with interests in common, with children. It's enough if you don't dislike him. Do you hate him?"

"Me? No, God deliver me. He's even nice. But I will only marry a man I love. This Pedro is as ugly as they come . . ." Flor was an avid reader of the novels in the Collection for Young Girls; what she dreamed of was a poor and good-looking youth, dashing and blond.

Dona Rozilda foamed at the mouth with anger and excitement; her shrill voice crossed the street, carrying the echoes of the argument to all the neighbors.

"Ugly? Who ever heard of an ugly or pretty man? The beauty

of a man, you fool, is not in his face but in his character, in his social standing, in his money. Who ever heard of a rich man that was ugly?"

As far as she was concerned she would not trade the homely Borges (and he wasn't all that bad-looking, tall and strong, even though his face was a little pimply—true) for that whole gang of fresh, insolent scoundrels of Rio Vermelho, without a cent to their names, no prospects, vagrants. Dr. Borges (she was taking the degree for granted) was a well-bred boy, one could tell it from his manners, of a distinguished family of Pará, distinguished and with money to burn. She knew for a fact that their house in Belém was a palace. Why, they had over a dozen servants! A dozen, you hear that, you ungrateful daughter, stubborn and crazy, with a head full of silly notions! All the floors of marble, the stairs of marble. She stretched out her hands dramatically: "Who ever heard of a rich man that was ugly?"

Flor smiled—her dimples were enchanting. She was in no hurry to get married. Her answer shut her mother up: "You are talking as though I were a strumpet who judges men by their money. I don't like him, and that's all there is to it."

The struggle between Dona Rozilda, irritated and irritating, with a nervousness that bordered on the psychotic, and Flor, who was as calm as though nothing were happening, a contest in which Pedro Borges was the objective and the prize, reached its climax with the graduation ceremonies that year. The candidate for the doctor's degree had invited them to the solemn act and to the dance afterwards.

For the conferring of the degrees, in the auditorium of the Faculty, Dona Rozilda dressed herself as became a mother-in-law, all decked out in taffeta, as majestic as a turkey with tail feathers spread, smiling to the very ruffles of her sleeves, and with a Spanish dancer's comb in her topknot. Flor was resplendent in lace and tulle, and did not have a moment's rest. Not a dance did she sit out, so many requests did she have. But not even so would she give any hope to the young graduate.

Not even when he, on the point of leaving for distant Amazonia, came to call on them, bringing along his father to impress them more. The father of the graduate from Pará was called Ricardo, a giant with a voice like a clap of thunder, his fingers covered with rings—Dona Rozilda almost fainted at the sight of so many precious stones. There was a black diamond the like of which she had never seen. It must have been worth at least fifty contos, God in heaven!

The old man talked about his lands, the harmless Indians, the rubber, tales of the Amazon River. He spoke, too, of his happiness at seeing his son a doctor, with his diploma in medicine. The only thing that was lacking now was to see him married, to a good girl, modest and sincere; money did not enter into consideration, he had made enough. He moved his fingers, the diamonds glittered, lighting up the room. He wanted a daughter-in-law who would give him grandchildren to fill with cheer and warmth that austere house of marble in Belém, that house where he, a widower, had lived all alone during the years when Pedro had been studying. He spoke and looked at Flor as though awaiting a word, a gesture, a smile; if that was not the prelude to asking her hand in marriage, then Dona Rozilda was a complete ignoramus. She trembled with emotion and eagerness; the blessed moment had arrived; she had never been so in reach of her objectives, and she looked at that simpleton of a daughter of hers, awaiting her timid but firm acquiescence. But all Flor said in her languid voice was: "There will be no lack of nice, pretty girls for Pedro to marry, for he certainly deserves it. I only wish it were here in Bahia so I could prepare the wedding banquet."

Without any resentment Pedro Borges pocketed the engagement ring he had already bought and old Ricardo cleared his throat and changed the subject. Dona Rozilda felt sick, short of breath, her heart thudding unevenly. She went out of the room in a fury of indignation, afraid she might have some sort of seizure, hoping to see her daughter dead and buried, the ungrateful thing, the stupid, conceited fool, the enemy of her own mother, the hateful wretch. How dared she refuse the hand of a doctor—now really a doctor—rich, the heir to islands, rivers, Indians, all that marble, the glittering rings, how did she dare, the shameless bastard?

Ah, what a wall of hatred and enmity, of unforgivable lack of understanding, of unsurmountable animosity would not have sprung up between mother and daughter, forever together and forever separated, if at the beginning of the year, after the departure of the flouted Borges, Vadinho had not appeared on the scene. Ah, by comparison with the degrees, the position, and the fortune of Vadinho—of which Dona Rozilda was amply informed by Vadinho himself and certain of his friends—Pedro Borges was nothing but a pauper, in spite of all the marble of his palace and his dozen servants, a beggar for all his lands and his waters.

6

With a quick, polite bow, Mirandão, his face radiating charm, asked permission to sit down beside Dona Rozilda. Cane-seated chairs encircled the room, alongside the wall. The chronic student ("Persevering," he corrected, if anyone happened to mention his seven years in the Agricultural School) stretched out his legs, carefully straightened the crease of his pants, studying the couples painstakingly dancing the Argentine tango, difficult steps, almost acrobatic, and smiled condescendingly; there wasn't one who could compare with Vadinho, not one. God bless him and keep him from harm. Mirandão was superstitious. A coxcomb of a light mulatto, about twenty-eight, the most popular figure around the brothels and gaming houses of Bahia.

Feeling Dona Rozilda's eyes following his, he turned to her, his captivating smile even broader, and examined her with a critical, perceptive glance. "Definitely an old hag, no good," he concluded regretfully. Not because of her age. Long since Mirandão had inserted in his code of behaviour vis-à-vis women a clause to the effect that none should be passed over because of her age or maturity; that could lead to fatal mistakes. Women already past fifty at times kept their figure and youth admirably and were capable of amazing performances, unforeseen capacity. He knew this from firsthand experience, and even now, gazing upon the ruins of Dona Rozilda, he recalled the twilight splendor of Celia Maria Pia dos Wanderleys e Prata—all those names to denominate a little wisp of a thing, a lady of high society, a flibbertigibbet, an imp. Admitting to being over sixty, and putting wreaths of horns on her husband's and lovers' heads, insatiable. With granddaughters approaching their forties and marriageable great-granddaughters, and she performing acts of charity—and what charity! She was a fiery and magnanimous female—to young, indigent students. Mirandão half closed his eyes not to see his neighbor, a worthless skeleton, and also the better to recall the unforgettable uterine furor of Celia Maria Pia dos Wanderleys e Prata, and the fifty and a hundred mil-reis bills which she, grateful, rich, and prodigal slipped into his coat pocket. Ah, those were the days; Mirandão beginning his initiation into the studies and mysteries of life, a freshman in agronomy, taking night courses. And Maria Pia dos Wanderleys used real French perfume on the wrinkles of her neck and under her arms, et cetera.

He reopened his eyes on the room, the fragrance of the unforgettable great-grandmother still in his nostrils; beside him, that old tub with the face of a witch—disgusting crone, sagging cheeks, her hair screwed up in a topknot—kept on staring at him with her little eyes. She was a scarecrow, how she must stink under her petticoats, reek of spoiled fish. Mirandão took a quick sniff of the French perfume of distant memory—ah, noble Wanderleys, where would you be now, septuagenarian? That old bag in the chair, what a hopeless hag!

But well-mannered, as he prided himself on being, the chronic student of agronomy never stopped smiling at Dona Rozilda. A harpy, the skin and bones of dry, salt fish, useless for any lecherous act or thought, not even on this account did she fail to deserve respect and attention; the worn-out mother of a family, a widow by the looks of her, and Mirandão was, at heart, a moralist who had strayed into gambling houses. Besides, his moment of well-being had arrived.

"It's a nice little gathering, don't you think?" he asked Dona Rozilda, thus initiating their momentous dialogue.

It always happened that way, every time he got drunk, which was frequently. First came the phase of overwhelming happiness. The world seemed to him good and perfect, life, gay and happy, and at that hour Mirandão could understand and evaluate everything, establishing between himself and others a climate of complete communion, even between him and that pestilential pisspot sitting in the chair next to him. He was courteous, chatty, overflowing of imagination. The figure of the poor student, "perpetual student and perpetually thirsty," the image he had created of himself and in keeping with which he lived, gave way to the triumphant young man of standing promoted to agronomic engineer when not a member of the faculty, listing his advantages, attaining important posts, and conquering women. He had a passion for narrating stories, and how he narrated them! He was a master of the oral narration, the creator of types and of suspense, a classic of good prose.

But if the binge went on, at the end of the night this optimism and well-being evaporated, and as it came to a close, Mirandão became enveloped in self-pity and lament, flagellating himself cruelly, in harrowing autocriticism, recalling his wife, the victim of his degradation, his four hungry children, the whole family threatened with eviction, and he, in gambling dens and brothels. "I am a miserable wretch, a debauched scoundrel," boasted a remorseful Mirandão, repentant and sincere, a moralist. But this second and lamentable phase occurred only on rare occasions, when he was really stoned.

At half past eleven, however, at the party being held in the home of Major Pergentino Pimentel of the State Guard, retired, Mirandão was at peace with the world, all ready for a cordial and profitable exchange of ideas with Dona Rozilda. They had just eaten and drunk their fill in the dining-room, tasting all the dishes, with second helpings of some. It was a feast of the first order, all the delicacies of Bahia were included—*vatapá* and *efó*, *abará* and *caruru*, marinated crabs, shrimp, fish, *acarajé* and *acaca*, chicken forcemeat, rice *haussá*, not to mention the piles of roast chicken, turkey, ham, slices of fried fish for those so devoid of palate as not to appreciate dendê oil (for, as Mirandão was thinking to himself, full of food and contempt, there are all kinds of dumb clucks in this world, no depths too low for them). And all this gorging washed down with pineapple shrub, beer, rum, Portuguese wine. The Major had been observing this celebration for over ten years, fulfilling strict *macumba* obligations, ever since the African deities had saved his wife, who had been on the point of death from kidney stones. Expense was no consideration; he saved up the whole year to spend it to his satisfaction that night. Mirandão had given himself over wholeheartedly to doing his part, both at the eating and, even more, at the drinking. Now, replete, glutted with so much food and drink, all that he needed was a nice chat to help digestion.

In the parlor the couples were renewing their efforts at the Argentine tango, with Joãozinho Navarro at the piano. For those in the know to say "Joãozinho Navarro" was to say everything; no pianist in Bahia was more sought out, and certain people, like a judge by the name of Coqueijo, who was an authority on music, turned on the radio just to hear him run through a program of popular songs. And in the early hours, in Tabaris, was not his piano the greatest contribution to the animation that reigned there? It was hard to secure him for a private party: he had no time for amateur performances. Invariably, however, he showed up for the Major's party, for he could not turn him down, owing him for old favors.

Mirandão watched the dancers complacently, nodded his applause to Joãozinho's playing—out of this world!—smiling at his neighbor and taking note of the fact that there had been no other gate-crashers with the exception of himself and Vadinho. No other heroes, for to gate-crash a party of Major Wild Boar (as the kids of Rio Vermelho had nicknamed the fierce Pergentino) was an impossible feat that had given rise to bets and dares. Mirandão felt himself really made; they had finally managed, he and Vadinho, to take the hurdle the Major had set up and have the heavy oaken door, locked and bolted, the entrance that opened to guests and

guests only—all of whose faces were known to the owners of
the house, friends of long standing—open to himself and Vadinho
and let them in. And not only that: the two of them received with
embraces by the Major and his wife, Dona Aurora—even more
persnickety than her husband about the station and the identity of
the guests. There outside, in the echoing darkness, uninvited dull-
ards tasted the bitterness of defeat as they saw them enter, after a
brief exchange of words with Major Wild Boar, crossing the
forbidden threshold to the animated exclamations of Dona Aurora.
How had they managed it?

Mirandão gave a crop-full sigh, smiled a beatific smile. There
went Vadinho whirling about the room with a pretty girl in his
arms, plump, brunette, well-fleshed—bones are for dogs—with
eyes shining like oil and skin the color of tea, beautiful thighs and
breasts.

"What a chick to lose your way with, that dark Venus!"
Mirandão commented, pointing to the girl who was dancing with
his friend.

The hag stiffened, raised her breastless bosom, and barked in
her embattled voice: "That's my daughter."

Mirandão didn't turn a hair.

"Then allow me to congratulate you, madame. It leaps to the
eye that she is a nice girl, of fine family. My friend . . ."

"That fellow who is dancing with her is your friend?"

"Is he my friend? Intimate, madame, like a brother . . ."

"And who is he, if I may ask?"

Mirandão straightened himself up in his chair, pulled out of his
pocket a perfumed handkerchief, with which he dried several
drops of perspiration on his broad forehead. He was smiling and
happy; there was nothing he enjoyed so much as making up a
cock-and-bull story, a real whopper.

"First let me introduce myself: Dr. José Rodrigues de Miranda,
agronomic engineer, on loan to the Assistant Commissioner," and
he held out his hand with great cordiality.

In a last touch of suspicion, Dona Rozilda looked her interlocu-
tor over with hostile glance. But the assured visage and the open

smile of Mirandão would have quenched any doubt, would have broken down any resistance, would have disarmed and overcome any adversary, even one as mean and mangy as Dona Rozilda.

7

PARENTHESIS HAVING TO DO WITH CHIMBO
AND RITA DE CHIMBO

That day, at the end of the afternoon, when the sultriness was at its peak, the air heavy as concrete, and Vadinho and Mirandão were in São Pedro at the Alameda Bar having their first rum of the day and discussing plans for the night's celebration in Rio Vermelho, suddenly there loomed up in the doorway the ruddy face of Chimbo, that important relative of Vadinho's, at the moment Assistant Commissioner—that is to say, the second highest police officer.

A notary public and the son of an outstanding member of the government, without respect for the hidebound austerity of his father, without any thought for social proprieties, this distant cousin of Vadinho's, a legitimate and wealthy Guimarães, was a playboy, an inveterate prankster, a master hand at drinking, dicing, and whoring—in a word, a screwball. Of late he had withdrawn a little from circulation, out of regard for his job. A job at which, for that very reason, he would not last long, preferring his freedom to public office, unwilling to trade it for the greatest benefice, for any title.

He had previously resigned from the government of Belmonte, the city where he had been born, where he had been put in as mayor by his father, a senator of feudal mentality, after a rigged election. He gave up the job and the title, duties and advantages; it was too high a price to pay. The people of Belmonte were not satisfied with his real administrative qualities; they demanded of their authorities unsullied behavior, which was an abuse not to be tolerated.

It gave rise to devilish rumormongering, an unheard-of scandal, just because he, bold and progressive, had imported a few agreeable girls from Bahia with the aim of breaking the monotony and boredom of the small city. He had brought in Rita de Chimbo, who had a reputation in Tabaris for making the night gay. De Chimbo, a nickname owing to the old and persistent infatuation which united them, a dalliance which had been sung in prose and verse by the local literati. They fought, quarreled, broke off for good; days later all was made up, and the idyll went on, unabated. For that reason Rita had added to her name the name of her love, just as the bride assumes the surname of her husband at the marriage ceremony. When she learned that he had been appointed mayor, the lord of noose and knife with authority of life and death over the defenseless inhabitants, she demanded, by telegram, a share in that authority. What pleasure in the world can compare with that of command, of power? The voluptuous Rita wanted to taste it. Chimbo alone in the nights of Belmonte, alone and with nothing to do, completely empty, hearkened to the ardent plea, and sent for the girl.

With Chimbo mayor, king of his city, Rita de Chimbo could not come ashore in this empire like just anybody. She was the favorite, the royal concubine. There you have the reason why she invited three beauties to escort her, all different, but each excellent: Zuleika Marron, a flighty, dissolute mulatta, whose swaggering haunches took up the width of the streets, bumping against the pedestrians; Amalia Fuentes, an enigmatic, soft-voiced Peruvian with mystical leanings, and Zizi Culhudinha, like a burgeoning ear of corn, fragile, golden, a flirt of the first water. This select and beautiful retinue, though it is sad to confess, did not receive the enthusiastic welcome it deserved in Belmonte; on the contrary, it was the target of overt hostility on the part of the ladies, and even of the gentlemen. If we except certain social groups—the beardless students, the rare night owls, the elbow-benders in general—and certain individuals, we can say that the population held itself aloof and suspicious.

And then Rita de Chimbo was seen at midnight on the balcony of the mayor's office so drunk she could not stand up, and calling the city every dirty name she could lay her tongue to. Dreadful pieces of news began to circulate: old Abraham, a merchant and a grandfather, was making a fool of himself over Zuleika Marron, squandering the patrimony of his grandchildren on orgies with that strumpet. Bereco, until that time an upright and chaste youth, an employe of the post office, president of the Society for Good Works, lost his head over Amalia Fuentes, revealing his roots of purity and religious faith by proposing marriage to her, to the despair of his biased family. The scandal reached its climax when Zizi Culhudinha became the sweetheart of all the schoolboys of Belmonte, their dream, their queen, their mascot and their pin-up girl. She went flaunting her blondeness in the nights of Belmonte, surrounded by the young fry, and the poet Sosígenes Costa dedicated sonnets to her. What ignominy!

Even that fairy of a vicar, an overbearing priest with a high-pitched voice, had delivered a sermon against Chimbo, a vehement denunciation of his scandalous behavior. He classified the chosen girls as "the dregs of metropolitan harlotry," as "allies of the devil," the poor things. A fiery sermon, with the church crowded at Sunday Mass, and the Father accusing Chimbo of transforming placid Belmonte into Sodom and Gomorrah, of ruined homes, broken families, an unhappy city which had the misfortune to have such a depraved mayor, that "Nero in underdrawers." Chimbo had a sense of humor and laughed at the virulence of the priest. The girls wept. Rita de Chimbo called for vengeance, and Miguel Turco, an excitable Syrian and the mayor's secretary, a supporter à outrance of the Guimarães clan and a notorious toady, proposed carrying it out: he would send for two ruffians whom he could trust to teach the subversive vicar manners, giving him the beating of his life.

Chimbo dried Rita's tears, thanked the Syrian for his devotion, rewarded the two bad men, two hardened criminals wanted in

Ilhéus. Under his outward nonchalance, Chimbo was a prudent and canny man who was not lacking in political acumen. Just imagine how the old senator would react if he got into trouble with the Church, beating up the priest to satisfy whores! Moreover, the Father had his reasons for that outburst. When he called him "Nero in underdrawers" he was referring to the night when, wearing nothing but striped shorts, the mayor had to cross the city in that fashion because the vicar had taken him in a flagrant idyll with trusting Maricota, an admirable servant who assured the reverend the services of board and bed, his chosen lamb.

Chimbo had no choice but to gather up his offended guests, give his arm to Rita de Chimbo, and send them off on a ship of the Bahian Line. With one swoop he relinquished job, emoluments, and a profitable cut from the numbers racket. Belmonte was deprived of his administrative gifts and he of the pleasure of the beauties of the capital. Bearing witness to Chimbo's efficient administration was the restored wharf, the increase in primary schools, and the repairs of the cemetery wall; as for the girls, the fleeting vision of them continued to upset the sleep of Belmonte for a long time.

Chimbo withdrew to the anonymity of a well-paid post in the service of justice, where nobody kept tabs on him. He renewed his night life from Tabaris (where Rita de Chimbo once more ascended the throne) to the Palace, from Abaixadinho to the House of the Three Dukes, from Carla's cathouse to that of Helena Humming Bird. From time to time his father the Senator withdrew him from his nocturnal celebrations and his remunerative and insignificant job—notary public sealed and sworn—to use him in political maneuvers, entrusting him with positions and salaries desired by others, not by him, who asked nothing but to live untrammeled, as he pleased.

Chimbo had a regard for Vadinho, not only because of their remote and spurious relationship, but also because of the qualities of his young comrade of the gaming houses and cabarets. On one occasion, when he heard someone call Vadinho a bum, without a job or way to earn a living, he fixed him up a modest post as Inspector of Gardens of Police Headquarters, for "a Guimarães

should have a definite place in society." "No Guimarães is a vagrant."

Contradictions in the nature of this agreeable Chimbo, so little
given to conventions and protocol, and, at the same time, with a
deep family feeling, zealous of the good name of the powerful
Guimarães clan.

That afternoon in question, Vadinho and Mirandão had met up
with Chimbo in São Pedro, when the Assistant Commissioner had
been on his way to Police Headquarters. A Chimbo for whom life
was a tiresome business, dressed in dark, hot clothing for ceremonial occasions, funerals, marriages—wing collar, starched shirt,
vest, spats, gold-headed cane—a formally dressed Chimbo on that
blistering February day, with the heat asphyxiating, dog days,
athirst for a cold glass of beer.

"Only a blizzard from the North Pole can save us," said Vadinho, embracing his relative and protector.

Chimbo cursed his fate in strong and expressive language,
reviling it in terms that gave vent to his bitterness: "A shit of a life
that's got me by the balls, a son-of-a-bitching job, having to
accompany the Governor to the most out-of-the-way places, to all
the ceremonies, to all that junk and rubbish." Look at the way he
was dressed up like a Portuguese Commander! That night, because
of the obligations of his job, he had to be present at the solemn
inauguration of a scientific congress—The National Congress of
Obstetrics—at the School of Medicine, with speeches and papers,
debates and opinions about childbirth and abortion, the most crash-
ing bore. Chimbo quickly gulped down his glass of beer, trying to
cool his heat and fury—his father with that insatiable mania for
using him in politics . . .

And on top of everything—what a piece of lousy luck—the
Congress had scheduled its opening for the very night of the
celebration of Major Pergentino, Major Wild Boar, of Rio Vermelho. He had done the Major a favor, he had released a hooligan
at his request, and now the Major wouldn't let him go, wanting to
entertain him, preparing an act of homage in his honor. The
celebration of Wild Boar, so it was said, was really something; you

ate and drank your fill there. And he, Chimbo, the guest of honor, just imagine the fun he was missing!

"Instead of that, I am going to have to listen to some doctor talking about labor pains . . . Honestly, the things my father gets me into . . ."

How could he persuade the senator to let him alone, tending to his own business, when the old man was a satrap before whom even the Governor trembled? Vadinho's eyes gleamed. Mirandão smiled. Chimbo had just opened to them the portals of glory and of the house of the Major.

8

That night, in front of the gala residence, the two imposters made a bet with other loafers of their ilk: they would gate-crash the dance and would be received as though they were guests of honor. They did gate-crash, and were welcomed with all honors, the red carpet rolled out for them, for Vadinho introduced himself to the Major and Dona Aurora as the nephew of the Assistant Police Commissioner, who was unable to attend, and Mirandão conferred upon himself the nonexistent post of private secretary to Chimbo.

"Doctor Airton Guimarães, my uncle, had to accompany the Governor to the Congress of Obstetrics. But as it is a point with him to honor your party, he sent me and his secretary, Dr. Mirandão, to represent him. I am Dr. Waldomiro Guimarães . . ."

The Major replied that he was touched by the Commissioner's politeness in sending his excuses, and having himself represented. He regretted that the Commissioner was unable to come to the party, it had been his wish to pay him homage but he received, he and his wife, the representatives of his valued friend with open arms. He held out his hand to Vadinho while Mirandão, in ecstasy and with great exaggeration, added his share to the explanation:

"Forgive me, Major, if I seem forward: I, Dr. José Rodriguez de Miranda, of the staff of the School of Agronomy, whose services have been requested by Dr. Airton, am here in representation of the Assistant Commissioner . . . My friend, Dr. Waldomiro, even though he is the nephew of the Commissioner, does not represent him, but the Governor."

"The Governor?" exclaimed the Major, overwhelmed by so much honor.

"Yes," Vadinho went on, quickly picking up his cue, "when the Governor heard the Assistant Commissioner ask his secretary and his nephew to go to the Major's party, he ordered me (I have served on His Excellency's staff) to embrace 'his good friend Pergentino and pay his respects to his worthy spouse.' "

The Major and Dona Aurora, highflown with vanity, made way for the new arrivals, introduced them, ordered drink and food served to them. Nothing was too good for Vadinho and Mirandão.

There outside, mouth agape, their scurvy comrades could not believe their eyes. What kind of chicanery had those two cynics invented to be received in that way? Nobody could recall that anyone had ever managed to cross the Major's threshold, for it was a point of honor with him to limit the party strictly to his guests, his friends, thus insuring his decency and reputation. Swearing by his glorious galloons, he boasted: "If anyone who has not been invited tries to come to one of my parties, it will be over my dead body!" And the most outstanding gate-crashers of the city, who were capable of sneaking into—and had done so—acts by invitation only, awe-inspiring, with a police guard, even entertainments at the Governor's Palace and the house of Dr. Clemente Mariani, compared with which those of the Major were mere surprise parties, a neighborhood shindy, nothing but a hop, had failed in their attempts, renewed every year, to gate-crash the Major's party. None of them had ever managed to cross the carefully guarded entrance.

To say none is not quite true. There had been Édio Gantois, a wily student, in cahoots with another who was equally crafty, the aforementioned Silver-Tongued Lev. Once while they were still students, the two of them managed, artfully, to get in and for half an hour, more or less, enjoy the party, only in the end to be thrown out, with pushes and punches, the athletic Édio in bodily combat with the guests, the bean-pole of a Lev trading kicks with the Major.

How did they triumph, and then afterwards fail in such lamentable fashion? Even though it is another story, it is worth telling here, the better to appreciate Vadinho's and Mirandão's feat. Around that time there had come to Bahia, with much newspaper fanfare, for only two performances in the Conservatory, an odd concert artist who played an instrument even stranger than himself: a saw which was as melodious as the best-tuned piano. The player was a Russian, with an unpronounceable name, the "Russian of the magic saw," as the posters and the advertisements in the papers dubbed him. Édio owned an old carpenter's saw, and Lev, the son of a Russian, the unpronounceable name. Both of them were crazy about playing low tricks, so they wrapped the saw in brown paper, tossed off a few glasses of rum to bolster their courage, and presented themselves at the Major's door as the Russian saw-player and his manager.

Major Wild Boar had a kind of extrasensory perception when it came to gate-crashers: he could sense them in the air, at a distance. He took one look at Lev and Édio and an inner voice sounded the alarm. But the guests, learning of the presence of the "Russian of the magic saw," were thrilled at the idea of hearing him play. In silence, devoured by doubts, the Major opened the door, and allowed the two scoundrels in. He remained, however, on the alert. They put the saw behind a piece of furniture, and the Major observed the haste with which they set out for the dining-room, their eagerness to eat and drink. Exchanging a glance with Dona Aurora, whom that whole act had impressed dubiously, too, the Major, supported by all the eager guests, demanded musical proof immediately. First the concert, then the refreshments. Édio, try as he would, with as hoodwinking a conversation as he could devise, to put off the hour of truth, was outmaneuvered. He obtained neither delay nor appeal.

Moreover, by some strange metamorphosis, Lev felt himself suddenly inspired; he played his role so well that he came to believe that he was the Russian of the concerts. And so, without further coaxing, he took up the old saw, to the sound of applause and bravos. He was so perfect—his long, thin body curved in an angle, his hair disheveled, his eyes looking off into space, a real artist—that he fooled them all, making even the Major and Dona Aurora wonder, until the moment when he scraped the belly of the saw with a coffee spoon. But the minute he touched it—as Édio told afterwards—all those present, without exception, realized that the whole thing was a farce. But Lev kept on, ever the more authentic artist, ever more carried away, making the saw vibrate to the touch of the spoon, without the Major, his wife, or the guests showing the slightest interest in all that effort and art.

The Major stepped forward, followed by certain of his friends, those most sensitive to jokes in bad taste. The crossing of the hall, the trajectory to the street door, was long and epic, truly unforgettable. Édio and Lev would remember it all their lives. Punches, kicks, jostles, falls. Dona Aurora would have liked to scratch their eyes out; the Major was content with throwing them into the street amid the watching crowd (and on the two fallen bodies they tossed the saw devoid of all sonority).

Nothing of the sort happened with Vadinho and Mirandão; neither the Major nor Dona Aurora had the slightest suspicion. After they ate and drank to their hearts' content, and Vadinho went waltzing around the parlor, Mirandão asked himself if it would not be fitting for him to propose a toast to the Major and Dona Aurora in Chimbo's name. He smiled in his chair as Dona Rozilda asked him who was the young man who was dancing with her daughter. For greater effect, he answered with another question:

"Didn't the Major introduce him?"

"No. I was there inside, and didn't see him when he arrived."

"Well, madame, it gives me pleasure to supply you with the information you desire. That is Dr. Waldomiro Guimarães, the nephew of Dr. Airton Guimarães, Assistant Commissioner, the grandson of the senator . . ."

"You don't mean Senator Guimarães, whom one is always hearing about?"

"That very one, my lady. The big shot, the top banana, the God Almighty of politics, that very one, my godfather . . ."

"Your godfather?"

"Of confirmation. And Vadinho's grandfather."

"Vadinho?"

"That's what he was nicknamed as a child. He is the senator's favorite grandson."

"Is he studying?"

"Didn't I tell you? Graduated, madame, a lawyer. On the staff of the Governor, an important municipal official, an inspector . . ."

"A customs inspector?" That information exceeded Dona Rozilda's wildest dreams.

"Gambling inspector, my dear lady"; and, in a whisper: "That is the inspectorship that pays the best, a fortune every month, not to mention the fringe benefits, a chip here, a chip there. And now, to top it off, a member of the Governor's staff . . ."

He was feeling very generous: "Perhaps you have some poor relative who is looking for a job. If that is the case, all you have to do is to say the word, give me the name." He took a deep breath, pleased with himself, and went on recklessly: "You see him dancing there? Well, don't be surprised if he is made a congressman in the next election . . ."

"So young?"

"That's the way things go, ma'am. He was born with a silver spoon in his mouth, everything done for him, his path strewn with rose petals." Mirandão was in a poetic mood that evening of glory. He improvised a monumental speech, bringing tears to the eyes of Dona Aurora herself, the spitfire of Rio Vermelho.

Dona Rozilda squinted up her little eyes, a yellow flame of ambition glowing before her. Joãozinho Navarro was winding up the tango with fancy flourishes. Vadinho and Flor were smiling at one another. Dona Rozilda shivered with emotion: she had never seen her daughter with that expression on her face, and she knew her well. And what about the young man, she asked herself, was he, too, roped for good? There was such an air of innocence, of candor, of sincerity on Vadinho's face that Dona Rozilda was moved. Oh, miracle-working Lord of Bonfim, could that be the rich and important son-in-law that heaven had reserved for her? Even richer and more important than Pedro Borges of Pará, with his miles of land and river, his dozens of employees? A son-in-law the grandson of a senator, closely connected with the government, he himself in the government! . . . Oh, My Lady of Capistóla, succor me! Grant me, my Lord of Bonfim, the grace of this miracle and I will walk barefooted in the procession of washing your temple, carrying flowers and a jug of pure water.

The Major came by. Dona Rozilda expressed her pleasure at meeting Mirandão, went over to the master of the house, and pointed to the group comprising Vadinho and Flor, Dona Lita and Pôrto, in a corner of the room. Mirandão observed the maneuver of the old busybody, and with an effort got to his feet and went off to look for a beer. Dona Rozilda was saying to the Major: "Major, will you introduce me to that young man."

"You haven't met? He is a relative of Dr. Airton Guimarães, the Assistant Commissioner, one of my best friends," and he smiled full of vanity, adding: "Known to those of us who are closest to him as Chimbo . . . He himself said to me: 'Pergentino, call me Chimbo, are we or aren't we friends?' A man without any nonsense to him, straight-shooting. He did me the biggest kind of a favor." He was now talking for all to hear, boasting of his friendship with the Commissioner.

Dona Rozilda shook hands with the young man, as Flor added: "This is my mother, Dr. Waldomiro."

"Vadinho to his friends."

"Dr. Waldomiro is very close to our eminent leader, the Governor. He is one of his staff."

"The Governor is very fond of you, sir. Just today he said to me: 'Give Major Pergentino an embrace for me. He is one of my best friends.' "

The Major was positively embarrassed with happiness: "Thank you, doctor."

Pôrto, whom such close contact with the world of power

frightened a little, remarked: "A great responsibility . . . But great importance, too . . ."

Vadinho put up a show of modesty: "Nonsense . . . I don't even know if I am going to stay on in the palace."

"And why not?" inquired Dona Lita.

"My grandfather, the senator . . ." Vadinho confided.

"Senator Guimarães," Dona Rozilda explained in an awed voice.

Vadinho smiled at her, an aura of candor haloing his face, and smiled melancholically at Flor, who was so pretty: "My grandfather wants me to go to Rio, he has offered me a post there . . ."

"And you are going to accept?" Flor's dewy eyes were dying.

"There is nothing to keep me here . . . Nobody . . . I am all alone . . ."

Flor sighed: "All alone . . ."

The Major called out from the dining-room; he did not give himself a minute's rest, looking after his guests continually, the perfect host. Then someone appeared clapping his hands, and requesting silence: Dr. Mirandão was going to offer a toast to the masters of the house. The pop of a champagne bottle was heard and the cork hitting the ceiling.

Vadinho and Flor walked smiling over to where they could hear. "A speech by Mirandão," Vadinho informed her, "is not a thing to be missed." Dona Rozilda, her heart going like a triphammer, remarked to Dona Lita and Thales Pôrto as she watched the two young people embarking on a definitive idyll: "Don't they make a perfect couple? Don't they look as though they had been born for each other? If God so wishes . . ."

"Good Lord, woman. They just met today and you are already fixing up a marriage." Lita shook her head—her sister was going crazy with that mania of a rich husband for her daughter.

Dona Rozilda raised her shriveled bosom, glaring arrogantly at the pessimist. From the dining-room came the voice of the orator, full-bodied, swimming in beer. The widow made her way toward him, full of hope. Applause greeting a felicitous phrase of Mirandão, he went on dauntlessly: "On the immortal pages of History, ladies and gentlemen, the honored name of Major Pergentino will go down in letters of gold, a citizen of exemplary virtues" (his voice vibrated as he spoke the high-sounding words) "and the name of his noble spouse, this ornament of the society of Boa Terra, Dona Aurora, an angel . . . Yes, ladies and gentlemen, an angel of unpolluted" (he repeated the word in his ringing voice) "virtues, a model wife, a virgin of bronze . . ."

In the middle of the parlor Mirandão, the gate-crasher, the glass of champagne aloft in his arm, had guests and hosts in his grip, all under the spell of his eloquence. The Major smiled beatifically; the model wife, the virgin of bronze, lowered her eyes, deeply touched. Never had a party of hers achieved such triumph.

". . . Dona Aurora, that lovable creature, that saintly, sacrosanct being . . ."

The eyes of the saintly being smarted with tears.

9

The courtship of Flor and Vadinho debouched straight into marriage, for there was no engagement, as will be apparent later on, with the cause and reason for this anomaly, which ran counter to the normal, time-hallowed procedures in all self-respecting families, duly set forth. A courtship, moreover, divided into two phases, perfectly delimited, each with its own characteristics. The first, placid and cheerful, everything rose-hued, the sky blue and unclouded, a real festival, all harmony. The second, confused and harassed, clandestine, tinged with vitriol and hate, hell on earth, enmity, dislike, open warfare. During the first phase Dona Rozilda was a changed person, all politeness and understanding, collaborating actively and devotedly with the success of the idyll. Later she became a fount of hatred, rancor, and vengefulness—a sight perhaps picturesque but unpleasant—prepared to use every means to prevent the marriage of her daughter to that foul creature—"worm, boil, sink of pus." All this putrefaction—"worm, boil, sink of pus"—was Vadinho, formerly the most desirable bachelor of Bahia, the ideal suitor, handsome, attractive, generous, a pearl of a youth, of unblemished character, none more upright.

In the gay deceit begun by the involved tale put in circulation by Mirandão at Major Wild Boar's party—confirmed and further developed thanks to fortuitous circumstances—Dona Rozilda basked for nearly two months, two unforgettable months when she trampled underfoot all Ladeira do Alvo and its environs, the Negress Juventina, with her airs, even Dr. Carlos Passos, with his numerous clientele. She vaunted her connections, her intimacy in government circles, among the upper echelons of Power, personified by Vadinho. And, above all, she made a display of the young man who was seeking her daughter's hand, with his dubious elegance, his engaging gift of gab, his chitchat, his airs. Vadinho took on the attributes of a divine being; he was everything to her. And nothing was too much for him; Dona Rozilda was unremitting in her desire to please, to captivate, to make sure of him.

A curious blunder contributed greatly to keeping Dona Rozilda enmeshed in this complete blindness. Among Flor's friends, there was Celia a schoolmate, who in addition to being poor was crippled, with a deformed foot, lame. With the greatest difficulty, using her handicap to soften people's hearts, as Dona Rozilda put it, she managed to finish Normal School and get a teacher's diploma. She had applied for a job in the public primary school, had struggled for months to be appointed without even managing to secure an interview with the Superintendent of Education. Dona Rozilda liked her and looked after her, perhaps because she was so pathetic and humble that compared with her she and Flor seemed millionaires. She listened attentively to the poor cripple complain of life and of the mighty of the earth, telling horrors about the officials, and revealing sordid details concerning those "vampires of education," whistling the words between her darkened, decaying teeth. The only ones who received an appointment were those who were willing to accept indecent offers, invitations for visits at night to Amaralina, Pituba, Itapoã, intimate festivities, harlots. A decent girl didn't have a chance; she mouldered in the leather chairs of the waiting room. From so much mouldering in them, Celia had become a spicy source of malicious anecdotes having to do with officials, bureau heads, not to mention the Superintendent of Education, an invisible being about whom, nevertheless, the rejected aspirant knew everything: his habits, his wealth, his tastes, his wife, his children, his mistress; nothing escaped her. But for all this she had never managed to be received by him and lay her sad case before him.

Now, following the first days of courtship, one night, the teacher in despair—the time limit for appointing new teachers ran out that week—came upon Vadinho in Flor's house, and was introduced to him. Dona Rozilda was eager to see the girl get the job, and even more eager to demonstrate to the neighbors the prestige of the young man, the aspirant to son-in-law, in charge of jobs and vacancies, with a hand in the administration of the state. A prestige to be utilized by her, Dona Rozilda, as she saw fit.

The widow was caught up in a web of errors concerning the scamp who was courting her daughter, but she did not make a mistake when, in describing to her acquaintances that model of virtues, she praised his kind heart. All suffering seemed to Vadinho unjust and hateful. And so, when Dona Rozilda told him Celia's sad story, dramatizing it, making a virtue of her handicap ("Even if she wanted to she could not accept the indecent invitations of those wretches in charge of the appointments—she's not up to that sort of thing"), expatiating on the injustice, exaggerating the hunger of the girl and her five brothers and sisters, the mother rheumatic, the father a night watchman, Vadinho instantly sympathized with the noble cause and made himself its champion. He really decided to talk the matter over with his gaming companions, some of whom had certain connections—he swore to Dona Rozilda and Flor that he would demand the teacher's immediate appointment of the Superintendent of Education the next morning when he had his session with the Governor. Not another day would elapse: Celia was to go to the Superintendent's office in the afternoon and get her appointment. The job was in the bag.

"You just leave it to me . . ."

"You can leave it to him," Dona Rozilda repeated.

Flor said nothing; she just smiled. It did not matter to her whether Vadinho enjoyed all that prestige or not; she would even have preferred that he be less influential and, consequently, less taken up with things. Days went by without his showing up, without his coming to talk at the foot of the stairs, and, when he did come, he was half asleep, drowsy, from the nights he had spent working with the Governor.

Vadinho took down the full name of the candidate, and all other necessary information. Once more Celia listed all that lifeless data on a slip of paper, without any hope; she had done it so many times. So many requests and recommendations, without any result. Why would that meddlesome fop, with his roguish, debauched air —a good-for-nothing if ever she saw one—how was he going to get her the job? Why, even Father Barbosa had given her a card for the Superintendent, and if the priest had achieved nothing, what was to be expected of this supposed suitor of Flor's; what could he do that others couldn't? Not much account could he be; you had only to look at his face worn out with carousing. Celia had stored up doubt and venom as she dragged her twisted leg through the hostile offices of the Superintendent of Education. The happiness of others did not soften her heart, nor even those rare beings willing to help her, touched by her bad luck. Her heart was dry and arid, and as she scribbled the names of her father and mother, the date of her birth, the year of her graduation, she had the certainty that it was a waste of time and effort—that coxcomb was not going to do anything for her, she was fed up with those stuck-up nobodies, full of promises and nothing more. But what else could she do? Dona Rozilda was in a tailspin over that braggart, Dr. Waldomiro this, Dr. Waldomiro that, and she, Celia, planning to sponge a lunch from the old witch. As for the suitor, you had only to take one look at him to see what he was up to: steal Flor's cherry and beat it, disappear without even saying "So long," and no one would lay eyes on him again.

Celia was being unjust to Vadinho, for to help her out he made a complete round of the gambling joints that night, with a double jinx. He lost every penny he had on him and did not meet up with a single acquaintance important enough to give him a rundown on the teacher's small drama and ask help for her. Neither Giovanni Guimarães, nor Mirabeau Sampaio, nor his namesake Waldomiro Lins, not one of them showed up, as though all his influential friends had disappeared, giving up roulette, baccarat, high stakes and low, blackjack, twenty-one. Vadinho spent the whole night making the circuit, and the most illustrious person he ran into was Mirandão, with whom he wound up going to partake of a stew of lights and liver in the house of Andreza, a devotee of Oxun, and a *comadre* of the student of agronomy.

"The dame is not only lame," Vadinho remarked, telling Mirandão about the business on the way to the shack of Oxun's devotee, "but she's knock-kneed, bare as a bone, and jinxed in the bargain. . ."

Mirandão advised Vadinho not to take it to heart; there are people like that, hexed, and there is nothing you can do to help them. Besides, worry spoils the appetite, and Andreza's stew was out of this world, eliciting praise even from Dr. Godofredo Junior, with all his authority. The next day Vadinho could try again. After all, the pest had already waited so long that one day more or less would not make her commit suicide. As for the stew of his *comadre* Andreza, just how did the phrase go, no not the phrase, the verse of Master Godofredo?

And whom did they find at the table of the deity's devotee but the poet Godofredo in person, doing honor to the meal of Andreza, sparing no praise of the seasoning and the cook, a wonderful hunk of Negress, a royal palm, the morning breeze, the figurehead of a ship. Andreza smiled with all her vainglory and stateliness, crushing peppers for the sauce.

"Well, look who's here!" Mirandão sang out. "My lord, my master, consider that I am on my knees before your intellectual gifts."

"We are all on our knees before this divine stew." The poet laughed, shaking hands with the two young fellows.

They sat down, and Andreza immediately took note of Vadinho's worried expression. He who was always so gay and full of fun, so shrewd and tricky, what had happened to make his face so overcast, melancholy? Come, my pet, tell all, relieve your soul, spit out your troubles. Andreza, dressed in yellow, with strings of beads about her neck and on her arms, was Oxun herself, outdoing herself in coyness and beauty. Come, white man, don't be in the dumps, here's your black girl to listen to you and console you.

At the table, over the cloth smelling of patchouli and the floor perfumed with pitanga leaves, between the stew and the first-class rum of Santo Amaro, Vadinho recited the rosary of misfortunes of the primary-school teacher, a child of ill fate. Sitting at the head of the table, the Negress Andreza was touched by the story, clasped her hand to her heaving bosom—poor girl with her deformity and her hunger, her eagerness to work and her unemployment. Was it possible that Godo, whose name appeared in the newspapers, who held a high official post himself, couldn't say a word on her behalf, do something for the poor thing? Andreza's lips quivered as she made her plea; Vadinho was right—how could one be happy when somebody was suffering so, so buffeted by life? Why had she asked to hear that sad story? She could never smile again until she knew the girl had got her appointment. The poet Godofredo promised to intercede, possibly he could obtain something. When was she going back to see the Superintendent? The next day . . . No, that very afternoon, for it was now almost morning, and Vadinho had so directed her. Then let her go, Godofredo would see. He did not go into the fact that the Superintendent of Education was a close relative and an intimate friend of his, and that a request of his was tantamount to an order. The poet did not like to show off; he only published his poems at rare intervals. All he wanted was to bring the smile back to Andreza's lips; without it, the night was sad and the world cold and bare.

So when, the next afternoon, Celia, pessimistic but persistent, dragged her lame leg up the stairs and went into the waiting room of the Superintendent of Education's office, imagine her surprise at being warmly and eagerly greeted by His Excellency's secretary, formerly so offhand and curt.

"Dona Celia, I was waiting for you. Congratulations, your appointment has just come through, it has been signed . . ."

"What's that you are saying?" The teacher trembled.

More and more courteous, the secretary grew confidential.

"Just as I tell you . . . It was the first thing the Superintendent did when he came in . . . Someone high up gave the order, without doubt. It was one of the last positions open and they were all bespoken . . . May I give you a word of advice? Go and present yourself right away. Don't lose time."

She presented herself, took over the post, collected her scrawny family and went to the first floor of Alvo to express her gratitude. "Someone high up," she said; and Dona Rozilda repeated the words rolling them over her tongue, savoring them, the taste of power. She was trembling with satisfaction; she had not expected such a quick appointment, such a lightning-like result. That urgency, that speed, could only mean direct orders from the Governor. From the Governor, my daughter, and nobody else. In other words, Vadinho worked his will in the government.

The news ran its course over the hillside, and when Vadinho appeared that night, with the hope of being alone with Flor in the darkness of the stairway, he was greeted by the neighborhood in what amounted to a manifestation of gratitude. He was overwhelmed with the thanks, embraces, praise, with Dona Rozilda practically hysterical. He had spent the day sleeping and had almost forgotten the misfortunes of the lamentable applicant. "Oh, that; that is nothing, please, you do not owe me anything."

The poet had kept his word, thanks more to Andreza than to Vadinho. But how explain the truth, set matters straight? Never would Dona Rozilda and her neighbors, never would the sour teacher and her shriveled, dingy family, the color of dirt, assembled there to thank him, understand the devious paths of the world and its ways, never would they believe that Celia owed her appointment to a colored cook, far poorer than she, happy in a shack on the seashore of Agua de Meninos, preparing meals for fishermen and stevedores, the Negress Andreza of Oxun.

Vadinho's fame grew and the requests multiplied. In less than a week there were eight appeals for appointments as primary-school teachers. From car conductor to tax collector there was not a candidate who did not fawn upon Dona Rozilda, knocking on the door of the house on Ladeira do Alvo. Even the job of sacristan in the Church of Conceiçao da Praia, reported about to be vacant soon, but which was not yet sure, even that they came to see about. If Vadinho had been Governor and Archbishop rolled into one, not even so would he have been able to attend to everything.

10

Dona Rozilda trod the summits of power, savored the incomparable taste of fame. Vadinho caressed Flor's firm breasts in the darkness of the stairway, felt the shy, timid thirst of her mouth, bit her lips. He revealed to her a world of forbidden pleasures she had hardly suspected, overcoming every night of their courtship a portion of her resistance and of her body, of her modesty, of her hidden feelings. Desire consumed her in a blaze of towering flames, but Flor did her best to control and contain herself. Feeling every day, however, less mistress of her will, her resistance weakening, the submissive slave of that bold youth who had already taken possession of almost all her body which was burning in a fever that had no cure, alas, no cure.

That insolent Vadinho! He did not tell her he was in love with her, did not make an avowal of ardent emotions, did not even ask leave to court her. In place of poetic phrases, high-flown terms, what she heard were phrases with double meaning, insinuations of randy intent. Coming up Ladeira do Alvo behind Flor (on her way back from Aunt Lita's house in Rio Vermelho a few days after Major Pergentino's party), the brazen scamp, reading the sign of the Cooking School, murmured in her ear, in a romantic whisper as one who pays an innocent compliment:

"School of Savor and Art . . . ," he repeated. "Savor and Art

. . ." and lowering his voice, his hairline mustache brushing her ear: "Ah, what I would give to savor you." And this was not just a joke in bad taste, but a clear statement of his intentions, a bold-faced avouchment of his idea of courtship.

Flor had never had a suitor like that, so different from the others, nor could she imagine a courtship of that nature. Why didn't she send him packing at once?

Flor was not one of those loose window-dawdlers, carrying on a scandalous idyll on the street corners, at the foot of the stairs, in the doorways. No seeker of her favors had even gone beyond a shy kiss. Pedro Borges had barely brushed her cheek; she did not stand for such intimacies. It was enough for some daredevil to reach out his hand to touch her, and Flor rose up in righteous indignation and ordered him out, as though she were saving herself wholly for the one she would really love. To this one she would deny nothing, and this one was Vadinho; there you have the reason why she did not send him away as she had done the others, without scene or scandal, but firmly and inflexibly.

She did not even rebuff him the first time in spite of the fact that they had known each other for only a few hours, for it was on the Sunday of the Annunciation Rehearsal, the day after the party at Major Wild Boar's house. In the company of several of her friends, Flor had come to see the groups, and Vadinho had showed up and joined them. The other girls went away giggling, certain that the moment had arrived for the indispensable proposal (a proposal more or less vehement and flowery depending on the temperament and gifts of the suitor; some of the shyer ones preferred to do it by letter resorting, if necessary, to *The Lover's Complete Handbook*). They had just been talking about the infatuation of the young man; he had not left Flor's side for a minute at the party, her constant partner. Now he was going to declare his love; it was a grave moment; the girl could either consent at once or ask for time to think it over, usually twenty-four hours. Flor had informed her friends of her plan to let Vadinho suffer a few days more, but the others had their doubts. Would she have the courage to do that?

Not a word that could be interpreted as a proposal passed his lips. The talk had to do with a number of amusing incidents. What a screwball that Vadinho was! Two lively carnival-like groups trying to out-do one another met by the wall of the Church of St. Anne, and taking advantage of the crush caused by the people rushing and crowding against one another, Vadinho caught Flor to him from the back, covering her breasts with his hands, avidly kissing the nape of her neck. She barely trembled, half-closing her eyes, and let him do his will, half-dead with fear and delight.

The early days of this courtship without formal proposal or formal acceptance were unforgettable. Every year in the summer, at the time of the neighborhood festivals, Flor was in the habit of spending some time with her aunt and uncle, of whom she was very fond. During the month of February the Cooking School of Savor and Art was closed.

She came for the procession in honor of Yemanjá, on the second of February, when the fishing smacks skim the waves, laden with flowers and gifts for Dona Janaína, the mother of the waters, of the storms, of the fish, of life and death of the sea. As offerings, she brought a comb, a bottle of perfume, a cheap ring. Yemanjá lives in Rio Vermelho, her shrine on a point of land stretching into the ocean.

In the company of the girls of the neighborhood, Flor enjoyed an intensive, gay holiday: sea-bathing in the morning; walks in the afternoon to the lighthouse of Barra and in Amaralina. At times they went as far as Pituba; the organization and rehearsals of the Carnival floats—a gay job; picnics in Itapoã, at the home of Dr. Natal, a doctor friend of Uncle Pôrto, or on the Lagoon of Abaeté, with guitars and songs; confetti fights. At night they made the rounds of Largo de Sant'Ana or Mariquito among the colorful booths when there was no dance planned in the house of some friend of the family, or they themselves did not invade and occupy a parlor in a surprise party.

The house of Pôrto, aflower with vines and acacias, was on Ladeira do Papagaio, and on Sundays her uncle invariably went out with another amateur painter who lived in the Square, one José de Dome from Sergipe, the most diffident person in the world, to paint groups of houses and landscapes. About two years before, when Rosalía and Antônio Morais had left for Rio, Flor, sad and lonely, had come to feel a certain tenderness for the painter, a man in his forties, though he looked younger, a stiff, taciturn caboclo. He had suggested to her one day, overcoming his almost morbid timidity, that he paint her portrait, and he had begun it against a background of violent ochres and yellows in which Flor's pale complexion was completely transfigured. "That's a crazy project, utter nonsense. Besides the man is not right in his mind," was the verdict of Dona Rozilda—whose horizon in matters of art was limited to calendar covers—at the sight of that explosion of color and light. However, José de Dome never finished the portrait. There was no time. Flor returned to Ladeira do Alvo and, although she promised to come to pose on Sundays, she never did; she did not understand the painting of the man from Sergipe either. She was touched by his smile and his loneliness. But that feeling never blossomed into love, for you cannot call love the long silence and brief smiles of the hours of posing. It never went beyond a passing tenderness which lasted only those days of the summer holiday, during which the artist's timidity never gave ground. Whenever she returned to Rio Vermelho, Flor greeted her uncle's friend with the same cordiality, but the attraction of earlier summers had disappeared as though nothing had happened between them. As for the unfinished picture, it is still on the wall of the painter's studio, on the third floor of an old house on the corner of Largo de Sant'Ana; anyone who wants to see it has only to summon the courage to climb the worm-eaten stairs.

So different from Vadinho . . . As though an irresistible avalanche were dragging her along, he dominated her and decided her fate. Flor understood, after those brief and perfect days in Rio Vermelho, that it was no longer possible for her to live without the warmth, the gaiety, the mad presence of that charmer. She did whatever he asked of her: at the parties she danced with nobody else; hand in hand they went down from the kermess of the Square to the dark beach, where in the blackness of the night they could kiss better, as he suggested; she shivered as she felt his caressing hand make its way under her dress, setting her thighs and haunches afire. As for Dona Rozilda, who would ever have imagined that she could be so democratic, so generous? She turned a blind eye to the clear overstepping of bounds in that uncontrolled courtship with no clear goal, to the point where Aunt Lita, so little given to grumbling, was nevertheless perturbed and warned her: "Doesn't it seem to you, Rozilda, that Flor is encouraging that young man too much? They go out together everywhere as though they were engaged; it hardly seems believable that they met only a few days ago."

Dona Rozilda's reaction was savage, her voice defiant: "I don't know what in the devil you and your husband have against Vadinho . . . Just because he is rich and holds an outstanding post, there is all this buzz-buzz about him; I can't understand why you people have taken this dislike to him . . . You got all steamed up over that poor devil of a painter; if it had depended on you, they'd have been married right away, as though I was going to give my daughter to that beetle. You don't have a good word to say for Vadinho. I can't see anything out of the way in his courting Flor—she's of an age to be thinking about marriage, and when the Lord of Bonfim, hearkening to my prayers, sends along a match like him, you and Pôrto set up such a to-do, calling him this and that . . . You let me handle my own affairs, woman . . ."

"I'm not trying to meddle in your business, my dear. I was just talking. You are the one who is always carping and criticizing. You only have to see a girl out walking with a fellow and right off she's a strumpet . . . And now you've made a complete about-face, you've turned the girl loose . . ."

"You think she is a strumpet? Is that what you are thinking? Out with it . . ."

"Calm down, Rozilda; you know that's not what I was saying."

Dona Rozilda summed up her position and put an end to the discussion: "I know what I am doing, she's my daughter, and, God willing, this year they will get married."

"Please God you are right!"

"That I am right? You just wait and see. And don't come to me with those warnings and so forth; it's just that you don't like Vadinho . . ."

No, nobody showed any dislike for Vadinho. He had them all hypnotized by his talk and his imagination, first the acquaintances in Rio Vermelho, and then those of Ladeira do Alvo. Dona Lita and Pôrto had already become friendly with him, and liked the idea of his being Flor's husband. As for Dona Rozilda, she seemed to live for nothing but to satisfy his desires, divine his whims.

As for whims, the only one he really had was to be alone with Flor, take her in his arms, overcome her resistance and modesty, making her his little by little with each encounter. Binding her with the ropes of desire, but binding himself as well, drowning in those liquid, startled eyes, in that frenzied, evasive body, burning with eagerness, held back by modesty. Above all, he was attracted by Flor's gentleness, by the home atmosphere, the setting that befitted the simple grace of the girl, her quiet beauty, an atmosphere which exerted a powerful fascination on him.

He had never lived a family life, never known his mother, who died in childbirth, or his father, who soon faded out of his existence. He was the offspring of a brief association between the eldest son of a middle-class family and a maid of the household, and his father, a distant connection of the Guimarães, had looked out for him as long as he was single. But when he made a good marriage, he did everything he could to rid himself of that bastard of whom his wife, ignorant and devoutly religious, had felt a virtuous horror—"the child of sin!" Vadinho had been put in a Catholic boarding school where, somehow or other, he had managed to reach the last year of high school, which he had not finished because he had fallen head over heels in love, one Sunday when he was on holiday, with the mother of a classmate, an attractive woman of forty, the wife of a businessman of the city, who had the reputation at the time of being the easiest bitch to make in the high society of Bahia—a devouring passion which was reciprocated.

Romantic, too. The illustrious lady rolled her eyes, sighed, Vadinho did not let her out of his sight on her visits to the patio of the school, which was as dismal as a prison, a lugubrious child's prison. She gave him chocolates and crackers from the package she brought for her son. On the sly Vadinho offered her an orchid which he had stolen from the friars' greenhouse. One day of recreation (the first Sunday of the month Vadinho never went out, nobody came for him, he had nowhere to go) she took him to lunch at her house, a mansion on Graça Square, and introduced him to her husband: "One of Zezito's classmates, an orphan, who has no family . . ."

Zezito was not too robust. He raised guinea pigs and on his free Sundays devoted all his time to them in the basement of the house. While the businessman snored away his siesta, Vadinho was lured off to a sewing room, covered with kisses and caresses, possessed. "My little boy, my student, I am your teacher, ah, my page," and fully aware of her gifts as a teacher, she taught him—and how! The affair grew, insatiable and brutal. She melted in sighs and vows —she would never love another, she repeated cynically and earnestly; Vadinho was her first lover, and she coveted nothing in the world except to go away with him so they could live their great love, the two of them, in some hidden corner. What a pity he was in a boarding school . . .

"If I were to leave the school, would you really live with me?"

He ran away from school, showed up early in the evening to take her away, to liberate her from that "beast of a bourgeois" who made her suffer so much, and humiliated her with his lechery. He had found a miserable room in a low-class boarding house; he had bought bread, sausage (he adored sausage), a pestilential brew that was sold as wine, and a bunch of flowers. He still had a few mil-reis —his most intimate friends, who knew how things stood and backed him up, had made a contribution to finance his flight and love. From their point of view, Vadinho was a he-man.

The esteemed lady almost collapsed with fright when he burst into her home, where her husband was sitting in the next room picking his teeth and reading the newspapers. Vadinho must surely have lost his mind, she said indignantly. Was she an adventuress to leave her home, her husband and son, her comforts and her reputation, to go to live as the mistress of a child, in poverty and dishonor? Vadinho did not have the sense he was born with. The thing for him to do was to go back to school. Perhaps they were not even aware of his flight, and on his next Sunday off, she promised him . . .

Vadinho did not want to hear her promise, overcome as he was with rage and chagrin. He had been made a fool of. Without taking into account the proximity of the businessman, he grabbed her by her long, bleached hair, gave her several slaps in the face, called her names, in a fracas of such proportions that it brought in, not only the husband and the servants, but also the neighbors of the fashionable Largo da Graça. According to Vadinho's subsequent account, that was the day he became a man, and a man who was not to be fooled again.

It was thanks to this scandal that Vadinho became a denizen of the night life of the city at the age of seventeen, under the sponsorship of Anacreon, a notorious cardsharper, a cheat of style and reputation. There was nobody better to teach an inexperienced youth the subtleties and intricacies of blackjack, twenty-one, baccarat, poker, to familiarize him with the dialectics of the roulette wheel and the mystique of dice, for Anacreon not only was competent, but also had a loyal heart, faced up to life, a kind of Don Quixote. Vadinho had a brief interview with his father in which he refused to return to boarding school, as a result of which the indecent Guimarães denied him his blessing and all financial aid: he "did not have the money to support hooligans." His wife's money had turned him into a miser and a moralist. Besides, at this juncture of his life, with his name appearing in the society columns, he began to entertain serious doubts concerning Vadinho's paternity. Could he really be his son? The late Valdete had accused him, between kisses, of having deflowered her and made her pregnant. But was the statement of a servant anything you could rely upon? She had never known another man but him, according to her friends weeping over her corpse. But was the word of these other housemaids, drifting from one job to another, proof of anything? All that had happened so long ago, had become the confused memories of youth, of irresponsible adolescence. Perhaps he was his son, perhaps he wasn't. Who could prove it, where was the certainty of it? What was certain was that Vadinho was a son of a bitch, and one of the worst: still a boy and trying "to violate a decent woman, the kindly mother of a schoolmate, in whose home he had been received as a son . . ." This father of Vadinho's was a Guimarães of "the rotten branch," as Chimbo classified him; he lacked the firmness and generosity of the family.

From that time on Vadinho had never breathed the scent of family feeling, had never again had a complex and varied interest. His sentimental life, active and diverse, for his multiple love affairs varied in age, social standing, and color, had run its course for the most part in brothels and cabarets, in brief infatuations with whores, cohabitation, in addition to a few adventures with married women. But none of these attachments could be called love. No infatuation had ever made him feel that his life was full and luminous, no separation, quarrel, or end of an affair had made him feel dull and empty or had brought the idea of suicide to his mind. He took off for the body of another woman just as he might have changed tables in a gambling room when his favorite number, 17, played him false.

The meeting with Flor at the Major's party had rekindled in him all of a sudden that old longing for a home, a family life, a table decently set, a bed with clean sheets. He did not even have a permanent address, changing from one cheap boardinghouse to another every month because he did not pay his bill. How was he going to squander money on rent when he had so little left for gambling?

Flor brought a new savor to his life—a repose, a tranquility, a longing for the tenderness of a family.

"I like you because you are tame like a little pet animal, sweetie . . ."

So beguiled was he by her that he even put up with her mother, the most awful and tedious, ridiculous and boring old harridan he had ever met. He loved the sincerity of the girl, her gentleness, her quiet joyousness, and her composure. Fighting every day to break down her resistance and destroy her chastity, he nevertheless felt happy and proud of her modesty and seriousness. For it was up to him, and no one but him, to overcome that shyness, turn that modesty into pleasure. Vadinho's friends noticed a gleam in his eyes, marveled at seeing him standing in front of the roulette wheel, forgetting to bet his chip, dreamy.

And the close friends, like Mirandão, were not surprised to see him at Carnival time forming one of the float of the "Gay Newsboys," a group organized by the families of Rio Vermelho, with decorations by Uncle Pôrto, girls and youths disguised as newsboys, selling the *Diario de Bahia* and *A Tarde*, the *Diario de Noticias* and *O Imparcial*. A carnival of confetti and cane syrup, of paper streamers and songs, in which the perfume squirters were for the lovers and not to be wasted on the air, a carnival without rum. The opposite of Vadinho's carnivals, which lasted from Saturday until Tuesday in one uninterrupted binge. Forming part of groups of masqueraders, fooling with the girls, dancing the samba in the middle of the street, drinking without letup. Falling in a drunken stupor at the end of the night in any cathouse of the district; and on like that for four days.

"Look who's there in that float with a tambourine in his hand! It's Vadinho, who would ever believe it!" said amazed passers-by who were accustomed to seeing him in a state of total debauchery during the merrymaking of Carnival. There was Vadinho, beside Flor, covering her with confetti and tenderness.

None of this prevented him, however, from slipping into utter dissolution, from taking aboard the heaviest load of rum once he had taken his leave of Flor, at midnight. He set out straight for Tabaris, or Meia-Luz, or Flozô. On Tuesday he made the excuse of pressing duties at the Governor's Palace, and left at ten, for he could not be late for the great dance of the Pinguelo Dance Hall, where Andreza and other superb creoles were dressed like ladies of the court of Marie Antoinette, in satin and velvet, with white cotton wigs.

Not even when his emotions were running highest, when he was carried away by thoughts of family life, domestic felicity, did it cross Vadinho's mind to change his way of being, to modify it, acquire new habits, regenerate himself. Mirandão threatened to do so every now and then: "Brother, I'm going to reform, beginning tomorrow . . ."

Vadinho never spoke like that. Crazy though he was about

Flor, planning to marry her, not even so was he prepared to elude his solemn responsibilities, his daily quota of gaming and raffishness, of drinking and disreputability, of gambling dives and whorehouses.

11

A sea of roses, an azure sky, a world of peace and good will toward men, Flor and Vadinho sweethearts. Then suddenly the tempest, the storm, a leaden sky, war without quarter, execration, Flor and Vadinho forbidden to see each other.

Mirandão, that moralist with aspirations to philosopher, felt a slight embarrassment over the matter. Hadn't he been the one who started the building of that house of cards, unable to resist the breath of the slightest investigation?

"There you are," he observed. "What guarantee does one have? None. Even when you have the motor of a truck repaired, you get a six-month guarantee. And when a person thinks all his life is fixed up, that finally everything is going for him, it comes apart, the saint falls from his float and turns into rubbish . . ."

In Mirandão's opinion, Vadinho had fallen from his float, the saint had become rubbish, with the remains scattered on the garbage dump, and there was no way of restoring the esteem of the ex-cabinet member in Dona Rozilda's eyes. An esteem equally damaged as far as Flor was concerned; how was she to accept the liar who had soft-soaped her that way? Mirandão was acquainted with gentle, meek persons of that sort; once they had been taken advantage of, they walled themselves around with stubborn pride, and there was no changing them.

"When they get mad, they stay mad for good," was his pessimistic conclusion.

Low, common, abject, infamous—Dona Rozilda found herself at a loss for terms sufficiently virile and vigorous to describe such a miserable specimen of humanity, who only the day before had been the ideal suitor, the saint on the altar all bedecked with praise. Her daughter could even marry a policeman, a criminal tried by jury and sentenced to jail, but never that worthless hound. Informed by the residents of Ladeira do Alvo of these heartless opinions, Mirandão shook his heavy, realistic head: if Vadinho thought he could get on with his affair, that was because he knew nothing about women. Always so wily, now that he was blinded by passion, he had lost sight of reality; he had loused everything up. Mirandão, disconsolate, called for another drink at the Triumph Bar to steady himself.

Vadinho could not have cared less about restoring his reputation in Dona Rozilda's eyes, placating her fury, that old she-devil, that insufferable hag, that dose of castor oil. He could not, however, endure the thought of breaking off with Flor, losing her gentle laugh, her calm tenderness, her sigh, which touched him to the soul. On the contrary, he now made up his mind to marry her. In the last analysis the only thing that mattered in that whole business was the love, the understanding, the affection that existed between them; all the rest was just a crazy joke. Whom did Flor love? Him, Vadinho, as he was, not the post he had invented, the job he did not perform, the money he did not have.

In that whole affair there was only one thing that annoyed him: having been unmasked by Celia, whom he had befriended, that gimp now a public-school teacher thanks to his intervention. She was the one who had started the whole ruckus, who had unfolded the plot, who had denounced him to Dona Rozilda. She had come hurrying to the first floor all of a swivet, so excited she could hardly talk. And so happy you had to see it to believe it.

"Someone of high standing? That faker never even went up the steps of the Governor's Palace. The only palace he knows, and he knows that one all right, is the 'Palace,' a gambling den and crib of prostitutes . . . Prestige? Only in the lowest streets of the red-light district, among the strumpets and crooks. Member of the Governor's cabinet? If he tried to go into the Governor's office, he would be arrested, thrown into the calaboose." Her appointment as a teacher? It was better not to think of that; God knows the shenanigans and rascality that scoundrel had resorted to.

And how was it that Celia, that insignificant primary-school teacher, had discovered all that fabric of deceit, bringing to light all the details of the farce, not leaving even the shadow of a doubt, a mere "perhaps" to which Dona Rozilda, shipwrecked in the sea of her sodden life, could cling? Why that effort to unmask and denounce the trickster, the cheap deceiver?

Vadinho was surprised, hurt: "Who would have thought it! What harm did I ever do her? On the contrary . . ."

Perhaps for that very reason. When Vadinho got her her job, Celia was at one and the same time grateful and offended. At heart she did not forgive him for having fooled her about him, for not being the gigolo her radar of bitterness and malice had picked up: her miserable existence had made her envious and mean. And with every passing day she was less grateful and more offended—there was something about him that did not convince her. Possibly she picked up a clue and had followed it up, tracked it down until she discovered all the details of the web of lies Mirandão had begun spinning in the Major's house, and for whose growth life was more responsible than Vadinho himself. Once she had got to the bottom of that exciting dime novel, Celia felt fulfilled. Nobody could fool her; she had eye and instinct; it took more than a job, appointment, and tenure to hoodwink her. Satisfied, happy with her scurrility, she did not even feel the weight of her dragging leg as she mounted the stairs to the first floor, where Dona Rozilda and Flor were at work on the trousseau. That pretentious bum was nothing but a gigolo; she, Celia, had never doubted it. Her dingy face glowed—she had rarely been so happy. Lots of tears would be shed that day; harsh words would be spoken; there would be grinding of teeth. And is there anything in the world as splendid and exciting, any display comparable to the suffering of others? Not for Celia. No man had ever looked at her to desire her. Nobody had ever smiled at her with love, and the children at school were terrified of her, fled her.

Dona Rozilda, on the verge of a fit, suggested killing and dying, and asked for a glass of water. Flor paid no attention to her, did not even hear her moans, occupied as she was with Celia: "Get out of here, you bitch, and don't ever come back."

"Me, Flor? Are you in earnest? Why?"

"Even if he were what you say, you had no business to come butting in. He found you a job. You should have kept anything you knew against him to yourself. You were dying of hunger and he found you a job."

"How do I know it was him? Who saw him do it? If you ask me, it was Father Barbosa's letter . . ."

Flor hardly raised her voice, but her words dripped disgust and hate: "Get out of here before I teach you not to meddle in other people's affairs, you stray bitch."

"Then stay with him, and much good may it do you. You were born to be a slut."

She went down the stairs vociferating against human ingratitude.

War, yes, what other term can we use, and war without quarter—the war between Dona Rozilda and Flor broke out there, at that very hour. At the sound of the door slamming in Celia's face, Dona Rozilda recovered her senses, came out of her fit, called for the teacher to go on with the talk about Vadinho, turning the knife in the wound.

"Celia, Celia! Don't go away."

Flor answered in a stern voice: "I sent her away."

"She came to do us a favor and you shooed her away, instead of being grateful."

"That troublemaker is never to set foot in this house again."

"And since when are you the boss here?"

"If she comes, I leave."

Mirandão was right in describing Vadinho's loss of standing with Dona Rozilda. He was wrong, however, completely so, with regard to Flor's reaction. Naturally, she was not happy; she was disappointed: such a worthless Vadinho. Why all those lies? But not for a minute did she think of breaking with him, of ending their affair. She loved him; his job or office mattered little to her, his position in society, his importance in politics.

That was what she said to him that night when, insolently defying Dona Rozilda's orders, she went to talk with him on a nearby corner. She listened to and accepted his explanations, shed a few tears, called him "crazy, senseless, my sweet idiot." For the first time Vadinho spoke to her of love, of how he hungered and thirsted for her, and as his wife. And to Flor this was worth all the irritation, all the pain of his having lied and tangled himself up without any need for it.

They would have to wait and have patience, Flor told him. At least the ten months until she reached twenty-one; she was still a minor, under her mother's control, and Vadinho might just as well forget trying to get Dona Rozilda's consent. She had never seen her mother in such a state. It was not even going to be easy for them to meet; they would have to figure out some way so the old lady would not suspect. Their courtship—that courtship which had met with so much approval, had been so well regarded by Dona Rozilda—had now been driven underground, was strictly forbidden. Vadinho's rating on Ladeira do Alvo was not worth the dust in the street. Vadinho dried her tears with kisses right there on the street corner, paying no attention to the passers-by.

Breathing fire and brimstone, Dona Rozilda was waiting for her, strap in hand, a strip of rawhide to discipline disobedient animals and children. It had not been used for a long time, not since the days when Hector sometimes fell behind in his studies. Rosalía had tasted of it. Flor had had an occasional whipping when she was a child. Hanging on the wall of the dining-room, the primitive whip was now little more than a cruel symbol of maternal authority which had fallen into disuse. When Flor walked in through the door, Dona Rozilda raised the strap, and the first lash crossed Flor's breast and neck, leaving a red welt which lasted for over a week.

She took it without a tear, covering her face with her hands, reaffirming her love. "You'll not marry him as long as I am alive,"

Dona Rozilda bellowed. The next day Flor could hardly get out of
bed. Her whole body ached, and that red welt on her neck. The
entire neighborhood commented on what had happened. The Negress Juventina, queening it in her window, supplied full details,
Dr. Carlos Passos severely criticized Dona Rozilda's educational
methods, though he did not deny her motives for exasperation and
the scolding.

Vadinho showed up at the usual hour; the whole first floor was
locked, the balcony empty, the doorway bolted and barred. Flor's
window opened on the side street; between the cracks of the
Venetian blind glimmers of light were visible. Then someone told
him about the beating of the night before; according to the neighborhood gossips Flor was languishing, locked in her room.

Vadinho agreed with the Negress Juventina when the mistress
of Antenor Lima said of Dona Rozilda justly and with a literary
flourish: "A bestial hyena, that is what she is, Mr. Vadinho"; he
listened to the news in silence, took his leave, and departed.

To come back after midnight, making all the windows in the
vicinity fly open, wake up the hillside and the neighboring streets
with the tenderest and most impassioned serenade almost ever
heard in this or any other city. Whoever heard it carried its
unforgettable memory in his ears and heart.

And with good reason. Vadinho had assembled in Flor's honor
the best there was. He had brought lanky Carlinhos Mascarenhas,
with his golden four-string guitar; he had gone looking for him in
Carla's cathouse, and had dragged him out of Marianinha Pentelhu-
da's soft bed. At the violin, Edgard Cocô, the *ne plus ultra*, whose
equal was to be found only in Rio de Janeiro or abroad. Playing
the flute—and with what dignity and skill!—the young lawyer,
Walter da Silveira. Vadinho had torn him away from his books,
for, recently graduated, he was diligently preparing himself for
examination for the bench; and before long, a judge of outstanding
reputation, he would no longer give public exhibitions on the flute,
depriving the masses of a heavenly delight. As for the guitar, it was
strummed by a young man whom everybody liked for his breeding
and gaiety, his modest and at the same time distinguished air, his
competence in drinking, his agreeable manners, and his music: the

unique quality of his guitar, his and only his, and his voice at once
mysterious and rakehellish. A wonderful guy. Of late he had
appeared and played and sung on the radio, and his success was
assured. His name was on everyone's lips: Dorival Caymmi, and his
close friends praised his as yet unedited compositions; the day they
became known, the Negro would be famous. He was a bosom
friend of Vadinho's: they had taken their first drinks together, and
had watched the sun come up. As a spare they had brought along
Jenner Augusto, a pale cabaret singer, and for good measure,
Mirandão, already tight.

At the foot of the hill they stopped for a few minutes; Edgard
Cocô's violin sobbed its first, heart-piercing chords. This was
immediately followed by the four-string guitar, the flute, the
guitar; and Caymmi began a duet with Vadinho, whose warbling
was nothing special. But his cause was good, his love forbidden; his
desire was to make amends to his beloved, cure her sadness, calm
her dreams, bring her the consolation of music, proof of his love:

> *Arching night, smiling sky,*
> *Silence that is almost a dream,*
> *And the moonlight on the forest*
> *Sheds its silver stream*
> *Resplendent in its glory,*
> *Only you, my beloved, sleep,*
> *Heedless of your troubador.*
> *Heedless of your troubador.*

The *modinha* of Cândido das Neves ascended the hillside more
quickly than they. Curious heads emerged from the windows,
fascinated by the music, the voice of Caymmi. The Negress Juventina clapped her hands in applause; she was on the side of Flor and
Vadinho, and crazy about serenades. Some woke up in a fury, on
the point of protesting, but the sweetness of the song disarmed
them, lulling them back to sleep with its call of love. Dr. Carlos
Passos was one of these: he jumped out of bed in a murderous rage.
He worked hard, he had to be at the hospital at six in the morning,
and there were days when he did not get home until nine at night.
But in the time it took him to get from his bed to the window, his

wrath became assuaged, and he was humming the tune as he leaned
over the sill to listen more comfortably:

> *Send your silvery light, oh moon*
> *To awaken my belovèd . . .*

They had now taken up their position under a lamppost on the
corner directly across from the house. Vadinho had stepped a little
ahead of the group to stand right under the electric light where
Flor could see him better. The sounds of Dr. Silveira's flute rose up
the wall; the moans of the guitar made their way to the balcony;
the violin of Edgard Cocô penetrated the windows of the girl's
room, drew her from her bed in a tremor. "God in Heaven, it's
Vadinho!" She ran to the window, raised the blind. There he stood
under the light, with his fair hair, his arms on high:

> *Would that I could kill my desires,*
> *Drown you in my kisses . . .*

A number of night owls joined to listen; Cazuza Funnel came
out wearing an old pair of pajamas, attracted by the music and the
hope of a bottle in the hands of the serenaders.

On the balcony of the first floor Dona Rozilda emerged from
the darkness, her wrath interrupting the music and the poem:
"Loafers! Vagrants!"

Higher rose the song, Caymmi's voice seeking the stars:

> *I sing . . .*
> *And my true heart's desire*
> *Hears me not, sleeps on . . .*

Where did Flor find that rose so red it was almost black?
Vadinho caught it in the air that romantic night of lovers, with the
yellow moon in the sky and the scent of rosemary, all the hillside
singing in chorus to Flor, a prisoner in her room:

> *There above the wandering moon,*
> *So pensive in the sky,*
> *And the stars so serene . . .*

Dona Rozilda rushed out of the street door, flinging it wide, her topknot askew, wrapped in a dirty bathrobe and hate. She made for the group in a wildness of fury: "Get out of here! You bunch of bastards! Out!"

But it lasted only a second. Immediately the flute of Dr. Silveira was heard in what seemed like a mocking laugh, like the whistle of a street urchin, a music that was more like a jeer and a jibe:

> *Fair one, please let me*
> *Come up this hill . . .*

Whereupon they all saw Vadinho advance toward his future mother-in-law, and in front of her, to the accompaniment of the flute, go through, with perfection and grace, with perfect motion of his feet and a swaying of his body, the step of *siri-bocêta*, the difficult and famous step of *siri-bocêta*. In utter confusion, panic, speechless, Dona Rozilda gathered up sufficient strength to rush up the stairs.

The serenade again took over the night and the street, continued until the approach of dawn. Night owls, in varying stages of drunkenness, reinforced the chorus, the night watchman who was making his rounds stopped to listen and applaud. The bottle Cazuza Funnel had felt must be there appeared; the repertoire was vast. Vadinho and Caymmi sang, Jenner Augusto sang, Dr. Walter sang in his basso profundo, the night watchman sang (his cherished dream was to sing on the radio). The whole street took part in the serenade to Flor, Flor leaning against her high window, all ruffles and lace, drenched in moonlight. Down below Vadinho, her gallant knight, with the red rose in his hand, so red it was almost black, the rose of her love.

12

It was in the house and affection of Aunt Lita and her husband Thales Pôrto in Rio Vermelho that the harried Flor sought and found protection when she ran away from home to marry Vadinho.

Pôrto had certain doubts; he wanted to avoid set-tos with Dona Rozilda, a termagant with a tongue like a knife. He was a man who loved to have peace, to live quietly in his corner with his insignificant job and his hobby of painting. His sister-in-law had already accused him and Dona Lita of opposing their niece's love affair during the happy days when she was seeing Vadinho as a compendium of virtues, a savior, a god, lacking only a halo to be a saint on an altar. A daft creature who thought she knew it all, presumptuous, spiteful, ill-humored; Pôrto wanted no part of such a petulant, undependable woman. But what could he do when Flor appeared, distraught, weeping, escorted by Vadinho, serious and solemn, very much aware of his responsibilities? They had come to confess what was now irremediable; he had fucked her, had stolen her cherry. They had to get married. With or without Dona Rozilda's consent, a minor or no minor, they had to get married. Flor was no longer a virgin, and only marriage could restore the honor of which Vadinho had despoiled her.

Flor, in a flood of tears, implored her uncle and aunt to forgive her. If she had gone to those lengths, disregarding her strict upbringing, overcoming her fear and modesty, surrendering her virginity to the dogged inspector of parks, the real culprit was Dona Rozilda, with her wiles, her intolerance, forbidding her to have anything to do with her sweetheart, locking her up in the house as though she, a grown woman, practically of age, were a child. She had even whipped her. Who could put up with such crabbedness? After all, Vadinho was no criminal, no desperado, no fugitive from justice or thug of Lampião's gang; nor was she, Flor, a teen-ager, an innocent who knew nothing of life. And who took care of the living expenses, rent and food, if not she? Her mother contributed very little; now that Rosalía was gone, the dressmaking was limited to an occasional order. But by way of compensation the cooking school was doing fine, and supported mother and daughter. Why, then, did Dona Rozilda take it upon herself to decide things, to condemn without right of appeal? Refusing to listen to sensible people like Aunt Lita, Mr. Antenor Lima, even Dr. Luís Henrique, Hector's godfather, whose opinion she had always set great store by before? Now she vehemently rejected his advice. Thales Pôrto shook his head; his sister-in-law had completely lost her bearings.

Neither Flor nor Vadinho could go on that way. For the young man the matter had become an out-and-out challenge. As in the case of the roulette wheel or the dice, he was staking everything on his luck. The desire for Flor had taken complete possession of him, from his head to his feet, beclouding his judgment, as though there were no other woman in the world, as though she—with her plump body and round cheeks—were the most beautiful and desirable woman in Bahia, the only one who could satisfy his hunger and thirst, dispel his loneliness. "No, never, not as long as I am alive," Dona Rozilda repeated each time Vadinho renewed his proposal of marriage, transmitted by relatives and friends.

Aunt Lita herself had intervened days before, as Flor reminded her. Dona Rozilda had answered her savagely, with a whole rigmarole of insults: "As long as God gives me life and health that bastard is not marrying my daughter. Not that she deserves this care, she's a fool, ungrateful, was born to be a nobody. But I will not give my consent as long as she is under my authority. I would rather see her dead than married to that tramp . . ."

Lita tried to argue, to persuade her sister, to break down that wall of hatred: love works miracles, why not admit the possibility of Vadinho's becoming regenerated? Dona Rozilda snorted reproachfully: "As though it were not enough of a shame for the family when you married Pôrto. Afterwards he straightened out, but suppose he hadn't? What if he had gone on being a good-for-nothing all his life?" and she pronounced the word "good-for-nothing" syllable by syllable, making it sound even more humiliating than it was.

She was referring to the fact that Pôrto had spent his youth in the theatrical circles of Rio de Janeiro, with stranded trips into the interior, playwright and choreographer of third-rate companies, and obliged to assume the role of actor, prompter, director, and designer. After marriage he had settled down and found a job in Bahia. All that remained of his career behind the footlights was an album of clippings and a few anecdotes. He never passed up an occasion to display the album or repeat the anecdotes.

"And didn't it work out?" Dona Lita came back, at heart proud of her husband's bohemian past. "Do you know of a happier marriage? Besides I am not the least bit ashamed of his having worked in the theater. He was not robbing anybody, or cheating anybody, or ruining virgins . . ."

"Ruining virgins? When every one of them was a slut—he might have been in a Mexican whorehouse. Where was he going to find a virgin in the whole lot? Not that he wouldn't have wanted to—he was no saint, believe me . . ."

Helpful and kindly, so different from her sister in many ways, Dona Lita, however, did not tolerate insults to her husband, and if anyone touched on the subject, it made her hot under the collar: "You just keep your tongue between your teeth, and stop slandering my husband. I did not come here to listen to your insults . . ."

Dona Rozilda took the rebuke to heart and muttered excuses. Dona Lita was the only person in the world for whom she had affection and respect, and with whom she never quarreled.

"I came here because I love Flor as though she were my own daughter. Why in the devil don't you let the girl get married? She likes the boy and he is crazy about her. Because he is not the big shot you got it into your head he was?"

"I didn't get anything into my head, as you know perfectly well; they took advantage of me, the wretches." The memory of the outrageous ridicule infuriated her. "And you know something?

It is better for us to consider the matter closed. She's not going to marry that blackguard as long as she is in my custody. After she is twenty-one, if she still wants to, she can leave and ruin her life. But before, I will not let her, and that's all there is to it."

"You're only looking for an itch to scratch. You just wait . . ."

And that was exactly what happened after the failure of this last mission. Flor made up her mind to listen to the voice of reason. That is to say, the whispered arguments of Vadinho persuading her of the only practical, viable, possible solution, and at the same time, delightful, tender, sweet proof of love and trust. Convinced, she lost no time in acceding: she let him have what he had so long begged and sought. To tell the whole truth, without omitting details (not even those having as their purpose maintaining the innocence and modesty of our heroine, unsullied in the eyes of the public, making her out the trusting victim of an irresistible Don Juan), it must be admitted that Flor was crazy to give, and give herself, yield to the fire that was burning her vitals and her shame, a raging flame.

A rich friend of Vadinho's, Mário Portugal, a bachelor and playboy of those days, lent him a little hideaway he had in the neighborhood of Itapoã. The sea breeze loosened Flor's straight, black hair, and the sun brought out its bluish tinges. To the murmur of the waves and the lulling of the breeze, Vadinho took off her clothes, piece by piece, kiss by kiss. Laughing as he undressed her and made her his: "I don't know how to fuck even covered with a sheet, let alone with clothes on. What is it you are ashamed of, my pet? Aren't we going to get married, isn't this what we're going to do? And even if we weren't, coupling is a blessed thing, it was God who ordered it. 'Go and couple, my children, go and have babies' was what He said, and it was one of the best things He did."

"Vadinho, shame on you, don't be a heretic." Flor wrapped herself in a red spread. Everything in that room appealed to the senses; pictures of naked women on the walls, reproductions of drawings in which fauns were pursuing and ravishing nymphs, a huge mirror in front of the bed. That Mário really lived it up, creating a sinful atmosphere, with perfumes on the dressing table, drinks in the refrigerator. A chill ran through Flor's vitals.

"If He hadn't meant for people to screw, he would have had them all gelded, and the children would have been born orphans, without father or mother . . . Don't be silly; take off that spread . . ."

Throwing aside the spread, Flor lay like an opening flower on the whiteness of the sheet. Vadinho gave an exclamation of joyous surprise: "Why you have hardly any hair, my pet . . . How odd and how beautiful . . ."

"Vadinho . . ."

His body covered her modesty, and she closed her eyes. The sea of Itapoã broke into a hallelujah, the breeze came to carry away the sighs of love, and amid the silence of fish and sirens, Flor's strangled voice broke into a hallelujah; hallelujah on the sea and the land, in heaven and in hell, hallelujah!

The morning of that day Flor had gone to help Dona Magá Paternostro, that rich woman who had been her pupil, with a birthday lunch, a feast for over fifty guests, and with trays of sweets and hors d'ôeuvre in the afternoon. From there she had left to meet Vadinho, and what was destined to happen had happened. While Dona Rozilda thought she was in Dona Magá's kitchen she was in bed with Vadinho in Itapoã.

From that day on Flor's life centered around ways to invent schemes to go to the beach house with Vadinho. She told all her friends and pupils: "If mamma asks if I went out with you, you say yes." They agreed to, for they were all fond of her and many of them sympathized with her cause. After the class one of them announced: "I am taking Flor with me to a matinée. The poor thing needs to forget . . ."

She seemed to be forgetting, to Dona Rozilda's great satisfaction. Of late Flor had not been so sulky, did not stay shut up in her room waiting for him to show up in the street—that bum—and then appear in the window, frankly defiant. The devil spent a lot of time exchanging chitchat with the Negress Juventina on the way. That shameless creature and others like her in the neighborhood encouraged the affair with their tittle-tattle. None of this escaped Dona Rozilda, and when the time came she would pay them back with interest. Flor tossed out notes to Vadinho, blew him kisses. Until Dona Rozilda lost her head and exploded in insults against her daughter and the scalawag, that scoundrel laughing on the corner.

In recent days, however, Dona Rozilda had had premonitions of a change. Flor's attitude was no longer the same. She did not go about singing plaintive *modinhas*, the revolting name of her suitor was not on her lips all the time, and he did not show himself on the street. Flor's smile had come back, she said good morning and good evening, and answered when Dona Rozilda spoke to her.

On Baixa dos Sapateiros a chance acquaintance said as she took her leave: "Watch your step," and laughed like an accomplice.

Flor and Vadinho laughed, too, as they slipped into a taxi—always the same, belonging to one Cigano, a chauffeur who had a taxi of his own, and was an old friend of Vadinho's—and drove quickly toward Itapoã, holding hands, stealing kisses. Cigano went to pick them up at twilight, they came back slowly, Flor's head resting on Vadinho's shoulder, her black hair fluttering in the breeze, and with a lassitude, a tenderness, the desire to remain together—why did they have to separate?

Vadinho kept demanding, with growing insistence, that they spend a night together. It was not enough for him to have her with him and possess her; he wanted to sleep beside her, lulled by her breathing. Flor, too, wanted this whole night, not to have to be thinking about the clock, counting the minutes, always too brief for her desire.

"But," she said to him one afternoon when he renewed his demands, "if I spend the night out I can never again go home . . ."

"And why go? We get tied up and that's all there is to it. You're the one who has not wanted to make a clean breast of things . . . I don't know why."

"And where am I going to stay until we get married?"

They decided on Aunt Lita and Uncle Pôrto's house in Rio Vermelho, which was like a second home to Flor. Once they had made up their minds, the next day she, after the cooking class, shut herself up in her room, and gathered up her belongings, filling two suitcases and a trunk. Then she locked the door, put the key in her pocketbook, and went out, saying she was going to Yansã's Market on Baixa dos Sapateiros. There Vadinho was waiting for her in the taxi; once more Cigano took them, but this time with instructions not to come for them until the next morning.

Dona Rozilda chatted with a friend who had dropped by for news and some sewing: "Flor went out to do some marketing. She'll be back soon. Fortunately, she has stopped talking about that character, she's not in such a fury any more . . ."

"She'll wind up forgetting about him . . . It always happens that way . . ."

"She has to forget him, whether she wants to or not . . ."

The visit lasted for some time, Dona Rozilda talking about a family that had recently moved into the neighborhood, people from Amargosa.

"Well, Flor seems to be taking quite a while, and I have to go. Remember me to her."

Dona Rozilda waited on alone. At first with vague doubts, then really uneasy, and by night with the complete certainty that Flor had lost her senses and had run away from home. She forced the lock of her room with a knife, saw the packed suitcases, and the trunk. The hypocrite had been fooling her, pretending that she had broken off with that scoundrel so as to rush headlong into misfortune of her own making. Dona Rozilda stayed up all that night with the light on, the whip in reach of her hand. Ah, if Flor had the impudence to come back . . .

When the next day, before lunch, her sister and brother-in-law showed up, Pôrto red with embarrassment, she staged an unforgettable scene, tearing her hair, beside herself: "I don't want to hear a word. No strumpet is to set her foot in here; the place for a whore is a whorehouse . . ."

Dona Lita did not take that meekly: "You will kindly show respect for me. Flor is in my house, and my house is not a whorehouse. If you care nothing about your daughter's happiness, that is your business. Thales and I care, and a lot. I came here to tell you that Flor is going to get married. If you wish, the marriage procession will set out from here, everything proper and in order, as it should be. If you don't, it will set out from my house and with my blessing."

"A whore doesn't marry; she shacks up."

"Listen, woman . . ."

All Aunt Lita's arguments and Uncle Pôrto's silent presence were of no avail. She would not attend or give her consent to the marriage; let them get permission from the judge, if they wanted to, bringing into the open all the indecency, making a public show of the thankless creature's dishonor. But they were not to count on her to cover up the chicanery, the shameless creature's behavior.

The next day she left for Nazareth, where her son received her without enthusiasm. He himself was thinking of getting married, and had not yet done so because his salary was still too low. But he intended to as soon as he was promoted and had a few thousand mil-reis saved up. He already had his eyes on a girl: a former pupil of Flor's, the one with the dewy eyes who answered to the name of Celeste.

13

While on her way to look at a house advertised for rent in Sodré, Flor ran into another former student of hers, a woman of distinction, the wife of a merchant in Cidade Baixa, Dona Norma Sampaio, a very gay, gossipy person, pretty, of whose natural kindness and good-heartedness we have already made mention. She lived in that neighborhood.

The house was suitable for Flor's needs as both dwelling and school, and besides, it was relatively cheap. So she decided to take it at once, Dona Norma providing the necessary references; the owner of the house was a friend of hers, and she was sure he would give her preference. Flor could leave it to her; she had nothing to worry about.

Dona Norma was a great comfort and consolation to her in that whole ordeal. She took upon herself the various problems that confronted the girl, and helped solve them, finding a way out of everything.

To begin with she raised her sagging morale. Flor gave her a detailed account of all that had happened to her. Dona Norma wanted to know all, she hated to be told things in a hurry, skipping over parts of it. Flor was suffering from the idea that the whole world was aware of her slip ("slip" was the term Aunt Lita had used out of delicacy), as though she bore the stigma branded on her face: a fallen woman who had known a man but was pretending to be a single girl.

"Come, my dear, stop being silly. Who knows what happened? Four or five people, at most, half a dozen . . . If you wanted to you could get married with veil and bridal wreath and who would have anything to say? Fortunately, your mother has gone away; she is the one who might come and make a scene at the church door."

Flor could not dissimulate her shame; she had behaved badly, but there had been no alternative. As far as Dona Norma was concerned all that horror boiled down to nothing: "This business of giving a little in advance happens to three out of two, and among the best people, my dear."

And she reeled off a long and curious list, comforting examples. The daughter of Dr. So-and-So, in the School of Medicine, hadn't she gone to bed with a friend of her fiancé's a few days before their marriage, breaking the engagement, running off with the other, marrying him on the double? And now wasn't she the cream of society, with her name in the newspapers: "Mrs. So-and-So held a reception for her friends . . ." and so forth and so on? And what about that other slut, the Judge's daughter, wasn't she caught with her sweetheart—he at least was her sweetheart—behind the lighthouse of Barra? The guard had taken them in the act, and the only reason he did not haul them off to police headquarters was because the quick-thinking gentleman had given him a generous bribe. But he had shown half the population the bold thing's panties (incidentally, a beautiful confection of black lace). Not even on this account, with all this display of underwear, had she refrained from getting married with veil and wreath, and a dress that was a work of art, for she had taste and money. And that other so-and-so—her father a real man-eater, ten times worse than Dona Rozilda, with the girls under his eye all the time, terrible scoldings, practically prisoners in their house—hadn't she been discovered in Ondina, in the woods, carrying on with a married man, a friend of her parents? Later on she had married some poor devil, and now she made free with all she had—"the more, the merrier" was her motto —to unmarried and married, acquaintances and strangers, rich and poor. "And lots of them don't do it before they are married, my child, because they don't know what they are missing or their suitor is too shy. When all is said and done, tell me, what difference does it make?"

Not only did she minimize Flor's fall from grace, restoring her spirits, but she also advised and helped her with the necessary purchases to make the house habitable, furniture and utensils. Including the iron bed, with the wrought head and foot, bought secondhand from Jorge Tarrapp, an auctioneer with an antique and old furniture shop in Ruy Barbosa Street, and, as was to be expected, a friend of Dona Norma. A good guy, this Jorge, a tall, red-faced Syrian, almost apoplectic; when he heard about Flor's approaching marriage he offered her in the bargain and as a present half a dozen wine glasses. Dona Norma contributed a set of bath and face towels from Alagoa, of first quality. And she gave Flor, for what she had paid for it, which was practically nothing, a spread of hydrangea-blue satin with clusters of wisteria in lilac, the last word in elegance. It had formed part of Dona Norma's magnificent trousseau, the *pièce de résistance*, the present of an aunt and uncle who lived in Rio. For some reason that crank Zé Sampaio had taken an aversion to the spread—according to him, the hydrangea-blue was a funereal purple, and the only thing that rag was good for was to put over a coffin. On account of that wretched spread they had almost quarreled on their wedding night. If Dona Norma had not been wild with curiosity to know what was going to happen, she would not have stood for Zé Sampaio's grumbling and rudeness. He was not satisfied until the spread was put away for good. She had never used it; it was brand new, and cost a fortune in Chile Street.

Speaking of spreads, Vadinho's sole contribution to the trousseau was a crazy quilt, the collective effort of the girls of Inácia's cathouse, all of them his admirers, beginning with the noble Inácia, a pockmarked mulatta, the youngest madam in Bahia, but not because of that less skilled. From time to time Vadinho turned up in her bed, his infatuation lasting days and weeks.

It was not his fault that his quota in the total of these endless expenses, which quickly consumed Flor's savings from years of work, was so small. Vadinho would greatly have preferred to shoulder the entire burden, or at least the main part of it, and he made every effort to do so. His friends had never seen him so nervous and persistent at the roulette tables, but 17—his number—was elusive, as though it had been scratched from the list. He tried everything, big and small, ronda, baccarat, but luck was against him; he was completely hexed. He exerted himself to the point where he no longer had anyone to put the bite on to ask for a loan, and he had to resort to his sweetheart, suckering her out of a hundred mil-reis note. "It is impossible for this luck to go on any longer, babe. I'm going to show up here tomorrow morning with a truckload of money. You can buy out half of Bahia, including a dozen bottles of champagne for our wedding."

He did not bring the truckload of money or the champagne; he was really perplexed, how long was that bad luck going to last?

So there was champagne only at the civil ceremony performed in the home of Aunt Lita and Uncle Pôrto. Thales Pôrto opened a bottle, and the judge toasted the newlyweds, and the family. The religious ceremony, too, was simple and short; a few close friends of Flor came: Mr. Antenor, in addition to Aunt Lita and Uncle Pôrto—not to mention Dona Norma, of course. Dona Magá Paternostro, the millionairess, could not come, but she sent an entire set of kitchen utensils that morning, and that was a useful gift. Representing Vadinho, only the Director of the Department of Parks and Gardens of Police Headquarters—whom the backsliding employe had touched for a loan, using his marriage as an excuse, as he had done with other colleagues—Mirandão and his wife, a thin, fading blonde, and Chimbo. The presence of the Assistant Commissioner led Thales to comment to Dona Lita that not everything was pure invention in the story trumped up by the scoundrels to take in Dona Rozilda. The relationship with the important Guimarães was a fact.

Dom Clemente, the chaplain of St. Theresa, officiated at the religious ceremony, thanks to Dona Norma's request. Vadinho was resplendent in his cabaret elegance. Flor wore blue, and was all smiles, with lowered eyes. Dona Norma was unable to persuade her to wear white with veil and wreath—the silly thing did not have the courage. The rings were lent by Mirandão at the proper moment. The night before, in Tabaris, they had taken up a collection and got together the money Vadinho needed for the rings he had already selected in the jewelry store of Renot. Half an hour later, Vadinho had lost his last penny at the House of the Three Dukes. Even so he could have got them on credit, if he had gone for them. The jeweler, shrewd as he was, was unable to hold out against Vadinho's smooth tongue; more than once he had lent him money. But after staying up all night, the groom slept through the morning, hurrying off for Rio Vermelho in Cigano's taxi.

As they were leaving the church, the banker Celestino appeared carrying a bunch of violets. He was introduced to Flor—Dona Flor henceforward, as befits a married woman. He kissed her hand, excused himself for being late—he had just heard about it, he hadn't even had time to buy a gift. He discreetly slipped Vadinho a note, and the guests, beginning with Chimbo and Dom Clemente hurried forward to greet the Portuguese financier.

The newlyweds took their leave of the guests in the patio of the convent; only Dona Norma accompanied them to their new dwelling on the façade of which the sign, SCHOOL OF SAVOR AND ART, had already been hung. At the door Dona Flor said to her neighbor: "Come in and let's talk a little while."

To which Dona Norma answered, with a teasing laugh: "I'd have to be awfully dumb," and she pointed to the dark clouds hanging over the sea. "Night is coming. Time to go to bed."

Vadinho agreed. "Neighbor, you talk little and say a lot. Besides, when it comes to that, I am ready at any time, day or night, I make no difference and I don't charge extra." And putting his arm around Dona Flor's waist, he led her down the hall, unbuttoning her and undressing her as they went.

In the room he tossed her onto the hydrangea-blue spread, pulling off her slip and panties. Dona Flor naked, stretched out on the bed, the first shadows of twilight falling upon her terse breasts.

"God help us!" said Vadinho. "This spread you got hold of, babe, looks like a shroud. Take it off the bed, and get that crazy quilt; on top of it you're going to be even more of a knockout. We'll keep this to take to the pawnship. They'll probably give a fortune on it . . ."

On the gay crazy quilt, silent in her modesty, covered only with the twilight, Dona Flor, finally married. Dona Flor with her husband Vadinho; she herself had picked him without listening to the advice of experienced people, against the express will of her mother, and even before marrying him, she had given herself to him knowing who he was. She might have committed an act of folly, but if she had not done it, her life would have had no meaning. A fire was consuming her which came from Vadinho's mouth, from his breath, and his fingers burned her flesh like flames. Now married, he had every right to undress her, and beside her, in the iron bed, he looked at her and smiled. Her handsome husband, with a golden fuzz covering his arms and legs, a heavy growth of blonde hair on his chest, the scar of a knife wound on his left shoulder. Stretched out beside him Dona Flor looked like a Negress, a hairless Negress. Bare within, too, seething with desire, trembling, in a hurry, a great hurry, as though Vadinho were undressing her soul. He said things, crazy things.

They satisfied their desire for each other until they were sated, and then she pulled up the quilt, covered herself, and fell asleep. Vadinho smiled and rubbed her head, Vadinho, her husband. Beautiful and masculine, tender and good.

At dawn Dona Flor awoke, the alarm clock at the head of the bed said two o'clock. Vadinho was not in bed. Dona Flor got up, and went looking for him through the house. Vadinho had disappeared, had surely gone to gamble the money the banker had given him. On their wedding night. This was too much. Dona Flor wept her first tears as a bride, writhing in the quilt, torn by indignation, gnashing her teeth with desire.

14

Seven years had elapsed between those first tears shed by Dona Flor on her wedding night and those on the tragic Lenten Sunday when Vadinho fell lifeless in the midst of a samba group of drag and masqueraders. As Dona Gisa well put it—and she was a person who put things well, thoughtfully and to the point—when she saw the young man's body stretched out on the stones of Largo Dois de Julho, completely and forever dead, his wife in those seven years had wept tears and to spare for her trifling peccadilloes and for those of her husband, the latter a heavy load of sins and wicked deeds. Tears of shame and suffering, of sorrow and humiliation.

Especially at night. Nights devoid of Vadinho's presence, sleepless nights of waiting that stretched out as though dawn had receded to the gates of hell. At times rain had crooned its lullaby on the roof, the cold had called for the body of a man, the warmth of a breast covered with hair, the shelter of strong arms. Dona Flor awake, sleep eluding her, the desire to have him at her side like an open wound. She shivered with chill, orphaned by sadness, in that bed which held only longing and loneliness.

When Vadinho was there—ah! When Vadinho was there, cold and sadness disappeared. He emanated a joyous warmth that went from Dona Flor's legs to her face, and the night flowered in rejoicing. Dona Flor felt herself courted and gay, a little tipsy as though she had drunk a glass of wine or sipped a liqueur. The presence of Vadinho at night made her drunk, wine of an intoxicating bouquet, how was it possible to resist the seduction of his words and his tongue? They were nights of delirious excitement, nights of delight, as in a fairy tale.

But those nights when she had him with her after dinner, stretched out on the sofa, his head in her lap, listening to the radio, telling her stories, his bold hand tickling her, fooling with her, leading her on, and then early to the iron bed, were scarce. This happened only rarely when he, in sudden and unforeseen surfeit, gave up for three, four days, a whole week, his sprees, his escapades, his drinking and gambling, and stayed at home. Sleeping most of the time, rummaging in the closets, shining up to the students, asking Dona Flor to come and have a tumble with him at any hour of the day, even the most unsuitable and indiscreet. These were brief, crowded days, with the rattlebrain putting his two cents into everything, his sly laugh echoing through the hall, chatting with the neighbors at the window, listening to Dona Norma's sermons, holding long discussions with Dona Gisa, filling house and street with movement and gaiety. They could be counted on the fingers of the hand, those nights of giddiness and well-being, of unrestrained laughter, tickling, endearing words, and the coming together of unleashed bodies in the iron bed. "My coconut kiss, my sweet basil flower, salt of my life, your cunt is my honeycomb," he said to her. Oh brother, what things he said to her. I am not even going to repeat them.

The nights of waiting formed an endless rosary. Dona Flor slept uneasily, waking up at the slightest noise, or did not sleep at all, lying on her pillow and her anger until she could make out his still distant step and hear the key in the lock. By the way he opened the door she knew the intake of rum and how the gambling had gone. She closed her eyes and pretended to be asleep.

At times he arrived at dawn, and she gathered him up in her tenderness, cuddled him until sleep came. His face gaunt, his smile worn, he rolled himself up like a skein of yarn in the hollow of her body. Dona Flor swallowed her tears so that Vadinho would not be aware of her weeping and sadness; he had had enough troubles, his nerves tense from the struggle with his bad luck. Nearly always liquored up, sometimes drunk, he would fall asleep almost immediately, though not without first running his caressing hand over her and murmuring: "My little furless pussy, today I really had a tough time but tomorrow I'll get even." Dona Flor continued wakeful and full of desire, feeling Vadinho's body tremble against hers in his sleep, going on with his gambling and still losing. As he fell asleep, he went on repeating numbers on which he had lost at roulette: "Seventeen, eighteen, twenty, twenty-three," his four favorite numbers. Or he shouted: "Banker's luck." Flor followed the variations of his dream, and she saw him bet on the "French hare"—that is to say, the three dice adding up to "4"; and the banker gathering up everyone's chips. She came to know all the terms, all the slang, the crazy calculations, and the secret seduction of the gambling racket. And, thus, at dawn, she protected him against the world, against the dice and the chips, the croupiers, chance. She nestled him to her breast and warmed him; asleep, Vadinho was a blond baby, a big child.

It sometimes happened that he did not come home, her vigil prolonging itself all through the day, into the next night, she rotting with humiliation. When they saw her quiet and sad, the pupils avoided all embarrassing questions in order not to bring tears of shame to her eyes. Among themselves they harshly criticized the behavior and loose life of that fraud. How did he have the heart to make such a good wife suffer so? But he had only to appear with his wily voice, his line of talk, his foxiness, and nearly all of them swooned over him, hot in the pants.

During the day Vadinho outdid himself running back and forth, at times in despair, trying to get the wherewithal for his gambling: no credit was extended at the roulette table; chips were cash on the barrelhead. He prowled around the banks, hanging about the tellers and clerks, trying to discount a promissory note; pulling out all the stops to convince hypothetical endorsers of this promised discount, or trying to cajole, almost by force and at absurd interest, a few hundred mil-reis from the niggardly fingers of some loan shark. He was capable of spending a whole afternoon with some miser, one of those who are hardest to persuade, deriving a certain satisfaction from getting the better of him, and seeing him finally pick up the pen and sign the promissory note, unable to hold out any longer. To discount a note or give the money was one and the same thing. Some of the more practical settled the matter in this way: Vadinho turned up with a note to be discounted, and the victim handed him a hundred or a two hundred mil-reis bill to get rid of him. Otherwise he ran the danger of signing, and thirty or sixty days later, he would find himself confronted with a note that had fallen due and was unpaid. This was a serious danger, for Vadinho was no pushover for anybody. To resist his wiles avarice was not enough; one had to be as hard as nails, of inexorable convictions, unfeeling where personal tragedies were involved, a fanatic, a heartless fanatic. Like the Italian Guilherme Ricci, of Ladeira do Taboão, famous for his tightness. He had intrepidly resisted Vadinho for years.

Another who had put up a brilliant opposition was the book-seller Dmeval Chaves, in those days nothing but the manager of the bookstore, not the tycoon he is today. But one day Vadinho showed up in the morning. They had lunch together. Vadinho went back to the store with him, pestered him for six hours without letup, timed by Mirandão with his real Swiss watch. Dizzy, his ears drumming, the shrewd Dmeval gave in: "Vadinho, I swear to you that this is the first note I have ever signed in my whole life."

"Well, you've made a good start, old man—you couldn't have done better. It is a first-class debut, now all you have to do is keep it up. Besides, anyone who signs a promissory note of mine never stops, he develops a taste for it . . ."

He rushed off to the bank, leaving the fat manager open-mouthed, bent over the counter, completely sunk, unable to understand how he had been hornswoggled into that crazy move, how he had given that signature.

In the days when gambling went on afternoon and night at Tabaris, Vadinho did not come home for dinner. He ate any old thing, a bean fritter, a sandwich, eating dinner at dawn when the last door of the lowest gyp joint had closed. The most recalcitrant —he, Giovanni, Anacreon, Mirabeau Sampaio, Meia Porção, the Negro Arigof, as elegant as a prince in a Russian novel—left in a group for Rampa do Mercado, Sete Portas, Andreza's house, for any greasy spoon where there was a vegetable stew, a fish soup, cold beer, strong rum.

On the rare occasions when he did come home to eat, it was to leave almost at once, before nine o'clock, always on the run. Defrauding Dona Flor's hopes of seeing him come in like other husbands returning from work, make himself comfortable, putting on his pajamas, reading the papers, talking over what had happened, perhaps suggesting that they go out for a visit or to the movies. How long had it been since she had been to the movies? If Dona Norma had not dragged her off to a matinée from time to time, she would almost never have gone, for months went by without her and Vadinho ever going out together. Nevertheless, she never failed to ask him, when she saw him take off his coat and loosen his tie: "You're not going out again today, are you?"

Vadinho smiled before answering: "I'm stepping out, but I'll be back in no time, sweetie. I have an engagement, but I'll cut it short." The answer, like the question, was invariable.

There were times when he arrived before dinner, but for a different purpose. These were days of complete failure, when, at the end of the afternoon, he had achieved nothing, all his attempts had been futile; his hunch about the numbers had been wrong, the managers of the banks had refused to listen to his blandishments, the note signers had disappeared, there was no one to put the bite on. On those hexed days he came home and was a cross to bear. On those afternoons he, who was such a glutton, who loved to taste the delicacies Dona Flor prepared, her incomparable recipes, ate in silence, restless, and ate little, quickly, without paying attention to what he was eating. He cast sidelong glances at his wife as though judging her mood, her receptivity. Because he was getting ready to ask for money; always a loan, naturally, with formal promises of repayment, all of them outstanding to this day. And she wound up giving him some, willy-nilly; on certain occasions under sad and even unpleasant compulsion. Those were the days when Vadinho was at his worst, resorting to brutality and anger, his charm and grace giving way to a cruel crossness.

Don Flor knew, even before he had spoken a word, his evil

intentions. He came in from the street exasperated by his failure, a dull anger stamped on his face. During those years she came to know him to the slightest detail, from the spring and cadence of his walk to the sneaky gleam in his eyes when he turned them on any woman—the chattering pupils, Dona Gisa's neckline—or, walking with Dona Flor down the street, on any who crossed his path, stripping them more or less bare, depending on how pretty or ugly they were.

Vadinho deployed himself during the afternoon in his search for funds, came or did not come for dinner, affectionate or brusque, and, at night, set out again on his ill-fated destiny.

Ill-fated? Such solemn, lugubrious adjectives suited neither Vadinho's nature nor his way of life. Nocturnal, yes, but not ill-fated. The shadows and gloom, the imprecations and dramas so frequently employed in the campaigns against gambling did not affect him. His hands did not tremble as he bet his chips, nor did he howl with remorse the next morning.

Suffering, undoubtedly, when the ball spun on the wheel, his heart constricted with anxiety, but a pleasurable anxiety. Never did the idea of suicide cross his mind; never did remorse gnaw at his breast; never did the grim voice of conscience upbraid him. He was immune to all this series of horrors that destroy the lives of those poor devils who let gambling get a stranglehold on them. A pity, perhaps, but that was the way he was. It is impossible to present Vadinho in that pathetic light, as a gambler enslaved to an irrevocable fate, hating himself, trying to free himself and unable to, redeeming himself by a bullet through his head as he came out of the casino.

Beyond dispute it was a harsh, tense fate—the fate of a real man. No weakling could have withstood that struggle every night and every minute of the night, but Vadinho never made of his emotional struggle a catastrophe of crimes and remorse, a sinister and irremediable misfortune. Sinister? His fate was exciting and amusing. Irremediable? There was always someone to lend him money; it was unbelievable what easy marks people were. Who knows? Perhaps they did that to run vicariously the risks of gambling without going to the forbidden casinos, to the dives of ill repute. It was a fate of deep and stirring emotions.

Like that August night that had started off so badly, with him trying to get hold of Dona Flor's money, and she holding out, for it was the money for household expenses, and the argument, the insults, the complaints, the shouting, the abuse. In Abaixadinho the dice were rolling in the "French hare." Vadinho had bet ten mil-reis on the big one—he bet only on the big one—and the game was under way. Believe it or not, the big one came up fourteen times in succession, and Vadinho, surrounded by a nervous crowd of players and whores, let his bets ride prepared to lay his money on the big one until the end of time. When Mirandão, who was in the other room where a game of ronda was going on, heard about it he came running like a madman, screaming at him: "For the love of your children, stop; your luck is going to change."

Vadinho did not have any children, and he was not going to stop; but Mirandão, who was a father, grabbed up the chips himself, and went to cash them in, pushing Vadinho away from the table. And how right he was, for the little one came up, and then the bank took all, and then the little one once more, and again the bank, while Vadinho departed against his will and in funds.

That night with his pockets bulging, and recalling Dona Flor's tearful remarks: "You are good for nothing, you don't amount to anything, and you don't love me the least tiny bit," he decided to go home early and take her a present, but something really worthwhile, not just any trifle. A chain, a ring, a bracelet, a good piece of jewelry. Where, however, was he going to get it when all the stores were closed? Perhaps, Mirandão suggested, he could pick up something from one of the trollops in the district. At times they received valuable presents when they were having an affair with a cacao colonel or some rancher from the backlands, and they salted away a nest egg, some of them even giving up their calling, and opening a beauty parlor or a little store. Mirandão had known two who wound up getting married, and turned out to be the most decent wives.

They went out looking, going from cabaret to cabaret, from

whorehouse to whorehouse, from crib to crib, and wherever they went beer, vermouth, and cognac were served liberally, at Vadinho's expense. They went over and examined the poor gewgaws of dozens of strumpets, without finding anything but junk, chromium-plated trash, glass, tin—and time was marching on.

"I want to get home early, make it a complete surprise." Vadinho was in a hurry, anxious, enjoying in his mind's eye Dona Flor's face when she saw him before midnight with a present in his hand. All that was lacking was the present, something really fine, eye-filling, not those peddler's odds and ends. They finally found it on Ladeira de São Miguel, in the boudoir—Mirandão pretentiously called it—of Madam Claudette, a courtesan whose day was over, and who managed to live thanks to a minimum clientele of schoolboys who visited her because she was French and because of her publicized refinements, all very Parisian, and economical.

A necklace of turquoise so exquisite that even Vadinho and Mirandão were impressed by its beauty and fascination. All set in gold filigree; the old jade held it tightly between her fingers as though protecting it. It was a family heirloom, she confided, which she had brought from Europe; it had belonged to her mother and her grandmother, which lent it double value. Only for a good price would she sell it, let go of that precious legacy of her lost world of Lorraine and her childhood. "Only for a good price, a very good price." "*Le petit Vadinho, le pauvre*" would never have that much money, and if, by chance, one day he did, he would not spend it on a gift for a woman. When had Vadinho ever made an issue of money, Madame? Even penniless, flat broke, without a plugged nickel, not even under those circumstances had he set store by money, and if he ran after it so madly, it was to throw it away at roulette. Suddenly, he began emptying his stuffed pockets, leaving them almost bare. Madame Claudette's little eyes lighted up with greed behind her mask of rice powder and face cream. That mummy trembled at the sight of the hundred and two hundred mil-reis bills.

Cigano's taxi left him at the door of his house at 11:40, before midnight, as he has wished. Dona Flor barely had time to close her eyes and give a faint snore when Vadinho was in the room, pulling off the sheet that covered his wife's body, laying the gleaming turquoises between her full breasts, and laughing reproachfully: "And to think that you did not want to lend me the money, you silly thing . . . ," as he scattered bank notes over the bed, for he still had more than two contos left.

So how was it possible to talk about a "harsh fate" in connection with anyone who was such a happy gambler, laughing in the face of luck and chance, filled with the joy of living?

A harsh fate perhaps in Dona Flor's opinion, from her point of view or, to put it better, from her waiting post. Harsh for Dona Flor, marking time in her lonely bed.

Waiting for him for seven years, a whole life. Dona Flor shed many tears during those years, as well as enjoying many tumbles in the hay, as though in those delightful moments of possession and tenderness she were seeking compensation for the bitter hours of absence and humiliation. One day Dona Gisa, with her presumptions of psychology, psychoanalysis, extrasensory perception, and other North American novelties, explained to Dona Flor that she had married an exceptional being—not exceptional in the sense in which Dona Flor understood the term, as a synonym for great, better, the best of all; nothing of that sort. But exceptional in the sense of being out of the ordinary, someone who did not fit the usual norms and could not be circumscribed by the mediocrity and monotony of daily life. Could Dona Flor understand him and be happy with him? Just more of Dona Gisa's jive, a good friend beyond a doubt, but with too much book learning, her head filled with nonsense and a tongue that was hung in the middle and swung at both ends.

What Dona Flor wanted was to be like everybody else, and to have a husband like other husbands. Didn't he have a municipal job that he had got through a rich relative, Dr. Airton Guimarães, nicknamed Chimbo? She wanted him to come home from work, the newspaper under his arm, a bag of cookies or coconut kisses, a package of fried beans or bean fritters. And having their dinner at a set hour like other people, going out with her on certain nights, arm in arm, enjoying the breeze and the moon. Loving, in bed, but early, before they went to sleep, on fixed days.

None of this could be, given the way he was; Vadinho's arrival could never be counted on; he often slept away from home, beyond doubt in the bed of trollops, some old or renewed passion; and wanting to ball around late and at the most unfitting hours, any old day, without regard for the clock or the calendar. Without schedule or system, or established habit or tacit agreement, nothing of the sort. It was a senseless anarchy, with him out all night without letting her know, and she in the iron bed, sick with jealousy, with a pain in her heart and a feeling of rejection. Why did all other married women get their due deserts from their husbands, and not she? Why wasn't Vadinho like all the rest, with a well-run, orderly life, without the uneasiness, the comments, the gossip, the endless wait? Why?

All that—the tardiness, the gambling, the drinking, the nights away from home, the shouts, the violence, the churlishness—became a habit as time went on, but Dona Flor had never grown completely used to it, and she never would till the day she died.

But the one who died was he, Vadinho, during Carnival. From then on, alas, from then on desire had not even the right to wait, to expect, to hope. Vadinho's absence took on another dimension. Suffering, too, acquired another quality. It would never again do Dona Flor any good to listen with bated breath to a noise on the sidewalk, her heart throbbing impatiently. Now it was a wait without hope; it availed her nothing to listen to the footfalls, those of the drunks, especially, to the cautious sound of the key in the door, to a scrap of song, to a tune lost in the distance.

Yes, to a tune lost in the distance. Because there had been nights during her seven years of marriage and waiting when Vadinho had come to awaken her with a serenade, with guitar, violin and flute, trumpet and mandolin, repeating that other unforgettable serenade on Ladeira do Alvo, when she had first learned the true nature of her love: poor, without a penny to his name, a petty employe, a chiseler, a deadbeat, a drunk, a libertine, a gambler.

15

Now, stretched out in the iron bed, Dona Flor tried to close her ears to the yackety-yak of Dona Rozilda at the street door in lively conversation with Dona Norma, the better to recall in faded memory, over the distance of years, the voices of the singers, the rhythm of the instruments, that moving serenade on Ladeira do Alvo, to fill up the hours, and calm her heart in those nights when waiting availed her nothing, for he had died, her husband. All she had left now was a world of recollections in which she took refuge, ashes with which to deaden the smoldering of desire. It was as though a wall had sprung up, separating her from the whispering and gossiping, the talk and comments, from everything that might disturb her recent widowhood, that new reality of separation. During the early days of bereavement, she had felt only pain and anguish, the need and the impossibility of having him there, beside her. Impossible now forever and ever.

Tuning out with the memory of the music and the songs the voice and sneers of Dona Rozilda, Dona Flor enveloped herself in memories of the past: of that night when she had gone over to the window at the sound of the first notes. Her whole body had ached, the rawhide had left a welt on her neck, she had been nothing but a rag, a beaten and humiliated rag. Vadinho had come up the hillside to sing, his arms stretched on high. She recognized the others: the unmistakable and incomparable voice of Caymmi, Jenner Augusto, paler than usual under the light of the moon, and accompanying them on their instruments and as a chorus, Carlinhos Mascarenhas, Edgard Cocô, Dr. Walter da Silveira, and Mirandão. She had run to get that rare dark rose which she had picked the evening before in Aunt Lita's garden. Everything in her life was snarled up, a complete clutter, out of control, and she under the iron authority of Dona Rozilda. The music had given her strength and courage. Suddenly, she felt happy that Vadinho was nothing but the most insignificant municipal employe, and she did not mind his being a confirmed gambler.

With the memory of those nights of tenderness and moonlight, Dona Flor, unable to sleep, tried to assuage her grief and despair at knowing that never again would Vadinho come to touch and kindle the embers of her body. In the long nights of waiting she would never again hear his off-key voice in the street in other serenades.

It sometimes had happened that Vadinho, having overstepped all bounds—night after night away from home, or, like that time when, while they were still recently married, gambling away the rent money without telling her, making her look like a deadbeat —wanted to make up, and on such occasions Dona Flor had refused to speak to him, ignoring his existence, as though she had no husband. Unhappy, Vadinho hung around her, all flattery, insinuations, trying to get her worked up and lead her to bed. Dona Flor resisted behind the trenches of her sorrow and exasperation.

Vadinho then played his big trumps: taking her to the movies, going to pay a long outstanding visit to Dona Magá or Hector's godfather, Dr. Luís Henrique. Or he organized a serenade, arousing her from sleep, overwhelming the street. By that time, however, he no longer brought Dorival Caymmi with his miraculous voice or Dr. Walter da Silveira. Caymmi had gone off to Rio, was doing programs for the Carioca radio and cutting records, famous singers were introducing his sambas, his revolutionary *modinhas*. Dr. Walter was completely out of the running; he was a judge in the backlands, his magic flute limited to lulling to sleep his little children, of which he had a cohort, one a year when not twins. It was not easy, in these frivolous times of indifference and screwiness, to find people who fulfilled their duties—all their duties, without exception—with a sense of responsibility befitting a painstaking and cultivated sense of their metier.

And now never again—alas, never again—would Vadinho

come. Neither his voice, nor his insinuating laugh, nor his searching hand, nor his thicket of blond hair, his impudent mustache, his dreams of chips and stakes. Not even the sad vigil was left Dona Flor. What would she not have given for the privilege of suffering while waiting for him, the anguish of fathoming the silence of the quiet street, trying to make out her husband's step faltering under the load of rum.

It availed Dona Norma nothing to plead with Dona Rozilda at the front door, to appeal to her for understanding: "The less you talk about Vadinho, the easier it will be for her to forget. Flor is still suffering deeply. Why keep raking up his shortcomings, making her miserable?"

It was of no use. Dona Rozilda had come with the intention of making a nuisance of herself; she knew no other way of comforting. How stanch those undeserved tears except by maligning the poor dead devil? She had already said and repeated: that was not a death that called for tears, but for rejoicing. In the evening conversation she flaunted her opinion time and again, almost shouting it; a lot she cared who heard her.

But it did not help her either because Dona Flor, amid noise or silence, could not forget. Neither his evil deeds nor his meanness, nor, above all, the good hours together, his engaging appearance, his crazy talk, and his masculine strength when he took her, his masculine fragility when he clung to her, shielding himself with her tenderness.

It was almost a morbid suffering, unhealthy, a bitter disavowal of life. However, by an effort renewed each day, Dona Flor managed to overcome her emptiness, restrain her tears, go on. After the mass of the seventh day, she reopened her cooking school. The students came back, at first avoiding their usual jokes, their malicious wisecracks, anecdotes, giggles intermingled with the lessons, and creating a cordial and sympathetic atmosphere in the classes around the wood and coal stoves. This mourning setting did not last more than two or three days; the gay normalcy reasserted itself, and Dona Flor herself was glad that it worked out that way; it distracted her, scattered the circle of ashes.

They all came back except little Ieda with her face of a wary

cat and her revealed secret. Was she afraid to confront her, Dona
Flor, or to face the house bereft of the charm of Vadinho, his
laughter, his guile, his impudence?

As far as Dona Flor was concerned, she could have come; she
no longer had any interest in knowing, arguing, and much less,
upbraiding. There was only one thing she would have liked to
bring into the clear: was she pregnant, the hypocrite, pregnant by
him, carrying a child of his?

Dona Flor had never conceived, but she knew that it was her
fault and not her husband's. Dr. Lourdes Burgos, her doctor, had
explained this to her, and Dr. Jair had confirmed her diagnosis,
suggesting a slight operation that might perhaps make her fertile.
But Dona Flor was afraid of surgery; besides Dr. Jair had not
absolutely guaranteed the success of such a step. So of all her
husband's deceits what most bothered Dona Flor was the possibility that he might have had a child by someone, some chippy, a
child being brought up any old way.

She had never been able to figure out whether Vadinho wanted
a child or not. Had her fear of the hospital and the scalpel
prevented her from talking more frankly about it, kept her from
really asking him how he felt? She could not say. True, she had
asked him several times: "Don't you feel the lack of a child?"

Perhaps because Vadinho knew she was sterile and afraid of the
operation, perhaps for that reason he had hidden his desire for a
child playing around the house, a little girl with blonde hair like
his, a boy with black hair and coppery skin like hers. Once when
she heard him praise the charms of a fat rosy child, a baby less than
a year old who had won a prize as the baby of the year and whose
picture was on a calendar, she prepared to confront the awkward
situation: "If you really want a child, I'll risk the operation. Dr.
Jair says it may work. The only thing is that he can't guarantee
it . . ."

He listened as though from a distance, as though lost in a
dream, and did not answer at once, making her raise her voice,
almost in anger, to get him out of his musing: "If it doesn't work
out, patience. At least nobody can say that you wanted a child and
I didn't do everything I could to have one . . . I'll put my fears

aside; it's up to you," and her last words came out drenched in tears, choked in sobs.

One thing he could never bear was to see her cry; he caressed her sad face, and smiled to cheer her up: "You silly, silly thing. What nonsense is this to want to have a doctor rooting around in your insides? Let your cunt alone, baby, I'm not going to have anyone meddling with it, leaving it all twisted inside, or no good. Forget about that business of a child . . ."

And as he wanted to put an end to the conversation, he put his arms around her, leading her to the bed for a good tumble without saying whether he wanted or did not want the child she could not give him and which he could so easily have with another. With this unexpected romp, he left no time for questions and answers, and blurred the presence of the nonexistent child which had arisen between them until he wiped it out completely.

As for liking children, he really loved them. And they preferred being with him to any kind of game, calling out his name, running after him. When he was with children, Vadinho was one of them, as though he were their age, and his patience was unlimited. Mirandão had asked him and Dona Flor to be the godparents of the youngest of his four; and from the time he was a baby the child was crazy about his godfather; the minute he laid eyes on him, he opened his big mouth like a frog's, waving his hands, struggling to get out of his mother's arms and into Vadinho's. The two of them played for hours, Vadinho imitating the howls of fierce animals, hopping about like a kangaroo, laughing with delight. How was it possible for anyone so wild about children not to want one of his own? But he never admitted it; perhaps not to make Dona Flor undergo the sacrifice of an operation whose results would be doubtful.

Dona Flor, in her widow's bed, felt a twinge of remorse. She could have gone through with the operation in spite of the manifest pessimism of the pair of doctors. Possibly she had let herself be influenced by the opinion of Dona Gisa, which was shared by other neighbors and even by her aunt and uncle—that Dona Gisa who was such a know-it-all, and who trotted out her theories about heredity to console her when she accused herself of being sterile and worthless. Even Aunt Lita, who was so kind, and was always finding excuses for Vadinho's carryings-on, had said to her more than once: "It's an ill wind that blows nobody good, daughter. What if you brought a child into the world that took after Vadinho, so irresponsible? Have you thought of that? God knows what He is doing."

Thales Pôrto backed his wife up: "That's a fact, Lita is right. To be happy you don't have to have children. Look at us. We never had any."

And they really were happy, devoted to one another, Porto with his Sunday painting, Dona Lita with the flowers of her garden, and with her alley cat, old and fat, as spoiled as an only child.

Surrounded by so many people to comfort her, Dona Flor gave free rein to her fear, her fear—and why not admit it?—her selfishness.

In her iron bed, hearing the sour voice of Dona Rozilda and the distant night-music of the serenade, the widow realized that what she had had was not just fear of the operation. If she had wanted a child as much as Vadinho, she would certainly have summoned up the courage to face the doctor and the hospital. She, however, had not felt the desire for a child to fill the house with its noise and laughter. She lived thinking about Vadinho, who was her child; it was he she wanted in the house, her husband and her child, her "big baby."

At the door Dona Norma was saying solemnly and with the best intention: "What she needs is to forget. That's all she needs. And she is so young she can make a new life for herself."

"She married that rogue because she wanted to," came Dona Rozilda's voice.

"If Vadinho was good for nothing, all the more reason not to talk about him. Why spend your time stirring around in the man's coffin? What we have to do is distract the poor thing, not leave her alone to brood. True, she has the school, but that's not enough. She has to go out, amuse herself, forget . . ."

And above the growls of Dona Rozilda, Dona Norma's kindly voice: "If only she had a child . . ."

The phrase reached Dona Flor's ears: "If only she had a child . . ." Yes, it would be much easier. She would not be so alone, so empty. Her life would not be so meaningless. In the street, among the neighbors at Mass and vespers, at the market and the fair, under Dona Rozilda's iron thumb, among friends and acquaintances, arose the chorus of maledictions of Vadinho's memory, no words to describe his meanness. Dona Flor closed her ears so as to hear nothing but the bygone serenade. In the iron bed, all alone with the irreplaceable absence of her husband. Without a child to console her.

In the midst of all that had happened during those seven years, nothing had upset her so much as the rumor that the child Dionísia, a mulatta living in the neighborhood of the Terreiro, had borne was Vadinho's. She had always been afraid that he might have had a child by another woman, who would lure him away. When she heard of some adventure of Vadinho's, an infatuation that had the look of a lasting relationship, an adventure that went beyond nights in the cathouse, her heart shrank at the thought of possible consequences, of a child that might be born, holding its arms out to Vadinho.

Of the women she was not afraid, only jealous: "Nothing but haybags to pass the time," as he said, not to excuse himself but so Dona Flor would understand and not be afraid. But what if a child came upon the scene? It would be impossible to fight against a child; it would mean the end of all hope. She almost went out of her mind, uneasy, not knowing what to do, when Dona Dinorá—it was almost always Dona Dinorá—where did she come by so much information?—brought her, amid roundabout phrases and lamentations, the name of the tramp and the details, some of them even intimate and indecent. She trembled with fear at the thought of a child, a son, that son she had not given him because she could not and also—alas—because she had not wanted to.

Imagine her distress, the impact on her when one day Dona Dinorá came over to tell her about Vadinho's "last caper." According to the news that was going around, he had had a son by one Dionísia, a mulatta who was considered a great beauty, who was at times a painters' model (she had posed for a modernistic canvas

dauber, known as Carybé, who, impudently and as a taunt to
society, had painted her dressed as a queen), at times the stellar
attraction and adornment of the democratic and well-patronized
cathouse of Luciana Paca, in the busiest section.

Dona Dinorá had come to tell her this out of the kindness of
her heart, not as a mischief-maker or gossip, for she was not one of
those. She was fulfilling an onerous obligation of friendship, so that
poor Dona Flor, so kind and so refined, would not be ignorant of
this, with everyone laughing at her behind her back.

"He had a child by a demi-rep."

She used the word "demi-rep" to avoid a stronger term. Dona
Dinorá was delicacy personified, and she had a horror of wound-
ing, of offending anybody, even a shameless, fallen woman who
had become pregnant by a married man, getting herself knocked
up by another woman's husband. "I am not a person who enjoys
gossip. I try not to do harm to anybody," Dona Dinorá asseverated, and there were those who believed her.

In her widow's bed, the last strains of the serenade having faded
away with the voices of the singers and the black rose, Dona Flor
shuddered as she recalled those days of fright and difficult decision.
Of what would she not have been capable to keep Vadinho at her
side, not to lose him, to have him as he was, gambler and chaser,
keeping a mistress, having children by anyone? Now she would
show who she was.

16

When the two women came out of the fashionable eleven o'clock
Mass at the Church of St. Francis one clear Sunday morning in
June, luminous and cool, and with resolute step crossed the Ter-

reiro de Jesus, making for the narrow old streets of Pelourinho, street urchins began dancing the samba in a circle, beating out the syncopated rhythm on empty guava paste tins:

> *Hey, lady*
> *With the big bum!*
> *Hey, the big bum!*
> *The fine bum!*

Dona Norma turned to her companion, grumbling: "Those brats—why don't they go and fool around with their mothers' bums?"

Perhaps it was a mere coincidence, and the kids had not been referring to their callipygous exuberance; but be that as it may, Dona Norma glared in terrifying fashion at the impudent mockers. A glare which instantly turned tender as she discovered in the circle a little boy of about three, ragged, bleary-eyed, and runny-nosed: "Look how cute, Flor, how pretty that little rascal dancing there is . . ."

Dona Flor looked at the gang of ragged children. Many others were scattered about the overflowing square, running between the legs of itinerant photographers, trying to swipe an orange, a lime, a tangerine, a hog plum, a sapote from the venders' baskets. They were applauding a barker selling miracle-working pharmaceutical products, with a snake coiled around his neck, a repulsive necktie. They were begging alms at the doors of the five churches on the square, practically assaulting the well-to-do parishioners. They were exchanging wisecracks with sleepy whores, young for the most part, patrolling the park in the hope of a hasty morning client. A swarm of ragged, bold children, the offspring of the women of the district, without father or home. They lived in a state of abandonment; they would soon be delinquents, for whom the police stations would hold no secrets.

Dona Flor shivered. She had come to carry away one of those children, newly born, and in that way protect it from itself and its mother. But on seeing the children running loose around Terreiro Square, her heart was filled with pity, with a pure and noble emotion; at that moment, if it had been in her power, she would have adopted them all, not just Vadinho's son. Moreover, Vadinho's son did not need her to get away from that life. Vadinho would never desert him. It was not in him to leave any child destitute, and least of all one of his own, flesh of his flesh. Instead of denying his paternity he would proclaim it, boast of it, delighted and proud.

Dona Flor had always known it, absolutely, beyond the shadow of a doubt, in spite of her husband's silence and reticence: to Vadinho to have a child would be the greatest thing that could happen to him, really hitting the jackpot, sweeping the board, breaking the bank. For that reason she had been so affected by the news Dona Dinorá had brought her. That was the greatest danger, the threat she most feared. When all was said and done, Vadinho had already been so little hers, what with his passion for gambling and his bohemian life, what would be left to her if there were the child of another woman between them, calling to him from some hidden alley, from a street corner, from a trollop's bed? The son that she had not given him.

The news had left her in such a state of despair, so beside herself, that Dona Norma herself had almost lost her head. She who as a rule was so efficient, finding a solution for the innumerable problems laid before her all the time, she, too, could not see any clear way out, confused and distressed.

"What if you were to tell him that you were expecting?" This feeble lie was the best thing she could think of.

"How would that help? He'd finally find out the truth, and that would be worse."

It was Dona Gisa who found the answer to the riddle; a measure not only honorable but also practical, a plan that would solve everything and perhaps many other things. The *gringa* was wonderful when it came to matters of psychology and metaphysics. Professor Epaminondas Souza Pinto himself took off his hat to her as "a woman of great erudition," and Professor Epaminondas Souza Pinto was not just anybody. He never made a single mistake in the proper place of a pronoun, and he had a column (for which he received no payment, naturally) of rules of grammar in Paulo

Nacife's weekly, a sheet limited in circulation but abounding in advertisements.

When Dona Gisa was informed of how things stood—Dona Flor on the verge of a breakdown, Dona Norma at her wits' end—she immediately set them straight and in her garbled Portuguese coached them as to how they should proceed. If Vadinho had wanted a child to the point of having it with a trollop, inasmuch as Dona Flor was sterile and could not conceive; and if this child born of another could draw Vadinho away for good, then Dona Flor had only one way of saving her husband and her home: to bring this bastard child of Vadinho's into her house and become its mother, raising it as though she had borne it.

And why not? Why was Dona Flor carrying on so, cursing like a North American millionairess—the simile was Dona Gisa's, amazed at her neighbor's reaction—swearing that never would she do this, bring up the child of another, of a shameless whore, of a bitch? Why all this scandal, when one of the most admirable things about Brazil, according to the opinion of the *gringa*, was its capacity for understanding and coexistence? It was such a common thing for married women to raise spurious children of their husbands; she herself had known of several cases, among poor as well as rich people. There nearby, in the same street, wasn't Dona Abigail raising a daughter of her husband by a good-for-nothing, and with the same tender love she lavished on the four children of her womb? That was a lovely thing, lovely; it was because of things like this that Dona Gisa liked Brazil and had become a Brazilian citizen.

And what blame attached to the child, what sin had it committed? Why leave the poor little thing, with the blood of her husband Vadinho running through its veins, to suffer a life of privations, undernourished, growing up in hunger and vice, a rat of the drains of Pelourinho, without right to an education and the better things of life? Besides wasn't Dona Flor afraid—as well she might be—that Vadinho would take up for good with the mother of the child so as to be near him, his child? If she, Dona Flor, went and sought it out and took it to bring it up as her child, what more

convincing proof of love could she give? That child, born of
another woman, would be the enduring bond between Vadinho
and Flor, freeing her forever from doubt and threat.

And who knows, who knows, my dear, with this child in the
house, growing up and learning decent ways from Dona Flor's
affection and example, being a permanent joy for Vadinho, and a
permanent responsibility as well, who knows but what the rogue
would mend his ways, giving up gambling and wildness once and
for all and becoming a model person? It was more than possible.
There were plenty of examples.

Indeed there were. Dona Norma enthusiastically backed her
up: "That *gringa* knows more than a book!" And she began to
quote names and addresses. Who could have been more given to
gambling and drinking than Dr. Cícero Araújo, who lived in Santo
Amaro da Purificação? His poor wife, Dona Pequena, had gone
through hell. One day she became pregnant, and before she had
even given birth, Dr. Cícero had turned into an exemplary citizen.
And what about Mr. Manuel Lima, crazy about a floozy? Why
that one, to tell the truth, had not even needed a child. Marriage
had straightened him out; a better husband could not be found.

Dona Gisa gave the answer to the puzzle: that child, in whom
Dona Flor saw such a threat to the stability of her home, could
become, as by the touch of a magic wand, her assurance, the
guarantee of her love, and, in the bargain, might even accomplish
Vadinho's regeneration. A pity, to be sure, Dona Gisa thought to
herself; once he had become a reformed character, Vadinho would
lose all interest, that aura of mystery, that dissolute charm.

Dona Flor's eyes opened wide as the idea penetrated her mind.
Her face lit up with happiness, and she threw herself gratefully
into her friend's arms. They worked out leisurely plans, detail by
detail. Not that it was easy; on the contrary. Without Dona
Norma's moral support Dona Flor might not have summoned up
enough courage to make her way to the red-light districts, to the
streets of "cheap whores," so frighteningly mentioned in the police
reports in the newspapers, on the trail of a certain Dionísia to
demand of her her new-born child, take possession of it, take it
away for good, legally adopted, entered in the notary's registry,

with witnesses and certified signatures. Dona Norma, who could not have been more like a solicitous sister, dropped everything, accompanied her, and encouraged her. A curious detail must be added; for a long time she had wanted to see one of the red-light district streets, where the women who took the wages of shame lived, to get a firsthand view of their sordid existence. She had never before found a valid excuse for the forbidden trip.

But how could she let poor Flor venture alone into those menacing labyrinths? She asked Zé Sampaio when her husband, aghast at the proposal, made an effort to dissuade her.

"I am not a flighty young thing. I am a grown, respectable woman. Nobody is going to try to get fresh with me." And she revealed the plans she had worked out to Zé Sampaio, who gave up, unable to resist his wife's impetuosity. "We're going on Sunday morning. I am going to pretend that I want to visit my godchild, the grandson of João Alves. Then I'll ask João to come with us to that so-and-so's house. And João, as you know, is a master of *capoeira* . . ."

And so they did. On Sunday they went to Mass at the Church of St. Francis (Dona Flor carried a candle decorated with flowers as she had promised, so all would go well), then they crossed the Terreiro and went to meet the Negro João Alves at his shoeshine stand in the street leading to the Medical School. He was surrounded by children, woolly-headed little Negroes, lighter or darker mulattoes, as well as blondes with hair the color of wheat. They all called him Grandpa. They were all his grandchildren, these children and others, running about the maze of streets between the Terreiro de Jesus and Baixa dos Sapateiros. The Negro João Alves had never had children either by his wife or by any other woman, but he managed to find godmothers for his grandchildren, food, old clothes, and even primers. He lived in a nearby basement, grumbling, with his African deities, his apparent ferocity, his rudeness, some of his grandchildren. The basement opened out over a green valley. From his lair the Negro João Alves was master of the panorama of the colors and light of Bahia.

"Holy Moses, look who's here! My *comadre*, Dona Norma. What a treat for sore eyes! And how's Mr. Zé Sampaio? Tell him

I'll be coming around to the store one of these days to get some shoes for the kids . . ."

The street urchins circled around the two friends. Dona Norma had come prepared, and she brought out a bag of candy. João Alves let out a whistle, a number of children came running, among them an Indian-Negro half-breed between four and five years old. The Negro stroked his head: "Ask your godmother for her blessing, you good-for-nothing . . ."

Dona Norma gave him her blessing and a nickel, while the old Negro inquired what favorable winds had blown her there.

"Well, *compadre,* I want to ask a favor of you, a very delicate matter."

"Delicate things are not for me. I am sort of a rough customer, as you well know . . ."

"What I mean is it is something very confidential, to be kept secret."

"There you are on safe ground, for I am not a blabbermouth or a troublemaker. Speak your piece, *comadre* . . ."

"Do you happen to know a certain Dionísia who lives around here? I am not sure, but I heard that she lives in this neighborhood."

"And have you some business with her?"

"Not me, exactly, no. It's this friend of mine who has a matter to talk over with her."

João Alves looked Dona Flor over from head to feet.

"She has a matter to talk over with Dionísia de Oxóssi?"

"It might be that very one. I have heard said that she is pretty."

João Alves scratched his nappy head. "Pretty? You can say that twice, if you will excuse me. Any white woman can be pretty, but there are only a few mulattas like Dionísia in the world—not even half a dozen, and that is stretching it a lot."

"One that had a baby not long ago . . ."

"Then it's her all right. She's just given birth, and has not yet gone back to work."

For the first time, Dona Flor opened her mouth to ask: "What does she work at?"

Once more João Alves looked her over, and in his glance there was a certain contempt for such ignorance: "Why, as a whore, which is her trade, Miss."

Dona Norma took the conversation into her hands again: "And do you know her, do you know where she lives?"

"Of course I know her, *comadre*. She lives close by, in Maciel."

"Then you will be good enough to take us there. My friend wants to talk with her, settle a question . . ."

João Alves once more studied Dona Flor at length, scratching his head as though all that seemed suspicious and dubious to him: "Why doesn't she go by herself, *comadre?* I'll show you the house."

"Come, *compadre*. Be a gentleman. Are you going to let two ladies go into these streets alone? Suppose some impudent fellow comes along and gets fresh with us?"

Nobody had ever appealed in vain to João Alves's gentlemanliness. "All right, I'll go with you, but I can assure you that nobody is going to try any funny business, for everyone here is respectful . . ."

He got up, left his shoeshine chair in the care of his grandchildren. He was a tall, well-built Negro, past fifty, whose hair was beginning to turn white. He wore a string of red and white beads, the beads of Xangó, around his neck, and only his bloodshot eyes revealed his weakness for rum. As he stood up, he asked: "Tell me, Dona Norma, what business is it that this girl"—and there was a mocking tone in the way he pronounced the word "girl"—"wants to discuss with Dió?"

"Nothing that is to her disadvantage, *compadre*."

"Because if it were anything that would do her harm, with all the respect I owe you, *comadre*, I would not go along. Nor would it do any good, for her divinity is a strong one." He touched the ground with the tips of his fingers, greeting the deity: "*Oké Aro Oxóssi!* There is no conjure or hex that can prevail against her; the spell would boomerang on the one who tried to work it."

"When are you going to take me to a macumba, *compadre?* I would like so much to go to a *candomblé*." This was another curiosity of long standing on the part of Dona Norma.

Thus, making their way through spellworkers and voodoo

centers, they entered the red-light district. As it was Sunday
morning—Saturday night's celebration had lasted until dawn—the
streets were practically deserted. An occasional woman sitting at
the door or leaning out of the window, more to see the light of day
than to snag a man. A silence and tranquility, one might almost say
a Sabbath peace. Dona Norma felt cheated; the time to come was
when things were jumping. On that sleepy morning it was not
very different from her own quiet neighborhood. Moreover, Dionísia's house was right on the corner of Maciel. They had barely
entered the district.

They ascended the rickety staircase, and a huge rat ran out of a
dark corner. Muffled words and phrases came from the various
floors. Someone was singing a melancholy *modinha* in a low voice.
When they reached the landing of the third floor, the smell of
lavender burning in clay incense vessels rose to meet them, announcing the arrival of a new baby. They came out into a hall, at
the end of which was the door of the girl's room.

João Alves knocked with the knuckles of his fingers.

"Who's there?" asked a warm, drawling voice.

"Friends, Dió . . . It's me, João Alves, and there are two ladies
with me who want to talk to you. I know one of them, my
comadre Norma, a fine person, for whom I have the greatest
consideration . . ."

"Then come in, and please excuse the way things look. I
haven't yet had time to tidy up the room."

The two women followed the Negro into the narrow room. It
held a double bed, a lopsided wardrobe, an iron washstand with an
enamel basin and pitcher, a chamber pot at the foot of the bed, all
very clean. On the wall a cracked mirror and a print of Our Lord
of Bonfim with ribbons that had been blessed hanging from it. A
window opened at the back of the room and through it came the
light and the sad *modinha*.

Leaning against the pillows, half-covered by the sheet, wearing
a robe of lace whose neckline revealed her turgid breasts, the
mulatta Dionísia de Oxóssi smiled cordially at her surprised visitors. In the curve of her arm, against the warmth of her breast, lay

her sleeping baby. A sturdy infant, very dark. On a chair, a clay holder of lavender smoldered, perfuming the garments of the new-born child, which were spread over the cane of the seat. In addition to the chair, two kerosene boxes covered with tissue paper served as stools. In a corner of the rear wall, the altar of Oxóssi, with bow and arrow, the *erukerê*, a picture of St. George slaying the dragon, a green stone, probably a charm of Yemanjá, and a string of turquoise blue beads.

"Mr. João," said the mulatta in her drawling voice, "please take those clothes off the chair, and put them in the wardrobe; they are to change the baby into after his bath. Give the chair to this lady . . . ," pointing to Dona Norma. Then, turning to Dona Flor, she explained with a smile: "And you, who are younger, please excuse it, but you'll have to sit on a box."

From the bed, lying back, she presided over the arrangements in the room, the movements of the bootblack dragging chair and boxes about, calm and smiling, not even curious about the reason for that untimely visit. Anyone who had seen her thus, ordering things so calmly, would have understood why Carybé had painted her dressed as a queen on a throne in a Carnival group.

Dona Norma, getting in front of the Negro, had gathered up shirt and diaper, had put them in the wardrobe, and as she did so she had taken a complete account of the mulatta's dresses, blouses, slippers, and sandals.

"Pull up a box for yourself, too, Mr. João, and sit down."

"I am all right standing up, Dió, just fine."

"The best way to talk is at ease and seated, Mr. João. Standing up and in a hurry never gets you anywhere."

The Negro, nonetheless, preferred to lean against the window looking out at the morning, which was becoming more and more luminous. A thread of song made its way into the room, dying out plaintively over Dionísia's bed:

> *In the chains of your love,*
> *A fettered slave,*
> *My master!*

Dona Norma and Dona Flor sat down; a brief silence followed which was soon filled by Dionísia's gentle voice. She turned toward the side where the day shone so beautifully, complaining that she had not yet been able to go out into the street: "I just hate to be shut in when the rain washes the day's face and then it is as bright as a new-blown leaf, so proud . . ."

The same thing happened to Dona Norma, and so the two chatted on about the sun and the rain and the moonlight nights in Itapoã, or Cabula, and heaven only knows how they got around to Recife, where Dona Norma had a sister, married to an engineer from Pernambuco, and where Dió had lived for several months:

"For over seven months; I followed a stowaway who must have put a spell on me, a nut. He abandoned me there."

Where would those two not have sailed off, to what far-away ports, in that dialogue without objective or aftermath—just talk for the sake of talking—if Dona Flor, hearing a church of the Terreiro ringing the noon bell, had not taken alarm, interrupting the friendly chat: "Norminha, I'm afraid we're taking too much time."

"Don't worry about me. It's a pleasure," Dionísia said.

"Some other day we'll come when we have more time," Dona Norma promised. "Today we came for a purpose . . ."

"All right, I'm listening . . ."

"My friend here, Dona Flor, has no children and cannot have them. There's a physical impediment."

"Yes, I understand, Her ovaries are out of place—isn't that it?"

"More or less."

"But she can have them straightened. Marildes, an acquaintance of mine, had that done."

"With Flor there is no way. The doctor has examined her."

"Doctor?" And she laughed an amused, contemptuous laugh. "All the doctors know how to do is to say nice words and write things you can't read. If the lady goes to see Paizinho, he'll fix her up in no time. What do you think, Mr. João?"

João Alves agreed: "Paizinho? He'll make a few passes over her belly, and a baby every year."

Dona Norma decided to ignore this new angle, avoid the spell-worker in spite of his fame, his reputation as a witch-doctor. She glanced toward the sleeping child. Wouldn't it be better, first of all, to clear up the matter of whether he really was Vadinho's son? He was so dark that it was hard to believe. But Dona Flor precipitated the conversation, raising her voice in that stubborn determination typical of timid persons: "I came here to talk about a serious matter, to make a proposal to you and see if we could reach an agreement."

"Go ahead, Miss, and I will do my best to answer you."

"The baby . . . ," Dona Flor said, and then was at a loss as to how to proceed.

Dona Norma took the floor again: "You had the baby a few days ago, didn't you?"

Dionísia looked at her child, and smiled in happy agreement.

"Well, my friend came here to talk with you. You see, she made a vow when she was at death's door: her first son would be a priest if Our Lord of Bonfim helped her to recover." Dona Norma proceeded cautiously; that story she had thought up the night before had never completely pleased her. "Well, God heard her, and she got well, miraculously."

The mulatta listened full of curiosity to see if she could find the connection between her child and the young woman's health and the miracle of Our Lord of Bonfim. Dona Norma speeded up her tale, a most uncomfortable task: "But as she has had no son, what can she do to keep her vow? Only by adopting a child, raising him as her own, and then sending him to the seminary to study for the priesthood. She had heard about your child, and picked him."

Dionísia smiled gently. Wasn't it a tribute to her child? Dona Norma took the smile as a sign of agreement, and went on: "She wants to adopt the child, really adopt him, with papers signed before a notary, all legal and permanent. To take him and raise him as her son."

Dionísia lay quietly, saying never a word, her eyes half-closed. Had she understood what Dona Norma said or was she listening to the distant song?

> *Would*
> *I might die in your arms,*
> *Rather die*
> *Than live like this.*

"Rather die" she murmured to herself, and when she reopened her eyes the cordiality in them had disappeared, and there was a different quality in her glazed expression, in the lines around her mouth.

"And why," she asked without raising her voice, "why did she pick on my child? Why mine?"

It must be an unbearable, an inhuman suffering, thought Dona Norma. What mother wants to part with her child? However poor, without means, in dire poverty, even so it was heartbreaking.

"Someone mentioned your son, that he was strong and pretty . . . and that you lacked the means to bring him up . . ."

If it had not been for the good of the child, if it had not been a question of Vadinho's son with all the implications this carried, Dona Norma would not have been there acting as go-between in this matter, forcing out her explanations. But was this really Vadinho's child? Dionísia must have a grimy womb, for the child had turned out even darker than she was. Where was Vadinho's blond hair? Dona Norma summoned up her forces for a new attempt: it would be better for the child, in that way his future would be guaranteed.

"The Terreiro is full of children, all the streets around here, and Mr. João Alves has countless grandchildren he has invented. I myself am the godmother of one of them. All of them are hungry, dirty, begging, even stealing. My friend is no millionaire, but she has enough to live on and can give the poor little thing a different kind of life, more comfort. He is not going to go hungry, nor wind up in jail. He will study to be a priest and say Mass . . ."

As though he had heard and understood Dona Norma's sermon, the baby woke up whimpering. Dionísia unfastened her gown, took out a breast, and settling the child comfortably, began to suckle him. She listened to her visitor in silence, as though she were weighing each of her arguments. Dona Norma gave her an outline of the future of her son, surrounded by comfort and affection, lacking for nothing. True, it meant a sacrifice on the part of the mother, but she would have to be selfish to condemn her child to a life of hunger and poverty when a kindly person was willing . . . Dona Flor was kindness itself, one could not find a better soul.

Dionísia accomodated her breast to the mouth of the child, who was almost full. As she answered, she turned toward the window where the Negro João Alves was standing, addressing herself to him as though the two women were not worthy of her notice: "Do you see, Mr. João, how they treat the poor? That one over there"—and she pointed to Dona Flor with her lip—"is unable to bear children and wants to keep her vow, so she goes sniffing around trying to find someone who has had a baby out of turn, and hears that Dionísia de Oxóssi, a strumpet who is in the best of health and the greatest poverty, has just had one. And so she says to her friend: let's go there and get it. She will even be grateful, the tramp . . ."

Dona Norma tried to interrupt her: "Don't be unfair . . . don't . . ."

Implacably, the languid voice of the mulatta went on, with a bitterness full of fire and ice: "But she didn't have the guts to talk herself, she asked this lady *comadre* of yours to act as her mouthpiece, to be her lawyer. 'Let's us go and get Dió's boy, who is a champion, so big and beautiful, and what a priest he will make. The mother is dying of want and she's nothing but a slut, first this one, then that one, and she'll probably be glad to get the kid off her hands. And if she doesn't want to give it up, it's because she's no account, is nothing but a hooker, all she is good for is a whore.' That was what she was saying, Mr. João, you heard her. Because she thinks the poor have no feelings, she thinks that because a person is a whore and has to lead this miserable life, one hasn't even the right to raise one's children . . ."

Dona Norma still tried to put in her oar: "Don't say that . . ."

The baby had finished nursing, and burped in satisfaction. Dionísia got to her feet with her child in her arm. Erect in all her beauty and fury, a queen radiating majesty. Even as she talked, she went about caring for the child, washing him in the enameled basin, changing his diaper, dusting him with talcum powder, and putting a dress perfumed with lavender on him.

"But they came to the wrong address; I am a woman who is more than capable of bringing up my son, making a decent person of him, I don't need anyone's charity. It is possible that he will not become a priest; he may even turn out a thief. Anything can happen. But the one who is going to raise him is me, and in my own way. He is going to be cock-of-the-walk of the neighborhood, and nobody is going to look down on him, and I am not giving him to any rich woman who doesn't want to go to the trouble of bearing her own children."

She smiled at the child, and said to him tenderly: "Not to mention the fact that you have a father to look after you."

At this point Dona Flor blew up, almost screaming, unexpectedly, her desperation lending her strength: "Except that his father happens to be my husband. I don't want your child, I want the son of my husband! You had no right to have a child by him. You enticed him because you wanted to. The only one who has a right to his child is me."

Dionísia wavered as though she had received a slap in the face. "You mean to tell me he is married to you? Really married?"

Having exploded and relieved her heavy heart, Dona Flor became her old timid self again, explaining in a low, hopeless voice: "Married for three years. Forgive me, that was the only reason I thought of bringing up the child as though he were my own, since I cannot give him a child. But now I see that you are right; the person to raise him is you who are his mother. And, after all, what would I accomplish by it? I came because I love my husband too much, and I was afraid he would leave me to go with the child. That is why I came. All the rest is made up. But after seeing you I realize that, with or without a child, he is never going to leave you."

"I am not a lady, I am a whore and nothing else. But I swear by the health of my child that I did not know he was married. If I had known that, I would not have had a child by him, nor have gone to live with him, leaving the life and setting up a house to live with him as husband and wife . . ."

By this time she had finished dressing the child. Dona Norma picked up the towel, and the atmosphere grew less tense. Dona Flor murmured: "I swear that Vadinho is my husband, everybody knows that."

"Vadinho never said a word to me about that. Why didn't he tell me? Why did he deceive me like that?" She had turned pensive, her rage was completely gone, and she spoke to Dona Flor with complete politeness, almost respect. "Everybody knows about the marriage, was what the lady said to me. Could be. But why didn't anyone tell me? And I know all his folks, all of them, even the mother . . ."

"The mother of Vadinho? His mother is dead."

"But I know his mother, and his grandmother. I know his brother, Roque, the one who is a carpenter by trade . . ."

"Then it's not my Vadinho!" Dona Flor laughed and she laughed and laughed, overcome with joy. "Oh, what a crazy, foolish thing, and how wonderful. Norminha, it is a different Vadinho! You know, I feel like crying."

Dionísia de Oxóssi, too, left the child on the bed, and went dancing around the room, the dance of a votary in the circle of the deity, dragging the Negro João Alves along with her to the shrine, greeting and thanking Oxóssi: *Ôke*, my father, *arô ôke!*"

"It's not my Vadinho—my Vadinho is not married. His one woman is Dionísia, his mulatta Dió."

Suddenly she stopped, looking at Dona Flor (Dona Norma had picked up the baby and was cradling it in her arms): "Didn't you tell me the lady was the wife of his namesake?"

"Which namesake?"

"My Vadinho and he call one another that, because they are both known as Vadinho. Except that mine is Vadinho for Valdemar, and I don't know what the other one's name is. He's crazy about . . ." She did not finish the phrase.

The one who completed it was Dona Flor: ". . . about gambling. That's the one. Vadinho for Waldomiro, my Vadinho . . ."

"And they came to you with the story that I had had a child by him. How can people be so low?"

The door swung open and in it stood a young, heavy-set Negro, his white teeth showing in a broad smile, his eyes like a bright Sunday: "Good-day, everybody."

Still dancing, the mulatta Dionísia de Oxóssi came toward him, and at his side recovered from all that fright, all that anger. She stretched out her arms, Dona Norma handed over the baby, and she put it in the hands of her man, the father.

"This is my Vadinho, a truck driver, the father of my child," and she said, pointing to Dona Norma and Dona Flor: "That lady there is a *comadre* of Mr. João, and guess who the other is."

"How should I know?"

"She's the wife of that other Vadinho, the one . . ."

"My namesake?"

"That very one! She came here with the idea that the baby was his child, the child of her husband, and she came for it, wanting to raise our little fellow, make a priest of him . . ." She laughed her gay laugh and finished up in a calmer tone: "What is your name? Flor? Well, you're going to be my *comadre*, you're going to stand up for my baby at baptism. You came looking for a child; I can't give you that because I have only the one, but I can give you a godchild . . ."

"My *comadre* Dona Flor," the truck driver said.

Picking up the child, Dionísia handed it over to Dona Flor. Birds zigzagged across the sky, coming to rest on the eaves of the archbishop's palace.

17

During the first epoch of her widowhood, days of sadness, of deep mourning, Dona Flor remained black and silent, in a kind of reverie that was neither sleep nor nightmare amid the steady murmur of acquaintances and the memories of her seven years of marriage. The acquaintances were ten, a hundred, a thousand, in a rumorous, steady solidarity; they came there on Dona Rozilda's trail, surrounding her with a court of gossips, their voices raised in a chorale of accusations against Vadinho, with Dona Rozilda as soloist, with Dona Dinorá as her understudy, their vituperous tongues indistinguishable.

Dona Flor, enshrouded in her sorrow and yearning, floated through that world of recollections, recalling the moments of laughter and the hours of bitterness, trying to keep in mind the image of Vadinho, his shadow still scattered through the house, thick in the room where they had slept and frolicked.

When all was said and done, what did they all want, the innumerable callers? Neighbors, acquaintances, students, friends, her mother coming from Nazareth to keep her company in that ordeal, and even strangers, like that circumspect Dona Ênaide, a connection of Dona Norma's? That worthy lady came all the way from Xame-Xame, where she lived—as though she had no husband, children, or domestic obligations—to recount Vadinho's shortcomings politely, pretending she was paying a visit of condolence. What did they want? What were they after, picking at barely healed scars, relighting the extinguished fires of suffering? Why did Dona Ênaide disclose in confidence, as though backing it up, the fact that she had known well that fatal Noêmia, today a fat married woman (whose husband wrote for the newspapers), but who still kept among her papers a picture of Vadinho?

Dona Flor lived with her good and her unpleasant memories, all of them helping her to bear the sadness, to live through that gray period of despair and loneliness, a desert of ashes. Even as she reviewed memories and images as detestable as that of her ex-student with her jeering laugh and cynical impudence, even as she pricked herself anew with those thorns, recalled those humiliations, she felt a kind of bitter consolation, as though memories and images, thorns and humiliations, all that she had undergone with him was a pallitive for the suffering that she was feeling now, boundless and hopeless. Because, in the last analysis, who had come off victorious, who had won the contest, who had kept him? Whom had Vadinho decided to stay with when Dona Flor, one day, reached the limits of her patience and issued an ultimatum: either she or the other one, but not both. He could go off with the slut if he wanted to (the indecent creature had spread the news of her approaching union with Vadinho to the four winds), but he was to do it right away, make up his mind at once. And what had happened, what decision had he reached?

Noêmia had come to learn the culinary art. She was engaged to be married, and her fiancé wanted a wife knowing the theory and practice of Bahian cooking. This fiancé was a snob, a fop full of pretensions about films and literature, all puffed up with himself and his learning, quoting authors and citing critics, a young genius shining in the sun of glory at the door of the bookstore. Because it took his fancy, he wanted Noêmia to become skilled in the art of preparing *vatapá* and *caruru*: "I want to see her proletarianized, that bourgeoise." She found the idea amusing and registered at the School of Savor and Art.

The daughter of a conservative family of Graça, rich and elegant, she felt it very chic to be the sweetheart of such a refined intellectual, and even more chic to fool around with Vadinho of the scoundrelly ways and dreamy eyes. When they realized what was going on—the distinguished family and the talented suitor—Noêmia had been taking lessons in shamelessness, barefaced shamelessness, with Vadinho at Amarildes's cathouse. What a row it set off, threatening to become a first-class scandal! Fortunately, the exceptional good breeding of the fiancé prevailed over his momentary mishap; he handled the situation with savoir-faire and diplomacy. He was not going to lose, because of stupid prejudice, that rich morsel, that coffer of gold. His comprehensive attitude and his understanding, however, were not enough, for the tramp in question did not want to give up that "adventure that carried no consequences," considering that she was getting a fine return on her investment in bed. To hell with the fiancé and the family: what Noêmia wanted was to run away with Vadinho, take off with him. Vadinho was the one who didn't want that. When the teeter-totter fell and the affair became public gossip, when Dona Flor in one of her rare but violent fits of anger demanded an immediate choice, either she or the other, he returned the girl to her fiancé, an even more snobbish and presumptuous esthete than ever, for to his talent and erudition he now could add horns, a first-rate suitor—it would be difficult to find another like him.

"All just haybags to while away the time," Vadinho had said to Dona Flor when, out of the depths of her suffering, she confronted him and told him he had to make up his mind once and for all. He had never even dreamed of going off with Noêmia. All that was nothing but her big mouth and showing off; in addition to being a floozy she was a liar to boot.

What more did the gossips want? Dona Rozilda, Dona Dinorá, that Dona Ênaide who had left her comforts of Xame-Xame, all the others, tens, hundreds, thousands, all joining in the vile chorus of lamentations and libels, what more did they want? Why recall this incident as proof of Dona Flor's marital unhappiness, proof that Vadinho had been the worst of husbands? On the contrary, it was the most complete proof of his love, of how he preferred her to any other. Didn't that Noêmia have money and position, a mansion in Graça, a checking account at the bank—Vadinho had lived high on the hog during that interregnum—a car with a chauffeur, ballet classes, rudiments of French, everything her heart desired, perfumes, dresses, slippers from Rio? And whom had he chosen, whom had he preferred when the moment of decision came? The checkbook was as nothing, nor the automobile at his disposal to take him and bring him, nor the dresses from Rio, the perfumes of

Paris, the refinement of language: *mon chéri, mon petit cocô, merde, quelle merde;* the smart way of talking, the *lòcé de parler,* as they say in the French of Bahia.

Vadinho gave no thought to the maidenhead he had enjoyed, or to the entreaties: "You have robbed me of my honor," or to the threats: "You'll see—my father will settle your hash. You will find yourself in jail." None of that had swayed him in the hour of decision. "How could you think such nonsense, that I was going to leave you for a bitch like that?" He boasted of the horns he had conferred on the fiancé, and went to bed with Dona Flor. Oh, what a night of peace and forgiveness! "All just haybags to while away the time; you are the only one I truly love, Flor, my sweet Flor."

In the opinion of the gossips, Vadinho was the worst of all the worthless husbands who ever existed in the world, Dona Flor the unhappiest of wives. She had no right to weep, to lament her loss. She should be giving thanks to God for having freed her in due time from such an ordeal. Beyond doubt Dona Flor was kindness personified, and only Dona Rozilda could have wanted her to rejoice, to celebrate Vadinho's sudden death. Worthless though he was, he had been her husband. But this persistence in her sorrow, this heavy mourning, this grief that was so deep, beyond all the accustomed ceremonials in the rites of widowhood, this vacant, expressionless face, the eyes turned inward or looking beyond the horizon, seeking out infinity or nothing—all this was unacceptable to the gossips.

On only one point were they all agreed, from Dona Rozilda to Dona Norma, from Dona Dinorá to Dona Gisa, true friends or mere gossipmongers: what Dona Flor had to do was forget, and as soon as possible, those unhappy years, efface the image of Vadinho from her life as though he had never existed. In their judgment, the period of grief was lasting too long, and for that reason they hovered over her to prove—with facts—that she had been favored by divine providence.

Even Aunt Lita, who was always ready to find excuses for Vadinho, could not conceal her surprise: "I never thought she would take it so hard."

Dona Norma, too, was amazed: "It looks as though she were

never going to forget him. The more time goes by, the more she suffers . . ."

Dona Gisa, backed up by her knowledge of psychology, disagreed with the pessimists: "It is only natural. It will take a while, but afterwards she will forget, and take up life again . . ."

"That's it, no doubt about it." Dona Dinorá was of the same opinion. "In time she will realize that God was looking after her."

They disagreed, however, on how best to help her. Dona Norma, leaning on the strong support of Dona Gisa, proposed that there be no further mention of Vadinho's name. The others, under the iron ferrule of Dona Rozilda—and Dona Dinorá was the sergeant of this combat troop—blathered on and on about ruses, abuses, laments, trying to convince her that now she could think of living a happy, carefree life, peaceful, untroubled, secure. By whichever route, whether that of kindly silence or noisy slander, it was her duty to seek out the paths of forgetfulness. She was still so young; her whole life was ahead of her . . .

"If she wanted to get married again, she would not be a widow long," prophesied Dona Dinorá, who, when it came to meddling in other people's lives, had a sixth sense, a gift of divination, a kind of second sight. Moreover, in her home (inherited from a Spaniard with a papal title), in flowing robe and a state of trance, she read fortunes with cards, and foretold the future while looking into a crystal ball.

Why, Dona Flor asked herself, did no one ever come to recall a single good act of Vadinho's? After all, despite his innumerable rascalities, on occasion he had showed kindness, generosity, a sense of justice, love. Why, then, did they measure Vadinho only by the yardstick of wickedness, weigh him only on the scales of curses? Besides, it had always been like that. When he had been alive, the talebearers had come, one on the heels of the other, to bring unpleasant news, to make her suffer, Dona Flor, poor thing, who deserved a kind and upright husband who would give her the treatment and consideration she was entitled to. Never once did it happen that a gossip, leaving her comforts, her duties and her idleness, hurried in, impatient and eager to tell her about something good that Vadinho had done.

"Listen, Flor, but don't say it was I who told you . . . Vadinho hit the numbers today and gave all the money to Norma to buy you an anniversary present. I know your anniversary is a long way off, but he was afraid of spending the money, he wanted to make sure you got your present . . ."

This had happened once, all the gossips knew it, and only Dona Norma had promised to keep it a secret. Nevertheless she, who was incapable of keeping quiet, had waited twenty days before telling her, for fear of breaking her promise. The others buttoned up their lips. Who is going to take the trouble to bear good tidings? For that there is no hurry or impatience. Nobody goes running into the street for that. Only when there is bad news. To carry that there is no shortage of messengers; there are those who are willing to make the greatest sacrifices, give up their work, interrupt their rest, sacrificing themselves completely. To bring bad news—what a delightful treat!

It was purely by chance that Dona Flor had not left that afternoon when Vadinho descended to the depths of ignominy, revealed himself in all his vileness. She had even packed her suitcases. There was always a room waiting for her in the house of her aunt and uncle in Rio Vermelho. It was touch and go that she did not leave, breaking with him for good. Nevertheless, the street was full of neighbors who had been attracted by the screams and weeping, and they all looked on when Cigano arrived, and all of them heard him speak with a broken voice and were witnesses to Vadinho's reaction.

Did any of them describe the scene to Dona Flor, repeat Cigano's words to her? What a hope! Not a single one, as though they had seen and heard nothing. On the contrary, all the gossip-mongers approved her decision, recognized her motives for breaking off for good with that hound. Some of them even helped her to pack her bags.

18

When Vadinho showed up that afternoon, Dona Flor immediately suspected the reason for his untimely appearance. The more she observed his behavior, the more convinced she became. He had never been so mannerly with the students, practically hiding in a corner of the living-room, letting them quietly finish up their practice test of a birthday cake in the kitchen. The girls who comprised the new group tittered without attempting to disguise their desire to meet the notorious husband of their teacher, for, in his way, Vadinho was famous. When the class was over amid "oohs" and "ahs" of praise, they were served slices of the cake and glasses of crême de cacao—a specialty of the house, and the pride of Dona Flor, whose skill at preparing egg-nogs and fruit liqueurs went hand in hand with her culinary gifts. She had introduced him, with a touch of vanity, a dash of pride: "My husband, Vadinho."

Not a single wisecrack, no phrase with a double meaning, not even a wink. Vadinho remained serious, almost sad. Dona Flor knew the meaning of that expression, and she feared it. Ah, if she could keep the students all afternoon and evening, drawing out the conversation, even running the danger of the scalawag overstepping the bounds of decency, becoming emboldened by their presence. Ah, if she could avoid the dialogue, the confrontation with that Vadinho unable to look her in the eye, crushed under the weight of the most evil intentions. But the students, girls and married woman on whom life made many social demands, gulped down their liqueur and took their leave.

The night before, Dona Lígia had sent her the money—generous payment—for the refreshments she had prepared for a huge reception in honor of some important visitors from São Paulo.

Ever since her marriage, Flor had limited herself to the work involved in her school, refusing private commissions. She made certain exceptions, however, for people she especially cared for. "I am devoted to Dona Lígia," she had said when she took on an assignment of that magnitude.

Extra money of this sort, which almost always came in when Vadinho was not around, was put aside by Dona Flor for unforeseen expenses, a special need, an illness, something urgent. She had even managed to get together several contos de reis, the bills hidden in secret places in the house. Savings for kitchen utensils, anniversary remembrances, the monthly payments on the sewing machine, not to mention the drain in the form of loans to Vadinho, a hundred and two hundred mil-reis at a time.

By mischance Vadinho happened to be resting from his labors in the living-room when Dr. Zitelmann Oliva took the trouble (he so busy with his eight jobs, all outstanding and remunerative) of coming in person to their house to pay the bill:

"I've been carrying this money around for three days. Lígia threatened to give me a beating today when she found out I had not yet paid you."

"Oh, doctor. Don't give it another thought! What nonsense . . ."

"Tell me, Mr. Vadinho," the big shot said teasingly, "what is it you do to keep your wife younger and prettier every day?" He had known Dona Flor since she was a child, and Vadinho, too, for a long time: from time to time the latter attempted to put the bite on him, but with minimal results, for Dr. Zitelmann was a hard nut to crack.

"The easy life, doctor, the easy life she lives. Married to a husband like me, who gives her no trouble. She lives in clover, no worries, happy," and he laughed his gay laugh. Dona Flor could not help laughing, too, at her husband's effrontery.

Vadinho did not ask her for money that day. Undoubtedly he had won the night before, still had reserves. But when he showed up unexpectedly the next afternoon, with lowered eyes, glum face, almost mournful, she immediately divined the reason for his appearance: he had come for money. While the pupils sipped the liqueur, tasted the cake, sprightly, casting furtive glance at the mute young man, Dona Flor, silent, her heart throbbing, swore to herself, taking a determined stand: she was not going to give him that money, neither all nor a part of it, not even a penny. It was to buy a new radio. Listening to the radio was Dona Flor's favorite pastime, her greatest diversion; she was crazy about sambas and love songs, tangos and boleros, comics, and, above all, soap operas. She, Dona Norma, Dona Dinorá, and other neighbors would get together to listen to them, all atwitter and wrapped up in the outcome of the countess's passion for the poor engineer. The one exception was Dona Gisa, with the disdain of a learned person for such trash.

The radio, which she had had since before she was married, was old and worn out; it was nothing but an expense, getting out of order every day, going off at the most dramatic moments, falling silent during the most moving scene. Repairs and more repairs, expensive and useless. This time Dona Flor's mind was irrevocably made up: she would not shell out her savings, no matter what happened. After all, she had to put a stop to such abuse.

The pupils departed in a flutter of laughter and somewhat disillusioned: was that glum customer brooding in a corner the touted husband of their teacher, reputed as dangerous, irresistible, the one who had been involved in that business with Noêmia Fagundes da Silva? Frankly, he was nothing to write home about; he seemed to fall far short of that spicy piece of gossip. Dona Flor found herself alone with Vadinho, face to face with her fear, her mouth bitter, her heart constricted. Making an effort, he got up, went over to the table, and poured himself a glass of liqueur: "This stuff tastes good but does it have a kick! It really knocks you out, and what a hangover. The only thing that leaves a worse headache is genipap liqueur . . ."

He was trying to act as though he had nothing on his mind. He came over to her offering her a sip from his glass, gentle and tender: "Taste it, babe . . ."

But Dona Flor refused, as she refused the caress of his hand moving down the neck of her blouse toward her breasts. "Hypocrisy, sheer hypocrisy, caresses to break down my resistance, to make it impossible for me to say no, playing on my weakness." She collected all her strength, recalled past grievances, her longing for a new radio, and got up, in a rage: "Why don't you say right off what you came for? Or do you think I don't know?"

Serious and sad was Vadinho's face; he had come because he had to, because he had not been able to get a cent anywhere, but he did not come happy, with his heart overflowing and full of laughter. Ah, if only he did not have to come.

He, too, knew what Dona Flor planned to do with that money. Mr. Edgard Vitrola had not yet shown up, for the old machine was still in the living-room as Vadinho discovered as soon as he opened the door. But he might appear at any moment with the eighth wonder of the world, a beautiful fixture of rosewood and chrome, the last word in engineering, waves and bands, megacycles and voltage, strong enough to pick up the most remote stations, those of Japan and Australia, of Addis Ababa and Hong Kong, not to mention the subversive programs of Moscow, all the more sought out for being forbidden. Dona Flor had sent an urgent message to Mr. Edgard through Camafeu, a *berimbau* player and inseparable companion of Vitrola's.

First in the street-car, with his hunch and his shame, then walking down the street, Vadinho came as though rent asunder. On the one hand, his haste to get home before the radio dealer arrived—never had he had such a strong hunch; on the other, the hope that Mr. Edgard had beat him there, and that there was no longer the old radio or the money paid by Doña Lígia, money earned by his wife in the sweat of her brow: she had spent the whole night and the next day over the stove without resting. Rent asunder, in the street-car, coming down the street, entering the house, opening the door. If Mr. Edgard had not yet come, what greater proof of the certainty of his hunch? But if he found the new radio installed, he would stay home that night, with Dona Flor, listening to the music, laughing at the jokes. Rent asunder, split in two, came Vadinho.

Why hadn't Mr. Edgard come sooner? Now he had no choice. "You think it is only to butter you up that I caress you?"

"Only for that and no other reason."

Self-interest, contemptible self-interest; Dona Flor entrenched herself in her position.

"Why don't you come out with it?"

A wall arose between them in that twilight hour when sadness floods from the horizon in gray and red, when everything and every being dies a little with the dying of the day.

"Well, if that's the way you want it, I am not going to lose any more time. You're going to make me a loan, even if it's only two hundred mil-reis."

"Not a penny. You're not going to see even a penny. How have you got the nerve to talk about loans? When did you ever pay me back one cent? This money is going from my hands straight into those of Mr. Edgard."

"I swear I will pay you tomorrow. Today I really need it, it's a case of life or death. I swear that tomorrow I myself will buy you a radio and anything else you want. At least a hundred mil-reis . . ."

"Not a penny."

"Don't be like that, babe, just this one time . . ."

"Not a penny," she repeated as though those were the only words she knew.

"Listen . . ."

"Not a penny . . ."

"Watch what you are doing! Don't fool around with me, for if not by fair means, then by foul . . ."

With this he looked around as though trying to locate the hiding-place. It was then that Dona Flor lost her head and, in desperation, threw herself toward the old radio; she had hidden the money beside the worn-out tubes. Vadinho came after her, but she had the bills in her hand, defying him with screams: "You are not going to gamble this away. You'll have to kill me first."

The screams echoed through the afternoon. The sharp-eared neighbors came out into the street: "It's Vadinho taking money from Flor, the poor thing . . ."

"That dirty dog. A regular hellhound."

Vadinho plunged after Dona Flor, blinded, his mind empty of everything but hate—hate of what he was doing. Grabbing her by the wrists, he shouted: "Let go of that crud."

She got in the first blow: pulling herself loose from him and not wanting him to grab her again, she hit him in the breast with her clenched fists, then in the face with her open hand. "You bitch, you'll pay me for this!" Vadinho said as Dona Flor screamed: "Let go of me, you scoundrel, don't you hit me. Kill me and get it over with." Whereupon he pushed her, and she fell over the chairs screaming: "Murderer! Assassin!" and he slapped her. One, two, four slaps. The sound aroused a chorus of protest and pity in the street. Dona Norma opened the door, and walked in without asking permission: "Either you stop that, Vadinho, or I'm calling the police."

Vadinho did not even seem to see her; he stood there with the money in his hand and an air of having lost his mind, his hair all tousled, looking in horror where Dona Flor lay, moaning and weeping softly. Dona Norma rushed over to defend her. Vadinho dashed out the door, the bills clenched between his fingers. The neighbors shrank back as he passed; it was as though they had seen the devil himself.

At that very moment the taxi of Cigano braked to a stop in front of the door. Recognizing him, Vadinho smiled, for that coincidence was still further proof of the infallibility of his hunch. He had been going along the street minding his own business, when he had had that certainty, but a total and absolute certainty, without any danger of mistake or bad luck, the certainty that that afternoon and evening he was going to break all the gambling banks of the city, one by one, beginning with the roulette wheels of Tabaris and winding up in the hidden den of Paranaguá Ventura. A certainty that grew within him, dominating him, demanding action, forcing him to every resort in his fruitless search for money, until he finally set out, against his will, to get the money from Dona Flor.

When he slapped her, however, the certainty left him, the hunch evaporated, he felt all hollow inside, not knowing what to do with that money, as though all that effort had been in vain. But

in the street, when the taxi of Cigano showed up as by a miracle—
for Vadinho was in a hurry to initiate that evening marathon of the
age—he grew calm again. A further indisputable proof of the
strength of the hunch. Vadinho's hands felt hot; he could not wait
to set out. Now the only thing that existed for him was the
roulette tables, the spinning wheels, the croupier, number 17, the
bets, the nervous surveillance of Mirandão on his left, who never
left his side, the chips—nothing but the gambling existed for him.
He opened the taxi door to get in, but Cigano vaulted out of it
among the women. His eyes were red with tears, his voice muffled.

"Vadinho, my brother, my poor old mother has died, my dear
mother. I heard the news in the street, I have just come from home.
I did not see her die, they said she called for me when the pain
took her . . ."

At the beginning Vadinho had not paid any attention to the
words of his friend, but as he took them in he clasped his arm.
What was he thinking up, what kind of a crazy story?

"Who died. Dona Agnéla? You're out of your mind or something?"

"Not three hours ago. My old woman, Vadinho . . ."

Often when he had been a bachelor, and even after he was
married, accompanied by Dona Flor, he had gone to eat the
Sunday bean stew of Dona Agnéla, at the end of the Brotas
street-car line. Fat and cordial, she had treated him like a son; she
had a weakness for that young gambler, forgiving him his dissolute
life. Wasn't he a replica, even to his blond hair, of the late Aníbal
Cardeal, an outstanding cardsharper, her lover and the father of
Cigano?

"The spitting image of the other. A pair of bums."

Once again Vadinho felt himself stunned, helpless. What a
loathsome, revolting day; first Flor, with that detestable stubbornness, and now Cigano jouncing through the darkness and bringing
the news of Dona Agnéla's death.

"But how did it happen? Was she sick?"

"I never saw her sick in my life. Today when I left after lunch,
she was at the tub, washing clothes. Singing, as happy as she could
be. Today was the day to make the last payment on the car, and

we had the money for it. Early in the morning we had been counting it, she and me. She handed over to me what she had saved during this month in ten tostão notes, two mil-reis. She was so glad because now the car was really mine." He paused, making an effort to hold back his tears. "They say that all of a sudden she got a pain in her breast. It gave her only time to say my name, and she dropped dead. It makes me feel so badly to think I wasn't there, that I was making the payment on the car. Isidro, who has the bar nearby, was the one who came to tell me in the square. I went running. Oh, my brother, she was all cold, her eyes rolled up in her head. I've come here now because I haven't got a cent, I put everything into the payment of the car. Both mine and hers, my poor old lady."

His voice was barely a whisper. Did the bystanders hear him? Even the worst gossips, dying a little with the sinking sun, had taken refuge in the shade when Vadinho handed over to Cigano the dirty money that he had taken by force and his indisputable hunch.

"It's all I have . . ."

"Will you come with me? There's so much to do."

"What a question! Of course I will."

Free of Vadinho's presence, the neighbor women went into the house, into Dona Flor's room with the suit-cases, Dona Norma trying to dissuade her. The busybodies could not understand Dona Norma's attitude. All the right was on Dona Flor's side, bushels of it. A chorus of buzzes: "What an unjust life, how can he torment her like that . . ."

"She ought to leave him once and for all."

"Imagine him striking her! What a horror!"

It did not enter Dona Flor's mind that they had not heard Cigano's conversation, his account of his mother's death. If it had not been for Mr. Vivaldo, of the funeral parlor, she would not have known about Dona Agnéla's attack, or what Vadinho had used the money for. Mr. Vivaldo happened to come by; taking advantage of the fact that he was in the neighborhood, he had come to bring her the recipe for a certain codfish dish, of Catalan origin, a delicacy he had savored at a pantagruelic lunch at the

house of the Taboadas, where they never served fewer than eight
or nine courses, just throwing money away. Observing Dona Flor's
eyes red with tears, he commented on the sad news: poor Dona
Agnéla. He had just heard about it; he had talked to Vadinho and
Cigano; he was going to provide the coffin, practically at cost.
Dona Agnéla deserved it; she had worked like a slave and was
always good-natured, an excellent person. Mr. Vivaldo had once
gone with Vadinho to do honor to her *feijoada*.

It was only then that Dona Dinorá and the other women made
the connection between gestures and words, the money changing
hands in the shadowy twilight. At least that was what they said;
whoever wants to can believe them.

Mr. Vivaldo took his leave, promising to come back and taste
the Spanish dish. It had taken both coaxing and a tip to get it from
the Taboadas' cook; Dona Antonieta was very reluctant to part
with her culinary secrets.

Dona Flor had come to know Dona Agnéla in those unforgettable days of the end of her love affair, just before her marriage,
when she spent the afternoons with Vadinho in the out-of-the-way
house in Itapoã. The playboy owner of the house, busy during the
day with his tobacco business, set aside the nights and the early
hours of the morning for womanizing. It happened, however, that
a real clock-stopper who had come through Bahia from Rio had
only one afternoon free. Vadinho got word that he was not to use
that discreet hideaway that day.

In the taxi they discussed where to go; she turned down the
idea of a movie, the afternoon show with its rubbing and squeezing; he was not going to take his future wife to a whorehouse.
Visit Aunt Lita in Rio Vermelho? And suppose Dona Rozilda
turned up there? Cigano suggested going to see Dona Agnéla, who
had already expressed a wish to meet Vadinho's sweetheart. They
spent the afternoon with the fat washwoman, talking and drinking
coffee, Vadinho kissing her in front of everybody, Dona Flor all
abashed. Dona Agnéla was charmed with the girl, and gave her a
lecture of warning and pity. "You're going to marry this scamp.
God help you and give you patience, for you're going to need it. A
gambler is the worst thing in the world, daughter. I lived for more

than ten years with one who was just like this one. Fair-haired, too, white and blue-eyed. Crazy about gambling, risked everything. Even a medal my mother had left me; the rascal sold it to use the money for his vice. He lost everything, and even got mad in the bargain, beat me . . ."

"Beat you?" Dona Flor's voice was incredulous.

"When he had drunk too much he even beat me. But only when he had drunk too much . . ."

"And you stood for it? That I would not do. Not for any man." Dona Flor quivered with revolt at the mere thought. "That I would never take."

Dona Agnéla smiled, understanding and experienced; Dona Flor was still so young, she had hardly begun to live.

"What could I do if I loved him, if that was my fate? Was I going to turn him loose in that tormented life without anyone to look after him? He was a cab-driver like Cigano, only he had to work for others, on commission. He never got enough money together to make the payment on a car, the spendthrift. What I managed to save he lost, taking it even by force. He died in an accident. All he left was a baby for me to bring up . . . ," and she looked at Dona Flor with affection and pity. "But I'm going to tell you something, my daughter: if he were to show up again, I would do it all over again. He died: I never had anything to do with another man, and let me tell you that I did not lack chances, even to get married. I loved him, what could I do, you tell me, daughter, if he was my fate?"

"He was my fate, I loved him . . ." What could Dona Flor do? "Tell me, Norminha, what can I do?" Empty the suitcases, put on a black dress to go to Dona Agnéla's wake. "What can I do if he is my fate, if I love him?"

Dona Norma went with her. Dona Norma loved a good wake. With tears, sobs, purple flowers, lighted candles, ceremonial embraces of condolence, prayers, stories, remembrances, anecdotes and laughter, hot coffee, cookies, a snifter toward morning; nothing to compare with it.

"It won't take me a minute to change my dress."

"What can I do, tell me, Norminha, if he is my fate? Cast him off, all alone, without anyone to look after him? What can I do, tell me, when I am crazy about him, and would not know how to live without him?"

19

Not to know how to live without him, nor be able to live. How could she get used to that life, when the light of day seemed tinged with ashes, a kind of leaden twilight in which the living and the dead were superimposed? So many images and figures surrounding Vadinho, so much laughter, so many tears, the confusion, the heat, the rattle of the chips, the voice of the croupier. Only on the basis of memory could life affirm itself, replete, with the light of morning and the stars of night; affirm itself victoriously above this coma-like twilight, this death rattle.

Sleepless in her iron bed, forsaken and alone, Dona Flor embarked on the route of the past, harbors of happiness, tempest-tossed sea. She evoked scattered memories, words, the brief sound of a melody, reconstructed the calendar. What she wanted was to break the fetters of this twilight, go beyond the day's work, the night's rest, live again. Not this colorless eking out an existence, not this vegetating in a smothering swamp of mud, this life without Vadinho. How could she break through this circle of death, cross the narrow door of this time devoid of meaning? Without him she did not know how to live.

At times Vadinho had been as mean as the neighbors, Dona Rozilda, Dona Dinorá, the other gossipmongers, had said. But on other occasions they had been unfair to him, accusing him without justification. Even she, Dona Flor, had behaved in that way more than once.

One day, for example, he had left in a hurry, and Dona Flor

had learned of it at the last moment, and imagined the worst, considering him gone for good. She did not believe he would come back from Rio de Janeiro, with its enchanted lights, its bustling avenues, its casinos, the hundreds of women from whom to choose. How many times had she heard Vadinho state: "One day I am going to get a chance to go to Rio; that's the life, and I'm never coming back."

Just another crazy thing, that trip. Needing money, Mirandão had invented a visit of a group of students of agronomy supposedly "to observe the centers of study of Rio de Janeiro" during vacation. He had visited the businessmen in the company of five colleagues, getting a contribution from everyone he could flim-flam for a Souvenir Booklet. He put the bite on bankers, industrialists, businessmen, storekeepers, merchants engaged in the most diverse trades, politicians of the governing party and the opposition. After a number of days he had collected a considerable amount of cash and found himself confronted by a problem: out of courtesy to the politicians, in sincere homage, he had changed the name of the delegation three times. Which of the three outstanding names to select now? Mirandão came up with an extremely simple solution: divide up the money they had received and forget about the trip, giving out that they had visited the centers of study. But his five colleagues disagreed as one; they wanted to make the trip, see Rio (being willing even, if a propitious occasion arose, to visit the School of Agronomy, at least go through its annexes).

Having received free passes at the request of the Secretary of Agriculture of the State, for the fourth time the group changed its name in honor of the generous Secretary of State. On the day of embarkation, almost as the boat was to take off, there was a dropout, one of the six grafters picked up malaria, the doctor forbade him to make the trip when there was no time left either to invite another student to take his place, or to sell the unused ticket for whatever they could get for it.

Vadinho had accompanied Mirandão to the dock, overheard the discussion. It was at this moment that he asked him, suddenly: "Why don't you come, take advantage of the ticket?"

"But I'm not a student!"

"What difference does that make! Now you are one. Only you'll have to step on it, the ship leaves in two hours."

Just enough time to rush home, gather up some underdrawers and shirts and his blue cashmere suit while Mirandão, a friend capable of any sacrifice, coped with Dona Flor's tears.

He was never coming back; she was sure of that. She was not such a fool as to swallow that crazy story about the student group on an educational tour. Why, Vadinho wasn't a student of anything, so how could he form part of a university group? The only thing Vadinho ever studied was the Book of Hunches, with detailed interpretations of dreams and nightmares, indispensable for any numbers player. He was undoubtedly leaving on the trail of some tramp for that abyss of depravity, Rio de Janeiro. The more Mirandão swore by the sacred memory of his mother, on the health of his children, the more dubious Dona Flor became. That story was not worth the breath that went into its telling. Why had Mirandão, her *compadre*, accepted that role, come to make her suffer so, making a mock of her deepest feelings with such a boldfaced lie? If he had no consideration or regard for her, why had he asked her to be the godmother of his child? If Vadinho had wanted to leave her, go off with some slut, move to Rio, at least he could have behaved like a man, come himself, telling the truth, and not send his *compadre* with that fairy tale to take advantage of their friendship and make her look like a complete fool. "But, *comadre*, it's the truth, the absolute truth. I swear to you we'll be back in a month." Why all that jive? Vadinho was never coming back, of that she was certain.

However, he did return on the date that had been set with the group—Dona Flor had come to accept the fact that it did exist, for the oldest son of Dona Sinhá Terra, a pupil of hers, was a member of the excursion, and in a letter had referred to Vadinho as a "swell companion." Not only did he come back, but he brought her a beautiful length of silk for a dress, imported, gorgeous, and expensive. Which, to Dona Flor's mind, meant that Vadinho had been lucky at the roulette wheel and had not forgotten her during the excursions, the carryings-on, the novelties of Rio, the nights of gambling and carousal. "How would I forget you, sweetie, when I only went to oblige the boys, not to leave the delegation incomplete." He came back wearing a vest, very *carioca*, talking very high-flown. He did a lot of name-dropping, people he had met: the singer, Sílvio Caldas, and Beatriz Costa, the famous actress.

He was introduced to Sílvio by Caymmi, at the Urca Casino, where the crooner had an engagement. Vadinho was extravagant in his praise of his simplicity, his modesty. "You'd never think he was who he is. He's just like anybody else. You'll see when he comes here. He told me he was coming in March, and I promised that you would cook him a lunch with every kind of Bahian dish. He sets himself up as knowing a lot about cooking." What a pleasure it would be for Dona Flor to prepare this lunch if the remote possibility ever arose; she was an enthusiastic admirer of the singer, listening to him on the radio. He had such a Brazilian voice!

Wrapped in the length of silk, slipping off her shoulders, covering and uncovering her, so happy over Vadinho's return, all laughs and sighs, Dona Flor climbed into bed with her husband. The sting of remorse made that manifestation of love even sweeter; she had been unfair to him, aggressive, unkind, doubting him, "the handsomest student of the lot . . ."

What Dona Flor never knew was the effort it had cost Mirandão to drag Vadinho out of Josi's arms and get him on the ship bound for Bahia. Josi was the *nom de guerre* of the Portuguese Josefina, a chorus girl of the Portuguese Review of Beatriz Costa who had lost her head over the young Bahian (and vice versa). They had met when the Student Delegation had gone to the show at the Republic Theater on complimentary tickets, and then afterward backstage to congratulate Beatriz and her supporting cast. Vadinho had taken a fancy to Josi while she was still wearing her fishwife's costume; she had looked the fake student over from head to heels, they had smiled at one another, and half an hour later they were eating slices of fried codfish together in a nearby tavern. Josi paid the check on that occasion and all the following, until he left. With his time divided between the Portuguese chorus girl and the casinos, Vadinho had completely forgotten the date and hour of their return to Bahia. Mirandão had to resort to firmness and appeal to his better feelings: "I have seen my *comadre* crying once, and I don't want to see it again. What will she say if I come back without you?"

Dona Flor never learned of this or of the true origin of the length of French silk; it was not bought in Rio, but won on board ship, in a poker game, the evening before the ship put in at Salvador, when the members of the delegation, all of them without a penny to bless themselves, staked their gifts and souvenirs of Rio on the deck of cards. From one of the students Vadinho had won the silk, from another, a pair of patent leather shoes and a blue bow tie, very high fashion. Against these belongings he had bet a superb photograph of Josi, big and in colors, with glass and a gilt frame, in which the country wench was got up like an actress, in a bikini and brassiere, with one leg on high, that farmer's daughter. She had inscribed it in her illiterate handwriting: "To my adored Bahian, his loving Josi." The photograph was finally acquired, after long bargaining, by a young lawyer, another traveling companion, who wanted to arouse the envy of his friends with tales and proofs of his sensational conquests in the big city. It was thus that Josi helped finance Vadinho's landing and contributed to Dona Flor's pleasure, Dona Flor panting in her husband's arms, the length of silk hiding and revealing her, finally rolling down to the foot of the bed.

How could she live without him? Smothered by his void, fighting fog, caught up in currents, how could she overstep the limits of impossible desire? How could she rediscover the light of the sun, the warmth of day, the morning breeze, the evening zephyrs and the stars of heaven, the aspect of the people? No, without him she did not know how to live, and she gathered him to her in that mist of sadness, laughter and emotions, in that world of his, always full of surprises.

The neighbors could recall the bad moments, the hateful arguments, the low ruses he employed to get her money, the nights when he did not come home, drunk, possibly with other women, his mad gambling. But why didn't they open their foul mouths to recall the exultant days when Sílvio Caldas had been in Bahia, when Dona Flor did not have a moment of rest or of sadness? A perfect week, without one ruffling detail—Dona Flor cherished every minute of it, the richness, the joy, a feast. During that week she was, so to speak, a kind of queen of the whole excited neighborhood; from Cabeça to Largo Dois de Julho, from Areal de Cima to Areal de Baixo, from Sodré to Santa Tereza, from Preguiça to Mirante dos Aflitos. Her house crowded with important people, really important, knocking at her door, asking permission to come in, for in spite of the fact that he was staying at the Palace Hotel it was in Vadinho's house that Sílvio really felt at home, receiving, talking, as though he lived there, and Dona Flor were his younger sister. Leaving out acquaintances like the banker Celestino, Dr. Luís Henrique, and Dom Clemente Nigra in person, the biggest swells of Bahia called, either because of the famous lunch, or on other days to greet the crooner, shake hands with him. Visits that would have thrown Dona Rozilda into an ecstasy, would have had her beside herself with excitement, had she not fortunately been in Nazareth das Farinhas making life a hell for her daughter-in-law, who, Hector had written, was finally expecting their first child.

Of that lunch Dona Flor preserved not only a vivid memory, but also newspaper clippings. Two journalists, friends of Vadinho, one that Giovanni Guimarães, so fond of jokes and tall tales, and the other a Negro Batista, a chaser who was famous in the whorehouses, both of them high livers, reported the event in their papers. Giovanni made mention of the "incomparable banquet in honor of the distinguished singer given by Mr. Waldomiro Guimarães, the diligent municipal employe, and by his distinguished spouse, Dona Florípedes Paiva Guimarães, whose culinary skill goes hand in hand with exceptional kindness and good breeding." As for the Negro João Batista, what he emphasized was the number of courses: ". . . an exquisite and abundant repast, in which the outstanding delicacies of the Bahian cuisine were served, not to mention twelve different desserts, all proof of the quality of our cuisine and of the divinely endowed hands of Mrs. Flor Guimarães, the wife of our subscriber Waldomiro Guimarães, one of the most devoted and efficient employes of our municipality." As is apparent, the two gluttons were so gorged and satisfied that they praised not only the meal, the culinary gifts of Dona Flor, but even transmogrified Vadinho into a devoted, efficient, and hard-working employe, an exaggeration that was a little hard to swallow.

Why didn't the neighborhood gossips recall that Sunday of the luncheon? The house so full one could hardly move, the tables loaded with food. Dr. Coqueijo, of the Supreme Court, an amateur musician, made a speech, praising Dona Flor's art; the poet, Hélio Simões, promised a sonnet in honor of the "enchanting mistress of the house, custodian of the great traditions, skilled in the use of dendê oil and pepper." And all the gossips were there, every one of them, whispering and taking in everything. They came when Sílvio picked up his guitar and let out his impassioned Brazilian voice. People gathered in the doorway to listen; and at five in the afternoon many guests were still there and a number of gate-crashers drinking beer and rum, begging the singer for more songs, and he refusing nobody.

The best of it all, however, superior to the spoken praises and those printed in the papers, to the speeches and verses, better even than the singing of Sílvio Caldas, in Dona Flor's opinion, was Vadinho's behavior, filling sky and sea with peace and harmony. Not only had he footed all the expenses of the lunch (where had he got hold of all that money on a moment's notice?—only Vadinho's gift of gab could have worked that miracle), but on that day he had not got drunk, had drunk sparingly, had been attentive to all the visitors, the perfect host. And when the crooner picked up the guitar without even being asked to, to show his gratitude for the lunch, calling Dona Flor "Little Flor, my sister," Vadinho went over and sat down beside his wife and held her hand. Tears rose to Dona Flor's eyes; it was more than she could bear.

How could she live without him? Without him, an inexhaustible fountain of amusement and surprise, how could she get used to it? She had read in the evening paper that the crooner had arrived for a short engagement at the Palace and at Tabaris. At the invitation of the municipality he planned to give a concert in Campo Grande, thus affording the people a chance to hear him and sing with him. Would Vadinho have gone to meet him, or would he not have been notified?

When he had returned from Rio several months before, he had never stopped talking about Sílvio Caldas, almost the only name he mentioned. He had even promised him a lunch prepared by Dona Flor. What a silly thing—a person as famous as that, making the headlines of the papers, the covers of magazines, visiting Bahia for a week. He wouldn't even have time to accept the attentions, the invitations of the rich; even if he wanted to, where would he find time to eat in a poor man's house? "A series of festivities is being organized by members of high society to honor the presence of the great artist in our midst," the paper announced. She would, however, with satisfaction, great satisfaction, assume the work of this lunch, prepared to spend her hard-earned savings, hidden in a post of the iron bed, to use up the money of the month, to go into debt if necessary, to receive a guest of such importance in her house and regale him with a real Bahian feast. She had no doubt about the cordial relations that had been established in Rio; wasn't the crooner omnipresent at the gambling tables? But from that to a visit of this celebrity to her house was a big step. But for Vadinho distances did not exist or obstacles of any sort. For him everything was easy, nothing in life was impossible. In a moment of dejection Dona Flor mentioned the matter to Dona Norma: "One of Vadinho's scatter-brained ideas! The things he thinks up. A lunch for Sílvio Caldas, did you ever hear of such a thing?"

Dona Norma, however, liked the idea: "Who knows but what he may come! In that case we'd even close the store . . ."

Dona Flor would be satisfied with much less: "I would be satisfied to go to the open-air concert. That is, if I had someone to go with. Otherwise not even that."

"Don't you worry about company, for I'll find a way to go. If Zé Sampaio doesn't want to, then he can stay at home alone. I'll go with Artur . . ."

The news program of the radio had announced the debut of the singer, set for that very night, singing at midnight in the room next to the gambling casinos of the Palace Hotel, and at two o'clock in the morning in Tabaris for the bohemians and the strumpets. Dona Flor went to bed thinking that in connection with all the activities of the crooner, only one thing was certain: there was no point to waiting for Vadinho; with Sílvio Caldas in town, it was as though she had no husband. When, at dawn, they left the cabaret, the last shade of night in Bahia would escort them to the mysteries of Pelourinho, the paths to Sete Portas, to the sea and fishing skiffs of Rampa do Mercado.

She fell asleep and dreamed. A troubled sleep in which Mirandão, Sílvio Caldas, and Vadinho were all intermingled with her brother Hector, her sister-in-law and Dona Rozilda. All of them in Nazareth das Farinhas, where Dona Flor was helping her sister-in-law, who was pregnant, tied to the raincoat of her mother-in-law by an iron chain. The news of the paper and the radio and the letter of her brother were jumbled together in a wild dream. Dona Rozilda, in a fury, wanted to know the reason for Sílvio Caldas's being in Nazareth. He had come there, he answered, for the exclusive purpose of accompanying Vadinho in a serenade to Dona Flor. "I loathe serenades," Dona Rozilda roared. But he picked up the guitar, and his voice of flower petals and velvet awoke the people of the Recôncavo beside the dreaming Paraguaçu. Dona Flor smiled in her sleep as though hearing a lullaby.

The voice in the street grew louder, awakening Dona Flor, but the dream miraculously went on, the song came closer. Dream or reality? People were getting up, hurrying to listen. Dona Flor quickly slipped on a robe and went to the window.

There they were, Vadinho, Mirandão, Edgard Cocô, the sublime Carlinhos Mascarenhas, the pale Jenner Augusto of the cabarets of Aracaju. And among them, the guitar against his breast, his voice loud and clear, Sílvio singing for Dona Flor:

> *To the sound of an impassioned melody*
> *On the throbbing strings of the guitar . . .*

There had been the serenade, the street in an uproar; there had been the lunch on Sunday, mentioned even in the papers; Sílvio came to prepare the second in person, brought everything, put on an apron, went to the kitchen, and he even knew how to cook. The other days he had no fixed hour for coming; he came and went, they all attended a *capoeira* match. But of all that happened that week nothing could compare with the public celebration on Tuesday, the eve of Sílvio's departure for Recife. There was a full moon, and he sang for the people, the multitude assembled in the square, from the reviewing stand of Campo Grande.

Dona Flor did not even ask Vadinho if he was going; he did not let his friend out of his sight. She merely informed him that she was going too, in the company of Dona Norma and Mr. Sampaio, for even the shoe-shop owner had laid aside his eternal weariness to go to the serenade.

Imagine Dona Flor's surprise when, after dinner, Cigano's taxi deposited Vadinho, Sílvio, and Mirandão at the door of the house. They had come for her. "What about your wife?" she had asked Mirandão. She had gone on ahead with the children; by that time she was probably in the square. While Dona Flor was getting ready, they mixed themselves a daiquiri.

Seats had been reserved for her and Vadinho among those occupied by the authorities. The Governor was not able to come, as he was confined to bed with an attack of grippe, but they set up a loudspeaker near the mansion so he and his wife could hear. The prefect of the city and his wife were among those near whom Flor and Vadinho were seated, the Chief of Police and his sisters, the Superintendent of Education, the head of the Military Police and the Fire Department, Dr. Jorge Calmon, and other persons of distinction. Dona Flor, in the midst of all those bigwigs, smiled at Vadinho: "I am only sorry Mamma cannot see this. She wouldn't believe it. Us sitting here with the people who run things."

Vadinho laughed his mocking laugh, as he answered her. "Your mother is an old harridan. She doesn't know that all that counts in life is love and friendship. All the rest is a waste of time, trumpery, not worth the trouble."

Suddenly the guitar struck a chord, and all the merry sound in the square died away. The voice of Sílvio Caldas, the full moon, the stars and the breeze, the trees in the park, the silence of the audience; Dona Flor closed her eyes and leaned her head on her husband's shoulder.

How could she live without him, how could she cross that

desert, traverse that darkness, lift herself out of that swamp? Without him everything was a waste of time, trumpery, not worth the trouble.

20

As Dona Flor lay there in her iron bed, one single thought tormented her, shattering her to the depths of her being: she would never have him beside her again, her Vadinho, all excitement; never again. That certainty pierced and undid her; like a poisoned blade it slit her breast, deadened her heart, snuffing out her desire to go on living, her youth eager to endure. In her iron bed, Dona Flor a suicide. Only desire bore her up and memory persisted. Why was she waiting, when it was useless? Why did desire light up like a flame burning her vitals, keeping her alive? It was useless. He would never come back, that shameless lover, to pull off her petticoat or slip, her lace panties, exposing her nakedness, saying such crazy things that she did not even venture to repeat them to herself, so mad and so indecent, but so sweet, ah! He would never touch her neck again, her thighs and belly, arouse her, and put her back to sleep, a whirlwind of desire, a cyclone bearing her along blindly, a breeze of tenderness, a zephyr of sighs and swooning, dying only to come to life again. Oh, never more. Only desire kept her living, and memory.

"Like a lost soul wandering about the damp and doleful house, a sepulcher." The smell of mold on the walls, the ceiling, the floor, a chill indifference to spiders and spider webs. "A grave where she has buried herself with the memory of Vadinho." Dona Flor in deep mourning, inwardly and outwardly, rotting away. Dona Norma, her friend, came to see her and said: "You can't go on like this, Flor. You just can't. Almost a month has passed, and you live like a soul in purgatory, shut up here in the house. And your home, which used to shine, is getting all mildewed. God forgive me, it's more like a tomb where you've shut yourself up. You must get yourself in hand, stop living like this, not give way to your grief."

The pupils dropped out; laughter and gaiety had a hollow sound in that atmosphere. How was the cordiality of the classes, the agreeable feeling that their study was a pastime, which was one of the main reasons for the success of the School of Savor and Art, to be maintained when the teacher laughed as though under constraint and making an effort? In her bygone days as a student, Dona Magá Paternostro, the millionaire, in a joking takeoff of a student reciting a piece, had declaimed from the threshold of the first floor of Alvo, a parody from *The Alsatian Student*:

> Long live the school so gay and free
> And its young teacher so merry . . .

Since then the number of pupils had grown, for each one became a free publicity agent, saying to her friends: "She is wonderful, nobody can match her cooking, she knows how to teach, and she's a darling. The classes are so entertaining: two hours of laughs, stories, jokes. There's no better way to pass the time." On occasion she had to turn down as many pupils as she accepted for the two courses. But now three girls had left the group and the word was going around that the school was soon to be closed. What had become of that "young teacher so merry?" Of the "two hours of stories and jokes"? In the middle of the class, when the girls were laughing, it was suddenly as though Dona Flor had taken leave of them, her eyes lost in space, her face drawn. Who likes to feel another's dead present all the time, day after day, as though there were no such thing as a cemetery?

Her *comadre* Dionísia de Oxóssi had come to visit her, had brought her that imp of a godson, had come all dressed in black as politeness demanded, but had come smiling, for almost a month had gone by, and with that she had completed her turn of three visits. The sadness Dona Flor's face revealed worried her; being so low-spirited was going to do her harm.

"Bury the man once and for all, *comadre*. Otherwise he will begin to rot and do away with everything here, including you."

"I don't know how. The only rest I have is thinking of him."

"Well, gather together all that is memory of him, gather together the whole load of it, and bury it in the bottom of your heart. Gather it all together, the good and the bad, bury the whole load, and then lie down and sleep a peaceful sleep."

With a load of books under her arm, wearing a light summer dress that showed off her freckles and her health, Dona Gisa, her adviser, scolded her: "What goes on here? How long are you going to carry on like this?"

"What can I do? It's not that I want to . . ."

"Where's your will power? You say to yourself: Tomorrow I begin a new life. I am going to close the door on the past and start living again."

The chorus of the neighbors, in a Gregorian chant: "Now, without that scourge of a husband she could be happy. She ought to give thanks to God."

Dom Clemente Nigra in the courtyard of the convent against the vast sea dyed blue-green touched her sad face, taking in her deep mourning and her thinness and dejection. Dona Flor had come to request the monthly Mass.

"My daughter," murmured the ivory-pale friar, "what is the meaning of this despair? Vadinho was so gay, he loved to laugh. Whenever I saw him, I realized that the greatest sin is sadness, the only one that is an offense to life. What would he say if he saw you like this? He would not be pleased; he liked nothing sad. If you want to be true to the memory of Vadinho, face up to life joyously . . ."

The keeners of the neighborhood kept on. "Now she can be happy, for the dog has gone to hell."

The figures moved about the rear of the room as in a ballet: Dona Rozilda, Dona Dinorá, the pious old hypocrites with their odor of the sacristy, and Dona Norma, Dona Gisa, Dom Clemente, Dionísia de Oxóssi, smiling with her baby: "Bury the load deep in your heart, *comadre*, and lie down and sleep."

But her body was rebellious and called for him. She reasoned, thought, listened to her friends, agreed with them that she had to put an end to this dying every day and each time a little more. Her body, however, would not agree and called upon him desperately. Only memory returned him and brought him to her, Vadinho, with his jaunty mustache, his jeering laugh, his impudence, his dirty and yet so sweet words, the hair on his chest, the scar of the knife wound. She wanted to go off with him, take him by the arm, grow angry over his misdeeds—and there were so many of them —moan shamelessly, fainting under his kisses. But she had to react and live, open up her house and her tight-closed lips, air out the rooms and her heart, make up a bundle of all the past, Vadinho, all of him, and bury it deep. Who knows? Perhaps in that way her desire would become assuaged. A widow, she had always heard it said, should be immune to such desires, to those sinful thoughts, all passion spent. A widow's wish is to go to the grave in her husband's coffin, be buried with him. Only a shameless creature, without love for her husband, could still think of such things— how revolting! Why hadn't Vadinho carried away with himself the fever that was consuming her, the despair that swelled her breasts, that roweled her unsatisfied womb? The time had come to bury her dead once more, completely: with all his ill-treatment of her, his meanness, his insolence, his gaiety, his humor, his generous impulses; and all that he had sowed in Dona Flor's meekness, the flames he had lighted, the burning desire, that frantic longing, ah, the unforgivable impulses of a brazen widow.

Before, nevertheless, at least once, for the last time she sought him out and found him, hanging on his arm. She went dressed as though she were rich, as in her unmarried days, when she and Rosália, two poverty-stricken young things, had gone to parties at the homes of rich people, and had been the best dressed there, vying with the others in luxury.

Ah, that night beautiful and terrible above all others, of wonder and surprise, of fear and exultation, of humiliation and triumph. With the emotions of the ballroom and the gaming-room, her nerves undone, her heart dancing, what a night.

To walk with him one last time. To reconstruct step by step the absurd itinerary of that starless night; the slipping out of the house, the two and Dona Gisa, the dinner, the tango, the show, the mulattas rolling their haunches, the Negresses singing, the roulette wheel, the baccarat table, the indignity, the tenderness, the return in Cigano's taxi, as in the old days, Vadinho impatiently kissing her right there in front of Dona Gisa, who smiled. Tearing off her best dress in a frenzy the minute they got into the room: "I don't know what there is about you today, my sweet, what a woman, and I am crazy about you. Come on, hurry up. You are going to see what screwing can really be, and today is the day, so get ready. I gave you what you wanted, now you are going to pay . . ."

Prone on the iron bed, Dona Flor shuddered. That night the gall turned to honey, once more pain became supreme pleasure; never had she been a mare so in heat covered by her potent stallion, such an eager bitch, a slave submitting to her own debauchery, a woman pursuing all the paths of desire, fields of flowers and sweetness, forests of damp shadows and forbidden ways, to their final conclusion. A night to enter the narrowest, most tightly closed doors, a night to surrender the last bastion of her modesty, Glory hallelujah! When gall is turned into honey and suffering is strange, exquisite, divine pleasure, a night to give and to receive.

It was the day of Dona Flor's birthday, and not long before, the preceding December, around Christmas.

21

PARENTHESIS HAVING TO DO WITH THE NEGRO ARIGOF
AND ZÈQUITO MIRABEAU THE BEAUTIFUL

Vadinho had awakened late, after eleven. He had come home early that morning as drunk as a lord. While he was shaving he realized how unusually quiet the house was, the absence of the morning pupils. Why were there no classes that day? One of the pupils, a golden young mulatta, thin and fragile, had fixed her eyes on him, had made drawling conversation with him. Vadinho had plans to take her for a walk when he had the time and inclination, to show her the wild beauty of the beaches, intoxicate her with the smell of the tides. A delicate reed, that silly Ieda, with her airs and shyness. She was on his list, waiting her turn. At the moment Vadinho was attending to the sexual-sentimental demands of Zilda Catunda, the boldest of the three forward Catunda sisters, but feeling that the end of his infatuation was approaching; the affected thing was growing demanding, wanting to boss him, control his goings and comings, even to the point of being jealous of Dona Flor, the hussy.

If it was not a saint's day or a holiday, why was there no class? When he came out of the bathroom, he was confronted with a festive atmosphere: Dona Norma helping in the kitchen, Aunt Lita polishing the furniture, Thales Pôrto installed in a rocking chair with newspapers and a glass of wine. There was an aroma of a company lunch, but what was the occasion for this celebration?

An abundant lunch, the house full of friends, a Sunday blow-out, that was one of Vadinho's pleasures. If his finances had been less fragile, he would have repeated with greater frequency oxtail stews, and *sarapateis*, *maniçobas*, and *vatapás*. Whenever he had a lucky break, he planned a *feijoada*, dried beef with manioc mush, guinea fowl in brown sauce, not to mention the classic *caruru* of Sts. Cosmé and Damian in September, and the corn pudding and genipap of St. John. But this lunch out of the clear sky, without warning or invitation, what the hell kind of celebration was this? Dona Norma answered him in an irate tone: "You've got the nerve to ask that, Vadinho? Don't you remember that today is your wife's birthday?"

"Flor's birthday? What day is this? The nineteenth of December?"

The neighbor stubbornly went on scolding him: "Aren't you ashamed of yourself? Come, now, tell us what you bought her for a birthday present?"

Nothing, Dona Norma, he had bought nothing and he deserved

the dressing down, the blame for his oversight; but was he a man to remember birthdays, to pick out presents in stores? What a pity, he had missed such a chance to cover himself with glory by bringing a gift. Dona Flor would have gone out of her mind with happiness, as on that other birthday, when he had handed over to Dona Norma, well beforehand, a big sum to buy "a swell gift, and not to forget a bottle of perfume, Royal Briar, which she likes very much."

It was a shame for him to have been so careless when he had been having a run of exceptional luck, winning large sums for four or five days straight. Not only at roulette, but at baccarat, dice, and the numbers, too; he had begun the week winning thousands two days straight.

So loaded that he had paid off a note the signer was on the point of protesting to satisfy his debt to a third party, saving his credit and reputation. And the rogue was not even a friend, just a pleasant companion, someone he had met at a bar and cabaret. It was, moreover, in Tabaris that the braggart, on a monumental bender, had agreed, with generous heart and unusual enthusiasm, to underwrite a promissory note for a month signed by Vadinho.

Shortly after the month had expired, Vadinho was called to the office of the manager of the bank where the note had been submitted for collection. He quickly answered the summons, as he maintained a shrewd policy of keeping on good terms with managers and assistant managers of banking establishments on which he was so dependent.

"Mr. Vadinho," said the executioner, who, let it be said in passing, was a good companion, Mr. Jorge Tarquínio, "I have here one of those chickens of yours that has come home to roost."

"Mine? I don't owe anybody anything. Let me see . . ."

"Here you have it. Now pay up," and he showed him the note. Vadinho recognized his signature and that of the co-signer.

"But, Mr. Tarquínio, if the note has a guarantor, why do you scare me like this, saying that I owe? . . . All you have to do is go to Raimundo Reis and collect; the man is filthy rich. He has a ranch, a sugar plantation, a law office, he goes to Europe every year. He's the one you should have sent for . . ."

"Naturally we went to him first, as he is the guarantor. But he says that under no circumstances will he pay. He refuses to . . ."

Vadinho was shocked and horrified at such effrontery: "He said he wouldn't pay, he refused to? But, Mr. Tarquínio, he has everything one could want in this world. How cynical and shameless can a person be? There he was in the cabaret boasting about his wealth, the leagues of land he owns, the herds of cattle, the sugar, what he does and doesn't do, how he took three women at one time in Paris, a blustering millionaire. He goes there, one trusts him, believes his swindling stories, accepts his signature as though he were a decent person. And what happens? The note falls due, is not paid and my credit is shaken, with you calling me in . . ."

"But Vadinho, when all is said and done it was you who took the borrowed money . . ."

"Oh, for heaven's sake, Mr. Tarquínio. If that embezzler was not prepared to guarantee the note, why did he offer to? After all, did he or did he not assume the responsibility, did he or did he not assume the obligation of paying the debt if I didn't? He assumed it, and I rested easy in my mind about it. And now . . . That's no way to do business. It's people like him who give folks a bad name with banks. When that rascal signed the note, it was because he was prepared to pay, Mr. Tarquínio. That Raimundo Reis should be in jail, that's where he should be, the old swindler . . ."

All that ridiculous indignation for the purpose of softening him up, of getting him into a frame of mind to extend the note that had fallen due, thought Mr. Tarquínio. Imagine his surprise when Vadinho put his hand in his pocket and pulled out a roll of bills.

"You see, Mr. Tarquínio, the harm that scoundrel does me. That's what comes of dealing with such riffraff. I always pick my guarantors carefully. Who would have believed it of Raimundo Reis? One lives and learns."

He did not even feel the outlay, with his luck at high tide without signs of diminishing, the money rolling in in red chips and going out in bills and coins, a week of dinners, quantities of liquor, unforgettable sprees.

An overflow of luck that had wound up in a real apotheosis the night before. Vadinho, who had dreamed of Mr. Zé Sampaio, did not even take the trouble to consult his book of hunches. What for? The bear, beyond doubt, and so it turned out; the bear coming up in every combination. The gains were multiplied later on in Tabaris at French hare and baccarat. It was a grim night for the bankers, for Vadinho spent it winning, without overdoing it, but with steady persistence, whereas the Negro Arigof, who must have had a pact with the devil in the early morning hours, won ninety-six contos at roulette in less than ten minutes.

The Negro turned up toward the end of the night, just as the croupier was about to announce the last play. He had come from the joint of the Three Dukes, with his tail between his legs; the games of *ronda* had swallowed up his last cent. He had been to Abaixadinho and the rat-trap of Cardoso Peraba, winding up in Tabaris, his last port of call on that unhappy journey.

Tabaris was a kind of topsy-turvy place, half casino, half cabaret, run by the concessionaires of the Palace Hotel. The good artists they brought in for the Palace gave shows there, and the second-class variety, from old women at the end of their careers to young girls, barely adolescents, all of them under the protection of Mr. Tito, the manager who had carte blanche. For the first, he felt sorry: there is nothing sadder or more tragic than an old actress out of work. He tried out the others in his office; if they were no good on the stage, they could work as whores, provided they did not offer too much competition. In the course of the night, the Tabaris was the gathering spot for those who frequented the Palace, as a rule persons of standing and money, and for the riffraff from the various taverns, from Abaixadinho, a bar with pretensions to being a casino, and even from Paranaguá Ventura's hidden den. They all came to wind up the night there, in one last try, one last hope.

Arigof came in and found Vadinho in all his glory, surrounded by a ring of spectators admiring his luck at baccarat, Mirandão on his left, snitching an occasional chip, and several women on his right, among them the Catunda Sisters. "Hurry up, give me a chip, brother, quickly, for he's going to close down," Arigof pleaded in a pathetic whisper. Holding tight to his cards, Vadinho put his hand in his pocket, pulled out a chip without even looking at it. It

was one of the small ones, five thousand reis, enough for the black.
He rushed over to the wheel, put his gift on number 26, which was
where the ball came to rest; twice the number came up. Ten
minutes later the game was over, Arigof was the richer by ninety-
six contos, Vadinho by twelve, not counting the conto and three
hundred mil-reis in Mirandão's friendly pocket.

That was the unforgettable night when the Negro Arigof, with
his English elegance and his manners of a grand duke, ordered and
paid for in advance the material and the tailoring of six suits of the
best white English linen. He had owed sixty mil-reis for a long time
to Aristides Pitanga, a tailor who was crazy about roulette and
afraid to play. His stinginess never let him go beyond two or three
bets a night, modest ones, but he circled the tables, thrilled with
the bets of others, suggesting hunches, kibitzing about luck and
chance.

For a long time the tailor had been saying a requiem for the
soul of the balance of the bill, but in the face of the spectacular
performance of that customer who was so demanding and such a
deadbeat, he disinterred the debit from the column of losses and
gains, and collected on the spot, in full sight of the other players
and the strumpets, an outright affront. The Negro did not turn a
hair.

"Sixty thousand mil-reis? For those suits? By the way, Pitanga,
what are you charging now for a white linen suit?"

"Regular linen?"

"English linen, eggshell. The best to be had."

"Around three hundred mil-reis . . ."

Arigof put his hand in his pocket, pulling out bills of five
hundred: "Well, there you have two contos. Make me six new
suits. Deduct your sixty mil-reis, and keep the change for your
trouble in coming to collect from a customer at the gaming table."

He threw the money in the tailor's face and turned his back on
him, while the other, in utter confusion, picked up the bills from
the floor amid the jeers of the women.

This Arigof was a gentleman in dress and manners, and like the
gentleman he was, he had done nothing his whole life but gamble;
as poor as Job, as black as coal, a master of *capoeira* fighting, he

was forbidden entrance to the Palace Hotel, where he had once got into a fracas with a young scion of an important family who, when he had drunk more whiskey than he could handle, developed race prejudices, and laughingly remarked to the group around him as he saw Arigof, impeccably dressed in white: "Look at the monkey that escaped from the circus." The room was turned into a shambles, and the big-mouthed fag still bears a knife wound like an open flower on his cheek.

The success of the two friends called for a celebration dinner under the illustrious sponsorship of Chimbo. The table was made up of Mirandão, Robato, Anacreon, Pé de Jegue, the architect Lev the Silver-Tongued, the journalists Curvelo and João Batista, and the lawyer Tibúrcio Barreiros, in addition to the hosts and a distinguished mélange of loose ladies and actresses, so to speak, thus satisfying the desires of the Catunda Sisters, zealous of the art and the elite of the brilliant society that gathered at fat Carla's cathouse. These Catunda Sisters, "actresses of polymorphous talent," according to the reporter João Batista of *O Imparcial* were three time bombs, daughters of the same mother, Jacinta Gold-Digger, and different fathers. The oldest of them was almost black, the youngest almost white, and the middle one an enchanting mulatta. All they had in common was their progenetrix and their inability to carry a tune. Weak in the musical register, but marvelous in bed, really polymorphous, according to the same João Batista, whose salary on the paper and a few cents he picked up here and there were spent on the enterprising sisters; he knew the three of them, one by one, and he was still unable to say which was the most skillful and polytechnical. The middle one, Zilda, had a weakness for Vadinho.

Lev the Silver-Tongued and the lawyer had wanted to bring the Honolulu Sisters to lend even more brilliance to the dinner, but in vain. These were not even sisters of the same mother, nor did they come from Honolulu; two North American Negresses, dingy of color but with perfect figures: the soft and deer-like Jô, the muscular panther Mô. In addition to their flawless bodies, they had pleasant voices and strange behavior; they accepted no invitations to parties, lunches, serenades, swimming in Itapoã, the moonlight

on the Lagoon of Abaeté; nor would they sit down and drink at
the table with any of the customers. Not even the banker Fernando
Goes, tall, handsome, elegant, a bachelor loaded with money, with
women throwing themselves at his feet; not even he could make
any time with them, even though he went to the Palace only to see
them and order bottles of French champagne. Jô and Mô sang
spirituals and jazz, danced with bare breasts and bottoms, but
stayed together and alone till it was time for them to come on
stage, half hidden at an out-of-the-way corner table, hand in hand,
sipping drinks from the same glass. After their number they went
up to their room; they did not want any talk with anybody.

The dinner was wonderful, with wine and champagne, the
Catunda Sisters at the height of their artistic prowess, a general
state of well-being, with the exception of the young lawyer Barreiros still smarting under the refusal of the Americans, "dirty
dykes," drinking furiously, indifferent to the warbling of Fat Carla
offering him consolation and poetry. When it came time to pay,
Arigof and Vadinho almost had a fight when the former refused to
let him share the bill, even if only as a token. The Negro, who was
still full of the old Nick, felt that any suggestion of financial
collaboration was a flagrant insult to his honor.

Dona Flor's birthday fell during this week of so much pomp
and wealth, with Vadinho really in the money, to the point of
expressing and fulfilling the praiseworthy intention of making a
contribution to the housekeeping expenses, a rare and notable
event. Dona Norma kept asking, reproachfully: "What is it you
are going to give your wife?"

Vadinho smiled at her, giving her tit for tat: "What am I going
to give Flor? Why, whatever she asks me for, no matter what it is
. . . whatever she wants . . ."

Dona Norma went in search of the celebrant: "Child, pick out
whatever you like"; Dona Flor came out of the kitchen, wiping her
hands on her apron: "Is it true, Vadinho, that you are going to
give me whatever I want? You are not just fooling me?"

"You just ask . . ."

"You won't go back on your word? I can really ask?"

"When I promise you know I carry it out, pet . . ."

"Well, the present I want is to go to the Palace Hotel for dinner with you."

She was almost trembling as she said this, for he had never allowed her into that world of his, and his gambling companions. The only one she was on terms of friendship with was Mirandão, her *compadre*, the only one who came to the house from time to time. She had seen some of them: once or twice; of the others she had heard only disagreeable epithets. Even Anacreon, whom Vadinho esteemed so highly, had come only five or six times during those seven years, and as for Arigof, she had seen him only one Sunday cadging a lunch. Dona Flor's world was the street, her own neighborhood that of her pupils or former pupils, reaching as far as Rio Vermelho, Ladeira do Alvo, and Brotas, decent people. She had nothing to do with the irregular life of her husband. Vadinho had never admitted Dona Flor to the dubious realms of gaming, those regions of roulette and dice. A wife's place was in the home. What in the devil would she be doing in joints of that sort?

"One person in the family with a bad name is enough. You are not cut out for that environment."

It did her no good to argue that the Palace Hotel was well known as an elegant spot, where the highest society foregathered. To dine in its beautiful room, dancing to the rhythm of the best orchestra in the state, watch the stars of radio and the theater, from Rio and São Paulo, was in the best tone. There the ladies of Graça and Barra came, displaying the latest fashions, and some of them, the most sophisticated, even had a fling at the roulette wheel. The gambling-room was like an extension of the dance hall; a long arched hall established a kind of nonexistent and ruinous frontier between them.

Why that stubborn refusal? Why, Vadinho? Dona Flor passed from pleading to demand, from entreaty to insult: "You're not taking me so I won't see your sluts."

"I don't want to see you in such places."

Hadn't Dona Norma gone to the Palace more than once with Mr. Sampaio when some sensational attraction was on? The Argentines in the ceramics business never missed a Saturday in spite of the fact that Bernabó was opposed to any kind of gambling. They went to eat, dance, applaud the artists. But Vadinho had never allowed himself to be persuaded, and, when all his arguments were used up, he took refuge in a vague promise: "There'll come a time."

And now finally the occasion he had always rejected had come. Dona Flor could hardly believe it when taken by surprise and without a chance to deny what he had promised, he agreed, though against his will. "If that is what you want. It had to happen some day."

Once he had made up his mind, the project was amplified to include her aunt and uncle, Dona Norma—and, with her, Mr. Zé Sampaio—and Dona Gisa. Aunt Lita was very appreciative, but declined; it was not that she did not want to go, but where would she get an evening dress, a toilette up to the standards of the Palace? Dona Norma was dying to go: an evening at the Palace was the last word as far as she was concerned, but Mr. Sampaio was adamant; Dona Flor was an excellent neighbor, a person for whom he had the highest regard, he even liked Vadinho. He thanked them for the invitation, but they would please forgive him, he could not accept. During weekdays Mr. Sampaio was in bed at nine o'clock, as he had to be up at six for the long workday in the store. If it had been on a Saturday evening or Sunday afternoon he would have gladly accepted. As for Dona Norma's going to the Palace without him, as Dona Flor had suggested, they must excuse it, but this was an absurd idea, not to be considered. The clientele of such places, what with gambling and drinking, was made up of the best and the worst, all intermingled and exposed to dissipated libertines without any notion of respect for decent folk.

One of the few times he had been there, dragged against all his will by Dona Norma, who had been anxious to hear a French faggot (Mr. Sampaio had never seen a more effeminate individual in his life, and yet the women were swooning over him), an unpleasant thing had happened. Mr. Sampaio had only left the table for a minute, impelled by an urgent need to go to the men's room, when some impudent rogue had showed up and tried to engage Dona Norma in conversation, inviting her to take a turn on the dance floor; praising her dress and her eyes, as though she were anybody. The only reason Mr. Sampaio had not made an example of the rascal was that he knew his family, his mother, Dona Belinha, and his two sisters, very distinguished people, excellent customers of his, as well as the blackguard himself, a notorious gambler and bohemian, Zèquito Mirabeau, also known among loose women as "Mirabeau the beautiful."

Thus their company was reduced to Professor Gisa, happy over the invitation, giving her the opportunity to hear the Honolulu Sisters and to observe with her psychological and psychoanalytical eye the infamous gambling world, giving it the proper metaphysical definition.

Dona Flor spent the rest of the day in a bustle, deciding with the help of Dona Norma and Dona Gisa the dress and stole, gloves and hat, shoes and purse to use. That night at the Palace she had to be the most beautiful of all, the most elegant, to whom no other could measure up or compare, neither the high-born lady from Graça with her dresses bought in Rio, nor a banker's or cacao planter's mistress with the latest in Paris fashions. That night she was finally going to cross the forbidden threshold.

22

When Dona Flor, timidly clinging to Vadinho's arm, crossed the entrance to the ballroom of the Palace Hotel, by a strange coincidence the orchestra was playing the same old but never outdated tango to which they had danced at their first meeting in Major Wild Boar's house, with Joãozinho Navarro at the piano, during the celebration in Rio Vermelho during the week of Yemanjá's procession. Her heart beating faster, Dona Flor smiled at her husband: "Do you remember?"

The room was dimly lighted, with a colored paper shade over each bulb, the height of bad taste. Dona Flor found it all so beautiful, that semidarkness, with paper flowers on the tables and the shade, how lovely. Vadinho looked around without any special recollection, it was all familiar and intimate, but nothing about it referred to Dona Flor.

"Remember what, babe?"

"The music they are playing. It is the same we danced to the day we met. At the Major's party. Remember?"

Vadinho smiled. "The very same," as he made for the table he had reserved beside the stage, right across from the passageway that joined the two rooms, the ballroom and the gambling-room. From there Dona Flor and Dona Gisa could observe all the motions, the steps of the dancers, the excitement of the players. Still standing up, Vadinho looked the dance floor over where there were only two couples, but each of such outstanding fame as tango dancers that nobody ventured to compete with them. The women were two of the Catunda Sisters.

The oldest and blackest had as her partner a tall, romantic-looking individual, dressed in the height of fashion, like the leading man in a South American movie, with the air of a gigolo. Vadinho learned later, when he was introduced to him, that he was from São Paulo on a visit to Bahia, Barros Martins by name, a respectable book publisher, and naturally, being a publisher, very rich. He was a knockout at the tango, with the air and ability of a professional, tracing letters, as the saying goes, with the execution of the most difficult steps.

The youngest and whitest was in the arms of Zèquito Mirabeau, that same "Mirabeau the beautiful," the delight of the whores who had given rise to the indignation of Zé Sampaio. With his eyes rolled up, biting his lip, lifting his hand from time to time to his floating hair, the Bahian was putting on just as good a show, performing his tango, a baroque version, with the greatest ease, mocking the *Paulista* with his flourishes and perfection.

Vadinho eyed the scene, and still smiling, held out his hand to Dona Flor and said, helping her out of the chair: "Honey, shall we show those jerks how it should be done? Shall we teach them how to dance the tango?"

"Do I still remember? It's been so long since I've danced, my joints are all stiff."

She had danced for the last time more than six months before when Vadinho, by some miracle, had gone with her to a surprise party in Dona Êmina's house, a birthday celebration. Vadinho was an outstanding waltzer, and Dona Flor danced well and enjoyed it. One of the reasons for her deep-seated resentment was that they almost never went dancing together, for it was once in a blue moon that Vadinho accompanied her to a party in the home of a friend. And without her husband, limited to comments, gossip, the re- freshment table, the subversive idea of dancing with another man, which a married woman can do only with the express permission and in the presence of her spouse, never crossed her mind. Va- dinho, of course, went about as he pleased to cabarets and dance halls, in joints of any sort, at the Palace, in Tabaris, in Flozô, with sluts and tramps of all kinds.

At the house of the neighbors he had given a veritable exhibi- tion of sambas and fox trots, *rancheras* and marches. Dr. Ives and Dona Êmina tried to follow them—everyone has his pretensions— but then they gave up. They knew the steps, but they were too restrained to compete with Dona Flor and Vadinho.

But it's one thing to dance at a birthday party, and something very different to get out on the dance floor of the Palace in the authentic movements of a voluptuous tango, and especially that one! It had all begun when, seven years before, he had invited her to dance that same dance at the home of Major Wild Boar. Would she still remember it after so long, and especially on that magic night when she was visiting the Palace for the first time? Never guessing that this first time would be the last, a first without a second, a night that would never return.

Only now, in the loneliness of memory and desire, did she realize the importance of every detail, even the most insignificant, of that chimerical night, from their entrance into the ballroom to the last moment of infinite pleasure, of shameless immodesty in the iron bed, with him covering her, in the roots of her being, her birthday present, the trip to the Palace.

Two gestures of Vadinho, the two equally tender and imperious, marked the beginning and the end of that enchanted evening for Dona Flor. The first, when he asked her to dance the tango with him, and held out his hand to lead her to the dance floor. The other in the tumbled, tempest-tossed bed when he turned her over by the shoulders. But she would recall this, this tremendous gesture, when its proper moment came, in that road she traveled with Vadinho the night of her birthday. She moved slowly, step by step, detail by detail, savoring each one; she would reach every door of joy, of fear, of lasciviousness.

On the dance floor Vadinho's arm had encircled her, and her body felt weightless in the cadence of the music. She sought within herself that girl who was vacationing in Rio Vermelho, quiet, without a sweetheart, timid in the painting of the painter from Sergipe, picking flowers in Aunt Lita's garden, and the sudden bursting into bloom the nights of the kermesse, when Vadinho's hand kindled her breasts and her thighs and seared her mouth once and for all.

In the ballroom of the Palace the two were going to dance a tango of sweetness and voluptuousness, suitable for innocent young lovers and equally for lecherous lovers. It was as though they had returned to the fascination of the Major's house, to the impact of the first glance, the initial laugh, the shyness, and yet at the same time they were the ripened lovers of seven years later, a long time to suffer and love. A chaste maiden, Dona Flor, an innocent girl; an unrestrained woman and ardent female, Dona Flor, in the arms of her husband, Vadinho. Such a tango had never been danced before, with such evident tenderness, so darkly sensual. People even came out of the gaming-room to watch.

The publisher from São Paulo, with all his experience of cabarets in São Paulo, Rio, and Buenos Aires, and Zèquito Mirabeau, with all his self-satisfaction, threw in the sponge and left the dance floor completely free to Dona Flor and Vadinho in that night of their passion.

"Who's that woman with Vadinho?" the habitués asked. Some

knew, the news quickly spread. "It's his wife, and it's the first time she has come here . . ." The most attractive of the Catunda Sisters, the middle one, gave a contemptuous gesture, stung by jealousy.

After the tango, when they returned to the table, where Vadinho, who had ordered drinks and dinner, answered Dona Gisa's questions, giving her information about things and people, the curiosity with regard to Dona Flor continued. It floated in the air, as though a halo of furtive glances and mumbled whispers surrounded her, as though she did not fit into the atmosphere of the room, made to the measure of the cream of society, the baronesses of Graça, the haughty ladies of Barra, and the most expensive harlots whose calling leaped to the eye.

Dona Flor felt a kind of faint dizziness sitting there in the room. A little giddy, half-pleased, half-fearful, of those sidelong glances, those elusive gestures; were those smiles friendly or scornful? She hardly took in what Vadinho was saying: "He's over seventy, and he plays nothing but baccarat with five-conto chips. There have been nights when he lost over two hundred. Once his children came—two louts and a slut accompanied by her husband —and they wanted to take him away by force, they raised hell. The worst of all was the daughter, a snake who kept egging the brothers on and her antlered husband. Now they have brought suit to prove that the old man is senile, irresponsible, unfit to control his money . . ."

Dona Gisa stretched her neck the better to see the old man with his fine white hair, almost nothing but skin and bones, but steady on his feet, resting on a cane, his face tense, with a last gleam of cupidity in his eyes, as though only the fascination of gambling kept him alive.

"After all, who but he worked to earn that money?" asked Vadinho, enraged at the old man's family. "What did the children do but spend it? They are rotten spoiled, good-for-nothings. And now they want their own father declared insane, to shut the poor old guy up in an asylum or old folk's home. I'd put the whole lot of them in jail, beginning with that cow of a daughter. I would have them all given a beating that would raise welts on them . . ."

Dona Gisa disagreed; this business of money had serious connotations. In her opinion the old man was not free to squander his fortune on gambling, for the family had legal rights.

Her lecture on economics was interrupted by the publisher from São Paulo, who made it a point to come and greet Vadinho and Dona Flor.

"Vadinho, my friend here wants to meet you; he has heard a lot about you and has seen you dance. He is a big shot from São Paulo . . ." Zèquito Mirabeau made the introductions. Turning to the stranger he said: "Vadinho, as you know, he is . . ." but the presence of Dona Flor restrained him. "Well, he is a great chap."

Vadinho, in an almost solemn voice, introduced the ladies: "My wife and a friend of hers, Dona Gisa. An American, a fount of learning . . ."

Dona Flor held out the tips of her fingers, suddenly turned into a country girl. The publisher bent over and kissed her hand.

"José de Barros Martins, your servant. Congratulations, madame; I have rarely seen a tango better danced. Admirable!"

Then he kissed Dona Gisa's hand, and as the orchestra was striking up a popular samba, he asked her: "Do you dance the samba? Or, being an American, would you rather wait for a blues?"

Vadinho undermined all the *Paulista*'s politeness: "What are you talking about. This *gringa* is a real swinger . . ."

"Vadinho, what is this you are cooking up?" Dona Flor scolded him affectionately.

Dona Gisa paid no attention; instead of being embarrassed, she left on the industrialist's arm, swinging her scrawny backside as though to confirm the words of the imposter. At this point a shadow came over Vadinho's face, and Dona Flor at once discovered the reason for it: one of the three mulattas at Zèquito Mirabeau's table, as pretty as a picture, had also come over, sizing up the situation. She looked Dona Flor over from head to foot as though challenging her, as she said to Mirabeau, half coaxing, half suggesting: "How about it, honey, here's our samba. I'm waiting. Let's go."

She gave Dona Flor a disdainful look, Vadinho a furious one, and smiled angelically and temptingly at Zequito: "Come on, sugar."

Dona Flor avoided Vadinho's eyes. An uncomfortable silence came between them. She turned toward the dance floor, her eyes closed, he looking toward the gaming-room. Why had she insisted on coming? Vadinho asked himself. It was because of women like that and others that he had always refused. And now, on her birthday, instead of being happy, the poor thing was biting her lips to keep from crying. That blasted Zilda was going to pay, and pay dear for this. Vadinho pulled his chair closer, taking Dona Flor's hand in his, and whispered to her with a tenderness she felt was sincere: "Darling, don't take it that way. You wanted to come. This is no place for you, my crazy little fool. Are you going to give a hoot now for these tramps here, do they cut any ice with you? You came here to be happy with me; just pretend the two of us are here alone, and nobody else. Forget about that piece of trash. I have nothing to do with her."

Dona Flor let herself be easily taken in: she wanted to be persuaded, her eyes brimming with tears, her voice a whimper: "You really don't have anything to do with her?"

"She's the one who's running after me, can't you see? Forget about it, sweetie, this night is ours, you just wait till we get home. I'm not going to gamble today, just to be with you."

The mulatta came whirling by, cheek to cheek with Mirabeau the beautiful, who was practically beside himself, biting her lip, his eyes on the ceiling. Dona Flor said: "Let's us dance, too."

They danced the samba, and then a two-step. She wanted to visit the gaming-room. Vadinho took her there, willing to satisfy her every whim. Dona Gisa went along, frisky and lively, wanting to know everything, what a horror! She did not even know the value of the cards, and had never rolled a die in her life.

Dona Flor moved silently, contrite, like one who has penetrated a secret temple, forbidden to the uninitiated. At last she had managed to reach and enter the mysterious territory where Vadinho was millionaire and beggar, king and slave. She knew she had barely touched upon this nocturnal realm, the mere fringe of this sea of darkness. There began a period of dream and suffering; the

rooms of the Palace were the rich and luminous capital of this
world, this sect, this caste. Farther on, in the byways of night in
the city, the terrain of ecstasy and agony, of cards and women, of
alcohol and drugs (cocaine, morphine, heroin, opium, marijuana, it
gave Dona Flor the shivers just to remember the names) came the
cabarets, the gaming tables, the cathouses, all those illegal spots, an
area is filthy and teeming as a flytrap. Along these paths Vadinho
moved completely at ease; Dona Flor, before the roulette wheel,
gingerly touched the hem of this world.

Beyond the Palace, with its "high class" reputation, according
to the advertisements, with its lights and shadows—a lampshade on
every table—the gleam of crystal, an orchestra of first quality, the
ladies of fashion, the sought-after sporting girls, the kept women
and mistresses and bedfellows of the cacao colonels, the ranchers,
the sugar planters, the rich men of the city, the young bohemians
and the crooks, beyond the Palace, at the crossroads of the poor,
untinseled night, stretched the mystery of Vadinho, his true
being.

In a rapid transition Dona Flor auscultated this mad geography,
the ocean of her tears, the valleys and mountains of her weary
waiting, her suffering love. Dona Gisa, on the contrary, was fascinated by the faces of the players, their gestures. One of them was
talking to himself, evidently furious with himself. If it had been up
to her, the teacher would never have left. But the waiter, out of
deference to Vadinho, his friend, came to announce that dinner
was served and the show was about to begin.

They returned to the ballroom and ran into Mirandão, who had
just arrived. What kind of a miracle was that, his *comadre* in the
Palace? Had she come to break the bank? Her birthday. Good
Heavens, how could he have forgotten? The next morning he
would send the missus with her godchild and a gift. "Your wife
and the baby are enough," Dona Flor answered, so he would not
feel under the obligation to buy her anything and because she had
already received her birthday present on that occasion—she did
not want any more. She was there with Vadinho; that was
plenty.

The meal was nothing to write home about; the rice was

undersalted, the meat had little taste, but how delicately Vadinho served it, putting into her mouth the best bits of his chicken! Dona Flor no longer felt fear or embarrassment.

The lights went out completely, and then came on again at once as Julio Moreno, the master of ceremonies, announced the attractions. First the Catunda Sisters (their voices were terrible, but what an exhibition of breasts and haunches)

> *I am going to dance the whole night long,*
> *Rancheira . . .*
> *Rancheira . . .*

The impudent one was the best-looking and most attractive of the three, Dona Flor could not fail to recognize, could not deny this almost naked truth. But Vadinho paid no attention to the mulattas, being more interested in the desserts. Now it was Dona Flor who eyed them with disdain; holding her husband's hand, the two of them sat talking and smiling, while the gracious sisters outdid themselves in the play of lights, their breasts blue, their haunches red.

They were followed by the Honolulu Sisters singing a sad, sorrowful song, the lament of Negroes in chains, the prayer of slaves, the suffering and humiliation of beaten men. Even the sex was sad, even the bodies which were so beautiful, thought Dona Flor. The mulattas Catunda, off key and jaunty, seemed like the tinkling of bells, the warble of a bird, a ray of sun, their bodies exuberant and healthy in comparison with Jô and Mô with their despairing sadness. The Catundas danced according to the dictates of the *orixás*, the gay and intimate Negro deities, come from Africa and ever more alive in Bahia. The American Negresses directed their plaint to the austere and remote white gods of the masters, imposed upon the slaves by the whiplash. The singing of the first was carefree laughter; that of the others desolate weeping.

"Look at them. They are lovers," Vadinho remarked.

Dona Flor had heard that there were such women, but she did not believe it; she even thought it was a joke of Vadinho's, some absurd invention, dirty talk.

"Aren't there men who are fags, sweet? Well, there are women who only like women."

"What a pity," Mirandão added. "Two knockouts like that who don't want any part of a man."

Dona Gisa backed Vadinho up: "Such cases are fairly common in the most civilized countries."

Dona Flor still tried to put in a kindly word: "I'll bet they are just decent girls." She wanted to hear their pure, sad song without mingling with its grandeur their flaws, their morbid state, their fate. It was the music of blood that had been shed, of searing lash.

"Sweetie, I am going over there and I'll be back in a minute."

Vadinho hurried over to the gaming-room, leaving Dona Flor alone with the harrowing song of the slaves.

The lights went up, there was a roar of applause, and Dona Flor saw Mô give her hand to Jô as they walked off to their doomed love. The publisher from São Paulo went back to the dance floor. Zèquito Mirabeau went to join the gamblers.

Mirandão would have liked to accompany Vadinho and Mirabeau; but his *compadre* had left him there to look after the ladies; he could not leave them. And that teacher with her idiotic questions. How the devil should he know whether or not gambling had to do with sexual impotence? "Listen, my dear lady, I was practically born at the gaming table, and I can only assure you that I am a man, a man from start to finish; and I've never heard that gambling sapped anybody's manliness."

Dona Flor could see Vadinho in the other room, moving about the roulette table, betting, surrounded by men and women. The little mulatta had come over beside him, and for a moment put her hand on his shoulder while Vadinho, tense as a wire, stood watching where the ball would stop at the solemn and decisive moment. Dona Flor almost got up from her chair, utterly indignant, feeling herself capable that night of scandal and violence, of acting, if necessary, like the most disreputable, shameless streetwalker. But then she smiled when Vadinho, after the croupier had called out the fatal number, became aware of the impudent gesture of Zilda Catunda, moved his shoulder, and must have said something very harsh to her, for the trollop disappeared as though she had been cuffed.

Vadinho, after looking at Dona Flor, came toward her, his hands full of chips. At the table, Mirandão, all entangled in Dona Gisa's sociological-economic-sexual questions, was drowning his ignorance in the remains of a glass of sweet vermouth—what a horror!

Vadinho bent over her, his mouth to her ear: "Listen, babe, just two or three bets and then we'll be leaving. I won't be any time at all, I've already sent word to Cigano to be here with the car. You get ready, for tonight you're going to get a real workout in bed . . ." And, bringing his mouth still closer, he bit her ear and licked it, breeze and flame.

Dona Flor, her body one damp shiver, gave a sigh. Oh, that crazy Vadinho, and if anyone had seen him, what wouldn't they say! The tyrant, the good-for-nothing!

"Don't be long . . ."

With the chips in his hand, he took his place at the table again across from the croupier. Bent over a little, with his blonde hair, his insolent mustache, his mocking smile. What a man!

Dona Flor eyed him fully, her Vadinho. Then she assembled one by one every detail of that night and every moment of her life with him, from beginning to end, omitting none, both the suffering and the happiness.

From the roulette table Vadinho made a sign; it was the last bet, Cigano's taxi had arrived a few minutes before. "No, my beloved, never again will I go with you to celebrate that night when the drop of gall turned into honey, a boundless sea of giving and receiving." Dona Flor took in Vadinho once and for all in front of the gaming-table, his chip on number 17. Then gathering up all her burden, she buried it in her heart. She turned over on her face in the iron bed, closed her eyes, and fell into a peaceful sleep.

23

A month after Vadinho's death, after attending Mass, Dona Flor set out for the flower market in Cabeça. It was the second time she had left the house since that unforgettable Sunday of Carnival when death came knocking at the door. The first had been to go to Mass the following week.

Everyone was watching her curiously as she came out of church. From the window of his bar, Méndez greeted her, and Mr. Moreira, the Portuguese who ran the restaurant, bellowed to his wife, who was busy in the kitchen: "Hurry up, Maria, come and see the widow." In the street, three or four men, among them the foppish Argentinian, Mr. Bernabó, took off their hats to her.

At the corner of the butcher shop, the Negress Vitorina got up from behind her tray of stewed beans and fritters: "Hail, my lady, *atôtô, atôtô!*" At the door of the Scientific Drugstore, Dr. Teodoro Madureira, the druggist, bent over in a deep bow, measured exactly to her sorrow and loss. Professor Epaminondas Souza Pinto, flustered and with his head in the clouds as always, a load of books and notebooks under his sweaty arm-pit, held out his hand: "My dear lady . . . life . . . the inevitable . . ."

The drinkers in the saloon having their morning apéritif, the customers of the store, the rancher Moysés Alves selecting spices for his famous lunches, came out to see her, bowing their heads in silence. The image-maker, Alfredo, a friend of Uncle Thales, who had his workshop nearby with its display of images, left the wood he was carving and came over to place himself at her disposal: "Good day, Flor. Can I be of any help to you?"

The sellers came over with their wares. She bought roses and carnations, tuberoses and violets, dahlias and scabiosas.

A tall, lean Negro with a sharply etched profile, an enigmatic expression, still relatively young, who was listened to with attention and respect by the mechanics and chauffeurs of the taxi stand, on learning who Dona Flor was and the reason for the purchase of the flowers, came over to her and asked her to lend a few of them to him for a moment. Somewhat surprised, Dona Flor did as he asked, holding out the bright bunch from which he himself selected, with religious care, three yellow carnations and four red scabiosas. Who could this man be and what did he want with those few flowers?

From the pocket of his coat he pulled a braided thread of African straw, a *mokan,* tying the carnations and scabiosas into a small bouquet with it, and making a knot.

"Untie them when you put them on Vadinho's grave. It's to propitiate his patron saint," and he added in Yoruba, lowering his voice: "*Aku abó!*"

This Negro was the *babalão* Didi, caretaker of the shrine of Ossain, a sorcerer of Ifá; and it was only much later that Dona Flor learned his name and his powers, his reputation as a fortuneteller, his post of *Korikoê Ulukótum* at the *candomblé* center in Amoreira.

Dona Flor was dressed all in black, from head to foot, deep mourning, for it was barely a month since her husband had died. But the thin veil over her hair, so black that it was almost blue, did not cover her face, and that expression of suicidal suffering no longer stamped her face. It was still sad, but not despairing nor expressionless.

Enveloped by the transparency of the air that morning, so beautiful in its light and so made to the measure of man that it was a privilege to live it, Dona Flor, raising her eyes from the ground, looked about to take in the sight of the street and the color of the day.

Among the heads with hat removed or bowing, receiving gestures and words of comfort and sympathy, amid the hubbub of the city, people passing, talking, laughing, Dona Flor walked with her bouquet of flowers chosen for the grave of Vadinho. She was going toward the cemetery, but she was taking up life again, returning, though still convalescent.

Not the same Dona Flor as before, to be sure; she had buried certain emotions and certain feelings—desire, love, matters of bed and heart, for she was a widow and a respectable one. She was alive, however, and could feel the light of the sun and the gentle breeze, could laugh and find joy, acceptance.

III

OF THE PERIOD OF HALF-MOURNING, OF THE PRIVATE LIFE OF THE WIDOW IN HER RETIREMENT

AND THE SLEEPLESSNESS OF A YOUNG AND BEREAVED WOMAN;
AND OF HOW SHE CAME, UPRIGHT AND GENTLE,
TO HER SECOND MARRIAGE WHEN THE WEIGHT OF HER
DEAD HUSBAND BOWED HER SHOULDERS DOWN

(With Dona Dinorá at her crystal ball)

COOKING SCHOOL
OF SAVOR AND ART

STEWED TURTLE
AND OTHER UNUSUAL DISHES

Someone asked a few days ago—I think it was Dona Nair Carvalho, for she likes to serve only the best—what to offer a special guest, one with a snobbish palate, highly demanding, in a word, an artist who wanted delicacies, unusual tidbits, nothing verging on the commonplace.

I would recommend to her that she serve stewed turtle, and here follows the recipe given to me by my teacher of sauces and seasoning, Dona Carmen Dias, a recipe that has been kept secret until now. You can copy it from the notebook. And, if I remember rightly, turtle is a dish served the gods at the *candomblé*, the favorite dish of Xangô, according to my *comadre* Dionísia, the votary of Oxóssi.

In addition to turtle, I would recommend game in general, and especially a fricassee of lizard, tender meat seasoned with coriander and rosemary. If possible, a whole roast peccary should be served, wrapped in aromatic leaves, one of the greatest of dishes, wild pig, meat with the taste of the forest and freedom.

But if your guest wants even finer and more unusual game, if he is looking for the *ne plus ultra*, the last word, the pleasure of the gods, then why not serve him up a young and pretty widow, cooked in her tears of suffering and loneliness, in the sauce of her modesty and mourning, in the moans of her deprivation, in the fire of her forbidden desire, which gives her the flavor of guilt and sin?

Ah, I know of such a widow, of chile and honey, cooking over a slow fire every night, just ready to be served.

TURTLE STEW
(Recipe of Dona Carmen Dias, as she passed it on to Dona Flor, who allowed her pupils to copy and taste it)

Take a turtle, killed by the (barbarous) method of sawing it across so the person handling it will not get hurt. Hang the animal by its hind legs, cut off the head, and leave it like that for an hour so the blood will run out. Afterwards turn the animal belly up and chop off the feet, taking care to save the legs, removing the thick hide that covers them. Then take out the meat, the giblets (liver and heart) and eggs (if there are any), discarding the entrails, an operation that calls for special care, doing each thing separately. Wash all, meat and insides, and put on a low fire with the following seasonings, until it takes on a golden color and a special odor: salt, lemon juice, garlic, tomato, pepper, and oil, plenty of olive oil. This dish should be served with white potatoes cooked without salt, or plain manioc mush garnished with coriander.

1

After six months of widowhood, Dona Flor went into half-mourning. Until then, whether in the street or at home, she had worn black high-necked dresses. The one nuance in her negritude was smoke-colored stockings.

For that reason, when her students (a new group, numerous and agreeable) saw her in a white blouse with dark flower print, a necklace of imitation pearls at her throat and a faint trace of lipstick, broke into applause for their "merry teacher." She still had to wait six months longer to use green or pink, blue, red, or brown, or the new and sensational colors then in fashion: royal blue, periwinkle blue, hydrangea, sea-green.

"Merry teacher," yes. As Dona Magá Paternostro, her rich pupil, had put it. Because the fact was that Dona Flor had laid aside her inner mourning, had cast off the funeral veils when, on the eve of the Mass a month after Vadinho's demise, she had buried within herself the accumulated burden of memories. She had continued to wear strict black out of respect for custom and the neighbors but, nevertheless, she had recovered her gentle smile, her warm cordiality, her interest in what was going on around her, her painstaking activities as housekeeper. Still, however, with a shade of melancholy making her pensive at times and giving her quiet beauty a new quality, a certain nostalgic charm; but in touch with life, and devoting great attention to her school, which she had neglected during that first month.

She had closed her lips over the dead man's name, seeming to have forgotten him altogether, as though after the crisis and her obsession, she had come to agree with Dona Dinorá and her fellow gossips, that the death of the rogue had been her certificate of freedom. Outwardly, at any rate, the widow and the gossips seemed to be in agreement.

On the occasion of the Mass at the end of the month, when she returned from the cemetery where she had laid the flowers and the mandate of the soothsayer, the *mokan* of Ossain, she opened the windows of the living-room, finally allowing the sun to light up the house, dispelling shadows and specters. She got the broom, the feather duster, cloths, and brushes, and went to work.

Dona Rozilda had intended to help her, but as part of this complete cleaning she, too, left, went back to Nazareth das Farinhas, just when her son and daughter were beginning to cherish the hopes of better days ahead. After all, who was more in need of the steady company, the affection, the help of a mother than Dona Flor, recently widowed and inconsolable? Dona Flor alone and defenseless, exposed to the countless dangers of her unhappy situation. It was only right that Dona Rozilda, an experienced and intrepid mother, should live with her bereaved daughter, helping her to run the house and with the solution of innumerable problems. Who knows but what a miracle might take place, and the couple and the city of Nazareth would be freed of mother and mother-in-law, more mother-in-law than mother? Celeste, the daughter-in-law and slave, had made a vow of great promise to Our Lady of the Sorrows.

But her prayers were not heard; Dona Flor's patron saint was more powerful, without her even knowing it, in the temples and gathering places of the *candomblés*, thanks to the king of Ketu, Oxóssi, deity of her *comadre* Dionísia. Thus it happened that it was the widow who was freed from Dona Rozilda who, moreover, had not left sooner because of sheer ill-breeding, cantankerousness, spite toward the neighbors. She longed for them to tyrannize over her, lay down terms for coexistence.

There in the capital she lived uncomfortably. The house was small, she had no room to herself, and slept on a cot in the living-room where Dona Flor gave her lessons in the theory of cooking, without a closet of her own for her belongings, whereas her son's house was large, with abundant space. But, above all, in Nazareth she, Dona Rozilda, was somebody. Her standing did not depend merely on her being the mother of Hector, an outstanding official of the railroad, the vice-secretary of the Social Club of Farinha, one of the best players of backgammon and checkers in the city (Mr. Gil's frustrated vocation having come to flower in him), a wonder at drawing: he did the likeness of any living being and reproduced in crayon pictures from the almanac. She was an ornament in her own right to the best society of Nazareth, where she boasted of her connections in the capital, the family of Marinho Falcão, Dr. Zitelmann Oliva, and Dona Lígia, the journalist Nacife, Dona Magá, the industrialist Nilson Costa with his country place in Matatu, and especially her *compadre* Dr. Luís Henrique, that "exceptional mind," the pride of his country.

In the capital, not even in that lower-middle-class world, circumscribed to a few streets between Largo Dois de Julho and Santa Tereza, not even there did they pay her attention or recognize her importance; on the contrary, they had taken an antipathy to her. The closest friends of her daughter, Dona Norma, Dona Gisa, Dona Êmina, Dona Amélia Ruas, and Dona Jacy, had no compunction about blaming her for the disconsolate frame of mind of the widow, laying it to her bad humor, her recriminations, her insults, her insatiable ill-will toward the dead man. Either she took a different attitude, stopping all that gibble-gabble and cursing of the memory of the dead, or she should leave. An ultimatum.

For that very reason, as a reaction to that unspeakable malevolence, Dona Rozilda prolonged her visit, in spite of the discomfort of the house and the censures of the neighbors. (Dona Jacy had even arranged for a maid for Dona Flor, a dark-skinned Sofia, a goddaughter of hers.) Nevertheless, she speeded up her trip, after the Mass, upon hearing from her *compadre* that she had been chosen by Father Walfrido Moraes for the distinguished post of treasurer of the Campaign for Improvements for the Cathedral of Nazareth, on whose executive committee gleamed the name of the wife of the District Judge (president), that of the Prefect (first vice-president), of the Congressman (second vice-president), and other social eminences of the area. For a long time Dona Rozilda had coveted a place on the governing body, even as the lowest member of the board; and then suddenly to be made treasurer! The Holy Ghost must have descended on Father Walfrido, hitherto so picky and choosy about his committee.

The priest had had his doubts and hesitations about this transaction, but the influential friend to whom he had resorted to obtain substantial funds had made one of the conditions of his help the investiture of Dona Rozilda in this desirable position among the church ladies. It was downright blackmail, thought the priest, but he had to accept it, for he needed the money, and without Dr. Luís Henrique's help, how could he speed up the bureaucratic machinery?

In the days preceding the event, Dona Gisela, with whom the doctor at times discussed the state of the world and the limitations of mankind, had told him: "If Dona Rozilda does not leave, poor Flor won't even have the peace of mind to forget. And she needs to forget, she has developed a complex, it's a curious case of a morbid fixation, my dear doctor, which only psychoanalysis can fathom. Moreover, Freud cites an example . . ."

Dona Norma, who had come with her, interrupted opportunely: "It's an act of charity on your part, doctor, getting rid of that pest, sending her to Nazareth, for nobody can stand her any longer . . ."

"Poor Hector, poor Celeste, poor children," the doctor and godfather lamented. But as between Dona Flor, widowed and Freudian, and the young couple who had been under Dona Rozilda's yoke for years, he did not hesitate; he sacrificed his godson and his nice wife, at whose house he ate, and always well, on his frequent trips to the Recôncavo.

Everyone has his cross to bear, he decided; Dona Flor had borne hers for seven years without letup. That husband had been a heavy load. It was not fair now, at the start of her widowhood, to dump Dona Rozilda on her, make her Calvary complete, cross, crown of thorns, gall, and wormwood.

Without Dona Rozilda, the gossips of the neighborhood would only bring up the rogue's name on rare occasions, out of respect for the demands of Dona Norma and Dona Gisa, and also because

Dona Flor had resumed the normal course of her life after crossing the limitless desert of separation. Not life as before, but a calm existence, without the presence of her husband, without his entanglements, the frights, the quarrels, the financial worries, the despair. Now all that was over, and Dona Flor had grown accustomed to sleeping from the time she went to bed till morning. She went to bed relatively early, after the usual chat with Dona Norma and the group of friends, their chairs on the sidewalk, commenting on happenings, radio programs, and films. She went to the movies with Dona Norma and Mr. Sampaio, with Dona Amélia and Mr. Ruas, with Dona Êmina and Dr. Ives, who was a fan of Westerns. Sundays she had lunch at Rio Vermelho at her aunt and uncle's house. Uncle Pôrto's enthusiasm for painting was unabated; Aunt Lita was beginning to show her age, though she kept her garden and her cats in splendid shape.

Dona Flor had not wanted to become one of the enthusiastic group of players of canasta and *tres-setes* at Dona Amélia's house; even Dona Ênaide came from Xame-Xame on the afternoon they played. The canasta fans, the enthusiasts of *tres-setes* did everything they could to win her over, but in vain, as though her late husband had consumed the entire quota of gambling in the family, leaving her nothing. The only one who disapproved more than she of gambling was Mr. Bernabó, of the ceramics factory, from Buenos Aires; Dona Nancy was crazy for a game of canasta, but her husband was a despot who would not give in; at most, and as a special favor, solitaire, and no more.

So Dona Flor's life moved calmly between her cooking school —two ever more numerous classes—and the discreet social activities that befitted her state. They were not trifling engagements, as might seem at first glance; they filled up her time completely, with no idle moments for sad thoughts. Not to mention the commissions she could not refuse for some special lunch, dinner, banquet or reception; from daybreak she was at work in the kitchen. Since she was highly self-exacting where her culinary art was involved, she was not only wearied but also worried.

A girl came in to help her, the sixteen-year-old daughter of another widow, Dona Maria do Carmo, heiress to a backwood cacao plantation, who had been living in Areal de Cima ever since the carnival and who had become one of Dona Norma's circle. The girl, Marilda, gave great promise in the field of sauces and seasoning, and she had taken a liking to Dona Flor and did not let her out of her sight, learning dishes and cakes in her leisure moments. Dona Flor smiled to see her moving about the house humming, her hair tousled, her face of a tropical adolescent, all up in the clouds or down in the dumps, so pretty; if Vadinho had been alive, no precautions would have been enough; he had had no bias about age.

As is apparent and leaps to the eye, there was no lack of things with which to occupy her widowhood; there was often not time enough. So many obligations, a world of things, the day completely filled up; at night there were times when she felt really exhausted as she undressed and got into bed. She fell asleep at once, as soon as she had put her head on the pillow.

Then if her life was so full, how explain that continual feeling of emptiness, as if all that activity which possessed and set her in motion was meaningless and empty? Given her modest way of life and her frugality, she had plenty to live decorously and even to hide away—the result of an old habit—some savings. If her life was peaceful, and even happy, why then was it meaningless and empty?

2

In the neighboring streets there was a superabundance of busybodies, old and young, for there is no age limit to that calling. Dona Dinorá was outstanding among these talebearers; she had achieved such success in her activities that there were those who believed she had second sight.

We have already seen her in action in this story, with her

complaints, accusations, and meddling, but without having really studied her in detail, leaving her practically anonymous, as though she were just a common gossip of the group. Possibly it had been the unaccustomed presense of Dona Rozilda, finally and happily banished to the Recôncavo, that had distracted the attention of the crowd. But there is always time to correct a mistake, to make amends for an injustice.

There were many who looked upon Dona Dinorá as the widow of Pedro Ortega, a rich Spanish businessman who had departed this life some ten years before. The truth of the matter is that she had never been married, and had been a virgin only briefly; when barely a teen-ager she had left her home to begin a lively and, after a fashion, brilliant existence, a spicy tale. However, there was nobody more high-minded or a greater defender of morality than Dona Dinorá from the time—God be praised—she met up with the Spaniard when she was already past forty-five, and the future looked grim to her, with her panic fear of poverty after having grown accustomed to comfort.

Without ever having been really pretty, she had a kind of obscene charm, which had been responsible for her success with men, but was growing diluted with age and wrinkles. She had had the thousand-in-one luck with the Spaniard, had hit the jackpot, as Dona Dinorá confided to her friends at the time. The Spaniard offered her respectability and security, not to mention the little house in the neighborhood of Largo Dois de Julho where he set her up.

Who knows but that because of the fear of finding herself old and poor, threatened by the lowest form of prostitution, Dona Dinorá, under the protection of the merchant changed quickly into the opposite of what she had been: became a respectable matron, a custodian of morality. A tendency that grew steadily after the death of Pedro Ortega. When he concluded his days on earth, amid speeches and funeral wreaths, the former demi-rep was over fifty—fifty-three to be exact—and during the eight years of concubinage she had taken a liking to virtue and family life.

The outstanding bastion of the conservative classes, grateful to his paramour for her fidelity and for the revelation of a world of pleasures he had ignored (What a fool he was! He had lost the best years of his life at the counter of a bakery and on the insipid and ignorant body of his devout and sour spouse.), left her in his will, in addition to a house of her own (the nest of their sinful love) stocks and government bonds, an income modest but enough to guarantee her a comfortable old age completely devoted to slander and intrigue.

There you have Dona Dinorá having rounded out her sixty years, with strident voice, ennervating guffaws, in a state of continual flurry. Outwardly the most sympathetic and understanding old lady; in reality, "a bottle of poison, a rattlesnake decked out with feathers," in the semipoetic words of Mirandão, the invariable target of this class of gossips. A phrase confided to the journalist Giovanni Guimarães, when he saw the crone go by, very much the widow and the upholder of morality on the occasion of the luncheon in Dona Flor's house in connection with Sílvio Caldas's visit. He had added, the philosopher and moralist: "The worse they are when they are young, the more sanctimonious they become when they get old. She has turned into a combination of a whore and a virgin . . ."

"That hag? Who is she?"

"She's not of our time, but she once had a name and fame. The one who talks a lot about her is Anacreon: he used to drink out of that jug. You've surely heard her mentioned. She was known as Dinorá of the Golden Ass."

Almost speechless, Giovanni managed to say in shock and amazement: "That piece of garbage? The Golden Ass who was so famous! My God!"

Proof of the vanity of the things of this world, the two observed, struck by the assumed air of virtue and the deplorable physical appearance of the talemonger: squat, thick-set, short-legged, flabby, big-headed, practically bald. She wore mourning like an authentic widow, with a locket containing a picture of the Spaniard, of whom she spoke as though she had really been his wife and he the only man in her chaste life. Creatures like Anacreon, a disgrace to the human race, did not exist as far as she was concerned.

Two-faced, she never came straight out with things, never a frontal attack; on the contrary, she bedeviled her adversaries gently, feigning to understand and excuse everything, praising this one, condoning that one. Whence her reputation as kindly and good-hearted, the flowers strewn along her gossip-littered path: "What a good soul she is . . ." When by accident she was caught in the act, she passed herself off as the victim; she had wanted to do a favor and in payment had received black ingratitude.

When Mr. Zé Sampaio, a peaceable soul, who retired early with his imaginary ailments, the daily paper, and old magazines (he adored reading old magazines and almanacs) heard the piercing voice of Dona Dinorá, he put his hands over his ears, seized by panic, saying to Dona Norma, in a tone of defeat, but unresigned, as of one who could stand no more: "That woman is a whore, the biggest whore in the whole neighborhood . . ."

"Now that is going too far. She is really kindhearted."

Proof of how astute Dona Dinorá was; she had managed to surmount that story about Dionísia's son, when her prestige had reached an all-time low, and had wormed herself back into Dona Norma's good graces. But not Mr. Sampaio's.

"A strumpet of the first order. Please see to it that she does not come poking her nose in here, in this room. Say I am sleeping, resting. Say I have died . . ."

But who was Dona Norma to stop Dona Dinorá from poking her nose in wherever she wished? She made her way, one of the household, into all the homes of people of distinction and money —toward the poor she was kindly, too, but aloof and distant, protecting those in need of favor, but keeping them in their proper place (inferior, naturally) without letting them get ideas. She came down the hall toward the room: "May I, Mr. Sampaio?" How Mr. Sampaio hated that big bleached head—"an elephant's head, the biggest in Bahia," the horse's teeth, the voice, and the pretended concern. "Always ailing, Mr. Sampaio? I tell everyone: 'Mr. Sampaio, who looks so strong, has very delicate health. The least thing and he is shivering in bed, with a table full of medicines alongside.' I say and I repeat: 'If Mr. Sampaio doesn't take care of himself, one of these days he'll kick the bucket.'"

Such talk affected Mr. Sampaio deeply, and he would have liked to order her out of the room.

"I'm as healthy as a horse, Dona Dinorá . . ."

"Then why are you always in bed, Mr. Sampaio, why don't you come and give us the pleasure of your company? Such a well-educated man, everybody says that you didn't graduate only because . . . Well, you know how people talk. If one were to listen to them . . . I pay no attention. What they say goes in one ear and out of the other . . ."

Mr. Sampaio knew what she was driving at: his disreputable years as a spoiled son who had done as he pleased. His father finally cut off his allowance, took him out of the university, and gave him a job as clerk in the store.

"Let people talk, Dona Dinorá. What difference does it make?"

"So you, too, agree that one should pay no attention to people's chit-chat? One really shouldn't." And she opened her big eyes, like those of an ox, fixing them on Mr. Sampaio, all attention, as though he were an oracle of our day.

"I, at any rate . . ." And, swelling out his chest: "You want to know something, Dona Dinorá? What I am looking for is peace and quiet. And to enjoy a little peace, I spend my time agreeing with those I know are wrong. And not even that way do I manage. They come pestering me here in my own house. If you will excuse me . . ."

And picking up his paper or magazine, he turned his back on the visitor. "Zé Sampaio has no more manners than a horse," Dona Norma said apologetically, "and with Dona Dinorá, who is so kind."

A harshness that was wasted, for Dona Dinorá did not consider herself ousted, and went on slyly: "Did you hear what happened to Mr. Vivaldo?"

What a diabolic being she was! Didn't she manage to arouse his interest? Mr. Sampaio put down the paper, beaten: "To Vivaldo? No I hadn't heard anything. What happened?"

"Well, I'll tell you. Mr. Vivaldo, an upright man, good-looking, too. Like a gringo, fair and light."

Always the same; after the praise, came the backbiting, the slander, the accusation of the extra drink, the roving eye, the name of a woman, nearly always a tramp.

Mr. Vivaldo of the funeral parlor, according to her, with complete disrespect for tombstones and coffins, gathered a group on Saturday afternoons, behind the red curtains trimmed with silver, for a poker game with high stakes and a tremendous consumption of cognac and gin.

"Doesn't that seem to you a lack of respect? They could find some other place for their immorality." A brief pause: "Don't you think, Mr. Sampaio, that gambling is the worst of all vices?"

Mr. Sampaio did not think nor did he want to think; all he wanted was a little peace, but Dona Dinorá really had a wagging tongue: Mr. Vivaldo, beyond doubt an honest taxpayer, an excellent husband, an admirable father, risked all this, for a gambler sooner or later loses control and bets even his wife and children. And when he doesn't bet them, he leaves them any old way, deserted, forsaken. What better example could there be than Dona Flor? While that wretch of her husband was alive, enslaved by his gambling, she had suffered the pangs of hell; mistreated, no thought taken of her, undergoing horrors. And now, see the difference. Free, at last, she could enjoy life without frights, without anguish.

And speaking of Dona Flor, what do you think, Mr. Sampaio, and you, Norminha, my dear, about her future? So young and pretty, wasn't it unfair for her to go on being a widow, and of such a good-for-nothing husband? For that was what he had been. Why didn't Norminha, such a good friend of hers, give her advice? In the meantime she, Dona Dinorá, would study the case in conjunction with the planets, the crystal ball, and her fortune-telling cards.

Not that she ever charged for this service, for she read the future out of friendship and a sense of camaraderie; but there were few professionals who could vie with her. Certainly to uncover indecencies of any sort she had a kind of intuition, a sixth sense, radar. A fortune-telling gift that verged on the prophetic. Wasn't it she who, a year before it happened, predicted that terrible scandal in the Leite family, with all their money and pride, locked behind the walls of their imposing mansion on the sea, near Ladeira da Preguiça? Had she read the greasy cards, looked into the false crystal ball, or had her sadistic instinct given her the clue?

No sooner had the angelic Astrud, with her unsullied air of a student of the Sacred Heart, arrived from Rio to live with her sister than Dona Dinorá, with no apparent basis for this judgment, foresaw the drama: "This is going to wind up badly."

These had been her words when she saw the girl in the automobile with her brother-in-law, Dr. Francolino Leite, the "satyr Franco," as he was known to his friends—the lawyer of top-rank national and foreign firms, a connoisseur of whiskey, a rancher in the backlands, and a member of the board of directors of prosperous concerns, a gentleman of standing and pride. At the wheel of his big American sports car, with a long cigarette holder and a gay neck scarf, the lawyer did not even notice the simple people of Sodré, Areal, Rua da Fôrca, Cabeça, Largo Dois de Julho. But Dona Dinorá noticed him, the attorney, she did not lose sight of him; she knew even the slightest details of the life that went on in that seigniorial mansion, close friend that she was of the cooks, the waitresses, the nurses, the gardener, and the chauffeur, her premonitory eyes discovering the thin edge of the wedge between brother-in-law and sister-in-law.

"This is going to wind up badly, you just wait and see. You don't put gunpowder near fire."

Nor was she in the least impressed by the innocent attitude of the Sacred Heart student: "A girl who doesn't raise her eyes is just a slut waiting for the right moment."

So unfair and absurd did what she was saying seem that a young neighbor, Carlos Bastos, not at all given to gossip and perhaps a little swept off his feet by the sweet Astrud, answered her with sharp vindictive words: "Don't sully the girl's purity with the slobber of slander."

When the scandal came to a head almost two years later—Astrud with her ingenuous air and some five months in the family way being ordered out of the house by her enraged sister, and the satyr Franco glutted with the succulent dish that the whole city had tasted—Dona Dinorá avenged herself on the romantic Carlos Bastos (perhaps still in love): "You see, you nincompoop? Nobody can fool me. It's not the slobber of slander that makes a baby; it's something very different . . ."

She had eyes that could see and foresee, a pointer that never missed its quarry, nothing escaped her alert senses. Moreover, the neighbors themselves came to tell her their problems, to ask her advice with the cards, the crystal ball from which nothing was hidden. For her past, present, and future were open books, easy to read.

Whether she possessed real supernatural powers, whether she was a fake who had no knowledge of astrology or of the occult science of the Orient, the truth of the matter is that she was the first to announce the coming second marriage of Dona Flor when the widow had barely put on half-mourning and was resuming her normal life, without surprises or problems, a circumspect existence, removed from all thought or idea of marriage.

She foretold the marriage, and discerned the face of the fiancé long before there was any talk of courtship, well before there was any indication of feeling or interest. And if there existed a remote inclination toward Dona Flor on the part of the suitor in question, nobody ever knew it, perhaps he did not even admit it to himself. Nevertheless, believe it or not, Dona Dinorá described him in detail: a dark-complexioned gentleman, tall, robust, distinguished, in his late forties, of serious and pleasant manners, carrying in his right hand, stem up, a wine-red rosebud. That was the way she saw him in the crystal ball. The queens and kings, the jacks, the aces of spades, clubs, and hearts all bore out his physiognomical traits and his upright intentions, the ace of diamonds underscoring his worldly possessions, economic stability, and university degree.

3

Now, in spite of his dark complexion, the Prince was anything but strong, tall, and in his mid-forties. In a way he was a distinguished and good-looking young fellow, but after his own wanton fashion. With the best will in the world, it was difficult to fit him into the frame of the fiancé envisaged by Dona Dinorá in the crystal ball and revealed by her to the inhabitants of Largo Dois de Julho, carrying the aggressive syndicate of gossips to the brink of excitement, almost subversion.

Delicate, pale, with that pallor of romantic poets and gigolos, black hair slicked down with brilliantine and lots of perfume, a smile that was a combination of melancholy and allure, evoking a world of dreams, elegant in bearing and attire, with large, pleading eyes, the Prince would have to be described by very high-flown words: "marmoreal," "wan," "meditative," "pulchritudinous," "brow of alabaster and eyes of onyx." Though over thirty, he looked barely twenty, and the sadness that shadowed his face was part of his instrument kit, as were the right word and the surreptitious glance. He was a highly competent and successful professional at his strange and special calling. It should be stated without further delay that he specialized in widows, having taken a complete course in the subject, theoretical and practical.

Generally known as the Prince in the circles of the underworld and the police (and where are the boundaries, if boundaries there be, between these two worlds so apparently dissimilar and in reality identical?), he deserved this name thanks to his good manners, his affability, his family pride. In the genial intimacy of the cribs, in the restricted circles of floozies, however, he was known by the mystical nickname of Our Lord of Calvary, a reference to his pallor and his gauntness. His name was really Eduardo, and he was one of the most gifted and agreeable rogues in the city, a real gyp artist. As for his last name, it is not given here because it has no bearing, one way or the other, on the tale of Dona Flor and her two husbands.

The Prince concealed it behind this alias; the police did not divulge it when they had dealings with this gallant youth, and the newspapers, when they mentioned him in their columns, alluding to his detention (generally of short duration) in jail, never referred to him by his last name, substituting it with a vague "So-and-so": "The disreputable Eduardo So-and-So, known in criminal circles as the Prince, was arrested yesterday in Sé Square charged with having deceived the widow Julieta Fillol, residing in Barbalho, promising to marry her, and thus being given the freedom of her house and making off with the jewels and two contos de reis belonging to the woman who had put her trust and love in him."

They all behaved in this fashion out of consideration for the family of the scoundrel, people of standing who were highly respected in Feira de Sant'Ana. If the authorities, the press, the grapevine, took this attitude, why should we make a sensational exception in this discreet account, bringing to public shame and the vilification of gossip and scandal the honor and name of the distinguished clan that merits so much respect from others? Imagine the horror if Dona Dinorá and her troop of gossips learned who the widow-swindler's family was; not even the grandchildren would manage to restore the name of their forebears, enveloped in shame even to the third generation, as Professor Epaminondas Souza Pinto would emphatically put it. Fascinated, the whole pious gaggle of them, notwithstanding, by the manners of the Prince and his languishing airs. Hadn't Dona Dinorá herself on one occasion attempted to modify the terms of her prophecy in order to make them coincide with the physical traits of the cheat? The rest were unanimously plunged into sadness when Mirandão, who had come to pay a visit to Dona Flor with his wife and two or three of his children, gave a complete rundown on him: "The only thing human about him is that he walks on two feet."

That whole story of the Prince making the rounds of the neighborhood, with his elegant rascality, was confused and mixed up from start to finish. Moreover, this was his habitual climate, his favorite atmosphere, in which he moved and had his being.

Friends and busybodies were all atwitter over the description of the future fiancé Dona Dinorá had seen in her crystal ball, and the information had been instantly transmitted from mouth to mouth when the Prince appeared, with the gait and sighs of a lover.

Dona Norma, Dona Gisa, Dona Amélia Ruas, and Dona Êmina turned it into a source of merriment; the old gossips made hay of it, untiringly trying to identify the gallant in question. Moreover, in honor of the truth we must admit that it was not only the gossips who engaged in this fruitless search. Dona Gisa herself cast her psychological eye over the masculine members of the neighborhood, looking for that fine figure of a man in his late forties. As for Dona Norma, except for a good wake followed by a fine funeral, she enjoyed nothing so much as a courtship and marriage. She had lost count of the number of young men and women whose marriages she had hatched out, bringing them into the presence of the judge and the priest, overcoming difficulties, surmounting obstacles and misunderstandings, strong family opposition. Her only failure had been with Valdeloir Rego, a vacillator without equal, and an attractive neighbor, Maria, who completely lacked get up and go. But not even so did she lose hope of marrying off Maria, perhaps, who knows, to Valdeloir in person.

Gossips and friends eagerly sought the hidden suitor, having at their command a complete description of his physical and moral virtues, for Dona Dinorá was not one of those close-mouthed soothsayers. In describing the future suitor she did not withhold a single detail; gay and prolix, she outlined a vast assortment of physiognomic qualities and traits. Perhaps for this very reason, because the portrait of the gentleman was so complete and faithful, it was difficult to identify him. To whom could such an abundance of minutiae be attributed?

The gossips mentally reviewed one citizen after another, in the neighborhood and even beyond, without finding a single one who summed up all the unknown factors. Some were university graduates, and had a certain financial standing, but did not meet the age requirements. Others did, but they lacked the dark complexion or the class ring, not to mention secondary considerations. Notwithstanding, numerous candidates were put forward, each gossip promoting her own, or more than one, just to be on the safe side.

Dona Flor joked at all this nonsense, smiling gently; only Dona Dinorá, with nothing better to do to fill in her time, only she could think up that crazy business of courtship and marriage. And especially in the case of Dona Flor, if for no other reason than that not a year had gone by since the death of her husband, the minimum time limit for a widow to grieve for and honor the memory of the departed.

Moreover, if she had reached one firm conclusion, after eight months of mourning had elapsed, it was not to remarry. Why should she, when she had what she needed, earned her living—food and dress—with her cooking classes; when her friends, so many and so kind, brought her the comfort of their affection and their pleasant company; she felt no need of a man; those things were over for good. So why marry?

With her somewhat melancholy laughter and with the assurance of this irrevocable determination, she confronted the cordial incitements, the onslaughts of Dona Norma add Dona Gisa, offering her, they, too, on the salver of friendship, the heads of possible candidates.

Dona Gisa's choice had fallen on the learned professor Epaminondas Souza Pinto, a born bachelor, a teacher at boys' private schools, and a historian in his free hours. He was always in a hurry and sweaty, shabbily dressed in a white suit with vest and spats, around sixty, somewhat vague and in the clouds. Dona Flor was fond of him and esteemed him, but if she was going to renounce her firm resolve to remain a widow, it would certainly not be to give her hand to a professor, too prissy and oratorical for her simple tastes (not to mention, out of politeness and discretion, the ungainliness of the grammarian). Dona Flor laughed banteringly:

even widowed and poor as she was, she was not that hard up.

Her friends laughed; Dona Norma, unable to make up her mind among various possible candidates, knew nearly everyone there was to know; Dona Êmina, upholding the cause of Mamede, a Syrian compatriot of hers, a widower and antique dealer, who was not around very much, spending a lot of time in the interior of the state buying worm-eaten images of saints, crippled chairs, unmatched glasses, and even old chamber pots. Mamede? Uglier than hunger, even worse than Professor Eparninondas, according to Dona Flor.

Even Dona Ênaide came from Xame-Xame with a suitor: a brother-in-law, a notary living at the end of the world on the São Francisco River, dark-complexioned, around forty-five, bald and somewhat beaky, but gay and entertaining, and with some money, a good catch, Aluísio by name. The one who most resembled the vision in the crystal ball as described by Dona Dinorá, if one is to believe in Dona Ênaide's word. He practically held a university degree, for he had acted as a lawyer for certain clients before he got himself messed up in politics.

He had just one drawback: he was single from the religious standpoint, but he was civilly married. He and his wife had not got along together, and he had been separated from her for over ten years. When young, being a Mason and anticlerical, he had refused to be married in the Church; but now he was willing to accept that if the bride insisted. Why wouldn't Dona Flor be satisfied with a religious ceremony which was, moreover, in the opinion of many people, the only one that was valid and carried with it the blessing of God, whereas the civil ceremony was nothing but a contract signed before a notary, almost like a business deal? Dona Ênaide had already even written her relative a letter full of praise of the beauty and charm of Dona Flor. "I would need to have my head examined. If I don't want to get married, much less do I want to be anybody's mistress, with or without the blessing of God." And on top of everything go to live in the boondocks, on the banks of the São Francisco River where there's all that malaria. Dona Flor pretended to be outraged: Dona Ênaide, who called herself her friend, coming from Xame-Xame to propose a shameful arrangement of that sort! It was all a big joke to laugh at and nothing more.

Each candidate had certain characteristics resembling those of Dona Dinorá's model. The Prince, however, was the least likely: he had neither money nor the university degree, nor the age, vigor, or height. When he appeared in the street, strolling slyly along the sidewalk of the Argentine's house, across from the windows of the School of Savor and Art, Dona Flor attributed the poetic apparition to his infatuation with some young student or an understanding with a sluttish married woman.

It was a frequent thing for one of the girls to come with her lover, and then the languishing youth would wait on the corner until the end of the class to escort the affected creature home. Others who were married utilized the school as a cover for their shamelessness, to screw a pair of horns on the head of their husband, utilizing the convenient schedule of the class for their frolicking. They appeared at one class, cut the next one or showed up at the start, when Dona Flor was dictating and they were taking down in their notebooks the ingredients of the delicacies, giving proof at home of their diligence and interest. The fact of the matter was that they spent half an hour at the school, and an hour and a half at the whorehouse.

For this reason, seeing him leaning against the lamppost, smoking incessantly, waiting, Dona Flor thought he was the light-of-love of one of the girls, one of the youngest, undoubtedly, for he had the face of a teen-ager.

As the days went by, not having surprised him in the company of any of the students, and always seeing him there at the most varied hours, and even at night, staring at her windows, she came to the conclusion, in view of that absurd schedule, that there was no connection between the persistence of the suitor and the students of oven and stove. If his steps were not directed toward one of the students, then who was the target of his glances and sighs?

Marilda, unquestionably; there could be no other explanation for his distressed presence. As the girl spent more time in the house of the teacher than in her own, the so-and-so probably imagined her the sister or niece of Dona Flor. They both had the same delightful color of skin, like a tea rose, pale and delicate, the result of the mixture of native blood with Negro and white to bring about that perfection of miscegenation.

Did Marilda encourage the suitor or did she disdain him? She had reached the age for falling in love; in two more years she would have finished her course in normal school and would be ready for courtship and marriage. Moreover, she had realized the interest the loafer was showing, but attributing it to some other girl: the uppity Maria, the pretty daughters of Dr. Ives, or the young teacher Balbina, perhaps. But none of them lived in front of the lamppost, their windows were not visible from there, whereas those of Dona Flor's living-room were where Marilda sat listening to the radio and reading novels of the "Maidens' Collection." Therefore the vigil and melancholy posture of the nitwit must be on her account.

Through the crack of the window they peeped out at the customer: "He's good-looking." Marilda sighed, her inconstant heart already prepared to sacrifice her flirtation with Mecenas, a classmate at normal school, a young whippersnapper her own age. Dona Flor agreed: "Really a handsome chap," still very young, not more than twenty-three or twenty-four years old, just the right age for the future teacher. They would have to find out more about him, what his profession was, how much he earned, or if he had a good job in a bank or office. Maybe he was rich, and it looked as though that might be the case, for he did not seem to have any definite hours, but was there in the street most of the time, holding up the lamppost in front of Dona Flor's house.

Marilda cast her smiles upon him, but in vain. She went out toward the square or to sit dreamily on the balustrade of the patio of the Church of St. Theresa—so ideal a spot to declare one's love never existed nor will it exist, so idyllic, with the heaven so close and blue, the sea below a dark green, the century-old walls of the temple, and, in addition, with all assurance, the comprehensive blessing of Dom Clemente for any stolen kiss.

But the prince did not follow her into the hubbub of the square or to the peace and silence of the belvedere over the waters. He did not leave the lamppost. It was as though he were chained there, with his eyes glued on the blinds of the school. Therefore, if Marilda was not the object of his longings, who could it be except Dona Flor herself?

This was the conclusion arrived at by the gossips and friends, and even by Marilda, in spite of her tender years and limited experience: "I think he's got his eye on you, Flor."

"On me? You must be crazy!"

Several days later, as she was going shopping with Dona Norma in Chile Street, he followed them, taking the same street-car, smoking one cigarette after another, and smiling so wistfully and tenderly. Dona Norma almost got mad at Dona Flor, thinking she was keeping secrets from her. "That's very nice. You've got a beau, and you don't even tell me about it!

"I don't even know who he is. He has been standing across from the house for several days. I never laid eyes on him before. I thought it was someone who was after one of the students, but I saw it wasn't. Then I said to myself: 'It must be Marilda,' and so it would have seemed, but it wasn't her either. The poor thing was even hurt about it. I don't know what to make of it."

Nearly beside herself with excitement, Dona Norma looked the fop over, studying him from head to foot in what she thought were mere glances. "Very good-looking. Only a little too young . . ." And then, after further study, adding: "He's not as young as he looks, and to be frank with you, he is too good-looking for my taste."

"Good-looking or homely, it's all the same to me."

They got off the street-car, and the character followed them. In the twinkling of an eye, Dona Norma had worked out a complicated itinerary which would settle the matter of whether the sap was really following them or not. It became clear at once that he was. Without attempting to approach them or say a word, maintaining a prudent distance with his coquettish smile and pleading glance, he did not lose sight of them for one minute. If they went into a store, he waited for them at the door; if they turned a corner, he followed them; if they stopped in front of a window, he watched them from the one beside it. How was it possible to doubt any longer?

The friends came by singly or in a group to observe him beside the lamppost. As he was attractive, and seemed unhappy, imploring tenderness, a glance, a smile, a hope, they all took his part, even fitting him in with the vision of the suitor the crystal ball had revealed. Was he not dark-complexioned and distinguished-looking, a doctor, perhaps, and well-off? As for the discrepancy in his age and other physical attributes, this may have been owing to Dona Dinorá's nearsightedness, seeing maturity where she should have seen youth, a strong torso where there was a frail chest, the picture of health instead of pallid languor. The best thing, in the opinion of the gossips, was for the soothsayer to consult the ball and the cards again, putting an end to those troublesome contradictions.

And so Dona Dinorá did, with the whole neighborhood in a state of commotion, with a growing wave of sympathy and solidarity surrounding Eduardo, the Prince of the Widows, anchored to the lamppost, eying Dona Flor's home, his next port of call for refueling and taking on supplies.

It so happened, however, that in the crystal ball and the deck of cards the same energetic profile of the important-looking man in his forties with his class ring and the rose the color of wine reappeared. Because the vision was hazy, as is always the case in the mystery of such revelations, Dona Dinorá could not tell exactly what the stone in the ring was, which would have thrown light on his profession. But she could, with absolute certainty, and a touch of sorrow for the pale youth pining on the corner, guarantee that there was nothing in common between him and the true suitor, the future fiancé, who had yet to appear.

Try as she would, bent over the transparent crystal or the colorful cards, concentrating on the Hindu effluvia of the Ganges, the secret legends of the temples of Tibet, she got nowhere: the hidden powers of Oriental magic were relentless in their decision to deny passage to Prince Eduardo (So-and-so). At the *candomblé* rites, in sacrifices of guinea hens and doves, cocks and a black goat, sacrifices recommended by Dionísia de Oxóssi to defend her *comadre* Dona Flor from evil spells and evil workers, Exu closed his

pathways, barred his crossroads to the gallant seducer, the unri-
valed specialist at consoling widows, stealing away their lonely
hearts, and, *en passant*, such savings as they might have accumulated, as well as rings and jewelry.

4

Dona Flor spent in a whirlwind of activities and innocent diver-
sions those eight months of widowhood following the first which
was so lacerating. Until she changed to half-mourning, she went
out only rarely—visits to her aunt and uncle in Rio Vermelho and
certain very close friends—spending her time in the house with her
school, special orders, the neighbors. In June, she cooked her pots
of corn pudding, her trays of corn fritters roasted in the husk,
filtered her liqueurs of fruit, her famous genipap cordial. The first
three months she did not open her house, not even on the eve of St.
Anthony and St. John or of St. Peter, the patron saint of widows.
The children of the neighborhood lighted a great bonfire at her
door, and came to eat corn pudding; with them, Dona Norma,
Dona Gisa, three or four friends, but quietly, without making a
party of it. All those dishes of corn pudding, the trays of fritters,
the bottles of liqueur were gifts for Aunt Lita, Uncle Pòrto,
friends, students, to mark the rites of June, the month of the feasts
of corn.

After the sixth month, until the appearance of the Prince in
December, her social activities increased greatly. She put on half-
mourning in September, on the eve of the first Sunday, a date
sacred to Sts. Cosme and Damian, to whom the deceased was
greatly devoted. When he was alive, the celebration began early in

the morning, with a reveillé of fireworks, ending late at night, with a real shindig, the house open to friends and strangers alike. In keeping with the precepts of the deities, Dona Flor cooked the *caruru* and served it quietly to certain neighbors and friends, thus honoring the obligations of the deceased. Mirandão came with his wife and children; Dionísia de Oxóssi with her baby, for Vadinho's namesake was eating the dust of the highways, driving trucks to Aracaju, Penedo, and Maceió.

Her friends took her shopping and for walks, visits to the movies, calls; she had gone to two shows in which Procópio acted when his company was at the Guarany Theater. To the first with Dona Norma and Mr. Sampaio, to the second with Dr. Ives and Dona Êmina, laughing both times till the tears came to her eyes.

At times she preferred to stay at home, refusing urgent invitations, for so many demands wearied her; and this weariness was responsible, in her opinion, for a certain disagreeable sensation that was hard to define; as though movement, work, and laughter were not enough to fill her life, bringing her a sudden lowness of heart; as though all that were more fatigue than she could bear. Not physical fatigue, which was always useful and beneficial, for it helped her to sleep at night, a sound sleep, free from dreams. It was an inner exhaustion, a dissatisfaction.

Not bitterness, however, or even a permanent state of melancholy; her life was gayer and pleasanter than it had ever been. She went out visiting, doing a hundred and one things, without neglecting the school, an entertaining responsibility. The dejection that came over her from time to time was like a passing cloud on a sunny day. She had her friends, her aunt and uncle of whom she was so fond, the constant company of Marilda, a kind of younger sister, almost a daughter, confiding her dreams to her, her desire to sing on the radio. She had her visits, her radio, with its music and serials, its humorous programs, the novels Marilda had given her a liking for, the chitchat of the neighbors, the forecasts of Dona Dinorá, the innumerable aspirants to her hand, according to the reports and wishes of her friends. What would the pseudo-aspirants say if they knew about that new slave market, that amusing farce, where they were offered up to Dona Flor for her to pick and choose, in a noisy exhibition and careful analysis of their virtues and defects, with comments and jokes to while away the time. Aspirants without knowing or wanting to be, and, moreover, systematically rejected.

"Mr. Raimundo de Oliveira? That assistant image-maker who works with Mr. Alfredo? Come, Jacy. He's a good man, but with that gloomy face and spending every spare minute in church. Find someone else, please!"

Neither were the others satisfactory; if they combined masculine attractiveness with the qualities a decent citizen should have, they were all married, without exception: Professor Henrique Oswald, of the School of Fine Arts, a relative of a family living in Areal; the architect Chaves, with a building under construction nearby, a real dandy; Mr. Carlitos Maia, with his not very successful tourist agency; the Spaniard Méndez; Mr. Vivaldo of the funeral parlor; and the one for whom the girls sighed in secret, for Dona Nair would have no carryings-on with her husband, not even in thought, Genaro de Carvalho, better-looking than any movie star, according to the women.

Dona Flor made such a joke of her second marriage that with time the joke was practically forgotten and the plans and candidates were discarded.

Thus her life went along, calm and at the same time full of interest until the month of December when, with the arrival of summer, the Prince, too, appeared on the scene at the foot of the lamppost as though he had sunk roots there.

Ever since that day when she had gone shopping with Dona Norma, up and down Chile Street, there had been no doubt left with regard to the muse that inspired the pale youth with sighs and languorous glances. Dona Flor felt herself burning with embarrassment, as though that interest carried with it a grave offense to her widowhood, as though she had not guarded the frontiers of the modesty and prudence expected of her. Could it be that she was such a forward widow that any impudent man felt he had the right to stroll past her door, peer into her windows? An insult and a disgrace—and what intentions lay behind it?

The worst, without doubt, groaned Dona Flor, locking doors

and windows, while Dona Norma advised her not to act too hastily. She, Dona Norma, did not like the person in question, true; there was something suspicious about that pale beauty, that choir-boy face, that foxy air. But who could say that they were not both mistaken, and that his intentions were the purest and the best, and that he was a very proper well-bred man, deserving of the esteem, and even the hand, of Dona Flor?

Deserving or not, the widow, content with her life, had no intention of marrying again. Much less did she want a suitor under her windows, courting her as though she were one of those frivolous floozies ready to bring shame to her husband's grave, taking off her mourning in a whorehouse.

Dona Norma tried to calm her. Why such a violent reaction, such rancor against the youth who, until then at least, had behaved respectfully, limiting himself to glances and keeping her company from a distance? After all, Dona Flor was no innocent young thing to imagine that she was beyond the gallantry, thoughts, designs, pure or impure, of men. She was young, pretty, alone in the world, and why shouldn't they desire her and try to obtain her favors? In a way it was a tribute to her beauty, proof of her gifts and charms. If Dona Flor was determined to remain a widow, fine; Dona Norma did not agree with such imbecility, but was not going to argue about it now. But why so harsh toward one who had approached her with respectable notions of marriage? Why not a polite refusal: "I am honored. However, I am a fool, my touch-hole is of no use for anything any more except to pass water. I don't want to hear about marriage!"

Dona Flor could not help laughing at her friend's wisecracking tongue, but when they got back from their shopping trip, with the suppliant still at their heels, she slammed the windows shut in his face. In vexation and disappointment, after a few moments of indecision, looking from one side to the other, he beat a retreat.

Through the cracks of the windows the neighbors surveyed the scene, all of them disapproving of Dona Flor's act. Even Dona Gisa, who had been a witness; Dona Gisa, so full of book learning, so ingenuous and even silly in her dealings with people. "Oh," she murmured in reprehension, as she saw Dona Flor's rude gesture, and her exclamation was balm to the soul of the offended Don Juan. "Poor lad; the victim of feudal habits, of prejudice and underdevelopment."

The poor lad wanted nothing better; right there, in the street, in a tearful and vehement unburdening of the soul, he laid before the *gringa* his upright intentions, his mad love, and his terrible suffering. He introduced himself: Otoniel Lopes, her respectful servant, a businessman of Itabuna, with a dry goods store and good credit at the banks, and starting a small cacao plantation, too. He was a bachelor but he wanted to get married; after all, he was thirty years old. He had come to the capital more on a pleasure trip than on business, and he had happened to see Dona Flor, and he no longer knew what rest and peace of spirit were; he was beside himself with love, to the point where life seemed meaningless if she did not listen to his entreaties. He knew she was a widow and an upright person; that was enough for him; nothing else mattered. If she were poor, better still; he had enough for the two of them to live comfortably.

Dona Gisa swallowed his story with delight. The Prince was sly, full of tricks; he led her on and Dona Gisa supplied him with information. Strictly speaking, Dona Flor was certainly no millionaire, but neither was she a beggar. With her school and without that husband who had squandered all she earned, she had her nest-egg, a certain amount of money which she—like so many other inexperienced people—preferred to keep in the house rather than put it to earning interest in a bank. People of backward mentality, Dona Gisa explained, unable to control her criticism of mistakes and errors. "Some day a thief will hear about the money, break in, take it, and it will serve her right."

He would have to be a real scoundrel to rob Dona Flor, answered the Prince, considering that the widow's behavior was proof of her good character, of her lack of interest in material goods, of her unworldliness. It was just such a woman that he was seeking as wife and companion, straightforward, simple. Little by little, bemused by his conversation, Dona Gisa furnished the thief with a complete inventory of Dona Flor, even her few pieces of jewelry, the necklace of European turquoises, the gold earrings with real diamonds, a family heirloom, Aunt Lita's only possession, aside from the cats, the garden, and the paintings of her husband. As she never wore them, and intended her niece to have them after she was gone, she had already given them to her. In that way Dona Flor could use them when she felt like it. She did not give them to her outright because they were the only guarantee the two old people had in case of need: a long sickness with a stay in the hospital and surgery, the house burning down, a disaster, for nobody can be sure of some unforeseen emergency.

Dona Gisa wound up as attorney and counsellor of the rogue. She would do all she could to get Dona Flor to receive and listen to the pseudo-Itabunan, even if the only result was a firm "No" to his proposals of courtship and marriage. The Prince asked merely to be received; he had complete faith in his cockiness, was experienced at flattery: blarney was his specialty. It never failed him. If he could only manage to get a hearing, the widow was in the bag, and the money was his. Not one had ever been able to resist his eloquence.

Early that evening, after the classes, Marilda lighted the lamp in the living-room of Dona Flor's house, turning on the radio and opening the window; she did not see the invariable loiterer beside the lamppost. Calling to her friend, she pointed out the vacant landscape.

Dona Flor brought her up to date, how the good-for-nothing had left after she had slammed the windows in his face. As she was telling the story, Dona Flor cast a quick glance down the street. At heart she was a little disappointed; the trifler's interest must have been very slight to grow discouraged at the first stumbling block. Dona Flor had done much worse things to Pedro Borges when she was single. The student from Pará had savored the bitterness of letters returned, gifts rejected, real insults, and he with an engagement ring in his pocket. That was a true passion, not this one which evaporated with the mere slamming of a window.

As the evening wore on, as though the matter had no importance, Dona Flor peeped out of the window three or four times to make sure of the consequences of her act; the fellow had disappeared for good.

When she got into bed, Dona Flor shrugged her shoulders in token of indifference. Better so. Since she did not want to marry again, why attach any importance to this meaningless courtship, to the volubility of the rogue? It was unbecoming to her state of widowhood.

For the first time in those long months, she did not fall immediately into a deep restorative sleep. She lay there with her eyes open, thinking. Really, was this determination of hers not to get married, to live out her life in quiet repose, without becoming involved in a new matrimonial venture as strong as she had thought? The matter had been decided, finished, and that was it. She did not even want to prolong the discussion with herself since there was no doubt nor decision to be taken. She was so prepared to carry out her resolution that she did not mind making a joke of the matter with her friends when they put forward candidates or when Dona Dinorá described her vision of the candidate for her hand. Why, then, was she losing sleep over the mere presence of a corner loafer?

Early the next day Dona Gisa came in, overflowing with news, giving full details of her conversation with the self-styled businessman of the boondocks. It had been impossible for her to come the evening before, as she would have wished; even at night she had students of English, three times a week, an intensive course, which exhausted her.

Dull from sleeping badly, with a headache, Dona Flor listened to her story. Receive him, listen to his proposal? But that made no sense at all; she was determined not to marry again, so why waste time with suitors? Dona Gisa outdid herself in arguments and appeals, finally getting her to put off a definitive "No." Out of consideration for her friend, Dona Flor promised to reflect on her answer and not send him packing rudely. As they were just about finishing up their talk, Dona Norma came in for some yeast for a cake and learned all about what had happened. A rich businessman from Itabuna? You see how mistaken a person can be. Dona Norma would not have given two cents for that sallow creature, and look how he had turned out, serious, established in business, a fine catch. But it was that shit-colored face . . .

"Excuse me, Flor, if I hurt your feelings. But honestly doesn't he look like that? The color of a baby's bowel movement . . ."

That afternoon the Prince resumed his watchpost, smiling, his eyes on the windows. Two or three times he caught a glimpse of Dona Flor with a coquettish bow in her hair, a good omen. That day the students had noticed a certain nervousness in the teacher, normally so calm and smiling. She had had a bad night, with a headache, insomnia. palpitations, the worst kind of a migraine. Dona Dagmar, pretty, excitable, big-mouthed, spoke up maliciously: "My dear, a migraine in a widow is the lack of a man at bedtime. There's a simple cure for it: marriage."

"Marriage! God deliver me!"

"That isn't really obligatory. You can take the cure without getting married; there is no lack of men, my dear," and she laughed with malicious implications.

She laughed all through the class; Dona Flor felt her face as red as the night before, like a thief taken in the act or a liar who had been unmasked. Could it be that, while thinking she was behaving like the most decent and retiring of widows, she was showing her desire for a man, her urgency for a sweetheart, longing for the street, all of a fire, offering herself? When she had been joking, laughing with the neighbors about candidates, crystal balls, they were probably thinking she was crazy to get into bed with a husband or a lover. It was a complete injustice; a more decent widow had never lived, behaving like a complete lady.

She put in a restless day, avoiding the windows where she had formerly leaned out to call to Dona Norma or Marilda, for now she knew that she was the reason for the presence there of the loafer, and also because never had she been so attracted by windows, as though the street suddenly were full of exciting goings-on. She was all mixed up.

So when Dona Amélia came to invite her to go with her and Mr. Ruas to see a very spicy and realistic French film, which for that very reason had enjoyed a controversial success, she gladly accepted, fearing another long sleepless night. She always came back from the movies dead for sleep, nodding on the street-car. The kind neighbors could not have chosen a more propitious occasion for the invitation, not to mention the film, which had been a fertile topic of comments and dispute in the newspapers and among those in the neighborhood who had seen it. Dona Êmina had loved it, Dr. Ives had detested it—out-and-out pornography! Dona Norma smacked her lips as she recalled certain passages: "There are scenes in it, honey, beside a lake, in which he strips off her dress, and plays with her breasts, and the two of them are wrapped around one another and do everything, so to speak, right before your eyes. All tangled together, she naked, with her little breasts standing up, and the young loafers in the audience—the things they say . . ." Marilda was out of her mind because the censorship (and Dona Maria do Carmo) would not let her see the film, which was forbidden to anyone under eighteen. Fascism's heavy hand against youth.

As invariably happened when they went anywhere with Mr. Ruas, they were very late; the news was on, and the theater was dark and filled to capacity. With difficulty they managed to find seats in three different rows, far apart. Dona Flor was well toward the back, in an end seat, beside a couple that was probably in love, for they were holding hands and their heads were close together. The booing of the students began as soon as the first scenes of the French film were shown, the action taking place in a Pigalle cabaret full of half-naked women. Dona Flor tried to ignore the kisses, the sighs, the rubbing against each other of the neighboring couple, and at the same time understand the complicated plot of the film.

Suddenly she felt a man's warm breath on her neck and a voice that was all delicacy murmuring gently in her ear above all that shouting, phrases that were like poetry, declarations she had not heard even when she was being courted, praise to her eyes, her hair, her beauty. She did not have to turn around to know whence came that gentle voice, those compliments. On the nape of her neck the breath of the man was like a tickle, a warm panting. In her ear the voice was praise and plea, a tender lulling.

Dona Flor moved forward in her seat, trying to put as much distance as she could between her row and that where the Prince was sitting. All she managed to do was to disturb the lovers; the scamp leaned over, keeping on with his ardent declaration. Dona Flor did not want to listen to him or watch the lascivious spectacle of the couple indifferent to the surrounding public. All she wanted was to follow the film, understand the plot, which was a difficult combination of sex and violence.

The audience kept shouting louder, for the exciting scene beside the lake had begun: the sensual star half-naked, her breasts on display, and the leading man, who had the air of a mentally retarded case, bending over her like a rutting goat, almost as shameless as the couple sitting beside Dona Flor, the like of which she had never seen.

And the voice of that clot behind her, making love to her, suggesting that they become engaged, begging for the favor of one single visit so he could give her a list of his possessions, his qualities, his intentions, laying at her tiny and adored feet the prosperous store of Itabuna and a loyal heart consumed by the flames of passion.

The warm breath of the man on her neck and the murmur of his voice, the phrases seeming verses, the caressing words . . . oh, that impossible film, with the audience bellowing, the actors behaving so indecently, as indecently as the couple sitting beside her, and that invisible disturbing presence behind her had Dona Flor encircled, stupefied, trapped. And to think that she was a decent, modest widow.

No sooner did he see her at the door, than he launched his supplicating glances at her. Her head low, Dona Flor came out with the Ruas, Dona Amélia vociferating against the film, her husband agreeing with the critics, but without real conviction, furious and not just with the carryings-on of those spoilsport students. What did Dona Flor think of it? She wished she had not come: the hoots and laughter had stupefied her, leaving her almost sick. She had hardly been able to follow the picture, and, to make matters worse, those two pigs sitting beside her—an old woman and a young scoundrel, she had seen them when the lights went up —behaving like degenerates.

Tired out by the movie and the previous night she had spent sleepless and unending, Dona Flor took a sedative to calm her nerves. But not even so did she liberate herself from that suitor, his breath, his voice, his entreaties, the problems of a man and marriage. She dreamed the whole night long. Such a crazy dream, which made no sense at all.

5

Dona Flor found herself in the center of a circle in the middle of the public square, as though she were playing a game of ring-a-round-a-rosy, but the ring was made up of the various candidates for her hand proposed by her friends and neighbors. All of them, from the perspiring and affected Professor Epaminondas Souza Pinto to the Syrian antique dealer Mamede; from the saint-maker Raimundo Oliveira to the pettifogger Aluísio, the brother-in-law of Dona Enaide, two-faced, from one point of view good-looking, from the other a clumsy backlander. In the foreground the *soi-disant* business man of Itabuna, the well-fixed Otoniel Lopes, that is to say our dear Prince So-and-So, the Widows' Lover Boy, making his way untiringly toward the lonely heart of Dona Flor and the pile of money (in his mind's eye it was always thick and covered with jewels), money she prudently preferred to keep in the house instead of risking at interest in some company or bank.

All this was taking place inside a gigantic crystal bowl; outside, displaying her false teeth and glasses, Dona Dinorá was watching the scene, directing the show. Slowly the ring turned, the candidates themselves marking its rhythm as they sang and danced around Dona Flor:

> *Ah Florzinha, ah, Florzinha,*
> *Come into the ring*
> *And you will be left alone . . .*

Setting out from the center of the circle, to examine the suitors one by one, Dona Flor replied:

> *I will not be left alone,*
> *Alone I will not remain,*
> *For I already have the professor*
> *As my partner. . . .*

With a big belly-bump she chose Professor Epaminondas Souza Pinto as her partner, and very clumsily and rearing back like a goat he came to the front, dancing with her in the middle of the ring, singing in his toneless voice:

> *I went to Tororó*
> *To drink water but found none,*
> *What I found was a pretty dark girl,*
> *Whom I left in Tororó.*

He offered her his worldly goods as a dowry: an expository grammar, a copy of *Os Lusíadas* with penciled notes, the *Second of July* and the *Battle of the Brook*. Aside from these, he still had a few days' salary due him, a bugle that had seen little use, and a ship inside a bottle ("We're going on a voyage in it, Dona Flor"). He tripped, however, over his own spats the color of ice, which played the devil with his dancer's elegance and his rain hat; Dona Flor was wetting herself from laughing so much at watching him try to keep his balance. He was simply too ridiculous; only the *gringa*, with no notion of the fitness of things, could have put him forward as a candidate.

As for Dona Flor, she did not seem herself; she laughed uncontrollably and without pity at the old fool stumbling about the ring, trying to steal her, her bridal veil, her orange blossoms. A beautiful brunette, lost to all decency, with another belly-bump she disabused the professor once and for all of his hopes for her pussy.

For Dona Flor had returned to her virginity, losing, however, at the same time, her modesty and circumspection. All dressed in white, lace, tulle, and taffeta, with the purity of veil and wreath, and the long full skirt of her wedding dress filling the entire circle, gathering up the candidates in her spoor of one who was offering herself, in her scent of virginity. With haste and anxiety Dona Flor offered herself in marriage to each and every one of them, as though she were a damsel in her death throes, without any hope of marriage. She went from candidate to candidate, inviting each to dance with her in the ring-around-a-rosy, the ring that was a challenge and a defiance; which of them would be capable of ravishing her of her orange flowers and her virginity, plucking her wreath apart leaf by leaf? All with benefit of law and clergy, naturally; a virgin doesn't give up her cherry as though she attached no value to it.

She wooed them with her siren song and held them fascinated with her whorish dance, her milling haunches, her hips and bust going through the suggestive movements of a slut, attracting them all to the center of the circle with belly-bumps, as though her depravity knew no limits. Cynical, dissolute, making herself so cheap that it positively turned one's stomach.

Rubbing belly-button and bottom against Mamede's paunch, she led him as her partner and excort, and he danced waggling his hips in a way one would never have expected from such a serious person. In one of his hands he held an old candelabrum, in the other a chamber pot of Macao chinaware, with a blue English landscape and a crack that was hardly visible, practically a perfect piece, like the candelabrum, which was solid silver. He offered the two for the virginity that was on the block, asking only a little change, a few mil-reis, about four hundred and fifty. But how was he to reach the flowers with his hands so full of antiques? Dona Flor danced around him, coming in closer, rubbing his belly, shaking the dust out of him, laughing loudly and banteringly.

Mr. Raimundo de Oliveira was really agile and a good dancer. His dowry: a cortege of prophets, the Bible, old and modern saints, in addition to the sacred animals, the donkey and the fish; and, as a special bonus, the eleven thousand virgins, with only three or four missing which he had given as a present to Mr. Alfredo, his employer, the image-maker in Cabeça. For the others, all intact and perfect, Mr. Raimundo had refused very flattering offers, cash down, from Mário Cravo, the architect Lev, the engineer Adauto

Lima, all of them on the look-out for good secretaries. If Mr.
Raimundo had so many virgins, why the devil was he trying to get
hold of another? Gluttony or a veiled interest? And was his
whorehouse that big, with all the clientele? "My whorehouse is the
sky, Dona Flor, and I only want to press a kiss on your lips of
honeycomb, I am an old sinner out of the Old Testament, and I am
on my way straight to the Apocalypse." Then beat it, Dona Flor
answered him.

Mr. Aluísio came, a staid backlander, an honorable inhabitant of
the boondocks, very proper in his dance and words, a gentleman
asking for her hand with the most delicate manners, practically
holding out wreath and flowers, almost picking Dona Flor's wild
flower. But Dona Flor, who was nobody's fool—quite the contrary
—did not swallow the chitchat of the pettifogging notary, so sly
and studied.

"Let us go to the church, madame, where I have everything
prepared, the banns and the episcopal blessing, I have even made
confession and been absolved of my sins."

"Ah, sir, do not try to soft-soap me; if it's the cherry you're
after, come with judge and priest."

"Do you mean to say that the priest is not enough, the blessing
of God and of religion? What is man's law worth when we have
God's within reach?"

"Put your blessing away, sir, your priest and your confession.
Without a marriage license, you will please excuse me, but there's
no cherry, no plucking of the petals of the widow's daisy."

"My little widow, my little widow," murmured the handsome
young man who had entered the middle of the circle, pale and
slender, languid and suppliant, his warm breath enveloping her, his
love song bemusing her:

> Take out, take out your little foot,
> Put it here by mine,
> And nobody can ever say
> That you will rue it.

He danced better than any professional dancer, a well-known
dance, which was it? Enveloping Dona Flor, his seductive voice:

> *Beautiful widow, make good use,*
> *One night is nothing,*
> *If you don't sleep now*
> *You can sleep in the morning.*

In the morning, a virgin or a widow. Suddenly there was Dona Flor divested of her bride's veil, of her white vestments of a chaste damsel on the point of being married, without the virginal orange blossoms. Now she was dressed as a widow, in deep mourning, wearing stockings the color of smoke, everything else the color of sadness, a veil covering her face, a lace shawl over her head, sadness and ashes. Just one flower, a rose so red that it was almost black.

She so wanted her white dress, her bridal dress—she had not used it when she should have, she had no cherry left when she signed the marriage license, a flower stripped of its petals by the sea breeze of Itapoã.

With the candidates of her friends and neighbors, with the visions of Dona Dinorá, one could have fun and jokes, calling oneself an immaculate virgin, without the touch, the brand of a man; all that was just something to laugh over.

But not with the gallant youth of the corner, a prince, a hidalgo, seeming so young and already so rich, with so many maidens moaning and sighing for him, and he moaning and sighing for Dona Flor, a widow and poor in worldly goods. With the prosperous businessman of Itabuna, a good match for any girl, and much more for a widow, it was not possible to indulge in mockery and jokes; his burning breath penetrated her flesh, covering her indifference with warmth, melting the ice, making one live again who had been dead to such things and for good. His breath made her faded, dry desire flower anew, destroying Dona Flor's peace.

She could not laugh at him or ignore his presence; he was not a matter for persiflage like the others, an invention of her friends, a machination of the gossips, but really standing there at the foot of the lamppost, sweeping her living-room with his eyes—he had only to take one step forward, and there he would be installed in the house of the widow and in her arms. Behind her when she went into the street; burning her with his breath and his words in the movies, his determination unshakable, fanning the flames of her desire.

Dona Flor now knew why, in spite of so much bustle, work, and diversion she felt so useless and empty, downhearted. About her the aspirant was dancing: "You will sleep in the morning." A dance that was very familiar to her, a dance of music hall and cabaret, not an ingenuous ring-around-a-rosy. But, Good Heavens, what dance was this, where had Dona Flor learned it?

The music and the dance, the hour or the place did not matter; in an impulse Dona Flor snatched the veil from her face, held her hand out to the suitor, and broke the crystal ball: "Beautiful brunette, don't stay there alone." "Come, pale youth, let us get married at once, at once, my nobleman, my enchanted prince."

Then suddenly she remembered: that music was the waterfront tango that she had danced as a girl in the house of the Major and seven years later in the Palace Hotel, and her partner was not a pallid youth, a suppliant, a suitor. He vanished into thin air along with the crystal ball and Dona Dinorá. The one who was with her was her late husband, whose memory she was not honoring as she should. Before her stood her husband, and he raised his hand in indignation and slapped her. Dona Flor fell upon the iron bed, and he pulled off her mourning attire and plucked away wreath and bridal veil. He wanted her naked, without a stitch on. Who ever heard of humping while dressed? Ah, what a tyrant! There was never another like him.

In desperation Dona Flor awoke, the room dark and she in a state of panic. The yowling of cats on the roofs and in the backyards, oh what a crazy dream, alas for her lost peace of soul.

6

The whole night long, thinking, thinking: weights and measures, loneliness and laughter, desire at the boiling point and a tear at daybreak. Very early in the morning, while the dawn was breaking the buttresses of doubt, Dona Flor sat down before her mirror to dress and comb her hair. She looked about for perfume, took out Aunt Lita's earrings and put them on, tried out various costumes, blouses and skirts, once again as vain as in the days on Ladeira do Alvo when she rivaled the rich in dress. So early in the morning and all decked out, the coquettish thing: more than once the pale youth had showed up before lunch. Besides, it was Sunday, and Dom Clemente was preaching the sermon.

The person who did show up before lunch and then stayed for lunch was Mirandão, one of his rare visits. He came with his wife and children, one of whom, Dona Flor's godchild, brought her plums and ambarellas, not to mention a crocheted yoke, the delicate work of his mother. But why all that, why so many presents? But, *comadre*, your wits must be wandering, don't say you don't remember that this is the nineteenth of December, your birthday? Oh, my friends, you are too kind; I had forgotten all about it, I have lost all taste for anniversaries. Mirandão's wife looked at her dubiously: "You mean to say you don't remember? Then why are you so dressed up first thing in the morning?"

Mirandão recalled with a note of sadness: "Do you remember, *comadre?* It's a year since that night in the Palace, but I will never forget that celebration."

It was a year, exactly a year. There was Dona Flor, dressed in her very best, her hair done, with a ribbon in it, diamond earrings in her ears, and exuding an exciting perfume from her breast, with-

out even being able to attribute all this to her birthday, for she had
forgotten about it. But her aunt and uncle had not forgotten, nor
Dona Norma, Dona Gisa, Dona Amélia, Dona Êmina, Dona Jacy,
Dona Maria do Carmo; they came one after the other with presents,
boxes of soap, bottles of toilet water, sandals, material for a dress.

"You look perfectly beautiful, Flor. What elegance!" Dona
Amélia remarked.

"It was last year that she was a knockout," Dona Norma said,
also recalling the visit to the Palace. "She got a present and a
half . . ."

"This year, too, she's getting a fine present . . . ," prattled
Dona Maria do Carmo's gossipy voice.

"Which present?" Mirandão's wife inquired.

Laughing, Dona Êmina and Dona Amélia whispered the secret
to her.

"You don't mean it . . ."

"A good man," Dona Gisa pontificated. "Honest, upright."

Mirandão had gone to the bar of Cabeça, where a group of rich
men from Ilhéus foregathered on Sundays to drink whiskey,
headed by the planter Moysés Alves. While her friends laughed
and gossiped in the living-room, Dona Flor in the kitchen, an apron
protecting her dress, and with the help of Marilda, was putting the
final touches to the lunch.

It was not until early in the afternoon that the Prince appeared
to harvest the fruits of the crop he had sown with a lavish hand the
evening before—Dona Gisa's intervention on his behalf, his avowal
in the movies. Resplendent of attire and pallor, never had he so
resembled Our Lord on his route to Calvary. The night before he
had said to Lu, his latest inamorata, in whose wild and amusing
company he was spending the last nickels of the preceding widow,
Dona Ambrosina Arruda, a hysterical mastodon: "Sugar, today I
storm the fortress, enter the living-room, and before you can say
scat I'll be in bed with the widow."

Lu snuggled her head against the consumptive breast of Our
Lord of Calvary: "Is she as ugly as the other? Or is she pretty?"

Jealous, without understanding the strict code, the ethics of the
Prince, she was not up to associating with a professional so compe-

tent and so devoted to his principles: "Ugly or pretty, I have already told you, you dumbbell, it's all the same to me. Can't you understand that it is a business, a financial enterprise, nothing more? I couldn't care less about the widow's tail, my little jackass, it's her money and whatever jewelry she may have."

Dona Êmina was the first to spot him. She ran to spread the news, bursting with laughter: "He's arrived."

All that noise, that excitement, that racing and chasing of the women disturbed Mirandão's happy drowse after his abundant lunch of shrimp soufflé and delicious roast chicken. When he awoke, he, too, went over to the windows, where the women were pushing one another out of the way to get a view. What he saw on the other side of the street leaning against a lamppost in front of the house of Mr. Bernabó, in a languid pose, was that scoundrel of an Eduardo So-and-So, the Prince, cleaning his fingernails with a match and smiling gallantly.

"What in the hell is Our Lord of Calvary doing over there?"

"Who is Our Lord of Calvary?" Dona Norma asked with her customary curiosity.

"I mean the Prince, that old trickster, the biggest swindler in town . . ."

He was on the point of adding: "The Widows' Lover Boy," but as he took in the dead silence of friends and acquaintances, he understood everything. As though he had noticed nothing, however, with that Bahian delicacy of his, he went on smiling: "That customer is one of the shrewdest sharpers that ever wore out shoe leather; he lives by fooling suckers with his yarns about a winning ticket, money he is collecting for a hospital, those master strokes you read about in the papers . . ."

"That guy never fooled me . . . all I needed was one look at his face," Dona Norma said.

"He must be staking out some house in the neighborhood, perhaps that of the Argentine or some other . . ."

"Without a doubt it is the Argentine's. I saw the two of them talking together . . . ," Dona Norma lied without blinking an eyelash. She was as good a Bahian as he was, with great delicacy of understanding and feeling.

Dona Flor silently left them chewing on the topic of how full life was of disappointments, shedding one tear, only one, hidden, for that humiliation and tawdry intent did not warrant any more. Mirandão, as though idly, crossed the street, heading for the sharper. Through the cracks of the windows that had been slammed shut the women saw him talking to the lowlife. Not for a minute did the Prince stop smiling, even though his explanations seemed a little confused. Mirandão made an energetic gesture pointing down the hillside. It was a quick scene from a silent movie for the women at the windows.

The Prince knew how to take defeat; only a moron would try to brazen it out and run the risk of jail or a beating. But what lousy luck to go and get involved with Mirandão's *comadre!* Thank God he was getting off with a whole skin. He was absolutely sincere in confessing his ignorance; if he had even dreamed of their relationship, he would not have set foot in the street, much less . . .

Without even raising his eyes to Dona Flor's house, he changed course, making for the open sea, rapidly descending the Ladeira da Preguiça. He had not even reached the lower part of the city when he discerned in the distance a widow, in full panoply of black and mourning veil, on her devout route to Conceição da Praia. He speeded up his pace, making for this newly discovered port, with the same languid smile, the pleading glance, Prince So-and-So, engaged anew in his arduous calling.

7

The wake of the Prince, who was never again seen in the neighborhood, was followed by comments, whispers, giggles, with claimants to reading the future, and gossips of all sorts, merriment and banter about Dona Flor's second marriage. But if before she had scoffed at all that, had made merry jest of it, now she avoided all talk on the subject, not hiding her displeasure and annoyance at the least reference to her widowhood and marriage, taking it as an insult and affront.

As though her friends and neighbors had signed a tacit agreement, for a while the topic was never mentioned, all of them in outward agreement with the widow in her firm opposition to courtship and marriage. When some old crone of a gossip felt her tongue itching to bring up the matter, the memory of the Prince at the foot of the lamppost sealed her lips; it was as though the cheat were still there making fun of the whole street. Not to mention the stern ban issued by Dona Norma, the lifelong president of the neighborhood, a government by and large liberal and democratic, but when the occasion demanded, pitilessly dictatorial.

For Dona Flor the weeks following that bizarre anniversary were perhaps the most active of her whole life; not a moment's rest did she have. One invitation on the heels of another, everybody trying to fill up her time, be kind to her. Movie after movie, countless visits, shopping with her friends. When her afternoon classes were over, she herself sought out engagements: "Norminha, honey, where are you bound for all dressed up? Why are you leaving so quietly, without saying a word?"

"An unexpected funeral, sweet. I just this minute heard about it." Lucas de Almeida, an acquaintance, a distant relative of Sampaio, cashed in his checks, died of a heart attack. Sampaio isn't going; you know what he is like; it's a shame. I didn't say anything to you because you did not know the deceased. But if you want to, come along. It's going to be a first-class funeral, really worth while."

She went with Dona Norma to wakes and funerals, to anniversary celebrations and baptisms. In sorrow as in joy her friend maintained the same efficiency and animation, insuring the success of any festival or funeral she attended. She took the helm, mapped the route, assumed charge of laughter and tears; consoling, helping, talking, eating her fill, drinking with pleasure (and prudence), almost always laughing, weeping if necessary. For gatherings of any sort, even for the deadly bore of lectures, Dona Norma had no

equal. Eclectic and willing. "She is a colossus," Dona Ênaide said of
her; "a monument" according to Mirandão, her admirer; "a saint"
in the words of Dona Amélia; "the best of friends" in the opinion
of Dona Êmina and many others.

"A hurricane," Zé Sampaio groaned, appalled at so much activity.

"You married the best woman in the world, Mr. Sampaio;
Norminha is mother to everyone in this street," Dona Flor answered.

"But I can't bear so many children, Dona Flor, and so much
annoyance." A pessimist—that is what Mr. Sampaio was.

Accompanying Dona Gisa, she visited the Presbyterian Church
in Campo Grande, the *gringa* singing hymns in English with the
same emphatic conviction with which she read Freud and Adler,
discussed socioeconomic problems and danced the samba, and was
scolded by Dom Clemente, with a friendly frown: "They tell me
you have become converted, Flor. Is that true?"

Converted? What nonsense! She had just gone with her friend
two or three times out of curiosity and to kill the time—the long
and empty time of widows, Father.

She went on an excursion trip by train with the Ruas, spending
the week end in Alagoinhas, their home town. With Dona Dagmar
she sent to a Yoga session, directed by a charming little woman, as
fragile-looking as a Dresden china shepherdess, who contorted her
body like a female acrobat at the circus. Because the schedule
conflicted with that of her school, Dona Flor, much as she would
have liked to, could not matriculate in the course and learn the
difficult exercises which, according to the beguiling booklet, maintained "the body agile and elegant and the mind clean and
healthy," providing "a perfect mental and physical equilibrium,
complete harmony between matter and spirit." Equilibrium and
harmony without which life was nothing but a "foul sump of
excrement," as the booklet stated and as Dona Flor had been
learning of late by her own experience. With matter and spirit in
conflict, life became "the Inferno of Dante."

In the company of Dona Maria do Carmo, she went with
Marilda, who had secretly inscribed herself in the "Talent Scout

Program" in which, on Sundays, for three months young men and women could try out for the title of "The Radio Company's Find" and a contract. The pretty normal-school student sang a Paraguayan air in Guarany, with deep emotion and bad pronunciation, and came out in second place, which was comforting and encouraging. She hoped to make a career for herself as a singer of folk songs, with a program of her own and her picture in the magazines. The hurdle in her path was Dona Maria do Carmo, who took a dim view of such projects, studios, and radio auditions. Only after much coaxing did she agree to that appearance, and that was because Dr. Claudio Tuiuti, a big wheel at the station, was an acquaintance of hers. It was not easy to persuade her, overcome her deep-rooted prejudices, against which Dona Gisa's logical arguments and Dona Flor's sentimental pleas were powerless. However, when she saw her daughter in front of the microphone, so attractive, her voice being carried over the air throughout the city, she burst into tears of pride and emotion. She was outraged at the decision, almost attacking bodily the master of ceremonies of the popular program, Sílvio Lamenha, or just Silvinho, for, in her opinion, Marilda deserved first place, and she did not get it because of partiality toward a certain João Gilberto, who could not carry a tune and hadn't an ounce of talent.

With her *comadre* Dionísia, she had planned to attend the festival in honor of Oxóssi at the *candomblé* of Axê Opô Afonjá, taking with her Dona Norma and the *gringa* (who was bursting with curiosity), and the only reason she did not go was because of a heavy cold and a touch of fear (a fear which turned the cold into a bad case of grippe). It is better not to get mixed up in those mysteries of *macumba* and *candomblé;* the streets are full of spells and conjures, powerful hexes, dangerous witch doctors, sorcery. Let whoever wants to believe, believe; whoever doesn't, doesn't have to. Dona Flor preferred not to investigate. Dionísia had said to her one day: "*Comadre*, your guardian angel is Oxun, I had a priestess cast the shells."

"And what is Oxun like, *comadre* Dionísia?"

"What I can tell you is that she is the goddess of the rivers; she is a woman very calm of face, and lives quietly in her house, you would think she was gentleness itself. But when you take a second look, she is over-proud, all affectation and has to be handled with velvet gloves. Outwardly, still water; inwardly, a squall. All I have to tell you, *comadre*, is that this two-timer was married to Oxóssi and to Xangô, and though the water is her element, she lives consumed by fire."

All this dashing about, all this running hither and yon, because with the departure of the Prince her peace had gone, too, her tranquility, that pleasant life, free of problems, that dreamless sleep at night, without a break, which had done her so much good.

Ever since that absurd dream of the ring-around-a-rosy, her peace had been cut short. Little by little, day after day, the restlessness of Dona Flor grew until it became a permanent distress, growing with her widowhood.

Nevermore since that night at the movies and her dream had that calm indifference returned, the complete feeling of a placid life, empty perhaps, but calm. Even though her life gave the impression of being serene and pleasant—a quiet pool—she never again had a day of complete rest; her breast was consumed by fire.

A modest widow, but forced to defend her modesty. Not against the insolence of an indecent proposal; who, knowing her, would even venture a flattering remark? As for strangers, bold street-corner loafers, these, for the most part, fell silent as they saw her pass, so proper and serious. But even if they made so bold as to let out a wisecrack, praising her figure ("What a swinging bum") or some detail of her body ("What firm little breasts") or even outrageous proposals ("Let's go make a baby, beautiful"), their words fell flat; they lost their cheek, their indecency, and their time. Dona Flor passed them by, deaf and dumb, enveloped in her modesty and her pride as a widow, forced to defend her circumspection against herself, against her errant thoughts, her unfitting dreams, against the aroused and ardent desire pricking her flesh like a goad. She had lost that "perfect equilibrium between mind and body" which was indispensable for a good life, according to the learned Yoga brochure, "the necessary balance between spirit and matter." Matter and spirit locked in a war to the death;

outwardly, an exemplary widow; inwardly, a fire that was devouring and consuming her.

Rarely at first, and only at night did dreams filled with lascivious images carry her to a world forbidden to virgins and widows, shaking her to the foundation of her being, arousing her instincts and desire. She awoke with a struggle, her hand on her breast, her mouth parched. She was afraid to go back to sleep.

During the day, busy with her classes, reading novels, listening to the radio, finding things to do, it was more or less easy to keep evil thoughts at bay, repress the throbbing in her breast. But how was she to control and restrain herself at night when her defenses were down, at the mercy of dreams she could not master?

With the passing of time, Dona Flor began to abandon herself to strange fancies even during the day, brooding and melancholy, disconsolate sighs. The danger lay in being alone. A cohort of memories invaded her; even the most lyrical and innocent led her to that bed of iron and fire, all craving and desire. And her widow's modesty?

She finally got to the point of imagining whole scenes, mixing passages from novels, items she had read in the papers, or the neighbors' gossip with the memories of her married life. The Prince's breath hot on the nape of her neck at the movies had filled her whole body with the tremor of desire; it had got into her blood and exposed her to sufferings worse than those of "Dante's Inferno" as set forth in the Yoga brochure.

There came a moment when she had to give up reading the silly novels, which were the spiritual pablum of young Marilda sighing over countesses and dukes in the tropical languor of a rocking chair. Dona Flor found the simplest pages suggestive, an overwhelming sexual drive in all that cheap sentimentalism, giving those vapid exchanges another dimension. She defiled the plot, the melodrama, and the characters, turning the virgin of the countryside into a lustful wench; the effeminate youths, almost eunuchs, into brutal stallions. The "Collection for Maidens" meant for adolescents became pornographic novels for reading in bed.

The same thing happened with the news of the city, the gossip of her friends, the pages of the newspapers. Seated in chairs on the sidewalk in the evening, the nocturnal gathering related and debated the latest crime of passion: the maid raped by her employer, she fifteen years old and one of eleven children: he fifty-three and the father of five, two sons, university graduates, and three married daughters, not to mention his wife and numerous grandchildren; the outraged father, arm in hand to avenge his honor; the three shots in the heart of the pillar of society, the upholder of civic virtue and morality, the leader of the conservatives; the mortal wound and the criminal in jail, in solitary confinement after a beating to settle his nerves; honor restored by blood, and the populace demanding justice, freedom for the avenger. Friends and fellow gossips were on the side of the father, driven out of his mind by the sight of his daughter with child, her honor swallowed down as though it were champagne. All except Dona Dinorá, who was always on the side of the rich: "Those wenches gladly go to bed with their employer to blackmail him afterwards." As for Dona Flor, all she took in was the indecent details, all that remained in her breast and her degraded thoughts was the vision of the girl in the arms of the lecher, moaning with pleasure, satisfied. All the rest, that vast panorama of horrors, was really a matter of indifference to her, in spite of the fact that she voiced her agreement with her friends' anger.

In this fashion her periods of inner peace grew briefer and briefer. However, anyone who had seen her in the classes, in front of the stove, or with her friends shopping, calling (never attending festivities inappropriate to her state of widowhood) would never have suspected the battle that was going on inside her, the mad bacchanalia of her nights, her anguish. There was nobody more respectable and upright; never did the name of a man cross her lips carrying a tone of interest: not even a passing reference to his qualities and virtues. And if earlier she had joked about presumptive candidates to her hand, going along with the neighbors' banter, now she refused even to hear their names, truly dead to any future marriage. So discreet and modest a widow had never been seen in the neighborhood, the city, or even the whole world; Dona Flor was the exemplary widow.

Outwardly, modesty personified. Calm-visaged and withdrawn, meekness itself; inwardly, a raging fire, "a roaring blaze," like Oxun, her patron deity. Ah, Dionísia, if you only knew how the fire of Oxun kindled the nights and the body of your *comadre*, her smooth belly, you would order a bath of herbs or a husband for her!

Ever more uneasy, Dona Flor spent her nights dreaming or lonely. When she managed to get a night's quiet sleep, it was a veritable benediction. As a rule, her untroubled sleep was only a brief beginning. Then the dreams began and led her to the infamy of obscentities, tossing about on the mattress, her breast aching, her womb mad. Every night her period of sleep and rest diminished, and the dreaming and desire grew. "The triumph of matter over spirit."

Shameles, wanton, what had become of her widow's modesty in dreams? She had never been like this before: even when she was married, in bed with her husband, she had never yielded easily. Every time he had had to break down the barriers of her chastity, overcome her natural modesty. But now, in dreams, she offered herself openly to this one and that one; at times, she was not even a widow, but a whore, selling her favors for money. What a shameful thing; at times she had awakened in the middle of the night and had burst into tears over the ruins of her former being, that chaste Dona Flor wrapped in her modesty and the sheet. And now enveloped in lustfulness, in the effrontery of dreams, an insatiable and cynical whore, a yowling vixen, a cat in heat, a harlot.

At times she was so worn out with the work of the day that she dozed at the movies, nodded while she was talking with her friends, dead for sleep. But she had only to put on her nightgown and stretch out in bed for all her need of sleep to disappear: sleep departed and her wandering thoughts overstepped the bounds of decency and all that made up her daily existence, the classes, shopping, a walk, the illness of a neighbor or acquaintance, Aunt Lita's asthma, which troubled her so much. That good soul spent nights without closing her eyes, threatened with asphyxiation by her heartless affliction.

Asphyxiated was Dona Flor, too, roweled by desire. She was no longer the mistress of her thoughts; she came back to Marilda's problems, her longing to sing over the radio, the insuperable obstacles—and suddenly there appeared before her the pale Prince repeating those phrases as finished as verses, words of love in the penumbra of the movies. Where were Marilda and her problems, her forbidden songs, her bird's voice?

Dona Flor had learned of the gallant's reputation in the harlot world. Dionísia, completely unaware of the ridiculous adventure, thinking her *comadre* had acquired her information about the cheat from the newspapers, entertained her with stories about the languid Lord of Calvary. When Dionísia had worked as a whore, the rogue had enjoyed high standing among the ladies of easy life. Because of his pale good looks, his romantic voice, his dreamy eyes, and his noteworthy accomplishments in bed, a real stud, one of those cut and come again, in the words of those in a position to know. He aroused wild passions, and on one occasion two sluts had set on one another, one going to the hospital with a knife wound, the other to jail charged with armed attack.

In dreams Dona Flor identified with the second, drunk and belligerent, her knife raised against Dionísia, jeering scurrilously: "Come on, if you are a woman, you filthy slut, and I'll slit your face and cunt." But Dionísia laughed shamelessly, as did all the harlots. A crazy widow. They did not tell her the handsome youth was the Widows' Lover Boy, taking from them only their money and their jewelry. Neither marriage nor fun and games in bed. Knowing this, why was Dona Flor still afire, unrestrained, shameless, offering him her naked body? What indecency, where was her widow's modesty?

She resorted to sleeping pills, guaranteed to give her a full night's rest. She consulted the druggist Dr. Teodoro Madureira, of the Scientific Pharmacy, on the corner of Cabeça. According to Dona Amélia, and this opinion was shared by all, Dr. Teodoro, though only a druggist, could give the back of his hand to many doctors; he was highly competent at his profession; nobody was better for minor ailments, a prescription he gave was unfailing, the cure guaranteed.

Insomnia, nervousness, sleeping badly? Probably nothing but

overwork, nothing serious, was the druggist's pleasant diagnosis, advising her to take certain tablets that were excellent to counter- act the effects of overwork; they relaxed the brain, steadied the nerves, inducing sleep. Dona Flor could take them without the least fear; if they did her no good, they could do her no harm, for they contained neither narcotics nor stimulants like certain new, expensive drugs in wide use. "They are extremely dangerous, madame, as much so as morphine and cocaine, if not more." The druggist was an encyclopedia, and so polite, somewhat ceremoni- ous, bowing gently as she took her leave. Above all, Dona Flor was not to forget to tell him what effects they had had.

No effects, Dr. Teodoro. She had slept all night long without waking, and then only in the morning when the maid had knocked at her door, frightened, for it was almost time for her class to begin. A long sleep, true, but the same as the others, the same obsession, the sensual delirium, the nocturnal ardor, the unending orgy; even worse than usual, for she could not interrupt it by awakening, and was crucified by it all night long, that unending dream, her womb aflame and athirst, an open wound, a running sore. In the morning Dona Flor was falling apart with fatigue. With or without tablets, sleep kindled the flames of desire in her. Obsessed, obsessed.

Obsessed, Dona Flor was in the throes of a ceaseless conflict. During the day, with her time occupied, she was blind and deaf to the appeal of sex that ran rife through the streets of Bahia; to the compliments, the inviting glances, the flattering or indecent phrases, the cupidinous male desire unclothing her and devouring her in a sigh as she crossed the street. A decent widow, an exem- plary widow in her work, when she went out, all circumspection. It was during the night that she collected from the street and the garbage the voice of men, their glance of possession, their cynical sigh, their indecent whispers, their mocking whistle, their obscene words, their invitation to share her bed. When it was not she who was doing the inviting, offering herself shamelessly to the men, wandering about the red-light district, the worst whore of the lot, the cheapest and easiest to come by. A foul pool of excrement. However, no man overtook and possessed her. When he was on the point of doing so, on the outskirts of her burning womb, Dona Flor rejected him, waking up suddenly in anguish and despair. A decent and modest widow in her night of despair and loneliness.

Nobody realized the shame and chagrin that were devouring her. Everybody thought hers a calm life, without problems, interesting, even happy. Formerly her husband had been a great source of suffering to her, a rogue, a gambler. Now she was a widow who accepted her status, satisfied with her life, completely indifferent to the thought of remarrying, with a total disdain for men. Calm to the point of arousing admiration and wonder. When she appeared in Cabeça, proud and serious, the men at the bar began talking about her: "There's a decent widow for you. Still pretty and young, she never looks at a man."

"No question about her being decent. Perhaps it's not because of her virtue . . ."

"What do you mean? Then why?"

"Maybe she's cold by nature. Cold as ice, feels no desire. There are women like that, beautiful statues, who do not know what desire is. Icebergs. There is no virtue in their chastity, nothing but frigidity. You may be sure she is one of those."

"Maybe yes, maybe no. Anyway, whether because of virtue or whatever other reason, she is the most decent widow in the city."

The other went on, skeptical and declamatory, the worst kind of subliterate: "Cold as an iceberg, you can be sure of that. Marmoreal, algid, glacial."

Dona Flor walked along circumspectly, dressed elegantly yet discreetly, with her simple, modest beauty, without looking to either side, answering the cheerful greeting of Alfredo, the image-maker, the sonorous "Good afternoon" of Méndez, the Spaniard, the respectful bow of the pharmacist, the warm laughter of Vitorina with her tray of bean fritters. It was not easy for her to put up that calm front, with her nerves twitching, the fatigue of her sleepless nights, her ignominious struggle against the fire seething within her. Outwardly, calm water; inwardly, a raging fire.

8

"There was no call for you to be so rude. Really insulting," Dona Norma said in all sincerity. "Ênaide is angry and she has a right to be."

It was a Sunday morning, sunny, indolent, after the uproarious festive celebration of Zé Sampaio's birthday the night before. Her friends surrounded Dona Flor, still exuding irritation.

"I will not put up with boldness."

"He was only joking . . . You took it the wrong way." Dona Amélia could see nothing wrong about Dr. Aluísio.

"It was a joke in bad taste."

Speaking firmly, Dona Norma reflected the thought of her friends: "Flor, excuse me for saying this, but you have become a touch-me-not. You get mad over the least trifle, your feelings are hurt . . . You never used to be like this, standoffish. I wasn't around, but even supposing he went a little too far, it was only in fun, you didn't need to get so worked up."

Dona Gisa had a complete scientific theory to explain the appearance and the approach of the notary of Pilão Arcado: "Mr. Aluísio is a typical man from the backlands, patriarchal, in the habit of treating women as though they belonged to him, a possession, an animal, a cow . . ."

"That's it exactly," Dona Flor agreed. "A cow. As far as he is concerned that is all a woman is. And he is a horse."

"Flor, you don't understand me and you don't understand Mr. Aluísio either. You have to judge him in terms of his background. A farming and cattle-raising background. He is a kind of feudal baron."

"A brazen customer is what he is . . . sly-handed. He takes yours in his and tickles it."

"Norma is right, Flor, you are a touch-me-not. All Dr. Aluísio did was to take hold of your hand," Dona Jacy added.

"To read it," Dona Maria do Carmo testified. "Why is it that every scamp uses that same trick of reading one's hand?"

"You, too, think he is a scalawag?"

"That Mr. . . . . Dr. Aluísio? Is he a doctor or isn't he?" and she added another dimension to the problem.

Mr. Aluísio or Dr. Aluísio? Dona Maria do Carmo, without meaning to, had given rise to a serious problem of address and protocol. In the region of São Francisco, from Juazeiro to Januária, from Lapa to Remanso and Sento Sé—the area where he exercised his legal functions, a self-made pettifogger, one of the most rhetorical pleaders to a jury—he was a doctor for all effects and purposes. In the capital, however, as he had never studied at the university, he was denied his assumed title. In the hope of maintaining this narration equidistant from the city and the backland, the two forms of address will be employed, thus satisfying the rigid formalists and the nonchalant liberals. As for the friends gathered in Dona Flor's living-room, the problem was of little interest to them.

"Whether he is a doctor or not, he is a charmer. He could talk a bird off a bush, foxy as they come." Dona Êmina, who up to then had said nothing, summed up the situation.

They talked over what had happened, almost a small scandal, the night of Mr. Sampaio's birthday. Since the shoestore owner took a dim view of parties and celebrations, Dona Norma, against all her inclinations, had limited the event to a dinner of numerous courses to which she had invited friends and neighbors. A glutton, though not a big spender, Mr. Sampaio had argued (as he did every year) that they should do nothing at the house, but go out to have dinner in a restaurant with their son. In that way they would eat well and without spending too much, thus also avoiding the noise and confusion. As she, too, had done each year since they were married, Dona Norma reacted in the same way to this prudent and thrifty suggestion: a buffet supper was the least they could do for their vast circle of friends.

In bed, his thumb in his mouth, Mr. Zé Sampaio marshaled his arguments in what seemed to him invincible array: "I am against the idea for numerous reasons, all of them valid."

"All right, let's hear them. But don't come to me with that old yarn about the sales of shoes falling off, for I have seen the books."

"No, I wasn't even thinking of that. If you'll just listen without interrupting. First of all, I don't like buffet dinners, with everybody having to stand up. I like to eat sitting at the table. With this American invention you have taken up now, everybody crowds around the table, and I, who as you know, am bashful, wind up getting the leftovers. When it comes my turn they have eaten up all the fritters, and all that is left is the wing of the turkey; the breast is all gone. Thirdly, it's even worse when we do it here at home. As the master of the house, I have to serve myself last, and everything is gone, I'm left empty-handed. Fourthly, this does not happen in the restaurant. One sits down, orders what one likes, and as it is a celebration, everybody can order two courses"—these two courses were his moving concession to his family and his gluttony.

It was an effort for Dona Norma to hear him out: "Zé Sampaio, do me a favor, stop talking nonsense. In the first place, there is not a birthday party of any sort we are invited to . . ."

"But I never go."

"Not often, but sometimes you do. And when you do, you eat like a harvest hand. Second, don't give me that guff about your eating little, your being bashful. At Mr. Bernabó's party, to which you went only because he is a foreigner, you served yourself nearly half the shrimp soufflé, not to mention the patties. As though you had a hole in your stomach . . ."

"Ah," sighed Mr. Sampaio, "Dona Nancy's cooking is so wonderful . . ."

"So is mine. We're even Steven. In the third place, here at home you are never the last, but the first to serve yourself. I never saw such bad manners. Imagine, the host! In the fourth place, there is never any lack of food at my parties, thank God. Fifth, restaurant food . . ."

"That's enough," the shoestore owner begged, wrapping himself completely up in the sheets. "You know I mustn't argue, I have high blood pressure."

Dinner at Dona Norma's was a banquet; if she invited twenty, she prepared food enough for fifty; no wonder all the poor in the neighborhood came to scrape the bottom of the pans, drink what was left in the decanters.

That year on the occasion of Mr. Sampaio's birthday all the neighbors were present, including the Bernabós, Dona Nancy trying to fit herself into the circle of the women, Mr. Hector talking about business and boasting of the progress of Argentina.

He was a formidable patriot, this Mr. Bernabó, always trying to draw comparisons between Argentina and Brazil and always, naturally, in his country's favor: pointing out in conversations and arguments Argentina's development, its wealth, its climate—four clearly defined seasons, not this insufferable heat the year around —the superb railroads, not this Toonerville trolley, the trains never on time, the excellent fruit of European stock, the wheat bread, all the meat one could eat, the pedigreed cattle. Dona Nancy wanted the floor to open up and swallow her when her husband took the bit between his teeth on the subject of civic pride, and emerged from her habitual silence to try to restrain him: "But, Bobo, there are good things here, too. Take the pineapples, for instance. They're just wonderful." She was crazy about pineapples and afraid of seeing her husband get into a hassle, at odds and perhaps blows with some patriotic Brazilian, one of the "don't tread on me" variety.

It had happened, moreover, and more than once. On one occasion, during one of these geoeconomic debates, Mr. Chalub of Mercado (the son of Syrians, a first-generation Brazilian, and, for that very reason, a rabid jingoist) had lost his head, comparing the ceramics factory to a brickyard, and following this remark up with the rude question: "If the industries there are so much better, if life is so pleasant, why did you come here to open your brickyard?"

The painter Carybé, too (the one who had painted the portrait of Dionísia de Oxóssi dressed as a queen, holding the *ofá* and the *erukerê*), who had gone on to discuss with the Argentine the possibility of firing certain folkloric pieces in his kiln, found himself involved in a polemic having to do with the tango and the samba, and wound up exploding: "To hell with it! A country where there are no mulattas, nothing but honkies, that's no place for anybody to live. Forget it!"

On Mr. Sampaio's birthday, however, the resolute defender of Argentina's greatness was cordiality itself. If he praised his own country, it was not to belittle Brazil's achievements. On the contrary, he lifted up his voice in a veritable hymn of praise to the people of Bahia, their temperament, their courtesy, their kindness. And so the birthday party of the shoestore owner was a social success, beclouded only by the incident (which had no repercussions outside the immediate circle of intimate friends) between Dona Flor and Mr. Aluísio.

Dona Flor had her doubts about whether she should attend celebrations of this sort. A buffet for so many guests, did it not take on the nature of a party, which was incompatible with her state of mourning? A year had not yet elapsed since the death of her husband; true, it fell short by only a few days, but a widow should abide by her principles, for the ideology of widowhood is sectarian and dogmatic. The slightest deviation can set off at one's heels the whole wolf pack of gossips, censuring and rebuffing.

Dona Norma laughed at her scruples; since when was a dinner, a simple birthday dinner forbidden a widow? It was not a dance or even a surprise party; and if Artur and his friends, fellow students, boys and girls, were to play a record and drag their feet around in a samba, that was nothing but a harmless diversion, an innocent pastime that was not going to interfere with the norms of etiquette demanded by widowhood and would not shock the dead man in his tomb.

Moreover, Dona Flor had spent practically the whole day celebrating Mr. Sampaio's birthday: in her kitchen, with Marilda's help, she had prepared the chicken and coconut milk friccassee—a huge kettle of it—and the fried fish, with its special sauce, simply

delicious, while Dona Norma had busied herself with the other
delicacies. Finally convinced, Dona Flor put in an appearance.
Would that she had not, for in this way she would have spared
herself aggravation.

When she arrived, the house was full, the tables were being
served, Dona Ênaide had come from Xame-Xame, bringing a tray
of coconut candy, a tie for Mr. Sampaio, and her husband's regrets,
for on Saturday nights he had a standing poker game which he
never missed for any other engagement. By way of compensation,
she had brought along Mr. Aluísio—Dr. Aluísio to many—the
well-known lawyer (so to speak) and notary of the banks of the
São Francisco, the half-bachelor, whom she had put forward as a
candidate for Dona Flor's hand. He was wearing a brand-new suit,
of a dark, hot material, all gussied up, his nose hooked and prominent, his bald patch gleaming, reeking of toilet water and talcum
powder, the glass of fashion. Dona Ênaide outdid herself in her
introduction of this important brother-in-law from the backlands:
"Aluísio, I want you to meet Dona Flor Guimarães, the prettiest
widow in Bahia."

"Ênaide, stop your joking."

Dr. Aluísio bent over to kiss her hand, and a wave of perfume
floated on the air, enveloping Dona Flor: "Madame, this is a
thrilling moment for me. My sister-in-law had already mentioned
you in her letters, heaping praise on you. But I can see with my
own eyes that everything she said fell short of the truth; it would
take a poet to do you justice."

Even as he said this, he stripped Dona Flor bare with a slow,
greedy glance, divesting her of dress and slip, brassière, and panties.
Never had Dona Flor felt herself so naked, with those eyes sizing
up the curve of her buttocks, the firmness of her breasts, measuring
her as with a compass. From appreciative, his glance turned to
complacent, and his pleasant social smile became a satisfied laugh.

All this, without letting go of her hand, holding it in his while
he stripped and appraised her.

Yes, because he was sizing up at one and the same time both
body and spirit, arriving at the conclusion that he had before him a
sure and easy catch. With his experience as a Don Juan of the

backlands, he classified her as a sham, and a sly one. He knew those women of meek air; nearly all of them were hypocrites, fakers; in bed they were the very devil, completely unbridled.

In the small cities of the backlands, where the woman has no rights, is a slave subservient to the will of her husband, her lord and master, and the confines of her home, Mr. Aluísio had been surprised on more than one occasion by the ardent response to his lubricous invitation concealed behind downcast eyes and feigned modesty.

Ah, how deep those still waters ran; under the outward seemliness and aloofness of mourning, what kind of inner storm would Dona Flor not be struggling against, a young, healthy woman? Dr. Aluísio had known others of equally modest appearance, in the shelter of their house, in the web of a medieval code of honor. Nevertheless, given the propitious occasion, they had got around difficulties and fears with amazing adroitness, showing their skill at planting a pair of horns on the brow of the most fearsome braggarts; at times a betrayed husband had laid down the law with bullets or dagger thrusts.

In his leisure hours—which constituted most of his day, for his notarial duties took up a small part of his time—he devoted himself to women, to their study and acquaintance (the more intimate the better), giving rise to the remark of the district judge of Pilão Arcado, Dr. Dival Pitombo, that he was "an outstanding psychologist, a shrewd judge of the feminine soul, and a learned reader of the classics." The classics boiled down to national or Portuguese translations of Greek mythology and episodes, for the most part licentious, of life during the Roman Empire. As for women, he had the expert diagnostician's eye, which brought him various adventures and widespread fame as the husbands' nightmare, the irresistible seducer. In spite of his baldness and prominent nose, there were women who were willing for his sake to run the risk of sin, the feudal code, the laws of vengeance.

Good and well; this lynx-eyed glance of the Casanova of the São Francisco River had plumbed Dona Flor's most intimate secrets, had pierced her every thought, after having divested her of her attire and adornments. Such a bold-faced gaze could have no other intention: Mr. Aluísio denuded her, body and soul, and found her to his liking, available and even easy. As far as he was concerned, Dona Flor was not the most modest, upright widow of Bahia, the one on whom the approval of the habitués of the bar of Cabeça fell, the one for whom the most malicious of all the gossips would put her hand in the fire, certain that it would come out unscathed.

And speaking of hands, the *soi-disant* lawyer held that of Dona Flor's between his lingeringly, pressing it lightly in a clasp that verged on a caress. Dona Flor took in at the same time the fact that he was laying her bare, the idea he had formed of her, and the handclasp that was in the nature of a foreclosure. What a bold hick, how conceited and self-assured! If Dona Flor did not react immediately, did not cut him short at once, he would feel free to carry his boldness to intolerable lengths. Frowning, she pulled her hand away from his. The backwoods seducer paid no attention to the rebuff.

"May I make a confession, my dear lady? Although I had a number of business matters to attend to here in the capital in connection with the government bureau I direct, and relatives to visit, my chief desire in coming to Salvador was to meet you. Ênaide, in her letters . . ."

But Dona Flor, seeing Dona Dagmar, her pupil and a friend of the Sampaios, arrive, turned her back on Mr. Aluísio: "If you will excuse me . . . I want to say hello to that friend."

Dona Dagmar, uninhibited and a blabbermouth, immediately asked: "Who is that bald parrot? A suitor?"

"Oh, for heaven's sake. That is Ênaide's brother-in-law, Dr. Aluísio, a political bigwig from I don't know where."

"So that's him! I have heard about him. They say he draws a lot of water around the São Francisco. Gosh, let me get something to eat."

In the dining-room the tables were being attacked by the guests to the clatter of plates and forks, platters of food arriving full and returning empty to the kitchen. Mr. Sampaio's birthday dinner was a resounding success. The house full, business friends, fellow members of the Club of Retail Dealers, relatives, neighbors, friends of

Dona Norma, in groups in the living-rooms and porch. The kitchen, too, was filled with godchildren and *comadres* of Dona Norma, the indigent of the neighborhood. In one corner of the dining-room, next to the main table, the guest of honor, Mr. Zé Sampaio, was eating with gusto and haste, casting sidelong glances at the table, fearful that the food might give out before he had a chance to get a second helping. He was half-hidden, out of sight, so that nobody would come to strike up a conversation and distract him. But the Argentine Bernabó, his lips yellow with dendê oil, giving a surfeited belch, came over to congratulate the master of the house: "*Macanudo*, my friend. What delicious food."

Dona Flor had been helping Dona Norma and the maids (all the maids of the neighborhood), but as the activity died down, she had found herself a chair in a corner of the porch, from which she watched the excitement of the party: Mr. Vivaldo, of the funeral parlor, was serving himself for the fourth time; Dr. Ives was gorging himself on desserts.

Mr. Aluísio, with a toothpick in his mouth, was drawing near as though unaware of what he was doing, until he was finally leaning up against the wall of the porch beside Dona Flor.

"A Roman banquet," he pontificated.

Dona Flor was on the point of not answering him, but she finally did; she had no reason to treat the backwoodsman so discourteously: "When Norminha gives a dinner, nothing is too good."

Mr. Aluísio looked about him, letting the conversation languish; Dona Flor was watching the other guests. It was at this point that the voice of the notary reached her in a low whisper: "Listen, beautiful, tell me something . . ."

"What in the world?" she answered in a startled tone.

"What would you think if we left to see the moon over the Lagoon of Abaeté? You go first and wait for me in the Largo . . ."

Dona Flor was already standing up, her voice choked: "Just who do you think I am?"

Dr. Aluísio smiled slyly, as though he knew how little value to attach to that indignation, accustomed as he was to those first sudden reactions. "Just a little stroll, nothing more."

Dona Flor could not even answer, indignation coloring her face and stifling her breathing. Were her longing for a man and her mad desire so clearly stamped on her face? Almost running, she came into the living-room.

"What is the matter with you, Flor?" Marilda asked, seeing her so nervous, her hands shaking.

"I don't know, I had a kind of palpitation of the heart. It's nothing."

"Sit down here. I'll get you a glass of water."

"Don't bother. I am going to sit over there with your mother."

Encircled by her friends, joking and passing remarks about the greediness of certain of the guests, Dona Flor recovered from her shock, from the taunting smile, the derisive words of the brash shyster. That cynic inviting her to go and see the moonlight on the lagoon on a night like that, as black as a pocket. In a little while she was taking part in the conversation, amused by the remarks of Dona Amélia and Dona Êmina. Dona Maria do Carmo had never before seen Mr. Sampaio in action at lunch or dinner; she was confounded. When the conversation was at its highest and most amusing, who should appear but the gallant from São Francisco, who apparently would not take no for an answer, arm in arm with his sister-in-law, Dona Ênaide, putting in his oar: "Is there room for two more? Or is this a talk for ladies only?"

"By all means, sit down."

Dona Flor paid no attention to the presence of the notary, who, in a few minutes, was reading Dona Amélia's palm, making them laugh with his nonsense. He was witty, the rascal: even Dona Flor smiled once or twice at his jokes. He foretold trips and wealth for Dona Amélia. Then it was Dona Êmina's turn. Very solemnly he assured her that she would have another child, very soon.

"The devil fly away with you. It's not enough that I had Aninha so unexpectedly? You go jinx somebody else."

"This time it's going to be a boy. I never make a mistake."

After reading Dona Êmina's hand, he turned his eyes on Dona Flor, as though nothing had happened before, eyes that undressed her all over again, the while he ran the tip of his tongue over his lips, in a gesture of such effrontery that she felt her heart stop. Just how far was he going? Fortunately, the others noticed nothing. Holding out his hand to take that of Dona Flor, he said: "Now it's your turn."

"I am not the least bit interested. That is all nonsense."

But the others insisted, chuckling and giggling. What would they think if she persisted in her refusal? It would be worse. Making a swift decision, she agreed. Dr. Aluísio smiled triumphantly, that specialist in the feminine soul; he never was mistaken.

He spread out on his Dona Flor's left hand, palm upward. With his well-manicured nail he began tracing the various lines, with a faint, subtle tickle, Dona Flor tense and rigid.

"A splendid lifeline . . . You are going to live to be over eighty." Then came a moment of silence while he scanned the widow's hand carefully. "I can see great things to come . . ."

"Things to come? What?" the friends asked in a chorus of excitement.

"The mount of Venus . . . I see a new love. An adventure, a passion . . ."

"Excuse me," Dona Flor said, trying to free her hand.

But Mr. Aluísio held it tight in his: "Just a minute. I have not finished. Listen to the rest. A gentleman from the backlands . . ."

Abruptly Dona Flor got to her feet, snatching her hand violently from those of the notary.

"I have not given you any excuse to go so far . . ."

She left the room like a whirlwind, her friends staring after her, and Dona Ênaide mortally offended: "Did you ever see anything so touchy! Now tell me: what did Aluísio do that was out of the way? Was he rude? It was just a joke to make people laugh. I can't stand people like that, putting on such airs. Who does she think she is? A princess?"

Only the notary was unperturbed, excusing Dona Flor: "Poor thing! It happens to every young widow who does not remarry. Hysterical . . . The small cities are full of cases like that. Old maids and widows, who take offense at the least thing, weep. Their lives are nothing but swoons and sullenness. In old age they become quietly mad . . ."

Dona Maria do Carmo interrupted him: "Just a minute, doctor;

I, too, am a widow, and I am going to feel myself offended . . ."
The notary looked her over with a knowing eye; a mulatta still
worth considering, well put together, firm-fleshed, good for a few
more rides. Doctor Aluísio was not a man to lose his time. Shifting
his attention from Dona Flor, he said: "Let me see your left hand,
please; there's something I want to bring into the clear . . ."

He took Dona Maria do Carmo's hand between his, looked into
her eyes with that lascivious glance of his: "May I tell the truth or
shall I lie?"

Dona Flor was going out the door; Dona Norma and Marilda
followed her home, where she gave way to a flood of tears, in such
a state of nerves that Dona Norma said to her, repeating the words
of Mr. Aluísio of Pilão Arcado: "What is the matter with you,
Flor. Are you getting hysterical?"

9

DONA FLOR'S ENTREATY IN HER CLASSES
AND IN HER REVERIES

Why don't they leave me alone with my mourning and my loneliness? Why do they have to talk about such things? Can't they
respect my widowhood? Let's go to the stove. A fancy and elegant
dish is *vatapá* of fish (or chicken), the most famous in the Bahian
cuisine. None of that nonsense about my still being young; I am a
widow who is dead to all those things. *Vatapá* sufficient for ten
(with some left over, as there should always be).

Take two fresh groupers—other fish can be used, but are not as
good. Salt and coriander, garlic and onions, several tomatoes and

the juice of a lemon. Four tablespoons of olive oil, either Portuguese or Spanish; I have heard said that the Greek is even better. I don't know. I have never used it, as I have not seen it on sale.

If I were to find a suitor, what would I do? Someone who would revive my desire, buried in the coffin of the dead. What do you girls know about the intimate life of widows? The desire of a widow is the desire for debauchment and sin. A seemly widow does not talk about such things, does not think about such things, does not bring the conversation around to such things. Just let me alone with my stove.

Sauté the fish in these seasonings and let it come to a boil with a mite of water, just a wee bit, almost none. Then all you have to do is strain the sauce, set it aside, and we proceed.

What if my bed is but a sad place to lay my body, with no other use, what does it matter? Everything in this world has its compensations. There is nothing better than a quiet life, without dreams, without desires, without being consumed by the flames of a burning womb. There is no better life than that of a serious, modest widow, a placid existence, free of ambition and desire. But what if my couch were not a bed in which to sleep, but a desert to be crossed, all fiery sands, and with no exit? What do you know of the secret life of widows, of their lonely bed, of their dead burden? You came here to learn to cook and not to find out the price of renunciation, the price in anxiety and loneliness to be an upright, modest widow. Let's get on with the lesson.

Take the grater and two well-fleshed coconuts, and grate. Grate hard. Go on—a little exercise never did anybody any harm (they say it dispels evil thoughts; I don't believe it). Gather up the grated white meat and warm it before you squeeze it; in that way the thick milk will come away more easily, the pure milk of the coconut. Put it to one side.

After squeezing out this first thick milk, do not throw away the coconut meat, don't be wasteful, for waste not, want not. Scald the meat in a quart of boiling water. Then squeeze it to get out the thin milk. After that you can throw the meat away, for by this time it is nothing but refuse.

A widow is nothing but refuse, limitation, and hypocrisy. In what country is it that they bury the widow in her husband's grave? Where is it that they set fire to her together with the body of her husband? It were better so than to be consumed in a slow, forbidden fire, consumed by longing and desire, outwardly hypocritical, a modesty of widow's weeds, veils hiding the rueful geography of fear and sin. A widow is nothing but refuse and suffering.

Cut the crust off stale bread, and then put the bread in the thin milk until it is moistened. In the meat grinder (well washed) grind up the bread moistened in coconut milk, and almonds, dried shrimp, cashew nuts, ginger, without forgetting the red pepper, bearing in mind the taste of the client. There are those who like their *vatapá* full of pepper, others who like just a pinch, the merest taste.

Ground and mixed, add these seasonings to the sauce of the grouper, mixing the one with the other, the ginger with the coconut, the salt with the pepper, the garlic with the cashew, and put it on the fire long enough to thicken the sauce.

Does not the *vatapá*, strong-flavored with ginger, pepper, almonds, affect people's dreams, lending them warmth and sensual seasoning? What do I know about such needs? I never needed ginger and almonds. It was the hand, the tongue, the word, his profile, his charm, it was he who stripped me of the sheet and my modesty for the wild astronomy of his kisses, to light me up with stars, in his nightly honey. Who bares me now of the veils of modesty in my dreams as a widow in my lonely bed? Whence comes this desire burning my breast and womb, if neither his hand nor his lip nor moonlit profile nor carefree laughter any longer exist? Why this desire, which is born of me alone? Why so many questions? Why this interest in knowing what goes on in the heart of a widow? Why don't they leave me with the black mourning veils on my face, veils prescribed by custom, to cover my divided face, divided between modesty and desire? I am a widow; it is not even proper for me to be talking about such things. A widow at the stove cooking *vatapá*, measuring the ginger, the almonds, the red pepper, and nothing more.

Add at once the coconut milk, the thick and pure, and at the very end the dendê oil, two full cups, flower of the dendê palm, the color of old gold, the color of *vatapá*. Let it cook for a long time over a low fire, stirring continually with a wooden spoon, always in the same direction; do not stop stirring or the *vatapá* will curdle. Stir it, keep on stirring, without stopping, until it comes to just the right point.

Over a slow fire my dreams consume me. It is not my fault: I am nothing but a widow divided in two, one half an upright, modest widow, the other a dissolute widow, almost hysterical, all swoons and sullenness. This robe of modesty is smothering me; at night I run about the streets in search of a husband. Of a husband to whom to serve the golden *vatapá* of my copper-colored body of ginger and honey.

The *vatapá* is now ready. Doesn't it look beautiful! All it needs is just a little dendê oil poured over it at the last minute. Serve it with ground hominy, and sweethearts and husbands will lick their chops.

And speaking of sweethearts, let me tell you so you will all know: there is a young widow endowed with a certain quiet charm and beauty, tea-colored, like gold and copper, a cook who can hold her own with the best, so hard-working, modest, and quiet that she had no equal in the whole city or in the Recôncavo, a first-class widow with an iron bed, the modesty of a virgin, and a fire burning her womb. If you should know of anyone whom this would interest, send him here on the run, at any hour of the day or night, in the rain, in the sunlight, send him at once, with the judge or the priest, with a wedding license, send him quickly, as quickly as you can.

I am launching this appeal to the four winds, to the mercy of undersea currents, to the phases of the moon and the tide, in the wake of any ship or coastwise vessel, for I am a port whose harbor is hidden, a secluded gulf, a refuge for the shipwrecked. If you hear of any unmarried man whose object is matrimony and who is looking for a widow, tell him that he will find Dona Flor here beside the stove, standing over a *vatapá* of fish, consumed by fire and accursed.

10

One day she could stand it no longer, and she opened her heart to Dona Norma: "Outwardly all chastity, inwardly, a pool of dung." Desire grew in her, in her breast, in silence, from loneliness, from reveries, in dreams. For no reason, without any point of departure, without seed or root. It came from her, "from my own evil, Norminha," from her febrile body, feeding on that flesh fertilized by absence, by destitution, by evil, a longing planted in the filth of her damnation.

"I am lost, Norminha; I do not want to think, and I think; I do not want to see, and I see; I do not want to dream, and I dream all night long. Completely against my will, against my desire. My body does not obey me, Norminha, the accursed thing."

The Yoga brochure, which she read and reread, explained that what went on was a "crucial battle between the fleshly matter and the pure spirit" joining forces within her, a frightening thing. The cursed matter of her body furiously and stealthily attacking the modesty of her spirit, destroying the calm of her life, her poise. There was no accord between her will and her instincts. All was confusion: on the one hand a widow, an example of dignity, on the other a young female consumed with desire. It was a serious situation calling for, according to the booklet, "a strong concentration of thought and daily exercises."

But the mystic literature and the difficult exercises—especially difficult for Dona Flor, who was plump and chubby—were of no avail. To see if she could achieve the elegiac equilibrium the booklet promised, for two weeks she underwent the most absurd contortions. Dona Dagmar, at her request, went over several of the classes with her, and Dona Flor submitted to them with patience and hope. Dona Dagmar extolled the Yoga principles, which, according to her, were wonderful; she had already lost eight pounds. But with Dona Flor they were a complete failure; she did not even lose weight. Instead of calm and poise, all she got in return was fatigue, an aching body, and not even because of this, less anxiety and boldness in her urgent demand.

Nor did the brilliant scientific analyses of Dona Gisa, mouthing words she had never heard of, as though she were a member of the university staff—libido, subconscious, repressed desires, taboos—help her: "For you, Flor, a widow full of repressed desires and complexes, sex is taboo."

Taboo or no taboo, consciously, unconsciously, or subconsciously, as the result of repressed desires and complexes or because of simple desire, that hideous noctural experience went on, with dreams that constituted a veritable bacchanal. The *gringa's* explanations had been no help at all. If Dona Flor were to follow her complicated talk, she would dash into the street to fornicate with the first male she met, doing away with repressions and complexes wholesale, putting an end to the miserable taboo in some whore-house bed, dishonoring forever herself and the memory of the dead.

Dona Norma was common sense personified, a wellspring of experience and human understanding. She went straight to the point: "This is the lack of a man, my saint. You are young, you are not seriously sick, you have not been spayed, so far as I know, so what is it you want? Even nuns get married to keep their vows of chastity, they marry Christ, and even so there are those who put horns on His head." And smiling at her memory: "Do you recall that cloistered nun who got pregnant by the man who delivered the bread, and wound up on the stage? It was a long time ago, maybe you don't remember it. People talked about nothing else."

Not even the image of the nun on the stage took Dona Flor's mind off her insistent, pressing problem. Without paying any attention to her friend's digression: "But, Norminha, I am a widow."

"So what? Or do you think a widow is not a woman? A

widow, to the best of my knowledge, thinks about a man, dreams about a man, looks at a man. Come off it!"

"You know very well that I am not one of those who is on the lookout for someone to marry. Once you even criticized me, calling me rude."

"And you were. I know that you are no hussy. But I am going to be frank with you: you are a widow who takes offense at anything, and you are getting unbearable. You have been a widow for a year, and instead of getting better, you are worse, as though you had just lost your husband yesterday. Before you used to laugh when people talked about courtship and marriage. Then you got so you could not take a joke, made a great ado about nothing."

"You know why. A swindler even showed up."

"And just because that Duke—Duke or Prince, whatever he was—was on the make, you have become worse than a nun! If he had his eye on you it was because he knew a good thing when he saw it. And now because Mr. Aluísio made a pass at you, nothing even worth mentioning, you have locked yourself up in the house, you hardly go out, you won't look at a man, as though a man were some wild animal. After all Mr. Aluísio only wanted . . ."

"I know perfectly well what he wanted."

"He wanted to go to bed with you, sweetie. Naturally, there will be many like that, just waiting for the chance. You are a knockout of a widow, you set plenty of eyes glowing."

"It must be that I look like a pushover for those scoundrels to dare . . ."

"Who ever told you that they want a shameless trollop to go to bed with? In spite of your face like a hangman . . ."

"But, Norminha, what can I do?"

"You need to quench that fire, woman. If you don't sleep well, if you don't rest, if you have no peace, it is because there is a fire burning your tail . . ."

"Good Heavens, Norminha, what a way to talk!"

"But isn't that your trouble? Isn't that the truth?"

"And what do you want me to do? To dishonor myself and become a slut? I am not a shameless woman, I was not born to take a lover; for me those things go only with a husband. Just because I dream of such crazy things I feel like dying. Is it that I look like a whore that you say these things to me?"

"Don't be crazy. What did I say that offended you?"

"Didn't you say . . ."

"I say and I repeat that your tail is on fire, or as the daughter of a friend of mine said to her mother: 'Mamma, my panties are burning.' That's more or less the trouble with you. But that does not mean that you are not a decent person. On the contrary. You are all that and more, but with that fire, your legs are spread. You are not only decent, you are aggressively so. You don't realize the expression that comes over your face when a man looks at you."

"Am I supposed to laugh, to say 'Come on to bed with me?' I'd rather die. I never went to bed with anyone but my husband."

"Nor should you."

"My husband died."

"Your first husband died. There is nothing in the way of your marrying again. You are still young, Flor, not even thirty."

"I will be on my next birthday."

"Still a girl. For what ails you, which is neither sickness nor foolish behavior, there are only two cures, my child: marriage or shamelessness. Of course, you could always enter a convent, but watch out for the bakers, the milkmen, and the gardeners. And even the priests, not to be unfaithful to Our Lord."

"Quit joking, Norminha!"

"I'm not joking, Flor. If you were a hussy, you could go on as a widow, wearing black, have a tumble with this one and that one, enjoy yourself, solve your problem. But as you are not that sort— you are decency itself—then you have to get married. There is no other way."

"A widow's desires, Norminha, should be buried with the dead; a widow has no right to recall the bed, the nights of humping, and even less, to dream of courtship, marriage, another husband. All of this is in the nature of an insult to the memory and honor of the dead."

"The desire of a widow is as urgent as that of a maiden or a married woman, if not more so, you crazy thing," Dona Norma answered firmly. "A second marriage is no insult to the honor of the dead. Any woman can cherish the memory of her dead husband and, at the same time, be happy in the company of her second spouse. Especially one whose first marriage was so out of the ordinary, and not always happy, to put it mildly."

It was a long and helpful talk the two friends had alone, in the intimacy of true regard for one another; two sisters could not have been closer. Dona Flor was finally convinced. Perhaps she had been all along during this cruel debate with herself, but had been unwilling to admit it until Dona Norma had torn away the veils of convention, of feigned mourning rotting in desire.

"But, Norminha, what good is it for me to be in agreement? Who is going to want me as a bride? Nobody wants the leftovers of a dead man, and I am not going out offering myself. I am going to die consumed this way."

"Take down the sign and I give you less than six months."

"What sign?"

"The one you wear on your face saying: 'I am a widow for good and all; I am dead as far as life and marriage are concerned.' Tear it off, learn to laugh again, to be like everybody else, and I'd be willing to bet that in less than six months . . ."

This conversation took place a few days after Carnival, which had fallen late that year, in March, more or less a month after the completion of Dona Flor's first year of bereavement.

On the morning of that sad anniversary, Dona Flor had set out for the cemetery, with tears and flowers, lingering beside the gravestone for a long time, as though it gave her comfort and calm. It was one of the quietest days she had had in all that turbulent period of her widowhood. It was sadness that she felt, just sadness, and a longing for the dead man. A deep, comforting loneliness.

The days of the Carnival festivities were more painful. With the music and songs, many of which were the same as those of the preceding year, the memories of that tragic Sunday returned. Leaning out of her window to watch a club or group of merrymakers go by, a crowd of drum beaters, a big bass drum or an *afoxé*, she recalled the dead man stretched out on Largo Dois de Julho among paper streamers and confetti, masquerading as a Bahian woman.

When the Club of the Sons of the Sea, in all the splender of its staging, stopped before the School of Culinary Savor and Art, at a signal from Camafeu's whistle, and the Negress Andreza de Oxun, carrying the banner of queen of the waters, went through the steps of a dazzling dance—the windows crowded, the street lined with people, applauding wildly—Dona Flor burst into a fit of weeping, and all the suffering and her sense of loss descended on her. A year before, with the body of her late husband stretched in the iron bed, she had still had the curiosity to watch the passing of the club from behind the shoulders of Dona Norma and Dona Gisa, though her breast had been full of life and death. So recent and so sudden had been Vadinho's death that it still held a tinge of life. But in this other carnival the glorious sight of the Sons of the Sea keeping time to the beat of their drums was more than she could bear. Ignoring the tribute that whistle represented, that interruption of their stroll, the voluptuous movements of Andreza like a ship gliding over the waves, the tribute of the club to their never-forgotten member and friend who had passed on a year before, Dona Flor could not remain at the window; all she saw was the naked and lifeless body, dead forever.

That Carnival was hard on her, and her life was ever more difficult. The dead man took advantage of the noisy rejoicing to intermingle himself with the pain of her unsatisfied desire. Her suffering grew so great that Dona Flor could no longer bear it in silence and loneliness. It was not possible for her to keep her secret to herself any longer, with her heart rent, her head dizzy, and her weariness. Dona Flor was a wreck. She opened her heart to Dona Norma.

Dona Norma guaranteed her wooing and marriage in a brief space of time, if she so decided, without mask or "Keep Off" sign. She sought confirmation in Dona Gisa, but the *gringa* attached slight importance to courtship and marriage, ridiculous legal, inhuman stringencies; she was reading Prince Kropotkin, and her thinking was a mixture of anarchy and psychoanalysis. With or without marriage, Dona Flor, in the opinion of the English teacher, had a "guilt complex" torturing her, from which she would free herself only when, breaking the taboos, "she would fulfill herself in some fashion." What crazy advice: a free love union, cohabitation, dalliance—an adventure, in a word, but right away. Dona Flor would have to be certifiable or the most cynical and hotpantsed widow in the world.

Dona Norma was a help and consolation; Dona Flor had to stop confusing modesty with hatred of the world, chastity with sourness, and Dona Norma would bet any amount of money that in less than six months the widow would have a ring on her finger, at least an engagement ring.

Dona Gisa laid no bets; why did Dona Flor have to wait six months steeped in suffering? Why all that nonsense, with so many men running around loose in the world? Besides, if she bet she would lose; almost always as between book knowledge and life knowledge, life comes off the winner.

Possibly because Dona Flor was growing more humane, her dealings with people becoming more than strict courtesy, and she was smiling again, talking to this one and that one, always discreet but nevertheless polite and attentive, or possibly it was mere chance (which is the most likely), but one day after this talk with Dona Norma and her discussion with Dona Gisa, what became evident to all and the subject of public discussion, was the upright interest and honest intentions of Dr. Teodoro Madureira, a partner in the Scientific Pharmacy on the corner of Cabeça. Twittering and triumphant, Dona Dinorá demanded recognition as the bearer of good tidings: "I foretold this months ago. I saw it in the crystal ball, and I told everyone: a distinguished man, a good man, a doctor, and well-to-do. Wasn't I right? Congratulations, Dona Flor!"

"What a match, how lucky she is!" The chorus of friends and gossips rose in wild, unanimous accord.

11

When the interest of the druggist began, nobody could say; it is not easy to fix the hour and minute of falling in love, especially when it is the definitive love of a man, the love of his life, all-absorbing and fatal, quite apart from clock or calendar. One day, when he opened his heart to Dona Flor, much later, Dr. Teodoro confessed with a certain smiling shyness that he had admired her for a long time, even before she became a widow. From the small laboratory at the back of the drugstore, he had watched her cross the Largo, following her steps along Cabeça with mute admiration. "If I should ever decide to get married, it would be to a woman like her, pretty and modest," he had said to himself as he handled the tubes he was heating, the bottles of medicines. A pure and Platonic sentiment, naturally—he was not a man to let his thoughts wander to a married woman and make her the object of ignoble passions, regarding her with lustful eyes or—to use the words of the druggist himself, precise and elegant, expressing somewhat flowerily those vulgar, low terms—"with the guilty eyes of concupiscence."

The first one to observe the druggist's inclination was Dona Êmina, a woman, moreover, little given to concerning herself with the life of others: she gossiped only enough to know what was going on around her. Compared with the others, meddlers of the first order, Dona Êmina was discreet and withdrawn.

It was the day of the hazing of the freshmen in the university, early in April, when the students crowded the main streets and avenues, celebrating the beginning of the new school year. In a long procession, under the baton of the older students, the freshmen—their heads shaven, wrapped in sheets, tied to one another like a string of slaves—wore placards criticizing the government and the administration, with wisecracks about the high cost of living and the incompetence of the politicians.

Coming from the School of Medicine, in the Terreiro de Jesus, the parade crossed the street toward Barra, stopping at certain spots such as Castro Alves Square, São Pedro, Piedade, Campo Grande. At these points of greatest concentration of the spectators, the older students put on a real show, with nonsensical speeches over the heads of their victims.

The inhabitants of the streets adjoining Largo Dios de Julho and Cabeça set out for São Pedro as soon as they heard the inaugural cornets and bugles coming from São Bento hill. Dona Norma, Dona Amélia, Dona Maria do Carmo, Dona Gisela, Dona Êmina, Dona Flor made up an eager group.

According to the information of Dona Êmina, precise and specific, Dr. Teodoro was comfortably installed beside the window of his drugstore, indifferent to the cornets, to the fools masquerading as professors and public figures, talking to the clerk and the cashier when he spied the group of women. He grew so nervous that Dona Êmina, puzzled by his behavior, kept her eye on him, thus following his strange movements one by one. The druggist, a man of serene bearing and respectful manners, no sooner laid eyes on the women than he quickly changed his comfortable position, moving away from the window, and assuming an almost rigid posture to greet them, wish them a cordial and sonorous good day. An important detail: pulling a comb out of the pocket of his vest, he ran it through his black hair—without any need for it, for his hair gleamed undisturbed under its layers of brilliantine. Gone was his serene bearing; he might have been a teen-ager. "I saw him put on his coat just to greet us," Dona Êmina said, asking herself the reason for all that concern and fervor.

With his immaculate white shirt and gray vest, a heavy gold chain running from one pocket to the other in an impressive curve holding a fine gold watch inherited from his father, his pants perfectly pressed, his shoes shining like a mirror, with his graduation ring, he was really quite a man, tall and agreeable. He bowed in greeting to the group.

The friends answered pleasantly; the druggist was one of the outstanding members of the community, highly regarded and admired. According to the further testimony of Dona Êmina—profuse in details, as is apparent—Dr. Teodoro's eyes were fixed on Dona Flor and on her alone; the others might not have existed. It was a glance, if not of concupiscence, certainly of longing. "He was devouring you with his eyes, he was eating you up," was the way the shrewd observer described that look to Dona Flor.

When he could no longer see them from the window, he went to the front door, then out on the sidewalk in front of the establishment, and, finally, after a moment's hesitation and a word to the employes, set off down the street after them.

He found himself a place close to them in the vicinity of the big clock of São Pedro, to size up the situation. Pulling on his gold chain, he smiled with satisfaction at the Swiss precision of his timepiece. Dona Norma and Dona Amélia, in order not to lose the slightest detail of the hazing, had climbed on to a bench in the little garden; the rest stood close by, on tiptoe. From where he was half hidden by the base of the clock, Dr. Teodoro was able to follow every movement of Dona Flor.

Keeping a watch on him, Dona Êmina was in a position to testify that the druggist had seen almost nothing of the amusing ceremony; the freshmen painted with red lead oxide, going through the steps of a macabre dance, the older students demanding beer and soda in the bars and stores. If Dr. Teodoro smiled, it was in response to the laughter of Dona Flor; his applause echoed that of the widow; he gazed at her in rapture. Dona Êmina tugged at Dona Norma's skirt as she was applauding from the bench the carryings-on of a student riding a donkey (the animal took advantage of the stop to eat the bits of refuse it found in the street). At first Dona Norma did not understand the message of vital import in the eyes and the fingers of her friend. Finally, discovering the druggist in shirt sleeves and ecstasy, she shared, astounded, her excitement. "Well, what do you know about that!"

Dona Amélia and Dona Maria do Carmo were quickly advised of the surprising behavior of Dr. Teodoro, half hidden behind the clock, getting an eyeful of Dona Flor. Only Dona Gisa kept out of it, reading the posters the students were carrying; according to her, such manifestations contained valuable material for the study of the collective soul. Dona Gisa lost no opportunity to study; she had been born for the purpose of knowing and explaining everything in the light of the most modern science. For the others, however, the strange behavior of the druggist was more precious and enlightening material.

"Girls, you would have to see it to believe it."

The procession continued to Piedade, and they followed. But, on the pretext of delivering a message, Dona Norma took a longer route, through a back street: "Let's get this clear, here and now." For a moment Dr. Teodoro hesitated in the shadow of the monumental clock, finally, however, following them at a nonchalant gait as of one who is in no hurry and just happens along.

Dona Norma and the rest of the group burst into laughter, all except Dona Flor, who was completely unaware of the whole affair, and Dona Gisa, holding forth on "the talent of the young for public causes." Suddenly they came to a halt in front of the door of a house while Dona Norma went to leave the message. Taken by surprise, with only a few yards separating him from the group, Dr. Teodoro was obliged to walk on. He passed them by, avoiding their glances, pretending not to see them, and he was so green at such things that it made one sorry for him. All infuriated, suspecting smiles and looks of mockery, not knowing what to do with his hands, a calamity. Abashed, he turned the corner, almost at a run. As he went by, Dona Maria do Carmo could not contain herself, and let out a peal of laughter.

"Ssh," Dona Norma reproved her.

"Where can Dr. Teodoro be going in such a hurry?" Dona Flor asked as she saw him disappear down an alley.

"You mean to say you don't know, you artful thing? What is going on here? Are you going to keep it a secret, or are you going to tell your friends? Don't you trust us?"

"Whatever are you talking about? You spend your lives making up things. Now what is it this time?"

"You mean to say you haven't yet noticed?"

"Noticed what, for heaven's sake?"

"That Dr. Teodoro has completely fallen for you."

"Who? The druggist? You need to have your heads examined. You are a pack of idiots! Who ever heard of such a thing! Imagine Dr. Teodoro, the politest of men. It's making a mock of him."

"A mock? He's put aside all his polite ways, my pet. He's all hopped up."

With this cutting up, joking, and laughing, they followed the procession of the medical students, poor Dona Flor not knowing quite what was happening to her. But when they got home, and Dona Norma was alone with the widow, she talked to her seriously. She brought up the manners of the druggist, a person who, as Dona Flor had rightly said, was all politeness, even if a little on the ceremonious side; never had anyone heard said of him that he cast sheeps'-eyes at his customers, and much less that he had followed one of them down the street in his shirt sleeves, running a comb through his hair, hiding behind a city clock, as shy as an adolescent. And with his eyes fixed on Dona Flor, as though glued to her. This was not just gossips' tittletattle or something they had made up. Dona Norma had had no part in the banter, for Dr. Teodoro was an upright, respected person, and it was not fitting to deal with so serious a matter in jest or jeeringly. A better match, my daughter, you will rarely find: a mature man, of suitable age, settled, a university graduate, the owner of a drugstore, the picture of health. You couldn't have asked for more if he had been made to order.

"You really think, Norminha, that he is interested in me? Or is it just a passing fancy, a taste for stale bread, spoiled meat, the leftovers of a dead man? Nobody would want . . ."

Dona Norma looked her friend over from head to foot: "God bless you," she said, with an approving gesture.

For Dona Flor, as a result of the excitement the news had produced, half-curious, half-abashed, hadn't the slightest resemblance to stale bread and less to meat that was not quite fresh. On the contrary: her delicate skin with a coppery sheen that came from her Indian blood covered a fresh, engaging face, her flesh was young and fragrant, smelling of Brazilian cherry, a real hunk of woman. Leftover, to be sure; she had had a husband; she had gone to bed with him, and they had had a time of it; more appetizing, however, than many a cosseted virgin, for a maidenhead is not everything, not by a long shot, in spite of all the todo that has been made over it. When all is said and done, it is nothing but a fragile membrane, a drop of blood, a moan, and, above all, an old prejudice, and if it is rated so highly that is because it has been in the hands of public relations agents for centuries, and they have been backed up by the army and the clergy, the police and the whores, all of them making of this pellicle the be-all and end-all. But how can a virgin, silly and unskilled in her desire, be compared to a widow, whose longing is compounded of knowledge and absence, of restraint and lack of satisfaction, of hunger and fasting, and is clear and unequivocal? "Forget it, Flor; not only Dr. Teodoro sighs for leftovers like you, but many others we do not know about." What Dona Norma wanted to know was something different: "How about you? How do you feel toward him? Could you love him?"

At first she did not even want to give thought to the matter of her feelings before being sure that the druggist really had an inclination toward her, that all this was not mockery or a mistake, unwilling to run the risk of new hoaxes and humiliation, as had already happened with that business of the Prince and the effrontery of Mr. Aluísio. But yielding to Dona Norma's friendly impertinence, demanding an immediate answer, Dona Flor confessed that she was not indifferent to the druggist. A gentleman whom it was a pleasure to deal with, extremely well bred, a man in whose good looks one could take pride. He reminded her of a movie star who was all the rage. A vague resemblance, but enough to arouse her admiration; in a word, if it was true, it was possible and even probable that Dona Flor might come to feel for him . . . what she had felt for the dead man? No, that was something very different. She herself was different, not the same as when, eight years before, almost a girl, she had met that rattlebrain at the Major's party, and had suddenly, without weighing the consequences or stopping to think, given him her heart (and, soon afterward, joyously, her breasts and thighs, that tumultuous night on the Largo, in the darkness of the beach). Crazy about him, lost to the point of giving herself to him, complete and asking nothing, throwing her worthless virginity in the face of Dona Rozilda, who had opposed the match and forbidden the marriage.

Now she was a widow with her place in the world, thoughtful, incapable of licentiousness, of hasty impulses and acts forgivable in a girl who was of an age to fall in love, but unpardonable in a woman getting on to thirty and in mourning (even though inwardly consumed by desire). If there was anything to it, time would tell whether liking would flower into love, in a peaceful tranquility of tenderness and understanding, without the youthful violence of passion in hidden corners, at the foot of the stairs. Perhaps a feeling of that sort, a mature, serene love might send up shoots in the soil of a discreet idyll. Dona Flor did not think this was impossible, for, as she said, Dr. Teodoro being neither antipathetic nor ugly, she had no aversion to him; on the contrary, she found him attractive, as she now realized. And there you have Dona Norma bringing to fruition courtship and marriage, foreseeing Dona Flor happy as she deserved to be and had never been.

"Ah, my pet, how lovely it will be. Now don't be foolish, don't lock yourself up in the house, take that frown off your face."

For Dona Flor, even though she admitted her interest in the druggist, had fortified her decision not to go out and show it, to offer herself, strolling past the pharmacy, revealing her longings, her eyes mournful as Lent, the result of bitter abstinence, of enforced fasting. That never, Norminha.

"And I am not going to let you lose a chance like this."

It took Dona Norma a long time to persuade the widow not to be foolish and stop playing hard to get. A person in her state, hot as a live coal, needing to marry, and marry quickly before she wound up hysterical or quietly mad or going out to give herself to the first man that crossed her path, in a brothel, a widow who covered with horns the skull of her dead husband, a remote and fertile cold frame for antlers in his honorable grave, one who so openly admitted her need for the warmth of a man, of a swaying bed, could not adopt the pose of a widow faithful unto death, of everlasting mourning and a crack to which she had thrown the key away, a cunt buried with the coffin of the dead, a faded flower at his feet, useless and wilted: "No good for anything but to pass water."

It was better for her to make up her mind once and for all to accept a husband, to live a decent, upright life with him, renewing herself in love and gaiety, maintaining honored, clean, and calm in his grave the memory and the remains of the first. Without talking too much about him not to offend his successor. Besides, in these last months it had been as though Dona Flor had forgotten the name of the departed. When the gossips had execrated him, insulted his memory, Dona Flor, bristling, had talked about nothing else all day long. Afterward she had locked him up inside her like a rare and precious jewel, when the neighbors and friends left him at rest in his tomb; if any of them recalled him, they never mentioned him. The thing was to go on in this fashion, naturally removing from the living-room the portrait of the rascal with his cynical, scampish smile (and, why not admit it? his irresistible charm), putting it away in the bottom of a trunk and in her heart. On the wall of the living-room—and you know where else!—the second, and what a second, my child, a beauty of a man in the flower of his years, and so distinguished.

Get married and quickly, have her husband, live a satisfying, decent life with him, in keeping with her nature and her duties, and not be consumed by dreams in her lonely bed, biting her lips, gritting her teeth, restrained only by fear and prejudice. She, Dona Norma, would not allow Dona Flor to lose this unique opportunity. There would never be a better, and all out of false modesty, stupidity, foolishness. No, no, and no.

Thus, when Dona Flor had finished her afternoon class, in which she taught her pupils how to make a dessert of gelatine and coconut known as "Male Cream," which gave rise to not a few wisecracks—"Never was there a more delicious cream"—Dona Norma came for her to take her along to Cabeça on the excuse of buying flowers. Such an involved transaction, having to do with the selection of a dozen tuberoses! But Dona Norma could not make up her mind, to the amazement of the flower-seller, the old Negro Cosme de Omolu, because Dr. Teodoro, occupied in the rear of the pharmacy, did not put in an appearance. After the flowers came the bean fritters of Vitorina, and the druggist still did not show up in the window. But Dona Norma was not easily discouraged: she dashed headlong, without previous warning, into the drugstore, dragging Dona Flor, on the verge of a nervous attack, after her, asking the cashier for a package of cotton. Dona Flor wanted the earth to open and swallow her up, with Dona Norma so noisy, calling attention to herself. Who ever heard of such goings-on?

In the back, in the small laboratory, behind big blue and red jars, like an engraving from a manual of alchemy, they could see Dr. Teodoro grinding salt and poison in a stone mortar. He had his glasses on, and with close attention, after the grinding, he weighed tiny amounts of the powder and salts in a small scale that looked like a toy. So concentrated was he on the mystery of filling the prescription that he failed to notice the presence of the ladies in his establishment, as though he did not hear the voice of Dona Norma recounting an item of news that had appeared in the papers.

Turning from the scales, the druggist put in a test tube the result of his pulverized minerals, in minute quantities, adding to them exactly twenty drops of colorless liquid, which then gave off a reddish smoke enveloping the dark, strong head of the doctor with wisdom and magic.

Dona Norma did not miss her cue, her voice echoed, flatteringly: "Look, Flor, my dear, Dr. Teodoro positively seems like a sorcerer all surrounded by sulfur. Gracious heavens!"

The doctor trembled as he heard the name—not his, but that of Dona Flor. Looking over his glasses (which he used only when he had to examine something close at hand), he became aware of the presence of poetry among his medicines, and he felt his foundations shake, with a chill in his lower stomach. He wanted to raise himself erect, but he stood confused and at his wits' end, the test tube falling to the floor in a thousand splintered pieces and the medicine, which was almost ready (to relieve the chronic cough of Dona Zezé Pedreira, an old lady in fragile health, in Forca Street), turned into a dark spot on the floor while the smoke screen still enveloped the austere face of the doctor.

"Oh, dear me," Dona Flor said.

And that was all that was said or happened, except that Dona Norma laughed as she paid for her roll of cotton, for the figure of the druggist, half-raised from his chair, his hand in the air, as though still holding the glass tube, his glasses slipping down his nose, mute and stupefied, was funny.

Completely embarrassed, not knowing what to do with herself, Dona Flor went out of the drugstore, while Dona Norma cast an accomplice's eye on the romantic druggist, as though throwing a rope to a drowning sailor. Dr. Teodoro tried to say something, but could not bring out a word.

Dona Norma caught up with Dona Flor at the corner. Did she still have any doubts about the druggist's feelings? Or did she perhaps want, she a widow consumed by desire, groaning under the weight of her mourning, did she perhaps cherish some absurd notion of a candidate of higher standing, class, and appearance? A better match was impossible, my pet: a doctor with a diploma and ring with a real amethyst, the owner of a flourishing establishment, good-looking, with vest and gold watch chain, in excellent health, of upright habits, a man of standing, a superb forty-year-old specimen.

12

Friends and gossips discovered in Dr. Teodoro, to the last detail, everything the crystal ball and the greasy cards had revealed to Dona Dinorá that afternoon when she had made her forecast. Well fixed, university degree, physical make-up, build, figure, bearing, distinguished manners, everything; and to think that in all that time they had searched the streets and squares, trying to find the face which matched that revealed by the clairvoyant, no one had thought of the druggist. How explain such an oversight, when he was right under their noses and one had only to look to see? Was it blindness on the part of the friends or a deliberate deception in this detailed narrative, a fatal mistake to rejoice the hearts of antagonistic critics? Neither the one nor the other, but a kind of collective obtuseness which impeded the friends and gossips from discovering him in the quiet rear of the pharmacy, his glasses slipping down on his nose, with his gold chain, bent over his drugs, mixing poisons to turn them into medicines, dispensing and delivering health at moderate prices.

The chronicler of Dona Flor's marriages, of her joys and sorrows, was merely faithful to the truth when he failed to place Dr. Teodoro in the list of aspirants whose candidacy the gossips put forward, for none of them happened to think of the druggist, as his name had not come up for consideration in the pleasant tittletattle dealing with Dona Flor's widowhood when they were all trying to cheer her up. Moreover, the druggist lost little by this oversight; at most, participation in the dream in which Dona Flor saw herself in a ring-around-a-rosy encircled by dolts aspiring to her hand. It was better for him that it should have been this way; thus, not even in dreams did he appear in a ridiculous role, losing esteem in the eyes of the widow.

But why this visual block, why did they forget him, why fail to discern him at the window of the drugstore, beside the blue and red jars, enveloped in that odor of medicines, with the hypodermic needle ready to pierce arms or buttocks of all the old women, his customers? If they saw him so frequently and had dealings with him, how was it they did not discern him?

Because they looked on him as a confirmed bachelor; for that reason when they listed possible candidates, they never put down the druggist's name, just as though he were married, with a wife and children. Not even Dona Norma, in her zealous search for a sweetheart for languishing Maria, her neighbor and godchild, had ever thought of him. Dr. Teodoro? He had not married and would never marry; it was a pure waste of time to think about him; even if he wanted to set up a home, he wouldn't be able to, the poor thing!

Because of what seemed a self-evident truth, in all this account of Dona Flor's widowhood, he was never the target of jests and gossip, like the other celibates of their acquaintance.

Dona Dinorá, queen of busybodies and fortuneteller, passed the Scientific Pharmacy every day; twice a week she uncovered her flaccid bottom (ah, how fleeting the vanity and grandeur of this world: that same withered backside which had inspired the satanic verses of Master Robato, when he was an adolescent bard of the diabolic school, and the sight and touch of which had cost checks, real shell-outs, by rich business men) to the druggist for a painful anti-arthritic injection. And not even so had her fortune-telling eyes, capable of reading the future, beheld in the dark gentleman, grasping the fold of her loose skin, the splendid forty-year-old subject of her prediction. Because she knew, and better than anyone else, why it was impossible for him to take a wife.

Not that he was a faggot, impotent, or a virgin whom women did not attract. For heaven's sake, not even remotely should such a thought occur, for Dr. Teodoro, a peaceable person, amiable, a bon vivant, was more than capable of laying aside his customary moderation and furnishing abundant proof of his masculinity, giving anyone who put his manliness to doubt a good sock in the nose.

He was a man who had plenty of *machismo*, though he made no display of it. If anyone wants precise and indisputable proofs on the subject, he has only to talk with the potent, tidy mulatta Otaviana das Dores or Tavinha Manemolência in Sapoti Alley, breaking down with a little change the reserve they owe their select clientele: two auctioneers, three businessmen of the city, an elderly priest, a professor of medicine, and our admirable druggist.

Because of her outstanding qualities of cleanliness, discretion, and propriety—she was more like a lady receiving guests in her hospitable home—Dr. Teodoro's choice and patronage fell on Otaviana, by whom he could always be depended on after dinner on Thursdays. Tavinha's clients, a select, close-mouthed elite, had their set day or night, each with his habits and tastes—sometimes as

strange as those of the auctioneer Lameira, which verged on copro-
philia—and, competent and comfortable, she took care of all, giving each complete satisfaction. Whether normal males without
problems, like Dr. Teodoro, or old satyrs, navel-lickers, high-
voltage fellatio performers, leaving them all satisfied and happy.

At eight o'clock on the dot, every Thursday, Dr. Teodoro
crossed the threshold, receiving a warm, special welcome. Sitting
in a rocking chair across from Otaviana as she knitted baby's
bootees, sipping a fruit liqueur, which was the speciality of the
nuns of a convent of Lapa, Dr. Teodoro and the lady of light
virtue engaged in an enlightening conversation, reviewing all that
had happened during the week, the news in the papers. In her
association with educated gentlemen, Tavinha had acquired a ve-
neer of learning: her talk was pleasant, she was by way of being an
intellectual, and in Sapoti Street her opinion was sought on any
subject. Moreover, she was highly moral, severely critical of the
habits of the day, those nonsensical ideas rife in the world, the
dissolute, unbelieving young people.

Thus the doctor spent an hour digesting his dinner and listening
to and agreeing with the edifying ideas of the mulatta that "The
world is headed for hell, doctor; there is no saint who can save it."
Afterward they went to her room redolent of aromatic leaves, and
Dr. Teodoro took Otaviana in the bed of sheets as white as snow,
with the privilege of an encore. How was it possible to put his
manliness in doubt, when he nearly always gallantly repeated his
excellent performance?

Without increase in price, it should be added, for Tavinha
Manemolência did not charge by time but by the night, her rates
being for the whole night even when her client, limited in his
freedom by family control, left early, utilizing only the brief space
that could be covered by a lie. An expensive rate, a high cover
charge, but the best service. All that courtesy and competence
justified the extravagance.

Dr. Teodoro stayed until midnight, at times dozing off in that
bed with its inviting mattress, soft and warm, with Otaviana
watching over his sleep. Before he left, she even brought him a dish

of sweetened hominy, rice pudding, or another glass of liqueur to "restore his strength," as the indulgent, dark, and worthy trollop put it.

The gossips did not include him in their lists or involve him in matrimonial plans because they knew he was devoted to his mother, old and paralyzed, to whom her son was everything. When she suffered her stroke, Dr. Teodoro, only recently graduated, promised her that he would never marry as long as she lived. It was the least he could do to show his gratitude.

His father had died when he, then eighteen, was getting ready to take his entrance examinations at the Medical School. He wanted to give up his studies, settle down for good in the city of Jequié, where they lived, taking over the small dry goods store, which was all his father had left them in addition to numerous debts and a reputation for kindness. But the widow, delicate of appearance, though highly capable, would not accept this sacrifice. The only ambition her late husband had cherished was to see his son graduate from college; and young Teodoro had showed himself to be an excellent student, his teachers predicting a brilliant future for him. He passed his examination and completed his studies, while his mother took over the store. There was just one change: instead of medicine, he studied pharmacy, a course that was three years shorter.

All alone, working day and night without letup, the widow managed the house and business, paying the debts and sending her son his monthly allowance. More than once he tried to find himself a job, but his mother put her foot down: the time for his studies was sacred; work would come after graduation.

When she saw him at the commencement exercises, a graduate, with ring and diploma in his black gown in the solemn setting attending the conferring of the degree, the satisfaction was too much for her; that same night, back in the hotel, she had the stroke. She came through by a miracle, but remained paralyzed.

Confronted by what seemed like her certain death, the young druggist, with a gesture befitting the hero of a melodrama, though completely sincere, swore that he would never leave her, would remain single as long as she lived. The next day, in the first minute

he could take off, he broke off his engagement to Violeta Sá, his
fiancée, and never had another love affair. His sole entertainment
and diversion was the bassoon, which he had learned to play as a
member of the Municipal Band while still in high school.

After selling the store in Jequié, he had entered as a partner in a
drugstore in Itapagipe which was badly rundown and belonged to
a doctor suffering from premature senility and commiting acts of
complete folly, so that his family had to put him in an institution.
Dr. Teodoro rented a house nearby and lived exclusively for his
work and his paralyzed mother confined to a wheel chair, her gaze
bewildered, her voice hoarse and almost unintelligible, jealous of
her son. Sitting beside her at night, he practiced his bassoon solos
to allay the sick woman's terrible loneliness.

For years and years he hardly ever left the neighborhood,
where he became popular and respected. Having made the acquaintance of the musician Agenor Gomes, he joined the orchestra
of amateurs which, under the direction of the competent director,
comprised doctors, engineers, lawyers, a judge, a clerk, and two
storekeepers. On Sundays, in the house of one or the other of
them, they gathered to play, happy with their instruments and
their compositions.

Under the management of the young pharmacist, the drugstore recovered its former prosperity, and Dr. Teodoro's reputation as an honorable, decent man spread and augmented.

Many aspirants to the hand of the young bassoon-playing
druggist appeared, but he, serious and incapable of taking up the
time of a girl whose object was marriage, gave none of them
encouragement or hope. All the attentions of a lover were lavished
on his mother: flowers, boxes of chocolates, little gifts, and a sonata
composed by the director in tribute to the devotion of the son to
his mother: "*Afternoons in Itapagipe* with motherly love."

The insane doctor died without recovering his mind. Dr. Teodoro drew up the inventory, settling the numerous problems as
though it were a question of his own family. Perhaps for that
reason, the widow dreamed of marrying him to her youngest
daughter, a tramp of the first water. Fortunately, his promise saved
Dr. Teodoro, for otherwise he might have found himself the

husband *malgré lui* of that slut, so importunate was the widow. She was already treating him like a mother-in-law, trying to run his life. In alarm, Dr. Teodoro saw only one way out: to dispose of his share in the business and withdraw from the drugstore and the threat of marriage.

When he made inquiries as to what he should do with the money he had received, an acquaintance of his (his and ours, for we have seen him on other occasions at the wheel in Chile Street, almost running Dona Rozilda down and, in the bargain, insulting her without mincing words, that sharp agent of medicines and laboratories, Rosalvo Medeiros) gave him a valuable lead: the Scientific Pharmacy, a prosperous establishment, excellently situated, which was the object of one of those sordid struggles among heirs, a disgusting family squabble. It was a marvelous opportunity for a person with money; he could make a first-class deal.

And so Dr. Teodoro did, buying up the shares of two of the five heirs, a down payment, with the rest on a short-term note. He had undertaken a large enterprise, a patrimony. He had bad times at the beginning, redeeming his notes at high interest. The person who was very helpful to him in those tight spots was the banker Celestino, to whom he had been recommended by another member of the amateur orchestra, Dr. Venceslau Pires da Veiga, almost as good at the violin as with the scalpel. The Portuguese immediately took in the fact that he was dealing with a decent person: he had the sight and scent of a bloodhound; he never made·a mistake. He assisted Dr. Teodoro in renegotiating his notes, helping him in every way.

A frugal person, whose luxuries were limited to a good nurse for his mother, his bassoon, and his weekly visit to Tavinha Manemolência, with the aid of the banker the druggist got through the initial period of the pharmacy without too many hazards, though he was still in debt. A year before he began courting Dona Flor he had paid, with a sigh of relief, the last note.

Now he was no longer a partner in a small drugstore in Itagipe, but in a pharmacy in the heart of the city. And even though a minor partner, as he had put up only two fifths of the capital, he did as he thought best in the business, for the three brothers did not get along and rarely set foot in the Scientific Pharmacy (except to ask for an advance on their monthly share).

Moreover, as a graduate pharmacist, he received a larger share of the daily profits. Calmly he waited, hoping to acquire the other shares sooner or later when the remaining heirs, a lazy and useless lot, had squandered the balance of their inheritance on high living. Meanwhile he won the respect and esteem of the neighborhood, including the gossips.

When he first appeared in Cabeça, impeccable in his dark suit, serious and competent, a bachelor approaching forty, the women swung into action. Then they weighed him in privacy, measured his capacity: "What a delicate hand for injections" . . . "Better at prescribing than many doctors," fine-combing the details of his life, his studies paid for by his mother in charge of the little store in Jequié, and including his bassoon solos, the art and pleasure of a bachelor, with tears when it came to the dramatic chapter of the hemmorrhage, when Dr. Teodoro swore that he would forego the love of a woman the better to look after his paralyzed mother.

Dona Dinorá, scrupulous and precise, unflagging in her search for details, extended her field of investigation to Itapagipe, where she interviewed the very nurse who had wheeled the old lady in her invalid's chair. That devotion of the son, which had elicited a sonata, melody, and poem triumphed over the slander of the gossips, who left the druggist in peace with his austere habits and ailing mother.

So accustomed were they to the solemn filial vow that they did not even take in the deep qualitative change that had occurred months before when the mother of Dr. Teodoro had died in the wheelchair in which she had spent more than twenty years, thus releasing her son from his binding promise, leaving him free to get married. As far as the gossips were concerned, the druggist did not exist as the object of their tittle-tattle and meddling. They gossiped about everyone except him, "that upright man, Dr. Teodoro."

Imagine their amazement, astonishment, sense of frustration, when the news of the druggist's interest in the cooking teacher exploded! Oh, the traitor! The neighborhood, in battle rank, occupied all the strategic positions between the Scientific Pharmacy and

the School of Savor and Art. Dr. Teodoro had to run the gauntlet
at his unhurried pace, between looks and smiles, in his gray or blue
double-breasted coat, with his austere composure, walking past the
window where Dona Flor answered his respectful though impassioned greeting with a brief, delicate smile. Ah, the traitor, indolent
and sly—the glances and gestures of the gossips reproached him.

Staying on in the distant house of Itapagipe, he was in no hurry
to take the car or the elevated after he had closed up the drugstore.
His crippled mother was no longer waiting impatiently for him.
He took to having lunch and dinner at the restaurant of the
Portuguese, Moreira, strolling about Cabeça, Maciel, Sodré, as
though reluctant to leave the environs of the widow. He courted
her at a distance, without imposing his presence on her, discreetly.
But how was he to keep within the limits of discretion, reserve,
with all the neighbor women on the alert, meeting one at every
step he took, hearing Dona Dinorá's insinuations?

Dr. Teodoro, who was nothing if not frank, who loathed fraud
and dissembling, was very uncomfortable; the situation was becoming unbearable. Dona Norma took this in: "It makes one feel
sorry for him."

Dona Flor smiled compassionately: "The poor thing . . ."

"This can't go on like this. I am going to have to do something."

Dona Norma prepared to have a frank talk with the impassioned druggist, to settle the matter once and for all. Even Dona
Flor admitted that she was interested, referring to him in terms of
affection, always at the window when the doctor crossed the
street.

"I'm going to talk to him."

"You must be out of your mind. Leave it to me."

But Dona Norma did not get a chance to take the initiative for,
that very afternoon, Dona Flor burst into her house, almost out of
breath, with the pages of a letter and the envelope in her hand.
Blue paper with a gold border and smelling of sandalwood, lovely.
A proposal in keeping with all the rules, gallant phrases in ultra-
correct Portuguese, a list of his worldly possessions and his qualities, all laid at the lady's feet, his upright intentions, in noble words

which nevertheless exhaled a breath of real passion, all within the limits of well-bred prudence, making of that document of his sentiments a declaration of love, too, quivering and intense.

"Swell," Dona Norma said, reading it eagerly and enthusiastically. "What a man!"

13

If Dona Flor's first marriage was carried out in a hurry, with a minimal, restricted ceremony, in the second everything took place as should be, with order and a certain display. There was no courtship in the first: falling in love led directly to marriage, with untimely sessions in bed. It was celebrated under those unpleasantly urgent conditions as a result of the necessary approval of State and Church for the loss of the girl's virginity, thus restoring, if not her maidenhead, at least the good name of the family.

The second was effected with printed invitations, a note in the social column of *A Tarde*, flattering reference to Dr. Teodoro, "our esteemed and outstanding subscriber," with music, flower, lights, and guests, many guests in the Church of St. Benedict, where the officiant, Dom Jerônimo, launched forth on the most eloquent of sermons; whereas at the civil ceremony the judge, Dr. Pinho Pedreira, with the elegance of phrase that characterized him, made a brief and pleasant speech, foretelling a life of peace and understanding for the new couple "under the sign of music, the voice of the gods." The gaunt and distinguished judge was a fellow member of the amateur orchestra directed by Master Agenor Gomes in which the magistrate played the clarinet.

Thus Dona Flor's second marriage had everything the first lacked; all under the control of Dona Norma—at the request of the newlyweds—with proficiency and attention to every detail, everything in its place at the proper hour, everything of excellent quality and at reasonable price, and with the enthusiastic help of the entire neighborhood in the whole enterprise.

What did Dona Norma not obtain? Even the presence of Dona Rozilda, her complete reconciliation with her daughter. Dona Flor's brother and sister-in-law, too, had come from Nazareth. The only ones who failed to put in an appearance were Rosália and Antônio Morais, the mechanic unshaken in his determination not to return to Bahia until his mother-in-law "had gone on a permanent vacation to hell."

This time Dona Rozilda had nothing to criticize; it was a marriage that met with her approval, the rites as well as the son-in-law. At long last a son-in-law who approached the model dreamed of in bygone days on Ladeira do Alvo: not entirely, of course, not the perfect prince, the ideal missed by a hair's breadth in the student Pedro Borges. But, nevertheless, a doctor, a man of means, a partner in a drugstore well stocked and well situated. A respectable man, well mannered, somebody, not a nobody earning his living by crawling around under other folk's cars, filthy with grease, like Rosália's husband; and, far less, a despicable vagabond, a rogue like Florípedes's first husband. She could show this Dr. Teodoro off to her most distinguished acquaintances: he did her credit, a man of substance, well-to-do.

In this second marriage there was no wooing, and this was as it should be, for it does not look right for a widow to be lovemaking in a corner or the doorway, cuddling, hugging, kissing, embracing, touching here, touching there, hand on breasts, slipping down to thighs. Brazenness and immodesty that can be overlooked in the courting of a girl if the suitor's intentions are serious, giving him the right to certain advances, but unforgiveable and demoralizing when it comes to a widow.

That is why, after the proposal of Dr. Teodoro, imparted by his noble epistle, the two parties agreed, with the advice and approval of relatives and friends, on a respectable and limited courtship, during which Dona Flor and Dr. Teodoro could learn to know one another better, and in this way measure their qualities and defects, thus deciding whether marriage was indicated for them. In the words of Mr. Sampaio, ambassador extraordinary, after Dona Flor's bitter experience she should not take such a serious step without full assurance of success.

Such a serious step: not even Dona Norma, for all her willingness and ability, ventured to take upon herself alone the answer to those blue and golden sheets, redolent of sandalwood and passion. In her opinion, close as she was to Dona Flor, like a sister, the confidante of her secrets, knowing her unhappy state as a young woman behind the bars of her widowhood, there were no doubts. That marriage offered the perfect solution to all her friend's problems. But the answer to that ardent and polite proposal could not be summed up in one word: "I accept." And then what?

What the situation called for was to bring everything into the clear, leaving no doubt as regards intentions, time limits, date, in such a way that Dona Flor would not be a subject of gossip, nor would the ridiculous situation in which the inexperienced druggist found himself be prolonged, for he was a man of standing and esteem who had suddenly become a clown and a source of merriment for the gossips who followed him down the street, keeping count of his glances and sighs, amusing themselves at his expense.

That was the reason Dona Norma summoned Dona Gisa, learned and a bluestocking, a devoted friend, as well as seeking the opinion of Mr. Zé Sampaio, and relying upon it. She had thought at first of Aunt Lita and Uncle Pôrto, since Dona Flor's mother was in Nazareth das Farinhas and her other relatives in Rio. But she and the widow were in agreement as to the uselessness of these kindly elders in the preliminary discussions of the matter. If they reached the solemn moment of announcing the engagement, then they would call in Aunt Lita from her garden, Uncle Pôrto from his bright landscapes, to hear from the suitor his intentions and his request.

It was a confused night; to make sure she could be present, Dona Norma had to get Dona Amélia to take her place at the bedside of a sixth or seventh cousin of hers who had just had a baby: "That Norminha had no call whatever to offer to stay with her; the girl has loads of relatives. She just likes to put her two cents into everything, so afraid she will miss something," Dona

Amélia grumbled on her way to the hospital against her will.

Dona Gisa had to break an engagement too: a musical evening in the home of some German friends where, with the lights low, they listened to records of Beethoven and Wagner in devout silence, sipping a drink. As for Mr. Sampaio, he was there against all his will, dragged in by main force; he had never wanted to get involved in other people's lives, and least of all in so personal a matter as marriage. However, because it had to do with Dona Flor, a person he truly admired, a widow and of exemplary behavior— and a real wow, a knockout (Mr. Sampaio could not control his low thoughts)—he decided to sacrifice his leisure and his principles to help her.

With a new reading of the letter, aloud and with comments from Mr. Sampaio, this historic summit conference (as the press would term it) got under way: "A man of noble feelings. I like him," the shoestore owner said.

This was followed by Dona Flor's timid assent: "Yes, so do I. Why not? He seems agreeable . . ."

"Agreeable? A man and a half, real groovy," Dona Gisa retorted, employing a phrase of Bahian slang in her foreign accent.

They finally decided, at Dona Norma's suggestion, to empower Mr. Zé Sampaio to discuss all matters with the druggist in the name of the widow, conveying her acceptance with certain conditions: no more public demonstrations or grotesque behavior, which became neither of the two parties and was to be replaced by a discreet courtship, after a meeting with Dona Flor's aunt and uncle at which the engagement would be officially announced.

Once this had been done, Dr. Teodoro could visit his fiancée in her home three times a week: Wednesdays, Saturdays, and Sundays. On Wednesdays and Saturdays he could come after dinner and stay until ten, these meetings taking place, naturally, in the presence of a third party so that there would be no breath of scandal about the widow's respectability. On Sundays the regime was more relaxed, beginning with a lunch in Rio Vermelho in the home of Aunt Lita and Uncle Pôrto and concluding with a visit to the movies in the company of the Sampaios or the Ruas.

The minutes of this memorable meeting should not be ended

without including in them the displeasure and disagreement of Dona Gisa over such limitations. She emphatically dissented from most of those ridiculous, foolish strictures, which, in her opinion, were deplorable, feudal remains of the Middle Ages. But Zé Sampaio, a man of the world, felt them necessary to protect the good name of the widow.

Everything indicated that Dr. Teodoro was an honorable man —his previous conduct, the elevated terms in which his letter was couched—yet, notwithstanding, the widow must be protected against any loophole. Just suppose the druggist, after spending day and night in the defenseless home of Dona Flor, after going about with her in the public gaze on trips and excursions, here, there, everywhere, the two alone, and then suddenly the scoundrel disappears, as had happened only too often in similar cases. Then what would become of the honor and the high regard in which the widow was held? From a widow who was exemplary in her seriousness and composure, Dona Flor would turn into the dead man's chamber pot, where anyone went to relieve himself and then kept on his way. Dona Gisa, with all her learning, could laugh at these customs, but he, José Sampaio, concerned with Dona Flor's moral well-being, was of the opinion that . . .

Middle Ages, feudalism, the Holy Inquisition. Who ever heard of a woman thirty years old, a widow, her own mistress, who earned her living thanks to her capability, having to have a witness on hand to receive a visit from her fiancé, a man past forty? Such backwardness was possible only in Brazil. In the United States it would cause hilarity.

Mr. Sampaio heard the *gringa* out in silence, looked at her steadily, and in his heart of hearts agreed with her: it was stupidity of the first water, all those precautions and witnesses; after all is said and done, when a person gives something that belongs to him to someone he wants to give it to, that is his or her own business. How good it would be if the *gringa*, so full of chatter and fancy ideas, were to put into practice her theories, her contempt for these conventions, for such childish notions. But what a hope! Lots of words and indignation, so much reading and learning, and she was a crag! At least until there was proof to the contrary. If she gave anything it was on the q.t., and how! Nobody, not even Dona Dinorá, had ever been able to adduce a suspicion that had any foundation, any fact, not even a suitor. Lots of talk, but no substance; the whole thing boiled down to nothing. The *gringa* smiling, pleased with life, with all the physical and moral signs of complete satisfaction, wanting for nothing, and the gossips wholly stymied, without being able to discover a flaw, no matter how much they pried.

God only knows, maybe she didn't, and was really a serious person, which was, after all, a kind of consolation, Mr. Sampaio concluded melancholically, at the same time he declared the meeting adjourned.

The next day, once more running counter to his usual habits, Mr. Sampaio set out for his shoestore late: he was waiting for Dr. Teodoro at the drugstore, discharging his obligation.

It was a cordial conversation, even though at the beginning it was a little difficult, awkward, reticent, Mr. Sampaio not knowing how to bring up the subject, Dr. Teodoro a novice in such situations. They reached an understanding, however, in mutual good will: the storekeeper completely sympathetic toward the cause, the druggist agreeable to any arrangement as long as it included marriage to the widow, for whom he felt the definitive passion of a mature man.

The meeting took place in the laboratory at the rear of the drugstore, seemingly protected from indiscreet glances and ears. But only seemingly; for at that very hour of the morning Dona Dinorá, in continual alert, observed the cautious approach of Mr. Sampaio, his lengthy visit in the alcove of the laboratory (not even a treatment for syphilis took that long), and stuck her nose in on the pretext of her injection for rheumatism (which, if the truth be told, was not due until the next day late in the afternoon).

The fright of the two conspirators on seeing her insolent face would have been confession enough; but, besides, she had caught a bit of conversation, a revealing statement by the dealer in shoes: "My dear doctor, it is a matter of congratulation for both of you, you and the lady. Both deserving . . ."

In less time than it takes to tell it, the news was making the rounds of the neighborhood, Dona Flor was receiving congratulations even before she knew the outcome of the mission so brilliantly accomplished by Mr. Zé Sampaio (who out of gratitude had, moreover, been chosen as best man at the religious ceremony).

On Saturday night, in tribute to the meeting of the suitor and the widow, a small, animated group had gathered in front of Dona Flor's house, the neighbors bold-facedly stationing themselves on the sidewalk in front of the Argentine's house, which gave them a vantage point directly into the living-room of the School of Savor and Art.

Dona Flor awaited the momentous visit smiling and calm, surrounded, as was proper, by her close relatives, in this case her aunt and uncle, and by her intimate friends (including Dona Dinorá, who had threatened war without quarter if she was not invited), three or four married couples, Dona Maria do Carmo and her daughter (as nervous as though she were getting engaged), and, in the best chair, Dr. Luís Henrique, an outstanding figure in public administration and national letters, a friend of the family, a rich relative, as it were. Outside, the group grew in numbers and conspicuousness.

Dr. Teodoro appeared on the dot, with the precision of his Swiss watch, with a swank that had to be seen to be believed, a flower in his buttonhole, a veritable fashion plate, sending a shiver of excitement through the gossips. Aunt Lita received him with a degree of formality. Then he greeted all the guests and took his place, according to strict protocol, on the sofa, beside Dona Flor.

Dona Flor was resplendent in a new dress, beautiful and unassuming in her modesty and blushes, all copper and gold. Nobody would have guessed, seeing her so calm, in such control of herself, how she was torn inwardly, consumed by suffering, how her desire had grown during those days of hope and doubt. At long last that grueling experience was approaching its end, the dark night, the desert of mourning and loneliness; once more she would help make the beast with two backs.

Dr. Teodoro sat down on the edge of the sofa, and the silence, the pause, the solemn moment that followed was unforgettable and very disconcerting. The druggist ran his eyes over the room full of people, Dona Norma smiled at him encouragingly. Then, getting to his feet again, and addressing Dona Flor and her aunt and uncle, he said how happy it would make him "if she would deign to accept him as her suitor, her husband after a brief interval, be willing to become his companion on life's road, a rocky road, full of obstacles and stumbling blocks, which would be turned into a paradise if he could count on her moral support and balm . . ."

It was the discourse of an orator, worthy of a university graduate or a politician, and revealed a hitherto unsuspected facet of Dr. Teodoro. "What a compendium of virtues," thought Dona Maria do Carmo who, of all those present, knew the suitor least. In the meantime, he went on, he felt himself on the threshold of paradise, merely at being there among her relatives and friends, who were the *raison d'être* of her life. What a pity her sister and brother were not present, her sister-in-law and brother-in-law, and, above all, that devoted and venerated woman, her saintly mother.

This unexpected reference to Dona Rozilda almost caused Dona Amélia to burst out laughing. "Just let him wait, and he will find out how saintly the old hag is." She covered her mouth with her hand, carefully avoiding meeting the eyes of Dona Norma or Dona Êmina.

In a word, Dr. Teodoro, in the presence of that distinguished assembly, was asking for Dona Flor's hand, asking that she become his wife. He put it so beautifully that Dona Norma could not restrain herself: she clapped her hands, to the indignation of Mr. Sampaio. Who had ever heard of applause at such moments, which call for the greatest sedateness? But Dona Flor restored order and harmony by getting to her feet, too, and holding out hand and cheek to her suitor, accepting his proposal: "I shall be happy to marry you."

He had barely brushed her cheek when there came an outburst of embraces, congratulations, good wishes, kisses from the women, the restless crowd in the street invading the house. And Dr. Teodoro had to listen to reproaches: "You deceiver! A saint of hollow wood!"

The neighbors, throwing aside all control, fell upon the table full of sweets and hors d'oeuvre. Marilda and the maid served homemade liqueurs of violets, currants, hog plums, guava, which led the druggist to make a teasing comment after tasting them: "Ah, these liqueurs are delicious. They were made by the nuns of the convent of Lapa, weren't they?"

By the taste he knew them, for they were identical with others he had tasted in other hospitable homes equally abounding in human warmth. People laughed, however, at his assurance, and even denied his hypothesis, considering it almost an insult: didn't he know Dona Flor's special gifts? She was not only a matchless cook, without rival at preparing sweetmeats, but also a mistress in the brewing of liqueurs: those of the nuns of Lapa, of Desterro, or Perdões, were syrups, drugstore syrups, doctor, not to be compared with those of your fiancée, not by a long shot.

The truth was, he confessed, he understood little about liqueurs, so he willingly accepted this criticism; as for her fame in the culinary art, that he did know. Not by chance was Dona Flor a teacher, and a highly competent one, a veritable artist when it came to seasoning. He had never had an opportunity to taste these delicacies, unfortunately, but now the hour of his redress was at hand. The trouble was that he would probably put on a lot of weight.

And so the engagement celebration moved merrily along. In the comings and goings of the guests, Dr. Teodoro happened to stop before the waiting-room of his hopes, the threshold of Dona Flor's bed. All embarrassed, he had no experience with courting and conquests, his intimate relations with women being limited to his weekly visit to Otaviana. If at one time the druggist had seen the tricky Tavinha Manemolência, receiving in addition to cash the flattery of sweet words, with the passing of time that arrangement had turned into a habit of politeness and cordiality, of agreeable attentions, with sweets and liqueurs, talk in bed, leave-taking of compliments and tenderness like a love affair or infatuation.

When it came time for him to go, Dona Flor held up her cheek for the chaste (or frightened or timid, but, above all, diffident) kiss of her fiancé. But she felt his hand tremble as she touched his damp fingers. She wondered if Dr. Teodoro was also aflame within, as she was.

That night Dona Flor dreamed of him, and only of him, and she saw him as a dark giant, strong, invincible, broad-chested, really groovy, as Dona Gisa had said, smacking her lips; he came and took her.

Thus the betrothal of Dona Flor took place. In all the neighboring streets this was the sole topic of conversation. Moreover, it aroused no discussion, merely unanimous approval. Not a dissenting voice was heard: everyone approved of the espousal of the druggist and the widow, made for one another, as the general consensus put it.

The first thing Dona Flor did was to set a date less than half a year away for their marriage. This was one of the few objections raised by her fiancé. Why such a long time, Dr. Teodoro wanted to know, when there was no trousseau to be prepared, and there were no problems to settle? Friends and neighbors shared his opinion, and finally Dona Flor came around to his way of thinking and reduced the period of timidity, of restrained desire to three months.

Three months of peace and harmony while they became accustomed to one another (easily, and better with each passing day). During this period, in their evenings of prolonged conversations shared with Dona Norma or some other friend, they decided all the details of their life together, which lay in the near future.

They were in agreement on remaining in Dona Flor's house, not only because it was very convenient for Dr. Teodoro, being close to the drugstore, but also because Dona Flor flatly refused to give up her school, as he had suggested. The drugstore brought in enough for them to live on in modest comfort—argued Dr. Teodoro—so why should she keep up that drudgery? But Dona Flor had become used to it and would not know what to do without her students, the noisy groups, the laughs, the diplomas, the speech and the tears when graduation day came, and without having her own money. No, she would not listen to another word about it.

Aside from that, they were in complete agreement. Even the iron bed, for which she had a secret affection, finding its old-fashioned air to her liking, and being a little fearful of its fate—perhaps the doctor would not like to sleep in the bed where her first husband had possessed her so many times—did not come up for discussion. When, as they went over accounts, they made up a list of things to buy to refurbish the house (a desk where the druggist could write out his notes and keep his papers, for example), they went over the house piece by piece before deciding; when they reached the bedroom, he suggested a new mattress, finding the old one full of bumps. There were new spring mattresses on the market, recently introduced, just wonderful. He had one of them, but it was for a single bed. As for the bed, wouldn't the thing to do be to paint it, as they were going to paint the house and certain pieces of furniture? And that was all there was to it.

They got used to one another, and Dona Flor already felt a tenderness toward that quiet, kindly man, a little on the solemn side, and systematic, expecting everything in its place and at a fixed hour, but who was incapable of rudeness, all attention and undoubtedly dying for love of her. Already, on arriving and leaving (and he came every day, that nonsense, so sternly criticized by Dona Gisa of three visits a week having gone by the board), he kissed her lightly on the lips. With his strong mouth he barely brushed hers. She felt a desire to bite him, give him a real kiss.

One night they had gone to the movies, but, as happened every time they went out with Mr. Ruas, they arrived late. The picture had begun, and the theater was so full they could not find four seats together. Dona Flor and Dr. Teodoro had to sit far forward, too close to see the film well, but they were alone and holding hands. There came a moment when he gently brushed her lips, but she opened hers and devoured him. It was the first real kiss they had exchanged, the caress of a man and a woman, the others had been mere osculation, not kisses. There was still a week to go, with the ceremony before judge and priest. That kiss, as it were, was the inauguration of their intimacy, doing away with the modesty and shyness of the most ceremonious courtship.

It was that kiss that Dona Flor dreamed of every night, giving, in her insomnia, full due to Dona Gisa: if they were to be married in a few days, why the devil could they not satisfy the hunger and thirst that devoured them? They did not do so, naturally, nor did they ever mention the subject or even remotely allude to it. That kiss, however, gave rise to others, and the hands clasped one another tighter, their heads came together in the movies. That night Dona Flor slept quietly, a refreshing sleep, after many months.

Thus Dona Flor, modest and gentle, came to the day of her second marriage. The house was simply beautiful, like new with the fresh coat of paint, a glittering wreath of lights shining over the sign of the school. A different arrangement of the old furniture, adding to it the new articles they had bought, with the desk and the swivel chair; the iron bed (blue now) with its spring mattress, marvel of marvels, a dream.

From the living-room walls the photographs in color of Dona Flor and her first husband had been removed. In their stead, the evening before the wedding, a picture of the druggist in the midst of his graduating class was hung, and he smiled down in his academic robes.

It did not look right for the dead man to preside over the household, Dona Norma told Dona Flor confidentially. She was right, but Dona Flor did not want just her picture on the wall, that picture taken when she was a girl, without any sense, a silly, anxious girl, at an age when she was suffering, the wife of a gambler; not the Dona Flor of today, a little plumper and more poised, the wife of a doctor, ripe for the conquest of happiness.

Everyone said the same without exception—the crowd of guests that filled the church to overflowing, including the banker Celestino, who was so busy, and who arrived late, just as at her first marriage—at that last moment in the Church of St. Benedict. At the beginning of that moonlit night, when the couple was about to enter the taxi that was to take them outside the city, to their honeymoon site in the quietude of São Tomé de Paripe, on the blue-green gulf of the Bay of All Saints, with countless stars, the chirping of crickets and the chorale of the treetoads, everyone, even Dona Rozilda, said: "This time she has picked the winning number. She is going to be happy."

This time, they all agreed, without exception.

IV

OF DONA FLOR'S LIFE,
ORDERLY AND PEACEFUL,
WITHOUT FEARS OR SORROWS

IN THE WORLD OF PHARMACOLOGY AND AMATEUR MUSICIANS,
GLOWING IN THE DRAWING-ROOMS AND THE
CHORUS OF NEIGHBORS REMINDING HER
OF HER HAPPINESS

(With Dr. Teodoro Madureira in a bassoon solo)

THE AMATEUR ORCHESTRA,
SONS OF ORPHEUS,

*takes great pleasure in inviting your Excellency and
distinguished family to the concert marking the sixth anniversary
of its founding, to be held in the garden of the mansion
of Mr. and Mrs. Taveira Pires, Largo da Graça, 5,
at eight thirty p.m. this coming Sunday.*

PROGRAM

Part 1

1

Berger. *Amoureuse.* Waltz.

2

Franz Schubert. *Marche Militaire.*

3

E. Gillet. *Loin du Bal.* Waltz.

4

Franz Drdla. *Souvenir.* Violin solo with piano accompaniment.

Dr. Venceslau Veiga, soloist. Mr. Helio Basto at the piano.

5

Oscar Strauss. *Waltz Dream.* Medley.

Part II

1

Francis Thomé.   *Simple Aveu.*

2

Othelo Araújo.   *Elegy.*   Violoncello solo, accompanied by orchestra.

Comendador Adriano Pires, soloist.

3

Graziano–Walter.   *Gemito Appassionato.*

4

Agenor Gomes.   *Lullaby for Florípedes.*   Romance
with bassoon solo and orchestra accompaniment.

Dr. Teodoro Madureira, soloist.

5

Franz Lehár.   *The Merry Widow.*   Medley.

Pianist-conductor: Master Agenor Gomes.

1

Having checked once more the complete order and irreproachable cleanliness of the room, Dona Filó went out slowly with her obese gait: "Now make yourselves at home, my angels. I do not need to wish you good night." Even when she was trying to be malicious, she was merely kindly and maternal. She had known Dr. Teodoro while he was still a student, a classmate of her son, Dr. João Batista. "Including you, do you know how many newlyweds have spent their honeymoon in this room since we have been here in São Tomé? Seventeen . . . or is it eighteen? I've sort of lost count."

Patting Dona Flor's cheek and giving the druggist a wink: "Sleep well, without waking up once," followed by a hearty laugh that made her jowls shake, echoed through the house, bringing a grumble from Dr. Pimenta in the room across the way: "There's Filó tormenting the guests."

"Go on to bed, woman. Let folks alone."

"I'm just making sure they've got everything," and with a last look from the door: "My turtledoves . . ."

Dona Flor and Dr. Teodoro turned toward one another in that enormous room, embarrassed, inhibited. An inhibition which had been growing throughout the day with the wisecracks of friends, the quips of the students. Such silly jokes, the double-meaning remarks of the neighbors. Both at the civil ceremony and in the church each of the guests had tried to outdo the other in sly witticisms. Those of the banker Celestino were fit to make your hair stand on end, that foul-mouthed Portuguese. Even as the taxi was moving off, he was still teasing and getting off dissolute jests. It was always so at the wedding of a widow, seasoned with rude merriment and spiced with coarse witticisms. Even Dona Filó, the kindest and most hospitable person in the world, laid aside her normal seriousness to make jokes, advising the druggist not to overdo things. There in the room their inhibition grew. Completely ill at ease, they stood silent, without even looking at one another, like two yokels.

Dr. Teodoro went over to the big French windows opening out over the garden, with the evident intention of closing them. Through them the night flooded the room: moonlight, glitter of stars, the croaking of frogs, the slithering of crabs, the phosphorescent glow of fish like blades of steel cutting the darkness of the sea, and the dark-blue moth, with gold spots, obstinately circling the light. The breeze came from among the coconut and mango trees, in muted puffs, bats knocking off sapodilla plums in their low flight of shadows and ghosts over the morass of crickets and frogs.

Dona Flor, impulsively—the barrier that separated them had to be breached, that first, silly impasse—came over beside her husband, leaning over the sill of the window. Dr. Teodoro, overcoming his timidity, clasped her to his breast. With his free hand, he pointed out the moonlit night, in the distance: "Do you see, my dear?" The "dear" came out with difficulty, he had to make an effort. "Way up there? That's the Southern Cross."

To think that she had always wanted to see it, ever since she had been a child!

"Where? Show it to me, my dear."

She raised her voice to say "my dear," and then repeated as though to herself: "My dear . . ." Dr. Teodoro enlightened her: "There . . . look . . . my dear."

Why, my dear, this fear, this shyness? Why don't you take me in your arms, kiss my mouth, carry me to the bed? Don't you see how impatiently I am waiting, can't you observe the hunger in my face, the uneven beating of my heart, can't you sense my eagerness? Dona Flor, too, was discovering stars in her nocturnal sky, a secret astronomy.

Beside her, at the window, holding her to his breast, Dr. Teodoro was wondering how to proceed so as not to hurt her, not to offend her by his indecency or crudeness. Take care, Teodoro, don't rush, relax: you can lose all by being a beast, you can give this model woman a shock from which she may never recover. Never confuse your wife with a shameless wench, with a prostitute whom you pay to satisfy your desires, your vice, of whom you can take advantage and toward whom you can behave without restraint of decorum or modesty. Whores and their miserable calling exist to satisfy man's licentiousness. Wives are meant for love. And love, you well know, Teodoro, is a blend of many things, all different and important. Including desire, but a desire of the spirit as well as of the fle .h; take care not to turn it sordid and obscene. A wife calls for prudence, especially when it comes to such delicate matters, and the wedding night is always a definitive point of departure for a happy or unhappy life. Especially when the wife has had the bitter experience of a previous disastrous marriage.

From what he had heard, that first experience had been not only bitter but also harrowing and cruel, all suffering and humiliation. For that very reason you must be so delicate and tender a husband as to efface from the heart of your wife all trace of the memory of villany or lack of respect. Yes, he would give her everything she had lacked and never cause for suffering and humiliation.

During that hour of contained desire, seeking understanding and tenderness, each with his deceptions, in a web of misunderstanding, feeling his path blindly, the courageous astronauts set out for the sky, and thus were able to find in the orbit of the stars the calm they needed and a certain intimacy.

Dr. Teodoro was familiar with the map of the heavens, the map of the world; he knew the names of constellations, satellites, and comets, the number and size of the stars in the galaxies. With his finger he pointed out in the far reaches of the infinite the purest star, then gathered it in, so to speak, with his knowledge and his large hand. There he put it, on the edge of the window, in the little hand of his wife.

That wedding night he gave her what no lover had ever presented to another: a necklace of stars with their divine light and size, weight, and measure, their position in space, their ellipsis and exact distance. With his doctoral finger he selected them from the sky, arranging them in the order of size; the diaphanous stars glowed on Dona Flor's neck.

That big star in your hair, almost blue, lifted from the edge of the horizon, the one that shines the brightest, the largest of all—ah, my dear, that is the planet Venus, wrongly known as the evening star when it lights up after sunset and at night, and as the morning star when it rises with the dawn over the sea. In Latin, my beloved, it is called *stella maris*, the star which guides the mariners.

This was not a lesson in cosmography, pedantic and naïve, no; it was the height of gallantry, his way of conquering his timidity and offering her the magic of the night and his love. Dona Flor, all covered with stars and learning, her head resting on the doctor's breast, now more at ease and taking delight in this knowledge, asked: "Isn't Venus the goddess of love, too? The one without arms?"

It was something quite different she would have wanted to say: "With her light over our bed, she is our lucky star; don't be afraid, my dear, you will not offend me if you take me with wild ardor, if you tear off without thought, in a burst of passion, this dress which Rosália sent me from Rio, if you stretch me out naked covered only with stars, and mount me and we set out, mare and stallion, through this field of mangoes and cashews, this sea of canoes and skiffs."

But where was she to find the courage to say this?

Smiling, the doctor pressed her hand boldly; it was trembling. "Yes, she was the goddess of love in Greek mythology, and that famous statue, the work of a classic genius . . ."

Dona Flor sensed once more that he, too, lacked the daring to be bold and wild enough to break the wall that separated them. Such a big man who knew so much and didn't know how to take her and make her his. As for her, ah, Teodoro, no matter how great her longing, it was not her place to take the initiative. She had already almost gone beyond the established limits, for it was not the role of the wife to urge on, incite her husband without being considered a hussy, a competitor of a whore, lost to shame. It is a husband's place, Teodoro, my love.

By fits and starts he continued his effort. Having already given her a necklace of stars with which to adorn herself, he now offered her the wealth of the monopolies of this world, and, in addition, the struggle of the people against the trusts.

"They say that near here there is a huge underground deposit of oil, huge, so rich that it could make our country immensely powerful . . ."

Rivers of oil, derricks, drilling, wells, all at the feet of Dona Flor; what would he not have given her that night of their wedding!

"I had heard about it, from Uncle Porto, who taught near here."

Dona Flor rested her head on the breast of her husband. There outside was the night, perfumed with jasmine, the same that had accompanied them on their trip from the mansion of Dr. Pimenta to the house of Dona Filó in the outskirts of São Tomé de Paripe. A moonlit night with the sky almost within hand-reach and alive with stars that seemed to spring one from the other, some anonymous, others classified in the polymorphous erudition of the druggist ("Only Dona Gisa can equal him in learning"):

". . . right there, above the genipaps, is Orion . . ."

The full moon creased the dark, thick water of the sea, as black as oil, the water of the gulf in quiet gentleness. The sailing lights of skiffs, wavering, red comets on the route to the plantations of green cane and tobacco, along the banks of the Paraguaçu River, where old cities and towns had been in a state of decline for years.

An inland sea, gently calm, listless, still, with a gentle breeze blowing between the jackfruit and breadfruit trees. Dona Flor feasted her eyes on the beauty of the moonlight on the water, the sand, the canoes, the skiffs. A sea of repose and peace.

Not the ocean-sea, beyond the bar, fierce and dangerous, with waves and underwater currents, deceptive tides, the open sea where the winds blow free, wild tempests—detouring on the way to the little houses of assignation in Itapoã, where love bursts out in hallelujah. A sea of boundless violence; not this sweet scent of jasmine, but of high tide, the bold smell of sargassum, of algae and oysters, of salt. Why recall it?

Why recall it, when that night in Paripe was so pleasant, with stars, a full moon, a dark, calm sea, and the peace of the world over the shy couple? Teodoro, show me quickly more stars, crush with your voice and your learning the memories of a dark past, dead and buried. Trace in your constellation of light our long and pleasurable pathway, this calm river, this backwater, this living in the shelter of a gulf, this happy life which we will slowly begin today. Dona Flor shivered, her eyes damp.

"You are cold, you are shivering, my dear. How foolish to stand here exposed to the night air; dangerous, really, one can pick up a cold, grippe. Let's go in and close the windows." Dr. Teodoro smiled his warm smile and asked a little abashed: "Don't you think it is time, my love?"

She, too, laughed, half hidden behind him, as though playing a game part shy, part provocative: "You are the boss, sir." He was so agreeable and polite, a kindly giant, she felt his support, his protection. She put her arm through his: he was her husband, a good man, strong, and self-possessed, such as she needed. A real husband, upright. Like that gulf, without storms, without violence, but— who knows?—perhaps with hidden stars, unsuspected riches, unforeseen.

They put the wooden bars across the windows, she helping him. The night became small and intimate in the room, a refuge adapted to the timidity of the couple. Dear God, now what is going to happen? Dona Flor asked herself as they finished.

To have something to do, Dona Flor started putting away her clothes and his in the closets. At the foot of the bed, the two pairs of bedroom slippers, the doctor's fine yellow pajamas and her nightgown of lace and ruffles, which was Dona Ênaide's gift to the bride, a masterpiece of cambric. Dona Ênaide was an artist, and with that delicate confection of embroidery she made peace with her friend, burying under forgetfulness that matter of Dr. Aluísio, country lawyer and lecher, a make-believe doctor.

Dr. Teodoro—ah, that was a real doctor with diploma and ring —watched her comings and goings to the closet. She had showed him the nightgown, holding it up to her shoulders. "Pretty, isn't it?" and he, looking at it and her, felt a chill at the back of his neck.

"Be careful, my lad, don't risk everything with a rough gesture, a strong word . . . ," the bridegroom told himself again and again. Prudence and tact must be the order of the day during those seven days of their honeymoon in the paradise of São Tomé, in distant Paripe, in the home of the Pimentas. Seven days there, of sea and garden, leisure and voluptuousness, but the honeymoon—that must last all their life.

He longed to say to Dona Flor: "Our honeymoon is going to last all our life." Why, then, so timid and shy? It was as though all that intimacy they had acquired with difficulty during their courtship had suddenly disappeared. Nevertheless, they were married, with the blessing of the friar of St. Benedict and the congratulations of the gaunt judge and musician, and before they were married they had exchanged kisses, avid, thrilling, in the movies, at home, feeling longing and ardor, consumed by desire. Why now this embarrassment, incapable of word or deed, like two blockheads, when here they were alone at last, man and wife at the moment of completing and effecting their union? What he wanted to say to her, to his love, was: "Our honeymoon will last our lifetime," and all he could bring out in the hope of undoing that knot of torment and silence was: "While you are undressing, I will go in there . . ."

He set off for the bathroom, carrying his pajamas and bedroom slippers, almost at a run.

Dona Flor got herself ready quickly in front of the mirror, listening to her husband running the water for his bath. As for her, she was perfumed with heliotrope toilet water and scent (which Dona Dagmar had told her went best with her complexion). Over her bare body, over her smooth belly, only the perfume and the black lace of the transparent cambric nightgown. An almost lascivious gleam of desire lighted up her normally modest eyes and made her tremble and fearful. She hid her desire and beauty, the transparent lace and ruffles under the chaste sheet to which the smell of lavender lent a touch of homeliness and innocence.

Dr. Teodoro returned, a study in yellow, fascinating; he looks bigger in his pajamas, Dona Flor thought. "He's really enormous!" He carried over his arm his wedding suit—striped trousers, a coat of heather mixture—and he put out the light of the crystal chandelier, leaving only the tremulous glow of the oil lamp before the saints in the old chapel.

"He's not going to see me when I take off my nightgown." He was not going to see her youthful body, like that of an untouched virgin, with its terse breasts, for she had never nursed a baby, a belly free from the laxity caused by pregnancy, without the discoloration often left by being with child, and its rose of copper and velvet.

But what did it matter? He would see her body when the night ride was over, when the dawn crept in with its pale morning light. Now all that mattered was that he feel her young, impassioned, and forever his. Feeling him near, Dona Flor closed her eyes, her heart beating wildly.

She imagined, however, what it would be like, for she had been married, and even before that, she had known a man in a tempest-tossed, sea-spray-scented bed. She knew exactly what it would be like, for she had a faithful, detailed memory of it in her thoughts and in every fiber of her body. In just a minute he, her new husband, crossing the frontiers of good breeding and modesty, jettisoning sheets and nightgown, in a whirlwind of caresses and words, wildly, in a gale of famished mouths, knowing hands, would withdraw her from her modesty and shame, reaching the subsoil of her moist truth. She felt her husband's body alongside hers in the bed.

She had always had to be conquered anew each time. She withdrew into herself, enclosing herself in shame that covered like gnarled bark the heartwood of her desire. It was a barrier that had to be overcome, bringing to the surface her woman's desire, her hidden craving. Now, however, after so many months of upright widowhood (oh, young and deprived), months that had been an endless waste of insomnia, when not tormented by harrowing dreams in streets filled with whores, lacerating nights, constantly on guard, now this hard outer sheath would be transformed into a frail, tenuous veil that would yield at the first touch.

Her heart leaping in her breast, her eyes closed, she waited for the abrupt gesture of her husband throwing off sheet and night-gown, revealing all. For, as she had learned at the price of her lost cherry, who ever heard of screwing in a nightgown, the body dressed or covered with even the most transparent cambric, who had ever heard of such nonsense?

Then she learned differently, not anything absurd, but something completely different. Instead of uncovering her, he covered himself too, and, under the sheets, took her in his arms. He drew her head over (the hair so black it was almost blue) and rested it against his breast as broad as the port docks, kissing her tenderly on the cheek and then on the mouth in a kiss such as Dona Flor had foreseen and awaited.

Taken by surprise, she let herself go, and with this kiss the frail, tenuous veil of her shame gave way. Her husband's hand descended from her hip to her leg, above the nightgown, till it reached the bottom; then, hardly giving Dona Flor time to put aside and forget her modesty, he lifted up lace and ruffles. Without wasting time undressing her and undressing himself, or in debauched caresses befitting a whore's bed, always under cover of the sheet, he mounted her and then possessed her with pleasure, strength, and delight. It was all very quick and modest, so to speak; completely different from what she had known before, and for that very reason she was lost and out of step with him in this silent, almost austere coupling. She had barely untethered herself in the pastures of desire when she heard the cry of victory of her husband at the far end of the meadow. Dona Flor was left with a sense of defeat, oppressed, almost on the point of tears.

That occasion of such lack of synchronization made it possible for Dona Flor to measure, with the yardstick of suffering and need, the gamut of emotions and the delicacy of Dr. Teodoro.

As has been pointed out, he had no experience in bed play with a wife (being a bachelor), and almost none with a mistress or lover, his dealings being only with whores, in which he ran no risk of a commitment that would make him break his promise. Even the dark, clean Otaviana, for a long time the only door open to his gratification, the vessel in which each week he left his masculine mite, never represented a tender attachment or an ardent passion, nothing more than a refined need, a habit that concorded with the monogamous nature of the doctor.

Moreover, it is also known that the doctor firmly subscribed to and was guided by that catechism, today (Praise be to God!) supplanted, which presented the wife as a sensitive flower, compounded of chastity and innocence, worthy of the greatest respect; for shamelessness, for unbridled pleasures of the body, there were the whores and that was what they were paid for. With them, paying the price, one could release all the brakes, without causing them offense or suffering; they were sterile ground, arid fields. But never with the wife; discretion was called for where she was concerned, pure love, beautiful and upright (and a little flat): the wife is the mother of our children.

But even so, hampered by these obsolete dogmas, in spite of his limitations and ignorance, he realized that he had left Dona Flor unsatisfied and tense.

Now, as has already been set down before, in his weekly visit to Otaviana, there were times when Dr. Teodoro gladly played a return engagement. And so he did with Dona Flor in that monumental bed of heavy rosewood, redolent of lavender, on their marriage night, in the house of the Pimentas. It should be added, moreover, that he repeated it with the greatest pleasure, not out of a sense of duty, and delighted to have the opportunity for this encore. Careful and thoughtful, this time he did not leave her on the outer edge of satisfaction, but full to overflowing.

He achieved this in spite of his minimal experience with such subtle calculations and measures, for he had never been the least bit interested in whether Otaviana or any other had been satisfied. What he had done then was to satisfy himself with complete expertise, for he had come for that and was paying for that, not for the wench's pleasure.

He knew, nevertheless, how to proceed step by step with Dona Flor as her passion grew, all this play giving him great delight, a pleasure such as he had never experienced, not even when, rather to humor Tavinha in nights given up to debauchery than on his own initiative, he had permitted himself certain lewd indulgences of the sort that can be practiced only with a demimondaine or a whore, never with a wife. With a wife it was different; one reserved for her a love comprised of things that were clean, a serene possession, almost secret, pure, modest. But not because modest, less pleasurable, as Dr. Teodoro could bear witness when he heard Dona Flor let out a grateful sigh as she murmured his name: "Teodoro, my love."

He hurried to overtake her, and so he did, and they finally met in a close embrace and a profound kiss. Enveloped in moans, sighs, lassitude, and cold, for the sheet, in the blaze of that meeting, had slipped off the bed, leaving them disconcerted, Dona Flor burgeoning in honey, her private parts visible (and how beautiful they were, as Dr. Teodoro took in at a timid glance, a mere peep).

Grateful for so many boons and pleasure, he kissed her feverish face and covered her body against the cold with the modest sheet and warm spread. Then, at last, he could tell her all he felt and he did so with the outpouring of his soul, a happy husband: "Our honeymoon will last forever. I will be faithful to you all my life, my dear, I shall never look at another woman: I shall love you until the hour of my death."

"Amen," repeated the toads and bullfrogs in that night of moon and nuptials in Paripe. "Amen, amen." It sounded like a bassoon solo.

"I, too, all our life," she answered, convinced of what she was saying, satisfied and delivered from her suffering, but not weary; quite the contrary, capable of new spurts if he set spurs to her.

But Dr. Teodoro, settling down under the sheet and spread remarked: "How funny! When a little while ago Dona Filó insisted on giving us something to eat, I wasn't hungry. Now, however, I would like something sweet, did you ever hear of anything so silly?"

"If you want me to, I'll go and get you something. She has all kinds of desserts and fruit. I'm going . . ."

"Indeed you're not! Don't even think of such a thing."

Then he realized what it was: not hunger, but the habit of eating some tidbit before leaving Tavinha at night; sheer indulgence. Imagine profaning his relations with his wife by continuing a

habit he had fallen into in a whorehouse! God forbid and stand
over him! In a last (and chaste) kiss, he bade her good night:
"Sleep well, dear, you must be dead tired. It has been a wearisome
day."

He was on the point of saying: "It has been a wearisome
night," but still afraid of offending her, he kept the remark to
himself, stretched out, and went straight to sleep.

Dona Flor did not go to sleep at once; the fact of the matter is
that she had counted on a white night, lasting until morning, blaze
following blaze, with her husband riding miles and miles astride
her body. Beside her Dr. Teodoro snored, breathing deeply, a
strong vibration. That snoring rounded out his manly figure: a
mighty, noble, handsome man, her husband.

She ran her hand over his broad chest, his calm face, lightly so
as not to awaken him. What she wanted was to wrap herself in
him, go to sleep in his arms, held between his legs. But she didn't
dare. Each man is different; there are no two alike, as she was
assured by certain of her students who had a vast experience to
draw upon, like that depraved Maria Antonia, who asseverated:
"There are no two men who are alike in bed. Each one has his own
way of killing fleas, his taste, his specialty. Some are skilled, others
are not. But if one knows how to make the most of them, ah, they
are all good, and with any one of them, foolish or wise, rough or
delicate, you can get your satisfaction and water the flower."

Another type of man, different, the opposite. All tact, understanding, so affectionate, tender! It was a wife's place to mold
herself to the manner and liking of the husband, fit into him
completely, exactly. It had been harder the other time, and she had
managed. So why not now, when it was much easier?

The two of them, Dr. Teodoro and Dona Flor, had all they
needed for a pleasant, happy life. Not only was that the general
opinion; Dona Flor was aware of it.

The perfume of the garden seeped in through the cracks of the
windows. Outside the serene night lay over the gulf, without
boisterous winds, sudden storms, disturbances, the unforeseen; all
calm. A happy life, stable, assured, without privations or waste,
without fear or bitterness, humiliation or suffering. Finally, after so

many ups and downs, Dona Flor was to know the taste of happiness.

"Teodoro," she murmured, her heart warm and confident. "All will be well; all will come out right."

The chorus of frogs answered on their enchanted bassoons: "Amen! Amen!"

This was the night in Paripe, with stars and the riding lights of the fishing skiffs.

2

Dona Flor always had been considered and had considered herself a good housekeeper, orderly and punctual, giving thought to everything. A good housekeeper and a good director of her cooking school, where she took on herself all responsibility, with the aid of a flighty, lazy maid and the friendly cooperation of young Marilda, eager to learn recipes and seasoning. She had never had a complaint about a student, which would have perturbed the calm of her classes. Except, of course, the incidents when her first husband was alive, for, as we already know full well, the departed had had no consideration for schedules or other people's obligations. Nor was delicacy his strong point; his carryings-on with the students had more than once created difficulties and problems for Dona Flor, headaches, if not actual infidelity.

But the truth was that she, Dona Flor, had not the least notion of order and method, was far from having the necessary guidelines and schedule in her house and the school, in her very existence. She had to live with Dr. Teodoro to realize that what she looked upon as order was anarchy, her concern niggardly and insufficient, that everything went along any old which way, without rule or control.

Dr. Teodoro did not lay down the law and set up the controls immediately and sternly; he did not even refer to them. Being a calm and wary person, with a good upbringing, he was not in the habit of imposing his authority. Nor did he. Nevertheless, he obtained everything he wanted without showing impatience, without anyone feeling offended; a gentle operator was our druggist.

You should have seen the house a month and a half after the honeymoon. What a difference! Different, too, was Dona Flor, trying to adapt herself to her husband, her lord and master, to measure up to his standards. If in her the change was an inner one, more subtle, less visible, it was apparent in the house: one only needed to look.

The change began with the maid. Dona Flor had taken her on at the advice of her neighbors shortly after she was left a widow: "Whoever heard of a young, decent widow living alone in a house, with nobody to look after her, protect her against thieves or good-for-nothings?" She was not happy about her choice, accepting, at Dona Jacy's urging, that Sofia, so thick-witted-looking, but at bottom as shrewd as could be at doing as little as possible, with the complete slovenliness of one who feels herself sure of her job, for Dona Flor was not a person to fire anyone, especially someone recommended by a neighbor and a friend. Even though she took a dim view of Sofia's laziness and incompetence, Dona Flor had got along with her, even feeling sorry for her; of little account, true, but not bad-hearted.

Now it so happened that the fifth day after their return from that tender week of their honeymoon in Paripe, Dona Flor had to hurry out to Rio Vermelho, where Dona Lita was having one of her bad attacks of asthma. That night Dr. Teodoro went to visit the patient and bring his wife home. But since her aunt was still suffering and as it was a Friday (there were no classes on Saturday), Dona Flor decided to stay on to look after the old people. She would not come back until Sunday afternoon when the spell eased and Aunt Lita could return to her garden.

Dona Flor was away for less than three days, and during that brief space of time the house had been transformed so that it seemed totally different. To begin with the maid, who really was different. Instead of Sofia, that dirty mulatta with her sad, feeble-minded air, there was in her place one Madalena, a dark, middle-aged woman, clean and strong. If it had not been for the darkness of her skin and the kinkiness of her hair, one would have said she was a relative of the doctor, as tall and active as he, courteous in her manners and diligent in her work.

Dr. Teodoro explained in his firm but polite voice that he had been obliged to dismiss Sofia. In addition to being very inefficient, she did not obey him, answering with a toss of her head and insolent grumbling his firm orders to give the house, which was never properly kept, a thorough cleaning. He had not consulted Dona Flor because he did not want to bother her with that trifle when she was so worried about her sick aunt, and, moreover, because the ungrateful creature needed to be thrown out at once, for he was not prepared to listen to insults or impudence on the part of a servant. When he gave orders for the house to be swept, the loud-mouthed creature had gone into the hall growling, calling him Dr. Physic.

Dona Flor was somewhat taken aback; it had never entered her head to dismiss Sofia in spite of her slovenliness and lack of manners.

"The poor thing." She felt sorry for her, and to dismiss her without first talking with Dona Jacy, who had sent her! At the same time, how could she overlook the fact that Dr. Teodoro was so right? It was not possible for her husband, a man of standing and position, to tolerate fits of sullenness on the part of a servant which she, a woman and a patient one, could overlook.

"Poor thing?" Dr. Teodoro repeated in wonder. "An impudent baggage, unworthy of your kindness, my love. At times, Flor, meaning to be kind one winds up being foolish."

And Dona Jacy? If anyone owed apologies to anyone, it was Dona Jacy to Dona Flor, for the impudence of sending her a worthless piece like that. Not satisfied with taking advantage of the kindness of her mistress, the creature had tried to make fun of her employer.

Dona Flor understood that the doctor had not brought up the subject for the purpose of arguing it; he was merely informing her how he had handled the matter: there was now a man in the house, the lord and master, she thought to herself. She smiled: "My husband, my lord." He had done right; she could not permit any lack of respect for her husband. "Dr. Physic!" Who ever heard of such impudence!

Moreover, one point admitted of no discussion; the new servant was a marvel. Dr. Teodoro had not taken her at the request of a neighbor; he had demanded references, which he had checked by telephone. This, indeed, was order and efficiency.

Not merely exemplary cleanliness. Every new broom sweeps clean. But everything in its place, really in its proper place, not here today, tomorrow there, never knowing where to find the objects of daily use, which Dona Flor found confusing in her classes: "Marilda, my dear, have you seen my recipe book? Sofia doesn't know where she put it. It's gone."

With her hands in the sauce, she would call out: "Sofia, where did you put the beater? Good heavens! Everything in this house disappears."

The doctor chose with unusual competence and taste a proper place for everything, and gave strict orders to the maid: when the classes were over and the kitchen cleaned up, he wanted every utensil in the place he had assigned it with a sign carefully lettered: "bread knife," "egg slicer," "grater," "mortar," etc., etc. and not only the things used in the school, but those of the house as well: "radio," "vase," "decanters," "drawer for Dr. Teodoro's shirts," "drawer for Madame's underwear."

"Good heavens," Dona Flor said, overwhelmed by so much efficiency. "And to think I thought I kept the house in order. It was a mess, a perfect jumble. Teodoro, my dear, you have worked a miracle."

"No miracle, my dear, just a little order that was needed. It so happened that with my mother paralyzed, I had to take charge of the house, and I got used to orderliness. In our house we have to be even more methodical, as it is both a residence and a school. And you are determined to keep up the school. As far as I am concerned, as I told you, I would give up this work. You don't need it. I earn enough for . . ."

"We have already talked that out, Teodoro, and we agreed to say no more about it. Why bring it up again?"

"You are right, Flor, and forgive me for insisting. I will not discuss the subject again unless you bring it up. Don't worry, my dear, and forgive me. I did not want to annoy you . . ."

It was "my dear" this and "my dear" that, all with affection and politeness, for Dr. Teodoro was of the opinion that gracious behavior and courtesy go hand in hand with love, are indispensable to it. He never addressed his wife except with affectionate attention, expecting the same affable treatment in return. He came over and kissed her cheek, apologizing for having alluded to the unpleasant subject.

While they had still been engaged, he had suggested to Dona Flor, as we have already mentioned, closing the school, putting an end to classes and students, diplomas and recipes, the morning and afternoon sessions. Presenting an itemized list of his holdings in the firm of drugs and medicines, Dr. Teodoro had showed her, leaving no room for doubt, how unnecessary it was to keep on with the school, for Dona Flor had no need of money of her own for expenses and even extravagances; fortunately, he was in a position to guarantee both the necessary and the superfluous, touches of modest luxury, without the prodigality of spendthrifts, to be sure, but without penny-pinching either. She had no call to work any more; when the druggist had asked for her hand he was prepared to support her, meet all her expenses. Which was not a difficult undertaking, as she was not given to squandering or waste.

Dona Flor refused. She stood her ground, kept up the school, suspending classes only during the brief period of her honeymoon in São Tomé. Let us take advantage of the interruption to say that, on the return of the couple, the flibbertigibbet students made the teacher the target of their jokes, indulged in a veritable spree of laughter and malicious remarks, at times indecent, and, in the case of Maria Antonia, frankly disagreeable, for the hussy wanted to know "which of the two could take the most and which had the stronger and sweeter gadget."

Coming back, however, to the doctor's talk during their courtship, Dona Flor put an end to the question: she would rather remain a widow than close the school. Accustomed to working since she was a child, she had got into the way of having her own money. If this had not been the case, how would she have managed during her first marriage and widowhood?

When she had run off with Vadinho, she had had a little money saved up, and with that she had paid for the furniture and the license and papers, the deposit on the apartment, and the expenses of the first days. And if it had not been for the school, what would she have done when she was so unexpectedly left a widow? The departed had left nothing except debts; not a branch of a bank in Salvador but held a note with his sprawling signature; no friend or acquaintance on whom the chiseler had not put the bite. Moreover, he had cashed in his checks during carnival, always a period of large, burdensome expenses.

If it had not been for the school, Dona Flor would have found herself destitute, without a penny for the funeral and other requirements. For all these reasons she set so much store by her work, her savings hidden in secret places.

So let's say no more, my dear, about closing the school. If you want me with the School of Savor and Art operating, I am yours; be patient; if I do not satisfy this wish of yours, ask me for something else. I will cover you with kisses, throw myself into your arms, but I am not giving you the school as a dowry: it is the wall at my back. Do you understand, Teodoro?

Besides it was not such a tremendous undertaking as to kill anyone. On the contrary, it was a pleasure, a diversion; it had helped her endure the empty days of her widowhood, and before that, ah, before that, during her first marriage, it had kept her from falling into despair. In the classes and the students she had found the comfort she needed to bear up under the dark, turbulent days. How many good friends had she not made around the stove and her book of recipes, more valuable even than the money? No, she would not give up her school, her livelihood and respectable pastime.

While the doctor was in the drugstore (and he left before eight, came home for lunch and a siesta, went back, and did not close until after six), the school was a gainful, pleasant occupation.

Without the classes, will you please tell me, sir, what I am to do with myself? Gossip and scandalmongering with the neighbors, at the orders of Dona Dinorá, in her offensive occupation of correcting everybody, prying into the lives of others? Or leaning out of the window, like a mannequin in a showcase, for the amusement of passers-by, listening to wisecracks, chatting with this one and that one, and then being talked about, getting a bad name?

There were those who enjoyed this conspicuous idleness, this attracting attention. Right in their street, on the corner, Dona Magnólia spent her time in the doorway, a high yellow passing herself off as a blonde with the help of camomile rinse, with her set smile like that of a celluloid doll, heavily rouged, with eyes like a dead goat's. There she stood like a lure all day long, following all the doings of the passers-by. A new neighbor, she had moved there not long before with her husband, a secret agent of the police, gallant in his bravery and cuckoldry. According to Dona Dinorá and other neighbors with piercing searchlights and exact information, the detective was her lover and not her husband. By inheritance he had obtained the tawny Magnólia from forerunners of diverse standing and position, but all without exception equally cuckolded with a constancy and steadfastness of purpose worthy of all praise.

As Dona Flor had never been given to window-watching, how was she to occupy her time, my dear doctor? Did he prefer to have her with the students in the school or flouncing about Chile Street, the invariable route, the short cut to the whorehouses nearby, in the side streets of Ajuda? Let him keep his whereases and wherefores, and not bring up the subject further. Dona Flor was proud of her school, its reputation, the esteem it enjoyed. This status had cost her effort and perseverance, represented a capital investment.

The doctor resigned himself, though making it clear that he would take charge of all the household and Dona Flor's personal expenses, he alone. The profits from the school were exclusively hers, and he refused to accept any part of them toward their expenses.

Moreover, as regards this money the doctor took further measures. It was ridiculous, an invitation to thieves to have it in the house, behind the radio tubes or in an old shoe box or behind the mirror of the dressing table or under the mattress. That was the way of gipsies, irresponsible people. Especially now, when this intact sum would acquire real importance. Dr. Teodoro went with Dona Flor to the savings bank and opened an account in the name of his wife, in which she was to deposit her savings: "In this way it will produce interest, my dear, three per cent, and that is not to be sneezed at. And in the bank your money is guaranteed, free from danger of thieves."

What to do with this money kept in the bank, for heaven's sake? Dona Flor suddenly felt that the money was meaningless, for she did not have it at hand, could not reach behind the radio to get it to pay for or buy something, use it for alms. But Dona Norma, who was experienced in such matters, laughed at her neighbor's prejudice against banks. Let her put her money in the savings account, and let her husband handle the expenses. As long as she had her passbook and checkbook, she was not dependent on the doctor for every pin, for indulging in an extra dress or hat. She did not have to go making excuses to her husband, haggling about money for such trifling expenses; money you had to beg for had the quality of a tip about it, was humiliating.

Dona Norma was familiar with this bitter unpleasantness, for Mr. Zé Sampaio was cantankerous and inclined to be tight. For that reason, thanks to a balancing of the budget worthy of an outstanding financier—with savings, hagglings, bargain hunting, measures of different sorts, mistakes in the bills, in the addition, the subtraction, the total, twenty mil-reis here, fifty there, a hundred and, if necessary, a search at night in her husband's pocket—Dona Norma possessed, she, too, her own private nest-egg, which allowed her certain touches of elegance, and looking after her enormous clientele of *compadres* and godchildren, aged, ill, unemployed, drunks, good-for-nothings, and the dozens of street urchins, for whom she had a weakness.

"For example, my pet, suppose it is the doctor's birthday, and you don't have a penny to bless yourself with. Are you going to ask him for money to buy him a present? Have you thought what it would sound like: "Teodoro, darling, will you give me something to buy you a pair of shorts for your birthday?' I would not do that with Zé Sampaio."

Dona Flor was in complete agreement with this, naturally; her reservation had to do with the money being in a bank, a sum set down in a book, not real money immediately at hand. Suddenly her nest-egg had disappeared from view; how could she handle it in that impersonal book, in that interest-bearing account? She had her habits, and now she had to change them, for, according to her friends, her former ways of doing things were those of a poor person, the wife of a poor state employe, and a gambler to boot, squandering the income from her school, living practically at her expense, more of a gigolo than a husband. They were the habits of a widow with no one to turn to, who had to support herself by her work, meeting the rent, the cost of food and clothing, and other expenses. The way of gipsies, irresponsible people, as the doctor had said; the habits of poverty, without money to put in the bank, carrying interest and checkbooks, according to Dona Norma.

Now, however, Dona Flor's social standing and her fortunes had changed. If she did not have money to burn, she was no longer the church mouse she had been; at least, and putting it modestly, she was well fixed. She had ascended the ladder various steps, from the bottom, where the poor were, to the rungs of her most important neighbors: the Argentines of the ceramics factory, Dr. Ives with his office and state job, the Sampaios with their flourishing shoestore, the Ruas with their enviable agencies, on an equal with the aristocracy of the neighborhood, to the rejoicing of Dona Rozilda, who at last had a son-in-law who came up to her expectations. According to Mr. Vivaldo of the funeral parlor, a reliable source, who was always curious about the financial situation of his friends, Dr. Teodoro, steady, serious, hard-working, would go far.

"It won't be long before the whole drugstore is his."

It was thus that Dona Flor opened her account at the savings bank, which grew every month, and it was thus that her life became truly organized. The druggist was quite right when he said that disorder, clutter, untidy habits cause arguments between husbands and wives, lead to misunderstanding, which is the first step toward conjugal discord, friction, and separation.

Dona Norma thought he overdid this business of system and method, demanding a place for everything and everything in its place, averse to anything done on the spur of the moment or by surprise, the sole flaw (flaw according to Dona Norma) in a man of so many fine qualities, so upright, kindly, well bred, handling his wife with kid gloves. Better so, rigidly systematic than messy like Dona Norma, always late, without hands on her watch, the mother of disorder.

Dona Flor laughed as she listened to her friend, to whom restraint and punctuality were unknown words, praise the order and methodicalness of the doctor, "a husband like that, you lucky creature, is one in a hundred, does not grow on bushes." Even Dona Gisa, educating the whole neighborhood in unvarnished truth, though she did call him feudal, admitted his virtues: "For you, Florzinha, who seeks security above everything else, you couldn't have done better."

Really, in an orderliness which was a wonder, under the wing and direction of her good husband, with every detail properly fitted in, a set day for everything, Dona Flor looked upon herself as the example of the happiest wife in the neighborhood.

Her life moved along calmly and without unforeseen developments, quiet and pleasant, her time fitted to a carefully thought-out schedule, perfect organization: the movies once a week on Tuesdays, the eight o'clock program. If some film was being shown that people were wild about and which *A Tarde* enthusiastically endorsed, they went twice; but that happened rarely, and never in the afternoon, for the doctor could not abide the noisy disorder of the young people, the boisterous crowd.

At least twice a week, after dinner, he practiced on his bassoon, preparing for Saturday afternoon, which was sacred, when the orchestra met at the house of one or another of the musicians. These were gay, cordial gatherings, around a refreshment table— the mistress of the house outdoing herself in honor of her guests— laden with cold drinks, and fruit juice for the ladies, plenty of beer for the gentlemen, and on occasion a glass of rum, if the weather was cold or sultry. The guests took their places, admirers of the master or the interpreters, "a select audience" of friends to listen to sonatas and gavottes, waltzes and romances, moved by the emotion of fugues and pizzicatos, sharps and flats, the carefully practiced solos; a supreme hour of art.

Other nights when they were free they went visiting or received calls. If Dona Flor had neglected her contacts during her first marriage, now she cultivated them with regularity.

Twice a month, for example, on a set day they were to be invariably found at Dr. Luís Henrique's, Dona Flor bringing the children a sponge cake, a corn cake, a tray of coconut kisses or candy, something to please them.

Filled with pride, Dr. Teodoro joined the group gathered in the living-room of the illustrious friend, all people of greatest distinction, like Dr. Jorge Calmon, former secretary of state, Dr. Jayme Baleeiro, attorney for the Chamber of Commerce, the historian José Calazans, a member of the Academy and the Institute, Dr. Zezé Catarino (the name speaks for itself), Dr. Ruy Santos, politician, professor, and author, and other outstanding figures of the administration, the Institute of History, the State Academy of Letters.

These were important nights for Dr. Teodoro, affording him spiritual pleasure when he was privileged to talk with "representative figures," listening to them with respect and passing prudent opinion on the weighty subjects under discussion. "The ideas gleamed amid the splendor of scintillating phrases," as he put it, "in these elevated tilts, this dialogue of privileged minds." While this was going on, Dona Flor, in the circle of wives, was talking about clothes and cooking or commenting on the latest crime news in the papers.

To Dr. Teodoro the visits to Dr. Luís Henrique were the last word, whereas Dona Flor's preferences were for the nights in the Garcia's mansion, the bungalow of Dona Magá Paternostro, one of the outstanding figures of society, her former pupil. There Dona Flor found amid the manners and refinement of these ladies of the city's elite the discussion of fashions, of protocol, of social events, together with pleasant incursions into other people's lives, not just those of her own everyday neighbors, but the vices of the rich, the wellborn, the high-toned. And what tales, what goings-on! A depravity of the highest order, all, without exception.

Of her old habits, those which had come down from her first marriage, the one they observed was the Sunday lunch in Rio Vermelho with her aunt and uncle, and no other (to be sure, during her first marriage they had had almost no habits, just confusion and disorder).

With the modification of their customs, their life took on not only activity but also stability, a placid, agreeable rhythm. A happy life in the general opinion of the neighborhood, and with Dona Flor's smile in agreement.

On Wednesdays and Saturdays, at ten o'clock, give or take a minute, Dr. Teodoro took his wife in upright ardor and unfailing pleasure, always with an encore on Saturday, optional on Wednesday.

Dona Flor, given the disorder acquired in earlier habits, at first was surprised by the discretion of covering and fulfilling the pledge of love in the iron bed upon the new (and marvelous) spring mattress. But later the native modesty and shyness that were part of her nature adjusted her feminine needs, her requirements, to the suitable and punctual manner, one might almost say respectful and distinguished of the doctor, having intercourse with her under the protection of the sheets but with unquestionable desire and lance at the ready.

In the marriage bed (in Dr. Teodoro's opinion) desire should not interfere with modesty or love be in contradiction with demureness. Desire and love are pure in their basic origin, even in the secret intimacy of marriage.

On Wednesdays and Saturdays, at the same unvarying hour, Dona Flor could discern the discreet and repeated movements of her husband in the shadows of the bed. Thus, half raised to take her, the sheet covering his outspread arms and his shoulders, the doctor seemed to her like an enormous white umbrella shielding her private parts, protecting them in that supreme moment of her yielding herself up to him. An umbrella—could there be anything more graceless, more inhibiting. So silly!

Closing her eyes not to see, Dona Flor then envisaged him as a bird with huge wings and powerful claws, an eagle or condor, pouncing upon her in its flight, to snatch her up and possess her in the air. Dona Flor gave herself over to the bird of prey. Feeling herself possessed by him, his huge claw in her gushing entrails, captive and free, he rose up with her in a sky of bronze in a joy they shared.

But not a wholly chaste pleasure, because Dona Flor, when she freed herself, released her thoughts, too, and off they went.

Thus were the nights of love of this model couple, with an unfailing encore on Saturdays, optional on Wednesdays.

3

When she returned to Nazareth das Farinhas, after a long stay in Bahia, Dona Rozilda, a careful observer of the first period of Dona Flor's new matrimonial life, confided to Dona Norma her worries and doubts.

An excellent son-in-law, from every point of view, was Dr. Teodoro. There was not the slightest doubt as to that. But would Dona Flor be the fit wife of a husband with such unusual qualities? Why not? Dona Norma, loyal to her friend, asked somewhat harshly, admitting no criticism of her. Dona Flor, in her opinion, deserved the most perfect husband, the best-looking and richest.

In Dona Rozilda, however, the flame of enthusiasm did not burn so high. In spite of being Dona Flor's mother, and therefore inclined to excuse and favor her daughter, she did not see in her the necessary élan for the social ascent that was now within reach: she lacked the eagerness to take advantage of the position of her husband, his financial standing, his connections, the esteem in

which he was held. Now, if she had taken after Dona Rozilda, on
the doctor's arm she would easily surmount obstacles, entering the
drawing-rooms, the gardens, the intimacy of mansions in Graça
and Barra, where the cream of Bahian society lived, the elite,
which the old lady had always dreamed of. Had not Dona Flor
already been introduced to the Taveiras Pires, had not the millionaire vulgarly known as the Pampa Mustang, kissed her hand? Had
not Dona Imaculada beamed her revolting, self-satisfied smile upon
her, she the first lady of society, the arbiter of fashion?

And what had Dona Flor done to repay these opportunities she
owed to her husband's degree, his flourishing drugstore, his sweet-
sounding bassoon?

Nothing, absolutely nothing. On the contrary, she went on
with her cooking classes like a poor nobody, in spite of the fact
that this activity redounded unfavorably to her husband's social
prestige (a husband whose wife works is either badly off, or a
miser, according to Dona Rozilda's maxims); she stayed on in that
little house when they could have a far more distinguished address
and on a different street.

Dona Norma would please excuse her, for Dona Rozilda was
not saying this to belittle anyone, but those streets, which in other
days had been elegant and select, were now just thoroughfares
inhabited by nobodies, with a few exceptions. In those alleys,
women of society and standing, the gossip went on venomously,
could be counted on the fingers of one hand. The wife of the
Argentine, Dona Nancy, really a lady of good family, and who
else? she asked with a provocative look at Dona Flor's friend: "As
for the others, just trash."

The only worse place to live was Rio Vermelho, so out of the
way, full of rogues, where her sister and brother-in-law insisted on
staying, at the end of the world, practically a suburb, and so
common, where on Sundays the men went out in the streets in
pajamas and bedroom slippers. Who ever heard of such a thing?
Once Dona Laurita, the wife of Dr. Luís Henrique, had gone
to call on Dona Lita, and had been scandalized by that indecent
morning parade, a pajama procession in obscene bad taste. Dona
Laurita had given vent to her indignation in words of disgust: "I

don't know how one can live in such a place, where even the rich seem poor, nothing but riffraff."

But coming back to her point of departure, what about the situation of the new couple? Dr. Teodoro was crazy to move, and she, Dona Flor, that silly thing, was determined to stay on in that mess of a place. Dona Rozilda shook her head: "He who is born to three pennies never gets a dime."

Moreover, it was to this idea of moving to another address that Dona Rozilda's sudden return to Nazareth was owing. One morning Dona Flor had said to her: "Mother, what is this business of telling Teodoro that I want to move? I want you to know, once and for all, that we, he and I, are completely satisfied with our house and we are not going to move."

Dona Rozilda, forgetting her pretensions of grande dame, spat out of the corner of her mouth in vulgar fashion: "And what do I care? Each pig to its own sty."

Dona Flor made an effort to keep her temper: "Listen, Mother. I know the reason for this yammering about a bigger house. What you want is to come here to live for good, but you can just forget about it. Come to visit us whenever you like, spend several days here. But not to live with us. I am being frank with you, Mother; you were born to live alone. Let me tell you . . ."

Dona Rozilda rose abruptly, without waiting to hear the rest, thus missing the pleasant part of Dona Flor's discourse, for, by way of compensating for her frankness, which bordered on the rude, she had decided to assign her mother a small allowance. "Pin money, Mother, for your charitable undertakings," as she was finally able to tell her when she accompanied her to the wharfs of the Bahian Line some days later.

She spoke once more of Dona Rozilda's plan of moving in with her. If she had not accepted the proposition when she was a widow, she would not want it now that she was newly married. At the first frustrated attempt, Dona Rozilda had taken great umbrage, practically breaking off relations with Dona Flor. Now she swallowed the affront; the temptation of this new life with her daughter, with the splendor of distinguished connections and gatherings, was too powerful. She was returning to Nazareth, true; but her visits to the capital became more frequent. Being taken in as a guest in that "end of the world" which was Rio Vermelho, she could then come early, before lunch, to her daughter's house, to snoop about in the neighborhood, commanding the brigade of gossips. She stayed eight or ten days, long enough to become insufferable, to quarrel with her sister, and then went off to make life a hell again for her son and daughter-in-law in the Recôncavo. In Nazareth she could embellish her various activities with the description of Dona Flor's social pomp ("She goes from lunches to receptions, is an intimate friend of Dona Imaculada Taveira Pires"), with praise of her son-in-law and his innumerable gifts, his intelligence, his enviable economic standing, his impressive performance on the unusual bassoon. Recounting in full detail the weekly meeting of the amateur orchestra, she melted in smiles, drooling commentaries: "That is what I call music."

She said this in praise of the arias, romances, concertos of their exquisite repertoire in which Handel, Lehár, and Strauss rubbed elbows with Othelo Araújo and Master Agenor Gomes, local composers less well known abroad, but none the less inspired. She said it, too, as an expression of her contempt for other music, such as sambas and folk songs, *modinhas*, that of the lower classes—a spate of contempt—and for the players of guitars and ukeleles, bagpipes and tambourines, a gaggle of vagabonds. With this she established a distance, pointed out the difference between the amateur orchestra, which comprised Dr. Venceslau Pires da Veiga, an eminent surgeon, Dr. Pinho Pedreira, a judge in the capital, and the millionaire and papal nobleman Adriano Pires—the Pampa Mustang—head of a wholesale firm, with a mansion in Graça, a car and chauffeur, the husband of the noble Imaculada, "the first among the first, the queen of society" (to use the felicitous phrase of Silvinho Lamenha, a radio announcer and the society reporter on the newspaper of the feared bard Odorico Tavares), Dona Imaculada Taveira Pires with her face like that of an old horse, her lorgnette, and her Swiss housekeeper, and the idlers with their disorderly serenades, drunks and lowlifes.

At the time of her daughter's first marriage (if that could be called a marriage), she had had to suffer the rum and obscenities of those good-for-nothings, rogues, with their depraved, debauched airs: Jenner Augusto, Carlinhos Mascarenhas, Dorival Caymmi. Occasionally, a man of education and background got in with that gang and turned out to be the worst of the lot, like that Dr. Walter da Silveira, whose sleek face Dona Rozilda recalled with hatred. She had heard praises of the legal knowledge of the aforesaid Silveira in Nazareth: devoted to the law and incorruptible. Let whoever wanted to believe this believe it; not she, Dona Rozilda, who had seen him accompanying the *siri-boceta* on the bagpipe, the scoundrel!

Thanks to this rabble, she had become so antimusical that she had reacted violently when she first heard of her son-in-law's gifts: "An imposter, a Jew's-harp player." Once again, without doubt, that imbecile of a daughter of hers, without judgment or pride, had tied herself up with a bum whom she would have to support, a burden on her shoulders, underwriting his vices and love affairs with the hard-earned money of her school. She had such an abiding hatred of serenades and songs that not even the title of doctor, which Dona Norma, knowing her weaknesses and preferences, had dangled before her when she told her of her daughter's wooing, not even that graduation ring had moved her. A doctor and of publicly acclaimed knowledge she had written her, but Dona Rozilda had not been impressed: "Another one of those sots! Carousing about the streets shamelessly all night. And for all we know, a gambler, too. What he wants is to live on the fat of the land while she works and he makes merry hell."

As for his doctor's degree, she had her reservations. "A druggist . . . A one-legged doctor!"

She distinguished between the different diplomas, not all of them possessing, in her opinion, the same class and standing: "A real doctor, first-quality, is a physician, a lawyer, a civil engineer. A dentist and druggist, agronomist, veterinarian, all those are second-class doctors, small potatoes, people who lacked the mind and the ability to complete their studies."

All this ill will toward her future son-in-law, whom she had not yet met and was already criticizing so severely, came from hearing that he was an amateur musician. Only later on, in Bahia, when she discovered the druggist's solid financial standing, the fact that he was a partner in such an establishment as the Scientific Pharmacy, at the corner of Carlos Gomes Street and Cabeça (the location alone was worth a fortune), saw how respectable he was, his manners and bearing, the splendid and vast circle of his friends, did her initial erroneous impression disappear, when she had confused the bassoon with a Jew's-harp and the amateur orchestra with serenades by the light of the moon.

Her son-in-law rose quickly and high in her estimation. He was not the enchanted prince she had one day envisaged in Pedro Borges, the student from Pará, with his rivers, islands, and rubber plantations, the riches of a thousand and one nights. However, what more could a poor widow, thirty years old, ask? Dona Rozilda, satisfied beyond her fondest hopes, confessed to Dona Norma: "Even I would marry him. An outstanding citizen, and what manners. This time she really hit the jackpot. And it was about time . . . a man of such breeding."

Exquisite breeding: Dr. Teodoro, cordial and respectful, addressed her only as "My dear mother-in-law," continually inquiring if there was anything she needed. He brought her lozenges for her cough, syrup for her chronic catarrh, and offered her a new umbrella when he heard her complain that she had lost her old one —dating back to the days of Mr. Gil—in the confusion of coming ashore.

Dona Rozilda had arrived planning to attend the wedding and stay on for a few days. But as she took in the qualities of her son-in-law, she glimpsed the possibilities of living with the couple, deciding to move in for good, giving up Nazareth das Farinhas, the good works of Father Walfrido Moraes, the club, the church, the presidency of the delightful, cruel local gossip center.

She liked it in that small city, as has already been mentioned. She was somebody, a person of influence, a busybody at large, trying her daughter-in-law's patience to the limit with her whims and bad humor. The daughter-in-law had lost all faith in miracles; Our Lady of the Sorrows had been blind and deaf to her appeals and vows; only death would save her. The death of her mother-in-law, of course. At times Celeste, who was so good-hearted, gave herself over to thinking of that joyful event. Oh, what an impatiently awaited wake! It would be the finest ever held in Nazareth, the sitting up with and encomium of the body of the old lady would be the talk of all the Recôncavo, the echoes reaching the capital. Celeste was prepared to spend whatever was needed.

She liked it in Nazareth, but with this new son-in-law, she preferred Salvador, and in order to stay there she worked out her campaign plan. She became flattering and ingratiating, kind and helpful, devoted to the druggist. Dr. Teodoro was touched at first. Talking with his friend Rosalvo Medeiros, the drug companies' representative, he said that with marriage he had acquired not only the most perfect wife, but also a second mother, his mother-in-law, that saintly old woman.

"Who?" The prosperous Rosalvo could not believe his ears. "Who is the saintly old woman? Dona Rozilda?" and he burst out laughing like Dona Amélia the day the engagement was announced. Honestly, the things one hears! Dona Rozilda, a saintly soul. You had to be naïve as Teodoro . . .

But not even Dr. Teodoro was taken in for long: the impertinence, the love of intrigue, the bad humor of Dona Rozilda soon prevailed over her honeyed smiles and her adulatory words, and the son-in-law began to understand the reason for Dona Amélia's and Rosalvo's guffaws. It was when Dona Rozilda came to talk to him, in a very roundabout fashion, of the disadvantages of a small house, with so few conveniences. Why not rent a house more in keeping with his means and connections? Larger, with more rooms.

She very cunningly gave the impression that Dona Flor was not satisfied with that house full of unpleasant memories. Only because she did not want to nag her husband she said nothing about her dissatisfaction.

Dr. Teodoro was surprised by the spendthrift suggestion of his mother-in-law, and, even more, by the supposed displeasure of his wife. Had not Dona Flor been the first to point out the conveniences and advantages of staying on there: the low rental, which had not gone up in eight years, and the location of the house, two steps from the drugstore, not to mention the well-known address of the School of Savor and Art, her kitchen adapted to her classes, with a gas and a wood stove? Why a bigger house when there were just the two of them? Why go looking for work and expense when they fitted in there perfectly, she, her husband, and her dream of happiness? These had been the arguments Dona Flor had employed even before they were married, modest and sensible.

Then why now this sudden change? Why come out with this wastefulness of a big house that involved work and expense? Why these luxuries beyond their means? Just to create an impression.

Dona Rozilda, in her confused harangue, had spoken of prestige, of "making a good impression." Dr. Teodoro was sensitive to this argument, zealous of his prestige and esteem, concerned about the criticism of others. But Dona Flor attached no importance to such things, and she had said to him, when they were discussing the school, that a person's value does not rest on outward appearances, but on his true merits, what he really is.

After all this, how could she be upset, bringing forth complaints and demands? Dr. Teodoro listened attentively to the rattling on of his mother-in-law, but he did not want to discuss the matter: "I did not know, my dear mother-in-law, that my beloved wife felt this way, and I do not want to discuss it. But I can assure you that everything will be settled to Flor's satisfaction."

Leaving Dona Rozilda floating on a cloud of optimism, he returned to the drug-store in an aggrieved mood. If Dona Flor's change of opinion surprised Dr. Teodoro, her approach displeased him. Why had she not come and talked to him herself, with loyalty and frankness? Why had she used Dona Rozilda as her envoy? The druggist wanted no doubt, no misunderstanding, however trifling, between himself and his wife. He was willing to give her everything he could, to satisfy all her desires, even when they seemed foibles, within his means and even making sacrifices. But he did ask for sincerity, good faith, confidence. Why resort to a third party, why intermediaries when they were husband and wife? Dr. Teodoro, in the rear of the pharmacy, employing the spatula, grinding ingredients, weighing minute quantities in the precision scale, felt hurt and sad. Why this lack of trust? Husband and wife should not have secrets from one another, or go-betweens in their dealings. Subnitrate of bismuth, aspirin, methylene blue, nutmeg, the exact amounts, not a grain more or less. The same with marriage. He prepared to bring the matter into the clear as soon as possible.

That night, alone with his wife in their room, while he was taking off his clothes behind the head of the iron bed, he said to her: "My dear, there is one thing I would like to ask of you . . ."

Dona Flor had already slipped between the sheets, waiting only for her husband's kiss to close her eyes and go to sleep.

"What is it, Teodoro?"

"I would prefer that when you want to discuss something with me you would speak to me directly, and not send anyone in your place." There was no anger in the doctor's voice, but rather a touch of melancholy.

Dona Flor sat up in surprise. Resting on her elbow, she turned toward her husband as he was putting on the pants of his pajamas: "What kind of a tale is this? When did I ever send? . . ."

"I feel that a husband and wife should be frank with each other; they do not need any third party."

"Teodoro, my dear please explain this, and quickly, for I do not make head or tail of it."

Wearing his striped pajamas, he came over and sat down on the side of the bed: "If you wanted to move, why didn't you tell me so yourself?"

"Move? Me? Who told you that?"

"Your mother, Dona Rozilda. She said you were complaining, were dissatisfied with the house, disliked it . . ."

Dona Flor looked very seriously at her husband seated on the edge of the bed, with a touch of sadness in his eyes. She felt like laughing: "A grown man and so easily taken in."

"Mamma? And you think I sent her? You don't know Mamma yet, Teodoro. I know exactly what she is up to. What would I want with a bigger house? The one who wants it is she, with a room of her own, to stay for good, God deliver me."

"But, if that is the situation, dear, to have room for your mother perhaps we should . . ."

Dona Flor restrained her laughter, and looked her husband in the eyes. "We should be frank with one another you said, Teodoro. Tell me, but I want the truth, would you like to have the old lady living with us for good?"

Dr. Teodoro was not a man who lied, but neither did he want to offend anyone, least of all Dona Flor's mother: "She's your mother and my mother-in-law, and if she so wishes and you are agreeable . . ."

"Well, I want you to know, my dear, that I do not want her and I am not agreeable to the idea. She is my mother. I love her, but here, living with us, I don't want her for all the money in the world. There is no one who can stand her, Teodoro, you don't know her well yet." She took her husband's hand: "Under this roof, my dear, only you and I, and nobody else. From here people go to their own homes. Moreover, the best thing, it seems to me is, when we are able, to buy this house."

The druggist gave a sigh of relief. He was prepared to make sacrifices for Dona Flor, even to put up with Dona Rozilda and her mischief-making. But, fortunately, everything had been cleared up. Dona Flor had not changed; she was still modest in her ambitions, frugal, sensible. As for Dona Rozilda, Dr. Teodoro's opinion had suffered a change; the saintly old lady had turned into a viper. Not for nothing did his brother-in-law, Morais, stay on in Rio, prepared to return to Bahia only when his mother-in-law gave up the ghost. Another whose only hope was death, for in the case of Dona Rozilda, as far as he was concerned, there was no alternative.

Dr. Teodoro, however, less experienced in the ways of his mother-in-law, and far more polite, better brought up, added an extenuating factor: "It's her age, poor thing. When you get to be that old . . ."

Dona Flor caressed her husband's hand. What a good man! "It's not a question of age, my dear. She was always like that. She is my mother, and it is not my place to criticize her—a daughter shouldn't. But she has always had that disposition, ever since she was a girl. Not even my father could bear it, and he was a saint. If she were to move in here, Teodoro, we would wind up quarreling."

"We two? Never, my dear, never." He looked at her with deep tenderness: "We are never going to quarrel. Nor hide anything from one another, no matter what it is. We will tell each other everything, everything."

He kissed her lips softly.

"Everything," Dona Flor repeated in a whisper.

Dr. Teodoro smiled, completely satisfied, got up and went to turn off the light. "Everything, Teodoro? Do you think that is possible? Even the most hidden thoughts, those which a person hides even from himself, Teodoro?" Dona Flor looked at the strong torso of her husband under his pajama; the broad shoulder-blades, the stout neck and muscles of his arms. Biting her lips, she tried to turn off her thoughts, for being Tuesday, it was not the day for such things. Systematic, the doctor observed in this as in everything else the most perfect order. So kind and generous, however, so delicate and thoughtful, so in love with her that he was even willing to put up with Dona Rozilda. Such devotion more than made up for his orderliness, his punctuality, his rules, his labels.

"Not everything, Teodoro. You do not know what a dark pool the heart is."

4

Dona Flor discovered new and unsuspected worlds which she entered on her husband's arm, coming to be a figure of distinction, "a charming ornament," as our exacting Silvinho, whose name invariably comes up, described her in reporting a party given by the Taveiras Pires.

It had never occurred to her that there existed a universe made up only of druggists, hermetical and fascinating, with its exclusive affairs, its special outlook on life, its own language, its atmosphere of nitrates and calomels. A universe whose capital and cupola was the Bahian Association of Pharmacy, with its own diocese, one whole floor, touching upon other worlds of greater or lesser importance such as that of the doctors who benefited from the work of others. For, the pharmacologists asked, what would be the value of doctors if there were no druggists? Why then did they put on such airs, assume such arrogance? Equally presumptuous were the agents of pharmaceutical laboratories; polite, even humble toward the great, especially at the hour of making a sale; indifferent to the lower members of the hierarchy, positively rude at times when a promissory note could not be met on the date it fell due. The traveling salesmen were pleasanter, with their cases of drugs and the latest stories. All these people, from the university and business, with their degrees, their money, their airs, rested upon the vast foundation of owners and clerks of the drugstores, who received a miserly stipend.

When walking past the Scientific Pharmacy, crossing its street to buy a tube of toothpaste or a bar of soap, Dona Flor had never before noticed that powerful emanation from the world of drugs.

It was the world in which her husband drudged, resting on his doctor's diploma (and even more on the knowledge he had acquired during his years in the laboratory and behind the counter), his devotion to duty and his honorability, always trying to assure himself a good financial position and a certain scientific standing. A modest fortune, a modest reputation, but nevertheless enough to open to Dona Flor the doors of that world of iodines and sulfates, make her the beneficiary of the cultural and recreational programs of the Bahian Association of Pharmacy: the meetings in their own hall, with the reading and discussion of theses and papers dealing with scientific or professional subjects; the luncheons on festive occasions—the inauguration of a new board of directors, the Pharmacists' Day—blowouts where directors and members (with their families) came together in a noisy "fraternizing of classes," as Dr. Ferreira inevitably repeated in his inevitable speech. Not to mention the dance at the end of the year, in December, before Christmas.

Dona Flor attended, but without overdoing it, the reading of theses and the repasts. She had relationships with the wives of her husband's colleagues; she visited certain of them, and was visited by them, and from this exchange of amenities she gained three or four friends and one pupil.

Dona Sebastiana, the wife and right arm of Dr. Silvio Ferreira, the secretary-general of the Association and its chief organizer, was a lively person with a voice like a peal of thunder and a contagious laugh. Dona Rita, the wife of Dr. Tancredo Vinhas, of the Santa Rita Pharmacy, was, with her husband, good company, he chain-smoking cigarettes, she with the dry cough of a chronic consumptive. Dona Neusa, the blonde Neusoca with the gay eyes, was the wife of R. Macedo and Co. The company consisted of the salesmen, Dona Neusa finding her attraction in young salesmen. She collected them and baptized them anew with the names of the medicines most in vogue. There was Yam Elixir, a fat mulatto. Bromide seemed a child, so young and delicate, still beardless and innocent, a precious jewel in that rare collection. Scott's Emulsion was pretty, a country boy who had recently arrived from Galicia in Spain, with cheeks as rosy as an apple. Female Restorative was the little Freasa, who kept her company when she was convalescing from hepatitis. There was the Laxative Gesteira, Caboclo Soap —a bluish Negro, Holy Mother!—the Dead Shot, the Wonder-Working Cure. The last represented a betrayal on the part of Dona Neusa of the drug salesmen in active service, to whom up to then she had been completely faithful; a gallant studying for the priesthood who was on holiday in the neighborhood, he held the spice for the insatiable Neusoca of a double sin against the law of man and God.

Dona Paula, the wife of Dr. Ángelo Costa of the Goiás Pharmacy, had enrolled in the School of Savor and Art, showing considerable aptitude. She was the only pupil from the ranks of pharmacy. Another, Dona Berenice, began the course, but soon gave it up, being unable to tell the difference between filet and top round.

Dona Flor was not on visiting terms with Dona Gertrudes Becker, the wife of Dr. Frederico Becker, the owner of the chain of Hamburg Pharmacies—four in the upper part of the city, one in the lower, and another in Itapagipe—the representative of important foreign laboratories, and the more or less perpetual president of the Association, king of magnesia and urotropine. Dona Gertrudes descended from her throne only once a year, for the December ball, allowing those petites bourgeoises, worried and long-suffering, with whom her husband had business dealings, to touch the tips of her fingers. As for Dr. Frederico, though he did not attend the lunches with soda water and wine from Rio Grande, he never missed a meeting of the Association, presiding, having the last word about any subject.

He was a short German, with gentle blue eyes and a grating accent. Stories circulated about his fortune and also about his degree, granted by some far-off German school when he was already the owner of three drugstores. He adored children, and stopped in the street to give them candy, of which he always had a pocketful.

Dona Flor had hardly been married for two months when she ascended for the first time the stairway leading to the hall of the Bahian Association of Pharmacy, on the second floor of a colonial building in Terreiro de Jesus. The lower floor was occupied by the Spiritist Center of Faith, Hope, and Charity, which carried on a fierce competition with the druggists, for mediums and astrologers obtained cures for all illnesses by means of metaphysical prescriptions, eliminating medicines, drugs, and injections.

Dona Flor was to have the unique opportunity of witnessing the sensational debate to take place that night at the Bahian Association of Pharmacy on the paper by Dr. Djalma Noronha, treasurer of the society entitled: "The Growing Use by Doctors of Manufactured Products, Thus Causing a Decline in Hand-Prepared Prescriptions, and the Unforeseeable Consequences Thereof."

The druggists were of two minds regarding that tendency on the part of the majority of the doctors, some of them being enthusiastically in favor of drugs prepared and packed in the laboratories of southern Brazil, while others were staunch supporters of traditional medicines, patiently mixed in the backrooms of drugstores according to written prescriptions, measured into bottles and boxes, and guaranteed by the druggist with the endorsement of his signature.

Throughout the week Dr. Teodoro talked of nothing else, he being one of the champions of the traditional school. "Of what use is a druggist if only manufactured products are employed? He becomes nothing but a clerk, a salesman in a drugstore?" he pathetically told the meeting.

On the opposite side, defending the industrialization of medicines (and even their nationalization) in keeping with modern times and advanced techniques, Dona Flor had occasion to listen to Dr. Sinval Costa Lima, whose discoveries of the medicinal properties of nightshade had given him wide fame, and to the eloquent, stirring words of the celebrated Emilio Diniz. Not because he happened to be his adversary in that debate did the upright Dr. Teodoro deny the brilliant talent of Professor Diniz: "He is a Demosthenes! A Prado Valadares!"

Equally endowed with minds of high order was the party in whose ranks our dear Madureira militated. It will suffice to cite the name of Dr. Antiógenes Dias, former director of the Faculty, the author of books, a man of eighty-eight, but still with the strength to proclaim: "A medicine made by a machine does not enter my drugstore."

He had not taken an active part in his drugstore for over twenty years, and his sons not only bought and sold manufactured medicines, but also were the representatives in Bahia of important laboratories of São Paulo. "The old man is in his dotage," they explained.

Perhaps the ingrates were right, and the old man was getting feeble-minded, laughing at everything. But there was no doubt as to the lucidity and competence of Drs. Arlindo Pessoa and Melo Nobre—privileged minds, both of them—and Dr. Teodoro, too, who should not be unjustly overlooked because he happens to be the hero of this unpretentious chronicle. Especially when he himself confessed to his wife that he was completely informed on the subject under discussion, pointing out once more the importance of the meeting. Dona Flor should count herself lucky to have the opportunity of being present at this historic debate.

Historic and academic, as Dr. Teodoro himself said to Dona Flor, for neither he nor either of the two other ardent defenders of prescriptions made up according to the doctor's instructions banned the laboratory products from their stores. How could they meet competition if they did not stock those damned drugs, which were so much in vogue? Their position was purely one of principle, gratuitous, theoretical, having nothing to do with the practical demands of trade, for, alas, my dear Flor, it is not always possible to reconcile theory and practice: life is full of ignoble conflicts.

Dona Flor did not want to delve too deeply into this contradiction between theory and practice, accepting the doctor's assertion that: "Just because of this the position of those who defend traditional prescription-filling is all the more praiseworthy." As far as she was concerned, it brought little cure and much well-being not to recall when she had been sick (aside from her insomnia as a widow).

It was truly a memorable evening, as Dr. Teodoro had foretold, and as the newspapers reported. A brief, limited account, our doctor complained when he saw his conclusive remarks and those of all the others whittled down to a colorless line: "Among others, Drs. Carvalho, Costa Lima, E. Diniz, Madureira, Pessoa, Nobre, Trigueiros took part in the discussion." They did not even give the complete names. Only the speech of Dr. Frederico Becker warranted a slight prominence, praise for his "clarity of exposition, his valuable knowledge, the logic of his reasoning." Why this disdain of the press for culture? Why such limitation of space? Dr. Teodoro protested, when there were pages and pages for the most revolting crimes, the nudistic scandals of movie stars, their absurd divorces, setting a deplorable example to our youth?

An extensive report, with a thorough analysis of the debate was to be found in the *Brazilian Review of Pharmacy*, São Paulo (Series XII., Vol. IV, pp. 179–81). Underwritten by the prosperous laboratories, the *Review* did not hide its position with regard to manufactured products. However, it did not fail to pay just tribute to "the brilliant interventions of Dr. Madureira, an unyielding and learned adversary, to whom we pay due tribute." "Unyielding and learned." These are the words of the *Brazilian Review*

of Pharmacy, with all its authority, not ours, for we are unconditional supporters of the doctor.

Dona Flor did her best to follow and understand the heated
debate, but in honor of the truth it must be said this was impossible. Out of love for her husband and her own pride, she would
have liked to keep her attention fixed on the speakers, but as she
was ignorant of the theses and formulas, finding those phrases and
words in dead languages rebarbative, she was unable to concentrate
on the speeches.

Her thoughts wandered off to less philosophical matters, such
as the problems of the school, the amusing tittle-tattle of Maria
Antonia (she even smiled in the middle of the cogent arguments of
Dr. Sinval Costa Lima concerning nightshade), her concern about
Marilda, more stubborn and eager than ever in her determination
to appear on the radio, an example—according to Dr. Teodoro—of
the lamentable influence of movie stars on the young. She had
become rude and disobedient, going around with someone in the
radio world, Oswaldinho Mendonça, and the good-for-nothing
was luring her on with the promise of programs, behind which
lurked a bed. Dona Maria do Carmo, in turn, kept a hawkeyed
watch over the girl's every step and gesture, punishing her, forbidding her to set foot out of the house.

When Dona Flor came back from her woolgathering, it was
not Marilda who was at the microphone, but Dr. Teodoro. She
tried to follow his reasoning, taking in the arguments with which
he confounded his adversaries. His expression solemn, his countenance circumspect, his gestures polite even when heated, he was
the image of the honorable man, the upright citizen fulfilling his
duty—at that moment those of the druggist doing honor to his
diploma, even though it ran counter to his business interests.

Always fulfilling his duty, always the upright citizen. The
night before, with equal competence and gravity he had fulfilled
his duties toward his wife in bed. Because she was nervous, on edge
(Marilda had had an attack of tears, sobbing, talking of committing
suicide: "Either the radio or death" was her fanatical ultimatum),
she had informed her husband, with caresses and wiles, that she

would enjoy a repeat performance that night, even though it was optional, being a Wednesday.

The doctor vacillated a little, but as she had already cast aside her timidity and modesty, revealing her desire, without further hesitation the doctor complied, fulfilling his pleasant duty for the second time.

Now in the meeting hall Dona Flor had understood the reason for her husband's hesitancy: he wanted to spare himself fatigue, giving his body and mind the rest they needed for the following night. He divided his time and effort among his various duties.

The encore the night before, however, had not tired him, for he spoke firmly forth in Latin (or would it be French?): "Lanataglucodide C is equal to acetic acid plus glucose plus 3 digitoxin plus digoxigenolid," formulas which fell on the ear like barbarous verses.

Seeing him so solemn and grave, with his Greek and Latin, his finger uplifted, his colleagues listening to him with attention and deference, Dona Flor realized how important her husband was. He was not a nobody, as Dona Rozilda well said. The neighbors were right: she should take pride in him, give thanks to Divine Providence, which had sent her such a good husband, a gift from heaven. Moreover, he had arrived at the precise moment when she could no longer endure her widowhood, running the risk of encouraging some adventurer, opening the doors of her house and her legs to the first pale, entreating vagabond who came by, like Prince Eduardo, the Widows' Lover Boy. Dear God, what she had been saved from!

If the druggist had not appeared in the window of the Scientific Pharmacy that day of the freshmen's hazing, she, Dona Flor, instead of being there, surrounded by consideration, in that hall where eminent doctors were discussing erudite themes, might have been going from bed to bed in a whorehouse, debauched, dishonored, her good name, her friends, her students, gone, winding up God knows where. She shuddered at the mere thought. Her applause at the conclusion of Dr. Teodoro's speech reflected not only enthusiasm but also gratitude. He had saved her, and was a man worthy of all respect. She should be proud of her husband.

From the directors' table to which he returned, Dr. Teodoro sought his wife out with his eyes and received the tribute of a smile, the greatest reward for his effort and brilliance. The discussion continued. Dr. Nobre had the floor: a man of great gifts, beyond doubt, but with a lisping, muted voice, completely soporific.

Dona Flor did her best to hold out, but her eyelids grew heavier and heavier. Her last hope was Dr. Diniz, a famous orator from his student days, an outstanding professor, author of GA-LENICA DIGITALIS—COMMUNIA AND STABILISATA, the definitive work on the subject. But neither he nor the rest who followed could keep Dona Flor from nodding. And not only Dona Flor. Dona Sebastiana was sound asleep, her mountainous bust rising and falling and the air coming from her mouth in a whistle. Dona Rita's eyes were closed; every now and then she blinked and came awake with a start. Dona Paula held out for a while, and then she gave up, her head on her husband's shoulder. Only Dona Neusa, with the deep circles under her eyes, was at ease and unperturbed; only she held out against the drowsiness of the formulas and ideas, as though all that erudition was an open book to her. Her eyes followed the movements of a young man who had been hired by the Association to keep the glass of water on the speaker's table filled. She had already thought up his nickname: 914, a famous injection that was infallible in cases of syphilis.

Dona Flor nodded; drowsiness crept up the back of her neck. As though in the distance she seemed to hear the voice of her husband. With a supreme effort she surfaced. Dr. Teodoro was talking for the second time. I don't understand a word of all this, my dear, chemical and botanical formulas, it's too much for me. Forgive me if I can't fight off this drowsiness; I am a housekeeper and nothing more, a dunce, ignorant; I am not made for these lofty heights.

The applause awakened her. She clapped her hands, smiled at her husband, threw him a kiss with her fingertips.

The session was almost over, and the wives, freed, gathered about in a smiling group to take their leave.

"Dr. Teodoro was magnificent," Dona Sebastiana commented (how did she know, when she had been asleep all the time?).

"What a marvel Dr. Emilio is!" Dona Paula repeated phrases she recalled from previous meetings. "Dr. Teodoro, a man of true wisdom."

Walking down the staircase on her husband's arm, Dona Flor said to him: "Everyone praised you, Teodoro. They all enjoyed it and said you had done so well."

He smiled modestly: "It's just their kindness. But perhaps I did contribute something useful. What did you think of it?"

Dona Flor squeezed his big, honest hand, her good husband: "It was beautiful. I did not understand much of it, but I loved it. And I was so puffed up when they praised you . . ." She almost added: "I don't deserve you, Teodoro," but perhaps he, for all his Latin and Greek, would not have understood.

5

If the world of pharmacists was *terra incognita* for Dona Flor, imagine the secret, almost cabalistic world of amateur musicians through which she penetrated by way of the strait gate of the bassoon.

Those grave, respectable gentlemen, all well fixed, with university degrees or stores, enterprises, offices—all except Urbano Poor Devil, a melodious violinist, who was nothing but a clerk at the Beirut Store—comprised a kind of closed society, with traits of a religious sect. "The sublime religion of music, the mysticism of sonority, with its gods, its temples, its worshipers and its prophet, the inspired composer and master Agenor Gomes," according to a report from the pen of Flávio Costa, a young journalist going through his apprenticeship (without pay) on *The Modern Shop-*

keeper belonging to the generous Nacife (who charged the cub reporter nothing for his training). The report on the amateur orchestra occupied the whole last page of the *Shopkeeper,* with a center photograph of the entire orchestra in formal dress in the gardens of the mansion of Commander Adriano Pires, who, moreover, the next day received a visit from the publisher, telling him the innumerable difficulties a newspaper such as his had to contend with. It was impossible for it to go on unless it could count on the understanding of men with a papal title, a heart and wallet appreciative of the rocky road journalism had to travel.

He showed him the page with the report of the meeting (an intelligent lad, the reporter, really gifted, but today, Commander, one has to pay them a fortune), and the millionaire opened his purse, moved at seeing himself beside the violoncello, surrounded by his coreligionists. A sect with its duties, its habits, a strict ritual, and a weekly rejoicing as of birds: their Saturday afternoon rehearsal.

Coming from the mixing bowls, the mortar, the capsule-compressors, the strainers, the earthenware jars holding oxides and poisons, mercury and iodine, Dona Flor's next step was among trills, pizzicati, pavanes, gavottes, solo or accompanied by violoncello, oboe, violin, clarinet, flute, French horn, percussion instruments, and the bassoon of her husband, all under the direction at the piano of the conductor Agenor Gomes, who was a charming person. She came from the company of Dona Sebastiana, Dona Paula, Dona Rita, the voracious Neusoca, devourer of clerks, to the far more distinguished society of ladies of high degree, the wives of those outstanding gentlemen. When the banker Celestino could not get out of going to one of their concerts (ah, a banker's life . . . and there are those who think it is a bed of roses, never imagining the boredom, the nuisances one has to suffer), he would invariably remark: "Every off-key note of one of those cranks is worth millions."

On Saturdays those important figures became gay, carefree children, relieved of engagements and obligations, of customers and business, of money calling for a quick turnover. They laid aside all social differences, the wholesaler fraternizing with the poorly paid municipal engineer, the famous surgeon with the modest druggist, the brilliant judge or the owner of the Emporiums of the North—eight branches in the city—with the clerk of a little store.

The women, too, so important and so chic, welcomed into their homes the wives of the other musicians without thought of their fortunes or social backgrounds, receiving them all with the same warmth, including *siá* Maricota (why *siá* and not *dona?* To which she proudly answered: "I am not *dona*, I am nothing but *siá*, and that is stretching it a lot").

Moreover, *siá* Maricota almost never put in an appearance, for she had neither clothes nor conversation that befitted those "shitty upper-crust ladies," as she explained to her neighbors on the street corner where Lapinha crossed Liberdade: "What have I to do there? They talk about nothing but parties, receptions, lunches, dinners, food, food—it's positively revolting. And me thinking about my children at home without enough food to fill them up. When they are not talking about food and drink, then it is the most bold-faced gossip: how So-and-so's wife is having an affair with somebody, that another is giving it away to the first one who comes by, that someone I never even heard of and don't want to was caught in a whorehouse. Apparently all those women know how to do is to eat and lap it up in bed. I never heard of such a thing."

In her disgust Dona Maricota ("I am not the mistress of anything; at most call me *siá* Maricota, like any servant, that's enough for me"), *siá* Maricota did not weigh her words, her judgments were harsh and realistic: "All they are interested in is luxury, fine clothes, the latest fashions. Let them stay up there in their shittiness, with their gossip, I can do very well without them. Urbano goes because he loves those rehearsals. If I had my way, he wouldn't go to the house of any of those rich people. He would play here, in Mr. Bié's tavern, with Mané Sapo and Mr. Bebe-e-Cospe." Here she opened her arms and let them fall helplessly. "But what can I do? He's just a poor devil!"

As a result of her repetition of the derogatory nickname, it stuck, and Mr. Urbano was known by that humiliating nickname.

As for Mané Sapo, he was a wonder with the bagpipe, and Mr. Bebe-e-Cospe owned an old accordion: the two of them, on Sundays, played their popular tunes and drank their rum in Mr. Bié's tavern, the meeting-place of high society in those side-streets. Mr. Urbano occasionally showed up and was applauded for his violin playing, though that public definitely preferred Mané Sapo's bagpipe and Bebe-e-Cospe's accordion. *Siá* Maricota, who understood nothing of music, grumbled at having to press her husband's blue suit, the only one he had, and with the pants beginning to get shiny in the seat, for the rehearsals: "If they can't rehearse without him, at least they ought to pay the presser. This damned orchestra is nothing but a headache; I don't see what the poor devil gets out of it."

He got peace of mind, flying away on the wings of music from his bitter-tongued Maricota, with her smell of garlic, her warts, and her complaints. At the rehearsals on Saturdays, going over the same music or trying out some new melody for the select repertory, Urbano Poor Devil had a reprieve from his miserable existence, and, like him, all the other members of the orchestra, the mighty, the rich. Some of them maintaining the solemnity of their manners, others doffing it as they took off their coats for the rehearsal and picked up their instruments, but all of them showing the same inner happiness, a pure inspiration that swept from their thoughts the daily shabbiness and squalor.

Dr. Venceslau Veiga, the egregious surgeon, after the first notes and the first glass of beer, smiled in content at life and mankind. All the fatigue of the week in the operating room, opening chests and abdomens, looking after the sick, bending over death, in an unending struggle, cruel and futile, all the accumulated weariness disappeared with the first chords as he drew the bow over the violin strings. Dr. Pinho Pedreira broke the chain of his loneliness, a bachelor and misanthrope, rediscovering in his flute the memory of a love affair of his youth, a pair of deceitful hazel eyes. Adriano Pires, the Pampa Mustang—white spots of leukoderma mottled his hands and face—the millionaire, the great wholesaler, the partner in banks, the director of enterprises and industries, the papal commander—grew humble in the presence of his mighty violoncello, making up to himself there for the week of fierce ambitions and fierce disappointments, the hours haggling with customers, competitors, employes—thieves, the whole lot of them—in his ambition to become richer, the agony of so little time in which to satisfy his ambition for money and power, as well as having to live with Dona Imaculada Taveira Pires, a calamity. He became not only humble, but even generous and human, smiling at the poor clerk at his side, the one liberated from the highborn Dona Imaculada, the other from *siá* Maricota.

Like *siá* Maricota, the wife of the papal commander rarely appeared at the rehearsals. Not for lack of clothes or conversation, naturally, but for lack of time. Her hours were taken up by a hundred and one obligations, being, as she was, the first lady of society, and also she found those rehearsals insipid, boring beyond words, the same chords repeated, the same music, month after month, unbearable.

Better so. Without her presence, without the sight of her bony face, covered with creams, her bust with jewels, her sagging jowls, and the loathsome lorgnette, it was easier for Mr. Adriano to efface her from his memory. Her and his daughters and sons-in-law. The daughters, complete flops, two poor creatures whose lives were bounded by clothes and dances. The sons-in-law, gigolos, one more useless and rascally than the other; one of them squandering in Rio, the other throwing away in Bahia the money which represented Mr. Adriano's sweat, blood, and life. The wholesaler found surcease from all this: from the millions he had made, from his competitors, the prosperous and the failures, from the emptiness, the selfishness, the unhappiness of his family. There in the violoncello he found rest. Beside Mr. Urbano, the two equal, just as, be the truth known, the highborn Dona Imaculada and the tattered *siá* Maricota were equal, both of them sour hags.

On Saturdays those outstanding gentlemen came together without fail, giving themselves over to music and beer, carefree and smiling. Each Saturday at a different house, and the mistress of the house providing lavish refreshments, a table with assorted delicacies, in the middle of the afternoon. Two or three wives always came, certain friends, and various admirers, for "there is no accounting for tastes" (as Mr. Zé Sampaio muttered when he returned from one of those Saturday festivities which he had attended at the druggist's request). Dona Flor, never-failing and in her place during the early sessions, was greeted with warm cordiality and was a gentle, sweet hostess.

In the select world of erudite music—and the adjective is used for what it is worth, even though Dona Gisa disapproved of it, as will be seen farther on—in this atmosphere impregnated with noble sentiments, no distinction was made regarding class and fortune among the members of the supercaste which the Sons of Orpheus formed, brothers in art. They were on the most fraternal terms; calling one another by their first names and nicknames—even the Poor Devil, who there was the Gifted Violinist: Lalau, Pinhozinho, Azinhavre, Raul das Meninas, Pampa Mustang. And the same thing, or nearly the same thing, happened with the women. They called one another Heleninha, Gildoca, Sussuca, Toquinha. Dona Flor was known as "my saint," "dark beauty," and her advice was sought in culinary matters. It was not their fault that sometimes Dona Flor was out of place in their conversation, ignorant of certain topics which were never-failing in that milieu. After all, she did not play bridge, was not a member of the clubs or indispensable at their social gatherings. During those hiatuses of silence, Dona Flor kept her eyes on her husband blowing into his bassoon, with his calm, happy face. She smiled then, the chatter of the women mattering not at all to her, feeling no sense of isolation.

When Dr. Teodoro informed her that their house had been chosen for the coming rehearsal, Dona Flor was really on her mettle. She was not going to play second fiddle to anybody. Before her husband knew it, she had invited half the city, prepared to spend her savings, if necessary, on a feast of major proportions. It was hard to hold her back. She wanted to show those society dames that even in the home of the poor, visitors were properly received.

Dr. Teodoro tried to limit the refreshments: at most she should serve some hors d'ôeuvres and sweets in addition to the

beer. If she wanted particularly to please the director, let her
prepare a dish of hominy cooked in coconut milk, which Mr.
Agenor was especially fond of.

"Besides he deserves it. He has a surprise for you. And what a
surprise!"

Even so, in spite of her husband's admonitions, Dona Flor
served a sumptuous repast and filled the house to overflowing. The
table was a sight to behold: bean fritters, fried fish vinaigrette,
coconut candy, hominy cooked in corn husks, peanut brittle,
codfish fritters, cheese tarts, all manner of dainties and tidbits. Not
to mention the kettle of hominy cooked in coconut milk, what a
sight! Méndez's bar supplied cases of beer, lemon and strawberry
soda, and *guaraná*.

The rehearsal was a success. Although only two of the wives of
the musicians put in an appearance, Dona Helena and Dona Gilda,
the house was full of people, the neighbors all excited, the students
nervous, the friends beside themselves (Dona Dinorá came within
an inch of dying from indigestion).

The orchestra assembled in the classroom, where, in addition to
the musicians, certain persons of quality were seated: Dom Clemente, Dona Gisa, Dona Norma, the Argentines (Dona Nancy had
really dressed for the occasion, elegant beyond words), Dr. Ives,
with something to say about everything, as he always had, emitting
opinions about music, alluding to operas and Caruso: "That was a
voice if there ever was one."

There came a moment's pause when Master Agenor Gomes,
baton in hand, said he had something he wanted to communicate, a
surprise for the lady of the house, a tribute. That afternoon, for
the first time, they were going to rehearse one of his compositions,
an unpublished romance, especially written "in honor of Dona
Florípedes Paiva, the adorable spouse of our brother in Orpheus,
Dr. Teodoro Madureira." A thrill ran through all those present,
and the silence, which up to that moment had been lacking in
respect, broken by laughter and talk, became total.

The kindly conductor smiled; for him those amateur musicians
were like a prolongation of his family, and with pavanes and
gavottes, waltzes and romances, he celebrated the happy moments

of their lives, the joys, the sadness. If the father or mother of one of them died, if a child was born to them, if one of them got married, as in the case of the druggist, the master unleashed his inspiration, and, whether it was an occasion for tears or laughter, manifested his solidarity in a page of music.

"*Lullaby for Florípedes*," the director announced, "with Dr. Teodoro Madureira in a bassoon solo." It was truly beautiful.

But a rehearsal is a rehearsal, not a concert, nor even an exhibition. If in other numbers, in which the orchestra felt itself polished, the conductor nevertheless from time to time interrupted this one or that one, in that unpublished work they went step by step, or, rather, note by note, including Dr. Teodoro in his bassoon solo. It was not easy to accompany the melody, to capture its grace, the beauty as gentle as the object of its tribute, meek and tender.

Even so Dona Flor was deeply touched, both by the gesture on the part of the conductor and by the devotion of the druggist, almost trembling as he sought the perfect scale to honor his wife. Before him the score, and he, with his nerves so tense, almost rigid, his forehead beaded with sweat, his hands cold, but prepared to express through the deep tones of the bassoon the happiness of a man who had triumphed, his life full and achieved, with his money, his drug-store, his knowledge, his oratory, his peace and order, his music, his chaste, comely wife, and the general respect he enjoyed. He had sought that unison, and had won it. Dona Flor lowered her head, overcome with so many honors.

Fortunately, the hour of intermission arrived and the master regaled himself at the table, taking a second helping of hominy, while the others stuffed themselves with those toothsome dishes, swimming in beer, soda, and *guaraná*. Everything perfect.

6

RONDEAU OF MELODIES

Dona Flor, unassuming and polite, glided through those worlds of pharmacy and amateur musicians, giving thought to her attire so as to be in keeping with the circles into which her new state had introduced her. When she had been a girl, before her first marriage, a poor guest at rich homes, in the mansions of magnates, she had been the best dressed. Only Rosália, her sister, could outdo her in fashion that was in the best of taste. No other, however rich or spendthrift she might be.

Different circles, different matters, different conversations, new acquaintances. Social demands, obligations, at times a tea, a visit, a rehearsal. In the residence of a director of the Association of Pharmacy or an important member of the amateur orchestra. Off went Dona Flor amid the admiring remarks of her neighbors, elegant in her perfect turnout, her bearing, an eyeful of woman. She had put on a little weight, was sleek and chic, made men's mouths water:

"Some dame," Mr. Vivaldo of the funeral parlor muttered between his teeth. "The extra flesh sits well on her, rounds out her backside. What a morsel! That Dr. Cough Syrup is eating a dish fit for a king."

"He treats her like a queen, gives her everything she wants, a nobleman." This was the comment of Dona Dinorá, who had foreseen Dr. Teodoro in the crystal ball and was his unwavering champion. "And what a picture of a man!"

A new neighbor, Dona Magnólia, a constant window watcher,

experienced in her judgment of the abilities of passers-by, re-marked: "I have heard it said that everything about him is big, that it's like a table leg. Now, who could have said that?" Nobody: she had taken one look and sized things up, thanks to her steady and useful practice.

Dona Amélia spoke up, "The two match in looks and kindness. Who ever saw a more perfect marriage? They were made for one another, and it took them so long to meet . . ."

"She first had to undergo horrors at the hands of the first one, that unfeeling worthless wretch . . ."

"Thanks to that she can better appreciate the one she has now. She can compare them."

Dona Flor did not want to measure or compare anything: all she wanted was to live her life. At long last a decorous, pleasant life, so well treated that it was a delight. Why didn't they let her alone? Before they had come to sympathize with her in litanies of pity, deploring her fate. Now it was all praise for her success, her admirable decision to marry Dr. Teodoro, the happiness of that exemplary pair.

The street was alert to Dona Flor's every move: her dresses, her society connections, the new order of her life, with visits, excursions, movies, and the coming election campaign in the Pharmaceutical Association. But, above all, the neighborhood was engrossed by music, a topic that came up almost at the same time as the sumptuous amateur orchestra rehearsal and the affairs of Marilda, the student of pedagogy.

At the beginning the discussion was limited to academic and pretentious concepts, a heated and harsh argument between Dr. Ives, an admirer of opera, and Dona Gisa with her inflexible standards, the two brains of the neighborhood. Dona Rozilda, tactless and sour, who was there on a visit, added her contribution. But it was young Marilda who gave the debate a dramatic and moving quality, shifting it from the purely intellectual plane to the reality of the gap between the generations, between parents and children, the old and the new (in the words of a philosopher of the younger generation).

While Dona Gisa, after the rehearsal of the amateur orchestra had rejected the classification "erudite music" (so pleasing to the outmoded prejudices of Dona Rozilda) employed by Dr. Ives with reference to the waltzes, military marches, and romances, young Marilda had been having clandestine meetings, disturbing the peace of her family and the tranquility of the street, with one Oswaldinho and one Mário Augusto, the director of Radio Amaralina, newly established and in search of talent at low cost.

To Dona Gisa, "erudite music" was the immortal music of Beethoven and Bach, of Brahms and Chopin, of a few sublime composers: symphonies and sonatas, music to be listened to in silence and self-communion, played by the great orchestras under famous conductors, with interpreters of international fame. For an audience capable of listening and understanding. She had been brought up on that music, and in her unyielding sectarianism, in her extreme formalism, she classified everything else as trash, "for those lacking in musical education."

(It should be pointed out, however, that in that sweeping definition—"Everything else is trash"—Dona Gisa did not include folk music, which was the expression of the people, ardent and pure. Sambas and *modinhas*, "spirituals," cocos and rumbas enjoyed her respect and regard, and it was amusing to hear her murder, in her terrible accent, the words of the latest samba in vogue.) She could not bear the fatuousness of that other music, lacking power and character, tailored, in her opinion, to the bad taste of the middle class, which was incapable of appreciating the beauty and being stirred by the great masters. Dona Gisa was stirred as she listened to such records, in the dim lights at the homes of her German friends, those nights of so much spiritual pleasure (and with tidbits, a good drink, and certain anecdotes).

Dr. Ives's mouth opened in protest: such pretentiousness on the part of that *gringa* running to flesh! What about the operas, professor, *Rigoletto*, *The Barber of Seville*, *Pagliacci*, *O Guarani*, by our immortal Carlos Gomes—you hear, Dona Gisa, ours, Brazilian, born in Campinas, bearing the name of our beloved country to the stage of foreign theaters amid applause? What about those marvels, with their arias, duets, their baritones and basses, their prima donnas? If that is not erudite music, then what is? Peradventure sambas and rumbas, *modinhas* and tangos?

Don't toss this aside lightly, Dona Gisa, for on this subject (as, for that matter, on any other) Dr. Ives is an authority. Raising his voice and in a triumphant tone he asked: where could one find anything more refined than a good operetta like *The Merry Widow, The Dollar Princess,* or *The Count of Luxembourg*?

The musical culture of the doctor rested on a firm basis, was the result of direct experience. As a student he had gone with a group to Rio, and had attended, seated in the second gallery on free passes, various of the operas presented and sung by the "Grande Compagnia Musicale di Napoli." He was bedazzled by the performance, the melodies, and the voices of baritones and sopranos, tenors and contraltos. And he had heard them, Dona Gisa, not on records, but in the flesh, on the stage, in all the splendor of their genius, Tito Schipa, Galli-Curci, Jesus Gaviria, Benzanzoni, in *La Traviata, Tosca, Madam Butterfly,* and *Il Schiavo* (also by our Carlos Gomes, my dear). Later on he had seen all the wonderful films—he had not missed a one—with the best operettas interpreted by Jan Kiepura and Martha Eggerth, by Nelson Eddy and Jeanette MacDonald. Has Dona Gisa by chance seen them? All of them, not missing a one?

In his enthusiasm Dr. Ives hummed parts of the best-known arias and even went through a ballet step. There was no soft-soaping him, downgrading him. They could forget records and poppycock of that sort, for when it came to musical culture he took a second seat to nobody.

"You call that culture!" Dona Gisa raised her hands heavenward, offended not in her pride but in her basic concepts. "Culture is a different thing, doctor, more serious. And this holds true of music, the true, the great. It is a very different thing."

Dona Norma called upon to act as referee, chose to remain neutral, confessing: "I don't understand any of all this. Aside from sambas, marches, carnival music—all of which I know—I am nine times zero is zero. I saw one opera, when the Billoro-Cavallaro Company (nearly all of whose artists had left) was here trying to scrape together a few cents. It was pitiful. Not even a whole opera, just some selections from *Aida*."

"I was there, too," the doctor said, adding this to his score.

"I don't understand anything, but I listen to everything, for anything amuses me; I even find the knell for the dead pretty. I take it all in: concert and opera, operettas I just love, and I am crazy about the musical programs on the radio. One thing is certain: there is nothing that can compare with, nothing equal to a *modinha* by Caymmi. But, as far as I am concerned, everything is good, everything entertains me, and I while away the time, even at those rehearsals of Dr. Teodoro, where you don't have to pay much attention."

To Dona Rozilda it was blasphemy to compare the music of the amateur orchestra, a special delight for refined ears, with that din of the street urchins on the guitar. A nice person, Dona Norma, well married, rich, but with low tastes. On the other hand, the teacher, just because she was an American was always giving lessons. Possibly Dona Gisa, there in her own country, had known something better, more erudite, superior to the Sons of Orpheus. But Dona Rozilda was not sure and had her doubts. In her opinion they were the last word until someone could prove the contrary. Gentlemen of quality, so distinguished . . .

Smiling and silent, Dona Flor listened to the argument, speaking out only to defend the rehearsals of the amateur orchestra which Dona Gisa considered the "ultimate in boredom."

"Don't exaggerate."

"But isn't it true? It can't be otherwise, for it is a rehearsal. When did one ever hear of being invited to hear a musical rehearsal?"

"It's not their fault, but mine, who did the inviting. Only those who want to, go to their rehearsals, members of the family. When they give a concert, I'll invite you and then you'll see . . ."

Dona Gisa's pessimism was unshaken: "Maybe at a concert. But even so I can't help thinking—and forgive me, Flor—that those dilettantes leave much to be desired."

They left little to be desired, if one were to believe the reporters and musical critics of the newspapers, whose obligation it was to understand such matters. They lavished praise on every performance of the orchestra—over a radio station, in the auditorium of the School of Music. One of these critics, by name Finerkaes, born, so to speak, in the lap of music, for he was of German origin, in a burst of enthusiasm compared the Sons of Orpheus to the "best orchestras of the sort in Europe, to which they owed nothing, quite the contrary." When he arrived from Munich, this Finerkaes was fairly restrained in his judgments. But the tropics conquered him completely: he lost his moderation and never regained his winter cool.

Dr. Teodoro owned an album in which he collected the concert programs, reviews, articles referring to the orchestra, much printers' ink. After their marriage it was Dona Flor who assumed the care of this storehouse of successes, these proofs of her husband's small glory. The last piece of news pasted in it was to the effect that Master Agenor had composed a romance in honor of Dr. and Mrs. Teodoro Madureira, his magnum opus, which was at the moment in rehearsal. The Sons of Orepheus planned to play it. "And speaking of the Sons of Orpheus, when will this excellent orchestra give us the privilege of the concert so insistently called for by the lovers of good music in Bahia?" the journalist asked. As is clear, the amateur musicians had their faithful friends, many of them and unconditional.

At the same time that she was listening to the discussion about the orchestra, Dona Flor was turning over in her mind Marilda's problems, which also had to do with music and singing forbidden melodies. The last information concerning the conflict between mother and daughter had come from the girl herself, and had to do with the significant fact that Marilda had met, through Oswaldinho, that Mário Augusto of the Menina Station, the Amaralina, and the so-and-so had promised her an audition, and, if he found her voice to his liking, would give her a contract for a weekly program. Oswaldinho, unfortunately, had not made any headway at the Radio Society.

Dona Flor was ignorant of later developments. She had been very busy during those days, and could not devote the necessary attention to Marilda. So it was that only after the drama did she learn of the girl's success in the microphone test. Mario Augusto was enchanted with her voice and (even more so) with her beauty, and drew up a contract for an important program, at a good hour, on Saturday nights. The salary was small, but what more could a beginner expect? With the draft of the contract in her purse, Marilda came running home, overwhelmed with emotion.

Dona Maria do Carmo tore the paper up. "I raised and brought you up to be a decent woman, to get married. As long as I live . . ."

"But, Mamma, you promised . . ." Marilda recalled the promise the widow had made the day she heard her sing on an amateur program. "You said when I was eighteen . . ."

"You're not eighteen yet . . ."

"I lack only three months."

"I will never let you, as long as you are living under my roof. Never."

"Under your roof? All right, you'll see."

"What will I see? Come, out with it."

"Nothing."

She even went looking for Dona Flor, a warm, friendly bosom, who could give her good advice and comfort. But she had left after the afternoon class, and Marilda was in a hurry, for evening was coming on and she would not endure such tyranny any longer. She ran away from home.

She collected a few clothes, several pairs of shoes, the collection of *Fashions of the Day*, the photographs of Francisco Alves and Sílvio Caldas, put them all in a suitcase, and took a street-car, all this while her mother was taking a bath.

She went straight to Radio Amaralina. When Mario Augusto learned that she was under age and had run away from home, he was very much upset, and did not even want her there in the building. She was to leave immediately: he was not looking for headaches. Marilda went into the street, aimlessly looking for Oswaldinho, from address to address, from the Radio Society to the office of a business firm, where he hung out. From there she went on to the lower part of the city where he had an appointment with one of the station's patrons, the important Magalhães. Oswaldinho? The one who works in the Radio? He had been and gone, perhaps to the studios, did she have the address? She set out again for the Radio Society, on Carlos Gomes street: she went up in the Lacerda Elevator, walked along Chile Street, and cutting across Castro Alves Square, finally, perspiring and bewildered, she stopped at the door of the station. Oswaldinho was not there, but the doorman let her wait, and even brought her a chair.

Tired and a little frightened, but still boiling with rage and prepared for anything, she stayed there hour after hour, seeing artists she knew pass, famous singers, among them Silvinho Lamenha, with a flower in his buttonhole, and a huge ring on his little finger. Some of them gave her the eye—who would that pretty young thing be? The doorman said to her from time to time, smiling (perhaps wanting to comfort her, pitying her distress and youth): "He has not come yet, but he won't be long. He should be here any minute."

Around eight o'clock, when it was completely dark, her eyes burning and her heart a lump of fear, she asked the doorman where she could get a sandwich and a cup of coffee. At the lunch counter of the Radio, he told her, and she went in. There, seeing and hearing singers and actresses, her idols, she regained strength, and decided to wait a lifetime, if necessary, to achieve her ideal of becoming a star.

She went back to the entrance and thought: "Mamma, poor thing, must be dying of fright," and sorrow and remorse began to infiltrate her anger and boldness. Soon afterward the day doorman left, and his replacement told Marilda not to expect Oswaldinho: "By this time he's not coming."

It was now nearly half past nine, and she was having trouble keeping back her tears, when a toothless individual approached, leaning against the door, and, after looking her over carefully, struck up a conversation with the porter, laughing, telling him about his gambling expriences there nearby, in Tabaris. Suddenly Marilda heard him mention Oswaldinho's name, and learned that her friend had been playing roulette since late in the afternoon. Very happy, according to the toothless visitor.

"Tabaris? What is that and where is it?"

The man laughed and looked at her with indecent desire: "Not far off. If you want me to, I'll take you there." He was dying to see the scene, enjoy the tears and recriminations. That Oswaldinho was death on girls.

They crossed the square, the toothless scoundrel making conversation, trying to find out if Marilda was wife, sweetheart, or just girlfriend. To be the wife, she was very young; for a girlfriend, she was taking it very hard. At the door of the cabaret, they ran into Mirandão, who was leaving for the Palace. He threw Marilda a passing glance, then recognized her, and turned back quickly: "Marilda, what in the devil are you doing here?"

"Ah, Mr. Miranda, how are you?"

Mirandão knew the toothless one all too well: "Cougar's Breath, what are you up to here with this girl?"

"Me? Nothing. She asked me to . . ."

"To come here? You're lying." Mirandão shouted.

Marilda excused the other; she had asked him to.

"To come here, to Tabaris? What for? I want to know."

She finally told him everything, and he took her home, which was not far off. There they found Dona Maria do Carmo practically out of her mind, crying, stretched out in bed, screaming for her daughter. Beside her were Dona Flor, Dr. Teodoro, Dona Amélia. Dona Norma had taken command of the search party, supported by Dona Gisa. They had dragged Mr. Zé Sampaio out of bed (in a rage) and set out for the first aid stations, the police department, the morgue.

When she laid eyes on her daughter, Dona Maria do Carmo threw her arms around her, hugging her, convulsed with tears. The two wept, kissed one another, asking mutual forgiveness. Upset, Dr. Teodoro withdrew almost brusquely, for, even going counter to Dona Flor, he had upheld Dona Maria do Carmo in her first and implacable determination to give the runaway daughter a whipping she would not forget.

Dona Flor tried to dissuade her, win her over to Marilda's side; she, too, as a girl had swallowed the same medicine and it had done no good. Why was Dona Maria do Carmo so obstinate in opposing her daughter's vocation?

Vocation, my eye! Dr. Teodoro backed up the widow. What the girl needed was a lesson to bring her to her senses and teach her to obey. They almost got into a quarrel, husband and wife, both unyielding, Dona Flor in defense of Marilda, the poor little thing, Dr. Teodoro in defense of principles, the duties of children toward their parents, a sacred cause. But it did not go too far, for the doctor checked himself and said: "My dear, you have your opinion, and I respect it without sharing it. I have mine, in which I was brought up, and it suits me, so let's each abide by our own. Moreover, we're not going to argue about this, as we have no children." Nor will we, he might have added for, while they were still engaged, Dona Flor had told him that she was barren.

There was not a trace of bitterness between them, as they leaned over the grieving widow begging to die if her daughter did not come back at once.

Marilda arrived, and we have seen what ensued. Dr. Teodoro, admitting defeat, withdrew. Dona Amélia and Dona Êmina left, too, only Dona Flor remaining with the mother and the daughter, and the question was settled once and for all: Marilda had won her right to the microphone. Dona Flor lingered only a minute, just long enough to make sure of the agreement, the mother's blessing on the future star's plans, and then she went home to find her *compadre* Mirandão waiting for her in the living-room.

"*Compadre*, why is it you have disappeared and not come to see me? Neither you, nor my *comadre*, nor the child? What did I do to offend you? I want to know even before I thank you for your kindness to Maria do Carmo and Marilda. Why have you quarreled with me?"

"I did not quarrel, why should I quarrel, my *comadre*? If I haven't been here, it's because I have been on the move every minute . . ."

"Is that the only reason, because you have been busy? Forgive me, *compadre*, but I don't believe you."

Mirandão looked out at the transparent night, the distant sky: "My *comadre* knows that nobody should come between a husband and a wife; even a shadow, a memory can do harm. I know that you are happy, everything goes well with you, and that is what I

want. You deserve all this and more. The fact that you don't see
me doesn't lessen our friendship."

This was true, Dona Flor smiled, and walked over beside her
compadre: "There is one thing I would like to ask you . . ."

"Don't ask, command, *comadre* . . ."

"It won't be long before the festival of Sts. Cosme and Damian,
that vow . . ."

"I had thought of that, just the other day I said to the missus: 'I
wonder if there will be a celebration this year at the *comadre's*
house?' "

"And what do you think, *compadre?* How do you feel about
it?"

"I can only tell you, *comadre*, that nobody can walk in two
directions at the same time, backward and forward. The obligation
was not yours, it was the *compadre's*, and it is buried with him, the
spirits are satisfied." After a pause: "If you feel the same way,
comadre, then set your mind at ease. You are not behaving wrong
toward the saints nor breaking a rule."

Dona Flor listened thoughtfully, concentrated as though she
were weighing ways of life: "You are right, *compadre*, but it is
not only to the spirits that one must render an accounting. I
wanted to observe the obligation which your *compadre* took very
seriously. There are things one cannot undo."

"So?"

"I had thought we could hold the feast in your house. I can go
there on that day, see the baby, take all the ingredients, prepare the
caruru, and we will eat it. I will ask Norminha and nobody else."

"As you wish, *comadre*. My house is yours, you have only to
give the orders. If I were sure of having the money, I would tell
you not to bring anything. But who can say whether that will be a
winning or a losing night? If I knew, I would be rich. You bring
the okra, to be on the safe side."

Having quieted down, Dr. Teodoro returned. He already knew
Mirandão by name, his reputation and his feats, and they exchanged brief greetings.

"This is my *compadre*, Teodoro, and good friend."

"You must drop in to see us," the doctor said, but it was not an invitation, merely a polite phrase; if Mirandão came, he would put up with him.

Mirandão returned to his harum-scarum life, Marilda arranged with her mother that they go to see Mr. Mário Augusto together the next day to discuss the terms of the contract and the date for her debut.

"Come, my dear," the druggist said.

It was late, but even so, to relax completely after all that excitement and letdown, Dr. Teodoro brought out his bassoon and the score. Dona Flor sat down and began to darn the cuffs and collars of his shirts, for the doctor changed every day.

In the quiet, warm living-room Dr. Teodoro practiced the solo of the romance composed in Dona Flor's honor. Bent over her sewing, she listened a little absent-mindedly, trying to order her confused thoughts. Her mind was far away, on other music.

Trying to capture the elusive notes on his instrument, bringing out the purest, most moving tone, triumphing over the scales of the difficult melody, Dr. Teodoro smiled, his calm restored. After all what did it matter to him how Dona Maria do Carmo dealt with her headstrong daughter? He was not the world's censor, and it would be foolish for him to quarrel with his dear little wife, so pretty and so good, for silly reasons that had nothing to do with them. He flew off on the right chord, touching the proper key, alone, harmonious and pure.

Dona Flor was finding her way back from other music, but not that of the recognized classics such as Bach and Beethoven, the symphonies and sonatas, which Dona Gisa thought so highly of. She was coming back from popular songs, the serenaders' guitars, the bohemian ukeleles, the crystalline laughter of the bagpipes. She must now adjust herself to the amateur orchestra, the solemn melody of oboes, trumpets, violoncellos, the resounding chords of the bassoon. Cast aside that other music which distracted her, leading her down dark pathways, the mystery of the crossroads. She must bury them in the rehearsals of the bassoon, the scales of the orchestra, all those memories of bygone melodies, of days now past, gone to come no more.

The sound of the bassoon vibrated over the doctor's shirts.

7

Of incidents involving women, there were only two. At least these were the ones Dona Flor heard about. She, nevertheless, would have put her hand in the fire for her husband, not believing that any other skirt existed in the doctor's life.

One of these two episodes, however, the one having to do with Mirtes Rocha de Araújo, the swinging *carioca*, never amounted to anything—nothing but a quid pro quo and a disillusion. An ephemeral disillusion, to be sure, for the brazen thing was not going to waste time on lamentations; she shrugged her shoulders. Better luck next time.

She was married to a bank clerk who had been transferred to Bahia with a better job and salary. Mirtes bewailed to her friends this exile to a city lacking in masculine attractions and without the freedom of Rio de Janeiro, where she had made a certain name for herself in adulterous activities. During her free and empty hours, having no children or other duties, she spent her time and her natural gifts on charitable amusement. Those were pleasant afternoons, in the company of kindhearted young men, highly competent and physically attractive, without running any risk, all so smooth and discreet. Where was she to find in Bahia that masculine prowess of one Serginho, for example, "a real stud," and the comfortable safety of a "rendezvous" at Dona Fausta's?

Inés Vasques dos Santos, a Bahian who was proud of the progress of her country, took offense at this disdain, with her city relegated to the condition of a village where there was nobody with whom to be unfaithful to one's husband nor any place to do it in safety. Why did Mirtes insult Bahia without even knowing it?

After all, Salvador was not such a hamlet or that underdeveloped.

Inés had begun her implantation of horns there, and could affirm, knowing exactly what she was talking about, that there were propitious opportunities for the tilling of these fields with the assurance of a rich harvest. Highly discreet bordellos, bungalows hidden among coconut trees on out-of-the-way beaches, with the breeze and the sea, a dream. As for young men, oh boy!

With dreamy eyes, biting her lip with her little teeth, Inés Vasquez dos Santos gave rein to her fond memories. Especially an insolent good-for-nothing, an idler, a gambler, but when it came time for the joust, what a knight errant! Inés, who was fickle but efficient, knew young men galore on the most intimate terms. "But let me tell you, girl: I have never yet met his equal. I can still taste his skin and feel the tip of his tongue behind my ear, his laugh when he took my money."

"Took money?" Mirtes had always wanted to know a gigolo.

Inés generously gave her information and address. School of Savor and Art, between Cabeça and Largo Dois de Julho. The teacher, his wife, was a nice girl, not bad-looking, with straight hair and coppery skin. Mirtes could register as a student: the classes helped pass the time and then the chaser would cast eye and hand on her, with his siren's song.

She was not to forget to write her afterward, telling what had happened and thanking her. Inés had no doubts about the delightful consequences of the association, which would be useful to all concerned, even the husband. With her diploma as doctor of the culinary art, Mirtes could serve him Bahian delicacies of the most delicious flavor. The teacher was first-class, really mistress of her art, with magic hands.

Never had Dona Flor suspected, neither at the time nor now, the affair that was going on between her late husband and that Inés, in those days a thin, well-behaved person, eager to learn the art of seasoning. If it had not been for the lack of discretion on the part of the tempestuous Mirtes later on, she might never have learned of that prank of Vadinho's. One more, one less, there had been so many, and now Dona Flor was married to a man of a different clay, with different standards, undefiled.

As for Mirtes, no sooner was she settled in Bahia than she looked up the school to register in it. Dona Flor tried to persuade her to wait until the new term began, but Mirtes was in a hurry, could not wait. She invented the possibility of their return to Rio in a short time, a brief assignment in Salvador, and she was not going to lose the opportunity to learn at least a few dishes: her husband was crazy about food cooked with dendê oil. Dona Flor, the silly thing, even promised that in her free time she would teach her at least how to cook *vatapá*, *xinxim*, and *apeté*.

She did not teach her either those or other delicacies, for Mirtes's transit through the school was of brief duration. Not having seen the teacher's husband during the first days, on the third she asked a fellow student about him, who said it would be difficult for her to see the doctor during classes, for he was in the drugstore at those hours. "Doctor? Drugstore?" She did not know he was a druggist, for that crazy Inés had only mentioned his sporting qualities, telling her nothing about his occupation outside the bed. Mirtes had been so full of hope: at last she was going to meet a real gigolo.

It so happened that that same day, shortly after this exchange, Dr. Teodoro needed a document and came to look for it. Excusing himself over and over again, very solemn and self-conscious, he walked through the group of students.

"Who is that?" Mirtes asked.

"Dr. Teodoro, the husband. And to think I had just told you it was hard to see him, and he showed up!"

"That's the teacher's husband? That one?"

"Whose did you think he was?"

Still excusing himself, with the paper he was looking for in his hand, he hurried back to the Scientific Pharmacy. Mirtes shook her head with its short platinum blonde hair (the latest fashion): either Inés was crazy as a bedbug or something had happened. Probably the teacher had got tired of the gigolo's tricks, and had kicked him out, unless he had run away with another woman. Be that as it may, Dona Flor had certainly chosen the complete opposite, a serious, respectable man, useless and impossible from Mirtes's point of view, vomit-making: the dolt had not even noticed the gleam of her hair, he had passed her by without even looking at her. Better so. That idiot was probably not any good to Dona Flor even as a husband, he might be one of those cuckolds without any sense of fair play, who avenge their honor with bullet or knife, obsolete and melodramatic.

She did not return to the school, nor did she feel she owed the teacher any apology. Besides, she watched her diet carefully to stay thin, in keeping with her "vamp" type.

Being a blabbermouth, she learned later on about the death of the fiery stud Inés had praised so highly and the widow's second marriage to that blind dullard. Blind, yes, indeed, and suffering from the worst kind of blindness, that of the person who closes his eyes to life, who cannot stand the light of the sun and hair the color of silver.

Flor learned the details of that comedy of errors from her friend Ênaide, who, in turn, had been a friend of Inés Vasques dos Santos since their school days, and, for that reason, the confidante to whom she told about Mirtes Rocha de Araujo's mistake in Bahia, summing up her disenchantment in a phrase that is almost literary: "That was my adventure with a dead man. It was all that was lacking in my dossier."

A phrase and a complaint: to meet Dr. Teodoro, "that milksop, that dunce," she had burned her fingers on Dona Flor's stove in the class for frying crabs. Of all the ridiculous things!

As for Dona Magnólia, that inverterate, intrepid window watcher, the fact that the doctor was serious and respectable did not divest him of interest, but even gave him a certain fillip, something different. In her sowing of horns, a task at which she was as proficient as the pedantic *carioca*, the secret-police agent's girl friend had learned that variety is the spice of life, in color, appearance, and age. She hated monotony. Whereas Mirtes, sectarian, thought only of callow youths, Magnólia, antidogmatic, refused to abide by a formula, a pattern. Today a black, tomorrow a blonde, the next day half-and-half, the restless adolescent followed by the graying fifty-year-old. Why always the same dish, with the same seasoning? Dona Magnólia was eclectic.

Four times a day, at least, as he came and went from his house to the drugstore and vice versa, the "splendid forty-year-old" (according to Dona Dinorá's crystal ball) passed beneath her window, where, in a low-cut robe, Dona Magnólia rested her insolent breasts, as big and round as they were enticing. The students of the Ipiranga Prep School, located on the next street, took to changing their itineraries, unanimously parading in military formation under the window on which rested those breasts that could have suckled them all. Dona Magnólia was touched: so sweet in their school uniforms, the smaller standing on tiptoe for the joy of seeing, the dream of touching. "Let them suffer so they will learn," Dona Magnólia reasoned pedagogically, shifting to exhibit still better breasts and bust (unfortunately the window frame somewhat limited the rest of her display).

The schoolboys suffered, the workmen of the vicinity groaned, delivery clerks, young men like Roque, who framed pictures, old men like Alfredo, occupied with his saints. People came from far off, from Sé, from Jiquitáia, from Itapagipe, from Tororó, from Matatu, making a pilgrimage just to see those celebrated wonders. A beggar, at three in the afternoon, sharp, under the hot sun crossed the street: "Alms for a poor man blind in both eyes."

The best alms was the divine sight in the window: even running the danger of being unmasked, snatching off his black glasses, he opened his eyes wide, feasting the two at the same time, staring at those gifts of God, the property of the police. Even if the secret agent should pursue him and throw him into jail on charges of imposture, panhandling, even so he would feel it had been worth while.

Only Dr. Teodoro, cravatted, his white suit stiffly starched, did not raise his eyes to the heaven exposed to view in the window. Bowing his head, in a greeting that indicated his good breeding, he raised his hat, to say "Good morning" and "Good afternoon," indifferent to the outburst of breasts which Dona Magnólia had surrounded by lace to heighten the effect, which should have rocked that man of marble back on his heels, undoing that insulting conjugal fidelity. Only he, that big dark brute, that handsome dog, undoubtedly with a tool like a table leg, only he went by without showing any signs of impression, delight, ecstasy, without seeing, without even looking at that sea of breasts. Ah, that was too much, an insulting offense, an unbearable challenge.

Monogamous, Dona Dinorá had affirmed, conversant with all the details of the doctor's life. He was not a person to be unfaithful to his wife; he had not even been so with Tavinha Manemolência, a prostitute, though restricted as to her clientele. Dona Magnólia had confidence in her charms: "My dear fortuneteller, take note, write down what I am saying: there is no such thing as a monogamous man, we know that, you and I. Look into your crystal ball, and if it is to be trusted, it will reveal to you the doctor in a brothel bed—that of Sobrinha, to be exact—with your humble servant, Magnólia Fátima das Neves, at her best, beside him."

So the doctor was not moved by the swooning eyes of his neighbor, by her seductive voice answering his greeting, with her breasts resting on the window sill, and the desire of the young men growing by day and by night, the drooling of the old men? Dona Magnólia had other arms which she could use, and she was taking the offensive at once.

Thus one sultry afternoon, when the air was heavy with desire, inviting to the delights of bed and lullabies, Dona Magnólia entered the swinging doors of the pharmacy, carrying in her hand a box of injections to be used as a new temptation of St. Anthony. In a thin summer dress she went lavishing her riches prodigally.

"Doctor, could you give me an injection?"

Dr. Teodoro was measuring nitrates in his laboratory, his starched white coat making him look even taller and giving him a kind of scientific dignity. With a smile she held out the box of injections. Taking it, he put it on the table and said: "Just a minute."

Dona Magnólia stood there, sizing him up, more pleased every minute. What a man, of good age, strong, brave. She sighed and he, leaving his powders and prescription, raised his eyes to her: "You have a pain?"

"Ah, Mr. Doctor," and she smiled as though to say that her pain was killing her and he was the cause of it.

"An injection?" He examined the bottle. "A vitamin compound . . . to keep your balance . . . these new medicines. What balance, madame?" and he smiled politely as though he considered those treatments a waste of time and money.

"It's my nerves, doctor. I am so sensitive, you have no idea."

He picked up a needle with a pair of tweezers, lifting it out of the sterilizer, while he drew the liquid into the syringe, calmly and without haste, one thing at a time, and everything in its place. A motto which hung over his worktable summed up his principles: "A place for everything and everything in its place." Dona Magnólia read it; she knew about a thing and the place for it, and she eyed the doctor maliciously. How sure he was of himself, that big shot!

He dipped a wad of cotton into alcohol, and raised the syringe: "Please roll up your sleeve."

In a voice both coy and malicious, Dona Magnólia answered: "Not in the arm, doctor, not in the arm."

He pulled the curtain across. She raised her skirt, displaying before the doctor's eyes riches even larger and more tempting than those exhibited every day at the window. What a backside, like that of a flying ant!

She did not even feel the prick of the needle, Dr. Teodoro had such a light and steady hand. The alcohol-soaked cotton the doctor rubbed her skin with gave her a pleasant sensation. A drop of alcohol ran down her thigh, and she sighed again.

Once more Dr. Teodoro mistook the meaning of that gentle moan: "Where does it hurt you?"

Still holding up the hem of her dress showing haunches nobody had ever been able to resist before, Dona Magnólia looked the distinguished personage straight in the eye: "Is it possible that you don't understand, that you don't understand anything?"

He really didn't. "Understand what?"

Furious now, she let her skirt fall, covering her disdained hindquarters, and said, between her teeth: "Are you blind? Don't you have eyes in your head?"

With his mouth half open, his face dull, his eyes staring, the doctor asked himself if perhaps she was out of her mind. Dona Magnólia, in view of such incredible stupidity, finished her question: "Or are you a complete nitwit?"

"Madame . . ."

She raised her hand and touched the cheek of the star of the pharmaceutical world, and with a voice once more swooning and coy, she confessed all: "Can't you see, you foolish creature, that I am nuts about you, head over heels in love with you? Can't you see?"

She came closer, her objective being to get him going right there, at least the preliminaries, and not even a babe in arms could have mistaken what she was up to with her lips pursed, her eyes languishing.

"Get out!" said the doctor in a low but firm tone.

"My beautiful mulatto," and she put her arms around him, clasping him to her.

"Get out!" The doctor cast aside those avid arms, that voracious mouth, fortified by his principles and unshakable convictions. "Get out of here!"

Majestic in his unswerving virtue, his white coat, syringe in hand, his expression of affront, if the doctor had been on a pedestal, he would have been the perfect monument, the luminous statue of morality triumphing over vice. But vice, in the person of the disconcerted and humiliated Dona Magnólia, did not look upon the unsullied hero with eyes of remorse and contrition, but with anger, rage, fury: "Fag! Freak! You're going to pay me for this, you old homo!" and she rushed out to make trouble.

Poor Dona Magnólia, the victim of disdain and bad luck, for she could not possibly have foreseen the results of her intrigue, her plans of vengeance toppling to the ground. Emphatic and insulted (in her modesty, in her honor as an upright concubine), she complained to the secret policeman of "the way that old goat, the druggist, ran after me," making her the most shameless propositions, telling her dirty stories, inviting her to go with him to see the moonrise on the beach of Abaeté. The hound deserved a lesson, a sound thrashing, maybe a hitch in the hoosegow, with a few smacks of the ferule to teach him to respect other people's wives.

She had not mentioned this before to avoid a row, and out of consideration for his wife, who was such a kindly person. But that day he had really got out of bounds. She had gone to the drug-store for an injection, and the scoundrel had run his hand down her breast, so she had to leave on the run.

Silently the secret policeman heard her out, and Dona Magnó-lia, who knew him well, could see the growing rage in his face. The doctor would pay dear for his boldness, at the very least a night in jail.

That afternoon the policeman had a dustup with one of his colleagues as the result of a mistake in the payoff of several mil-reis extorted from the numbers bookies. During the somewhat harsh dialogue that preceded the punches and slaps, Dona Magnó-lia's lover having called his colleague a pickpocket, he heard revela-tions from the other which left him appalled: "I'd rather be a thief than a cuckold, two-timed without even knowing it, like my dear friend here." And he proceeded to enlarge upon certain recent incidents in Dona Magnólia's love life. In short he informed him that, among his police colleagues alone, there were five who took turns at putting horns on him. Not to mention the commissioner. If a light bulb were put on each horn, it would illuminate half the city, from Largo da Sé to Campo Grande. He might not be a thief, but he was a disgrace to the force. And then the punches began.

His honor cleansed by the fight, he made peace with his com-rade, and from him and others he heard further dismaying news. Had he never heard talk about a certain Messalina? No, she did not operate in the district, she belonged to history, and what a reputa-tion she had. But compared to Dona Magnólia, she was an unsullied virgin . . .

Crushed, the policeman swore vengeance, incidentally plagiar-izing Dona Magnólia's threat to the druggist: "That cow! She's going to pay me!"

So he listened skeptically to all that rigmarole, and no sooner had Dona Magnólia mentioned how she had defended her breasts against the pseudoadvances of the doctor than the detective grabbed her by the nose, and demanded a full confession.

It was a beating administered by an expert, one with experience and a liking for the job. Dona Magnólia told all she had done and had not done, even bygone affairs that antedated her acquaintance with the policeman, and, for good measure, the whole truth about her relations with Dr. Teodoro. The whole truth in terms which though they established his innocence did not fail to reflect her opinion of him: impotent, all façade and nothing behind it, for nobody had ever insulted her to the point of resisting the sight of her ass ready for combat.

What a hubbub in the street, a real ruckus! The slaps and screams, the oaths drew a curious twittering mob of neighbors before the policeman's house, gossips and students of the prep school. The gossips and the neighbors, for the most part, approved of the beating, which was well administered and well deserved, having only one defect: it had been too long in coming. The boys from the school felt each slap, each yank as though it were in their own flesh, all of them having possessed that tender, inviting body in their lonely adolescent beds. There were nights when she slept, ubiquitously, the omnipresent shepherdess of youths, goddess of love, in more than forty beds at the same time.

The ones, however, who entered the house of the policeman were Dona Flor and Dona Norma, the others limiting themselves to approving or criticizing. Nobody wanted trouble with a cop.

"Mr. Tiago, what goes on here? Are you trying to kill this poor woman? Let her go," Dona Norma shouted.

"She deserves to be killed, this cow," the agent answered, giving her a few last blows.

"The poor thing. You are a monster," Dona Flor said, bending over the battered victim of fate.

"Poor thing, indeed." The policeman choked on the injustice. "Do you know what the 'poor thing' cooked up about your husband?"

"About my husband?"

"She came telling me that the doctor was running after her and tried to have a go at her in the drugstore today. When I pinned her down, she admitted it was all a lie, that she wanted to make trouble between us, so I would go looking for satisfaction, and that it was she who led him on and he wouldn't bite. Not to mention other things." In a saturnine voice he asked: "Do you know what they call me? 'The disgrace to the police force.'"

That night, when they were getting ready to go to the movies and Dona Flor was powdering herself in front of the mirror, she said smiling at Dr. Teodoro: "So you try to make the patients who come to the pharmacy for an injection? You wanted a fling with Dona Magnólia . . ."

He looked at her and saw that she was joking. Dona Flor could not keep a straight face, it all seemed so comical. Try as she would to be moved by her husband's loyalty, she could not get the picture out of her mind of Dr. Teodoro with the syringe in his hand, and the bosomy Magnólia, lost to all shame, trying to kiss him. That was a decent husband if ever there was one. But how could she help it if that incident struck her as funny, ridiculous rather than heroic?

"That crazy thing! What ever gave her the idea that I would profane my laboratory, take advantage of a customer?"

"In this case it wasn't taking advantage, it was she who was asking for it."

He lowered his voice: he had never completely lost his shyness toward his wife in matters of this sort. "How could I even look at another woman, when I have you, my dear?"

A more loyal, upright man did not exist. Dona Flor raised her lips to his, and he kissed her lightly.

"Thank you, Teodoro, I feel the same way about you."

In the street, on the corners, over their drinks at Méndez's bar, the men discussed the beating, the reasons for it, and its effects. Dona Magnólia had sought refuge in the home of relatives, taking baths in water mixed with salt, and the secret policeman was numbing himself with rum.

Mr. Vivaldo of the funeral parlor raised the question: was Dr. Teodoro impotent or wasn't he? Not only had the slut affirmed this at the top of her lungs, but, to tell the truth, only a eunuch would be able to resist the temptation of Magnólia, her abundance of riches. There was reason to doubt his manliness, there really was. Moysés Alves, the cacao planter, got all worked up defending the druggist: "Fag? That's a lie of that indecent slut. What he is is a serious man, with a sense of responsibility. Did you expect him to start screwing that hussy on the counter?"

Mr. Vivaldo was not wholly convinced: "To turn up your nose at a dish like that . . . in the drugstore or wherever it was. If she should show up here, at the 'Flowering Paradise,' I'd be more than willing, even if we had to use a coffin."

What they were in agreement on was one detail: whether because he was impotent or austere, Dr. Teodoro had behaved badly in chasing her out without giving her another appointment: "God gives nuts to those who don't have teeth."

Echoes of these discussions, going on at street corners and bars, growing heated over beer and rum, reached Dona Flor's ears, as did the general praise of friends and neighbors.

"If only all husbands were like that, it would be a different story."

She got cross with this slandering of her husband, and said to Maria Antônia, a former student, garish and intriguing, who came to see her only to pry: "If anyone has any doubts about his really being a man, just come here and I'll have him prove it . . ."

"You really would!" laughed Maria Antônia, who found it a great source of merriment.

Dona Flor laughed, too. Even though she was annoyed by the gossip, she could not help laughing at the grotesqueness of the situation.

One morning, some time afterward, the person who appeared was Dionísia de Oxóssi, carrying her roly-poly little boy to receive his godmother's blessing. She had come only rarely of late. She told of the suffering she had undergone on discovering that her husband was mixed up with another woman: traveling about in his truck, stopping here, stopping there, he had got entangled with some trollop in Joazeiro. Dionísia had found out about it from a letter from the good-for-nothing, she had made a big scene, and had threatened to throw the treacherous husband out. Only threatened, *comadre*, for where is the man who doesn't have a roving eye, who doesn't two-time his wife? But she had taken it hard, she had even lost weight, and only now was she beginning to feel better, for her husband had not only put an end to the affair with that slut, but didn't even spend the night any more in Joazeiro.

Dona Flor consoled her; who was there who had not suffered

such disappointments? Not long ago she, Dona Flor, had also made a discovery which wounded and hurt her.

"The doctor, too, has been up to no good? Even he? You see why I said nobody could avoid woman trouble . . ."

"Who? Teodoro? No, my annoyance comes from a very different thing. Teodoro is the exception that proves the rule. He is a truly upright man; I would put my hand in the fire for him."

Dona Flor suddenly realized, and she almost confessed it to Dionísia, that of the two incidents having to do with Dr. Teodoro, the only concrete one, with a beginning and an end, and the only one that had wounded and hurt her deeply had occurred not with her second, but with her first husband: that old story, now come out, about Inés Vasques dos Santos and the late Vadinho. When Dona Flor thought about Magnólia or Mirtes, it was the skinny, silly Inés who arose before her, that hypocritical bitch, that hussy!

8

The rehearsals of the *romance* lasted almost six weeks before the exacting conductor considered it ready to be performed. He was especially exacting in this case, for it was his own composition and dedicated to the charm and kindness of Dona Flor, *Lullaby for Florípedes*, his favorite work.

Every Saturday afternoon, rain or shine, in one home or another, the members assembled to repeat the chords for the concert whose date and site had been set: in a week at the residence of the Taveira Pires.

Those months had gone by peaceably, without anything worth special mention, unless perhaps the debut of Marilda "at the microphones of the people, those of Radio Amaralina, Menina Station, the newest and with the most listeners," which was the talk of the neighborhood. It was as though all those streets and alleys were making their professional appearance through the voice of the girl carried on the airwaves, so great was the excitement and nervousness.

Dona Norma, in her role of leader, commanded the noisy delegation of fans which appeared at the station on the festive day. The neighbors took up a collection for a suitable gift to commemorate the occasion. From Mr. Samuel, Jeweler—he sold jewelry and everything one could think of: worsteds, tropical suiting, linens, furniture, perfume, all smuggled and all practically for nothing—they bought a wristwatch, very high fashion and unusual, guaranteed for six months. "Swiss, seventeen jewels, for half of what it is worth," Mr. Samuel giving the impression that he was selling it only as a favor to his good customer, Dona Norma.

That night, when the great bargain was shown to Mr. Sampaio, he realized that his wife had been swindled once more by the old peddler, which had been happening now for twenty years and would go on until one of the two cashed in his checks: "And if she should be the first to go, at the hour of her death old Samuel would try to sell her a last rites he had smuggled in."

It was neither Swiss nor had that many jewels. It was made in São Paulo, but not on that account was it a bad watch. "We've got to get over this mania of downgrading Brazilian industry, which is as good as any other," the nationalistic Zé Sampaio wound up.

On the day of the debut, as was natural and understandable, Dona Maria do Carmo had a brief fainting spell when she saw her daughter at the microphone and the master of ceremonies praising her gifts, "the melodious voice of a tropical bird." Dona Flor, too, wiped away a tear. She felt a maternal tenderness toward Marilda; she had helped the girl all she could to achieve her ambition and on one occasion had had a difference of opinion with Dr. Teodoro because of her. If Marilda's victory belonged to the whole neighborhood, Dona Flor had a major share in it. To celebrate it, she prepared the desserts for the buffet that was given at the girl's house that night, when a bottle of champagne was even opened (Oswaldinho's contribution).

In addition to the debut of the young singer, acclaimed by radio critics and the public, there was the sudden trip of Dona Gisa to the United States, giving rise to fervid comments. Not even Dona Dinorá with her extrasensory perception had had the slightest inkling of this event. A certain Mr. Shelby had died in New York and had left all his property to Dona Gisa. Who was this Mr. Shelby, and why had he made this teacher of English who had lived in Brazil for so many years his heiress? They could not ask Dona Gisa, for she had left overnight, without notice and without observing the protocol of leave-taking.

The most harebrained rumors sprang up in connection with the dead man and his fortune. There was the theory that he was her husband, divorced or not, an old passion, an undying love; myriad versions, some decent, others not. All were in agreement on one point: Dona Gisa had come into possession of a colossal fortune, an inheritance from the greatest of millionaires of the United States, a millionaire in dollars, not in mil-reis.

All that gossip crashed to earth when Dona Norma received an air-mail letter which she examined carefully before she opened it, with those air mail stamps and Dona Gisa's well-known handwriting, heavy and hard to read, like that of a doctor.

She wrote from New York telling her that she would soon be back: she was taking flowers to the grave of her cousin ("Cousin? Let whoever wants to swallow that! He was her husband, or something else," the gossips and loafers commented on street corners and in bars), and settling up her affairs. To be sure, she had inherited something—she was the only relative—but the inheritance consisted of an old car, some personal effects, a few shares of oil companies in the Middle East (not worth much, given the state of things there). She had sold everything and the return would hardly cover her traveling expenses. The real inheritance the dubious cousin had left her was a thoroughbred basset, Monsieur, who would soon be seen in the streets of Bahia, for Dona Gisa was already getting his papers ready.

And there you have all that took place in those months which deserves mention in this chronicle of Dona Flor and her two husbands. Aside from this, the rehearsals, the meetings of the Pharmaceutical Association, the cooking classes, visits to relatives and friends, the movies, and love-making on Wednesdays and Saturdays.

Dona Flor did not attend the rehearsals with the same assiduity as at the beginning. Not, however, that she considered them a bore, an annoyance, as did the wives of certain members of the orchestra, who made no bones about it. Despite her affection for her husband, and her solidarity with his duties and tastes, at times she was reluctant to go and begged off. Because really only they, who were mad about music, were able to find inner peace and boundless pleasure in that monotonous repetition of melodies.

Neither could she be counted on for the learned meeting of the Pharmaceutical Association, with its theses and debates. Why make herself go? To struggle all evening against an insidious drowsiness, doing her best to stay alert, only to be overcome by shameful nodding. She could not stand a whole meeting, not even when Dr. Teodoro presented his controversial thesis about barbiturates ("On the substitution of brews by organic products in the treatment of insomnia"), despite the fact that that was an impassioned session, with violent debates, the doctor's scientific reputation at stake. It was almost dawn before the discussion ended, and when her husband, trembling and happy, offered her his arm, she, who had awakened with the applause, almost asked his forgiveness for having fallen sound asleep, as though she had taken doses of teas and barbiturates that would have put a horse to sleep. Even so she said: "My dear . . ."

But he was in such a state of euphoria that he did not notice her red eyes, her face only half awake.

"Thank you, my dear. What a triumph!"

He had demolished the barbiturates, once and for all, fulfilling his duties as citizen and druggist. To be sure, he sold them, those dangerous toxins, at his drugstore, making a handsome profit on them, for they were all the rage. A learned and studious pharmacist and, at the same time, the owner of a well-stocked, prosperous drugstore, he felt no pangs of conscience or duplicity over the contradiction this position of his represented, for he was observing with the same adamant conscience the noble morality of the scientist and the no less noble dignity of the astute businessman.

A real event was the concert of the Amateur Orchestra of the Sons of Orpheus given in the mansion of the papal commander and virtuoso of the violoncello, Adriano Pires. It reechoed in the society column of the newspapers, was a topic of conversation in high circles, in dress shops, tailors, whose mention is obligatory here (who knows but what in the ups and downs of life we have to have recourse to Commander Adriano Pires, the king of money?).

To describe that revel of art in all its splendor seems to us an impossible task, beyond our power and limited style. If somebody wants to know, for instance, about the dresses the ladies were wearing, their beauty and their incomparable chic, we would have to refer them to the collection of the poet Tavares's newspaper, where they can read the coverage by the ever-brilliant Silvinho Lamenha, an authority in these delicate matters. As for the concert itself, those who are interested can find the opinions of music critics such as Finerkaes and José Pedreira, in addition to the article by Hélio Basto, a man of multiple accomplishments who, in addition to being a pianist, cultivated letters and the fine arts. Dona Rozilda collected the clippings in Nazareth, nearly all of them praising Dr. Teodoro and his "superb rendering of the bassoon solo in the romance of Agenor Gomes, one of the high points of the concert" (cf. Coqueijo: "*Pizicatos de um concerto*" in *The Gazette of Bahia*).

That night Dona Flor reached the peak, the top rung of the social ladder. She not only ascended it, but special mention was made of her: "that beautiful ornament, and who could have been the Paris couturière who designed her dress of *moiré fauve* with draped décolletage, outdoing many of our great ladies?" to quote Silvinho, the fair-haired boy of society. The cream of society was there, the most important people of Bahia, political bigwigs, financiers, intellectuals, from the Archbishop to the Chief of Police, and among them, snobs and bores, those crooks and swindlers, beginning with the Commander's sons-in-law.

In the neighborhood of Largo Dois de Julho, aside from Dr.

Teodoro, only Mr. Zé Sampaio, a fellow member of Pampa Mustang's in the Retailers' Association and his old classmate, received invitations. Zé Sampaio refused to go.

"For God's sake, no. Let me alone. I'm having trouble with my spleen. I need to rest. You go by yourself, if you want to, Norma."

Naturally Dona Norma went, not by herself but with Dona Flor and Dr. Teodoro. (How could one turn down an invitation that was a privilege? Only that husband of hers, morose and antisocial, a wild animal.)

The Commander said to Dona Imaculada: "I want everything of the finest and the best."

And so it was. Dona Imaculada might be a cruel burden to bear, but, let it be said in justice, she was a perfect hostess. They had engaged the services of the architect Gilberbet Chaves (and at what a price!) to decorate the gardens where the orchestra would perform.

"Don't take expense into account. I want the best, with platform and everything. Spend whatever is necessary." The Commander, so niggardly with his employes and with regard to small expenses, opened his wallet wide, reached for his checkbook.

Those words fell like honey on the ears of Master Chaves. He loved not having to take expense into account. He spent a fortune, but how beautiful it all was. It looked like a garden out of a fairy tale, and the little amphitheater was of an architectural audacity never before seen in Bahia: "Gilberbet—learn the name correctly; it is Gilberbet and not Gilberto or Gilbert, as certain parvenus pronounce it— has given proof of his ultramodern genius." (This was Silvinho again, and not the last time.)

As Dona Flor walked in, her mouth opened in admiration and astonishment. Dona Norma had only one word to say: "Dreamy."

Dona Imaculada and the Commander received the guests, she enveloped in rags come from Europe, her lorgnette in her hand, he ungainly, in spite of his tuxedo, his stiff-bosomed shirt, his wing collar. When he saw Dr. Teodoro with his bassoon in his hand, his mottled face opened in a smile: "My dear Teodoro! We're really going to hit the high notes today!" He was happy about the concert and the play on words.

Drawn to her full height, Dona Imaculada held out the tips of her fingers for the men to kiss, awaiting the bows of the women as though they had all come to ask her blessing.

"What a hag!" Dona Norma said, as soon as she was out of sight of the lorgnette.

"But very charitable. She's the president of the Society for the Conversion of the Heathen of Africa and Asia. She even wrote me about it." Some time before, Dr. Teodoro had received a circular asking help for the Catholic missions in those continents, signed by Madame Commander.

Then they saw Urbano Poor Devil, a sight in his rented tuxedo (paid for by the Commander when he learned that the violinist could not take part in the concert for lack of a proper suit), with his violin case in his hand. He had left his house to the jeers of his wife, and was looking for a place to hide under the trees so that nobody would notice him. Dr. Teodoro led him over to the amphitheater, where they left their instruments.

Though the concert was supposed to begin at eight thirty, it was past nine when Master Agenor Gomes managed to get his musicians together and start.

The guests, tippling through the parlors and gardens, showed no haste, and the Commander himself had to grab the microphone and roar into it angrily: "The concert is about to begin. Please take your seats! Come on, come on!"

Who was there bold enough not to heed that summons, an order, not an invitation? The noise died down, ladies and gentlemen took their seats, many of the men standing up, hoping to be able to slip away. It was a veritable fashion parade, the women displaying expensive jewelry and plunging necklines, all the men in evening clothes, the conductor in tails. In the first row, close to Dona Imaculada, sat Dona Flor and Dona Norma. And the Archbishop, on the point, so it was said, of being made a cardinal.

Master Agenor Gomes, deeply moved ("I ought to be hard-boiled by now, but I am as nervous as though each concert were the first one"), raised his baton.

The first part was listened to with attention and applause. Schubert's *Marche*, played with *brio* and accuracy, and then the admirable violin of Dr. Venceslau Veiga, in Drdla's *Souvenir*, drew applause and even "bravos" from certain appreciative listeners such as Dr. Itazil Benício "who doubles in medicine and art" (Silvinho). Master Gomes perspired happily.

During the intermission, the guests, like famished barbarians who had not eaten for months, threw themselves upon the sumptuous refreshment table where, for the first time in their lives, Dona Flor and Dona Norma saw and tasted caviar.

Dona Flor, with her experienced palate as a cooking teacher, found the highly praised caviar—each gram cost a fortune—to her liking: "It's strange, but it tastes good." Dona Norma was not in agreement, and said to her friend laughing (what she did like was champagne, and she had already had two glasses): "This stuff has a rancid taste. I don't know how to describe it . . ."

Dona Flor laughed, too, and, as Dr. Teodoro had gone off in search of Urbano Poor Devil to make him come and help himself to the refreshments, recalled a phrase of her late first husband on his return from Rio. On the trip, Dona Flor never knew where, he had had his fill of caviar, and said to her, when she asked him what it tasted like: "It tastes like tail . . . and it's very good."

Dona Norma burst out laughing, a little giddy with the champagne: the departed had been a rascal, foul-mouthed, hopeless, but so gay, unforgettable. "Sweetie, Vadinho was witty, and he understood those tastes . . ."

Dr. Teodoro came back, leading Poor Devil by the arm, and Dona Flor hurried to fix his plate, not forgetting to include a helping of caviar.

It was somewhat difficult to assemble the guests in the amphitheater for the second part of the concert. The lovers of music took their places, but they represented the minority in that mass of people whose minds were more on eating and drinking than music. The Commander, however, gave stern orders to the servants and finally the maestro and the orchestra attacked *Simple Aveu*.

After François Thomé's music came the culminating moment of the concert: the violoncello solo by Commander Adriano Pires, the Pampa Mustang. Then there really was complete silence: even in the pantry and the kitchen the servants stopped work and the waiters served no drinks until the number was finished. Dona Imaculada had personally given orders that the strictest silence was to be observed.

Everything forgotten, the world and its inhabitants, the papal commander, the crusty millionare, during that hour at the violoncello knew the meaning of happiness and kindness, suddenly became a human being.

Interminable applause when he finished. Standing and bowing his gratitude, Mr. Adriano pointed to the conductor and his fellow members of the orchestra. There were shouts of *"bravo, encore,"* and not only from the enlightened, those of the musical circles. All applauded, and the loudest among them was the moneylender Alírio de Almeida, who knew absolutely nothing about music; but his business depended on a word from the Pampa Mustang.

As Poor Devil said later, the Commander's number should have been the last on the program, for after it many of the guests left the orchestra in the garden and went into the house to drink and talk. Those who occupied seats and did not venture to leave listened to the rest of the concert inattentively, some even impatiently. From time to time one of them plucked up his courage, and excusing himself, walked by his neighbors and went inside the mansion to enjoy its delights.

The Sons of Orpheus, however, did not notice these defections, pursuing their program to the end with unvarying pitch and quality. The lovers of music, however, were annoyed by the growing restlessness and whispering. Dona Norma went "s-s-h," turning around when Dr. Teodoro began his bassoon solo (his eyes on Dona Flor). Dona Imaculada, the thoughtful hostess, turned, too, raising her lorgnette. That was all that was necessary; complete silence followed and nobody else had the temerity to get up from his seat.

The tones of the bassoon filled the air, floating over the garden, weaving a halo of love around the hair—so black it was almost blue —of Dona Flor.

Dona Flor half closed her eyes, hearing and recognizing in that romance solo all that he had given her, her good husband. There she was, where she had never dreamed of being, seated in the garden of the most aristocratic house of Bahia, with his Eminence, the Archbishop, in purple and ermine, at her side, listening complacently.

He had given her so much: peace and security, tranquility, order and comfort, everything she wanted and he could think of, protection, and never a bad moment, never a worry. Now he was seeking in the lean belly of the bassoon the deep note of his love, his devotion. Nobody could ask for a better husband.

When it came time to applaud, Dona Norma looked at her friend: there was a tear on Dona Flor's cheek. "Tears of happiness," smiled her kind neighbor, she, too, happy over the doctor's success.

"Dr. Teodoro played divinely . . ."

Even Dona Imaculada, from her nearby chair, deigned to remark: "Your husband did very well."

In the big reception room dancing began as soon as the sound of the orchestra died away in the medley from *The Merry Widow*, the final number. In the garden the audience, with the Archbishop at its head, complimented the director and the musicians, gathering around the Commander. Dona Flor had not dried the tear on her cheek, and the doctor, seeing how touched she had been, felt more than compensated for his six months of rehearsal.

They came out of the parlor in search of Hélio Bastos to pound out sambas and fox trots, tangos and boleros at the piano, improvising a dance. Dr. Teodoro, his bassoon in his hand, suggested that they leave; it was after midnight. Dona Norma asked for just five minutes more, long enough to gulp down another glass of champagne: "I just adore it."

She lapped up two glasses, and in the taxi she laughed for no reason at all, satisfied with life. Dona Flor took the hands of her husband, her good husband, in hers. They commented on the concert and the party, both magnificent. So many things to eat and drink, all of the finest quality; the Commander must have spent a fortune.

"That was overdoing it," the doctor said. "Even caviar. The real kind, Russian."

Dona Norma, in the state of well-being the champagne had

produced, winked her eye at Dona Flor, and asked Dr. Teodoro in a malicious voice which only the two women understood: "And did you like the caviar, doctor?"

"I know that it is a delicacy for the gods, and I tasted it today, because one should not miss an opportunity to taste such an expensive dish. But, to tell you the truth, Dona Norma, I did not find it altogether to my liking."

"And what did it taste like to you?"

Dona Norma smiled mischievously, in a state of happiness that had got out of hand. Dona Flor lowered her head, perhaps to hide a mocking smile. Dr. Teodoro tried to find a comparison for the tidbit, but was unable to: "To tell you the truth, I can't recall anything that tastes like it. Here among us, where nobody can hear us, I thought it tasted awful."

"Awful!" Dona Norma doubled up in laughter. "So did I. But there are those who like it, aren't there, Flor?"

But Dona Flor did not laugh. In the darkness her face was sober, perhaps sad, or just moved. She looked out at the night as though she did not hear the laughter of her friend. Squeezing her husband's hand, she said in a low voice: "The music was beautiful, and your playing, Teodoro."

"I did the best I could. You must remember I am only an amateur."

Why better? Who am I to ask of you, my dear, more than you do? What did I bring you, what dowry did I put in my side of the marriage scale that could even begin to match yours, full to overflowing, from money to the romance on the bassoon, from knowledge to good breeding, and that uprightness, that decency? I brought you nothing, added nothing to you, and I am not so clear and constant, I lack your noonday light, I am made up of shadows, too, of dark, changing matter. I am very small for your heights, Teodoro.

At the street-car stop, waiting for his to come, Urbano Poor Devil saw them go by. In his hands, his violin case and a package of delicacies for *siá* Maricota.

9

Professor Epaminondas Souza Pinto, circumspect and self-assured, loved proverbs, stereotyped phrases, finding in such expressions a resumé of the wisdom of centuries, the distillation of eternal truths.

"Happiness leaves no history. A happy life is not the subject for a novel," he answered when Chimbo, that important relative of the late Vadinho, inquired about Dona Flor, whom he had not seen for years, since that tragicomic Carnival ("How many years ago, two or three?") and the funeral of the dissipated scamp.

"Well, she married again and is happy. About a year ago, she joined her fate to that of Dr. Teodoro Madureira."

"And what else has happened to her?"

"As far as I know, nothing." And not to let an occasion of that sort slip by he added the proverb: "As the saying goes: happiness leaves no history."

Chimbo, experienced in life, agreed: "That is really true. When something happens it is nearly always unpleasant. If I were to tell you . . . Just listen."

And he opened his heart. At his age, getting on in years, he had to pick up with a girl of nineteen—not quite a virgin, but almost. Some rascal, pretending that he was courting her in earnest, had stolen her cherry, but had done it so fast, so helter-skelter, that there was some left over which Chimbo, in the process of consoling and protecting her, had finished off. "And the result, my noble professor? The girl is in the family way and I am responsible."

Professor Epaminondas Souza Pinto, of blameless life, had no advice nor consolation for the distress of this illustrious public figure, and for lack of a fitting remark, he congratulated him on this "auspicious pregnancy."

Nor do we have comfort or prudent advice for Mr. Chimbo, neither time nor space, and we introduce the episode merely to highlight the truth of the proverb; in the happy life of Dona Flor and Dr. Teodoro nothing further took place that needs to be set forth in this narrative, which we have no desire to prolong (it is already substantial) with the day-to-day account of quiet happiness, monotonous and insipid antiliterary material.

Even Dona Flor, a narrator of trifles in her scant correspondence with her family, in a letter to her sister Rosália on the eve of the first anniversary of her marriage to the druggist said she had nothing of importance to tell her.

She filled the pages with news of relatives and neighbors (during those years Rosália had come to know all those people by name through her sister). She told her about Aunt Lita's attacks, how Uncle Pôrto seemed ageless. Dona Rozilda stayed on in Nazareth —poor Celeste! Marilda, enjoying one success after the other, now with Society Radio and the promise that she would cut a record. She told a story about Dona Norma, so funny ("You really have to meet Norminha, it is worthwhile"); she was invited on Wednesday to go to a baptism the next Saturday, and she excused herself "because on Saturday I have to go to a funeral." "How could you know that there was going to be a funeral on Saturday, Norminha, when it's only Wednesday?" How? An acquaintance of hers was ready to cash in his checks, and he would surely do it between Friday evening and Saturday, to take advantage of the weekend, and have a bang-up funeral. Dona Gisa, who had returned, had brought a dog from New York, one of those that look exactly like a sausage, and as a present for Dona Flor a pretty pin. But: "Can you imagine, Rosália, what that crazy *gringa* brought for Teodoro? One of those shirts covered with naked women. Can you see the doctor putting on a thing like that? Being the well-bred man he is, he didn't say a word, he even thanked her without showing his displeasure, but I put the shirt away in my bottom drawer so he would not have to look at it and get mad at Dona Gisa every time he saw it, for in spite of everything she is really very good." The person who was sick, too sick to go out, was Dona Dinorá: "Imagine how she must suffer with her joints all swollen, a wicked attack of rheumatism, having to find out things secondhand." All she could do was to lay out the cards for her visitors, and foretell misfortunes for everybody, she was in such a foul humor. She had even warned Dona Flor, as she read her fortune: "She tells me to be careful, for there's no happiness that lasts forever; I never saw a mouth so full of curses. God be with us."

Aside from this humdrum news, there was nothing to relate: "Nothing happens, nothing worth mentioning." The doctor had thought of buying the house where they lived, but one of the heirs to the pharmacy had decided to sell his share and move to Rio. Dr. Teodoro had talked the matter over with Dona Flor: "Which did she think wiser: to buy the house or the share of the pharmacy?" And, he had added, that extra share would give him control of the firm, would make him the chief holder. As for the house, they would buy that later on, when they could afford it. The owner had no choice but to sell it, the rent they paid was ridiculously low.

The truth was that the doctor had already made up his mind and decided what was best to do, and if he asked Dona Flor's advice, it was out of politeness and good breeding. "Time goes on, and the doctor does not change; the same politeness, the same routine, the same behavior, always the same, day after day. I can tell beforehand what is going to happen every minute, and I know every word, because today is the same as yesterday."

With life going along like that, gentle and placid, in this slow, unchanging rhythm, how was she to fear change, how take seriously the warning of that crippled once-by-twice fortuneteller, more of an amateur at her decks of cards than Commander Adriano Pires at the cello?

Why, Dona Flor would not take it amiss if something were to happen, something unforeseen to break the monotony of those days all equally happy and equally placid. "It is positively a sin, sister, to talk like this when I am blessed with this life I lead, after having eaten such bitter bread; but the same thing every day gets cloying, even when it is of the finest. Just between us, my dear, there are times when this blissful life, which everyone envies me, causes me such torment, absolutely idiotic, which I can't even

explain, I don't know what it is. It must be the vile nature of this
sister of yours who does not know how to appreciate as she should
how much she owes heaven without her deserving it: such a
tranquil life and such a good husband."

At about this time, one Sunday she went to Mass at the Church
of St. Theresa. The theme of Dom Clemente's sermon was: "Why,
Oh Lord, does not peace dwell in men's hearts?" After the services,
she went to the sacristry to invite the priest to the first anniversary
of her marriage to Dr. Teodoro. It was not to be a real celebration;
just a few intimate friends in to have a liqueur and some refreshments, honoring at the same time the selection of the druggist as
second treasurer of the recently elected board of directors of the
Bahian Pharmaceutical Association.

"It will give me great pleasure to come, to congratulate you on
this year of conjugal harmony, this example of a union blessed by
God."

Dona Flor departed, and the ivory-pale priest, in a somewhat
pessimistic autocriticism of his sermon, smiled happily: now there
was a person, Dona Flor, whose heart was the dwelling place of
peace, a human being satisfied and happy with her life, giving the
lie to his gloomy, doubt-ridden sermon.

Halfway down the hall, Dona Flor stopped in front of the
strange group made up of the baroque image of St. Clare and the
old wooden folk-sculpture of that angel of cynicism and innocence
so like the late Vadinho, with his insolence and irresponsible
charm.

Poor saint: her sanctity, however strong and fortified, however
great in virtue, could not hold out against the lascivious eyes of
that devil, the poor blessed creature succumbing to him, handing
over to him her decency and her life, risking for him her salvation
already gained, trading heaven for hell, for without him, what was
heaven or life worth?

There, in front of that strange assemblage in wood and plaster,
Dona Flor stood for a long time, and the nave of stone and mortar,
a huge ship, lifted anchor and set out, cutting the blue sea of
clouds, heavenbound.

10

Dona Flor spared no effort, and the little party was most distinguished, a complete success crowning the first anniversary of the "happy union of twin souls," in the words, so well befitting the occasion, of Dr. Sílvio Ferreira, General Secretary (reelected) of the Bahian Pharmaceutical Association, who raised his glass in a toast to the couple, "to our highly esteemed Second Treasurer and his admirable lady, Dona Flor, an example of talents and virtues."

Dona Flor had told Dom Clemente that the gathering would be limited to "a few close friends," but, when he entered, the priest found the house full, and not only of neighbors. The prestige of Dr. Teodoro and the affection Dona Flor inspired had brought to that intimate gathering a number of people: important figures from the field of pharmacy, colleagues from the Amateur Orchestra, representatives of drug firms, students and former students of the School of Art and Savor, in addition to old friends, some as important as Dona Magá Paternostro, with all her money, and Dr. Luís Henrique, that "privileged mind." Even before greeting the doctor and his wife, Dom Clemente embraced that "celebrated belletrist." His *History of Bahia* had just been honored by a prize awarded by the Institute, "the much-sought laurel which sets the seal of recognition on an authentic value" (cf. Junot Silveira: "Books and Authors" in *A Tarde*).

In the cultural field, in addition to the speech of Dr. Ferreira abounding in rhetorical figures, there was also a little music. Dr. Venceslau Veiga performed two arias on the violin, and was enthusiastically applauded. Also applauded—and loudly—was the young singer, Marilda Ramosandrade, "the ardent voice of the tropics," in

spite of the fact that she had no accompanist, only Oswaldinho
beating out the time on a tambourine.

During this impromptu hour of art, Dr. Teodoro made his
contribution, a number which caused a veritable sensation: he
played the entire national anthem on the bassoon, which was
received with the most enthusiastic hand clapping.

Aside from this, they ate and drank, laughed and talked. The
men gathered in the living-room, the women in the other room, in
spite of the protests of Dona Gisa, to whom this separation of the
sexes seemed a "feudal and Mohammedan" vestige. Only she and
two or three women ventured to join the circle of the men, where
the beer flowed freely and stories met with Dona Dinorá's disap-
proval who, though still suffering and weak, was unshaken in her
convictions: "That Maria Antônia is a dissolute creature . . .
There she is among the men listening to filth. And she has even
dragged Dona Alice and Dona Misete along with her. As for the
gringa, she is the worst of the lot. Look how she stretches out her
neck not to miss a word . . ."

By way of compensation, there was Dona Neusa Macedo (and
Company), setting an example of good behavior in the circle of
women, sedate, discreet, paying attention to Ramiro, a lad of
seventeen or eighteen, the son of the Argentines of the ceramics
factory. If not for her, the adolescent would not have had anyone
with whom to pass the time, for the other young men were
gathered around Marilda, asking her to sing sambas, waltzes, tangos, and *rancheras*, while all he wanted to talk about was his
fishing: "I caught a red snapper that weighed over ten pounds!"

"Oh!" she answered admiringly. "Over ten pounds! What a big
one! And what else did you catch?" And all the while she was
wondering what name to give the bold fisherman—"Cod-liver Oil"
wouldn't be bad—and Neusoca's eyes lighted up.

When the Argentine arrived with his wife and son, he stopped
by the door with Mr. Vivaldo of the Flower of Paradise funeral
parlor. They went in together to congratulate their hosts, and as
they made their way into the room where the men were, the
Argentine from Buenos Aires, with his frankness which bordered
on the rude, remarked on the elegance of Dona Flor, whose dress

was making all the women green with envy, and, in the bargain, Miltinho, the nervous fag who served at times as chambermaid— excellent, incidentally—at Dona Jacy's, who had lent him for the celebration. ("Dona Flor is taking an unfair advantage today, she looks good enough to eat.")

"It's money that makes a woman pretty," Mr. Hector Bernabó commented. "Look how smart Dona Flor is, and how handsome . . ."

Mr. Vivaldo looked. This was no hardship for him, for he liked to look at women, measuring contours, curves, angles.

"If the truth be told, she was always elegant and attractive, but not really pretty. Now she is more of a woman, a knockout, but I don't think it's the money. It's her age, my dear fellow, she's at exactly the right age. Anyone who goes for teen-agers need to have his head examined. Ten of them together are not to be compared with a woman at the peak of her vigor, bursting her buttons . . ."

"Look at her eyes," said the Argentine, who apparently also knew a good thing when he saw it.

Dreamy eyes lost in the distance, as though given over to voluptuous thoughts. Mr. Vivaldo wondered how the druggist could inspire such tender thoughts to the point of leaving Dona Flor so bemused. She went from one room to the other, looking after all her guests, polite and pleasant, the perfect hostess. But she was doing it all mechanically.

Mr. Vivaldo laid his hand on the Argentine's arm: it isn't money that makes a woman pretty, Mr. Bernabó, it's the way she is treated, the peace of spirit, happiness. Those dreamy eyes and those voluptuous haunches were the result of the calm happiness of her life.

That expression of her eyes was strange. When had he seen her before with that same brooding look, as though she were looking into her own heart? Mr. Vivaldo riffled through his memory, and he came up with it: it was the look she had had at the wake of her first husband. The identical expression, that lost gaze with which she received condolences then and congratulations today, her eyes looking beyond time, as though neither tears of sorrow nor laugh-

ter of celebration existed for her, only loneliness. Her beauty, Mr.
Vivaldo realized, also came from within her, from some dimension
that he could not hit upon.

In the room where the women had gathered, the theme of
Dona Flor's present felicitous life came up again. Several of the
ladies who were there, wives of members of the orchestra or of
pharmacists, knew little of that first disastrous marriage and that
rogue of a husband.

The neighbors and gossips asked nothing better than to tell and
compare, and so they did, to their hearts' content. As far as they
were concerned, there was no greater diversion than the pleasure
of gossip, neither the off-color stories the men (and tramps like
Maria Antonia) were laughing their heads off at in the other room
nor gathering around Marilda begging for old sambas, old waltzes,
nostalgically, like Dona Norma, Dona Maria do Carmo, Dona
Amélia, and all the young bucks (crazy about Marilda, every one
of them). That first marriage, dear friends, was hell on earth.

This happiness in her second marriage was even greater and
more to be prized when contrasted with the mistake of the first, an
ordeal, a disaster, a calamity. What that poor martyr had not
suffered at the hands of that monster, who was a combination of
every vice and meanness, a devil; he had even struck her.

"Dear God!" said Dona Sebastiana, shocked, raising her hand to
her vast bosom.

What she had suffered! Everything a devoted wife can suffer in
humiliation along the street of bitterness, working to support the
house and even the gambling of the debauchee, for gambling, as
everyone knows, is the worst and most expensive of vices. If she
was happy now, she had been good and miserable before.

From the pantry Dona Flor, her eyes in a distant haze, overheard these reminiscences of her former life. With Dona Gisa in
the storytelling group, Dona Norma in that of the singers, nobody
said one word in defense of Vadinho.

Around midnight the last of the guests took their leave. Dona
Sebastiana, still moved by the account of that martyrdom which
had lasted seven years—how had she stood it, the poor thing?—
patted Dona Flor's cheek tenderly and said to her: "How good

that now everything has changed and you have what you deserve."

Marilda, dazzling the young students with her stellar light, left singing a tango which was a favorite of serenaders: "Arching night, smiling sky, silence that is almost a dream . . ." the one Dona Flor had laid to rest in the coffin of her dead.

Dr. Teodoro, aglow with satisfaction, accompanied the last guests to the door, a noisy group involved in an interminable argument having to do with the effects of music in the treatment of certain ailments. Dr. Venceslau Veiga and Dr. Silvio Ferreira were not in agreement. In order not to miss the end of the argument, the master of the house accompanied his friends to the street-car. Marilda's song had died away.

Alone to herself, Dona Flor turned her back on all that: the refreshments, the bottles of liquor, the disorder of the rooms, the echoes of the conversations on the sidewalk, the bassoon in a corner, mute and solemn. She walked to the bedroom, opened the door and turned on the light.

"You?" she asked in an ardent voice, but without surprise, as though she had been expecting him.

There in the iron bed, naked as Dona Flor had seen him the afternoon of that Carnival Sunday when the men had brought the body from the morgue and turned it over to her, lay Vadinho, stretched out. Smiling he beckoned to her with his hand. Dona Flor answered him with a smile; who could resist the charm of that scapegrace, that combination of innocence and cynicism, those knavish eyes? If not even the saint in the church could, what was to be expected of Dona Flor, a mere mortal?

"My darling." That beloved voice, languid and drawling.

"And why did you come today?" asked Dona Flor.

"Because you called me. And today you called me so many times that I came," as though saying that her summons had been so insistent and intense as to fuse the boundaries of the possible and the impossible. "So here I am, my darling, I just this minute got here . . ." And half-rising, he took her hand. Drawing him to her, he kissed her. On the cheek, for she turned her mouth away: "Not on the mouth, no. You mustn't, you crazy thing."

"And why not?"

Dona Flor sat down on the edge of the bed, and Vadinho stretched himself out at his ease, spreading his legs a little, showing everything, those forbidden (and beautiful) indecencies. Dona Flor was moved by every detail of that body; she had not seen it for almost three years, and it was as though time had stood still.

"You are exactly the same. You haven't changed the least bit. I have put on weight."

"Oh, you're so beautiful, you can't imagine. You're like an onion, firm and juicy, so good to bite into. That scoundrel of a Vivaldo knows what he is doing. He doesn't take his eyes off your backside, that dirty dog . . ."

"Take your hand away from there, Vadinho, and stop lying. Mr. Vivaldo never looks at me—he has always been respectful. Come on, take away your hand."

"Why, sugar? Why take away my hand?"

"Have you forgotten, Vadinho, that I am a decent married woman? The only one who can lay a hand on me is my husband . . ."

Vadinho winked a dissolute eye: "And what am I, sugar? I am your husband. Had you forgotten? And the first, too; I have priority."

That raised a new problem. Dona Flor had never thought of it, and could not find an answer: "The things you think up! You leave no margin for a person to argue . . ."

The firm footsteps of Dr. Teodoro on his way back echoed in the street.

"He's coming, Vadinho, go right away. I am happy, so happy, you can't imagine, to have seen you. It did me so much good."

Vadinho, completely at ease, did not move.

"Get out, you crazy thing. He's coming into the house now. He's going to lock the door."

"And just why should I go?"

"Because he's coming and will see you here, and what am I to say?"

"You silly thing! He can't see me, the only one who can see me is you, my flower of doom."

"But he'll be getting into bed . . ."

Vadinho gave a gesture of nonchalance: "I can't stop him, but, squeezing a little, all three of us will fit . . ."

At this she got really angry: "What do you think I am, or don't you know me better than that? Why do you treat me as though I were a whore, a streetwalker? How dare you? Have you no respect for me? You know perfectly well that I am a decent woman."

"Don't get cross, pet. After all, it was you who summoned me . . ."

"I just wanted to talk to you."

"But we haven't had a chance to yet."

"You come back tomorrow and then we'll talk."

"I can't be coming and going. Or do you think it is just a short excursion, like from here to Santo Amaro or Feira de Sant'Ana? You think all I have to do is say: 'I'm going there, and here I am back'? My darling, now that I have come, I am staying for good."

"But not here in this room, here in bed, for the love of God. Look, Vadinho, even if he can't see you, I would die of embarrassment. I am no good at that sort of thing." And tears came into her voice. (He could never bear to see her cry.)

"All right, I'll sleep in the living-room, and tomorrow we'll settle the matter. But first I want a kiss."

They could hear the doctor washing in the bathroom, the running of the water. She held out her cheek, modestly.

"Oh, no, sugar. On the mouth, if you want me to go."

The doctor would soon be there. What could she do except submit to the demands of this tyrant, surrender her lips to him?

"Ah, Vadinho, ah," and she could say no more, for lips, tongue, and tears (of shame or happiness?) were devoured by that hungry, knowing mouth. Ah, that was a kiss!

He went out completely naked, so beautiful and manly! The golden fuzz covering his arms and legs, that mat of golden hair on his breast, the knife scar on his left shoulder, that insolent mustache and shameless eye. He left her with the kiss burning her mouth (and her vitals).

As he came into the room, Dr. Teodoro gave her the praise she deserved: "It was a lovely party, my dear. Everything as it should be, nothing lacking, all perfect. That's the way I like it, without any hitch." And he went behind the iron bed to change his clothes while she put on a nightgown.

"Fortunately all went well, Teodoro."

In honor of the anniversary, she put on the nightgown of lace and ruffles she had worn on the wedding night in Paripe, Dona Ênaide's gift, which she had not worn since. She saw herself in the mirror, pretty and desirable. She wished Vadinho could see her, even if only for a glance.

"I'm going to get a drink of water, I'll be back in a minute, Teodoro."

The other might already have gone to sleep after the fatigue of his long journey. Not to wake him up, she tiptoed down the hall. She just wanted to see him for an instant, touch his cheek if he was asleep, show him (at a distance) the transparent nightgown if he was awake.

She arrived just in time to see him going through the door, naked and in a hurry. She stood there frozen in her tracks, with a pain in her heart: she had offended him and he had gone away, and she would be alone forever. Never again his delicate face on which to rest her lips, never again to be able to show herself before him in her nightgown (so that he would stretch out his hand and pull it off, laughing), never again. He had taken offense and had left.

But perhaps better so. Certainly better so. She was a decent woman—how could she look at another man, even that one, when there was her husband in bed waiting for her in a new pair of pajamas, an anniversary present. Better so, that Vadinho should leave at once and forever. She had seen him, she had kissed him, that was all she wanted. Better so, she kept telling herself, better so.

She went back to the bedroom. Why had he left so suddenly? Why such a swift departure when, in order to come, he had had to traverse space and time? Maybe he had not gone for good. Maybe he had gone out for a walk, to look at the night in Bahia, to see how the gambling was going on, what had been happening while he was away—perhaps just an inspection trip, from the Palace to the Three Dukes cardhouse, from Abaixadinho to Zezé de Meningite's place, from Tabaris to the den of Paranaguá Ventura.

V

OF THE TERRIBLE BATTLE BE-
TWEEN THE SPIRIT AND MATTER,
WITH UNIQUE HAPPENINGS

AND ASTOUNDING CIRCUMSTANCES, WHICH CAN HAPPEN
ONLY IN THE CITY OF BAHIA, AND LET HIM
WHO WILL BELIEVE THE TALE

(To a chorus of drums and bells and with Exu singing a mocking song:
"I had closed the door
I have now ordered it to open.")

COOKING SCHOOL
OF SAVOR AND ART

CULINARY LIKES AND DISLIKES OF THE DEITIES

(Information supplied by Dionísia de Oxóssi)

Every Thursday, Xango eats *amalá* and on special days, turtle or mutton.

Ewá, goddess of the springs, cannot stand rum and chicken.

Iyá Masse eats guinea hen.

For Ogun they set aside the goat and *akikó*, which means cock in the language of the candomblé centers.

With mirror and fan, all touchy and affected, Oxun likes fried bean cakes and yams cooked with onion and shrimps. And with goat, which is her favorite meat, serve her cornmeal cooked in dendê oil and honey.

Oxóssi, the most highly respected diety, king of Ketu and a hunter, is very picky. He faces the wild pig in the forest, but he does not eat fish that does not have scales, he cannot bear yam and white beans, and he does not want windows in his house—his window is the forest.

For the female warrior who does not fear death or the spirits of the dead, for Yansā, do not serve her squash, nor give her lettuce or sapodilla. What she eats is bean cakes.

Beans with corn for Oxumaré, for Nanan well-seasoned mustard greens.

Dr. Teodoro is one of Oxalá's, as is apparent in his serious behavior and composure. When he is wearing a white suit and carrying his bassoon, which is like a *paxoró*, he resembles Oxolufan, old Oxalá, the greatest of the divinities, the father of them all. What he eats is *ojojo* of yam, mustard greens with white corn, snails and porridge. Oxalá does not like spiced things; he uses no salt or oil.

They says it was Asobá Didi who cast the shells for the departed, and three times they came up with the same answer: Vadinho's patron deity was Exu and no other. If Exu is the devil, how did he get in there? Perhaps Lucifer, the fallen angel, the rebel who defied the law and cloaked himself in fire.

Exu eats anything in the way of food, but he drinks only one thing: straight rum. At the crossroads Exu waits sitting upon the night to take the most difficult road, the narrowest, the most winding, the bad road, it is generally held, for all Exu wants is to frolic, to make mischief.

Exu, the great mischief-maker, Vadinho's patron deity.

1

The croupier was on the point of announcing the last play: dawn was breaking and everyone was dead tired. In desperation Madame Claudette went from player to player, holding out a begging hand to each. She could no longer bring to her eyes and voice a hint of suggestiveness, a seductive tone, a promise of sweet repayment. She had not a vestige of self-respect left, nothing but fear of hunger, of dying of hunger. She no longer said in her pure Parisian accent: "*Mon chéri,*" "*Mon petit cocô,*" "*Mon chou.*" In her voice reeking of decayed teeth all she could do was plead for a chip, at least one of the little ones, five mil-reis. Not to gamble, but to redeem it, thus insuring her food for the next day.

If she had found any takers when she first came in, eluding the watchful eye of the doorman (who had orders to keep her out) or touching his heart, she would have staked the chip in the hope of winning the money for the rent due on the pigsty she occupied in a tenement of Pelourinho in the company of rats and roaches (black, hard-shelled roaches that crawled over her in bed, such a horror). Every morning she was awakened by the shouts and coughing, by the threats of immediate eviction of Stinkpot, the agent of Dona Imaculada Taveira Pires, the owner of that and many other tenements, the rent of which the Commander assigned her for her charities.

The rent—who knows, perhaps she might still get a stay of a day or two if Stinkpot were inclined to "satisfy his needs," as he put it. It was a terrible price to pay, according to those who knew

Stinkpot (even taking into account Madame Claudette's complete decadence; compared to him, Madame was perfume and flower).

Getting on for seventy, if not that already, almost bald, with a few wisps of hair, shards of teeth, cataract-blurred eyes, she was no longer able to follow that honorable profession in which one day she had been a star, when clients had lined up in the parlor of the sporting house which she enhanced with her refinement. She had disembarked in Salvador in the full vigor and charm of her forty years (nobody would have said she was more than twenty-five) via Buenos Aires, Montevideo, São Paulo, Rio, "the sensation of Paris" and of harlotry of the highest class in Bahia, in days so long past that Madame Claudette had only the faintest memory of them, so that that bygone splendor was not even a source of pleasure.

She had descended step by step, street by street, from the Pension Europa, on Theater Square, which was the last word in chic, where the cacao "colonels" threw away five hundred mil-reis notes, and took an intensive course of lessons in the Gallic variants of pleasure, sinking in standing and price, until, in the course of years and years, she had landed in the deepest filth of the hillsides, the cribs of Julião and Pilar, in the Alley of Rotten Meat. And finally, not even that. On the darkest corners, in a hidden hallway, she offered herself for a nickel *"michê de Paris, mon cocô."* On one occasion a Negro who had had a couple of drinks said to her almost kindly, giving her a nickel: "Go look after your grandchildren, Granny; you are no good as a whore any more . . ."

She did not have grandchildren; she did not have a relative, a friend, nothing. Neither did she have fine dresses to wear; her latest outfits were a mixture of patches and dirt. She had sold, piece by piece, everything she owned. The last piece of jewelry, the one she had held on to longest (it was a family heirloom) she had got rid of one morning some ten years before (more or less; Madame Claudette had long since lost track of months and years) when she was practicing her declining trade in São Miguel Street, a cheap ass peddler. Vadinho, a crazy gambler, but polite, had offered her a pile for the turquoise necklace.

At that moment, there in front of the roulette table, at the very moment of making the bets, as the last ball was spinning, Madame

Claudette, without chips, a penny, or hope, recalled Vadinho. Winning or losing, on a lucky or jinxed night, he had never failed to offer her at least a ten-tostões chip and his hunch. On one occasion, he had almost broken the bank at the Tabaris Casino, leaving with his pockets stuffed with money, and had gone to the red-light district with a gang of friends, to celebrate. There he had distributed among the women, like a king of fairy tales, five and ten thousand mil-reis bils, some of twenty and even of fifty. What a night! The trollops carried him on their shoulders like a saint.

If Vadinho were alive, if he were there, he would certainly give her a chip, thus guaranteeing her a piece of meat and beans and a pack of cigarettes, doing it, moreover, with that rascally smile of his, with insolent charm, saying: "I am at your orders, Madame, yours to command." And Madame would answer: "*Merci, mon chou*," and go and play it. But, alas, he had died young, during a carnival, if her worn-out memory did not deceive her.

It was at the very moment that she was remembering him that it happened: Chastinet, the perfect croupier, was gathering up and paying for the last spin of the ball, with his hands full of chips—those of a hundred, two hundred, five hundred mil-reis; those of five hundred were big, of mother of pearl, really beautiful—when he had an attack, a kind of seizure. He gave out a short, hoarse cry, raised his arms, opened his hands, and the chips rolled over the carpet.

Without losing a second, the rascals were scuffling for them, men and women bent over grabbing them. Only Madame Claudette, so confused and in such despair, lacked the strength to join the rough-and-tumble, and stood by motionless, while Chastinet, recovered from his attack, got down on his knees to gather up what there was left. Granuzo, too, the guard, came running to save what he could. There were chips for everyone except for her.

Down the décolletage of her droopy bosom, Madame Claudette felt a hand slipping her one of the chips, a big one of mother of pearl, worth five hundred mil-reis, more than enough to pay her rent and assure her food for two weeks. "At your orders, Madame, yours to command"—it seemed to her she heard that shrewd, sly voice. "*Merci, mon chou*," she answered as she had so long before.

She went over to the cashier to redeem her fortune, too old and too buffeted by fortune to seek an explanation. Undoubtedly one of the players had slipped one of those dreamed-of chips down her bosom. "*Merci, mon vieux,*" whoever he was.

2

Dona Flor awoke with a start; Dr. Teodoro had already bathed and shaved, and was beginning to get dressed.

"I overslept . . ."

"My dear, you must be exhausted, it's only natural. It's no joke preparing a party like yesterday's and receiving so many people, looking after them. You need rest. Why don't you stay in bed? The maid will get my breakfast."

"In bed? But I'm not sick."

She leaped out of bed, got herself ready in a hurry, for they always had their morning coffee together, and Dona Flor insisted upon fixing the porridge herself, since she was the only one who did it exactly to her husband's taste, light and fluffy, adding a pinch of powdered tapioca to make sure of this.

Tired, true, but not because of the party; tired because of her sleepless night, her ear alert until nearly dawn, as in bygone days, to the footsteps in the street. Another source of concern: had Teodoro, perhaps, noticed any difference in her manner during that celebration marking their anniversary? It was not Wednesday or Saturday, but Dona Flor had put on her wedding nightgown, and the doctor had said: "What a delicate reminder, my dear. There are occasions when one has to forget about the calendar, and you must forgive me if I take unfair advantage tonight." He was always so prudent and thoughtful—what woman would not be charmed by his good breeding?

Dona Flor complied, but her emotions were in conflict. Her bruised lips, her mouth on fire, her burning tongue still held Vadinho's mordant flavor, his bold taste, and so the kiss with which the doctor invariably began his transports seemed to her dull and insipid.

Completely confused, she was out of step, and the perfect coordination that had made them one in their chaste yet impetuous pleasure, was broken. All upset, she did not accompany her husband stage by stage as she usually did, and he came first, whereas it was only in the encore (for there was an encore) that Dona Flor managed to release her taut nerves. They had never bungled things so—it was almost a repetition of the errors of that first night in Paripe. Fortunately, if he found her strange and aloof, he attributed the mischance to fatigue, to the work the observance of the anniversary had involved.

Around daybreak, when the light still dimmed by night began to color the walls, Dona Flor heard steps in the distance, and then she fell into a heavy sleep, as though she had taken a sleeping pill.

Slipping on her bedroom slippers, her flowered robe over her nightgown, she ran a comb through her hair and went out into the kitchen. When she got to the living-room, however, she saw that devil stretched out on the sofa, in all his shameless nakedness. She had to wake him up even before she started the porridge (from the kitchen came the fine smell of coffee that the maid had brewed). Dona Flor touched Vadinho on the shoulder. He opened one eye, grumbling: "Let me sleep. I got in just a little while ago."

"You can't sleep here, in the living-room."

"What's wrong with that?"

"I told you, I am embarrassed."

He gave an impatient gesture: "What's that got to do with me? Will you let me alone."

"You've started up your bad manners again. Please, Vadinho . . ."

He opened his eyes again, and smiled at her lazily: "All right, you silly thing. I'll go into the bedroom. Has my colleague left?"

"Colleague?"

"Your doctor—aren't we both married to you, both your husbands? Bed colleagues, my pet . . ." And he looked at her shrewdly and impudently.

"Vadinho! I will not stand for jokes of that sort."

She said this out loud, and from the kitchen the maid asked: "Were you talking to me, Dona Flor?"

"I was saying I was coming out to prepare the porridge."

"Don't get mad, sugar," Vadinho said, getting up.

He reached out his hand to take hold of her—what indecent nakedness!—but she evaded him.

"You have no sense."

In the hall the two men passed one another, and as she watched, Dona Flor felt tenderness toward both of them, so different, but both her husband by church and law. "The two colleagues," and she couldn't help laughing at the coarse joke. But she quickly checked herself: "Dear God, I am getting as cynical as Vadinho." Moreover, the cynic winked an abetting eye at her, sticking out his tongue at the doctor at the same time and making an indecent gesture with his hand. Dona Flor really got mad.

No, that wasn't right and she could not tolerate such low behavior, those suggestive jokes, the manners of a loafer, the coarseness and insults. It was time for Vadinho to learn how to behave himself in a decent home.

The doctor, clean-shaven, buttoning his vest and coat, spic and span, said: "We're a little late today, my dear."

"Good heavens, the porridge!" Dona Flor flew to the kitchen.

3

At the close of the morning session, when they were drawing lots to see who would win the dish of coconut custard to take home, Dona Flor felt his presence even before she saw him.

Until then she had not quite taken in the fact that it was only she who could see him, and when she found Vadinho there beside the table, naked and with everything in view, she shuddered. But as the students showed no reaction to his unseemly behavior, she realized that only she and nobody else was privileged to see her first husband. Thank heaven for that.

The students went on laughing and joking as though there were not a totally naked man in their midst, looking them over and measuring them with an experienced eye, lingering over the prettiest ones, an outrage. Once more he was there upsetting her classes, fooling with the students, the same as before. And speaking of that, Vadinho owed her an explanation, the settling of old, overdue accounts: that treacherous Inés Vasques dos Santos, the sneak.

The complete coxcomb, entirely at ease, with a light foot, almost like a dance step, three times circled the voluminous Zulmira Simões Fagundes, a majestic creole, with sumptuous hips, free-moving, independent, breasts of bronze (at least, so they seemed), the private secretary of the powerful tycoon Pelancchi Moulas, very private, if one were to believe what one heard.

Having thoroughly appraised and praised her haunches, Vadinho wanted to clear up once and for all the mystery of those breasts: were they really of bronze, or just unusually firm? To do this he levitated himself into the air, and with his feet up and his head down, peeked down the opening of the dress of the princess of the Yorubas.

Dona Flor stood speechless, utterly dismayed: she had not yet seen him rise up as much at his ease in the air as on the ground, assuming the position that best suited him: with his legs stretched out either horizontally or vertically, head down, as he was at that moment to get a look at those proud breasts.

Though, to be sure, the students were not privileged to see him, nevertheless they must have sensed something in the atmosphere, for they were more nervous than usual, laughing and talking for no good reason, in a kind of presentiment. Dona Flor was getting furious. Vadinho was overstepping all bounds.

He really overstepped them when, not satisfied with looking, he put his hand down the front of Zulmira's dress to find out, once and for all, what raw material had gone into the making of those divine creations: were they of flesh and blood, or was it something miraculous?

"Ay," Zulmira groaned, "somebody is touching me."

Dona Flor lost her head in the face of that shameless effrontery, and burst into a scream: "Vadinho!"

"Who? What? What happened? What is the matter with you?" The silly and excited students gathered around their comrade and teacher. "What was it you said, Dona Flor? And you, Zulmira?"

Zulmira explained with a prudish sigh: "I felt something take hold of and squeeze my breast."

"A pain?"

"No, it was rather pleasant."

Dona Flor made an effort and collected herself. When she had let out that cry, Vadinho had disappeared.

4

Two or three times late that afternoon Vadinho repeated in a sly voice, with a mocking smile: "We'll see who can hold out longer, my saint. You with your doctor and your pride, and I . . ."

"You, with what?"

"Me with my love."

It was a challenge, and Dona Flor, fortified by the discovery that he had done little to her until then (he would not take her by force, but only with her consent), prepared to accept it, willing to run the risk, trusting in her moral integrity and strength of will. A person who has undergone the hell of widowhood without getting burned, my bully boy, is not afraid of wiles or seducers: "I put my decency above all."

"You are talking just like the doctor, my love. All ridiculous, high-falutin', as though you were a teacher."

It was her turn to laugh: "I am a teacher. I was before I knew him and before I knew you. And, incidentally, a highly thought of teacher."

"A teacher of cooking not of putting on airs."

"You really think I am putting on airs? That I have changed?"

"You're never going to change, sweetie. Your one pride is your honor. But I already ate it once, and I'm going to do it again. However much of a teacher you may be, when it comes to humping, you are my student. And I have come to finish your education."

In this backchat, with laughing, jokes, and tenderness, they kept on until it was almost time for dinner. Dona Flor was all puffed up and self-assured; never would Vadinho overcome her determination to be an upright woman or infringe on her chastity as a wife. That other time she had been an ignorant young thing, had not known how to control the emotions of her first love, and had lost her honor in the sea-breeze of Itapoã. But now she was a woman who had lived sorrow and happiness: she knew the price and the meaning of everything. Vadinho was going to get tired waiting. But he set little store by that invincible resistance: "You are going to give yourself to me when you least expect to, just like the other time. And do you know why?"

"Why?"

Arrogantly and insolently, he explained: "Because you like me, and deep down in your heart, so deep that not even you are aware of it, you are crazy to give yourself to me."

Vadinho full of guile, of bluster. Dona Flor firm in her basic decency: "This time you're going to lose your time and your big talk."

This was the end of a serene, enchanted afternoon. It had begun, however, under unpleasant auspices.

When, after her afternoon classes, Dona Flor came out of the bathroom and began to perfume herself and comb her hair, half-naked, wearing only a brassiere and panties, a whistle of admiration came from somewhere in the room. Before she went into and when she came out of the bath, she had looked the room over carefully, making sure that neither of her two husbands was there; the doctor was still in the drugstore, and Vadinho had evaporated after the hubbub in the morning class.

But there the devil was, on top of the wardrobe, swinging his legs. In the dusk, the half light, he seemed made of the same wood as the angel in the corridor of the Church of St. Theresa. His eyes rested on Dona Flor's shoulders with the same lasciviousness, gluttony, running over her, over her damp body. "Dear God!" Dona Flor murmured, snatching up her robe and throwing it on.

"What are you doing that for, sugar. Do you think I don't know you, inside and out? Where haven't I kissed you? What foolishness is this, what stupidity?"

With the leap of a dancer—his movements were weightless—his naked body crossed the light and the shadows, coming to rest elegantly on the iron bed with its new spring mattress.

"Pet, this new mattress is like a cloud, just wonderful. Congratulations."

He stretched out lazily, a ray of light illuminating the satisfied smile on his sensual tempting face. Dona Flor, in the shadows, observed him.

"Come here, Flor, come and lie down beside me, let's do a bit of screwing. Lie down here, let's have some fun on this swell mattress."

Still furious at what had happened with the students—that incredible business of Vadinho's running his hand down Zulmira's breast, and the devil enjoying it, which she knew without even looking at him, embarrassed to the point of almost fainting—Dona Flor reacted sharply: "You're not satisfied with what you did? You have the cheek to hide here to watch me? Your manners have not improved in all this time. You could have made better use of it . . ."

"Don't be like that, darling! Lie down here, beside me."

"And you even have the nerve to ask me to lie down beside you! What do you think I am? You think I have neither decency nor self-respect?"

Vadinho did not want any arguing: "Sugar, what are you so

mad about? I didn't do anything out of the way. I just took a quick look at the girl's build, just out of curiosity to know what it was that took Pelancchi Moulas's fancy. They say he nurses those breasts." He laughed, and then lowered his voice. "Come, babe, sit down here beside your hubby, since you don't want to lie down, you are afraid. Sit down and let's chat a little; wasn't it you who said we had to talk?"

"I sit down and then you try to grab me . . ."

"If only I could! Do you think that if I could grab hold of you, without your consent, I would be here flattering you, wasting time? I am never going to take you against your will: you can write that down, I give you my word."

"Are you forbidden to take me by force?

"Forbidden? By whom? Neither God nor the devil can forbid me anything. Don't you know that, or did you live with me for seven years without learning to know me?"

"Then why?"

"Did I ever take you against your will? One single time, tell me?"

"Never."

"So? I am the one who forbade it, I never had to take a woman by force, and once when Mirandão tried to latch on to a little colored girl on the beach of União, I did not let him. This guy you're talking to, pet, wants only what is given to him, and given wholeheartedly, willingly. How could anything taken by force fail to have a bad taste?"

He gave her an appraising look, smiling again: "You are going to give it to me, my lovely little Flor, and I am crazy for the moment to come to get my piece. But it's got to be you who wants to give it to me, you who wants to spread your legs, for I only want you when you want it, too. I don't want you with any taste of hate, my sweet."

She knew that what he was saying was the absolute truth. Pride flamed in the breast of her (first) husband like an aureole, a glow. Not exactly of a saint, but of a man a he-man through and through.

Then Dona Flor sat down on the edge of the bed with Vadinho

stretched out beside her, watching her. With her nerves relaxed, at ease, disarmed against him. But she had no more than sat down when the trickster was slipping his hand from her waist to the amphora of her belly. She got to her feet indignantly:

"You are plain no good. I began to think that you were talking sincerely, that you were a man who kept his word. And then you contradict yourself, you start putting your hand . . ."

"And am I taking you by force, assaulting you? Just because I put my hand on your bellybutton? Sit down here and listen, my love: I am not going to take you by force, but that does not mean that I am not going to do everything, everything, that I am not going to use every means I can think of so you will give yourself to me of your own free will. Every time I can touch you, I will; every time I can kiss you, I will. Don't fool yourself, my Flor, I am going to do everything, everything, and quickly, for I am crazy to get at you. I am dying of hunger."

It was a challenge: her honor as a decent woman against Vadinho's fascination, his gift of gab, his boasting, his roguishness.

"I am not fooling you, Flor, I am giving it to you straight, and when that doctor of yours least expects it, he is going to have a crown of horns on his head. Moreover, my pet, with that big head of his and tall as he is, he's going to look real pretty. He is going to be a tree of horns of the finest class."

A challenge? Very good, my first husband and a stud of great fame, the Don Juan of brothels and the red-light district, the sly seducer of maids and wives, the wise guy, the hot number; but sly as you are, you are not going to bamboozle me again. With all your guile, with all your gab, with all your bag of tricks, I am not going to let myself be conquered or taken in. I am a decent woman, I am not going to befoul my name or that of my husband. I accept the challenge. And having so thought and made up her mind, she sat down on the mattress again.

"Don't talk like that, Vadinho. It is ugly. Respect my husband. Leave off such conversation, and let's talk about serious things. If I called you, as you say, it was to talk with you; at times I had such a longing, a desire to see you, to hear your voice. But not for anything indecent. Why do you hold me so low?"

"Me? When did I ever think badly of you?"

"I was your wife for seven years. You ran around the town, and it was not only to gamble: you climbed into the bed of every whore in Bahia, and not content with that, you had affairs with girls and married women, trollops who were worse than honest whores. And speaking of those artful hussies, I only recently discovered that you had had a crush on one of them, Inés, a consumptive-looking thing that came to the school a long time ago . . ."

"Inés? A thin one?" He searched the files of his excellent memory, that of the deadbeat, and came up with name and figure of slender Inés Vasques dos Santos with her insatiable mouth and appetite. "That one? Nothing but skin and bones. Don't give her another thought, my sweet. She doesn't count. A haybag, and one of the worst. Besides, this happened so long ago, why do you bring it up now, a forgotten slip like that, all over."

"A forgotten slip, all over, but I only heard about it the other day. Can you imagine the shame, Vadinho? You dead and buried, I married again, and your rascalities still pursuing me. Because of that and other reasons I called to you, because we still have accounts to settle. It was not for what you think."

"But, pet, no matter what it was for, since I am here, what's wrong about us screwing just a little? Let's take advantage and rid our bellies of their suffering. You could stand a little, and, as for me . . ."

"You ought to know me. Am I a woman to deceive her husband? For seven years you played Cain with me, you tormented me in every way. Everybody knew about it, it was the talk of the street."

"And do you care what that gaggle of old hags thinks?"

"You tormented me, and not a little, but a lot. If I had been a different woman, I would have left you or I would have made you a laughingstock with other men. Did I do that? No, I took it all, because I am a decent woman, thank God. I never looked at another man as long as you were alive."

"I know that, my love."

"Then if you know that, how is it that you want me to deceive

Teodoro, who is as much my husband as you, and a good, upright
man. He can't do enough for me, he would never be untrue to me.
Never, Vadinho, never. Once, even . . ." and she broke off in the
middle of the phrase.

"Once even what, darling," he asked in a gentle voice. "Tell me
the rest."

"Well there have been lots of women after him, and he pays
them no mind."

"Lots of women? Don't exaggerate, my dear, there was only
one, Magnólia, the biggest cow in Bahia, and did he make a fool of
himself! Who ever saw a grown man, a doctor and everything,
behave like a kid, scared of a woman. He practically called for
help. What a shame. Do you know what they called him after that
fiasco? Dr. Clyster, my dear."

"Vadinho, you shut up. If you want to talk in a decent fashion,
all right, but to come here to make fun of my husband—that I
won't have. I want you to know that I am very fond of him, I am
more than grateful for the way he treats me, and I shall never
dishonor his name."

"The one who brought up this conversation was you, pet. But
tell the truth: whom do you like better? Don't lie. Me or him?" He
laid his head on Dona Flor's shoulder, and she caressed his hair.

Lost in thought, she did not answer this compromising question. "I am never going to deceive him, Vadinho, he does not
deserve it."

Vadinho sighed, with the innocent smile of a child. Dona Flor
pressed him to her breast, touched that mat of golden hair, so soft
and warm. He said, and it was a statement, not a question: "You
like me better, sweetie. I know that for sure."

"He deserves all my love."

Dona Flor ran her hand over the knife scar: it gave her pleasure
to bring to mind the memory of the quarrel that had taken place
before she knew him, the long, deep gash, a fight in his youth after
which he had run away from school. What a swashbuckling rogue
that Vadinho! So good-looking.

The sweetness of the afternoon entered the room half in light,
half in shadow, on the wings of a drowsy breeze.

"My love," he said, "I had such a longing for you, so great that it weighed on my breast like a ton of earth. I have been wanting to come for a long time, ever since you called to ine the first time. But you had me fastened down with the *gri-gri* which Didi gave you, and it is only now that I could free myself and come. Because it is only now that you really called to me, wanted me, needed me . . ."

"I longed for you all the time. It did not matter that you had been bad, Vadinho; I almost died when you died."

Dona Flor felt something strange within herself. She did not know whether she wanted to laugh or to cry, but quietly, softly. The caress of Vadinho's hand on her arm was so gentle, on her nape, on her face, with his head resting on her breast, seeking a more comfortable position, and heavy and hot against her thighs, giving her warmth and drowsiness. Such a pretty head with its golden hair. Dona Flor gradually lowered her head, Vadinho raised his, and suddenly his mouth was on hers, and not by force.

Dona Flor wrenched herself from the kiss and the arms in which she felt herself swooning. "Oh, God! Dear God!"

It was not going to be an easy duel. She could not allow herself one moment of carelessness, the slightest negligence, if she did not want the devil to get the better of her.

Whistling, on top of the world, Vadinho got up with a mocking smile and began monkeying around in the bureau drawers. Sheer curiosity, or, perhaps, to give Dona Flor a chance to collect without too much effort the remnants of her strength of will, of her stoutly proclaimed decision.

5

When the doctor got home for dinner, Dona Flor had completely recovered her innate decency, and her determination was stronger than ever to keep herself worthy of him, maintaining his name and reputation unblemished, his brow—where ideas gleamed, knowledge abounded—unencumbered. "I shall never besmirch the name you bestowed on me, nor put horns on your head, Teodoro; I would rather die."

The important thing was not to falter, not to give the sly rogue a chance to play on her feelings, securing the complicity of the vile, contemptible matter capable—as she remembered from the days when she had taken up Yoga during her famished widowhood —of betraying her pure sentiments and selling her honor. If Vadinho hoped to go on seeing her, he had to keep within the bounds of decency, of Platonic relations, for Dona Flor and her former husband could allow themselves no others.

Dona Flor did not hide from herself—she did not even try to—the tenderness she felt for her ex-dead husband, her first and her great love. It was he who had awakened her to life, making of that silly young girl of Ladeira do Alvo a fire of leaping flames, who had taught her what joy and suffering were. She felt a deep, touching tenderness for him, something difficult to analyze and impossible to explain even to herself, a compound of good and evil.

She was glad, happy to see him, the rascal; to talk with him, to laugh at his mischievousness, his way of looking at things; happy even with the sufferings of her heart, once more anxious, waiting for him throughout the endless night, listening, sleepless, for his steps in the silence of the street; taking the bad with the good, as before. But now all this did not go beyond an affectionate friendship, without further implications, binding compromises, without the indecencies of bedding down together. The bed—ah, there lay the danger. A mined area, full of traps and time bombs.

Now, remarried, happy with her second husband, she could have only chaste relations with the first, as though that shameless, boundless passion of her youth had been converted, by Vadinho's death, into a modest encounter of romantic lovers, divested of the violence of the flesh to become pure incorporeal spirit (which, moreover, was called for because of these and all the other reasons). Bed and bodily pleasure only with her second husband, with Dr. Teodoro, on Wednesdays and Saturdays (with an encore) and with devoted affection. For Vadinho there was more than enough time during sleep, an empty stretch in the midst of so much happiness or—who can say?—so much happiness that had elapsed.

If Vadinho was willing to accept this situation, respecting this agreement, fine; this platonic sentiment full of sweetness and the discreet, gay presence of the young man would be a source of pleasure and charm in Dona Flor's life, so regulated, compensating in this way for a kind of dull monotony which seems to form an integral part of happiness. Mirandão, a philosopher and moralist (as has been abundantly proved) said on one occasion in his typical Bahian manner: "Happiness is pretty boring, hard to take—in a word, a pain in the neck."

But if Vadinho was not willing to abide by these restrictions, then Dona Flor would never see him again, breaking off relations and feelings—even that spiritual affection which was so innocent that it could not be looked upon as a sin or lack of consideration, a threat to the limpid brow of her upright, respected husband.

Thus, calmed by these reflections, strong of spirit, and having sucked a peppermint tablet to get out of her mouth the taste of honey and pepper left by that indecent kiss, Dona Flor received Dr. Teodoro with the same gentle affection, the same soft kiss as every evening, taking from him his coat and vest and bringing him a cool pajama jacket. When the doctor was having dinner or working at his desk, or practicing on his bassoon, he put his pajama coat on over his shirt and tie. It was his form of negligee.

During the meal, Dona Flor noticed in the voice and manner of her husband a gravity that was unusual, verging on the solemn. The druggist was inclined to be somewhat formal, as we know. But that afternoon, his gloomy face, his silence, his eating without paying any attention to his food indicated worry and uneasiness. Dona Flor watched her husband as she passed him the platter of rice and served him stuffed pork loin (with a dressing of eggs, sausage, and pepper). The doctor was confronted by some serious problem, undoubtedly, and Dona Flor like the good, devoted wife she was, became worried, too.

When they came to the coffee (accompanied by tapioca cookies, manna from heaven), Dr. Teodoro finally broke his silence, and it was an effort for him:

"My dear, I want to talk with you about a very important matter that concerns both of us."

"I am listening, dear."

But he hesitated, looking for the right words. What a difficult problem it must be, Dona Flor said to herself, to make her husband so unsure of himself. Concentrated on his uneasiness, she had completely forgotten her own problems, her dual marriage.

"What is it, Teodoro?"

He looked at her, clearing his throat: "I want you to feel absolutely free to decide as you think best and most convenient."

"For heaven's sake, what is it? Speak up, Teodoro."

"It's the house. It's up for sale."

"Which house? This one we live in?"

"Yes. As you know I had the money saved up to buy this house as you wanted. But just as we were about to close the deal, everything ready . . ."

"I know . . . the drugstore . . ."

". . . there came that chance to get another share of the drugstore, which made me a majority holder, guaranteeing us the ownership of the Scientific. I couldn't turn it down."

"You did right, just what you should. Remember what I said: 'The house can wait till later on.' Wasn't that what I said?"

"What has happened now, my dear, is that the house is up for sale at a bargain price."

"Up for sale? But weren't we supposed to have the first choice?"

"We were, but . . ." And he explained in detail what had happened. The owner had bought a ranch in Conquista and had gone in for cattle-breeding, putting a fortune into calves and heifers: he had entered the zebu bullring. Did Dona Flor know what the "zebu bullring" was? Had she ever heard of it? Well, in this fight he had lost even his house, and had put it up for sale at a ridiculous price. As for their having first choice, according to him although she was an old and excellent tenant, Dona Flor had forfeited this privilege when she' had given up the purchase, with the terms already settled, with the papers waiting to be signed before the notary. He could not wait for Dr. Teodoro to finish buying up all the shares of the heirs to the drugstore and then consider buying the house. What he wanted was to sell it at once. What good was that property to him paying him that ridiculous rent, the Madureiras occupying it practically for nothing? What was good business was to raise zebus, a disease-resistant breed of cattle, the pound of meat selling for a big price. Buried there on his ranch, he had turned the sale of the house over to the real estate department of the bank of their friend Celestino. And there would be no lack of offers, given the attractive price.

How did Dr. Teodoro know all that? Very simple: Celestino had told him about it in his office at the bank. He had called the druggist by phone—"Forget about your medicines, and come right over"—and had told him how things stood, finishing up by asking why Teodoro didn't make an effort and buy the house. It was the chance of a lifetime: you couldn't ask for a better stroke of business—the crazy fool was offering the property practically for nothing, the price of a lot of calves he wanted to buy in that zebu nonsense.

"When the zebus stop running, Dr. Teodoro, a lot of good people are going to lose their shirts. Here at the bank we won't lend a nickel for that speculation. Buy the house, my friend, don't think about it twice."

The Portuguese was right in all he said about the house and the zebus. The doctor, too, had his misgivings about that craze for calves, cows, and bulls. But where was he to get the money, when only a little while before he had put all his savings into buying up the share of the pharmacy and had borrowed money from the bank, lent him by Celestino himself, with notes payable when they fell due?

The banker looked the druggist over. An honest man, scrupulous, incapable of rooking anyone, no matter whom. He was not a man to apply for a bank loan unless he was absolutely sure he could repay it—Dr. Teodoro was no gambler. Celestino smiled. Life was a funny thing! That gentle Dona Flor, so timid of appearance and such a marvelous cook, had married two men who were completely the opposite of each other. Imagine him offering to lend money to Vadinho, as he was now doing to the druggist. The rascal's nervous hands would pick up the pen and sign any paper that was put before him, just so those signatures brought him some money for roulette.

"You scrape up some money for the down payment, and I'll get you the rest through a mortgage on the house. Look here . . ."

He picked up a pencil, and began figuring. If the doctor could get a few contos de reis, the rest didn't matter. He would give him a long-term mortgage at low interest, every facility. What the Portuguese was proposing was the kind of deal a father offers a son. Celestino had known Dona Flor since the time of her first marriage. He had eaten food prepared by her, thought a lot of her. Just as he did of Dr. Teodoro, a decent man, of excellent character. In his remarks he did not allude to Vadinho out of respect for the second husband and because the rogue was dead. But at that moment he recalled his profile and his roguery, and the memory made him smile and extend the maturity date of the mortgage by six months.

"I appreciate your offer, and I will never forget your generosity, my noble friend, but at this moment I do not have the money to put up as the down payment. Neither do I know where to get it. It is a great pity, for Florípedes wants to buy the house badly. But there's no way . . ."

"Florípedes," Celestino said to himself, "what a silly name. Tell me one thing, Dr. Teodoro Madureira, when you are with her do you call your wife Florípedes?"

"No, not when we are alone. I call her Flor, like everybody else does."

"Very good," and he interrupted the explanation the doctor was about to give him with a gesture. A banker's time is money. "Well, I happen to know that Dona Flor or Dona Florípedes, whichever you prefer, has a considerable amount in her account in the savings bank. More than enough for the down payment on the house . . ."

The druggist did not even remember about his wife's money. "But that money is hers, the fruit of her toil. I will never touch it. That is sacred money."

Once again the banker took a long look at the druggist sitting across from him. Vadinho had taken every cent he could get from his wife to gamble it away, and at times by force, brutally. He had even hit her, he had heard tell.

"Admirable sentiments, doctor, worthy of the lunkhead you are." The Portuguese shifted effortlessly from the greatest politeness to utter rudeness. "A numbskull is what you are, like those fellow countrymen of mine who carry pianos and break rocks in the street. Tell me: what good is that money of Dona Flor's in a passbook of the savings bank? She wanting to have her own home, and this fine gentleman out of respect for his shitty scruples—yes, I said shitty—passes up an opportunity of this kind. Aren't you married? Isn't what you have community property?"

Dr. Teodoro had swallowed without protest "lunkhead," "numbskull," and "shitty," for he knew the Portuguese well, and owed him many favors. "I don't know how to bring it up to her."

"You don't know how? Then do it when you go to bed, which is the best occasion for discussing business with one's wife, my dear fellow. I only discuss matters of this sort with the missus when the two of us are in bed, and they always turn out well. Listen: I am giving you a twenty-four-hour option. If tomorrow at this same time you don't show up here, I shall give instructions to sell the house to the highest bidder. And now, let me get back to work."

Not in bed, but at the table, as night was falling, in front of the snowy tapioca cookies soaking in coconut milk, Dr. Teodoro repeated his conversation with the banker to Dona Flor, omitting the dirty words and "lunkhead."

"If it were up to me, you would not touch that money in the savings bank."

"And what am I to do with it?"

"It's for your own personal expenses."

"What expenses, Teodoro, when you don't let me pay for anything? Not even the allowance to my mother. You pay for everything and even get cross when I object. In all this time I've been putting money in the bank, I only drew on it twice, nothing worth mentioning, to buy two remembrances for you. Why keep this money which is doing nothing for us? Unless it's for my coffin when I die . . ."

"Don't talk nonsense, my dear. The truth is that it is my obligation as a husband . . ."

"And why don't I have the right to contribute to buying us a house? Or don't you consider me your helpmate in everything? Am I only good to clean up, look after your clothes, cook your meals, and go to bed with you?" Dona Flor was in a temper. "Just a servant and a strumpet."

In the face of this unexpected explosion Dr. Teodoro was left speechless, his heart thudding, the fork with the piece of cookie motionless in his hand. Dona Flor lowered her voice, plaintive now: "Unless it's that you no longer love me, despise me so that you don't even want me to help you with the purchase of our house . . ."

Probably in all the time they had been married, over a year, Dr. Teodoro had never been so moved as at that dinner. With the sudden impulse the timid sometimes reveal, he burst out: "You know that I love you, Flor, that you are my whole life. How can you doubt it? Don't be unjust!"

Still excited, she went on: "Am I not your wife, your spouse? All right, if tomorrow you do not go to the bank, the one who will go is me and I will settle the business with Mr. Celestino."

Dr. Teodoro got up, went over to her, and clasped her to him in a passionate embrace. Dona Flor snuggled against the doctor's broad breast, moved too. They sat down on the sofa, Dona Flor in her husband's lap, cheek against cheek, in a tenderness that was almost sensual.

"You are the most upright, the most loyal, and the prettiest wife of all!"

"Not the prettiest, my Teodoro."

And she looked into his eyes, swimming with happiness.

"Not the prettiest, but loyal, that I can assure you, I will be and I am."

And as she said this she sought her husband's lips and took them in hers in a kiss of love: her kind husband, the only one who was entitled to her tenderness and the pleasure of her body.

The full night had suffused the room, and from the shadows Vadinho observed the scene. He ran his hand over his head, uneasy; then he turned his back and went out in the street, disgruntled.

6

After that conversation between Dona Flor and Dr. Teodoro, events took on an accelerated rhythm, ever more rapid and confused.

Things happened in the city capable of astounding (and they astounded) even those beings most familiar with wonders and magic, like the clairvoyant Aspásia, who arrived every morning from the Orient, her true habitat, at the Portas do Carmo, where she was "the only one to employ the system of spiritual science in motion"; like the famous medium Josete Marcos ("phenomena of levitation and ectoplasm"), whose familiarity with the beyond was more than well known; like the Archangel St. Michael de Carvalho, with his booth of miracles in Calafate Alley; like Dr. Nair Sacá "with her diploma from the University of Jupiter," who could cure each and every illness with magnetic passes in the Street of Fifteen Mysteries; like Madame Deborah, of Mirante dos Aflitos, recipient of the secrets of the monks of Tibet, perpetually with child as the result of spiritual coitus with the living Buddha, she herself being the "supreme revelation of the future," her gifts of foresight making it possible for her to "predict and guarantee rich marriages in a brief space of time and reveal the winning numbers of the lottery"—not to mention Teobaldo, Prince of Baghdad, by then somewhat in his dotage.

And not only were these competitors astounded. The amazement affected even those on closest terms with the cults of Bahia, those who created and preserved them, their custodians throughout the years: priests and priestesses, temple votaries and caretakers. Not even Lady Mother, seated on her throne in the Axé do Opo Afonjá *candomblé* center, or Menininha do Gantois, with her court in the Axé Iamasse center; or Aunt Massi of the White House in the venerable Axé Iá Nasso center, not even she with her hundred and three years; or Olga of Yansā dancing proudly and arrogantly in her center of Alaketu; or Nézinho de Ewá, or Simplica de Oxumarê, or Sinhá de Oxóssi, the votary of the late priest Procópio do Ile Ogunjá; or Joãozinho do Caboclo Pedra Preta; or Emiliano do Bogum; or Marieta de Tempo; or the half-breed Indian Neive Branco in Aldeia de Zumino Reanzarro Gangajti; or Luís da Murioca—none of them could control the situation nor explain it to his satisfaction.

They saw war break out among the deities at crossroads on nights of *macumba* rites, on the temple grounds and in the expanse of the sky, in the form of black arts which had no precedent, witchcraft, death-dealing spells, sorcery and conjures on every corner. The deities were infuriated, all united, complete in their attributes and the races from which they came; confronting them was Exu, alone in protecting that rebellious spirit of the dead, to whom no one offered red clothes or the blood of cocks and sheep, or a goat, not even a Guinea hen. He was bedecked in the apparel of desire, with the tinsel of imperishable passion, and as a sacrifice he asked only the laughter and the honey of Dona Flor.

Not even Yansã (*epa hei!*), who scares away souls, who has no fear of the spirits of the dead and stands up to them, who commands the departed, the warrior woman whose shout ripens the fruit and destroys armies, not even she could impose her authority and fearlessness. That votary of Exu had taken from her her scimitar and her horsetail symbol. Everything was upside down, inside out, all backwards, just imagine, midday at night, the sun of daybreak.

There came a moment when, prostrated at the hour of sacrifice, the priestesses and priests no longer wanted to intervene. It was up to those who were under the spell to find the decision in the fire of combat. Only the sorcerer Didi, because he was the Asobá de Omolu, magician of Ifá, keeper of the house of Ossain, and, above all, because he held the post of Korikoe Ulukotum in the center of the spirits of the dead in Amoreira, tried once more to envelop in the straws of the charm the spirit aroused from his sleep by love. He did this at the request of Dionísia de Oxóssi, but it was in vain as we shall see farther on.

Let it not be said that Cardosa & Sa. was astounded. He was not one to be astounded, nor was he given to frights and shocks. But he did have a jolt, and there's no way of hiding it, and merely by saying that Master Cardoso & Sa. was surprised, all is said and the measure of the unusual, the absurd atmosphere of the city is given. It was during those days that the people, lucidly and furiously, attacked the headquarters of the foreign monopoly of electric power, demanded the nationalization of the mines and oil wells, routed the police, and sang the *Marseillaise* without knowing French. It all started on that occasion.

Dona Flor did not realize the situation at once, unlike Pelancchi Moulas, whose Calabrian blood warned him and then gave him the clue to the meaning and direction of events that same baleful night. It took only a few days to convince Pelancchi. Terrified—yes terrified, this man without fear or feelings, this bandit of Calabria, this gangster after the manner of those of Chicago, this sky's-the-limit gambler—sent his chauffeur Aurelio, in whom he had complete trust, to the *candomblé* center of Mother Otavia Kissikbi, a priestess of the Congo, while he himself went looking for the mystical philosopher and astrologer Cardoso & Sa., the only ones who could help him in that terrible emergency, save his empire and majesty.

Empire and majesty, for Pelancchi Moulas was the ruler of the most powerful trust of Bahia, king of gambling and bookmaking, legally running the roulette games, the French hare, baccarat, *lasquiné*, at the Palace, in Tabaris, in Abaixadinho, in the large and small establishments where his managers were alert to the dice and decks of cards, to the croupiers and overseers, and brought him every day the rich intake from *ronda*, twenty-one, black jack. There were very few joints that were not under his control, one or two, such as that of the Three Dukes, of Meningite, the den of Paranaguá Ventura. His claws, avid and hooked (through well manicured by his exclusive manicurist, a young mulatta sired by old Barreiros, the father of that lawyer Tibúrcio, a specialist; he had modeled thirty-seven mulattas by different mothers, each more wonderful and exciting than the other) reached out over all the others.

And what about the huge illegal (seemingly so) empire of the numbers racket? Pelancchi alone was permitted to act as banker with the backing of the police, and if some unwitting fool tried to compete with him, the zealous authorities applied the full rigor of the law to the infamous intruder: *dura lex sed lex*.

There was no one in all the state of Bahia who enjoyed more power, civil or military, whether bishop or macumba priest. Pelancchi Moulas gave orders and countermanded orders.

Administrator, governor of the most complex and richest empire, that of the gambling world, at the head of an army of subordinates, masters of ceremonies, croupiers, bookkeepers, bankers, pimps, spies, secret police agents, bodyguards, he was the pope of a sect with thousands of faithful followers, fanatical slaves. With his pay-offs he supported and enriched illustrious figures in government, intellectual circles, and the public order, beginning with the Chief of Police, was a contributor to good works, and helped pay for the building of churches.

Compared with him, who were the Governor and the Prefect, commanders of land, sea, and air, the Archbishop with his mitre and his ring? There was no earthly power that could frighten Pelancchi Moulas, an old Italian with white hair, a warm smile and hard, almost cruel eyes, continually smoking a cigarette in an ivory holder, and reading Virgil and Dante, for, in addition to gambling, he loved poetry and mulattas.

7

The Negro Arigof was depressed. Bad luck of that sort was too much. It had been on his back for almost a month, ever since the time when he had run down the stairs of the tenement where he had his bachelor's room, and had stumbled over a bundle with a hex in it. A fierce piece of sorcery, put there to louse up his life. The paper had torn open, scattering yellow manioc meal, the black feathers of a hen, charmed herbs, two copper coins, and pieces of a knitted necktie of his, still fairly new. The necktie gave him the unmistakable clue: it was the revenge of Zaíra, a heartless cow, who never suffered an outrage without getting her own back.

One night Arigof, losing his calm and his patrician elegance, had slapped her a couple of times in Tabaris in sight of everyone so she would learn manners and not try his patience further. Zaíra was *mucurumin* by race, but she practiced voodoo and Guinea rites and had power with the *inkices*.

It must have been a hex of the strongest kind, a terrific hoodoo. Who could have prepared such a powerful conjure for Zaíra?

Undoubtedly someone who knew the requirements, was good with herbs and powerful in evil. There was no counterspell that did any good; the hex had dragged the Negro's luck to the bottom of the well, and he went about like a beggar from gambling house to gambling house, losing in all of them. He had hocked all his best possessions: his silver ring, his gold chain with amulets from Guinea and a little ivory horn, the watch he had bought from a blond sailor who had probably stolen it from a millionaire's state-room. It was so pretty and unusual that the Spainard in Sete, with all his knowledge of jewelry, had whistled at the sight of it, offering him over five hundred mil-reis if the Negro would sell instead of pawning it.

That devil-pacting creole, born in witchcraft, had dried up his luck. Deeply worried, Arigof asked himself where the rest of his knitted tie could be. Beyond doubt, tied to the feet of an Indian god or an *inkice* together with his picture, that little one, taken for his identification card, with the Negro smiling, showing his gold tooth. Arigof had given it to that heartless witch as proof of his love, and now he could imagine his face stuck full of pins on the altar of the divinity so that the hex would be renewed every morning and put out his lucky star quickly and forever.

He had taken a bath of herbs and been prayed over by Epifania de Ogun. Three times the priestess had to renew her packet of leaves, for they fell withered as soon as they touched his body, so great was the load of sorcery on Arigof's back.

During the harrassment of this hoodoo, the Negro was walking along Chile Street, turning over the vicissitudes of life in his mind. He had come from the restaurant, and his immediate destination was Teresa's house. Waldomiro Lins had taken him to dinner after that disastrous afternoon in Zezé de Meningite's joint, where the Negro lost his last cent. Arigof, in a fury, ate his breakfast, lunch, and dinner all at the same time.

"You are choked with hunger, Arigof. What's the matter with you?" the other asked in view of that insatiable appetite.

The Negro answered with boundless pessimism: "I don't know if I will ever eat again."

"Are you sick?"

"Bad luck, brother. They have put some kind of a spell on me, some caboclo hex, or a god of Angola, for that treacherous beast uses black magic. I am dead broke, brother."

He told him how he was jinxed: his infallible hunches came to nothing; not one worked. Whether at dice or cards or the roulette wheel, he always lost. The other players were beginning to look askance at him, as though his hex were catching.

He went on with his story in lengthy detail, hoping that Waldomiro Lins, a young fellow of means and a gay companion, would help him out of his tight spot, lending him a few bucks to play that night. But the plan did not work; instead of money, his friend gave him advice: there was only one way to outfox the conjure, and that was to give up gambling for a while. Let the tide of bad luck run out and the power of the hex wear off, unless he was crazy. If he kept on he would wind up having to pawn his shorts. He, Waldomiro Lins, had learned to respect luck and chance, and on one occasion he had spent over three months without looking at a deck of cards, dice, or a roulette table.

Walking along Chile Street, Arigof realized that his friend was right; that stubbornness was sheer stupidity, the obstinacy of a person out of his mind. It would be better to go to see Teresa da Geografia, a white girl who was crazy about strong Negroes and the cause of his slapping Zaíra. In Teresa's house, stretched out in bed alongside her, sipping a rum with lemon, he could forget all those losses, rest from his bad luck at the gaming table. Yes, this time the Negro Arigof had been defeated. All that was left him was a shameful retreat. Waldomiro Lins was right: he was a man of experience who gave good advice. Prepared to set out for his visit to Teresa, the Negro-lover, Arigof nevertheless did not feel completely satisfied. It was not his way to flee from battle even when the situation was desperate, defeated before he started. He recalled another Waldomiro, his exemplary and unforgettable friend: Vadinho, unfortunately dead, capable, bold, unequaled at gambling and in almost everything. He was the one who could help him if he were alive.

One night many years back, after weeks of the toughest luck, without a cent and without anywhere to find it, Arigof had gone into Tabaris, where he had run into Vadinho, overflowing with pride and chips, betting high. The Negro took a chip from him and the example of his triumph: in a few minutes he had won ninety-six contos. Nobody had ever seen anything like it. It was a dream night: Arigof ordered half a dozen suits at one time, throwing bills of five hundred mil-reis in the face of the tailor. A fantastic night of a never-to-be-forgotten orgy in Carla's cathouse, he paying all the expenses, a legendary night in the gambling annals of Bahia.

Wasn't it funny: he had only to recall Vadinho and his boasting and it seemed to him that he could clearly hear that insolent voice: "So, you scary Negro, what's become of your guts? Up the white girl's ass? The person who doesn't pursue luck doesn't deserve it—you know that. Since when did you become Waldomiro Lins's pupil? Weren't you already a professor when he laid his first bet?"

Arigof stopped in the middle of Chile Street like a simpleton, so live and close did he seem to hear Vadinho's voice. Emerging from the sea, the moon began to turn the city to gold and silver.

"Leave the white girl's bones for later on, you cowardly Negro. You afraid of a conjure! Aren't you the son of Xangó? Leave the white girl until you've cut the hex in two! Tonight is your night to celebrate."

Vadinho had the craziest hunches, and was the same whether he won or lost, always wore the same sly, insolent smile. Who knows, Arigof asked himself, from beyond the moon Vadinho might be seeing him with the spell on him, divested of his gold chain, his silver ring, the watch the Spaniard of Sete coveted.

"Where's your mettle, black man? What's become of the Negro Arigof, a *macho* three times over?"

Waldomiro Lins, a careful, canny player, had advised him not to go against his luck, to wait, hidden in the bed of his girl friend, so white and so learned: Teresa could recite the names of the rivers of China, the volcanoes of the Andes, the mountain peaks. When she saw the Negro Arigof, huge and naked, she greeted at the same time the peak of Mt. Everest and the axis of the earth. That shameless Teresa. With all this hoodoo and Teresa waiting for him, one would have to be crazy to go back to gambling that night.

"Go! I guarantee your luck, you shilly-shally Negro," came the voice of Vadinho in his ear.

Arigof looked all around for him, for he could even feel the touch of Vadinho's breath. It was as though his former friend were taking him by the hand and leading him to the stairs of Abaixadinho, so close by.

Teresa would be waiting for him eating chocolates, enveloped in the lakes of Canada, the tributaries of the Amazon. Without a cent in his pocket, Arigof went into Abaixadinho and walked over to the table of *lasquiné*.

Antônio Dedinho, the croupier, was opening the box of six decks to start the new game. The faces around the table were those of losers. None reflected enthusiasm: all the luck was with the house. Not one friend whom Arigof could touch for a chip or money. Antônio Dedinho announced that the bank was for a hundred contos, and turned up two cards on the table: the queen and the king.

"The queen," Arigof heard Vadinho order.

And nobody to lend him at least five mil-reis. There was a man there, well dressed, very well turned-out in a white suit, with chips in his hand and the air of a habitué, but a stranger; perhaps from the interior. Arigof pulled out of his tie the showy stickpin, a key over a heart, the gift of Teresa. But the gold was plate, and the diamonds nothing but glass; the Spaniard of Sete had turned up his nose at it, refusing to give him anything on it.

Displaying the pin, Arigof turned to the man in the white suit: "Sir, lend me a chip, of whatever value, and keep this jewel as a guarantee. I will pay you back. My name is Arigof, and everybody here knows me."

The fine gentleman held out a chip worth a hundred mil-reis: "Keep your pin. If you win, you can repay me, and good luck to you."

With his chip on the queen, Arigof waited, the only one, for among those around the table nobody wanted to risk his money. They were completely discouraged. Not even the man in the white

suit, who preferred to kibitz. Antônio Dedinho turned up the first
card and it was the queen. Arigof picked up the chips. Dedinho
turned up another set of cards, and they happened to be the queen
and king again. Once more Arigof put his money in the hands of
the queen.

Antônio Dedinho pulled a card out of the deck and—what a
coincidence!—the card was the queen again. A new deck, and the
coincidence repeated itself, and this was unusual: for the third time
the queen and the king lay on the table. Arigof kept on with the
queen and, together with him the man dressed in white, laid his
bet. The first observers came over. Antônio Dedinho drew a card
from the deck and, impossible as it sounds, the first card, for the
third time, was the queen. Of diamonds, incidentally, bringing
Teresa to mind. "My God," a whore said nervously.

Nervous not only because the queen had come up three times,
but because it was always the first card and because three times
running the same cards had come up on the gambling table; the
queen and king.

Not three times, but a dozen the queen and king were dealt on
the table, and a dozen times the queen responded to Arigof's call,
and was always the first card to be turned up. Now not only the
man in the white suit but several others followed the Negro's
hunch, who was laying three contos on every bet, the maximum
allowed.

Pale as death, his heart full of fear, Antônio Dedinho prepared a
new deck. Lulu, the supervisor of the room, was now standing
beside Dedinho carefully watching the shuffling of the cards.
Around the table the crowd grew. People came over from the
baccarat table and the roulette wheel.

Antônio Dedinho held out the deck to the players' view, and
drew two cards from it. His pallor increased, his hands trembled,
for the cards were the queen and king. Arigof smiled; he had
changed his luck, broken the spell, and had gone to seek his fortune
with his hands and teeth and with the memory of Vadinho. If
there was another world, if the dead were up there, wandering
through the sky or space, as certain specialists in such matters say,
then perhaps Vadinho was watching him from the height of the

moon pouring itself out in gold and silver over the sea and the houses. Proud, without doubt, of the bravery of his friend Arigof, a black man who was all man, rendering spells and charms powerless.

But evidently Vadinho was right there in the room, beside Arigof, and stubborn as hell, for when the Negro had decided, after deep cabalistic calculations, to change cards and back the king (it was impossible for the queen to come up again, absolutely impossible), he heard the angry voice of his friend ordering him harshly: "On the queen, you son-of-a-bitching Negro."

And Arigof's hand, independently of his will, as though obeying some superior force, laid his chips on the queen.

Gritting his teeth, his eyes wild, Antônio Dedinho turned up the first card: a queen. There was a stir, exclamations, nervous laughter, and more and more people came over to see the impossible happening.

Gilberto Cachorrão, the manager of the joint, with his distrustful air of a watchdog, took his place beside Lulu, prepared to unmask the swindle (for what else could it be but a gyp and a big one?). Right under his nose the same incredible thing happened several times, and the bank of a hundred contos broke. Riotous and gay, the queen was always the first card. What kind of a gyp was it, brash or subtle, Cachorrão?

Antônio Dedinho turned to the manager, defeated, awaiting his orders, but Cacharrão merely gave him a suspicious look and said nothing. The croupier got out new decks slowly, in plain sight of all, and said almost choking: "The stakes are one hundred contos."

He turned up two cards: queen and king. There was a dead silence, and now everybody wanted to bet on the queen. People came in from the street and from Tabaris, where the astounding news had already been heard. The new bank did not last.

At Gilberto Cachorrão's orders, Lulu rushed to the telephone. In the gambling hall the impossible had become routine, the queen always coming up first. The man in the white suit spoke out: "I'm leaving now before I have an attack, my heart can't stand this. I have been playing for more than ten years in Ilhéus and Itabuna, in

Pirangi and Água Preta. I have seen many skin games, frauds of every sort, but this takes the cake. And I might add that I cannot believe what I am seeing."

Arigof wanted to repay the chip he had loaned him and invite him to dine at Teresa's house, but the man declined: "God keep and watch over me. I am afraid of witchcraft, and this can only be witchcraft. Keep the chip and let me redeem mine before they light out or declare themselves bankrupt."

Lulu came back, and before long he and Cachorrão were joined by a circumspect elderly creole, wearing glasses, very calm, Professor Máximo Sales, the number one stooge of Pelancchi Moulas, the person he most trusted.

When he received the telephone call from Lulu, the tycoon refused to believe that harebrained tale. Beyond a doubt Lulu had started drinking again and was now doing it during work hours, which was unforgivable. His gray head resting on the warm bosom of Zulmira Simões Fagundes in sweet intimacy, Pelancchi sent Máximo Sales to get the straight of that crazy rumor. Probably the whole thing was nothing but a snootful Lulu had got.

"If he should be drunk, professor, please don't hesitate; fire him on the spot. And telephone me to let me know what happened."

The right hand man of Pelancchi had barely time to take in what was happening and the fact that Lulu was completely sober when the stake of a hundred contos had disappeared into the hands of Arigof.

Antônio Dedinho, wiping the sweat from his pale forehead, looked at the three observing him. He had children to bring up, and he was not trained for any other kind of work. Oh, Lord! The three looked him over up and down, and Professor Máximo Sales whispered: "Go on." In his blue suit, his rimless glasses, his ruby ring, Máximo Sales had the appearance of a respectable professor with woolly hair whitened by study and nights of scientific experimentation. He was so formal and dignified that everyone called him Professor, including Pelancchi, even if his training had been exclusively in smuggling, chips, and cards. In this field he was really outstanding, indisputably competent, knowledgeable, a *doctor angelicus*.

Antônio Dedinho, a plaything of destiny, got out another deck and everything happened just as before, like a nightmare. As Amesina said (her pretty name was a combination of "Ame" from that of her father Americo, and "Sina" after her mother Rosina), a whore given to the reading of the *Almanac of Thought* and other esoteric materials, this marked the "long awaited sign of the end of the world." Máximo Sales asked Cachorrão and Lulu several questions (taking in at the same time the innocence of their breath). Then, making his way through a flood of women, he got to the telephone.

That is why Pelancchi Moulas showed up in the room, with Zulmira at his side. A path was opened for him to come through and thus see at first hand how his money was disappearing. The bank of a hundred contos blew up in his face.

With a regal gesture, Pelancchi Moulas pushed Antônio Dedinho aside, and in view of all had a look in the drawer: the twelve kings piled up in the bottom of the box the last cards. The three employes—Máximo with his doctoral air, the watchdog Gilberto, and Lulu, the overseer of the hall—exchanged knowing glances. Antônio Dedinho knew he was innocent but doomed. Pelancchi Moulas, his eyes cold, blue with cruelty, looked first at the croupier and the three employes, and then at the crowd gathered about, their faces avid and tense, gamblers of the-sky's-the-limit variety. At the head of all of them, the Negro Arigof, a peak of the Himalayas, incredibly tall, the axis of the world, according to the learned Teresa, geographer and Negro-lover. Arigof smiled, covered with sweat and chips.

Pelancchi Moulas, too, smiled at Zulmira, bringing up his rear, and he himself opened a new deck and announced the bank as though he were declaiming a verse: "A bank of two hundred contos."

Not because of him, Pelancchi Moulas, the lord of gambling, of noose and knife, ruler of all that is known and not worth repeating, not on this account did luck change, which was no longer luck but a miracle: out came king and queen, the queen the first card. When the bank broke before half the deck had been dealt, Pelancchi Moulas examined the drawer with the rest of the decks: there at the bottom ("the end of the world," repeated Amesina, the prophetess) were the twelve useless kings.

Throwing down the cards, Pelancchi Moulas whispered something and Gilberto Cachorrão repeated his words aloud: "Play is over for today."

Arigof withdrew amid demonstrations of applause, followed by admirers and ardent, fawning women. He redeemed his chips, bought champagne, and set out for the house of Teresa, the Negro-lover, a *summa cum laude* in geography and bed-play. The Negro was highflown with conceit and pride; the hex and the jinx and the anger of the Mali spell-worker were powerless against him.

Pelancchi Moulas gave himself up to thought. Lulu rubbed his hands together. Gilberto Cachorrão could come up with no explanation, but he agreed with Máximo Sales: there was a gyp, a swindle in that business, and a big one. Shipwrecked in a sea of women, Antônio Dedinho awaited his sentence. The whole thing had to be cleared up, the professor said solemnly. Pelancchi Moulas shrugged his shoulders: let them take whatever steps were necessary, inquiries, investigation; let them even call in the police if that would help. As for him, he had misgivings, his Calabrian blood was attuned to the irrational, the emanations of the beyond.

So were the breasts of Zulmira Simões Fagundes, bronze and velvety. The first secretary, the prima donna, the favorite of Pelancchi Moulas, suddenly writhed giving a coy giggle: "Something at my breasts, Pequito, something is tickling me, oh what a crazy thing! It almost seems a ghost . . ."

Pelancchi Moulas made the sign of the cross.

8

Those were days of confusion, days filled with emotion. Dr. Teodoro and Dona Flor in a bustle, running hither and yon, from the bank to the notary's office, from the notary's office to various government bureaus. She had to cancel her classes until the end of the week; he hardly put in an appearance at the pharmacy. Celestino, with his customary Lusitanian frankness, told Dona Flor: "If you really want to buy the house, forget about that rubbish of your classes. Otherwise, you can kiss it goodbye."

Another customer had showed up, and if it had not been for the kindliness of the banker, they would have lost the chance to make the deal. Now everything was practically finished; all they had to do was put their signatures to the deed, and in a few days the notary would have it ready. But they had already made the down payment to the former owner, and for that purpose they had used the money Dona Flor had to her account in the savings bank.

On her husband's arm, confiding in his strength and knowledge, Dona Flor had traversed half of Bahia during that weekend. She had spent hardly any time at home except to eat and sleep, and even during those hours she had been unable to rest. How could she with Vadinho present, stationing himself at her elbow the moment she appeared, and bolder with every passing minute, prepared to drag her into dishonor, adultery?

"Adultery? How adultery?", the wretch asked, "when I am your husband? Who ever heard of a woman becoming an adultress because she went to bed with her legitimate husband? Didn't you promise obedience before the judge and the priest? Who ever heard, my passion flower, of a platonic marriage of this sort? It's crazy . . ."

The devil had a honeyed tongue, a clever lip, logic and rhetoric. He knew all the arguments that could confuse her, and his voice was like a lullaby: "Darling, wasn't it to sleep together that we got married? What have you got to say to that?"

Dona Flor still felt against her arm that of the doctor. She could still smell the odor of his sweat as they climbed the hills in their trips from government office to office. Vadinho's voice upset her —how could she rest when she had to be on guard, when she could not relax her vigilance for a second without danger? The danger of succumbing to the music of his voice, dizzied by his words, the touch of his treacherous hand, his lips. Before she knew what was happening, she was in his arms and had to free herself violently. She did not yield to him; nor would she ever.

She did not yield to him or, at least, she did not yield completely, though she did allow him certain liberties during those weary days: slight and innocent caresses. Or were they so slight and innocent?

One afternoon, for example, when she got home worn out from the various bureaus and the notary's office (the doctor had gone to the drugstore to fill prescriptions), Dona Flor took off her dress, pulled off her shoes and stockings, and stretched out in bed, wearing nothing but her brassiere and slip. There was silence and a breeze in the empty house, and Dona Flor gave a sigh.

"Tired, sweetie?" It was Vadinho lying beside her.

Where had he come from? Where had he hidden that Dona Flor had not seen him?

"So tired . . . to get a paper at one of the bureaus takes a whole afternoon. I wouldn't have believed . . ."

Vadinho touched her face: "But you are happy, aren't you?"

"I always wanted to own my own home."

"I always wanted to give you this house."

"You?"

"You don't believe me? I don't blame you. But I want you to know that it was the thing I most wanted: to be able to give you this house one day. The time would come when I would win so much on number 17 that I would be able to buy it. I was going to come with the deed without saying a word to you. Except that there wasn't time. Otherwise . . . you don't believe me, do you?"

Dona Flor smiled: "Why shouldn't I believe you?"

She felt Vadinho's mouth level with her face, and she tried to free herself from his enveloping arms. "Let me alone."

But he begged so much that she let him rest his blond head beside hers, and allowed him clasp her to his bosom. Innocently, of course.

"You swear that you are not going to try . . ."

"I swear."

It was a delightful moment, Dona Flor feeling Vadinho's breath against her neck, and those hands defending her rest. One of them caressed her face, touched her hair, banishing her weariness. She was so exhausted that she fell asleep.

When she awoke, the shadows of night had arrived and so had Dr. Teodoro: "Did you have a nap, my dear? You must be dead, you poor thing! On top of spending your money, all this drudgery."

"Don't talk nonsense, Teodoro," and she modestly covered herself with the sheet.

She looked about for Vadinho in the semidarkness of the room, and did not see him. Undoubtedly he had left when he had heard the doctor's footsteps. Could it be that he was jealous of Teodoro, Dona Flor asked herself, smiling. Vadinho had denied it, naturally, but Dona Flor had her doubts.

Dr. Teodoro put on his pajama top, Dona Flor her robe, and got up. Her husband took her hands in his: "What a bother, isn't it, my dear? But it was worth the trouble, for now we own our house. I will not rest, however, until I pay off the mortgage and put back in your savings account all the money you used in this transaction."

Together, the druggist's arm encircling Dona Flor's waist, they came out of the bedroom into the dining-room. There they found Dona Norma, longing to hear all the details about the purchase of the house.

"You look like two lovebirds," the neighbor said, when she saw them so affectionate, whereupon the doctor grew bashful, and drew away from his wife.

The next morning Dona Norma came back to talk over some matters having to do with sewing. Pointing to Dona Flor's bare neck, she said jokingly: "This love affair with your husband is becoming scandalous."

"Hm? What are you talking about?"

"You think I didn't see the two of you yesterday coming out of the bedroom, still embracing one another?"

"Are you talking about me and Teodoro?" asked Dona Flor, still frightened.

"And whom would I be talking about? Are you trying to cover up? The doctor is losing his seriousness. And before dinner, too. Did the party go on afterwards? To be sure, the purchase of the house called for a celebration."

"What a way to talk, Norminha! There was no party."

"Ah, my saint, you don't expect me to swallow that. What about all those marks on your neck, and you tell me nothing happened. I didn't know the doctor was the blood-sucking type."

Dona Flor ran her hand over her neck, and hurried over to the mirror. There were red marks, turning purple, all down one side of her neck. How shameful.

Ah, what a lying, crazy tyrant that Vadinho was. She had felt the caress of his lips and had protested. But he had asked what harm there was in touching her neck; it wasn't even a kiss, just running his mouth over her skin. While that had been going on Dona Flor had fallen asleep—ah, that hopeless Vadinho.

She turned away from the mirror and put on a high-necked blouse to hide the guilty marks. What would the doctor say if he saw those red signs of lips that were not his, he who was incapable of such debauchery and deprivation? She came back to the living-room:

"Norminha, my dear, for the love of God don't make jokes to Teodoro about such matters. You know how easily embarrassed he is. He is so shy."

"Of course, I am not going to josh him about it, but Florzinho, there's no doubt that he is loosening up. He was shy in bygone days, but now he is relaxing. He's even acting like Vadinho; the only difference is that he doesn't do his stuff in front of the neighbors."

Dona Flor sensed a laugh and a presence of which Dona Norma was fortunately unaware. The rogue was floating through the air and, as though that weren't enough, had put on that shirt covered with naked women which Dona Gisa had brought back from America for the doctor. But the shirt covered only his chest, leaving everything else in plain sight, making it look more indecent than ever.

9

"What's wrong with that, my darling? What am I doing to you? Leave my hand there. I'm not pinching you or stroking you—my hand is still, what's wrong about that?" He kept his hand discreetly on her rounded hips, but no sooner had he received her silent consent, than it did not remain quiet, but went moving up and down her flanks, from rump to thigh, a vast territory that it went conquering bit by bit.

Thus, with hands, breath, lips, soft words, looks, laughter, jests, complaints, quarrels, insinuations, Vadinho was beleaguering the fortress which Dona Flor had assured him was invincible, undermining walls of dignity and modesty. In a relentless advance, in stubborn assault, he was conquering the field hour by hour.

In each engagement he occupied a new position and bastions fell, overcome by force or astuteness: the knowing hand or the lips that uttered a thousand promises, all of them sham: "Just one kiss, darling, just one . . ." And then followed breasts, thighs, neck, hips, the satiny backside. Now all that was his, terrain free from reprimand for Vadinho's hand, lips, caresses. By the time Dona

Flor took in what had happened, her decency and the doctor's honor were hemmed into the last redoubt, the only one still holding out. The rest, that burning battlefield, he had conquered almost without her being aware.

Dona Flor came prepared to make a complaint about those red spots on her neck, those incriminating, dismaying signs, but he enveloped her in an embrace, whispering explanations or making fun of her modesty and seriousness, and in a little while he was biting her ear, in a blandishment that sent shivers through her.

She had to put an end once and for all to those dubious relations which were already far from the tender affection, innocent loving friendship, the platonic sentiments which she had thought were possible on Vadinho's return. As she weighed the full extent of the danger, the virtuous wife was filled with fear and courage, prepared to put an end to that absurd situation. Who ever heard of a wife with two husbands?

Sitting on the sofa, Dona Flor reflected on the delicacy of the affair. She had to handle the discussion with great adroitness so as not to hurt Vadinho, not to offend him; after all, he had come in answer to her call. And there before she knew it the knave had appeared and had her in his arms. While Dona Flor was seeking the way to bring up the problem, Vadinho had slipped his hand under her dress, trying to reach that final and still unyielding redoubt, the strongbox that held her dignity as a wife and the honor of the doctor.

"Vadinho!"

"Let me see the hotbox, sweetie! I am dying of longing for the pussy, and it's mine . . ."

Dona Flor leaped up in an explosion of rage, violent and furious. Vadinho got mad too, and the squabble was harsh and disagreeable. Probably Vadinho had not expected such a sharp reaction from Dona Flor by this time; he thought he could count on victory.

"Take your hand off me! Don't you touch me any more. If you still want to see me and talk to me, it must be at a distance, like acquaintances and nothing more. I told you that I was a decent woman, and I am very happy with my husband."

Vadinho answered mockingly: "Your husband, that dumbbell, that sap! All he's got is his size. What does he know about these things, that nance?"

"Teodoro is not an ignorant thing like you, or a no-account. He is a man of great learning."

"Great learning. Maybe he is able to mix up a cough syrup. But for what really counts, for screwing, he must be the biggest nitwit in the world. All you have to do is look at him: he's been altered . . ."

Dona Flor looked Vadinho in the eye; he had never seen her so angry: "I just want you to know that you are very much mistaken, and who is a better judge of this than I? I am more than satisfied. I have never met a better man than he. You are not fit to tie his shoelaces."

"Pff," Vadinho answered, with a contemptuous and vulgar sound.

"You just let me alone! I don't need you for anything. And don't you dare touch me again."

She had made up her mind: she would not allow him any further intimacies, embraces, innocent kisses, or let him stretch out beside her "to talk more easily." She was an upright woman, a devoted wife.

"If you were so satisfied, why did you call me?"

"I have told you it was not for that, and I am sorry I did it."

Later on, when she was alone, she asked herself if she had not been too rude and violent. Vadinho was furious, offended, his head hanging. He went out the door and she did not see him for the rest of the day. When he came back at twilight, she would explain things to him with kind words. Cynical and insolent though he was, at times Vadinho had unexpected reactions, was capable of understanding Dona Flor's scruples and of keeping his relations within the limits laid down by decorum and honor.

Always in the afternoon, when her day's work was done and after her bath, Dona Flor, redolent of toilet water and talcum powder, lay down for a few minutes' rest. Then Vadinho invariably stretched out beside her and they talked about the most diverse subjects (and while they talked he kept undermining her defenses, holding her to his breast, bending her to his will). When she was on the point of reprimanding him, he distracted her by telling her of the places from which he had come, and Dona Flor, consumed by curiosity, full of questions, lacked the power to enforce her bans.

"And what is the world like seen from there, Vadinho?"

"It's all blue, my dear."

And the tempter let his hand slip down her thigh or breast while Dona Flor asked: "And what is God like?"

"God is fat."

"Take your hand away from there! You are making fun of me . . ."

Vadinho laughed, his hand holding her firm breast, his lips seeking Dona Flor's mouth. How could she tell if it was the truth or a lie? That breath of flame, that burning breath of pepper, the sweetness of the breeze, the zephyrs off the sea, oh, that lying, worthless Vadinho. Thus he went conquering her little by little, only the last redoubt holding out, her ultimate rear guard.

That day, however, she waited in vain. He did not come. Uneasy, Dona Flor moved restlessly from side to side in bed, torn between anxiety and doubt. Could he have gone away again, hurt in his pride, offended? Could he have gone away for good?

The thought made Dona Flor shudder. How was she going to get used to living without seeing him? Without his zaniness, his wit, the temptation he represented?

But be that as it may, she had to learn to get along without him if she wanted to remain an upright, virtuous woman. It was the only possible solution; that impasse left no other way out. It was a rigorous measure, a test that was almost unbearable, but what could she do? A drastic rupture was in order; if Vadinho stayed there, all the strength of decency and virtuous determination would be unable to stand up against the irremediable. Dona Flor did not fool herself: what were the talks except excuses for caresses, for that struggle, so grueling and so delicious?

How was it possible to resist Vadinho's gift of gab? Hadn't he convinced her, and hadn't Dona Flor let herself be convinced, that provided no sexual intercourse was involved, all the rest was a harmless joke, like games between cousins, not implying dishonor or even indecency? As long as there was no screwing, there could be no dishonor, and her dignity and the distinguished brow of the doctor remained unblemished.

For the second time Vadinho had lulled her scruples to rest with the same lullaby, the same *modinha* with which he had gulled her in the far-off days of their love affair in Rio Vermelho and on Ladeira do Alvo. She had let herself be taken in and when she had opened her eyes, he had eaten her cherry and her honor there by the sea in Itapoã.

Now once more Vadinho had come to the keys of her last citadel, the most hidden resort of her being. At the least oversight on her part, in a second of uncontrollable desire, he would eat not only her cherry but also the honor of her husband and her decency as a wife.

Of a model wife, of a husband who was an example of good husbands. When the poor soul least expected it, horns would burst forth on his head, and it would be the greatest of injustices. The seeds of these unjust horns were already planted by the hands of Vadinho, by his kissing mouth, by his masculine ardor, which aroused longing and sin in Dona Flor.

Yes, there was only one solution, safe and sure: for Vadinho to go back where he had come from. Only in that way would her decency as a wife and the druggist's head be protected. It would break her heart, she would suffer terribly, but what other way was there, what other solution? She would politely explain her reasons to him: "Forgive me, my love, but it is impossible for us to go on like this. I can't stand it any more. Forgive me for having called you! It was all my fault, farewell, and leave me in peace."

In peace? Or in despair? No matter which, but at least virtuous, loyal to her husband.

Vadinho did not show up. Neither in the bedroom as twilight was falling nor later in the living-room at dinnertime. He was in the habit of coming and cutting monkeyshines, so Dona Flor often had to bite her lips to keep from laughing when, wearing the shirt with the naked women, he came out dancing and showing off. Or not to get angry when she saw him behind the doctor's chair, putting horns on Teodoro's head with his fingers, the wretch.

Nonexistent horns, for she had not given them to him, protecting unyieldingly the redoubt where real honor exists (all the rest was nonsense, as Vadinho had told her, and as all who have given thought to this matter can certify).

She waited until bedtime, but he did not come. Beyond doubt Vadinho had left offended; he was proud and hard, capable of meeting the rudest provocation with head high. Who knows? perhaps he had left for good. Oh, God, he had not even said good-bye.

10

Vadinho's disappearance took place on Wednesday morning, and Dona Flor spent the day utterly lost, in the pain of not seeing him, in the fear of having lost him again, and with the conflicting hope that this was the case, for she knew that this definitive departure, for good and all, was the only thing that could save her happy home.

Now, on Wednesday and Saturday nights, as we have said and repeated, the methodical doctor honored his wife and took his pleasure with her, fulfilling his matrimonial obligations, a gratifying task. With an encore on Saturdays (we must not forget that), and with the established ritual in which pleasure did not exclude respect, a pleasure enveloped in modesty, circumspection (and the sheet).

After the bungling of the night of their marriage and the night of Vadinho's return, the bed relations of Dona Flor and Dr. Teodoro had resumed their normal state, she giving herself to her husband with demureness and tenderness and receiving from him complete, abounding satisfaction, repeated on Saturdays.

Moreover, Dona Flor had never felt such keen pleasure with the dauntless druggist as of late. To tell the truth, she gave herself to him now with more tenderness than modesty, the doctor felt her more desirous and impassioned, losing at times her discreet restraint, moaning and sighing, all in a turmoil. The doctor was delighted with these proofs of love and satisfaction. The love of his wife had increased with the passing of time, and he, too, loved her even more, if that was possible.

There was even an extra session of love-making, not provided for by the calendar, on the night of the day they wound up the transactions for the purchase of the house in Celestino's bank and the office of the notary Marback. The doctor fulfilled joyfully the celebration of this event, finding it fitting to break the systematic order of their night life for this reason.

He himself, as he came out of the bedroom into the living-room that afternoon, with his arm around Dona Flor's waist, and his wife's head resting on his shoulder, as he took in Dona Norma's mocking smile had sensed a vague appeal for love in the atmosphere, coming from Dona Flor, and it had moved him. He himself had already thought of celebrating the event on the grounds that "a touch of folly on occasion does not represent an abuse of or threat to the physical or moral well-being of the consorts (provided it does not become a habit, naturally)."

If the purchase of the house had affected Dona Flor, leading her to arouse her husband and obtain his agreement and collaboration in that "extra," she had not been aware of it. The fire burning in her had not been lighted by the trips to the bank, the mortgage, the notes, and the deed. The purchase of the house undoubtedly drew her closer to the doctor, added to her affection. But what led her to seek extemporaneous pleasure and possession was the fire kindled by Vadinho, his caresses, his fondling hand, his mouth overflowing with kisses, that insolence of his at twilight, and the marks he had left on her neck. Now as the doctor rose over her, wrapped in the sheet and as she closed her eyes, Dona Flor did not see a huge bird, but Vadinho, finally taking her, making her moan and sigh. What a diabolic mix-up!

Dona Flor avoided giving further thought to that knotty problem; she already had enough to worry her. For his part, the doctor seriously made up his mind to schedule an extra session every two weeks.

On that Wednesday night of her quarrel with Vadinho, Dona Flor was perplexed and agitated, in need of something to quiet her nerves. She kept thinking of Vadinho, departed perhaps for good. This represented the return to her former calm existence, the end of days of tension, when she was torn between two husbands, both with the right to her love, and she not knowing what to do, at times even mixing them up and confusing them, in the worst kind of jumble. Who could say whether now she could return to the quiet routine she had led before Vadinho's return, when her body had come to life only on Wednesdays and Saturdays?

And so that Wednesday night, hiding under the sheet the marks of Vadinho's kisses on her neck and locking her heart against the fear of his absence, Dona Flor received her husband, with him beginning the sweet and discreet rite. But the doctor had no more than risen over her, like a comfortable umbrella, when Vadinho's laugh echoed in Dona Flor's ears, making her shiver.

First it was the joy of seeing him there, balanced on the foot of the bed. He had not gone away for good, as Dona Flor had feared! Then her joy turned to rage, at the sight of his lewd smile, that feigned air of pity in his mocking, derisive face.

That hateful creature was having fun, lifting up the corner of the sheet the better to see what was happening and jeer at it. Dona Flor could hear his voice within her breast, his debauched, bantering laugh: "And you call that screwing? And this is Dr. Know-it-all, the teacher of whores, the king of fags? This half-assed stuff? I never saw anything more insipid! If I were you, I would ask him to bring me a bottle of cough syrup instead of this; it's good for a cold and is pleasanter. Because what he is doing, my pet, is the sorriest thing I have ever seen . . ."

She even tried to say: "Well, I like it," but she couldn't. The doctor had shot his bolt and she was lost in Vadinho's laughter, dying of shame (and desire).

11

Dona Flor so unhappy, beside herself, fearing for her honor, her happy home, all endangered. Then what of Pelancchi Moulas? His empire was tumbling down as though shaken by an earthquake or a revolution.

The like had never been seen since the beginning of the world and of betting. To be sure, there had been cases of amazing luck as well as of unbelievable bad luck, and on more than one occasion a daring and lucky player had broken the bank of a casino. But those were rare and infrequent events. Aside from that there were gyps. But skullduggery always comes to light, especially if it is persistent and repeated. In this uncertain world, nothing is surer than that the revenue and profits of the gambling houses and the numbers racket go to the concessionaires: they win from many, lose to a few; they are big shots, living on the fat of the land. The only better business, the only more profitable racket, is to be the president of the republic.

However, decks of cards, dice, the roulette wheel had all turned against Pelancchi Moulas; everything that had no explanation was happening. The absurd, the incredible, the impossible—one had to see it to believe it, and even so, seeing it with one's own eyes, there were many who repeated the words of that man from Ilhéus, when he witnessed Arigof's tourney of queens: "I see it, but I can't believe it."

When it came to gambling, Professor Máximo had seen during his lifetime everything there was to be seen, including a man who dropped dead of heart failure when every number he had bet on came up at roulette, and another who killed himself by swallowing a tablet of poison, an ugly death. But he had never thought he would come up against the inexplicable—he was a skeptic, with his feet firmly planted on the ground and with a cool head. As a young lad he had sold numbers tickets in Porto Alegre, in Manaus he had been the manager of an unlicensed joint, a croupier in Rio, a confidence man in Recife, a banker of *ronda* in Maceió. He had lived by poker playing in the diamond fields. There was not a secret, not a trick but he knew it.

"All right, professor, what do you have to say to me? What are your findings? The straight goods." Pelancchi's eyes were evil, and there was fear in his voice.

Absolutely nothing in the way of straight goods. Máximo Sales had to face the music. Dice and cards had been given the most thorough examination, as had tables and drawers. Not a sign. The police had come in, a district commissioner with the reputation of being highly competent, several plainclothesmen, who had questioned the employes under Máximo's instructions. Exhaustively, without taking into consideration the posts they held, their ages, not even their connections with the boss. Not even Domingos Propalato, foster-brother of Pelancchi, had been spared. Only Zulmira had been saved this humiliation, but not because she was who she was did the professor give her a clean bill of health: "For all we know she is one of the gang."

In Máximo's opinion only a gang, and one of the very best organized, could have arranged a gyp of that sort. An international gang, for the local crooks lacked the necessary ability, and the same went for those of Rio or São Paulo. Only European or American specialists, from Monte Carlo or Las Vegas, would be capable of pulling a stunt like what happened with baccarat: for two nights running at the same table in Tabaris, the punters had won every time against the bank, and old Anacreon had made a fortune. He and everyone else, for a veritable crowd had joined the game with the lucky dog. Lucky? In Máximo's opinion, Anacreon was nothing but an accomplice of the gang.

The banker of the house was one of the best in the city, perhaps in all the north of Brazil, Domingos Propalato. Not just a paid employe, but a fellow countryman, *compadre*, and foster-brother of Pelancchi Moulas. They had been born in the same village, only a few days difference between them, and the mother of Domingos had nursed the future millionaire at her full ·breast. Propalato, who was capable of killing and dying for his brother, was above any suspicion. Opposite him, old Anacreon. More than suspect.

Where had he got the money and the hunch for the game? Everybody knew the miserable state he had fallen into: so low that he was reduced to selling numbers tickets in Raimundo Pita Lima's café.

Moreover—and Máximo ticked his accomplishments off on his fingers—the old man had audacity and experience. Long before Pelancchi Moulas had set up his empire in Bahia, Anacreon was already a well-known figure in unlicensed gambling, harried and robbed by the police. Skilled in the handling of the deck, in the throwing of the dice, who was an older and steadier habitué of the roulette table, the games of baccarat, faro, black jack, twenty-one? A patriarch.

The years went by, old generations died off, new ones appeared, only old Anacreon was indestructible, with his ups and down to be sure, but never had he exercised any profession other than gambling.

Young fellows who had grown up in his shadow no longer gambled. They had been transformed into serious and respectable persons like Zèquito Mirabeau, Guerreiro, Nelito Castro, Edgard Curvelo, and even Giovanni Guimarães. One of his earliest companions, Bittencourt, had quickly risen to be director of the waterworks, an able engineer. He had not forgotten his friend, offering him a steady job, which would guarantee his old age. Anacreon was so touched that he embraced Bittencourt with tears in his eyes, but he never went to sign the contract: "The only thing I am any good at is gambling, nothing else."

Some (fortunately, only a few) holding important positions or married to rich women did not even venture to recall those bohemian days of youth. Others had died while still young, and Anacreon was always recalling their names and deeds: that gay Ju, prince of wit and refined devilishness; that beautiful Divaldo Mi-

randa, rich and elegant; fat Rossi, what a wonderful guy, crazy
about the samba and rum; once, when he was drunk, he had passed
water in the foyer of the Palace, in plain sight of the ladies, and if
he had not been not lynched, it was because Anacreon, pulling out
a knife, had stood guard and covered his retreat; Vadinho, the
unforgettable, his favorite friend, the craziest and most amusing,
one swell guy.

One swell guy, the swellest. Even dead and buried some three
years back, he could not stand the sight of old Anacreon selling
numbers tickets in the back of cafés, in that poverty-stricken state,
his morale shot. He had appeared to him in a dream—a dream that
was more like reality, for Anacreon did not even sleep, just at most
a doze after his meager lunch—and had advised him to go without
fail to Tabaris that same day and the next, and at Domingos Propalato's he was to bet on the same point, and only on the point, all
night long. Always on the point, never on the bank. Where was he
to get the money? He was to borrow some from Raimundo on the
sly; he was a good soul, the café owner, and would not make an
issue of a few mil-reis. Moreover, the next morning Anacreon, his
pockets filled with gold, playing the numbers, and not the employe
of a numbers runner, would repay with interest the few cents he
had taken from Raimundo's café.

An old and experienced player, Anacreon respected dreams,
giving a good hunch the value it deserved, especially when it was
provided by a friend as loyal as Vadinho. At the end of the
afternoon, when turning in his accounts, he managed to keep back
a little change, and Raimundo, that kindly soul, said nothing.

Then it happened, to the amazement of the city. Nobody
talked about anything else: that sensational happening at the baccarat table, with the point coming up every time two nights
running, Domingos Propalato losing his cool for the first time in
his long years at the job, Máximo Sales, with a dumbfounded air,
running out to find Pelancchi Moulas.

Anacreon himself, in all his glorious chronicle as a lawbreaker,
had never seen anything to compare with his luck and the ill fate
of the bank. But it was not up to him to discuss what had
happened; a hunch of Vadinho's was to be respected and not

dissipated in foolish discussions. A man of broad horizons, Anacreon believed in fate and in his lucky star, and for him, when it came to dice and cards, the impossible ceased to exist.

As for Pelancchi Moulas, the minute he came into the room he read the panic in Domingos Propalato's bewildered eyes. He came over beside his foster-brother, and heard him say in a voice of despair which was like a death sentence: *"Dio cane, Pecchiccio! Siamo fututi!"*

A mere tool in the hand of fate, Propalato turned up a card. It was the point.

12

"Sono fregato, sono fututo!" Pelancchi Moulas repeated when, immediately after Anacreon, Mirandão's turn came.

Of all those of his generation, Mirandão was the only one who remained the same jovial bohemian as though time had stood still, spending his nights amid the excitements of gambling.

One Sunday morning, when he was home cleaning out the birds' cages, Mirandão picked up clearly a message from Vadinho: that night, at the roulette wheel of the Palace, number 17.

Mirandão had never had a better friend; he and Vadinho were like twins, so inseparable had they been. Nor was Vadinho's name ever out of his thoughts or words. How could he forget him, when he had never had such a friend?

That day, however, was different. The memory of Vadinho took on the quality of actual presence, as though he were there helping Mirandão with the cages to get the finches and canaries to start singing.

Mirandão had been invited by the Negress Andreza to a lunch

of pigs' lights and liver. On the way the voice kept repeating the
hunch, as it did at the table covered with a white cloth on which
the appetizing dish and the pepper sauce exhaled their aroma.
Seventeen was Vadinho's lucky number, but it had never favored
Mirandão.

During those three years, in tribute to his dead friend, Mirandão had several times staked his scanty capital on 17, and had
invariably lost. He would do it again, if Vadinho so desired, for his
friend was deserving of this and more.

But it happened that that Sunday he was flat broke, and among
Andreza's guests—the carpenter Waldemar, Zuca, an employe in
the government rural service, behind in his salary, the mason
Rufino and the *capoeira* teacher Master Pastinho—only Robato
Filho might be able to lend him a little change. Vadinho's name
came up in the conversation, and Robato declaimed an ode of the
poet Godofredo, raising on high his glass of beer, but as for
money, he did not have a thin dime.

With a full stomach and a light heart (nothing like a good
lights-and-liver stew to uplift the soul of a Sunday), Mirandão
trudged the streets uselessly, in search of someone he could put the
bite on. If he could only get some money together, he was prepared to lose part of it on 17. His number was 3, and 32 was good,
too. It was just throwing money down the drain to play on 17,
and he did it as though he were taking flowers to Vadinho's tomb.

But where was he to get money on a Sunday? Everybody was
at the soccer game or the movies: the streets were bare. The two
or three friends he did run into refused to finance his hunch. They
were pessimists.

When he had just about lost hope, he remembered his *comadre*,
Dona Flor. He had never asked her assistance in matters having to
do with gambling, but only when it was a question of the health of
the children, and once to fix the roof of his house, for the landlord
had refused to comply with his duties, showing himself mean and
heartless: "So the rain is coming into the house? Wetting the
children? As far as I am concerned, Mr. Mirandão, it can rain all it
likes on anybody; walls, roof, ridgepole can fall in, what do I care?
Is the house mine? It seems much more as though it belonged to

Your Lordship, my dear friend. For over six years I have not seen a cent of the money you owe me."

And what if Dr. Teodoro was in? Since Dona Flor's second marriage, Mirandão had visited her only once, not wanting to obtrude on the druggist, who would surely not enjoy seeing him, given his resemblance to Vadinho, his copy or picture, not physically—the one blond, the other mulatto—but morally, or, to put it as some did, amorally.

But that afternoon Mirandão had no choice: he either inconvenienced his *comadre*, or he could not play.

"Well, look who's here," said Dona Gisa to Dona Flor, the two of them sitting in chairs on the sidewalk.

"Good God, he has revealed himself to Mirandão!" Dona Flor thought terrified, for alongside the *compadre* came the ex-departed, all self-satisfied and naked (he had given up the shirt covered with enticing women).

No, Mirandão did not see him. Fortunately. Greeting Dona Flor and Dona Gisa, the *compadre* inquired about the doctor's health.

"He's fine. He went to a meeting of the Pharmaceutical Association."

"I did not know you were here alone," Vadinho said, but only Dona Flor heard him, and she paid no attention to him.

Dona Gisa talked a little while longer and then excused herself, on the pretext of having some English papers to correct. Mirandão sat down in the empty chair: "*Comadre*, please excuse me, I have come here to bother you, but my need is urgent."

"Somebody in the family sick?"

He was on the point of inventing an illness, one of the children running a fever, requiring a doctor and medicine. But why upset Dona Flor, in addition to swindling her out of some change? "No, *comadre*, nobody is sick. It's that damned gambling . . ."

"That's better."

And suddenly Mirandão was pouring out the whole story: ". . . his very voice, *comadre*, ordering me to play today without fail. Under no circumstances was I to miss going . . ."

Dona Flor could see him; there, seated on the window ledge, in the fading light of the afternoon, Vadinho was looking her over with his insolent eyes. She tried not to look at him, but, even not wanting to, her gaze wandered to his nakedness, to his white, smooth skin, the golden fuzz of hair, the knife scar, his proffered mouth.

"How much do you need, *compadre?*"

"Not much . . ."

She went to get the money. Vadinho followed her, and in the bedroom clasped her in his arms and kissed her. Dona Flor, the poor thing, could not even scream, with her *compadre* at the door, waiting. Her resistance fell to pieces under his kiss.

"Oh, Vadinho," she moaned, and then it was she who was offering him her lips, bereft of sense and modesty.

Vadinho was leading her toward the bed, trying to undress her at the same time. If it had not been that she heard the footsteps of her *compadre* in the house, Dona Flor might have relinquished then and there her honor as a married woman and an upright wife. But at the last minute she got control of herself, brought her legs together, and shaking off the kiss and her vertigo, got out from under Vadinho: "What kind of insane behavior is this . . . with Mirandão there? . . ."

"He's outdoors."

"He's in the living-room. You let me go! what a shame!"

She smoothed her hair with her fingers, and composed herself. Mirandão was drinking a glass of water in the dining-room, and she handed him the bill wet with the perspiration of her hand.

"Thank you, *comadre*, I don't know how to repay you. If I don't win today I never will. I am certain of it, it's as though Vadinho were beside me and bringing me luck."

At the street door, Mirandão laughed and revealed his plan: "Only he wants me to put my money on 17, and I am going to put it on 3 and 32. I am not crazy. Once I won four times running on 32, it was a sensation."

"You idiot!"

"Did you hear that, *comadre?* Did you hear him speak? Was it his voice or wasn't it? Tell me . . ."

Dona Flor, her body lax, her heart unsteady, her mouth dry and hot, said in a low voice: "Don't pay any attention, *compadre*, there are times when he makes attempts on me, too."

Mirandão did not understand. Besides, everything that day had been so confused, without sense or explanation. Like the night which had come on suddenly to the west, ahead of its usual time, without the usual twilight reds, a completely blue night. By Mirandão's watch it was time for gambling: he could not miss one single turn, one ball. "Goodbye, *comadre*, tomorrow I will come and pay you."

"Don't bother, *compadre*. If you win, buy the children some candy in my name."

And after a pause she added, lowering her voice: ". . . and in that of your *compadre*."

Vadinho's kiss brushed her cheek as though it were the breeze of that blue night.

"Be seeing you, my love! Tonight I'm coming to drag you out of bed. Wait for me, as you undoubtedly will.

13

It was Sunday night, and the rooms were full of people. The orchestra struck up a fox trot, the couples moved out to the dance floor. Mirandão recognized the Argentine Bernabó and Dona Nancy. At the cashier's window he exchanged Dona Flor's hundred mil-reis for chips. He put two in his pocket, two of the smaller ones: "These are for Vadinho's 17 later on." He divided the rest equally into two groups: one for the 3 and the other for the 32.

At the roulette table he smiled at Lourenço Mão-de-Vaca, the croupier, an old acquaintance. With unerring aim, he tossed one chip on the 3, the other on the 32. And, lo, the two swerved in the air and both came down on the 17, at the very moment that Lourenço announced that play had begun.

Naturally, the 17 came up. And it would never have stopped, forever and without fail, if, a little after midnight, on the excuse that something was wrong with the wheel, Pelancchi Moulas had not ordered play suspended.

14

In Zulmira's apartment, his head in the lap of the mulatta, under the benediction of her full breasts, Pelancchi Moulas listened to the report of Professor Máximo Sales: the roulette wheel and the table had been taken apart piece by piece, submitted to every possible test, and showed no sign of tampering or defect, no evidence of trickery.

"I knew it! It's a waste of time," the poor king groaned.

There at that address known only to a few, the great man, the king of the city, the power behind the government, hid himself away to avoid nuisances and botheration. In his office (Pelancchi Moulas, Entrepreneur) there was a steady stream of people coming and going, from morning to night: individuals of the most varied sorts, commissions of every kind, each with his list, his letter, his request, his problem, his blunder, his swindle. They all came looking for money.

Money to build churches, to buy bells, contributions for good works and hospitals, for old people's homes and juvenile reform schools, help for trips of students in the south and the north of the country. Journalists and politicians, avid, insatiable, all in search of money to save the country, Christian morality, civilization, the regime, from the dark and fatal menace of subversion and atheism. Writers with plans for magazines and manuscripts of books: "You, sir, are a friend of culture, of arts and letters, of poetry, the new Maecenas." (Pelancchi felt like saying: "Maecenas is the whore who bore you," but instead of this he came up with a twenty or fifty mil-reis bill, depending on whether the one who was putting the bite on him was a young genius or an old sonneteer). Reformers, moralists, Catholics, Protestants, people of the most esoteric faiths, all who combated anarchy and disorder, the danger of Communism and free love, the shameful neglect of the rules of Portuguese grammar (the indefinite pronoun at the beginning of a sentence) and the indecent bathing apparel to be seen on the beaches (showing everything, even the belly). The Association of Mothers in Constant Vigil against Alcohol, Prostitution, and Gambling, the mothers being chiefly that Antônio Chinelinha, at the beginning of his promising career; the Society for the Protection of Missions in Oceania; the Campaign against Illiteracy, of Major Cosme de Faria; the Devotion to St. Januarius, and the Carnival Club of the Gay Brunettes of Cabula. Persons afflicted with every type of ailment, from leprosy to cancer, from the bubonic plague to beriberi, from Chagas's disease to St. Vitus's dance, and the hordes of blind, lame, and halt, not to mention the crazy coots and those who came simply to ask for money, without any pretext, as bold as brass.

Pelancchi rested from all this in the apartment and on the bosom of Zulmira, refuges now more precious than ever; only there could he combat the panic fear that was coming over him. There he heard from his helpers: prattle, twaddle.

Unwilling to admit defeat, Máximo Sales outlined a bold and simple plan: why not take advantage of the fact that the roulette wheel was dismounted, and bring everything into the open? How? Very simple. Tilting the wheel so it would be impossible for the ball to fall into the 17 compartment. A trick as old as the game itself. Dangerous, sure; dishonest, certainly; but how could they secure the definitive proof otherwise?

Máximo stuck to his opening guns: all those absurd suppositions, in which Pelancchi saw the black hand of dire luck, were nothing but a monstrous gyp, the work of a gang—foreign, of course—in combination with cashiers and croupiers, with Arigof and Anacreon, with Mirandão.

Forget about the gangs and the foreigners! *Sono fregato, sono fututo!* As far as Pelancchi Moulas was concerned, all that blather of Máximo Sales's was just a waste of time. There was no gang or gyp. It was something far worse: his enemies, to work his ruin, had invoked supernatural powers, uncontrollable, of the other world.

In his rise to power, which had not been easy, Pelancchi had sowed profound hatreds, mortal enmities. When necessary, his hand was heavy and hard, leaving in his wake curses and vows of vengance. Now he found himself at bay, surrounded by witchcraft and spells.

Pelancchi was not afraid of men or of fights: he was a ruthless adversary. But that modern gangster, that son of the age of Enlightenment and technology, hid his head under the covers at the first clap of thunder, fearful of the glare of lightning, nothing but a child of Calabria, a little peasant child of superstition and poverty.

"*Maledetto, sono stregato!*"

"Very good," said Máximo Sales, who feared only men and did not believe in souls of the other world, a freethinker and skeptic, always looking for the rational, logical explanation of every phenomenon, "very good, we're going to get to the bottom of this. We will tilt the table and then we'll see. It is illegal and dishonest, that I know, and you do not like monkey business of this sort. Neither do I. But it is a question of drastic measures, and what they are doing to you is more dishonest, isn't that so? If with the table tilted, 17 still comes up—and you know that is impossible—then I will have to agree with you: the devil has a hand in it, and we will have to get the *macumba* priests to help us."

Pelancchi Moulas shrugged his shoulders: if it was just a test and nothing more, let Máximo do what he pleased, make the wheel cheat, but with the greatest care and discretion.

"I'll handle the work myself, don't you worry."

"And only for one night."

"That's right, only for tonight."

Rubbing his hands in satisfaction, Máximo left to carry out his delicate job. To Pelancchi Moulas all that seemed useless. The moment had come for him to put his fortune and his fate in abler hands than those of Máximo and the police. If anyone was capable of finding the answer to that enigma, that person was Cardoso e Sa., that charismatic philosopher, whose sublime mind extended to the beyond, to the vast spaces of the infinite, a clearing in cosmic space, unveiling past and future, for he lived at one and the same time yesterday, today, and tomorrow, on the sublime heights, in the black abysses.

Neither did Zulmira have any doubts: this was witchcraft, the devil on the loose. She did not tell him before because she did not want to add to his worries, of which he had so many; but the night before, at the Palace, when play had stopped, just as had happened before, some invisible being had touched her breasts and tickled her. And not satisfied with this, he had got under her skirt and pinched her bottom.

"Just look, Pequito. Here."

She raised up her robe. Beneath it her copper-colored skin glistened, and on it he could see at the spot she indicated, the reddish-blue mark of Vadinho's fingers, definitive proof of the unknown.

"*Accidente!*" the Calabrian said, and, summoning up all his strength, plunged into that dark mystery.

15

Senseless and shameless. Vadinho had always been like that, and the years of absence had not changed him: "Tonight I'm coming to drag you out of bed. You wait for me . . ."

As though Dona Flor were the lowest of ass-peddlers, so dissolute that she would give herself over to depravity in front of her sleeping husband. In the iron bed Dr. Teodoro slept the well-known sleep of the just, his noble figure placidly relaxed, his breathing even, as though he were snoring in time to the bassoon.

Dona Flor gazed on the honorable countenance of her husband, and a wave of tenderness enveloped her: no better man existed, such a perfect husband. Courageous, of unblemished character (also called adamant). Dona Flor made up her mind to break off once and for all that dubious, inexcusable entanglement, unworthy of her state and her chastity.

It would be better to wait in the sitting-room, hold her vigil there, and safer, too; she would not run the risk of finding herself in the arms of Vadinho in the room where her other husband was sleeping (the good and upright one). Because, the slave of her senses, with the vile matter of her body wanton, Dona Flor was fearful of yielding to him instantly. Her will was no longer under her control; her strength disappeared at the sight of Vadinho, and when he approached her, a kind of giddiness came over her and she was at the mercy of the seducer. She was no longer the mistress of her body; the rebellious matter no longer obeyed her spirit, but the desire of Vadinho.

Even so she had not yielded, to be sure, but perhaps this was because in these last days Vadinho had hardly appeared; given over once more to gambling, a wild life, he had not shown up.

And so it was that night. He had been so categorical, so clear-cut: "Wait for me, wait for me without fail, I will be coming to bed for you." He did not even have the least consideration for her; he had promised to come and had stayed on gambling. Or maybe he was in a sporting house. Dona Flor paced the room, opened the window, looked out into the street, counted the minutes.

All those vows of love, that boundless passion, nothing but lies. There was Dona Flor waiting for him, and he was incapable of giving up a single play. Perhaps he would still come when the last ball had stopped spinning.

But the gambling was over. Dona Flor was familiar with the schedules; all the details of the casinos were perfectly familiar to her; this waiting for Vadinho had begun years before. Where would he be, what kind of shindig would be keeping him, for whom had he broken the promise made to her? Vadinho, why do you take this advantage of my feelings, why don't you come when you promised to come and I waited for you, hating myself for doing so? What do honor, decency, home, upright husband matter to me? The only thing that matters is your being here. Why did you arouse my desire for you?

That morning in the cooking class Dona Flor, nervous and distrait, almost let the rice overcook. In the rear of the room she could hear the voice of Zulmira Simões Fagundes, all excited: "Girls, it is some kind of spell, I am so scared. Don't you remember that the other day here in class I felt something stroking my breast? Well, that's not the end of the story . . ."

The students gathered around her in the greatest turmoil: "What happened? Come on. Give."

"Last night I was at the Palace . . ."

"You don't miss one night at the Palace."

"That's part of my work."

"Boy, would I like a job like that!"

"Go on, Zulmira . . ."

"Well, last night I was at the Palace with my boss, and something was going on with the roulette wheel; only number 17 came up."

Dona Flor listened thoughtfully.

"When the excitement was at its peak I felt the same invisible hand touching my breasts and afterwards"—here she lowered her voice—"it pinched my bottom."

"An invisible hand pinched your bottom? Don't tell me," a woman said in a dubious tone of voice who was little given to mysteries and had an untempting bottom.

"You don't believe me? I can show you the mark."

The idea of being thought a liar annoyed Zulmira, so she lifted her skirt, displaying a thigh that aroused envy even in her fellow students best endowed with haunches. A little faded, but there was the mark of Vadinho's fingers. Silently Dona Flor left the room.

All that day Dona Flor waited for him, merely sad. Vadinho

did not come. Nor the next day. All that passion was a lie, that frenzy of love, false and hypocritical. Dona Flor sleepless and waiting for him, and the scoundrel enjoying himself at the gaming table or under Zulmira's skirts, pinching her backside. Vadinho cynical and irresponsible, disloyal, heartless. Dona Flor free of all inner conflict, released from both chastity and desire, merely sad.

16

At the hour of triumph, Professor Máximo Sales did not become puffed up with pride; on the contrary, he attributed his success to the old adage which never failed: "Set a thief to catch a thief." A scholar without self-importance, a true humanist.

But he did not want to hear another word about souls from the other world and nonsense about charms and hexes. It was enough to tilt the roulette table for all the witchcraft to disappear as nothing but double-crossing. Now all that had to be done was to discover the leader, the head of the gang, and settle accounts with him. Lourenço Mão-de-Vaca, who was completely innocent in that conspiracy, was the one who set the ball rolling on the table. The night before only 17 had come up; today not once in the whole evening.

The tension on Pelancchi Moulas's face eased. He was afraid only of the supernatural, nothing else. But what cabalistic power was this, incapable of outdoing the wile of the roulette table? Máximo had ripped the mask of mystery from the swindle, and Pelancchi, with his long, influential arm, would get hold of the one who was responsible, making him pay with interest the money he had stolen, the audacity, the insolence, and, above all, those pusillanimous hours, his fear in plain view of all, the terror gnawing at his heart. Between Zulmira and Domingos Propalato, once more at peace with the world, Pelancchi smiled at the players; nobody had a more cordial, affable smile.

During all this, Mirandão, a deserter and drunk, was sleeping in Carla's sporting house, in the beautiful and discreet boudoir done in pink. The evening before, when Pelancchi Moulas, visibly beside himself, had ordered play suspended, Lourenço Mão-de-Vaca, the croupier, and Domingos Propalato were not the only ones there who had found themselves free of that undecipherable nightmare. Mirandão, surrounded by piles of chips, felt no less relieved, for that whole business was absurd and terrifying.

As long as the roulette kept coming up on 17, Mirandão was in a state midway between euphoria and terror. Euphoria, thanks to that boundless luck, and terror because there seemed to be no limit to his diabolic good fortune. That night the dikes of fortune collapsed, and all the chips of the casinos came into Mirandão's possession. But was that good luck really his, Mirandão's?

It was all very suspicious and strange: Vadinho's voice in his ear, from the morning when he was fussing over the birds, at the lunch of lights-and-liver stew, and then in the street. The visit to Dona Flor, the strange words, the obscure remarks, and he hearing the insult of the dead man, as though, in addition to Mirandão and Dona Flor, Vadinho were taking part in the conversation. Afterward that magic with the chips, falling on 17 when he had laid them on 3 and 32. In the middle of the night Mirandão, out of stubbornness and as a test, once more put his chips on his favorite numbers. But the chips, of their own accord and without anyone knowing how, turned up on 17. When all was said and done, what was Mirandão? A player or a plaything of fate?

When he left the Palace, a mighty millionaire but heavy of heart, he made his way to Carla's sporting house, a suitable place to celebrate successes of that sort and, in hours of tribulation, a welcoming home. He handed over his money to the fat Italian, a person of integrity and scruples (authorizing her, naturally, to spend whatever was needed for the celebration, without thought to expense). He was afraid of excessive affection on the part of the women or the sudden liking of his many friends when he passed

out. For that night Mirandão was determined to go on the bender
of a lifetime, drowning in it the terms of that enigma, the sum of
that madness.

The celebration, directed by fat Carla, lasted until the next day,
and those with the most resistance, such as the writers Robato
Filho and Áureo Contreiras (always with a flower in his buttonhole) and the journalist João Batista, had lunch in the sporting-
house the following noon, a marvelous, overflowing *feijoada*, with
rum and white wine. It was not until after that marathon that
Mirandão passed completely out and was carried by the girls on a
stretcher as though he were dead. Thoughtfully, they undressed
him and gave him a warm sponge bath; they powdered and perfumed him, and finally laid him to sleep in the best bed, the one
in the boudoir reserved for guests of honor, all decorated in pink
and satin.

Mirandão and some of the more sensitive guests, such as the
aforementioned Amesina—Ame for her father Americo, Sina for
her mother Rosina—had been aware of an irresistible force in the
atmosphere, directing the celebration. How was it possible to
explain otherwise the number of Carla dancing the dance of the
seven veils, a sublime and monstrous sight?

Máximo Sales, too, skeptic and realist though he was, freethinker, had the impression that he was being watched when that
afternoon in the gaming-room (assisted only by Domingos Propalato, Pelancchi's foster-brother) he carried out, skillfully and con-
scientiously, with the perfection of an artist, the difficult enterprise
of tilting the wheel. There were moments when the strange sensation was so strong that he had to stop work and run his eyes about
the room in search of the invisible witness.

Around midnight, when gambling was at its height, through his
leaden sleep, heavy with fatigue and alcohol, Mirandão heard the
same voice as the night before. At first blurred, then clear and
exactly like that of Vadinho, ordering him to return at once to the
Palace, without delay, and to put his money on 17. On 17 and only
on 17. Shake it up!

Opening his eyes, Mirandão found himself alone with the
shades of night and that voice. Cowering under the sheets, scared

to death, he covered his ears with the pillow, he did not want to hear. At the height of the celebration the night before, Anacreon had asked him: "Did you, too, hear Vadinho's voice whispering in your ear? There will never be another friend like him. Even after death he does not forget one."

Mirandão did not want to hear, but he heard, he heard distinctly: he was possessed, bewitched, with the spirit of a dead man on his back. He had to go as soon as he could to Our Lady's *candomblé* center to be purified of body and offer a cock to the gods, perhaps a goat.

Even through the pillow the voice went on domineering him, almost threatening. Mirandão saw no other way out, more worthy, less humiliating, than to scream, call for help, upset the whole house. Excusing herself to the highly esteemed judge, an illustrious and slow-paced client, the kindly Carla went to look after her frightened guest. When she put her arms around him and clasped him to her bosom, Mirandão swore to her, on the soul of his mother and the well-being of his children, that never again would he gamble, never in his whole life. There was no human (or superhuman) power that could make him touch a chip again.

17

When the telephone rang, Giovanni Guimarães had been asleep for over two hours. After his marriage he had got into the habit of going to bed early and getting up early, habits, in the opinion of his wife, very healthful. For good health and a successful career there is nothing so useful and necessary, expecially for one who had wasted so many nights in his wild, dissipated life.

There was a man—the well-known journalist Giovanni Guimarães—whose life had undergone a complete change, and in a short time. From one day to the next, as it were. Proof of the benefits of marriage to a devoted, energetic woman, unwilling to tolerate insolence and effrontery. Giovanni had kept his gaiety, his spontaneous laughter, his lies, his exaggerations. Outwardly he was the same, a pleasant person to talk to, who knew all the ins and outs of what was going on in the city—political, financial, adulterous, everything. But only outwardly. For the incorrigible bohemian, the night owl, the gambler, all that was washed up, to the amazement of many who knew him.

On a certain occasion the family, alarmed by the news that reached the latifundium of Urandi, sent a cousin who was a tax collector and had the reputation of being an old fogy, to Bahia to see what was going on with the prodigal son. The collector stayed with Giovanni in his bachelor's apartment in Piedade, and in order to carry out his delicate mission faithfully, he accompanied him wherever he went for a week that was unforgettable. On his return he summed up his diagnosis in one word: "Hopeless!"

And so, at any rate, it seemed: he was squandering his salary and the income he had inherited in gambling-dens, and, on top of this, he had turned day into night, showing up at the government bureau he worked for only to collect his wages. Debt-ridden, sympathizing with subversive ideas. Of what use was his reputation as a journalist, his gifts of intelligence, that charm which made everybody his friend?

Back in his collector's office, his religion and his family, the cousin considered Giovanni's regeneration extremely improbable: he would have to be a downright fool to renounce those delights, especially one of them, an outstanding ornament of Zazá's place, Jucundina by name, but better known as Sweet Meat. His mouth watering, the cousin said to the weeping family: "Give up your hopes. He is crazy. He's never going to straighten out."

Well, he did. When everybody considered him a lost cause, incorrigible, he fell in love, and in two months he got married. There were those who pitied his bride: "Poor thing, she is going to curse the day she married him: that Giovanni is a screwball."

That was because they did not know the girl, but were taken in by her quiet air, her almost timid ways. Six months after the marriage, the old fogy of the backlands, who had gone back to the capital, shook his head: "*Poor* Giovanni!" and hurried off to Zazá's place. Possibly Sweet Meat was still available and would be willing to adapt to the rural setting , to country living.

Giovanni was a different man; nobody ever again saw him at the gambling table or in a carousal of any sort. Beautiful women, only on movie screens. Aside from that, he was the most dignified gentleman, the perfect civil servant, the ideal family man, walking along the street with his wife on one arm, his daughter Ludmila, who had the makings of a beauty, on the other. A touching sight!

Baldness was setting in, conservative ideas, old-fashioned habits and the ambition for land and cattle. As is apparent, a man completely reclaimed for society, the family, and landed estates.

Giovanni had been asleep for over two hours when the telephone rang. He got out of bed, still drugged by sleep, and reached for the receiver. Who could it be?

"Is that Giovanni?" asked the voice at the other end.

"Yes, it is. Who is talking?"

"It's Vadinho who is talking, Giovanni. Come to the Palace as quickly as you can, and put your chips on 17, don't be afraid, it will come up, I guarantee you it will. But come as fast as you can."

"I'm on my way."

Avoiding making any noise, he got dressed quickly. Luckily his wife had not awakened, for he did not have time for explanations, he was in such a hurry to get away that he forgot his keys, documents, and his billfold. A taxi was coming by on the corner, he hopped into it, and it was only when he went to pay, at the door of the Palace, that he realized he did not have his wallet.

"I forgot my wallet . . ."

"Don't give it another thought, doctor. You'll pay me afterward." Giovanni recognized the chauffeur Cigano, always on duty in the late hours.

He recognized the chauffeur, but not himself, Giovanni Guimarães. What the hell was he doing there in front of the Palace, at one o'clock in the morning? A telephone call had awakened him, Vadinho urging him to bet on 17. But Vadinho had died some years back, before Giovanni had married. A dream, beyond doubt, a kind of hallucination.

But, dream or nightmare, as he was already there and the mischief had been done—he had slipped out of the house at night, and it would be impossible to avoid the consequences—he might as well take advantage of the hunch. The night air and freedom enveloped him, and Giovanni felt himself almost a hero as he walked up the stairs to the gaming-room.

In spite of the hour, the excitement in the room was great, especially around the roulette table. Giovanni was greeted with real enthusiasm: "What a sight for sore eyes!"

"What miracle brings you here?"

Going over to Pelancchi, the journalist asked him: "Will you take an IOU? I left in such a hurry that I forgot my wallet and my checkbook."

"For as much as you like. The cash register is at your service . . ."

"I just want enough to test a hunch. I dreamed of 17."

"17?"

A broad smile came over Máximo Sales's face, but Pelancchi Moulas felt a misgiving, a presentiment. Giovanni wrote out the IOU, and gathering up the chips, laid two on 17.

"It hasn't come up once today," someone remarked.

"The game is on," Lourenço Mão-de-Vaca announced.

The ball spun on the tilted table. It was impossible for it to land on 17. Máximo Sales's face had the meek expression of a saint. Pelancchi Moulas's was tense.

"Black. Seventeen," Lourenço Mão-de-Vaca called out.

18

It was a Saturday afternoon, melancholy and rainy. It was so hard to be alone with her sadness. Not even that was permitted Dona Flor.

In his raincoat and carrying an umbrella, Dr. Teodoro had gone off with his bassoon to a rehearsal at Dr. Venceslau's house. Dona Flor excused herself: she had a headache and that talk about fashions and other people's doings did not amuse her. Nor was she willing to endure the monotony of the rehearsal. Naturally, she did not say this to him; on the contrary, she lamented not being able to hear again Master Agenor Gomes's new composition, of which he was so proud, a slow waltz in honor of Dona Gisa, with whom the musician had made friends: *Sighs in the Moonlight on the Mississippi.*

Moreover, Dona Gisa had been over a little while before to invite Dona Flor to an exhibition of *capoeira* fighting on some empty lots over near Amaralina: that bold *gringa*, into everything. How was she to go when she had even refused to accompany her husband to the rehearsal, her body limp, her spirit undone? She had turned down the invitation of Dr. Yves and Dona Êmina, who never missed the Saturday matinee and nearly always at the same movie house. Dona Norma had also tried to take her with her: "Come and watch the game of *bisca*. Play does not interfere with conversation."

"Thank you, Norminha. If I felt better, I would have gone with Teodoro. I let him go alone."

"Yes," Dona Norma said, "I saw him go by to take the car. His face was as long as though he were going to a funeral. That husband of yours adores you, Flor."

It was unfair for her not to have accompanied him to the rehearsal; he asked so little of her in return for so much love and devotion. As for the other . . . she did not even want to think about that devil, that scoundrel. Why is a person's heart so contradictory? Why, in the last analysis, did she want to stay alone? Dr. Teodoro's greatest pleasure was to play the bassoon at the rehearsals, with Dona Flor there to listen to him and encourage him. And she, why had she stayed home if not in the hope that the other one would come, even for a moment, from his everlasting night of gambling?

Well, perhaps she had, but it was to tell him the whole truth, to send him away for good and all, to break off all and any relationship with him. Was this really the reason? To tell him this truth, or the other: "Take me, Vadinho, all of me, I can wait no longer." Which of the two truths would she tell him? Ah, in this battle between the spirit and matter, she was nothing but a poor creature in despair.

From the house next door came the voice of Marilda in a love song. She was practically engaged, this student of pedagogy, this new radio star, although the engagement had not yet been officially announced, for the suitor, a rich cacao planter and full of prejudices, demanded that she give up the radio. She was to sing only for him and for nobody else. It had been no small effort for Marilda to reach the microphones, her small melodious voice being heard throughout the city. Why pay such a high price for a suitor? Trustingly, she had come to ask Dona Flor's advice. But Dona Flor was in no position to advise anyone, not even herself, confused as she was. She was no longer one single person, whole and upright; she was split in two, the decent and the unseemly, her decorous spirit on the one hand, the desirous matter on the other. Completely discordant.

Dr. Teodoro had set out in the rain, his bassoon protected by his raincoat. There were only two sacred things in this world as far as he was concerned: Dona Flor and music. For his wife and the melody of the bassoon he would sacrifice, if necessary, drugstore and profits, scientific papers and his reputation. An upright man, an exemplary husband.

The other was a rogue, a vagabond, nothing more. Prepared to dishonor her for the second time, while at the same time unwilling to sacrifice anything for her, not even a minute of his dissipated time. He had been that way the first time, ungenerous, yielding not an inch. All she had got was the crumbs of his debauched life. "You wait for me, I'll be right back," and then not coming back. Beelzebub, full of tricks and wily words.

Marilda was kneeling at Dona Flor's feet: "Florzinha, tell me what I should do. Singing is my whole life, but Mamma says my life should be marriage, a home, husband, and children, that all the rest is just a childish whim. What do you say?"

What could Dona Flor say? "You get out, you cursed rascal, leave me upright and happy with my husband," or "Take me in your arms, enter my innermost redoubt, your kiss is worth the price of any happiness." What could she say? Why is everybody two different people? Why is it necessary to be torn between two loves? Why does the heart hold at the same time two emotions, contradictory and opposed?

"You have to decide between one and the other: a career or marriage."

"And why do I have to decide? Why can't I get married and go on singing, when I love both him and singing. Why do I have to choose when I love both? Just tell me why?"

Why, Dona Flor? Through the open window came the voice of the lover calling for Marilda, and she raised her face, beautiful as a medallion, and ran out. Dona Flor followed her with her eyes: Vadinho was the wind blowing her hair about and encircling her legs.

"Vadinho! Not with Marilda! I will not allow that."

Laughing he squatted at her feet, where Marilda had been and put his arms around her legs, laying his head in her lap.

"You let me alone," Dona Flor said in a petulant voice.

"Why do you treat me like that, my sweet? Always scolding?"

And he had the nerve to ask why, as though he had not said: "I'll be right back. You be sure to wait for me." What sleepless

nights, bitter days, agonizing waits. The only news she had had of
that scoundrel had been written in the pinches on Zulmira's bottom. And he still had the nerve to ask why.

"But you said you didn't want to see me any more, that I was to
get out, didn't you? So I went to have a little fun with Pelancchi.
What a kick—I almost died laughing."

"With Pelancchi or with his secretary?"

"So you're jealous, my pet? How right I was when I thought:
I'll disappear for a few days, and she'll be praying to God for me
to come back—she is crazy to have me, she can't stand it any
longer."

"Who told you that? Well, it's a lie. I am a decent woman, take
your hand away from there."

Hand and lip were burning her flesh, lip upon her mouth, hand
in her most secret spot, her last redoubt. With the rain her body
grew more lax, her last resistance crumbled. At the very moment
when she affirmed her honor and invincibility, she was yielding her
mouth to him without even charging him for his absence and the
sighs of Zulmira. That dizziness was overpowering her; she lacked
the strength to oppose Vadinho's advances, to defend the ultimate
limits of her honor. Ah, if there were only someone she could call
on for help. Vadinho was in a hurry, eager to get back to the
gaming table; he had come on the run. "Let's do it in bed, my
love." She got up, in his arms, unable to hold out no longer. What
did husband and honor matter to her. "Wherever you like, my
love."

"May I come in, *comadre?*"

Dionísia de Oxóssi was entering the doorway, and as she looked
at her she said: "Aren't you feeling well, *comadre?* You are so
pale."

Sitting down again, saved by a miracle, Dona Flor murmured:
"It was God who sent you, *comadre* Dionísia. Only you can help
me. Sit down, here beside me."

Dona Flor took the hands of the votary of Oxóssi in hers:
"*Comadre,* I need somebody to find a way to rid me of Vadinho,
to send him away, and not let him upset me any more, for he has
been troubling me for a long time, and I am no longer myself, I

don't know who I am or what I am doing, I have no will any more?"

"You mean my late *compadre?*"

"Do whatever is necessary so he will return to his rest, for otherwise, *comadre*, I don't know what is going to happen. I can't begin to tell you. He is trying to take me with him, just now when you arrived he was trying, and I was so overcome by idiocy that I almost went. If he keeps on, he will finally win out."

Dionísia covered her mouth with her hand not to scream: "Oh, *comadre*, we have to hurry, something must be done at once. I am going this very minute to talk to Father Didi; fortunately I know where he is performing a rite. This business of the spirits of the dead is not for just anyone. Only for the one who uses the cane of Ojé. Oh, God, *comadre* . . ."

"Didi?" Dona Flor suddenly recalled the gaunt Negro in the flower market who had given her the fetish for Vadinho's tomb. "Go, *comadre*, go quickly, if there is anyone who can save me, it is he. Otherwise, *comadre*, I am lost, a dreadful misfortune is going to happen."

"Right this minute."

Dionísia left, protected by her necklace of Oxóssi, shrinking with fear of the spirits of the dead, but determined to do all she could to save the life of her *comadre:* a dreadful misfortune was about to happen. What could that be except death. Quickly, Dionísia, more quickly, down the narrow hidden paths to the gates of the kingdom of Ifá. At its crossroads you will find the *candomblé* priest with all his power.

"My father," the votary said, as she kissed his hand, "the dead husband wants to carry off my *comadre*. Save her. Secure the spirit in his death," and she told him the story, what she knew of it.

At that very hour Dr. Teodoro returned, all wet. Because of the rain, there had been no rehearsal. He took a swallow of liqueur as a precaution against grippe, put on his pajama coat, and played for Dona Flor music from his select repertoire for the bassoon. Listening to him, little by little Dona Flor recovered from her fright and depression, her disgust with herself, a married woman whose virtue was so fragile. You have nothing more to fear,

Teodoro: I love you, and I am yours, yours alone, this Saturday (with the right to a repeat) and tomorrow and forever. No heart should hold two loves at the same time. I have ordered half of myself torn away, and here I am, once more inviolate and upright, listening to you playing the bassoon, Teodoro, your chaste wife.

On the other side of the Bahian night, a clearing in the wood lighted up, and within it the priest cast the shells at the entreaty of Dionísia, the votary of Oxóssi. The rain turned into a tempest, the thunder roared, the lights went out, the sea rose up in fury, and the gods, mounted on lightning and flashes, came in response to the call of Asobá. All of them said yes, except Exu, who said no.

19

Pelancchi Moulas's message reached the mystic Cardoso e Sa. in the Church of the Episcopate, visiting his tomb as he did each anniversary of his death. His death when he had been known as Joaquim Pereira, a potentate of Bahia, who passed away in his manor house on the Corredor da Vitoria, on the Ides of March of 1886. A sumptuous wake was held, his funeral was attended by a cortege of his fellow Masons and his colleagues in the wholesale business, with the Governor of the province and professional mourners present, and a Mass was said over the open coffin.

The tombs of Cardosa e Sa. multiplied throughout the world. A mummy discovered in the Great Pyramid, a museum piece, a body buried under the eternal snows of the Alps when Hannibal's vanguard crossed them, and in the sands of the Araby desert, Zalomar on his chestnut horse. He died in France at least twice, the same number of times in Italy, and the Inquisition tortured him to death in Spain as an alchemist and heretic; rich and poor, beggar and cardinal, he had sold dates in Egypt, at the market gates on the banks of the Nile in the days of Rameses II; he had scanned the stars of the Oriental hemisphere, a Hebrew with woolly beard, the celebrated mathematician Allhy Fouchê, who was born and died before the Christian era.

In Bahia, in addition to his perpetual resting place in the black Church of the Episcopate, he also had a tomb in the Church of Baiacu, on the island of Itaparica, where he died in the war against the Dutch, at the age of thirty-three, in the figure of the handsome, strong, and libertine servitor of the king of Portugal, Francisco Nunes Marinho d'Eça, First Captain-Major of the Coast, an authority on Indians.

All this vast experience—and much more, for it would take various volumes to relate the multiplicity of his life or lives, all of them full of feats and love—was now stored in the frail framework of Antônio Melchiades Cardoso e Silva (Cardoso e Sa. to the elect), a modest employe of the municipal archives, the master of occult sciences, the heir to Solomon's seal, a universal and Hindustani philosopher, and captain of the cosmos.

"Come, Mr. Cardoso, the boss has told me to bring you to him without fail. He is really in a bind," said Aurélio, Pelancchi's chauffeur.

"Come on, I was waiting for you . . ."

"You mean you knew I was coming?"

The sage laughed at the question, a clear ringing laugh. There was nobody happier and more satisfied than he, so completely happy: "And what is it I don't know, Aurélio? I know the negative and the positive."

As for Aurélio, he had no intention of arguing about either the negative or the positive, but the mere presence of Cardoso e Sa. made him nervous.

In the car, sitting beside the chauffeur, the captain of the cosmos greeted invisible beings: "Good afternoon, brigadier . . ."

Where was the brigadier? There, sitting looking out over the sea, enjoying the cool of the afternoon. Where, Mr. Cardoso? Aurélio could not discern anyone, either in uniform or in civilian clothes. "It is not given to all to see, my dear fellow, only a few."

"My compliments, madame, I kiss your feet."

"You don't see her, either? So elegant, in her feather-trimmed hat and dress with a train. She was the beauty of her day, other days. Because of her, two young men, in the flower of their years, killed each other. Now along the beach there go the three, arm in arm, all gallantry and laughter. Your eyes are blind, miserable material eyes, for you don't even see her, in the splendor of her royal beauty."

"Gove save and protect me, Mr. Cardoso."

The master laughed his hearty laugh. the street was peopled by specters; the chauffeur was tense at the wheel. He did not enjoy driving in all that mystery.

"So things are not going well in gambling?" Mr. Cardoso suddenly asked.

"Then you knew?" Could it be that he really knew everything?

When, lo and behold, Cardoso hid his face and crouched down. Hid from whom? That blonde swinger on her way to the beach? That very one, my dear chap. You know who she is? She is Joan of Arc, and you know who Cardoso e Sa. is? He is none other than the French Cardinal Pierre Cauchon, the papal legate, whose trembling hand signed the death sentence of the Maid of Orleans. He sees her everywhere, her innocent eyes, her blonde profile as she went to the stake.

"I was hesitant, frivolous, immoral, cowardly . . ."

In Zulmira's apartment Pelancchi was impatiently awaiting the magus of Hindustan, the only one capable of adding up the fragments of the impossible.

"You took a long time, Cardoso."

"I never arrive too early nor too late, always at the exact moment."

He greeted Zulmira, who was enveloped in floating chiffon. She knew Cardosa e Sa. from other days, when at the head of the Amazon women she had crossed the valley in spirited hunting expeditions, revealing her one full breast. It still remained bounteous (that one, and the other too), but no longer in full view, more the pity, thought Master Cardoso, almost pure spirit after having passed through so many incarnations, but not, however, to the point of being unaffected by certain excellences of this gross material life from which one must redeem oneself.

"I have been trying to get hold of you for two days."

"What is it you need. Haste or help?"

His eyes unmoving, fixed on the beyond, his broad forehead covered with sweat, surrounded by an aura. Intense concentration: "The roulette failed you, didn't it?"

Pelancchi turned toward Zulmira, as though saying: "See how he divines everything." The rumors going about the city reached even the spiritual shack where Cardoso dwelt with his poverty and his five children (he never charged a penny for doing good), and during those days the one topic of conversation in the city was what had happened at the Palace, at Tabaris, at Abaixadinho, and the tables of roulette, baccarat, and faro. A mystery or a swindle, a miracle or a gyp, nobody had ever heard of such a streak of bad luck as that which Pelancchi Moulas had suffered. To be sure, these comments had reached the ears of the master. But even if he had not heard them, would this have prevented his knowing them? Since when did Cardoso e Sa. have to hear to know?

"This morning, talking to myself, before I left the house, I said: Pelancchi is going to send for me. He's submerged in darkness, he needs a little light."

"A little? A lot! I feel like doing away with myself, Cardoso, like wiping myself out, get it over with . . ."

He described all those incredible events. Cardoso e Sa., sitting opposite him, listened undismayed to the alarming account. He shook his head, perhaps to confirm some idea or glimpsing a certainty. Through the transparent chiffon of her peignoir and out of the corner of his eye, Cardoso e Sa. took in a handspan of Zulmira's thigh and was moved by it, though he kept his mind on the dramatic account of the gambling king. This carnal vision did not disturb him, for beauty does not affect a sage, nor is it immoral or opposed to the spirit. On the contrary, it relaxes the spirit.

His sight was weary; his incorporeal eyes saw through space, the past and the future. When Pelancchi finished his tale of dismaying misfortune, Cardoso e Sa. had everything worked out, the terms of the problem and its unknown quantity. He had the answer and the solution: "It's the Martians," he answered categorically.

And he laughed his hearty laugh, as though all that were nothing but a good joke, as though it were not costing Pelancchi a fortune every day.

"Martians? What Martians? Mr. Cardoso, don't come to me with crazy stories. I have put my trust in you, don't let me down. What do the Martians have to do with all this? It's my enemies, it's a hex of some sort. Who ever saw a Martian, nobody knows if there is such a thing. But witchcraft does exist, and malign spirits, and the evil eye."

"You have never seen them because you are burdened by flesh. It is the Martians, as I have told you. Not enemies or spells. The Martians are very curious, they spend their time monkeying around all kinds of machinery, they want to find out everything, and for them, who are of a superior mentality, there is neither good nor bad luck."

"Martians?" Zulmira asked, always eager to learn. "On the earth? Since when?"

Now we must be on our guard not to confuse and compare Cardoso e Sa. with fortunetellers or occultists like those to be found by the dozen everywhere gazing into crystal balls, or clairvoyants of limited vision, or cheap soothsayers, petty chiromancers. Cardosa e Sa. was a professor of mystery, a sage of the obscure, a scientist far beyond astrophysics and relativity.

"It was a long time ago that the first Martians landed on the earth. Only three human beings witnessed the landing."

"And you, sir, were one of those three?"

He smiled modestly and went on: "One of these days, they will reveal themselves, and mankind will receive a shock." He laughed his hearty laugh, finding the fright of mankind infinitely amusing. "For the time being they are invisible. Only a few of the elect . . ."

Zulmira was consumed by curiosity. "You who can see them, tell me what they are like. Are they pretty?"

"Compared to them, we are loathsome beasts."

The mulatta was absorbed, thoughtful, in a daydream: "Do you mean to say, Mr. Cardoso, that it was a Martian who ran his hand over me and pinched me? Are they, too, like that?"

"Like what?" Cardoso was eager to learn all the details. What hand, what pinches, and in which spots of her anatomy?

Zulmira told him, still frightened, the innocent victim of this interplanetary debauchery, this ectoplasmic nudging. "I showed Pequito, he saw the bruises. I showed them to the other girls at Dona Flor's class at the cooking school. Dona Flor was so impressed that she almost fainted."

She had shown them to everybody except Cardosa e Sa. Why this prejudice against him? Without an examination *in locus* (as Cardinal Cauchon would have said) it was impossible to define the phenomenon. A little irked, Cardoso e Sa. answered: "The Martians? I don't think so. With them it is merely transmission of thought."

Only transmission of thought? Let anyone who wants to buy that, Zulmira thought to herself, going on doing her nails.

As for Pelancchi, he still had his doubts. "Martians? And suppose it's not?"

"You leave it to me and I'll take care of everything."

Pelancchi had great faith in Cardoso e Sa.: he had had occasion to verify the vast scope of the man's learning. But perhaps in such a complicated matter it would be worthwhile not to limit himself solely to the magus of Hindustan, but to consult others possessing magic powers, Mother Otávia, for instance.

Cardoso e Sa., refilling his pipe, his eyes lost beyond the window and the horizon, took his leave with the last ray of light, his voice coming as from afar: "I have great prestige among the Martians. It is not yet four days that I went with them on a visit to Mars. I walked all around the planet. They have one city that is all silver and another that is all gold. The fish there fly through the air and the sea is a garden of flowers."

Now he did not even look at Zulmira's legs or at her full bosom showing through the lace of her negligee. He was taking off for Mars in a ship of light. He's in a trance, Pelancchi whispered respectfully, and Zulmira put the lace of her peignoir in order.

20

The gates of hell swung open and the rebellious angel crossed the threshold of Dona Flor's bedroom (and love room), his lustful eyes gleaming, his mouth inviting, and completely naked. If even the saint could not resist those eyes, the charm of that laughter, that naked breast, how could Dona Flor? Where are you, *comadre* Dionísia with your *gri-gri* prepared by the witch-doctor? Quickly, come quickly Dionísia, with the high priest and the charm to find the devil in his eternal repose. If he remains alive, Dona Flor cannot answer for her honor and for the doctor's brow. A whole upright life, exemplary behavior, decency, respectability—all this enviable capital in danger. Tomorrow the name of Dona Flor, the symbol of virtues, will be a laughingstock, dragged through the mud, an object of contempt. Tomorrow she will be a different woman, pointed out, covered with remorse and shame.

Dona Flor received the lustful glance in the center of her being and responded to the invitation.

At the same time she was the vigilant, watchful Dona Flor, aware of the danger, upright and austere, unyielding, and the Dona Flor eager to give herself, before it was too late. Which of the two was the real Dona Flor? The one who slammed the door of her body noisily shut or the one who opened it crack by crack? And the rain pattering on the roof.

That Saturday night after her headache in the afternoon, her dizzy spell, the visit of Dionísia, the bassoon concert—it all seemed so far away. Dona Flor's time was the time of battle, not to be measured by hours and minutes, a time of rejection and desire, long and painful. Saturday night, the doctor's night, with a repeat performance. He was in the bathroom getting ready for that discreet and delectable feast of the body. Dona Flor lay waiting for him, a submissive and grateful wife. But, oh, the rogue was there at the foot of the bed, ordering her with his finger in the air: "Tonight you are not going to sleep with that turd, I won't let you. Not even if I have to rip the joint apart."

It was absurd, an abuse, ridiculous, but—let who will understand the human heart—Dona Flor felt a surge of satisfaction to the point of laughing and asking him (instead of ordering him out, offended and indignant): "So you're jealous of him, eh? The tough guy is jealous."

"It's that I want you, babe," he answered smoothly, stretching himself out comfortably in the bed. "I've already waited too long. Who ever heard of a man having to conquer his legitimate wife, with whom he slept for seven years? It's over and done with, I'm not waiting any longer. Me jealous of that druggist doctor of yours, when I have no quarrel or competition with him? He married you, he's your husband, and, aside from screwing, at which he is a complete flop, he is even a good husband. I admit that. I am not questioning his rights. But today, and I hope he will excuse it, he's going to be up the river without a paddle, the one who's going to do the screwing is this expert here, who knows what it is all about and when to come and when to go."

"You are going to have a long time to wait."

Completely naked, his mouth hot, his eyes lustful, and his hand traveling the routes he knew so well, he overcame her: Dona Flor, the slave of Vadinho, free only when it came to words, pure boasting. Pride and shame, decency, morality, dignity—what did all that amount to when he desired her and had come because of her (you know from where, from the invisible regions).

"I was in the depths of hell, bound hand and foot there, and the effort it took to get loose and come to see you, my pet! But you called to me and I came, passing through fire and ice, void and obstacles. I have come and you cannot refuse me bread to eat and water to drink, can you?"

"Oh, Vadinho . . ."

"Why do you treat me like this, like a dog? But this is the end, my sweet. Either today or never. When that cockroach comes out of the bathroom, you tell him you don't feel well, that you're not up to it. Then afterward we're going to really give the pussy a workout."

"Oh no, not that! I am a decent, respectable woman, I am not going to betray my husband, how many times have I told you that?"

The doctor emerged from the bathroom in a pair of clean pajamas, giving off the scent of soap. He was of agreeable appearance; his smile was sincere, his eyes were honest. Vadinho had his hand on Dona Flor's dark rose. Oh, Dona Flor, how can you have sunk so low?

"Teodoro, my dear, you will forgive me, but I don't feel well tonight. Let's leave it until tomorrow if you have no objections."

Not well? The doctor was disturbed. She had already complained that afternoon. Would it be nothing but a simple indisposition? Where were the thermometer, the syrup, the box of medicines? "I don't need anything, my dear, don't you worry. You go to sleep and tomorrow I will be well, completely well . . ."

". . . and at your command," she vowed to herself.

How could she suddenly become like that, so unfeeling, so shameless, so indecent, so lacking in pride? Dona Flor asked herself, feeling a pleasant tenderness for her worried husband and a certain satisfaction in the farce she was playing: she kissed his cheek. But Dr. Teodoro was not satisfied. She ought to take a tablet, some drops, at least a sedative to get a good night's sleep and wake up calm and refreshed. He went to get the medicine and a glass of water. No sooner had he gone than Dona Flor felt Vadinho embracing her.

"You must be crazy. Let go of me! He's coming right back."

Vadinho remarked thoughtfully and impartially: "He's not a bad fellow, this second husband of yours. Quite the contrary. Would you believe, my sweet, that I like him better every time I see him. Between the two of us, you are well cared for. He, for troubles and problems, me, for screwing . . ."

The doctor came with a pitcher of cool water, two glasses, and a little flask of colorless liquid. "Tincture of valerian, twenty drops in half a glass of water, and you will sleep soundly and rest, my dear."

He picked up the dropper and carefully and calmly added the sedative to the water. Did somebody change the glasses while the doctor turned his back for a moment? Who? Vadinho or Dona Flor? But, if that was the case, how was it the doctor, being the competent druggist he was, did not recognize the taste of the valerian? Did a miracle occur? If it did, at this stage of the game, one miracle more or less doesn't impress us, causes us no surprise. Maybe there wasn't even a miracle, and Dona Flor just didn't take the sedative, and the doctor's deep sleep was the consequence of the patter of the rain on the roof and his easy conscience. He barely had time to kiss his wife.

"He's growing horns," Vadinho said, using the fitting term. "Now it's our turn, babe."

"Not here," Dona Flor begged, expending the last remains of shame and respect for her second husband. "Let's go into the living-room."

In the living-room the doors of heaven opened wide, and a song of rejoicing burst forth. "Who ever heard of screwing in a night-gown?" Dona Flor as naked as he, each dressing and completing himself in the nudity of the other. A fiery lance ran through her. For the second time Vadinho had made off with her honor, the first when she was a virgin, now that she was married (and had there been other opportunities he would have taken advantage of them). Off they went through the meadows of the night to the edge of dawn.

Never had they found such pleasure in one another: so free, so fiery, so gluttonous, so delirious. Ah, Vadinho, if you felt hunger and thirst, what about me, on that limited bland diet, without salt or sugar, the chaste wife of a respectful, restrained husband? What do I care about what people think of me? What do I give for my honor as a married woman? Take all this in your burning mouth, which tastes of raw onion, burn in your fire my innate decency, rend with your spurs my former modesty: I am your bitch, your mare, your whore.

They came and went, and hardly were they back when they

were off again, going and returning. So much longing and so many goals to achieve, all won, all repeated.

Insolent and beloved, foul and beautiful, Vadinho's voice was in her ear, saying so many indecent things, recalling the joys of other days. "Do you remember the first time I touched you? The Carnival groups were coming through the square, and you leaned up against me . . ."

"It was you who put your arm around me and ran your hand down me . . ."

He ran his hand down her and recognized her: "You have the tail of a siren, your belly is the color of copper, your breasts of avocado. You have put on weight, Flor, you are more filled out, you are delicious from your head to your feet. Let me tell you, I have picked a lot of cherries in my life, a good crop, but there is no cunt that can compare with yours, it is the best of all, I swear that to you, my Flor."

"What does it taste of?" Dona Flor asked, shameless and cynical.

"Of honey and pepper and ginger."

He talked and Dona Flor dissolved in sighs. Vadinho, crazier, more overbearing than ever, fire and breeze. Vadinho, don't go away, never again. If you should leave, I would die of sorrow. Not even if I beg or plead with you, don't go away; even if I command and order you to, don't leave me.

I know I will only be happy if you are not here, if you go away. I realize that with you there can be no happiness, only dishonor and suffering. But without you, however happy I might be, I do not know how to live, I cannot live, oh, never leave me.

21

They always got up later than usual on Sundays, and when Dona Flor opened her eyes that Sunday morning when it was still raining, she saw the doctor's face bent over hers, gazing down on her devotedly, his hand on her cheek.

"Did you sleep well, dear? You don't have any fever."

Dona Flor smiled as she stretched, happy to have such a good husband, to be the object of so much solicitude; she put her arms around his neck, and gave him a kiss of gratitude.

"I feel fine now, Teodoro. It was just some silly passing thing."

Just a silly thing, laziness, the pleasure of doing nothing, wanting to stay in bed, enjoying the warmth and dedication of her husband, a saint if there ever was one. She cuddled up against him: "How lazy I am, dear."

"And why don't you rest. You had a bad day yesterday; today you stay in bed as long as you like. If you want me to, I'll bring your coffee here."

So worthy and endearing: "Only if you stay too. Only with you here beside me."

What Dr. Teodoro was was a big boy, devoid of malice, a boy in spite of his standing, his knowledge and his age: "If I stay here in bed beside you"—and he laughed bashfully—"I won't answer for the consequences if . . ."

Dona Flor answered coyly: "I'll take the risk" and hid her face in the pillow.

She was still a little indecorous, one breast exposed, the curve of her thigh showing through the sheets, the color of molasses. The voice of the doctor, timid and hungry, his hand curbed: "You have been tossing around in bed, my dear, see where you have bruised yourself. In more than one place. You slept badly."

She shrank within herself and her heart stopped: "Where?"

"Here. You poor little thing," and the eager hand moved up her thigh and beyond it.

Between her husband's legs Dona Flor effaced those blemishes of a good or bad night's sleep (or no sleep at all). Their mouths met and she trembled: the taste of that pure (but ardent) kiss, the unexpected pleasure of that embrace, the rain pattering on the roof, the warmth of the bed, the timidity of Dr. Teodoro, his hand inexperienced but perhaps for that very reason more delectable, the desire in her husband's lowered eyes, in his panting breast, and all in the light of day, what a confusion. Dona Flor quivered again: such delight. "For suffering and cares, her good husband." Only for that? Every man has his own special flavor, Maria Antônia, her former student, well versed in men and bed play had said: "Each has his own thing, some are wise, others are not. But if one knows how to make the most of them, they are all good." Dona Flor felt herself flooded with desire, a different kind of desire, born of laziness, of Teodoro's timidity, of his diffidence.

"You are in debt to me, my dear."

"Me? What are you saying?" the doctor asked, an innocent offender, a big silly boy. That long head of an intellectual, a brow filled with outstanding thoughts, and such a silly man. Dona Flor ran her hand over his head as though in curiosity, and laughed gently, never had she been so enticing and so coy: "Yes, sir, you are in debt to me. What about yesterday?"

"Don't be unfair, my dear, it was you . . ."

"Then if I am the debtor, I am prepared to pay up, for I don't like to be in debt," and she covered her face with her hands, laughing teasingly.

What better could the noble druggist ask for? He even laid aside his seriousness: "Then I am going to collect, and with interest."

A methodical man, observant of laws and rites, Dr. Teodoro assumed his customary position, and took hold of the sheet to cover their lovemaking with the modesty and respect married people owe one another. But Dona Flor did not give him time: she threw the sheet off the bed, along with the modesty and respect, and the doctor found himself in her arms. He would never forget that rainy morning, that blessed Sunday, that holy, celebrated day, that unequaled encore, encore and more, to state and define everything exactly.

Afterward Dona Flor rolled herself up like a ball of yarn, a smile on her lips, and fell asleep to the lull of the rain, a sound sleep, so quiet and satisfied that it was a marvel to behold.

22

Nothing changed, there was no difference: it was a Sunday like every other Sunday, and Dona Flor was the same person as always. She had undergone the pangs of hell, certain that it was going to be the end of the world. What surprises this life holds!

However, as it was the Scientific Pharmacy's turn to be open that Sunday, it did make the day a little different, for the doctor had to attend to many customers—imagine only one drugstore open for so many people! So when Dona Flor came out of her room she did not find her husband. Nevertheless, it was a very active morning.

First Marilda, with the crisis of her engagement, and Dona Maria do Carmo, practically in hysterics: was the girl to go on singing or get married? The women of the neighborhood were practically of one accord, with the exception of Dona Gisa. But the American was known for her unconventional ideas, all right perhaps for the United States, but screwy, if not downright dangerous, for Brazil. Not only did she defend divorce, but on one occasion, in a discussion with Dona Jacy and Dona Ênaide, she had

gone so far as to state, loud and clear, that virginity was not only
obsolete, but bad for the health: according to the *gringa* the
insane asylums were full of women who had never had sexual
relations. Can you imagine!

The others repeated, full of moral conviction, that marriage
was the only legitimate objective of woman, ordained by God to
look after her house, her husband, bear and bring up children,
happy and willingly. At the head of this dauntless army, Dona
Maria do Carmo, looking to see her daughter settled, said: "This
girl must be settled in a home of her own. The radio offers no
guarantees and is dangerous."

Dangerous? The group became excited: not one but many
dangers lurked in wait for the singers, artists, a species, moreover,
somewhat ambiguous, of suspicious conduct, in the opinion of
Dona Dinorá, a person, as we know, of severe and rigid conduct, of
mounting intransigence in her struggle against impropriety and
looseness. She was always on guard when the talk came around to
artists, stage, radio. As for directors, singers, musicians, they were
all lowlifes, wolves preying on the poor young artists, with sharp-
ened claws.

Only a little while back a young singer, a girl of excellent
family—connected with Dona Ênaide, "highly distinguished people"—had to be rushed to the hospital, bleeding to death, and when
the doctor examined her he found that the cause of the hemor-
rhage was an abortion she had undergone, and very poorly done by
some woman who lay in wait for poor creatures like that. The girl
had not died, thanks to the timely care of Dr. Zezito Magalhães,
whose reputation was outstanding. She did not die, the doctor
saved her life, but as for her cherry, not even Dr. Zezito, competent though he was, could restore that. Neither he nor anybody,
for, as Dona Dinorá put it, "nobody has yet invented a spare
maidenhead."

"Can you imagine," Dona Norma reflected, "how rich the
person who invented that would become. If it was nothing but
going to a drugstore, the Scientific Pharmacy, for example, and
saying: 'Dr. Teodoro, please give me two new hotboxes, one for
me and one for my sister . . . and a cheaper one for the maid.'"

They all laughed, even though none of that had anything to do with Marilda, who in the opinion of the neighborhood was a decent girl. For that reason she should not vacillate between marriage to the rancher and the poorly paid radio work.

Therefore it caused no little surprise when, that Sunday, Dona Flor, consulted again by Marilda, advised her to send her square, despotic suitor packing, and to stay on at the Radio, where before long she would be getting a better salary. Dona Maria do Carmo, seeing her daughter strengthened by the unexpected support, prepared to break off the engagement, came to demand an explanation, almost quarreled with Dona Flor: "If it were your daughter, I doubt very much . . . you are not even behaving like a friend . . ."

The argument grew heated, involving the neighborhood, but Dona Flor stuck to her guns: "This is just being hidebound."

The jawing wound up in tears, Dona Maria do Carmo herself torn between the success of her daughter and the security marriage offered. Dona Flor had the majority support. Dona Norma summed the situation up in these words: "Maybe she can boss things around like that in hell. Slave days are over."

Dona Flor went into the kitchen to prepare lunch—when the doctor had to be on duty at the drugstore on Sunday they did not go out to Rio Vermelho—and there Dionísia de Oxóssi found her: "With your permission, my *comadre*."

She had come for money and was in a hurry, for the spell was being prepared and the circle of votaries was waiting to dance in the afternoon and far into the night. Before, however, there were many things to do, the undertaking was one of the most serious, and the measures were complicated. The priest had cast the shells and the deities had answered. To assure her tranquility, protect her from the evil eye, from any illness, from the menace of the spirit of the dead, which was dissatisfied at not taking her to her death, Dona Flor had to fulfill a costly vow, not a simple charm, an insignificant hex. Exu, the guiding spirit of the dead man, was opposed, and was on a war footing. Dionísia had told the witchdoctor not to take expense into account. Being a case of life or death, and with Exu up in arms, contrary and not yielding an inch, money did not count, and what mattered was speed, great speed: her *comadre* Dona Flor could barely stand up. In the face of all this, Asobá himself had advanced the money out of his own pocket for the most urgent expenses: a ram, two goats, a dozen cocks, six Guinea hens, twelve yards of cloth. Not to mention the other things, a long list written on wrapping paper in pencil. Each item with its price and twenty mil-reis extra for the shrine of Ossain so that he could open the paths to the forest where Exu was hidden.

But when she arrived, Dionísia found Dona Flor so hale and hearty, so satisfied with herself, that she did not even seem the same person as the afternoon before. Had she done wrong to justify all that expense?

No, she had done right, for the evening before Dona Flor herself, terrified, had ordered her to take those steps. I thank you, *comadre*, for all the work I gave you. Now, however, nothing mattered, everything would work itself out one way or another.

"Has the departed stopped bothering you?"

Trying to hide her embarrassment, Dona Flor smiled and said: "Or I got over my fright. I don't need anything more."

And now what? To call off the work was impossible. During the night and the early morning they had sacrificed the animals, and with the first rays of the sun they had set before each deity the wooden trough with its ritual food. All Sunday, during the afternoon and the night, the prescribed rites would continue, with the deities there in the center. Call it off, stop halfway, not go on, undoing what had been done was impossible, *comadre*, with a spell in a center of such importance. Who would escape alive the fatal, unforeseeable consequences of the cruel punishment by the sorcerers? Not even she, Dionísia, in spite of the fact that she was a mere intermediary.

There was no choice but to see it through. Even if Dona Flor felt herself free of threats, the spell was a further guarantee of her peace of soul. The money had been spent; the gods had drunk the hot blood of the animals at the hour of their slaughter and at daybreak had accepted the pieces of flesh they liked best; they were decked out in their arms and emblems, and the cry of Yansã had already echoed through the woods. Dona Flor would now have the assurance that the dead man would never return to disturb her, but would be bound forever by his death.

Dona Flor counted out the money, added a little more, thanked Dionísia once more for all the trouble she had taken, and invited her to stay for lunch: chicken in brown sauce and pork loin cooked in brandy, corn meal dumplings, and mangoes and sapote plums for desert. But Dionísia was in a hurry to get back to the temple, where, to the rumble of the drums, Oxóssi was calling for the services of his favorite mount.

On Sundays when he was on duty, after lunch (the druggist eating so fast he did not even notice the flavor of the delicacies she had prepared, in his hurry to get back to the drugstore, which was entrusted to the delivery boy), Dona Flor changed her clothes, and without listening to her husband's protests, went along to keep him company, lighten his work on that day of rest. She sat beside him at the counter, helping him with everything, all dressed up, as elegant as though she were going to pay a visit to Dona Magá Paternostro, the millionariess, or go to a reception at the home of Commander Taveira Pires. All that elegance, all that beauty, just for him; Dr. Teodoro felt himself paid and well paid.

And so that Sunday, all charm and beauty, bewitching and coy, Dona Flor had put on that old turquoise necklace which Vadinho had given her. Nothing had changed; it was a Sunday like any other when the drugstore was open. Everything the same: the street, the people, the doctor and she, Dona Flor. Nobody pointed a finger at her, nobody noticed anything, nobody saw in her the guilty adulteress, not even Dona Dinorá with her pretensions of being soothsayer and her malignance. The same sun as before, the same rain (now just a misty drizzle), the same conversations, the same laughter, the unaltered respect for her. She had thought it was going to be the end of the world, without her and within her, that her heart would break, that death was better. And instead of this, everything the same. How people deceive themselves in this life!

From the counter, attending to a customer, Dr. Teodoro smiled at her, all conceited and puffed up at seeing her so lovely. She smiled back at him and cast a glance at his brow as she did so: not a sign of horns. How foolish, Dona Flor! What is the meaning of this sudden pleasure in being party to a farce?

Nor had anything changed between her and the doctor. Only the recollection of the morning in bed, which made that afternoon in the store with him more intimate. What remained, too, was the memory of the night on the sofa, that gluttonous, violent love, that shameless ride under the patter of the rain, the victorious cry of Vadinho. In that calm afternoon, in the peace of that Sunday, the goad of desire again pricked her body. When would he come back again, that screwball, that tyrant, that devil, her first love? That night, without fail, when the doctor, worn out, slept the sleep of the just and the happy.

In that calm happiness she was the good wife, one with her second husband, fulfilling her duty by helping him, and awaiting the lewd night with her first husband. A disturbing thought suddenly assailed her: Dionísia had said that Vadinho would never return to trouble her, tied forever by the bonds of the spell. My God, what if it were true?

23

Mother Otávia Kisimbi prayed over Pelancchi's body, and both he and Zulmira took a bath of leaves with coconut soap. The feathers of the cocks that had been sacrificed were placed at the crossroads of the pathways. Mother Otávia ringed Pelancchi with defenses on all sides and against the seven gates, and told him to await results. But the king of the numbers racket was in a hurry, and he went off to visit other specialists.

The clairvoyant Aspásia had just disembarked from the Far East, traveling on the zephyrs of dawn, and had hardly donned her fortuneteller's uniform (somewhat the worse for wear) when she received the visit of Pelancchi, displaying a wad of money. Although the seeress was indifferent to the tinkle of gold—she lived on the bounty of heaven, completely detached from the pleasures of this world—how could she refuse the bill when, moreover, it was such a difficult task that was asked of her?

Availing herself of the "system of spiritual science in movement," her own, exclusive patent, she took off for the beyond, groaning hoarse words, threshing about as though she were being strangled. It was not one of the most edifying sights, and Professor Máximo Sales, skeptical by nature, hard-headed, felt like leaving. But Pelancchi stayed on, holding Zulmira's trembling hand, for she had developed a great awe of the supernatural since those invisible creatures had demonstrated an interest in her breasts, her bottom (and, who knows?, the rest). Zulmira, secretary and confidante, loyal at the side of her boss, the consolation of his sufferings, and what a consolation!

Slobbering disgustingly, her eyes popping out of her head, the seeress of the Far East returned from outer space, and as she looked at Pelancchi, her body writhed, a scream rent her scrawny breast —like an ironing board, a sad sight to behold. She requested more money. Ah, that was an extenuating task, everything as dark as pitch in the realms of the beyond, so dire was Pelancchi's fate. A small sum for candles. Perhaps with that reinforcement of light, she might be able to unmask the whole conspiracy. She put the bills in a drawer, lighted the symbolic candles, and, by their light, her penetrating eyes recognized Pelancchi's enemies: "I see three men beside a road and the three of them hate you . . ."

"Ah," Pelancchi groaned. "Tell me, *signora*, what they look like."

She took a while to examine them carefully, but Pelancchi was in a hurry: "See if one of them isn't bald, and the other isn't fat. The third . . ."

"Let her tell herself what the third is like," suggested Máximo Sales, the biggest buttinsky ever known. "When all is said and done, who is the fortuneteller?"

The seeress, even in a trance, shot a withering glance at the dog who was making her charitable endeavor more difficult; who had ever said that she came by her money easily? She grunted, snorted, bit her wrists, pounded her head; was this money of Pelancchi's a bargain? It was hard and risky.

"The first of the three," she said in a voice that seemed to come from beyond the tomb, "is bald."

"A real piece of news," muttered Máximo, the scoundrel.

"The second is a fat man, very fat . . ."

"And the third one, what is he like?" Máximo inquired scoffingly.

"I still can't see the third clearly, he's in the dark . . ."

Pelancchi could not keep quiet: "That's him, that's the one, always hidden, *maledetto!* See if he doesn't have a mustache and a broken nose . . ."

But the pythoness assuredly did not hear him off in the beyond endeavoring to discern him: "Now he is coming clearer: he has a mustache and . . . wait a minute . . . I am beginning to see . . . he has a broken nose."

"They are the Strambi, I haven't the least doubt." Pelancchi wanted to know what to do to get them out of his pathway, those implacable Strambis.

To expel them from Bahia, to inspire in them the noble sentiments of forgiveness, and lead them to the distant East, Aspásia, exhausted, would need more money. Pelancchi was already reaching for his wallet, but Máximo Sales, the foul rascal, once more sticking his nose into other people's business, secured a considerable reduction.

Thanks to the hands of Aspásia, the Strambi disappeared, but not the bad luck at gambling. Pelancchi continued his Calvary, his Via Dolorosa from fortuneteller to occultist.

Josete Marcos was at least pretty and young, as Máximo Sales could bear witness; she proved an exception to the general run of the sorority, made up for the most part of unappetizing hags. Why —the professor of illegal activities asked himself—did the other world make use of such scarecrows? Why were their waiting rooms so dirty, their temples of revelations, the stench of mystery so offensive, the B.O. of the souls? The skeptical Máximo reached the conclusion that the beyond must be somewhat fetid and foul.

Josete Marcos was the exception, slender, blonde, and clean! The small reception room in which she met them had a vase of flowers and cuspidors. After listening to them, she left them with her husband and aide and went to the levitation and clairvoyance room to pray. The husband, Mr. Marcos, also young, with the agreeable air of a Ph.D. in rascality, explained that Josete charged nothing for the benefits she conferred on people thanks to her mediumistic gifts. It was all voluntary, the spirits accepted nothing, and Josete accepted only what she absolutely needed for injections and medicines (everything was so expensive nowadays, with the cost of living going up all the time) to restore her health, weakened by every session. When the ectoplasm departed from her— and she spared no effort as the visitors would see with their own eyes—her organism, fragile to start with, became so weak that her life was endangered. Pelancchi, full of hope and pity, was generous, and Mr. Marcos pocketed the money.

In the other room, the one where the wonders took place, the darkness was almost complete. It was completely curtained in red. In a white robe, stretched out in a chair, Josete lay amid her extrasensory fluids, and the husband ordered the four of them—Pelancchi, Zulmira, Domingos Propalato, and Máximo—to hold hands to establish the current of thought. So they did, and a little lamp, the only one in the room, went out.

Then there came the tinkling of bells and the sound of squeals like cats' miaows, and a light moved through the air around the curtains, eliciting a hysterical scream from Zulmira. As for Pelancchi, he could not even scream, and Propalato was sweating, shivering, his teeth clenched. That light and those bells were Brother Li U in person, a Chinese sage of the Ming dynasty, absolutely authentic. In the opinion of Máximo Sales, who was incorrigible, instead of the sage Li U, that light and sound were nothing but the work of that scamp Marcos, a sharp customer who enjoyed a satisfying life at the expense of that attractive ectoplasm. But inasmuch as Máximo Sales was a big mouth and incredulous, his opinions are of no value and not worth taking into consideration, and if we mention them here it is merely to maintain the accuracy of this narrative.

Credit and confidence were due Josete, completely converted into ectoplasm and speaking in a strange language, like that of a child, perhaps old Chinese or more possibly the Portuguese of Macao, for it was difficult to understand her. According to the sage Li U, the cause of all that trouble was a woman, an Italian and full of spite, to whom Pelancchi had been unfaithful.

"Blonde or brunette?" the Calabrian asked.

"Brunette and pretty, about twenty-five . . ."

"Twenty-five? Closer to forty, and she was a snake. I was not to blame. Please, my dear, tell the Chinese that I was not to blame."

Her name was Annunziata, she seemed a harassed and ingenuous young woman, looking for protection. But a whore to end all whores. He, Pelancchi, had been a boy at the time, a poor young boy of seventeen . . .

Carried away by the impulse of those jeered-at seventeen years, he had left a knife mark on the betrayer's cheek and several cuts on her jaw for good measure. As he was under age, Pelancchi was not sent to jail, but Annunziata, in the hospital, vowed vengeance, alive or dead. Now, so many years later, she had come to fulfill her promise in that Italian drama. Annunziata, his first love, so inconstant, such a whore.

Even today Pelancchi did not regret what he had done. A woman who is his is his alone, not for another. Zulmira shrank into herself in the darkness: what a dangerous place this world is!

The Chinese sage, thanks to the price of a few more boxes of injections, freed Pelancchi from the memory of Annunziata and her hatred. As for the material details, such as sum and payment, Mr. Marcos acted as intermediary, go-between of souls and spiritual manager of that spiritual nook. Annunziata disappeared with her bleeding cuts, but not the bad luck.

The Archangel St. Michael of Carvalho, enveloped in a kind of sheet, with a turban on his head, did not describe faces or mention names, but he was positive and wasted no time. Taking Pelancchi by the hands, he looked him in the eyes: somewhere in space a cruel enemy was pursuing him, a man whom the Calabrian had deeply offended, and who had departed the flesh not long ago. The Archangel immediately observed him with his angelic lantern: "He is standing up, right behind you."

Everybody recoiled, and even Máximo Sales, just to be on the safe side, stationed himself beside the door.

"Was it a little while ago that he died?"

"Yes. And the quarrel was over a woman," the Archangel went on, having taken a deep breath of his magic powers.

Pelancchi identified him as Diógenes Ribas. He had taken away his wife, the most pretentious mulatta, an honest-to-God knockout, magnificent and wily. Diógenes, the aggrieved and dissatisfied owner, had made a show of dagger and threats. Pelancchi, now the mighty gambling king, to shut him up and at the request of the mulatta—whom Diógenes was tormenting with abuse and calumny —ordered him given a beating, assigning the job to a team of experts. When the doctors finally released him, Diógenes Ribas disappeared for good. It was only by chance that Pelancchi had heard of his sad recent death, completely destitute. As for the mulatta, the pivot of the drama, with the passing of time she became unbearable. Pelancchi had traded her to a Swiss for a gross of decks of cards.

With his flaming sword the Archangel swept away Diógenes, who was all words, no guts, a third-rate spirit, a cuckold in the bargain. He had not been expensive, for he did not exploit believers but did what good he could to mankind, as he explained to his audience. The cuckold vanished with his horns, but the bad luck grew worse.

Nair Sabá, a doctor of general medicine and surgery, graduated with honors from the University of Jupiter, in her forties and as ugly as sin, cured the sick by magnetic passes. In the conjunction of the planets, and at a fitting price, she discovered at least six enemies of Pelancchi, whom she identified at once without any possibility of mistake. The Doctor of Jupiter liquidated the six in record time, and in the bargain cured Pelancchi of a duodenal ulcer and Propalato of a persistent rheumatism. The only thing she could not cure was the bad luck.

Madame Deborah, some sixty years old, in Máximo's opinion was not worth the money even as a spectacle: she gave no assurance, complained about pains in her stomach (she had been in the family way for over thirty years, having conceived and being about to give birth to the Apocalypse), reeked of rum, had a chronic cold, and was enveloped in the rags of a gipsy. The only thing she really brought to light was one Carmosina, an old flame of Pelancchi's, deserted by him without compassion or pity. The gambling king did not keep ugly bags of bones. Madame Deborah had difficulty in getting rid of that dame, but she finally managed to do it with the help of a few swigs of rum she kept in a cough syrup bottle. Afterwards she tried to sell Pelancchi some infallible hunches for the numbers game. The bad luck kept on, it goes without saying.

The only one who charged nothing was Teobaldo, Prince of Baghdad, a wizened old codger all dressed in white, his eyes blue and steady, his face smiling, his mouth enigmatic. He did not want money or gratuity of any sort; he did not reveal any invisible enemy, male or female. If he saw them around the gambling king or in infinity, he kept it to himself. All he said, touching Pelancchi on the shoulder, and with tears in his eyes, was: "Only the Master of the Absurd can save you. He alone and no one else."

"And where can I find that gentleman?"

More than eighty years old, ever since he had been a little over twenty he had been announcing the end of the world, undeterred by incredulity and persecution, jail and the insane asylum, never giving up, the implacable prophet of the Old Testament. Teobaldo, Prince of Baghdad informed him: "Where you least expect him, there you will find him." And having said this, he closed his eyes and went to sleep.

In Zulmira's apartment, in the isolation a thinker requires, Cardoso e Sa. set in order the final details of his battle plan: he had arranged an interview with the Martians, he had friends among them.

"And then?" he asked Pelancchi.

Tired out and pessimistic, the gambling king shrugged his

shoulders: "Do you by chance know where I can find a certain Master of the Absurd? Have you ever heard speak of him?"

"The Master of the Absurd? You want to meet him?" And the mystic's hearty laugh ran through the room.

"As soon as I can."

"Well, here you have him, in front of you. I am the Master of the Absurd."

At baccarat, at lasquiné, at roulette, Arigof, Anacreon, Giovanni Guimarães, and a crowd of others followed their hunches, breaking bank after bank. Not once did they lose, never.

"You? Well, you'll have to work fast. If this lasts another week, I am ruined."

"Fast, Cardosinho," Zulmira, too, pleaded.

The Master of the Absurd smiled at the intimate address and at the zealous secretary: "Set your minds at rest. It shall be done immediately."

"He has the eye of an eagle, irresistible," Zulmira thought to herself.

24

Arm in arm, Dona Flor and Dr. Teodoro arrived from the drugstore at lunchtime. After a brief siesta, he would return to work, for his shift lasted until ten at night, really rough.

"Poor dear," Dona Flor said.

"Today you are going to bed early, my dear, you were feverish yesterday," her good husband counseled.

Dona Flor was feeling so satisfied, suddenly whole and of a piece, no longer contradictory, rent apart, spirit and matter contending with each other. She had only one fear: what if he did not come back, her first husband? Suppose he did not return?

But he did, as soon as the druggist had left for his store (in raincoat and carrying an umbrella, for the rain had become heavier), and in less time than it takes to tell it there were Dona Flor and Vadinho in the iron bed, on the spring mattress, sexing it up.

"You look pale and tired, and you have got thin. You haven't been sleeping, with all this gambling and jazzing around. You have to rest, my love."

She said this to him during an interval of gentle caresses, after the encounter of fire and storm. Vadinho was pale, very pale, as though his blood were ebbing away, but he smiled: "Tired? Just a little. But you can't imagine the laughs I have had at Pelancchi's expense. In a little while . . ."

"In a little while? You're going back to the gaming rooms? You're not going to spend the whole night with me?"

"This is our night, now. Afterward, babe, it's my colleague's turn, your other husband."

Dona Flor's mettle was aroused, and she reformulated dramatic decisions: "Never again with him. How could I? Never again, Vadinho. Now it's just us two, don't you understand?"

He smiled gently, stretched out at his ease in the bed. "Don't say that, pet. You love to be faithful and upright, I know that. But it is over, why fool yourself? Not only with him, not only with me, with both of us, my deceitful Flor. He is your husband, too, he has as much right as I. He's a good fellow, I like him better all the time. Besides, remember when I got here I told you that we were going to get along well, the three of us . . ."

"Vadinho! You don't mind my putting horns on you with Teodoro?"

He ran his hand over his livid head. "Horns? No, there are no horns involved in this. He and I are tied, babe: we both have our rights; we were both married by priest and justice of the peace, weren't we? The only thing is that he doesn't make much use of you—he's a nitwit. Our love, darling, may be perjurious if you want to call it that to make it more exciting, but it is legal, and so is his, with certificates and witnesses, isn't that true? So, if we both are your husbands, having the same rights, who is deceiving whom? Only you, Flor, you are deceiving the two of us, for you are no longer deceiving yourself."

"I am deceiving the two of you? I am no longer deceiving myself?"

"I love you so"—oh, how that divine accent echoed in her ears —"my love was so great that to see you and hold you in my arms, I broke the bounds of not being and I exist again. But don't ask me to be Vadinho and Teodoro at one and the same time, for I can't. I can only be Vadinho, and I have only love to give you. Everything else you need, he gives you: your own house, conjugal fidelity, respect, order, consideration, and security. It is he who gives you this, for his love is made up of these noble (and tiresome) things, and you need all of them to be happy. You also need my love to be happy, this impure, wrong, crooked love, dissolute and fiery, which makes you suffer. A love so great that it could resist my calamitous life, so great that after not being I came back from the beyond, and here you have me. To bring you joy, suffering and pleasure. But not to stay with you, to be your companion, your thoughtful husband, to keep faith with you, to take you visiting, with a set day for going to the movies and an exact hour for humping, not for that, my sweet. For that you have my noble colleague, and you'll never find a better. I am the husband of poor Dona Flor, the one who comes to stir up your longing and provoke your desire, hidden in the depths of your being, your modesty. He is the husband of Madame Dona Flor, who protects your virtue, your honor, your respect among people. He is your outward face, I your inner, the lover whom you don't know how and can't bear to evade. We are your two husbands, your two faces, your yes and your no. To be happy you need both of us. When you had only me, you had love and lacked everything else, and how you suffered! When you had only him, you had everything, you lacked for nothing, and you suffered even more. Now you are Dona Flor, complete, as you should be."

The caresses grew, the bodies became ignited: "Hurry, my pet, for our night is brief. Let us make haste, for in a little while I will be leaving for doom, which is my fate, and it will be the hour of my colleague, my partner, my brother. For me your longing, your secret desire, your deep-buried wantonness, your hoarse cry. For him, the leftovers, the expenses, the day on duty at the drugstore, your grateful respect, the noble side. All perfect, my love, I, you, and he. What more can you ask for? The rest is deceit and hypocrisy. Why do you still want to deceive yourself?"

Just as he was on the point of taking her, he added: "You think I came to dishonor you, when the truth of the matter is that I came to save your honor. If I had not come, I, your husband, with all legal rights, tell me, my Flor—speak the truth and don't deceive yourself—what would have happened? I came to prevent you from taking a lover and dragging your name and honor through the mud."

"You never thought, you never even admitted the idea of a lover, an upright woman like you, a chaste widow, an honest wife, faithful to your husbands? Then what about the Widows' Lover Boy, Eduardo So-and-So, also known as Our Lord of Calvary? You don't even remember him standing by the lamppost? You were at the window crack, and if I had not sent Mirandão on the double, you'd have been screwing with him, sowing a garden of horns on my grave."

His heavenly voice, his desire, and the burning taste of ginger, pepper, raw onion, and the salt of life (and what he was saying was true).

"Now, love, forget everything, everything, this is the time for humping, and you know very well, Flor, that humping is a sacred thing, invented by God. Come, my pet."

Vadinho, you greatest cheat, greatest heretic, greatest tyrant, let us lose no time.

25

With his head resting on the breasts of velvet and bronze of Zulmira Simões Fagundes, the mystic Cardoso e Sa. . . .

Cardoso e Sa.? Yes, this is no error or misprint, no confusion of names, but the real (and lamentable) temporary substitution of physical presences. It was not Pelancchi Moulas, the gambling king, the emperor of the numbers racket, the patron of the government and of Zulmira, who was reposing, as was his exclusive right, on the breasts of the mulatta, enjoying the warmth and the comfort of these jewels. The one who was doing it, moreover making himself surprisingly at home about the whole thing, was our ever unpredictable Master of the Absurd and daring Captain of the Cosmos, that almost pure spirit.

How had Cardoso e Sa. attained such heights and grandeur? By asking for it. During the time he was seeking the solution to Pelancchi's problems, he had taken to visiting the gaming rooms, holding successive conferences with the Martian leaders (he had even interviewed the Genial Guide, the gloomy and meritorious dictator of Mars, who, up to then, had been inaccessible to any human being), and he had asked Zulmira, insistently and flatteringly, and the old trick had worked again.

To begin with, and out of pure and praiseworthy scientific curiosity, he had asked to see the bruises left by those invisible beings on "your magnificent Amazonian haunches." The bruises had disappeared, she told him, were nothing but a memory. Even so Cardoso e Sa. wanted to see the spot (study the phenomenon "in loco"). Without doing that, he could not make a proper diagnosis. Science is exact.

So she showed him the extensive locale, and he took his time (haste is the enemy of science) studying it: the color, the firmness, the architecture, all really first-class. Zulmira let him get his fill, smiling and shy: wasn't Cardosinho practically a pure spirit, free of the baseness of matter? Almost.

"Like the mountains of Mars, in its promontories and abysses," commented the Geographer of the Planets.

Having satisfied (partially) his curiosity concerning that territory, and having heard of the incidents involving the breasts, he asked to see those marvels, the slopes and the peaks, invoking aesthetic as well as scientific reasons. Accustomed as she was to Pelancchi's cult of beauty and poetry, how could she refuse this dogged but polite request, free of all tinge of lewdness, coming from such an upright person? Zulmira asked herself, and gave in.

Master Cardoso e Sa., the respectful artist, had said he wished to gaze only for a moment on those "masterpieces of the Supreme Artificer of the Universe," but when he saw them bared, his aesthetic pleasure was so great that he lost his head instantly and completely. If he, practically pure spirit, yielded to the lack of restraint of matter, how could one demand firmer conduct on the part of Zulmira, a frail mortal? So, in this asking and giving, it happened.

Moreover, if Pelancchi Moulas had really been of a generous nature, he would have wanted to reward fittingly the colossal efforts of the astrologer and alchemist on his behalf, and would have given Zulmira as a present to Cardoso e Sa., freeing her of all duties and commitments toward gaming and her boss, reserving for himself only the gratifying pleasure of guaranteeing the expenses (which ran high) of the opulent charmer. Because the Great Captain, honoring his promise, had settled the gambling problem, saving the Calabrian's fortune, freeing him from that bad luck and the confusion of the Martians.

One thing is certain and indisputable, at least: during those days Giovanni Guimarães deserted, the last to leave.

The first was Anacreon. The old patriarch, the master of generations, a man of respect and gray hairs, one night set out for the den of Paranaguá Ventura, and in that gyp joint, where every card was marked, he felt himself a gambler once more. Because to win and win without end is not gambling, is not a contest between a man and luck, a battle against the banker and the roulette ball, against the cards and the dice. He picked up a chip, laid it on a card, on a number, and gathered in his winnings. What pleasure was there to that, a magic without any fun to it? What had he, Anacreon, the perfect gambler, the pedagogue of the roulette wheel, done to deserve this irreversible luck?

That was winning, not gambling. The emotion of gambling is the not knowing, the risk, the fury at losing, the joy of guessing the right number, winning and losing. It was following the roulette ball in its wild spin and not knowing where it would come to rest, each time on a different number. When by chance it repeated itself, what a thrill! Now Anacreon did not even look at the ball as it fell obediently on the number on which he had staked his chips. And what about the cards? And the dice? What crime had he committed to deserve such punishment?

Old Anacreon was an upright man, honest, decent, a gambler for the joy of gambling, the pleasure of not knowing, of running risks. Now there was no risk, it was all cut and dried from the start. A shame.

He gathered up the easy money he had come by, and went to Paranaguá Ventura's joint.

"This isn't Pelancchi's casino," the Negro said to him. "Don't you come here trying to show off."

The two of them laughed. One needed more than luck there: one had to have mettle and an alert eye not to be cleaned out. But that night Anacreon did not mind losing, whether as the result of bad luck or of being gyped. What he did not want was that miraculous good luck, profit without amusement, struggle, pleasure. Human nature is like that.

Arigof, who had begun sooner, still delayed a few days before taking off for the dive of the Three Dukes, the den of Zezé da Meningite, where gambling was really gambling. Why the delay? We might as well tell all: the easy money was beginning to corrupt Arigof's upright character. He had picked up the mania of keeping a woman, of spending money on a mistress, which constituted a

total about-face of good habits. He drowned Teresa with presents, bought her a globe of the world in relief and a bird to sing
her to sleep. He was hell-bent on taking over the rent, everything.

Offended and frustrated, the geographeress pointed out to him
the absurd and ridiculous situation he was putting her into: it
was up to her, Teresa Negritude, to support her house and her
Negro: she had her pride, her honor to defend. An occasional
present, good and well; the bird had really touched her, but from
that to contributing to the rent, et cetera, nothing doing.

Thanks to Teresa, Arigof had seen the abyss yawning at his
feet in time; he was no longer going to the casino to gamble, but
just for the money. What had become of his integrity as a man and
his pleasure in gambling? He found himself once more in the joint
of the Three Dukes, in Zezé da Meningite's dive, and Teresa gave
him entrance again to her foaming sea, her white latitude.

As for Mirandão, we already know what happened to him, the
vow he took in his hour of terror. He went on being a bohemian,
filling the nights with his yarns and smile, his prolonged drinking,
but he never gambled again. He never again wanted to feel himself
so close to the presence of the impossible.

Giovanni Guimarães, after his return from the gaming rooms
of the Palace, was no longer the gambler he had formerly been. He
stuck to his duties as an important government official and a
rancher. Even so, if it had been up to him, he would have spent the
rest of his life winning on 17, putting Pelancchi's money into land,
cattle, pasture. But his wife and society frowned on his return to
gambling, and the agreeable journalist, who had recently joined the
ranks of the conservative classes, yielded to the demands of his
home and his credit at the bank, and took to retiring early again.
He did not go from the Palace to the Three Dukes, Zezé, or
Paranaguá Ventura's dive. He went back to his marriage bed, to his
respectability. He was undoubtedly moved by excellent and worthy reasons, but not of the same moral tenor as those of Anacreon
and Arigof.

Thus the three acts ran parallel and arrived at the same destiny:
the interplanetary agreement between the Captain of the Cosmos
and the Martians, the game of asking and giving, an innocent

amusement with which the mystic and the Amazon entertained themselves to while away the time, and the ennui of Vadinho's friends.

However the victory of Cardoso e Sa. did not vanquish the materialistic convictions of Professor Máximo Sales, dogged and stubborn. It was all clear to him: that Cardoso, with his seemingly foolish behavior and those yarns you would have to be crazy to believe, was, beyond doubt, the head of the gang and Zulmira his accomplice. The two had known each other for a long time and were lovers. Only Pelancchi, that old cuckold, was unaware of this. Otherwise, how explain what had happened?

And who would have believed that Cardoso e Sa.—Cardosinho to his intimate friends like Zulmira—was so amazingly, unexpectedly versed in matters of love? Not just the love of our miserable, miniscule astral body, but also that of the more progressive planets, the richer galaxies? A professor of the delightful branch of knowledge which he imparted to his attentive student. Attentive and inquisitive: "Tell me what it is like on Saturn, Cardosinho. How do they kiss when they don't have mouths, how do they embrace one another if they don't have hands?"

The Master of the Absurd laughed heartily. "I'm going to show you right this minute . . ."

Zulmira was afraid that Pelancchi might find out about that spiritual affection, that mystic bond between two kindred souls, taking as evil and vice what was nothing but scientific curiosity and aesthetic delight.

"What if Pequito should come in and find us like this? He is capable of killing us. Once he swore . . ."

The Master of Light answered: "I will make this motion with my hands and we'll become invisible."

He made that motion with his hands and taught her certain habits of the dwellers of Neptune. Boy, oh boy!

26

Paler every day, more listless. Dona Flor bent over him: "What ails you Vadinho, my love?

"I am so tired."

His voice faint, his eyes lack luster, his hands gaunt. In Dona Flor's opinion, it was that dissolute life he was living: no organism could endure that steady, unremitting wear and tear.

The other time the same thing had happened all of a sudden: when everyone thought him strong and healthy, full of energy and vigor, Vadinho had collapsed among the Carnival masqueraders, decked out in the costume of a Bahian woman, all animation. He had suddenly fallen, dead as a doornail. Still so young, so young and handsome, a braggart, a carouser, and all the time his heart was shot to pieces, completely worn out. Dona Flor had come making her way among the masqueraders and Carnival groups, supported by Dona Norma and Dona Gisa, and she had found him dead, smiling at death. Beside him, standing watch, Carlinhos Mascarenhas, in gipsy outfit, his marvelous guitar silent; the mourners were decked out in bells, sequins, and bright colors.

But now death was approaching day by day, death or whatever it was. First, pale and fleshless, then wan and fluid. Yes, fluid and almost transparent. It was not the thinness of a sick person: he had neither pain nor fever. He was losing density, becoming incorporeal, disembodied, disappearing.

At first Dona Flor had attached no importance to the matter. Being the teaser he was, always up to mischief of some sort, a wag, this might be just a hoax he was setting up, to laugh at her fright and joke at her fear. Vadinho had not lost his old habits; he was the same scoundrel he had been from the start, gibing at everything, amusing himself at the cost of others. Just ask Dona Rozilda, terrified; a riot.

The old lady had showed up without warning, with her big suitcases foretelling a long visit. Dr. Teodoro mastered his shock, and with his customary politeness, graciously greeted his mother-in-law, "who was always welcome" in his house. With the years Dona Rozilda's meanness had increased until she was a veritable sink of poison. She had no more than arrived when the malevolence filled the house and the street: "Your brother is a milksop, a cockroach, has no backbone. His wife is the boss, that bleary-eyed thing. I have come to stay."

"Dear God, give me patience," Dona Flor prayed, and Dr. Teodoro lost all hope. If that monster had "come to stay," there were only two ways out: either to poison her, and he did not have the courage to do that, or a miracle had to happen, and the days of miracles were over. The doctor was wrong, as we well know and he was later to verify.

Less than twenty-four hours after she came ashore, Dona Rozilda was on her way back to Nazareth, hurrying to the boat as though all hell were at her heels. Not all hell, but certainly Satan or Lucifer or Beelzebub, whatever name or title you want to give him: the devil, the worst of them, the one who had been her son-in-law, unfortunately for her and her daughter. He pulled her hair and once knocked her down; he spent the whole day whispering dirty words in her ears, obscene abuse, threatening her with blows and kicks in the ass, proposing utter indecencies to her.

"This house is betwitched. Curses on it! I am never going to set foot in it again," she complained, collecting her suitcases.

A miracle had happened. We are still in the days of miracles, the doctor thought humbly, not feeling himself deserving of so much grace, such a boon.

"The devil is on the loose. He tried to kill me." Having completed her information, Dona Rozilda set out in the greatest haste.

"She's getting senile," Dr. Teodoro diagnosed with relief and assurance.

Dona Flor smiled in agreement with the doctor, feeling the same alleviation as he did, and in answer to Vadinho's wink. In the door the scamp was laughing his head off, even though he was almost immaterial and fluid.

That pallor of his increased. Vadinho became less and less tangible, almost gaseous, transparent, and there came a moment when Dona Flor could see through his body.

"Oh, my love, you are vanishing into nothing . . ."

For the first time Dona Flor felt Vadinho powerless, confused and lost. What had become of his ardor, his arrogance, his rascality?

"I don't know, my darling. They are taking me away. And I don't want to go. Can it be that you don't want me any more? Only you can send me away. As long as you want me, desire me, have me in your mind, I will be alive and here. Flor, what have you done?"

Dona Flor remembered the charm. Her *comadre* Dionísia had warned her. It was all her fault, for she had resorted to the African gods and begged them to take Vadinho back to the dead.

"It was the charm."

"Charm?" The voice was like a trickle of water, the merest murmur.

She told him all, going back to that Saturday afternoon when, with her already in his arms, Dionísia de Oxóssi had saved her honor, and in desperation she had entrusted the spell to her. The high priest Didi had taken charge of working it: it was Didi who had his hand on Vadinho's head. What did you do, Flor, my lost flower, and why?

"To save my honor."

It had been of no help. What was to happen, happened. Stronger than the spell had been the desire unleashed by Vadinho's words. After what had taken place, Dona Flor tried to halt the spell, but it was too late: the sacrificial blood had been shed.

Ah, so you have sent me away, you, and I have no choice but to go. My strength is your desire, my body is your longing, my life is your love; if you do not love me, I cease to exist. Good-bye, Flor, I am going, they art fastening me down with a *mokan*, and it's all over.

He disappeared little by little from her sight, dissolving into nothingness.

27

Vadinho was gone, the combat zone of the deities, the spoils of the *orixás*, a dead soul without a grave.

Dona Flor, why don't you take advantage of the situation? It is your last chance, your final opportunity for the honor, the decency, the chastity, the moral strictures of your neighborhood, your people, your social class. You still have this door open to you, with the charm ordered by Dionísia and carried out by Didi, the Asobá. Even though we are reluctant to resort to spells and strange gods, errors of the lower classes, the safety of morality is in danger, virtue, and the precepts of society, of civilization, so what choice do we have? The important thing, Dona Flor, is for you to save yourself in the eyes of God and your own conscience, the strayed sheep returning to the fold, purified. Fortunately, it is not necessary in the eyes of men, for they are unaware of your misstep.

If you let Vadinho go, it will be easy for you to forget those few shameless nights, that mad ride and the moans of love. All this may have been nothing but a dream, the delirium of fever, a hallucination, or merely foolish thoughts in the idle hours of a whole life of decency and happiness. It will cost you nothing. You will have no remorse. You will live at peace with your husband and your conscience. Your last chance, Dona Flor, to put your virtue in practice, to continue to be the pillar of morality and upright living. Leave Vadinho to his eternal peace. Are you or are you not a decent woman?

Where are you headed, Dona Flor, and what powers are you counting on? Why free him from nonbeing?

Without love I cannot live, without his love. It were better to be dead with him. If I cannot have him with me, I will go seeking him desperately in every man that crosses my path, I will try to find the taste of him in every mouth, howling, a famished wolf running through the streets. He is my virtue.

28

The city rose up in the air, and the clocks marked midnight and noon at the same time in the war of the gods. All the *orixás* had assembled to bury Vadinho, that rebellious spirit of the dead and his burden of love, with Exu alone defending him. Lightning and thunder, whirlwind, steel against steel, and black blood. The encounter took place at the crossroads of the final pathway, on the boundaries of nonbeing.

On the crest of the ocean waves, Yemanjá, dressed all in blue, with her long hair of foam and crabs. Her tail of silver held three different sexes, one white of seaweeds, the other scum green, the third of black powders. With her metal fan, the *abebé*, she called up the winds of death. She commanded a fleet of hulls of ships; an army of fish greeted her silently: *odóia*.

The forests bowed down before Oxóssi, the hunter, the king of Ketu. In that war he rode three horses. In the attack of the morning a wild boar; the white horse of the waning moon; and in the midnight hours his mount was Dionísia, the most beautiful of his votaries, his favorite. Wherever he passed, with his *ofá* and *erukerê*, the animals died, all of them, in that war without quarter.

In the form of a huge snake, Oxumaré displayed the colors of the rainbow, male and female at the same time. Covered with snakes, the rattlesnake and the pit viper, the coral snake and the adder, and followed by five battalions of hermaphrodites. They caught Vadinho up in one tip of the rainbow; he was a male in all his masculinity when he entered; he emerged a timorous female, a wilting maiden. With his trident Exu dissolved the rainbow. Oxumaré put its tail in its mouth, ring and enigma (subilatorio).

Ogun beat the iron and tempered the steel of the swords. Euá with her fountains, Naná with her venerability. Xangô, king of war, encircled by *obás* and *ogans*, in a court of splendor, sending out flashes and rays of lightning. Beside him, Oxun, vain, in all her coyness. Omolu, with his terrifying army, commander of smallpox and leprosy, filthy mucus and pus, all the ailments. Vadinho, consumptive and pestilential, blind and deaf. Exu charmed away the ailments, one by one, a witch-doctor of African tribes.

Brandishing his silver *paxorô*, an invincible lance, Oxalá was two: the youthful Oxoguiã and the old Oxolufá. As he danced past, all bowed down. Ahead of him came Yansã, the ruler of the dead, the mother of war. Her cry silenced the onlookers, and slit Vadinho's bared heart like a dagger.

They came in closed rank, with their arms, their emblems, their ancient ritual. Finding themselves few, they invited the deities of the Grunci and Angola, of the *inkices* of the Congo, and the Indian divinities. All the peoples, from south to north, against Exu and his departed spirit. They set out for the last battle.

It was then that the maidens of the city undressed themselves and went out to offer themselves in the streets and squares. Then the children were born, thousands of them. All alike, for they were all the children of Vadinho, all devils and born on the wrong side of the covers. Out to sea floated houses and mansions, the lighthouse of Barra and the manor house of Unhão; the Fortress of the Sea was transported to the Terreiro de Jesus, and fish sprouted in the gardens and stars ripened in the trees. The Palace clock marked the hour of terror in a crimson sky with yellow spots.

Then a dawn of comets came into being above the whorehouses, and every prostitute acquired a husband and children. The moon fell upon Itaparica above the mangrove swamps, and the lovers picked it up, and in its mirror kisses and desire were reflected.

On one side the law, the armies of prejudice and backwardness, under the command of Dona Dinorá and Pelancchi Moulas. On the other, love and poetry, the fearlessness of Cardoso e Sa., laughing between the breasts of Zulmira, the lieutenant-colonel of dreams.

The people came running down the hillsides with javelins of kerosene, and a long list of strikes and uprisings. When they arrived in the square, they set fire to the dictatorship as though it were a piece of dirty paper, and lighted the torch of freedom on each corner.

The commander of the uprising was the Devil, and at thirty-six minutes past ten, order and feudal tradition crashed to the ground. Only the shards of what had once been accepted as morality remained, and these were later gathered up and guarded in the Museum.

But the cry of Yansã maintained in men the fear of death. Of Vadinho, without hands, without feet, without gadget, there was very little left: dingy smoke, scattered ash, and a heart broken in battle. Almost nothing, a worthless thing. It was the end of Vadinho and his load of desire. Who ever heard of a dead man in an iron bed, humping, starting all over again? Who?

The turn in the battle had come. Exu, powerless, surrounded on all sides, all paths blocked. The dead man in his cheap coffin, in his bare tomb, good-bye, Vadinho, good-bye forever.

It was at this moment that a figure traversed the air, and bursting through the most tightly sealed paths, overcame distance and hypocrisy—a thought free of all shackles. It was Dona Flor, completely naked. Her cry of love outdid Yansã's cry of death. At the last moment, when Exu was rolling down the hillside and a poet was composing Vadinho's epitaph.

A fire lighted up the earth, and the people burned the time of lying.

29

On that bright, transparent Sunday morning the habitués of Méndez's bar, on Cabeça, saw Dona Flor pass by, the last word in elegance, on the arm of her husband, Dr. Teodoro. The couple were on their way to Rio Vermelho, where Aunt Lita and Uncle Pôrto were expecting them for lunch. Her face gay, but her eyes downcast, discreet and serious as befitted an upright, married woman, Dona Flor answered the respectful greetings.

Mr. Vivaldo of the funeral parlor looked Dona Flor over from head to foot: "I would never have thought that Dr. Cough Syrup could be so satisfying. He doesn't look it, but it just shows you never can tell."

"Doesn't look what? As a druggist he is better than lots of doctors," interrupted Alfredo, the image-maker.

"Just get a load of her. What a handsome, beautiful woman! A knockout, and you can see that she lacks for nothing either at board or in bed. She even looks like a woman with a new lover, putting horns on her husband."

"Don't say that," exploded Moysés Alves, that spendthrift cacao planter. "If ever there was a decent woman in Bahia, it is Dona Flor."

"I agree with you. Who doesn't know that she is a virtuous woman? What I am saying is that that doctor, with his dopey face, is a sly customer. My hat is off to him. I would never have thought he was up to the job. For a woman like that, curves here, curves there, you have to have a lot on the ball."

His eyes aglow, he added: "Look how she swings it. Her face so modest, but oh that backside. Just take a look at it: you'd even think someone was tickling it. A lucky guy, that doctor."

On the arm of that lucky dog of a husband, Dona Flor smiled gently. Oh, that mania of Vadinho's for feeling her breasts and buttocks on the street, fluttering about her like the morning breeze. That clear, rain-washed Sunday morning, with Dona Flor strolling along, happy with her life, satisfied with her two loves.

And with this we come to the end of the tale of Dona Flor and her two husbands, set forth in all its details and mysteries, as clear and dark as life itself. All this took place; let him who will believe. It took place in Bahia, where these and other acts of magic occur without startling anybody. If anyone has his doubts, let him ask Cardoso e Sa., and he will tell him whether or no it is the truth. He can be found on the planet Mars or on any poor corner of the city.

Salvador, April 1966.

FOREIGN WORDS AND EXPRESSIONS

abará. Dumpling of cow peas, soaked, peeled, mashed with salt, onion, olive oil, wrapped in banana leaf, and cooked in a double boiler.

abebé. Metal fan used by Yemanjá, goddess of the waters.

aku abó. Words to propitiate spirits of dead in Yoruba.

acaça. Dumplings of soaked and ground corn cooked in banana leaves.

acarajé. Fritters of mashed cow peas, served with hot pepper sauce.

afoxé. Carnival group with African influence typical of Bahia.

akikó. Rooster. (Nago.)

aku. Funeral ceremony or first anniversary of death. (Nago.)

amalá. Dish made of okra, similar to *caruru.*

ambarella. English: umbrella.

apetê. Boiled yams, with olive oil, shrimps, onions and peppers.

arô ôke. Words of praise to deity Oxóssi in Yoruba.

arroz hausa. Rice boiled to a mush-like consistency.

atôtô. Greeting to God Omolu in *candomblé.*

babalão. Priest in *candomblé* center.

bahiana. Woman of Bahia.

berimbau. Word of unknown origin (also spelled *berimbão, birimbão*) used in Brazil for two musical instruments: a musical bow of which the string passes through a gourd resonator held against the player's chest or stomach and is tapped with a small stick; and a form of Jew's-harp.

bisca. Name of various card games.

caboclo. Usually half-breed of white and Indian. At times loosely applied to inhabitants of backlands of whatever race.

capoeira. Style of fighting brought from Africa by Negroes of Angola in the sixteenth century, in which they use hands and feet and head-butting, although at times they resorted to use of razor and dagger. As a graceful as a ballet.

candomblé. Strictly speaking, each of the great annual celebrations of the Afro-Brazilian cult. Also used to describe voodoo ceremonies in general.

carioca. Native of Rio de Janeiro.

caruru. Dish of mustard greens, or similar leafy vegetable, cooked with fish or jerked beef.

chayote. Small squash that grows on trailing vine.

comadre, compadre. Literally, godfather, godmother, in relation to godchild's parents. By extension, intimate friend, crony.

conto (de reis). One thousand mil-reis.

cruzeiro. The Brazil money unit that replaced the mil-reis in 1942.

dendê. The African oil palm grown in Brazil from whose fruit *dendê* oil, which is much used in cooking, is extracted.

efó. Dish made of mustard greens cooked with onion, salt, shrimp, red pepper, and olive oil.

epa hei. Greeting to god Oxalá.

erukere. Kind of short whip made of ox tails carried by the god Oxóssi.

feijoada. Typical Brazilian dish made of black beans cooked with pork sausage, dried beef, and peppers and served with rice and manioc meal.

gri-gri. An African charm or amulet.

gringa. Name used in Latin America for woman (*gringo,* man) of the United States.

guaraná. Brazilian shrub from whose pounded seeds a paste is prepared for medicinal use and also for flavoring a stimulating and refreshing drink.

ibejes. Twins. St. Cosme and St. Damian.

inkice. Same as Orixa, a god or divinity of one of the Afro-Bahian sects.

iya moro. Assistant to priestess in *candomblé* center.

Korikoe Ulukotom. Honorary title in *candomblé* center.

lasquiné. Game resembling twenty-one, except that the winner is the one who comes closest to making thirty-one points.

macanudo. Argentine slang: wonderful, tops, great.

macumba. Brazilian version of voodoo or fetishism. Cf. *candomblé.*

macho. Male.

machismo. Showing off "malesness."

maniçoba. Ground young cassava leaves, boiled with dried beef, pig's head, bacon, and seasoned with laurel, pepper, and mint.

mil-reis. Former Brazilian money replaced in 1942 by cruzeiro.

modinha. A sentimental ballad or folk song.

mokan. Charm to propitiate and quiet spirit of dead.

moqueca. Fish fried in slices and served with sauce of red pepper, coriander, lemon, tomato, and onion.

mucurumim. Person of Mali origin.

obá. Male dignitary in *candomblé.*

odoia. Salutation to goddess Yemanjá.

ofá. Bow and arrow carried by Oxóssi.

ogan. Dignitary of the *candomblé.* It is the duty of *ogans* to look after the ceremonial site.

ojojó. Cake of ground rice, served in honor of Oxalá.

orixá. General term for Negro god or divinity.

paulistà. Native of São Paulo.

paxoro. Kind of cane, one of the attributes of Oxolufá, the elder Oxalá.

ranchera. Song, probably of Argentine origin.

ronda. Patrol, also round dance.

sapotes. Sapodilla plums.

siá. Abbreviation for Senhora.

siri-bocêta. A lewd, indecent dance.

Tres-setes. A card game.

vatapá. Chicken stewed in coconut milk and seasoned with sliced shrimps, onion, red pepper, and olive oil.

xinxim. Chicken stewed with shrimp, onion, crushed squash or watermelon seeds.